WHAT MAKES A FATHER SPECIAL?

He chases the monsters away.
He holds your bike for you.
He looks so sad when you disappoint him.
He teaches you to drive—maybe!
He fixes your toys.
He gives you what you need to grow up.
He cries when you hurt.
He laughs at your jokes.
He frames your drawings.
He's a hero in every sense of the word!

And no matter how he becomes a father,
or where his child is,
he'll always love you.

KATHLEEN EAGLE

is a transplant from New England to Minnesota, where she and her husband, Clyde, make their home. After fourteen years of teaching high school students about writing, the mother of three saw her own first novel in print in 1984. Since then, she's published many more novels with Silhouette Books and Harlequin Historicals that have become favorites for readers worldwide. She also writes mainstream novels, and has received awards from the Romance Writers of America, *Romantic Times* and *Affaire de Coeur.*

❧❧❧

CHERYL REAVIS

is an award-winning short-story author and romance novelist who also writes under the name Cinda Richards. A former public health nurse, Cheryl makes her home in North Carolina with her husband. Her Silhouette Special Edition novels *A Crime of the Heart* and *Patrick Gallagher's Widow* both won the Romance Writers of America's coveted RITA Award for Best Contemporary Series Romance.

❧❧❧

JACKIE MERRITT

and her husband live in Arizona. An accountant for many years, Jackie has happily traded numbers for words. Next to family, books are her greatest joy. She started writing in 1987, and her efforts paid off in 1988 with the publication of her first novel. When she's not writing or enjoying a good book, Jackie dabbles in watercolor painting and likes playing the piano in her spare time.

Kathleen Eagle
Cheryl Reavis
Jackie Merritt

The Father Factor

Silhouette Books

Published by Silhouette Books

America's Publisher of Contemporary Romance

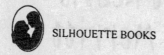

SILHOUETTE BOOKS

by Request

THE FATHER FACTOR

Copyright © 1998 by Harlequin Books S.A.

ISBN 0-373-20147-8

The publisher acknowledges the copyright holders of the individual works as follows:

GEORGIA NIGHTS
Copyright © 1986 by Kathleen Eagle

A CRIME OF THE HEART
Copyright © 1988 by Cheryl Reavis

RAMBLIN' MAN
Copyright © 1990 by Carolyn Joyner

This edition published by arrangement with Harlequin Books S.A.

Printed in U.S.A.

CONTENTS

Dear Reader,

What does it mean to be a father?

No, this isn't a Father's Day card, but it is a good question for a spinner of romantic tales like me, because the answers can be wonderful story seeds. There are all kinds of factors to be considered in defining fatherhood: biological fathers, father figures, surrogate fathers, *real* fathers—unreal fathers? How about uncles? In my husband's culture—the Lakota Sioux—uncles take a fatherly interest in their brothers' children, and great-uncles are called "Grandpa."

Connor Ryan is not Lakota. He's a man who's had little love in his life, even though he's adored by millions of music fans. His brother's sudden death left him with no close family ties, so when he receives a letter from a fan and a photograph of a child who looks just like Kevin, he follows his heart. He knows his duty. The trouble is that the letter didn't come from the child's mother but from another uncle—Sarah Benedict's errant brother. Sarah is doing quite well on her own, thank you, and little Dannie won't be needing her rich and famous uncle's financial support. Or his life-style.

But what about his love? The man who pours his heart out in his music hasn't thought much about what's missing in his own life, but Connor soon realizes that to know Dannie and Sarah is to love them. Shy Sarah's fear of his larger-than-life persona is understandable, but what about the real Connor Ryan? Surely there's a place for him in their quiet lives, a role for him to play in their little family.

Enjoy Connor's love song to Sarah and Dannie!

All my best wishes,

Kathleen Eagle

GEORGIA NIGHTS

Kathleen Eagle

For Mary, my mother, whom I have always loved,
and for her special friendship with Jean,
whose determined efforts on behalf of her son
became a frontline onslaught
in the battle for special education

Chapter One

Connor Ryan felt a twinge of something that reminded him of stage fright. The windshield of the car framed a house in the October twilight. It was one of those big, old New England homes, looming amid the sycamore trees like a proper Puritan with its sternly whitewashed face. Connor filled his cheeks with a mouthful of air, which he released in a reluctant sigh as he stretched his long legs over the low-slung edge of the rental car's door frame and planted his western boots in the gravel driveway. The thunk of his car door settled it. He was here now, and he'd finish this. Absently fingering his breast pocket, where the hard outline of a photograph recalled the images of a woman and a child, he told himself he'd see it through for Kevin's sake.

It was the photograph that had brought him here, not the letter that came with it. He'd gotten at least a hundred letters from people who made every claim and declaration imaginable. Nor was it the face of the blond child, a face that certainly resembled his own. No, it was the woman's face—a perfect, porcelain oval that could have graced a hundred-year-old canvas. He could have had the letter checked out without coming here. He could have made whatever arrangements seemed appropriate. He could certainly do without kids. But he wanted to see *that* face in the flesh.

The front window brightened with lamplight and the face appeared. He'd already mounted the steps, and he knew she couldn't see him. She peered past the filmy curtains and spotted the car as he rattled the brass door knocker. The door swung open, and they stood face-to-face in the half light of evening.

"You must be Sarah Benedict."

At the sound of his voice, she took a step back, astonished. He stepped up and crossed the threshold, putting him almost a head above her. She took another step back, and she let the doorknob pass from her hand. He almost enjoyed the shock in her widening dark eyes. It was well-done. He could almost believe she thought he was a ghost. And her frosty New England coloring almost had him believing he was looking at one.

With her next step Sarah backed into the newel post. "Oh, my," she managed in a small voice. This face seemed a bit harsher, certainly more deeply tanned, and the straw-colored hair was longer, more stylish, but the resemblance was astounding. She shook her head slowly, trying to make some sense of what she saw. "You look just like...*remarkably* like..."

Connor felt a stab of pity even as he reminded himself that this beautiful lady was out to get him with the innocent-eyed shock treatment. "Kevin Ryan," he supplied. "Yes, I know. But I'm not a ghost. My name is Connor Ryan. Kevin was my brother."

Sarah stared at the proffered hand, which had never touched her but could easily have been the one that had. She watched her own hand disappear into his and found it to be smooth and warm inside. "Brother?" Allowing herself another look at his face, she told herself to stop talking like a half-wit.

"Yes, I remember Kevin saying he had a brother. I don't remember mention of a *twin* brother. You must be...must have been..."

"No, we weren't twins." Her eyes were brown, he noted, and her mouth was a classic bow. Her hair was ranch mink, its shiny length reaching past her shoulders. He realized, when her hand slipped out of his, that he'd held it longer than necessary. Suddenly self-conscious, he stuffed his hands in the pockets of his jeans. "Kevin was a year younger," he explained quickly. "We were often mistaken for each other, though, after we got to be about the same size. I guess we looked a lot alike."

"Yes, you do," Sarah breathed.

"I'm sorry. I should have called first. I came...sort of on the spur of the moment."

"How did you know about me?"

He quirked her half a smile. She was good at this. "From your letter. Or your *brother's* letter."

"Jerry wrote to you? He..." Understanding dawned slowly, and embarrassment followed hard upon it. "You're the singer, aren't you? Kevin said his brother was a singer."

"Musician is what they put on my tax returns."

"And Jerry thought you might be part of a rather famous band."

"The group is pretty well-known, yes."

"He didn't...Jerry didn't..." Her distress imposed itself on her tongue, and she couldn't form the words. "I hope he didn't give you the idea that I..."

Connor glanced in the direction of the living room. "Look, maybe if you invited me in, this would be easier."

"Of course. Please..." Sarah took his soft suede jacket and hung it on the coat tree near the door. She paused while he thought to retrieve a pack of cigarettes from the jacket and watched him shove them in a shirt pocket. Then she led him into the living room, where the overstuffed furniture was all slipcovered. The room was done in blue and white, with splashes of rose. None of the tables matched, and they were all different shades of old. There was a fire in the well-used brick fireplace, and the room held a feeling of warmth and comfort. Sarah indicated a chair, but he joined her on the couch. He intended to watch that incredible face at close range.

"I suppose Jerry told you about Dannie," Sarah sighed.

"He mentioned a child—a girl." Connor drew the picture from his shirt pocket. "Is this my brother's daughter?"

Sarah glanced at the picture—the one she'd had taken at Sears during its Mother's Day special. Damn that Jerry, she thought. "Yes. She's Kevin's daughter."

"Did Kevin know about her?"

Sarah shook her head.

"Why not?" His voice carried a gruff edge.

"The last time I saw him, I suspected but I wasn't sure. I wanted to be sure. Then they sent him on one of those missions. I had a feeling…" She remembered the feeling as though it were yesterday. She was in Paris, and he'd called her. He said he was at the officers' club, and she knew he'd had a few drinks. He was gearing up for something. Kevin told her he'd be gone for a while and wouldn't be able to make it down to see her this weekend. No, he didn't know when he'd be back. No, he couldn't tell her where he was going. He'd call her as soon as he could, and they'd get together then. But she had something important to tell him. No, not over the phone. Yes, it *would* have to wait, then, wouldn't it? It would have to wait forever.

"I had a feeling, too," Connor said, his voice so much like Kevin's that Sarah could have sworn she was still on the phone. "Had a feeling he was in the wrong business." He pulled another picture from his pocket, this one of a man and a woman who could have been the two sitting on the couch. "I'd seen you before," he said, handing her the picture. "He sent that to me. That is you, isn't it?"

"Yes. It was taken in Paris…that summer." She smiled at the memory.

Connor had to hold on tight to keep his heart from going out to her. She looked quite forlorn, all right—the very picture of the girl left behind, still not quite over her soldier boy's death even after all this time. "I recognized the Eiffel Tower right away. You're going to be amazed at how observant I can be, Sarah Benedict. How long did you know my brother?"

His piercing blue eyes made her uncomfortable. She remembered that Kevin's eyes had always put her at ease. "Almost a year. We met when I was teaching adult-education classes at the post in Wiesbaden. When the class ended, I went back to Paris, but we...we saw a lot of Europe together that summer."

"I'll bet you did. Kevin always loved traveling. You were over there teaching?" He had pulled the tip of a cigarette from the pack in his hand, and she was watching him, disapproval apparent. "Do you mind?" he asked, just before the filter end reached his mouth.

"I don't have any ashtrays," she said stiffly.

The pack hesitated, and then a forefinger pushed the chosen cigarette back in its place. "I guess that means you mind."

She saw no reason to allow him to increase the discomfort he was causing her. "I guess it does."

He stuffed the cigarette back into his pocket and leaned back, slouching into the plump cushions as he draped both arms along the back of the couch like a great-winged condor settling over a buoying current of air. As if testing its resilience, he patted the ledge of the backrest with both hands several times before attempting another conversation launch. "So what's her name?"

"Whose name?"

"The little girl. My brother's daughter."

She returned with a level gaze. "My daughter's name is Danielle. She was named for my landlady in Paris, who was very good to me after..."

"Was she born over there?" he wondered.

"No. I came home, and she was born here." She offered him a self-deprecating little smile. "The birth of my daughter marked the end of my Paris period. Being a starving artist in

Paris was an adventure, but the prospect of being a starving mother with child was something else.''

"Artist, huh?" Somehow he couldn't picture Kevin with an artist. "How old is Danielle?" He knew, of course. Just thought he'd confirm it.

"She's going to be five...in March."

That figured right. Almost five. "It's been five years, hasn't it?" he said, absently marveling at the number. How could it have been that long?

"Yes. Five years. Do you know...did the army tell you what happened?"

What happened. Kevin was killed; that's what happened. Kevin came back from his grand and glorious tour of duty in a regulation army casket. Connor simply shook his head, staring past Sarah into a fire that danced in the blackened brick box across the room. The body, they'd said, was charred beyond recognition.

"I never even knew where it happened," Sarah explained. "His friend Chuck told me Kevin's helicopter went down and that his body had been shipped back to his family. Of course, I had no claim on him, but I think it would have helped to...to have gone to a funeral or something."

Connor shrugged, turning his mouth down in disagreement. "Didn't help me one damned bit. I wanted to take him home, back to California, but my father insisted on Arlington, with all the military pomp and circumstance. So there we were, putting this box in the ground, and where was Kevin? He was alive last time I saw him."

He gave her a look that told her he'd never quite made his peace with it. "Somewhere in the Middle East was what they told us. Highly secret operation. We have no idea what he was doing—whether he was shot down or what. Those big choppers he flew—they can be involved in most anything, I guess."

For the first moment since he'd arrived, Sarah shared a plane of feeling with Connor. For a moment they occupied that place, the feeling of emptiness, together. "It doesn't matter how it happened, though, does it?'' she noted. ''He *is* dead, isn't he? That's what it comes down to.''

''Yes, that's what it comes down to.''

Sarah watched the fire dance in his eyes and wondered if his memories were anything like hers. Despite the physical resemblance, this man reminded her of Kevin only in incidental ways—a gesture now and then, the way his hair caught the light. Kevin had been a small-talk artist, a genius at livening things up—the kind of person everyone sought for good company. He'd had only one mood—good-natured. His brother, Connor, was obviously a man of many moods, and he hadn't made any small talk.

''Would you like to see her?'' Sarah asked, gently disturbing some reverie.

''Hmm? See her?''

''Dannie. We've been out all day, and she's exhausted. She fell asleep right after supper.''

''I don't want to wake her, but I would like to see her, if that's okay with you. Just to look at her, I mean.'' He didn't believe he'd heard himself say that. Best thing to do was find out what the woman wanted and get the hell out of here. But he was already following her upstairs to the little girl's room.

A small lamp with a wooden-pony base filled the room with soft light. Treading awkwardly across the floor on the balls of his feet, Connor felt like a gorilla in a poodle's cage. Everything in the room was pink and white and miniature. The small braided rug by the bed thankfully muffled his footsteps, and he sank his weight back onto his heels. Looking down at Dannie, her blond curls cast about her little face in disarray, he saw Kevin. The only concession her visage made to her mother was the perfect bow of a mouth. She was Kevin's daughter.

Connor wasn't thinking as he sank to one knee beside the bed. He forgot about the woman standing behind him when he reached past the glassy-eyed teddy bear and touched the fine wisps of cottony hair that framed the child's face. He caught himself smiling, and then he pulled back. He'd probably awaken her and she might start to cry or something. Swallowing convulsively, he headed for the door.

Several steps down the hallway, Connor felt more than heard Sarah at his back. He knew he should smile casually and toss off a compliment. What would Kevin have said to smooth things over? Kevin, of course, would never have gotten choked up when he wanted most to keep his cool.

"She's...she's a pretty little kid, Sarah. She looks just like Kevin."

Who looked just like you, Sarah thought. It must have been a strange moment for this man, seeing his dead brother's only child for the first time. "Do you have any children of your own?"

"Me? No. No children. I'm not married." And neither was Kevin.

Sarah paused at the top of the stairs to watch Connor hurry to the bottom, his feet passing over each step with hardly a touch of the soles. He seemed relieved to reach the floor, and he strode directly into the living room. Following, Sarah saw him go for his cigarettes again before he thought better of it. She offered him a carnival-glass dish she'd picked up at a rummage sale.

"That's not an ashtray," he noted.

"No, but it's washable." He took the dish and gratefully lit up a cigarette. "Would you like some coffee?" she asked. "I'd offer you a drink, but I don't have anything in the house."

"Figures." He blew a quick stream of smoke toward his right shoulder, away from her face. "Coffee's fine."

While she was out of the room, he busied himself with looking around. The room was homey and comfortable, but everything seemed more used than she, in her years on her own, could have made it. He wondered if the house belonged to her parents—grandparents, even—and whether they still lived here.

The paintings on the walls were the only furnishings that weren't either worn or obviously refurbished. They were originals, and they were unique in character. Connor didn't know much about art, but these looked like the kind a real art buff might like. They were certainly better than those huge things the interior decorator had put in his own living room in Santa Cruz. He took a closer look at an unframed still life of purple and white cut flowers. It had her signature in the corner.

"What do you think?"

Connor turned toward the sound of her voice, feeling almost as though he'd been caught peeping into her closet. He shrugged, smiling sheepishly. "Very nice. I don't know much about art, but I'd gladly hang these on my wall."

"That's as good a measure as any," she said. "If you enjoy seeing it every day, it's a good piece."

The tray she set on a side table bore two steaming stoneware mugs and cream and sugar. He took his coffee black, returning to the couch while she doctored hers up. Her rich brown hair, hitched back over her shoulder and draping along the side of her face as she bent toward the table, was an exotic contrast with her fair face. Below the neck it was hard to tell what she might look like. In her T-shirt and man-size flannel shirt over loose-fitting jeans, she was hardly dressed to kill. Must be her artist's outfit, Connor thought, hoping she didn't always dress like that.

"So Paris is the place to go if you want to be a starving artist," he reflected. "What do you do when you're tired of starving?"

"You come back to the land of opportunity, where you either find a job or improvise one." The opposite end of the couch offered the best view of the fire, she reasoned as she rejoined him there.

"How do you improvise a job?"

"When you have a baby to look after, you figure out what kind of employment doesn't preclude having her with you."

"And?"

"And—the obvious. Housekeeping. I have a housekeeping business."

"A housekeeping business?" He squinted at her through a lazy haze of smoke. "You mean you're a maid?"

She didn't like the sound of the word the way he said it. "I do housekeeping for a number of clients. I set my own hours, and Dannie goes with me. The pay is pretty good, and it allows me to set aside blocks of time for my painting."

"You can't make a living as an artist?" he asked. "From the looks of these, I'd say you're too good to waste your time…"

Sarah laughed, shaking her head. "After I'm dead, someone will probably realize that. But right now it isn't steady. The gallery sells a piece once in a while, but we can't depend on it. I *can* depend on people's houses getting dirty." She watched him over the rim of her cup. For some reason he appeared to be dissatisfied with that answer. Who was he to judge the worthiness of her livelihood? It was time to discuss something else. "What kind of music do you play?"

"I'm with Georgia Nights. Heard of them?" Say no and I won't be able to keep a straight face.

"I think Jerry mentioned the name of your group to me once, but it wasn't one I recognized. You're not from Georgia."

That gave him the excuse he needed to laugh. "Only when we're on tour, honey," he drawled. "Then I'm jest as down-home as suhthun fried chicken an' black-eyed peas." He enjoyed laughing with her and forgot how she'd precipitated it. "Actually, I've lived so many places, I could say I'm from anywhere. When Mike introduces me—Mike Tanner, the lead—he uses the town I've lived in that's closest to the concert city, says that's where I'm from. Works pretty slick. When I play my solo, they go crazy for the hometown boy."

"Maybe they just go crazy for your music," she suggested. Her remark seemed to surprise him, but he said nothing. "Your father was in the army, too, wasn't he? Is that why you moved around so much?"

"Yeah. I had enough moving to last me a lifetime."

"But your business must keep you on the move quite a bit."

His left hand signaled a correction. "I have to travel, maybe, but I don't have to *move*. I have a house of my own now, and it's always in the same place, always there for me to go back to. I spend a lot of time there, believe it or not. No crowds, no schedules—just me and my music."

"Is it country music your band plays?"

She certainly was working hard to convince him she didn't know who he was. He sank back into the cushions again, taking a last pull on the cigarette he'd all but forgotten and wondered why she'd decided on this ignorant tack. All it took was one look at the kid. Surely she could see she'd gotten him with that. He was good for a reasonable amount of support for Kevin's kid. What the hell?—he had the money and nothing better to do with it. And she'd already told him she was a *maid*, for God's sake. Now she was going to feed him some highbrow I'm-not-familiar-with-pop-music routine? "Country rock," he answered, crushing his cigarette into the pink dish she'd given him.

"And you sing?" she asked.

"Not usually the lead, but, yeah, I sing—play lead guitar, a little banjo, fiddle. I write some of our music."

That caught her interest. "You write music? What have you written?"

He smiled only with his mouth. Now he was cool. Now he was creative—an artist, just like her. "You remember 'Gentle On My Mind' and 'Me and Bobby McGee'?"

"Yes," she answered brightly.

"I didn't write either of those."

"Oh."

He chuckled. "I wrote 'Dressed For Dancing' and 'Your Soft Voice.'" She shook her head slowly. "How about 'Misty River Morning'?"

"Oh, yes. That's a lovely song. I've heard it. You wrote that?" He dipped his head in acknowledgment, surprised to find that her recognition of his song pleased him. "Then I have heard your music on the radio. I'm sorry—I guess I don't pay that much attention to the names of the groups, but I remember the song well.''

"That song did well for us," he admitted. "What kind of music do you like? Classical?''

Sarah lifted a shoulder. "I listen to whatever suits my mood. I'm not very trendy. I guess I'm not much for real hard rock or...or the real twangy country stuff. When I hear something I like, I listen.''

"Sort of like me with the painting," he observed.

"Exactly. I don't buy records, though, so I don't always take note of the...artists' names.'' She smiled around the word that gave them a common bond.

"Yeah, well, I bought some paintings that this decorator lady said I needed, but I like yours a whole lot better. Think I'll throw that stuff out and start over.''

Throw it out! Why did money have to be wasted on the rich? "Is your group as popular as Jerry claims?''

Connor stiffened visibly. That's right, Sarah, let's see your true colors now. "We had the best-selling country album last year. We're doing pretty well.''

"Funny. Kevin said you were a singer, but he didn't tell me you were...''

"I wasn't then." One of life's great unfairnesses was that Kevin hadn't lived to see Connor's success. He took his cup up from the end table and drained what was left of the luke-warm coffee. "And obviously I've yet to make an impression in...what town is this?''

"Amherst.''

"I've yet to win some of the prominent hearts in Amherst, Massachusetts. Let's see if I can remedy that, shall we? What do you need, Sarah?''

"What do you mean?''

"What do you need for Dannie? And for yourself, too. Hell, Kevin owes you. Do you want a trust fund and a monthly allowance? That's probably the best way in the long run, al-though...''

"What are you talking about?" Sarah bit out, each word pronounced more precisely than the last.

"Listen, I'm not going to be able to fill in for Kevin, much as I'd like to." He gave her a quick but appreciative once-over. "But I can handle being a rich uncle. Kevin was my only brother. Far as I know, this is his only kid. I *would* like to be able to see her sometimes, if that's—"

"You are way out of line, *Mr.* Ryan," Sarah said quietly. If Connor had known her better, he'd have recognized her growing anger. The angrier she got, the quieter and more measured her words became. "I don't care who you are or what you do for a living. I want *none* of your money."

"What do you mean, none of my money? What do you want, then?"

"Mr. Ryan, you are the one who came to *my* home. You came to see *my* daughter, which I have allowed you to do."

"Right. And there's no doubt in my mind now—she's my niece. I'm willing to pay...."

"There's no charge, Mr. Ryan. You are, as you say, her uncle. I won't charge you for admission into her life. With my supervision, you may visit my daughter. She has precious little family, and if you want to take your place as part of that, then fine. But we neither need nor want your money."

Connor couldn't figure this one out. She really didn't sound like she was angling for anything. In fact, she sounded downright mad. He'd never had much patience with being tactful. "Listen, Sarah, I'm not saying you aren't doing fine on your own. You're obviously working pretty hard, and you deserve a break. I really don't mind helping out with Kevin's kid. Hey—" he punctuated his innocence with an open palm and a single-shouldered shrug "—you wouldn't believe the way people come after you with all kinds of stories. I've been threatened with more than one paternity suit. I've had letters from at least a hundred high-school girlfriends. Somebody forgot to tell me what a great adolescence I had." He shook his head in mock disbelief. "I must have been a hell of a stud."

That got a sudden burst of laughter out of her, and Connor

felt the muscles in his back relax. He hadn't realized he'd tensed up that much. Laughing with her, he continued the story, hoping he was facilitating a mood change. "I pretty much discount the ones who remember how witty and charming I was. I figure that must have been Kevin using my ID."

He had her smiling, mainly because she imagined there were lots of Jerrys in the world, and people like Connor must have dealt with the best of them. Jerry was such a bungler, and he'd answer to Sarah for this one. "But you don't discount all the letters, and you're willing to donate your money," she surmised, "when you think someone deserves a break."

"When the request is reasonable and the grounds are legitimate, yes."

"And how are those conditions determined?"

"Usually my accountant determines 'reasonable' and my attorney decides 'legitimate.' But in this case…"

"And just what was my brother's request?" she asked quietly.

"He didn't come right out and ask for anything, really. He said he knew I was coming to Springfield for a concert, and he thought I might like to meet my brother's daughter. He had all the right details and sent the right picture to pique my interest."

"I see." Maybe Jerry wasn't such a bungler after all. It sounded as though he'd researched this quite carefully.

"It's a nice picture," Connor noted, leaning slightly toward her now because she was talking so quietly.

"Dannie's very photogenic."

"It's a nice picture of you."

His eyes caught hers, and again the sharp blue gaze seemed to rivet her soul, penetrating more deeply than Kevin's ever had. He held her that way for a time, then released her at his leisure. "So nobody's asked for anything," Connor concluded, "but I'm offering anyway."

"Thank you for the offer."

"You know, you could have gotten child support from the army. Under the circumstances…"

"I know that," she assured him, reaching for his cup. "More coffee?"

"No, thanks. You wouldn't have to feel like that was charity or anything. It would be more like you were giving Kevin a chance to support his child. He was a career officer, you know. Bound to have been a thirty-year man like his father."

"I wasn't married to Kevin," Sarah reminded him patiently. "Danielle has my name."

A slight frown clouded Connor's face. "But if Kevin had lived, you would have been married."

The cups were deposited on the tray, which gave Sarah the opportunity to hide a smile. For all his contemporary fame, there was something about Connor that rang with the charm of old-world propriety. He was here to do the right thing by his brother's child because Kevin had died before he could do the right thing himself. It wouldn't surprise her if Connor proposed marriage once he was fully convinced she wasn't an opportunist, tossing his freedom to the wind to save the Ryan name.

"I don't know what would have happened if Kevin had lived." It was as honest an assessment as she'd ever been able to come up with in all her "what-if" deliberations since Kevin's death. "We were two very different people, but in that situation, living overseas, the mere fact that we were both Americans gave us common ground. Here, of course, that would have meant exactly nothing."

"You mean...you didn't love him?" For some reason, that possibility set uneasily in his stomach.

"Oh, yes, I loved him very much. What's not to love with Kevin?" Sarah smiled, knowing Connor would understand. "He was everybody's friend—always pleasant, always optimistic, always had a good story to tell. But he belonged to the army. We saw Europe together—Paris, Nice, Venice, Florence—the most romantic cities in the world. That part was all my romantic fantasies come true. But if I never see the inside of another officers' club, that'll be fine with me. That was one part of Kevin's life I could never have shared. I loved him, but I don't know whether I could have lived with him.''

"Yet you had his baby,'' Connor pointed out.

Sarah heard his indignation and thought only that it was understandable under the circumstances. "Yes, I did. What do you say about the untimely birth of the child who's become the light of your life? That she was a mistake? I know now that I was very careless and that I was foolish in my relationship with Kevin. I only knew how I felt. I didn't think ahead. I had no business letting myself get pregnant.''

And Kevin had no business getting you pregnant. I heard the same lectures he did. "You could have terminated it,'' he said flatly.

"Oh, but I thank God I didn't. I can't imagine being without Dannie. She's very much like Kevin, you know…always cheerful and friendly.''

"And you can live with that?''

She detected a teasing sparkle in his eyes, and she refused to take offense, laughing instead with, "I can handle the budding stages. Her husband will have to live with the admirers when she becomes a full-blown crowd pleaser.''

A click in his cheek and an engaging wink punctuated his agreement. "The crowds can be hard to take.''

"I'm sure yours are more pressing than Kevin's ever were.''

"I used to think more would be better.'' I used to think outdistancing Kevin would make it better. "I was wrong. I like to think there are people out there who enjoy my music, but crowds…'' He smiled sheepishly with the admission. "I have to swallow my stomach every time I go out onstage.''

"And when you get out there?''

"When I get out there, I don't see the crowd. I see a few faces in the front row.''

"But you hear them.''

"They approve, so I like hearing them. What about you? How do you feel when you sell a painting?''

"I feel a few dollars richer. Oh, yes,'' she agreed, studying her hands, suddenly noticing that they were speckled with paint and wishing she looked a little more presentable, "I want my work to be recognized, praised by the critics, exhibited in the best galleries." She glanced up, smiling. "I don't want a crowd, but I'd like to see a few faces in the front row."

He returned the conspiratory smile. "Yeah, well, wait till the old boyfriends start coming out of the woodwork." He slid to the edge of the couch and braced his palm on his knees. "So...are you going to take my money or what, Sarah Benedict?"

"No, Mr. Ryan, I am not going to take your money." This time she gave him a merry grin when she called him "Mr. Ryan."

"Then sell me a painting."

"What painting?"

"Any painting. They all look nice from up here in the front row."

"You don't need a painting," she protested.

"If you saw the junk in my living room, you'd eat those words, Sarah Benedict."

His eyes were dancing, and in this mood, as in the others, she'd seen the life in them was far more intense than his brother's had been. "Choose one, then."

"The one with the purple flowers," he said, tossing his chin back over his shoulder.

"It's yours, with my compliments."

"Compliments, hell," he roared, but he toned his voice down when she shushed him. "I said I wanted to *buy* it."

"Would you deny me the satisfaction of making my first donation to a culturally deprived living room?"

The squeak and slam of the front door cut the conversation short. "I didn't hear anyone drive up," Sarah said, puzzled.

"I hope Dannie's a sound sleeper," Connor mumbled, following Sarah's lead as she stood to investigate.

"Hey, Sister Sarah, I need a bunk for the night." The voice was Jerry's, and Jerry was drunk. "Pepper threw me out again."

"It's Jerry," Sarah offered in a low whisper. "Listen, I

know you have every right to be furious with him, but please, not tonight. I'm afraid he's...''

Connor raised a hand in protest. ''Hey, I'm not mad at anybody. I came of my own accord. What's a Pepper?''

Sarah stifled a laugh, letting it escape through her nose. ''I should answer with a jingle, but I can't sing. Pepper's his girlfriend.''

Jerry did a little fumbling at the coat tree before propping his shoulder against the archway and peering curiously at his sister's guest. Recognition dawned gradually through the fog. ''Are you...is it real- ly...Connor Ryan?''

''Mr. Ryan, this is my brother...''

''Jerry Bendict.'' He'd lost one syllable of his name, but the handshake was there. Curly brown hair, dark eyes, underweight, Jerry looked like a twenty-five-year-old teenager.

''Connor Ryan.''

''Connor Ryan! Oh, wow.'' Having accomplished the handshake, Jerry managed a feat of even greater agility as he spun a full circle on one foot, catching himself at three-hundred-and-sixty-five degrees. ''I can't believe it. Connor Ryan. You're the best there is, man! If I could play the guitar like you do...''

''Jerry...'' Sarah warned.

''I really appreciated your letter, Jerry. We had no idea that Kevin had a—''

''I knew you'd feel that way, Connor. When I found out that you were little Dannie's uncle, I knew it was my duty to get in touch with you. 'Course, I suspected it for some time, but I checked it all out just to make sure. I tried to tell Sarah, but she doesn't know anything about music, and I knew she wouldn't go along with the idea of getting in touch, so I just...hell, man, I knew you'd wanna...''

''Jerry...'' Sarah tried again.

''You did the right thing, Jerry,'' Connor assured him.

''See, Sarah? I did the right thing. For once I did the right thing. And here's Connor Ryan, standing right here on your very own floor, just as casual as you please.'' Jerry's attempt at giving Connor a friendly punch in the shoulder missed its mark as he whirled off balance, landing in Connor's arms.

Sarah was mortified. Connor laughed as he deposited Jerry in a nearby chair. "See now, Sister Sarah," Jerry spouted, wagging a finger at her. "We're sittin' pretty now. For once I did the right thing."

Afraid of what her brother would say next, Sarah turned pleading eyes on Connor. "You'd better go now. He can be such a blubberer when he's drunk."

"You sure you don't want me to help you get him to bed?"

"I don't think he'd go to bed as long as you're here. He'll just fall asleep in the chair, which is what he deserves."

"Pretty hardhearted of you, Sister Sarah." But Connor's sympathy was obviously for Sarah.

"Hey, Connor, ol' buddy, your concert is sold out, did you know that?" Jerry was trying to sit up straight in the chair with little success. "And you know, I couldn't get any tickets."

Humiliated, Sarah closed her eyes briefly, hoping Connor would close his ears to that familiar whine of Jerry's. Her hands found Connor's arm, and she urged him toward the door. "Really, I don't mean to be rude, but I wish you'd go now."

He covered her hand with the warmth of his, offering a reassuring squeeze. "I'll call you."

In a moment, he was gone. Her hand still tingling from the touch of his, Sarah turned an accusing glare on her brother.

He gave her that infuriating cockeyed grin of his. "I guess you're mad at me, huh?"

Chapter Two

Mad at him, yes, and Sarah stayed mad until Jerry packed up his hangover and crawled back to Pepper's. His flying eyebrows over his silly rolling eyes didn't get him anywhere with Sarah, so he finally gave up, the act causing him more pain than it was worth. He left the house reasonably happy. He'd met his idol, and though the previous night's scene came back to him only in snatches, he remembered shaking hands with "the Man."

Connor's call came midmorning. Over the phone his voice was an aural déjà vu, but Sarah's mind saw Connor, not Kevin, and that surprised her. If Dannie was awake, he wondered if he could see her. He'd flown in ahead of the group just for this purpose, and since the others wouldn't be in town until tomorrow for the concert, he had the day free. If Sarah had plans, he'd like her to go ahead with them and include him. Great! He'd be there in an hour.

"Mommy, look what I found in my closet. A big envelope with a string tied around it, just like a present."

Sarah hung the receiver on its hook and turned to watch her daughter drag a portfolio into the kitchen and plunk it down next to the table. "That was way back in the cubbyhole, Dannie. What were you looking for?"

"My pink-elephant pants. I wanna wear them today."

Sarah sighed, lowering herself to sit cross-legged on the floor by the portfolio, which Dannie was busy unlacing. "Those are much too small for you, sweetheart. I put them in with the giveaways."

Dannie flashed blue-eyed dismay at her mother. "Don't give my pink-elephant pants away! I can still fit in them. I wanna wear those today."

"Dannie, today of all days would not be a good one to wear clothes that look too small. You can wear your new corduroy bibs with the Tinker Bell on them."

Dannie brightened just as the long brown lace on the portfolio came undone in her hands. "My new ones? I don't have to save them anymore?"

"I think today's the day we were saving them for." Sarah smiled, cupping her daughter's cheek in a gesture that said, "You and me, babe." It was a sticky situation but one she and Dannie could help each other handle. "You're going to meet your uncle today, Dannie." Dannie's face puckered into a question. "Not Uncle Jerry—he's my brother. This man—Uncle...Uncle Connor..." It sounded so strange she decided she'd better practice it a few times before he came. "Uncle Connor is your father's brother. He's come all the way from California to meet you, and we're going to..."

"I thought we were going to climb the mountain today," Dannie groaned.

"We are. Uncle Connor's coming with us."

"Oh. Okay," she agreed, returning to the investigation of the portfolio. "Look, Mommy, pictures." Pulling her face back from the envelope, Dannie produced a handful of charcoal-and-pastel sketches, their colors long ago fixed with spray. "Did you make these, Mommy?"

Sarah took them from her hand and leafed through the stack.

Until last night she hadn't thought about those Paris days in a long time. The sketches looked almost alien to her now, done, as they had been, by a wide-eyed ingenue who wanted nothing more than to steep herself in the great works of art and to mingle with the artists at Montmartre. She'd perfected her French as a sidewalk portrait painter. She was better than most, but the American tourists wanted their portraits done by "real" artists, which meant Frenchmen. She'd also learned the best defenses against the French flirt and the occasional ugly American. Kevin had called it classy slumming, but it was an education Sarah couldn't have gotten anywhere else.

"Who's that?" Dannie wondered, pointing to the smiling face in Sarah's hand.

"It really looks more like your Uncle Connor than your father." A tilted view of the portrait didn't change anything. "Isn't that funny? Frailty, thy name must be woman."

"My Uncle Connor?" Dannie mused, studying the pastel sketch.

"No, honey, this was your father. But your Uncle Connor looks very much like this."

"My father who was killed in the war?"

Dannie's upturned face still looked for a reasonable explanation of that term, one she'd substituted for "killed in the army" after she'd heard it recently in a movie. Sarah knew none of the words could make any sense to a four-year-old, and there wasn't much point in trying to alleviate any minor misconceptions yet. "Yes, your father who was killed. When you see your Uncle Connor, you'll know what your father looked like."

Dannie was quiet for another moment as she perused the picture again. Then she uncurled her legs one at a time and hopped to her feet. "I'm going to put my new pants on now," she decided, and she scampered around the corner and up the stairs.

The house looked infinitely better this morning. Maybe it was the sunlight. Or perhaps it was the red-and-yellow-leaf show, which was best performed by New England trees on just such an October day. Connor's heavily treaded running shoes greeted the gravel driveway like a rubberized track. The car door sang out the announcement of his arrival, and he leaped over three steps to the porch. With a conscious curb on his exuberance, he rapped the door knocker.

When the door swung open, the perfect porcelain face he expected at eye level wasn't there. He had to drop his expectations several feet to find his greeter. Hair a few shades lighter than his, eyes exactly his shade of azure, she squinted up at him against the morning sun and inquired quite efficiently, "Are you my Uncle Connor?"

"Yes, ma'am, I am."

"Then you can come in."

Connor closed the door behind him and hunkered down on his heels to greet this young relative at her eye level. For Connor, relatives were in short supply, and the more complicated his life became, the more he wished he had a close relation or two. This one looked pretty harmless, and her smile promised to be a bright spot in this day and maybe in more to come.

"You're my father's brother," Dannie instructed.

"That's right," Connor confirmed.

"And you look just like him."

"Right again."

"But he's dead and you're not."

Bull's-eye. Leave it to a kid to squeeze everything into a nutshell. No glib reply for that one.

"I'm glad you're not dead because that means you can climb the mountain with us. When I get tired of walking, you can carry me." Dannie surveyed his shoulders and mentally assessed the possibilities. "You think you can carry me?"

"Let's see if I can even lift you." Connor scooped her into his arms, and she rose on a child's favorite elevator. "You're a pretty big girl, but I'm a pretty strong guy," he assured her.

"You think we'll make it up the mountain?"

"How big a mountain is it?"

"Really big," Dannie emphasized, lifting a small hand above her head.

"Well, I'm *really* strong," Connor drawled back.

Both heads turned for Sarah's descent on the stairway. Connor felt his mouth go dry as he watched. The soft violet turtleneck under a thick plum pullover and matching slim-fitting jeans were a vast improvement over yesterday's artist's outfit. Her hair was pulled neatly back into a French braid exposing a little widow's peak, which he hadn't noticed before. She was an artist with makeup, too, for though he detected hints of pink gloss and blush and a touch of mascara that hadn't been there the night before, her appearance was soft and natural.

She looked up smiling, feeling his appraisal. "I see you two have found each other."

His sense of where he was came back to him. "Oh, yeah, recognized each other right off. I'm told my job is to carry little girls when they get tired, so we're trying it out. Do I pass muster, Dannie?"

Dannie eyed Connor as though he'd suddenly become a very strange bird. "Mommy made all the sandwiches with mayonnaise. You don't put mustard on chicken. Yuk!"

Laughing as he lowered her to the floor, Connor had the feeling that whatever this little girl came up with would delight him. "I have to get my jacket," she reported, spinning away like a dervish.

Sarah collected the backpack she'd already prepared, then loaded it and Dannie into the back seat of Connor's rental car and directed Connor along the winding road over "the Notch" and into South Hadley. The car was left in the parking lot of an isolated tavern chinked into the hillside, and Sarah led the way along the easy grade of the path in the woods. Dannie chattered as she darted out ahead, squealing at squirrels and stuffing the pockets of her jacket with acorns.

Connor carried the backpack and admired Sarah's brisk gait when she went on ahead in her attempt to keep up with Dannie's explorations. Sarah spun toward him, smiling happily and motioning for a quicker pace. He picked it up a little, noting that she hadn't lost a step, but he thought better of telling her that he liked the view from a few paces back.

He felt good. He felt youthful and exhilarated as he drank autumn's air like a draught of crisp, tangy beer. He'd forgotten that New England had an exclusive contract for top quality with the Maker of Autumn and no other place did it better. Nowhere else had he seen reds, yellows and oranges this vibrant. The smell of the woods' rich humus was one he hoped he could store in his nose, to be used later when he was stuck in some stuffy hotel-room party. This was a day for keeping in your memory—a Saturday-afternoon-football-game day, a joyride-in-the-country day...a walk-in-the-woods-with-two-pretty-girls day. He'd enjoy these moments many times over.

They had veered off the footpath at Dannie's insistence, and Sarah seemed to know where her daughter was headed. Connor ducked a low-hanging branch and shuffled through the accumulation of brittle brown leaves.

"Are you girls gonna try to tell me this is the *mountain* you were talking about?" he challenged in his best cowboy drawl. "This here ain't no *mountain*. Why, where I come from, we'd call this jus' a lil' blister on ol' Atlas's back."

"Leave it to you westerners to call this lovely place a 'blister,'" Sarah scolded. "This is Mount Holyoke, a princess of a mountain, fine boned and delicately featured—not like your big rugged peaks."

Dannie had found what she was looking for, and they slowed to a halt while she proceeded to rummage around in the rocks at the base of a gray shale ledge.

Connor plucked a mottled leaf from a tree and studied its veined red, yellow and green pattern. "Princess, huh?" He glanced down at Sarah's upturned face. "She's a pretty one; I'll grant you that. I can go along with princess of a hill. But if you want to play King of the Mountain, you have to go west, young lady."

"I like rugged peaks, too," Sarah said quietly, her eyes on his face.

"And I like delicate features," he returned.

Dannie's voice severed their eye contact. "I can't find any, Mommy."

Connor hunkered down beside Dannie, who squatted with her chin between her knees as only a four-year-old can manage. "What are you looking for, Princess?"

Dannie responded with a broad smile. Being a princess was special. "This is where I found a trilobite once."

"Oh, yeah?" Connor dug into the rock pile with her. "What's a trilobite?"

"It's a bug. About a million years old."

"You sure it's not a fish?" he asked, carefully examining a piece of shale.

"Well, maybe a bug fish," Dannie compromised.

"How about an arthropod?" he offered, tossing the shale and reaching for another.

"What's an arthropod?"

"It's a sort of a...bug fish," Connor agreed, extending a find in his hand. "How about this?"

"What?" Dannie peeked over the blunt tips of four large fingers. Sarah knelt to join the pair, curious.

"It's a fossil, too," Connor said.

Dannie took it, studied it and pocketed it. "It's just a fern. They're easy. I wish I could find another trilobite."

"Kevin and I used to hunt for arrowheads. I've got a whole box full." Uncurling himself and offering Sarah a hand, Connor concluded, "Kevin never had much patience with it, though. All he ever found was pottery shards."

"Kevin," Dannie echoed. "My father's name was Kevin, wasn't it?"

Connor and Sarah exchanged glances and dropped hands at the same instant, Connor wondering how often the name had been mentioned and Sarah realizing she said "your father" more often than "Kevin" and both more rarely as time went on.

"That's right, Princess. His name was Kevin," Connor affirmed. "Now, when are you going to show me the top of this so-called mountain?"

Connor was puffing when they reached the peak. Smoking had been cutting his wind lately, and it bothered him. He knew he'd have to quit before it also cut his vocal range. But he retreated to a spot with a good view and lit up a cigarette while Sarah took care of the contents of the backpack, which he hoped meant food. Chicken with mustard, even. He was hungry.

In his plaid shirt jacket and tight blue jeans, Connor looked as strong and hard as he'd sworn to Dannie he was. Sarah wondered how he moved with the rhythm of his music. Every rock singer seemed to have his own moves. She wondered if the young girls in his audiences went wild when he did his act for them. His hair caught the early-afternoon sun in white-gold snatches as the breeze ruffled it over his tanned forehead. Watching this man grind his hips against the back of an electric guitar would probably drive her wild, too.

With his heel he dug a hole in the dirt, took a last drag on the cigarette before he squatted and buried the last of it, killing the ash with a twist of his foot. Brushing his hands on his thighs, Connor looked up and caught Sarah staring at him. A slow smile spread across his face. The porcelain lady did a little sight-seeing herself now and then.

"Uncle Connor, will you take me up on the fire tower?" Dannie pleaded as though for the hundredth time. "Mommy won't let Uncle Jerry take me up because she says he's too silly. But you could take me, couldn't you, Uncle Connor?"

Connor helped himself to a second sandwich as he sized up the eighty-foot steel structure that stood in the clearing behind them.

"I don't want this, Mommy," Dannie said.

Sarah received the remnants of a sandwich and sacked them, saying, "Dannie, the tower is too tall."

"But you could take me, couldn't you, Uncle Connor?"

"Sure I could. You wanna see what's up there, Princess?"

"Oh, yes!"

"Oh, no!" her mother wailed. "It's too high."

"It's perfectly safe, Sarah. Look—there's a fence around

the platform and a railing all the way up the steps. Let's all go up when we're done here."

Jerry had often tried to get her to climb the tower and she'd always refused. But for some reason she wanted Connor to think she was a good sport. He took her silence to be assent, and Dannie was beside herself until the leftover pumpkin bread was rewrapped and the apple cores were in the garbage sack.

"You go first, and I'll be right behind you with Dannie," Connor instructed, standing to one side with Dannie in one arm and his other hand on the rail.

"Oh...I don't think I..."

"Sure you can. I'll be right behind you. Just don't look down until we get to the top."

"Ohhh," she moaned quietly, but she'd made up her mind she was going to try. This fear of heights had crept up on her as she'd gotten older, and she didn't like it. When she was a kid, she could climb any tree her brother could. Gripping the railing, Sarah planted first one foot on a clanging step and then the other. She concentrated on the top and did pretty well until she let herself sneak a glimpse of her feet. Her stomach dropped right through the grillwork of the step and tumbled to the ground.

Connor heard her gasp. "Don't look down," he reminded her. "You're doing fine."

Don't look down. That's what they always say, she thought. Sarah's knees became glutinous, but she lifted her chin and resolutely pressed on. "'Atta girl," she heard him say. "Straight to the top, honey, you can do it."

Sarah headed for the middle of the platform immediately. When Connor and Dannie joined her, she grabbed his arm and stared ahead, never up, never *never* down. She wondered when her knees would go. Her stomach was long gone. Connor, meanwhile, was enchanted with the perfect horseshoe bend in the Connecticut River, with the blaze of color that burned across the valley like Moses' bush, with the...

"Sarah, are you all right?" The color had drained from her lips. Not a good sign.

"If we could just go back down now..." The voice was too small to be hers.

"Sure we can. We've seen enough, haven't we, Princess?" Dannie nodded happily. "We'll go first." Three steps toward the stairs, and Sarah froze in her tracks. Connor worked his arm loose from her grip and quickly draped it around her, pulling her against his side. She latched on to his jacket, a hand in front and one in back. "This isn't going to be easy, is it?" Connor mumbled. In the pocket of his shoulder he felt her shake her head.

"Okay," he resolved. "We do this in stages. Sarah, you're going to sit right down in the middle of this thing and stay put until I get Dannie down."

"Oh, no," she whispered. "Please don't leave me alone up here. I'll die."

"Mommy's gonna—"

"No, she's not." Tension on his left, and now tension on his right. "Sarah, you're scaring the k-i-d. Tell her you're all right."

"I'm fine, sweetheart." Not very convincing.

"Okay." Connor was repeating himself. "Now we all sit down together. Easy." Halfway down he became everybody's sole support. "Good going. It doesn't seem so bad now, does it?" He drew back and watched Sarah shake her head. She'd sprouted saucers for eyes and gone all chalky. Still not very convincing. Connor kept talking as he moved away from Sarah and started down the steps. "Keep your eyes right here, Sarah. Straight ahead. I'll disappear for just a minute, and then I'll be right back."

"Hold on to Dannie," she called out with what sounded like the last of her voice. Connor disappeared with Sarah's daughter, but his voice reached back to Sarah. She strained to hold on to it even as it faded with his footfalls down the stairs, and she took heart as it picked up in volume again.

"Holding on to Dannie. Be right back...I'll have you down

on the ground in no time—standing on your feet, of course! You're gonna be just fine, honey…we're almost at the bottom…just two more steps…here we are! Hang in there, Sarah! I'm on my way up, baby, hold on…just a few more steps, honey, I'm flying…here—'' he gasped ''—here I am, Sarah.''

Getting her to the top of the steps was difficult, but getting her to take the first step down presented real problems. They were steep-graded fire-escape steps, and negotiating them without looking down would be next to impossible. He should have realized that, but hindsight was…hindsight.

''We're going down the way we came up, honey—you looking up and me right behind you.'' She shook her head quickly. Her voice *was* gone. ''Yes, we are. Listen, I know what I'm doing. I was an ironworker once.'' He was prying her left hand off the rail and turning her around. Always one step below her, one arm around her waist, the other hand on the rail, he guided her down, looking out for both of them.

''I'm a regular Spiderman. No kidding. Look up, baby. Keep looking up. I won't let you fall.'' Their feet scraped the metal grillwork with each slow step, and as they neared the bottom, her stiff tremors became spasmodic shudders. Finally, she sobbed.

He stopped for a moment and put both arms around her. ''I won't let you fall, Sarah. Trust me. I'll get you down.'' His quiet reassurance steadied her, and when he asked, ''Are you ready now?'' she nodded, and they worked their way to the ground.

Connor braced his back against a steel support and pulled Sarah into his arms. She was shaking so badly she'd never know that he was, too. He felt small arms wrap themselves around his leg, and he reached down to pat Dannie's head.

When Sarah found her voice, it was to say, ''Oh, Connor, I've never been so scared.''

''Me, neither,'' he whispered, ''but don't tell the k-i-d.''

''I'm sorry I acted so foolish. I could have gotten us b-both—''

"Not a chance," he said quickly, cutting off the predictable last word for Dannie's sake.

"I c-couldn't help myself," she said, her words couched in a sob muffled in the front of his jacket.

"I know. I should have taken you seriously when you said you were scared. I wanted to be the one who could get you to go up there." He didn't know why, but he knew it was true.

"And I wanted to be able to go. I don't like being such a ni-ni-ninny." She lifted her head and began wiping furiously at her eyes. "I don't know why I'm acting like this. I've never *done* anything so ridiculous, never...."

"Hey," Connor said, catching her hand before she rubbed off her mascara. "It's okay. From now on, you're allowed to be scared of heights, and I'm going to punch out anybody who calls you a ninny."

She smiled and tried to laugh, her eyes glistening brown puddles. "Thanks," she managed to say.

"Besides, something good has come of all this." He settled her hand back on his chest and brushed a loose strand of hair over her temple.

"What?"

"You called me by my name." She gave him a puzzled look. Hadn't she been calling him by his name? "You hadn't called me Connor, and I was beginning to wonder if you wanted to call me something else."

"No. I'm glad you're Connor."

Connor smiled as he watched Sarah bend down to cuddle her daughter. It had taken a while, but he'd learned to be glad of that, too.

Solid ground felt better than it ever had before, and Sarah found the rocks, leaves and yellowing grass to be new wonders, situated as they were in the foundation of security. She wished a bluejay lots of luck, and she admonished Dannie not to disturb the hooded jack-in-the-pulpit in the woods. And, no, she didn't want any purple asters plucked from the meadow for her. Let everything keep its roots in the ground today.

Yes, Connor thought, she's rooted in the earth, deeply rooted—nothing shallow about his woman. Nothing about her screams or shouts. She's as quiet as these woods, plunked right here in the middle of a valley teeming with people. Dry twigs cracked under his feet, and the sound echoed in the woods' close womb.

Connor held Dannie on one arm, and it seemed natural that he held Sarah under the other as they drifted back to the car in the late afternoon.

"Is there a good place to eat around here that'll take us dressed the way we are?" Connor wondered as he buckled Dannie into the back seat.

"These are my new bibs," Dannie said proudly. "I got to wear them today because Mommy says my pink-elephant pants are too small. But my pink-elephant pants are my favorites. They have pink elephants right here—" two chubby hands indicated her knees and then trailed along her shins "—with trunks that go all the way down to here."

"Pink elephants, huh?" Connor tightened the seatbelt and patted Dannie's knee. "When I start seeing pink elephants on girls' knees, I know I've been on tour too long. How does Uncle Jerry like your pink elephants?"

"He gave them to me. He thinks they're funny. But now—" dramatic sigh "—they're too small."

"Don't worry, kid," he said, gently clipping her chin with a fist, "Uncle Connor will come up with something better."

"Uncle Connor's *time* is something better," came the rejoinder from the front seat.

Connor smiled at the brown eyes that peeked between the bucket seats. "Uncle Connor's got all night. Name a restaurant."

"We could go home," Sarah suggested.

"You girls did lunch. Supper's on me."

Connor protested against the diner that Sarah's often one-second-too-late directions led them to, but after three-quarters of an hour of "Oh...we should've turned there," he figured the silver-streak affair was at least at hand.

"Lots of college kids come here," Sarah explained, sliding into a booth upholstered in cracked vinyl.

"Looks like the joints I frequented as a starving guitar picker," he noted, retrieving the plastic-covered typed menu from a clip behind the napkin box.

"You were once a starving musician?" Sarah asked.

"Just another gaunt-gutted hopeful," he confirmed. "But I imagine it's classier starving in an artist's garret than in a cheap motel room."

"Someday we should compare notes. How did you get your big break?"

He shrugged, studying the menu. "I got lucky. I met someone who liked my style and introduced me to someone who had the right contacts."

The scene flashed right up on the screen for her. "And the original someone was...?"

Mmm-hmm, this was fun. "A very chic lady. The kind who never looks for a price tag on her clothes but always puts one on her favors."

"Ah, yes. A true patron of the arts." *Frailty, frailty. Well, just to see if he remembers...* "What was this lady's name?"

"Her name—" blue eyes flashed merrily over the menu "—was completely forgettable." He glanced down at the menu. "Just tell me what's safe on here."

"Everything's safe. How can ten-thousand college kids be wrong about anything as serious as food?"

"We like clams," Dannie offered. "They come in a bucket like chicken."

"Fried clams?"

"Steamed," Sarah clarified. "Right in the shell."

Connor's face became a dried prune. "Slithery, slimy steamed clams?" He got two enthusiastic nods. "Yech! I'll have Swiss steak and hope to God I can keep it down while I watch you eat those things."

He tried not to watch but he was teased unmercifully by both dyed-in-the-wool New England gourmets, who finally coaxed him into trying just one clam. It slid off the shell and into his mouth easily enough, but when Dannie warned, "Don't chew it too much; you'll get sand in your teeth," the blubbery stuff was relegated to a wad of napkin.

"Tastes like Boston Harbor," Connor growled, retreating to his beer.

"Exactly." Sarah slid another clam down her throat with practiced ease. Then she smiled sweetly as Connor rolled his eyes in disgust. "And the next time you open your mouth to do one of those accents of yours, you'll get your cheers from the *Hahvahd* contingent. Those clams stick in your throat."

"They have to get past my teeth first. Anyway, I already do that one, as you'll see tomorrow night." Her look of surprise prompted him to add, "You're coming, aren't you?"

"I don't have any—"

"I do." He patted his shirt pocket. "Right here. For you and Dannie and Jerry and what's-her-name. Down front."

"Oh, I don't know, Connor. Dannie's too young to..."

"It's just music, Sarah. We don't tell jokes or take any clothes off. We just play music."

"But it's so loud."

"The speakers will be above you, suspended from the ceiling. Just don't look up this time."

"And the crowd..."

"They won't bother you. You'll be sitting down front with the press and the jocks and the mayor. Very sedate company." He turned his offer over to Dannie, where he was sure he'd get better reception. "You wanna see what your Uncle Connor does for a living, don't you, Princess?" He got the nod he was angling for and returned to Sarah with an arched eyebrow. "I have a feeling your mother thinks it's akin to devil worship."

"I do not, Connor," Sarah protested. "I just don't want to damage her eardrums."

Connor reached across the table and cupped his hands over Dannie's ears. "You think I'd damage these eardrums? No way!"

"Oh, well, I guess...I do want to...and Jerry would kill me if I..."

The advantage was suddenly his. "And after the concert, Jerry pays me what he owes me by taking the k-i-d home so you can party with me. This is the end of the tour."

"Oh, no, Connor, I don't know those people, and I wouldn't..."

"I'm the only one you need to know. The rest are just window dressing," he proclaimed, suddenly feeling so good he knew it had to be the truth.

It was so quiet on the way home Connor thought both of his girls were asleep. *His girls.* Well, okay, maybe he was presuming too much. Dannie was Sarah's, and Sarah had been Kevin's and Connor had never been much inclined to be *any-body's.* So the thought might be a hell of a bad notion. On the other hand, right now, parked here in her driveway with that soft face so close by, everything felt just right.

Carrying Dannie up to her room felt right to Connor, too. For Sarah the sight of her little girl being carried up the stairs by a man who showed every sign of caring for her was an unexpected balm for an ache she'd felt so long she'd simply allowed herself to adjust to its constancy. She'd always re-sented that pain, and now maybe she resented the balm a little, too. But if this man had love to give Dannie, Sarah was de-termined not to begrudge either of them.

Sarah made coffee, and without asking permission Connor got a fire going in the fireplace. He didn't feel that he had to check with her, and Sarah smiled her approval when she brought the coffee and saw the blaze. He sat next to her on the couch, closer this time than he had the night before.

He took the coffee and thought about a cigarette. He wasn't planning on one, just thinking about one, and what he thought was that he didn't need one. He tilted his head to look at the back of Sarah's head and the intricate braid that marked its midpoint. His hands wanted to be busy with other things. Sip-ping the hot coffee, he caught her eyes with his, and his smile drew a tentative little one from that bow of a mouth. His mouth wanted to be busy with other things, too.

Sarah felt a surging tingle inside her skin, and it made her uneasy. She wanted simply to be quiet and comfortable with this man. She wanted him to confine his pulse-rate manipulations to the teenyboppers, or whoever his fans were. They could handle that sort of thing. Sarah couldn't. Sarah was a very private person who...who was tingling, hot and cold at the same time inside her skin. He'd just slipped the elastic from her braid.

Defenses, to the front line. "Don't say something corny like, 'I've been wanting to do this all day,'" Sarah warned.

"I'm not going to say much," he promised, beginning the unbraiding near the bottom. "I just like to touch the things I admire. I'm like a kid—very tactile."

He continued to sip his coffee and to play at the process of unbraiding her hair. When he had it undone, he used his fingers as a comb, enjoying the way the zigzagging waves felt as they slipped between his fingers. He glanced at her coffee. Since she'd hardly touched it, he assumed she didn't really want it and he set both cups aside.

His hands carried her face closer to his, and he heard her draw a shaky breath. One soft kiss fell at the corner of her mouth. "I just want to kiss you, Sarah." Another teasing kiss, and then he murmured against her mouth, "And, yes, I've wanted to all day."

It began tentatively, his mouth testing hers, asking what she wanted, what she needed. Her lips responded with a tiny flutter. *I want closeness. I need gentleness.* He took that flutter, rising slowly on its promise, and gave a more tangible caress. Their lips danced briefly, taking the first lessons in an unfamiliar step. Then there was a sharp intake of breath, a soft moan and a sudden lack of patience to come to know the taste of each other. Connor's hands dived deep into her hair, and Sarah's arms reached under his to surround his back, pulling him closer. His kiss was hard and wild. His tongue sought a mate, and hers met it.

Intentionally entangled in her hair, his hands were not free to touch any other part of her. He would know her with his mouth now, and he would tease himself a little because his gambit had suggested just a kiss. I just want to devour you, Sarah, he thought. I just want to be absorbed in your softness while you take all the world's hardness away.

Sarah lifted her chin to welcome the sweet wet touchings on her neck. If she voiced the welcome that rang in her ears as it coursed throughout her veins, she knew it would be all over but the recriminations. But how good it was to feel this much life in her every nerve. How sweet to have someone to cling to, however briefly. Connor, hold me closer. Connor, touch me. Connor, don't let me give this a second thought because if I do... "Connor, this could lead to real... complications."

He nudged a kiss into her ear. Complications. A euphemism for involvement without commitment. Who could blame her for fearing that kind of thing? "I'm just kissing you, Sarah. Kisses aren't complicated."

"Yours are," she groaned.

"No, they're not," he protested, nuzzling the sleek hair at her temple. "Very simple. Just you and me and our kisses tonight."

"Your kisses are very...sticky." She let her hands slide down the cool cotton of his shirt and rest at his sides.

He chuckled softly near her ear. "Dannie's are sticky, honey. Mine are just a little wet."

"Dangerous when wet."

He drew back, smiling as he untangled his fingers and smoothed back her hair. "Slid right into my arms, didn't you?"

"I'm afraid I—"

"Don't be." He touched her cheek and shook his head. "Don't be. I know you haven't got it straight in your head who I am yet. There are lots of things I've wanted to do all day, Sarah Benedict, but I'll wait until you know, until you're sure."

"Too many people know who you are, Connor. That scares me." He put his arm around her and cuddled her against him, and that didn't scare her.

"Not as many as you think. When you're part of a group, you can usually walk down the street just like anybody else—unless you're in town for a concert. People are kind of looking for you then."

"You do pick high-profile jobs, Connor Ryan. If you'd stayed an ironworker you could've taken that literally."

"Ironworker?"

She leaned back for a look at his face. "You told me you'd been an ironworker." He grinned. "You mean you weren't?"

"I've been a lot of things, honey, but I've never been *that* crazy."

Chapter Three

Sarah was faced with what she knew psychologists called an approach-avoidance conflict. She paced. She brooded. She ransacked her closet and all her drawers. Then she brooded some more. Sarah wanted to go to the concert, but she had nothing to wear. She wanted to see Connor perform, but she didn't want to watch from a front-row seat. She'd prefer some isolated little projectionist's booth or a box in a private opera house, like the sumptuous one she'd seen when she toured Versailles. *Really, Sarah. Country rock at Versailles.*

Admittedly, knowing Connor had been very nice so far. He was a very attractive man with a warm personality and a fine sense of humor. But then there was also this vague notion that elsewhere he'd be something larger than life, a fantasy that everyone wanted a piece of. Here in her house he was simply a man, and that was complicated enough.

In the back of her closet she found a skirt she hadn't worn in a long time. A leather-craftsman friend of hers had made it in trade for a painting. Sarah had a number of handmade treasures she'd acquired that way. The skirt was butternut kidskin, and she could wear it with the matching boots she'd bought in Italy and her pale yellow Italian silk blouse.

Dannie wasn't sure what all the excitement was about, but she knew that her new uncle was somehow involved, and he'd already assumed hero status with his little niece. She thought he'd like her blue calico smock with the white pinafore because it was a pretty dress, and princesses wore pretty dresses. She scolded Uncle Jerry for not dressing up, but he told her that T-shirts and blue jeans were all he had.

"That's all the roadies ever wear," Jerry protested.

Sarah withdrew her all-weather coat from the front closet near the stairs, only half-interested in an answer when she asked, "Roadies?"

"Roadies are people who travel with the group to take care of equipment, sell souvenirs, run errands, that sort of thing," Jerry explained. "Wouldn't I make a great roadie?"

Sarah's eyes narrowed. "Jerry, if you even hint at asking for favors from that man again, I will never forgive you. You've caused enough..."

"What have I caused?" The arm he draped over his sister's shoulders wasn't intended to be patronizing. "I've gotten some people together. What's the harm in that? The man deserved to know about his dead brother's daughter."

She's *my* daughter, Sarah's brain screamed, but Dannie was sitting at the bottom of the steps buckling a shoe, and she couldn't be expected to understand why Sarah took exception to all this sudden talk of *Kevin's* daughter. "All right, now you've told him. But I don't want him to think we want anything from him. Not *anything*, Jerry."

Jerry smiled his sweet, crooked smile. "I won't ask for anything. But wouldn't it be fun to travel with a band like that, Sarah? Wouldn't it be a great life?"

With a motherly, one-armed squeeze, Sarah drew back to put her coat on. Jerry lifted a hand in one of his typically ineffectual overtures of assistance, managing, as always, to be just a little late. Lifting her hair at the back to free it from her coat, Sarah clucked an indulgent "tsk" at Jerry, adding, "At twenty-five you're still trying to decide what you want to be when you grow up."

Jerry laughed. "I know what I want to be. I want to be rich and famous. I just haven't figured all the angles yet."

There was no point in commenting. Jerry would go to his grave believing there were easy angles he'd missed out on. "Are we picking Pepper up on the way?"

"Pepper's not coming," Jerry said, a twinge of guilt nudging his chin toward his chest.

"Why not? I gave you her ticket."

"I know. I scalped it."

"You…Jerry, you have absolutely no…no conscience," Sarah stammered.

"Hey, she kicked me out the other night, Sarah. I had to hitch a ride over here. I don't like going back with my tail tucked between my legs every time I get a little buzzed. I don't need that, Sarah."

"Maybe not." Taking Dannie by the hand, she headed for the door, tossing back, "But you do need a place to stay, don't you, Jerry?"

The truth struck Jerry as funny. "Yeah, I do. And if you don't want me back here, don't say anything to Pepper about that ticket."

From behind the stage, Connor witnessed their arrival. Sarah was a classical beauty, simply stated. He'd seen too many groupies in their blue jeans—blue jeans with T-shirts, blue jeans with fancy blouses, but always the blue jeans. He tucked his thumbs into his western belt behind his back. Blue jeans for him, too. It was part of the image—comfortable, casual, one of the folks.

Smiling in Sarah's direction, though there was no possibility that she could see him, he turned her name over in his mind a few times. She wasn't a groupie; she wasn't even a fan. She was here as a friend, just to see him. That bit of consideration was what he'd wanted from his parents, what he would've had from Kevin if things had been different. But that was water under the bridge, and this was someone else. This was Sarah.

He watched her sit down, fuss over Dannie's hair a little bit and then respond to something Dannie pointed to in the program book. Unless she had him totally buffaloed with the fierce independence she professed, Sarah wasn't interested in images. She was here just to see him. He'd show her how good he was at what he did. She'd like his music because he knew how to make great music, and tonight he'd make it even better than great.

"What's out there, Connor?" The hand on his shoulder belonged to Scotch Hagan, the big, redheaded, bushy-bearded drummer for Georgia Nights. "See any pretty faces in the front row?"

"One," said Connor, and then he amended. "Two, but the second one's wearing ruffles and ankle socks."

"What's the first one wearing?"

Sarah turned wide eyes over her shoulder as one boisterous fan hooted a greeting at another behind her. Connor chuckled. "A nervous smile."

The house lights went down and then out, and the crowd quieted, waiting, watching the dark stage. Movement on stage brought forth a low buzzing from the audience, one anticipatory "Yeah!" from the bleachers, then a high-pitched "Whoa!" from the opposite side. At once the stage was flooded with white light and the imperative of a rock-hard downbeat. Cheers from the audience melded with the music, and the electrical connection was instantly complete. Four microphones, four voices, four instruments, one sound—one complete circuit with the audience.

The intro was a pacemaker for those whose hearts beat in four-four time. The lead singer's rhythm guitar tagged into the drummer's beat while Connor's guitar laid down a track for the lusty male voices to ride on. Head tilted back in amazement, Sarah watched Connor's hands wrench the hard-driving melody from the taut strings, heard him belt out the demands in the chorus, saw him lean over the neck of the instrument and squeeze roller-coaster sounds out of the bottom end. She tried to remember the man who'd knelt by Dannie's bed and tentatively touched her hair. There was nothing tentative about those fingers now.

The first songs pitched the crowd forward in their seats and kept them speeding over the hills and around the curves of each tune. Then came the introductions, handled by the lead singer, who introduced himself as Mike Tanner from Waycross, Georgia. That drew an enthusiastic response. Then there were the jokes about Scotch Hagan's red beard and bassist Kenny Rasmussen's low voice, and then...

"The three of us, we're all from south of the Mason-Dixon line, but we got this here Yankee—" a few stray cheers "—in our midst. Ol' Connor, he's kind of a wandering minstrel. Plays lead guitar, banjo, fiddle, whatever else he can get his hands on." A female catcall. "Don't ever let him get his hands on *you*, honey, lemme tell ya..." Female shrieks. Connor shuffled a little uncomfortably. "No, Connor was raised up around these parts. You know these hill folk pretty well, doncha, Connor?"

Connor waited for the laughter to settle to the floor before he leaned close to the microphone and asked, "Anybody climbed the fire tower up on top of Mount Holyoke lately?" Assent came from the applause. He looked straight at Sarah, grinning with their private joke, the message that he knew she was there. "Scary, ain't it?" Sarah felt her face grow hot, warming her smile as the crowd cheered in agreement.

"Connor Ryan writes most of our music," Mike continued. "Like this one. 'Misty River Morning.'" Applause greeted the introductory chords, and Connor assumed the role of lead singer, his voice pouring over the words of the slow song like warm golden honey. Sarah felt her chest tighten as he sang the last lines—"You and me and the river, babe, makin' misty mornin' love." The sustained last note was a plea that elicited a second's silence before thundering applause.

It was Connor Ryan's night. His double-necked guitar argued with itself like a two-headed creature, provoked by fingers that could not possibly be connected with any human hand. On a bluegrass number, his sassy bow played a fast seesaw on the fiddle, the high-pitched music whirling around the stage and tumbling out to the crowd like a spinning Cossack. Mike Tanner set his guitar aside and did a mountain jig while Scotch and Kenny clapped along with the crowd. Sarah was close enough to see Connor's sweat and feel his exhilaration. The audience was his.

He sang the lead on two more songs, attesting to the pleasure of "givin' my woman all I got" and pulling at the heartstrings with memories of "the dusty echoes of a lie, a lonely, hollow, aching sigh." All of the music was a natural extension of Connor and his instrument. Even the songs the lead singer sang seemed to be showcases for Connor in one way or another. Sarah would not remember what Mike Tanner had sung in the shadow of Connor's performance.

"Hey, you Georgia boys, I got an idea!" Mike shouted through the speakers.

"Yeah?" came three practiced replies.

"What say we...scare up some brew..."

"Yeah?" Scattered cheers.

"And some tunes..."

"Yeah?" Anticipation.

"And some Springfield boys and girls..."

"Yeah?" Whistles. "I like that last part," Scotch put in.

"And see if Springfield knows..."

"Knows what, Mike?" Scotch prompted amid a growing volume of yells.

"Knows how to par-ty!"

The lyrics, what were distinguishable, reveled in the prospect of "gettin' a rockin'-good party goin' tonight," and there was hand-clapping, foot-stomping pandemonium in response. Connor's euphoria was no less dramatic than the rest, and the party seemed to have started already. Sarah stood with the crowd while Jerry bounced Dannie in his arms and sang along. The foot stomping in the bleachers became deafening. Sarah felt raw panic rising in her throat. Uniformed policemen kept the crowd from swarming the stage, but Connor didn't seem to notice that there wasn't much between him and this growing madness except a few stern faces. He continued to pour total enthusiasm into the song. Sarah envisioned an army of crazed music lovers pouring from the bleachers to descend upon the band the minute this was over.

But it didn't happen. The group obliged the roaring crowd with one encore and then another, but with the dawn of the house lights, the single-voiced crowd began to break apart into individual pieces. Several thousand cars would have to be moved into the streets of Springfield. Therefore, since no one accepts the challenge of cutting into traffic quite like the Massachusetts driver, it was every man for himself.

"Miss Benedict?" Sarah turned to find a young man in a black Georgia Nights T-shirt looking like the proud bearer of an official message. "Will you follow me, please?"

"Follow you where?"

"Right this way. You have a friend backstage." His eyes hinted at connotations suggested by the word "friend."

Sarah complied, and Jerry brought up the rear with Dannie in his arms. The young man swung him an unwelcome look, but Jerry informed him, "I'm with her."

"Yes, he is," Sarah agreed, reaching for Dannie.

Shouldering his way past fans and security guards, the young man led them down a corridor, obviously quite taken with his own privileged status. Jerry caught Sarah's attention and widely mouthed the news that this was a roadie. Sarah nodded without the enthusiasm that Jerry would have considered appropriate.

The roadie's knock brought Connor to the dressing-room door, which he swung open with a smiling flourish. "This the right lady, Connor?"

"*These* are just the *ladies* I wanted to see. Thanks, Rob." The roadie took his leave as Dannie readily transferred herself into Connor's waiting hands. "Hey, Princess, what'd you think?"

"That *was* you, Uncle Connor! You were very loud. I wish I could sing that loud."

"Loud, huh?" Connor laughed. "I don't know how to take that. Was I any good?"

"Oh, yes, very good—and wonderfully loud. Did you take a shower with your clothes on, Uncle Connor?"

"Not yet, but it sounds like a good idea. Here..." He lowered her to a padded swivel chair. "I'm getting your pretty dress all wet. Lights must've been pretty hot tonight."

Jerry was about to burst with excitement as he bounced on the balls of his feet and split his face with a grin. "That's honest, working man's sweat, Connor. You really know how to make that fiddle sing, and that double-neck... I never heard anything like it."

The compliments were nice, but they hadn't yet come from the right quarter. Connor felt Sarah's eyes on him, and he tingled with the need to hear her voice. He looked past Jerry to find her eyes ashimmer with unspoken praise.

She hung back, feeling awed, feeling shy. His plain white western shirt, sleeves rolled just below his elbows, stuck to him in opaque wetness. His hair was a shade darker damp than it was dry, and it formed more waves and curls. He looked exhausted, but the excitement lingered in his eyes.

"Did you like the concert, Sarah?"

She stepped closer, ignoring Jerry's presence, hardly noting Dannie's. She saw that her answer was important to him. "The concert was a little overwhelming, Connor. But you...you were *completely* overwhelming. I became...totally absorbed in your music."

"Are you tempted to buy a record?" he wondered, and she nodded, smiling. "Terrific! If we've made a fan of Sarah Benedict, we must have the rest of these pilgrims in the palms of our hands. I'll see that you get autographed copies of all the albums," he promised. "And something decent to play them on."

"Oh, no...actually, I think we'll get a stereo soon—maybe for Christmas this year."

"I think so, too." He turned a winning smile on Dannie. "Did you know Santa has a reindeer named Connor, Princess?" Dannie matched his smile and shook her head. "Sure. Comet, Cupid, Connor and Blitzen. Big, strapping brute. They use him to pull the sleigh when it's full of stereo equipment."

"I want a dollhouse for Christmas," Dannie announced.

"He's the one who brings the dollhouses, too." Connor gave her a chuck under the chin. "So you leave him some oatmeal cookies, okay? He likes oatmeal cookies."

"Connor…"

He cocked an eyebrow at Sarah along with gift-giver's eyes. "Oatmeal cookies," he emphasized. "With lots of raisins." Turning to Jerry, he laid the charm in double layers. "Listen, buddy, I really appreciate your staying with Dannie for a while so I can have a date with her mother. We won't be too late. I promise."

"Bet that's gonna be some party," Jerry said, his voice convincingly wistful. "Sarah's never been much for parties. Don't know how she got related to me."

"Well, I'm not much for parties, either," Connor said, "but these are my friends, and I want them to meet Sarah." Connor's hand on his shoulder pumped Jerry up to double his size, and the "Thanks, man, I knew I could count on you" was the clincher.

A limousine sped Sarah, Connor and Scotch Hagan to the hotel in dark-windowed anonymity. Such luxury made Sarah uneasy, and she couldn't bring herself to let her back relax against the plush upholstery. She assured Scotch that she'd enjoyed the concert and expressed appropriate appreciation for his compliments on her beauty, which struck her as so much Southern charm. Clutching her purse in her lap, she watched the familiar streets pass by the car window with dread anticipation of what was to come.

"Sarah's an artist," Connor told Scotch. "You should see her paintings. Really fine work. I've been trying to get her to sell me one, but she doesn't believe I'm a real connoisseur."

"He's not," Scotch said with a nod in Sarah's direction. "I

gave him a hand-thrown pot once, and you know what he did with it? He filled it with horse feed.''

"What else do you do with a pot that size?"

Sarah understood immediately. "Are you a potter, Scotch?"

Shrugging a bit sheepishly, Scotch nodded. "I kind of putter, I guess. I have a wheel and a kiln. I like to mess around in the clay."

"You mean you made that?" Connor asked, amazed. "You never told me...."

"Not after you filled it full of horse feed, I wasn't gonna tell you." Scotch glowered for a moment and then burst out laughing. "Some connoisseur. If you can't play it on the guitar, our boy here don't know nothing about it. Unless it's a pretty girl. And then ol' Connor sure can pick 'em." Sarah was treated to a red-lashed wink.

Connor took Sarah to his suite, where she listened to the radio while he showered and changed. The pop-music station was featuring Georgia Nights in honor of their visit to Springfield. She remembered the way Connor's body moved with the music, the slight roll of his hips and the occasionally emphatic swing and sway of his shoulders as he pounded out the climax of a song. She'd never be able to listen to this music without remembering the sheen on his forehead and the bright excitement in his eyes, an excitement that translated into wattage in Sarah's own bloodstream even now.

Connor burst from the bedroom on the tail end of the hurry he'd been in to avoid keeping her waiting. Sarah interpreted it as a rush to get to the party, and she sat up straight in her chair, her spine stiffening.

"Did I tell you how great you look tonight?" he wondered. "That skirt is terrific."

"Thank you," she murmured, brushing at the spotless leather. "A friend made it. You...um...you look very nice, too."

Laughing off the sudden awkwardness, Connor reached for her hand and drew her to her feet. "Nice" was an understatement, and she wondered whether he knew it. He seemed totally unconscious of his looks, unaware of the fact that everything he wore seemed to accommodate itself perfectly to his frame. His pearl-gray pullover with stylish satin insets at the shoulders and open-flap neckline flattered his broad shoulders and long torso. Gray jeans and boots hardly gave him a California look, but then he was hardly Californian—or maybe he was truly Californian. He was the man from all over America.

"Connor, I know most people, including my impossible brother, would give their eyeteeth to go to this party, but I'm afraid I'm going to be such a dud. I just don't do well at parties."

"You don't have to do anything, Sarah. Just make it very obvious that you're with me, and we'll both be fine."

Sarah found that to be a taller order than it had sounded. The party was already under way in a large suite. The private bar was open, and it was apparent that they'd certainly managed to scare up some Springfield girls. Sarah was introduced to Mike Tanner, with his dark hair that hung to his shoulders and a neatly trimmed beard. His woolly chest completed the hairy look, since he'd not found time to button his shirt. Mike seemed more than pleased to meet Sarah, as did Kenny Rasmussen, whose low-pitched Southern drawl was a startling contrast with his fair-haired, boyish appearance.

Besides Connor, Sarah quickly decided she liked Scotch the best. Everyone else seemed too quick with a laugh. Mike asked her where she was from and gave a high sign over her head to someone behind her just as she opened her mouth with an answer. Over her head he proceeded to effect a bushy raised brow, a wounded frown and a mimed denial before recovering his end of the conversation.

"Whereabouts did you say, hon?" A slurp of beer drew his interest next.

"I didn't."

"Ahh, mystery lady. I like that. This one's cool, Connor. Real New England-style cool." Even as he gave Connor a friendly slap on the back, Mike's eye was scanning the crowd. "See if I can find me one just like her."

"I wish you luck, my friend," Connor offered, shaking his head after the man.

"He's already outta luck." The hand on Sarah's shoulder gave her a start, but she relaxed somewhat when she caught Scotch's smile. He'd hooked his other wrist over Connor's shoulder. "Not a one like our Sarah. I already checked."

"*Our* Sarah? I never heard you say *our* Maggie," Connor said.

"I let her feed you once a month, though," Scotch reminded him, turning to Sarah with the explanation, "This is Connor's way of letting you know that I'm the only one of the bunch who's respectfully married and perfectly harmless."

Connor gave Scotch's beard a playful tug. "Faithful as an ol' red setter."

"Gotta be. You oughta see my ol' lady. Big as a Louisiana bayou and twice as snaky. Her daddy was an alligator, and she's got the teeth to prove it." He was gratified by Sarah's small laughter. Scotch knew the poor girl was terrified of this whole scene—anybody could see that. Maggie had never warmed up to it, either. "This boy's got no manners, Sarah. Lord knows we've tried to teach him the meaning of Southern hospitality, but he just can't seem to get it down. What can I get you to drink?"

"I'm just fine, really."

"I'll bet you'd like a little white wine or maybe a spritzer?"

"Yes, actually I think I would."

Scotch moved toward the bar like a gentleman with a mission, never sidetracked. "I'd have offered first," Connor said, "but Scotch likes to play host. Keeps him busy."

"And I'll bet his wife isn't big or mean or snaky," Sarah guessed.

The light in Connor's eyes told Sarah that Maggie was special to him, too. He shook his head, smiling. "Maggie's a gem. He'd have hell to pay if she heard him call her his 'ol' lady.' They have two redheaded rascals, one Dannie's age. And they have…" Sarah caught a wistful look, a quick wish. "They have a nice home in Nashville."

"And you visit them once a month?"

"We record in Nashville, and I have an apartment there. When I'm in town, Maggie puts the welcome mat out." Scotch was back with a beer for Connor and Sarah's glass of wine. "Thank you, my man," Connor said with a nod, repeating, "She's a gem, that wife of yours, Scotch."

"That she is," Scotch agreed. "And our Sarah's a lady, Connor. You don't wanna keep her hangin' around this party too long. I have a feeling we'll be paying for damages again."

Connor scanned the room and nodded in agreement, but the idea seemed to amuse him. Sarah didn't think it was a funny prospect at all.

Guests included roadies, technicians, local disc jockeys, people who knew the right people, and the right people themselves, whose sphere of influence was not always altogether clear. Among them were several attractive women who were obviously aware that they were there simply by that virtue.

One persistent brunette tried to strike up a conversation with Connor, offering Sarah a plastic smile and a perfunctory nod before putting her wit on the line with, "You were wonderful tonight, Connor. I felt your energy pouring directly into my body and I thought, 'A Leo. He has to be.' I'm totally compatible with Leos, and I know one the minute I see one. Can you guess what sign I was born under?"

Deadpan expression, absolute innocence. "The sign of the spider. That's one, isn't it?"

"If you want it to be," she tried.

Connor leaned closer, and her eyes fluttered to half-mast before the promise of his slow smile. "Go try Mike, then. I think he was born under the sign of the fly." Her eyes followed the direction of Connor's nod.

The interest in Connor wasn't all as obviously sexual, but most of it seemed no less opportunistic. The right people were interested in him nowadays because he was money. Sarah was introduced to a woman named Sally, who seemed to be in charge of seeing that Connor and the other members of the band greeted the people who expected to be greeted. Connor smiled and nodded and answered most of their questions, appreciated their praise. Sarah remembered the way Kevin had enjoyed this kind of scene. But while Connor was pleasant, he wasn't glib, and he kept Sarah close to him. She wondered if he could be as uncomfortable as she was.

Sarah became increasingly awkward as the sea of eyes around her got glassier and the grins became loose and rubbery. She didn't want to think about what might be responsible for those fish-eyed looks.

"Ready to go?" Connor's face was blessedly sober. Sarah answered with a grateful nod.

"Hey, Connor, come on over here and pick some with us."

Connor's face clouded slightly as he sighed. Mike needed Connor to make him look good. This was the point at every party where Mike plugged his hose into Connor's guitar and depended on Connor to inflate him. Mike had a good voice, but he hadn't grown with his success. It was getting harder to keep Mike sober before a performance and harder still to tolerate him afterward.

"Come on, boy, we need those magic fingers. Sheila here needs a little orientation in country music." Mike saw Connor's reluctance, and he wasn't above a little subtle pleading. "Come on over; we'll give her the short course. Ten minutes."

Ten minutes. He could give Mike that. Ten minutes would buy Mike a whole night of the kind of fawning he enjoyed. Connor checked his watch. Still pretty early by Georgia time. "Ten minutes," he agreed.

Sarah's heart slid down a mental rain gutter. She'd seen what the music did to Connor. In ten minutes he'd just be getting warmed up.

In twenty, he was hot. Where earlier there'd been genuine friendship apparent only between Connor and Scotch, now with the music the camaraderie among the four was tangible. They used folk guitars now, and Scotch tapped out a beat on a practice pad. Seated in a loose circle on a couple of stools and folding chairs, they swung together from rhythm and blues to rockabilly, Connor carrying Mike like a broad-shouldered brother. The essence of the relationship was couched in the scene.

But for Sarah, there was more than the music. There was the distance between herself and the man who'd brought her here. And she felt out of place among the sweaty, seamy, suffocating party crowd. As the bodies pressed toward the music, she drifted back near the bar. The faces around her became leering, distorted, inhuman. They were like the faces in a funhouse mirror. This was surrealism for Sarah at its most gruesome. It was time to call a cab.

"He's incredible, isn't he?"

The brunette had crept to her side without Sarah's notice, and she was in the process of draping all eight of her long, lean appendages over the bar stool next to where Sarah stood. She splashed a shot of vodka in a hotel glass and lifted the glass in Sarah's direction. "May he turn out to be as good as he looks," she said, her long, wine-colored nails coddling the glass. She read the look in Sarah's face and thought better of downing the shot. "You aren't staying with him tonight, are you?"

Sarah said nothing. If real spiders could smile the way this one did, flies would get nervous.

"You aren't a pickup." Confidently lowering the webs in front of her eyes, the spider lady tapped her glass with a red nail. "He's going to take you home. And I'll be here when he gets back. A man like that has different women for different reasons, doesn't he?"

Sarah had nothing to say. She would defy the webs.

"You're very pretty and very sweet. I'd say you've served your function, wouldn't you?"

Sarah didn't feel the vodka dribble down the front of her skirt or drip on her boot. She looked down when she smelled it. Horrified, she watched the soft butternut leather turn yellow-brown. Her dignity never faltered, but she felt like a wilting sapling. She turned a wordless glare at the creature who was responsible, refusing to acknowledge the existence of such a low form of life with a verbal condemnation. Sarah simply turned from the absurdity of the scene and walked away.

She did not take the time to mop herself up or to announce her departure. She found her coat on a rack, put it on and left the party. At the front desk she called a cab. The expense would destroy her budget, but she had gotten herself into this, and she had to get out. At this time of night, there was no other way.

The cost of the cab nearly destroyed more than Sarah's budget. The cash she had stashed in the freezer for emergencies had been "borrowed" again. She had less than half the fare in hand, and the cabbie refused to accept a check.

"Listen, lady, nobody takes a cab from Springfield to Amherst unless she's loaded one way or another. I should've guessed what kind of loaded you were. You smell like you fell into the punch bowl."

"I'm not loaded—" Sarah spat disgustedly "—either way. I wouldn't have called you unless I had the money. At least, I thought I had the money. You will be paid."

"When?"

A pair of brazen headlights swung into the driveway. Sarah squinted as they swept past her face, and the arriving car took a berth on the opposite side of the cab. The engine was abruptly shut off, and the car door was slammed. "You all right, Sarah?"

The voice struck a mellow chord, a welcome sound in the night. "Yes, I'm all right."

In the dark, his face was a twice-familiar one that caused her a quick catch of breath each time she saw it. It was no longer a face for public consumption but one reflecting private concern. He couldn't imagine what had possessed Sarah to take a cab home.

"Sarah, you should have said something. What are you doing? Did something…"

"She's telling me she doesn't have enough cash to pay her fare, that's what she's doing," came the grumble from inside the cab.

Without a word, Connor pulled out his wallet and handed some bills through the open window. "Thank you for waiting. This should make it worth your while."

"Yeah." Grinning up at Connor, the cabbie pocketed the money. "Glad somebody around here's loaded. G'night, folks."

They stood together in near darkness listening to the cab's retreat into the night, making certain of the silence, and comfortable in the knowledge that neither could see the depth of feeling in the other's eyes. It had been a near miss. He almost hadn't come, not knowing why she'd left. He'd almost indulged himself in an angry assumption. She'd almost let him go without a word of explanation. They might have let it end right there. But now he'd found her, and each one rejoiced privately.

"I wanted to take you home myself," he said quietly. "You should have told me you were..."

"I did."

"But *I* suggested we leave. You agreed, but I didn't realize it was this urgent."

"Connor, I told you I was no good at parties. You weren't ready to go. It wasn't necessary that you..."

"It was necessary," he insisted, catching her shoulders in his hands. "I got carried away and left you to fend for yourself among the—"

"I've been fending for myself quite well for some time now," Sarah informed him on a soft note of indignation. "I knew the way home, and if Jerry hadn't raided the freezer, I'd have paid for my own ride. As it is, I intend to pay you back, but I'm not responsible for your flashy tipping."

Connor took that as a sign that she wasn't completely opposed to his help or overly angry about his negligence. He dropped an arm over her shoulder, and they walked toward the front door. "No, but you're at least partly responsible for my headache, so you can pay me back in aspirin, and a little coffee on the side. And maybe we could talk awhile."

"Talk? I wonder how you can have any voice left at this point."

They'd reached the front door, and Connor took the keys from her hand. "This the right one?" It proved to be. "I get keyed up for a performance, and it takes me a while to come down. I'll talk until you fall asleep, and then I'll slip quietly away. I want to know all about Jerry and the freezer and whether you do windows and why you left without telling me."

"How about if I fix you some breakfast?" she whispered, hooking her coat on the coat tree alongside his jacket.

"Love it. Just don't forget the side order of aspirin."

Sarah shed some light on her brown-and-yellow country kitchen and took a bottle of aspirin down from the cabinet. "I hope you came by this headache honestly," she said, handing him a tall glass of water. "I'd say most of your glassy-eyed guests are in for some headaches when they come down, too. Is that all...par for the show-business course?" Her eyes phrased the question more personally.

"I had a couple of beers, which is par for *my* course," he told her. "The rest doesn't interest me. I don't need any more brain damage." The question in her eyes was rephrased. "Forget I said that." He shrugged quickly. "Poor joke. What're we having, now? I do terrific omelets. Got any mushrooms?" He rubbed his hands together briskly, dismissing the "poor joke" with serious cooking talk.

Connor allowed no interference with his omelet, so Sarah busied herself with coffee and a fruit compote. When all was ready, she hung her apron on its hook, and he noticed the front of her skirt.

"What happened there?"

Having forgotten about the stain, she wished she hadn't uncovered it now. "Spider Woman got a little clumsy," she answered lightly.

Connor remembered that about the time he'd realized Sarah was gone, the Spider had staged a second come-on, more direct than the first. He'd felt as though he'd walked into a room full of cobwebs, and he couldn't find the door fast enough.

"Is it ruined?" he asked.

"I think so." She joined him at the table.

"Damn, I liked that skirt. I'll buy you another one."

Sarah's frown lacked patience. "You can't buy another skirt like this, Connor. It was made for me by a friend. There *isn't* another skirt like this."

His shrug said otherwise. "I'll have another one made. What do you think?"

She sighed, rolling hot cheese, mushroom and eggs over her tongue. "I don't think you understand."

"I know *you* don't understand. What do you think of the omelet?"

"It's delicious. And I am not going to become your special charity. The skirt is not replaceable, and it wasn't your fault anyway, so don't worry about it."

"Of course it was my fault. It was my party. Is that why you left?"

"Yes...no, not entirely. But sometimes it takes a cold splash to bring me to my senses."

He didn't ask what her senses had told her about him after she recovered them. She was afraid of him; he knew that. He'd have to cure her of that. He found her shyness to be lovely and painful at the same time—lovely because it was so honest, and painful because he felt it, too. As long as he was making music, he didn't care if there were five or five thousand people around, but just hanging out and rubbing elbows in a crowded room was something else. He'd never quite overcome the fear of suffocating while everyone else in the crowd took all the air. He never knew when the conversation would turn to him and he'd draw an absolute blank. Most of his party appearances were brief—arrive late, meet the people, play a few tunes with the boys, exit quietly.

They ate in thoughtful silence, and when the food was gone and only the coffee was left, Connor spoke. "Are you going to give me a hard time every time I want to do something for you and Dannie?''

"Every time?" Her eyes grazed his face. "How many times will that be, Connor? After a few extravagant gifts, then what?"

"I offered you money," he reminded her quietly. "That offer still stands."

"And I offered to let you see Dannie, and if she's more than a novelty to you, that offer still stands."

Connor held his cup in both hands, studying its contents thoughtfully. "That's really all you want from me?"

Was that really more than he wanted to give? "Dannie has one very self-centered uncle and one rather eccentric mother. That's a very limited family for a little girl. You told her you were her Uncle Connor, and that's all she wants from you."

"But what do you want?"

"I want you to be careful not to make promises you can't keep, not to dazzle her with expensive gifts, not to spoil her." Too many negatives, Sarah. Give him a positive. "We don't want your money, honey, but if you've got some time..." she recited with a smile.

Connor grinned. "Got a little country in your soul after all, haven't you, Sarah Benedict?"

"I think I can match *you* hayseed for hayseed, Connor Ryan."

She watched his grin relax into a soft smile as he leaned slightly forward on his elbows and gazed across the rim of his cup at her, his eyes skylight blue. "I've got plenty of time. When can you come out and see me—both of you?"

Sarah lifted naturally delicate eyebrows over a mocking brown-eyed smile. "To California? When gas prices get back down to forty cents a gallon. To Nashville, maybe sixty cents."

"I can't send you a couple of plane tickets?" Sarah shook her head, still smiling. "They're cheap, you know, coast to coast." The head continued to shake. "Hey, what is this? I haven't always had the kind of money I have now, and this is hardly noblesse-oblige time. You know what kind of family I've got?'' He set his cup down patiently, noticing that she was listening now, no longer shaking her head. ''I've got parents, whom I see infrequently because we can hardly think of anything to say to each other, and I think I've got a couple of aunts and cousins somewhere, though we pretty much lost touch over the years with all the moving we did. So things are pretty limited on the Ryan side of Dannie's family, too. Sarah, I've got time *and* money on my hands. Let me spend some of it on my brother's daughter.''

Oh, Lord, this man was charming and here he was in her house again. The image of the spotlighted stage star was quickly fading from Sarah's mind as she listened to him talk about family and watched him dawdle over eggs and coffee. She had to recall that party and those fish-eyed people and remember that his life-style was one that was bound to be filled with weeping and wailing and teeth gnashing. And deep down she knew the charm threatened her own peace of mind more than it did her daughter's...*her* daughter's.

''Our door is always open...to Dannie's Uncle Connor,'' Sarah told him quietly.

Connor took that as a rejection. Grimly admonishing himself to say no more, he remembered the offer he'd made a couple of years ago to his parents—a trip for their anniversary. They had talked about taking a cruise when, as his father had always said, ''we can go in real style.'' Connor had consulted a travel agency and presented them some options in the form of a gift when he took them out to dinner for their wedding anniversary. The meal was a custom that Kevin and Connor had started many years ago and that Connor observed whenever possible for reasons still not quite clear to him. His father had declined the trip, assuring Connor that they were just too busy to get away. He then remembered thinking of all of his gifts that had never brought quite the pleasure that Kevin's had, and that if this had been Kevin's gift...

His watch comfirmed his growing suspicion that he'd stayed long enough. He helped Sarah clear the table but made no further offers. He was ready to leave—had his jacket on, his hand on the doorknob. Another minute and she'd say something at least, give him something to take with him. He didn't want to go without…some sign of…

He was leaving, and she had no idea whether she'd see him again. A raft of suggestions raced in her head, some totally ridiculous, others totally unacceptable, but she had to say something before he was gone and it was too late.

"Connor, if you have no family commitments, maybe you'd like to come for Christmas," Sarah said quickly.

There was a bright flicker in his eyes, but it faded just as quickly. "I have…we have a concert in Austin—a benefit. It's going to be televised."

She smiled sadly, sensing shared disappointment. "I'll be able to see you on TV, then." And she quickly amended, "*We* will."

He dropped his hand from the doorknob now and looked at her earnestly. "I'm glad I came, Sarah. I told myself I was coming to negotiate a settlement, but if that had really been the case, I'd have sent my lawyer. I wanted to find some part of Kevin still alive. That's really why I came. There was a lot of water under the bridge between him and me, but Kevin was my brother, and he was my friend, and I miss him."

At that moment Connor looked more vulnerable than Sarah was certain Kevin had ever been. Kevin had never revealed any such personal feeling to her. She'd sometimes wondered if Kevin had ever experienced doubt or anger or pain. But Connor's eyes said that he had known all three. And Sarah, who had known them also, wanted nothing more at this moment than to reach out to Connor, to speak of Sarah and Connor, but the words failed her. She chose, instead, to affirm the one emotional cornerstone she knew they shared.

"I miss him, too," she said. *I will miss you* was what she wanted to say.

And *I will miss you* was what he wanted to hear.

Chapter Four

Can't spare a minute or a tinker's damn
Got nothin' left over for Uncle Sam
But she don't care if I'm rich or not
Cause I'm givin' my woman all I got.

"Dannie, I've told you not to touch the stereo." Sarah sighed as she pulled the vacuum-cleaner plug from the wall. The voice on the radio was a welcome sound, displacing the empty roar of the vacuum, but Sarah resolutely pushed the warm feeling aside and persisted with the reminder, "This isn't our house."

"That's Uncle Connor's song, isn't it, Mommy?" Returning to her baby doll and its assortment of small clothes, Dannie watched the vacuum cleaner suck up its cord like a piece of spaghetti. Her mother dismantled the machine, seeming not to have heard the question. It was not until the song was over that Sarah turned the radio off and carefully closed the doors on the stereo's fine cherry-wood cabinet.

"I remember he sang that song in his show," Dannie concluded, hoping her mother would remember, too.

Sarah smiled. "Isn't it nice that we can turn the radio on and hear his voice? Not every little girl can hear her uncle's voice at the flip of a switch."

"Is that his real voice?" Dannie studied the silent cabinet. "Was he really singing at the other end of the radio?"

"No, they were playing his record at the other end. But it was his real voice on the record." If that voice gave Dannie a feeling of wonder, she had a right to it. She was not yet five years old. Sarah, on the other hand, was privately embarrassed about the pattering sensation that voice caused within her. She was really too old to be a groupie.

"Put your toys in your tote bag now, Dannie. I think Lady Lavinia's house is ready to receive guests." Pushing Connor's voice to the back of her mind, Sarah surveyed Lavinia Porter's living room. Tomorrow morning it would be strewn with empty glasses and ashtrays full of cigarette butts, and Sarah would be paid to restore it to its present condition—immaculate except for Dannie's crayons still on the side table.

Sarah picked Dannie's drawing up from the table. Dannie had taken an interest in drawing quite early on, Sarah thought, and now her shapes were recognizable. She had a real feel for color and texture. Indulging herself in a proud-mother smile, Sarah noted Dannie's rather original bent for putting things in an unexpected order; her flowers grew under the vase, and the man in profile had eyes in the back of his head. It was nice that children were free to experiment. Sarah believed in providing paper and pencil or crayons—never a coloring book, which might cramp Dannie's budding style.

A purple tote bag stuffed with doll clothes dropped at Sarah's feet. "I like these pictures very much, sweetheart," Sarah said. Dannie's tiny teeth shone brightly in her smile. "You're really into purple lately, aren't you?"

"Those are like the flowers you painted. I'm going to give them to Uncle Connor when he comes back." One by one, Dannie returned her crayons to their little box. "He likes your pictures," she reported, trying to jam a yellow crayon among its fellows. "Do you think he'll like mine?"

"I'm sure he will." On second thought she asked, "How do you know he likes my pictures?"

"He told me. Up on the mountain he said it was as pretty as one of your pictures. And he said *you're* pretty and *I'm* pretty." The yellow crayon had been jammed into the box, and she was working on an orange one. Her puffy little frown betrayed frustration, and she was grateful when Sarah took the box from her hand. Mother's magic fingers easily coaxed the crayons into straight rows, leaving space for one more, which Dannie slid into place with a triumphant smile. "And he doesn't have a little girl, except now he's got me, and he's glad he found me."

The innocent joy shimmering in Dannie's blue eyes squeezed Sarah's heart like a fruit press. "Dannie, you have to understand that Uncle Connor isn't going to be...he won't be able to..."

Wide eyes waited expectantly, innocence at the fore. "Won't be able to what, Mommy?"

Sarah brushed a stray wisp of blond hair back toward Dannie's curly ponytail. Experience would shatter her expectations all too soon. A few disappointments, a rejection or two, and this beautiful quality of childhood would be gone. "Uncle Connor lives very far from us, sweetheart. You probably won't see him...very often."

Dannie smiled confidently. "He lives in California. He has a horse named Ginger, and he's going to teach me how to ride it."

Promises, promises. Didn't he realize that children believed in them? "I'm sure he'd like to do that, but you must remember that California is...just so far away from us." Far away from us in every way possible. Light-years away.

"I know that. But airplanes take you there."

Beautiful innocence.

Through his glass wall Connor Ryan watched a white-lipped, blue-gray wave roll over his stretch of beach. The clouds overhead were steely gray, angry and anxious to release some tension. Coolness penetrated his back as he leaned against the stonework in the corner of the room where stone wall met glass wall. The stone wall housed a fireplace, which offered some sense of home, while the glass wall gave him a sense of freedom.

He had a tight-fisted hold on both ends of the towel that hung around his neck. The wall felt hard and hurt slightly, but it was cool. He'd worked himself into a heated sweat at the weight bench, sat in the sauna, showered, and now the cool stones felt good on his back.

Dropping his head back against the wall, he dragged heavily on the cigarette he held in a cupped hand and then blew a gray cloud of his own. Why did he hammer his body into shape with weights and then tear it down with cigarettes? Something gnawed at him from the inside, something like the bark-boring worms he used to find in the trunk of his tree house when he was a kid. He would poke at them and kill them because they made his tree weep in the crotch of its branches while they turned its wood to pulp. Now he would smoke out the gnawing gut borer with a smudge pot full of tobacco.

From the multitude of hidden stereo speakers, a Castilian rhythm of classical-guitar music filled the room. Pushing away from the wall on a burst of restlessness, Connor flicked the last inch of the cigarette into the cold cavern of the fireplace. He shoved a hassock aside with an impatient foot and dropped into a plush chair, swiveling it to face the sea. He'd chosen this house for its beauty and solitude, and now, as evening shadows and dark clouds drew in around him, he saw that the beauty could be hauntingly hollow and the solitude was bleak.

He'd always been a loner, but he'd never wanted to be truly alone. Kevin had known that. Scotch understood it, too, and so did Maggie. They both loved Connor, and they hoped he'd find what they had together. Unlike Mike, he'd quickly tired of the parade of women through his bedroom, and so this kind of solitude had become more the rule of his off-tour life rather than the exception. His friends accepted that as part and parcel of his creative nature. But those close to him knew that he was lonely.

Lonely, yes, but not miserable. Not pacing with the physical ache that had plagued him since he'd come home this time. The house seemed bigger, emptier, colder than he remembered. He was surrounded by the starkness of white, and the ocean echoed endlessly. The garish painting over the fireplace had to go, and those on the opposite wall were meaningless. He wanted some warmth in this room. He wanted something of Sarah's. His hand dropped over the phone and hesitated, as it had a hundred times in the last week. He needed something of Sarah herself.

> *It's a misty river morning, babe*
> *The sun's just blinkin' through the trees*
> *White mist risin' on the lazy river's bend*
> *And white light seepin' through the window shade.*

The telephone jangled more insistently than usual, and now Sarah set brush and palette pad aside in disgust, gave her hands a cursory wipe on a rag and picked up the receiver. "Sarah Benedict," she clipped, reaching to turn down the volume on the radio.

"Sarah Benedict, you gorgeous struggling artist you, this is Barbara from the Tate Gallery. Are you deaf, Sarah? I've been calling all morning, and I know your schedule. You're home on Wednesdays."

"I'm home, but I'm working. What's up, Barbara?"

"What's up? Not you, I hope. You'd better be sitting down. I've got news, lady. Big-bucks news."

Barbara Tate should have owned a football team rather than an art gallery. Over the phone she always rattled the eardrum with her news, which was always couched in a directive. Sarah simply waited quietly for the point.

"We sold three of your paintings yesterday out of the clear blue. You won't believe this, Sarah. The *price* we got is unbelievable! And, of course, my commission is wonderful. We're on our way."

Sold three pieces all at once? Sarah let that sink in before she got to the next part. "What kind of unbelievable price?"

"Three grand!" The two syllables burst over the wires. "Can you believe it? *Three* grand."

"Which ones?" Astonishment gave way to ecstasy. "Who bought them?"

"Let's see...*Apple-Pickers*, *Girl by the Pond* and *Destinations*. Great pieces, Sarah. Wonderful work. He wanted earthiness—bronze, sienna, gold—with soft-color accents."

"Who? Who wanted...?"

"Some broker from California. I must be advertising better than I thought. Bought them for some rock star, I guess."

Oh, Connor, you didn't! "Did you *ask* for a thousand dollars apiece, Barbara?"

"No, no, Sarah, he paid *three* thousand apiece. And I should tell you I got it for you, but I didn't. He offered two, and when my mouth dropped open, he said three was his final offer. And he wanted Sarah Benedict, no one else. The word must be out on you at last, my friend. I didn't know you were showing anything out on the West Coast."

"I'm not. I think it's someone I've...met."

"The broker?"

"No, the...uh...the musician." Sarah really didn't want to get into this, certainly not with Barbara.

"A rock star? *You?*"

"He's sort of a friend of a friend. A friend's relative, actually. Look, Barbara, this isn't real. I mean, this man is very eccentric, and I'm sure he doesn't intend..."

"The money's real, Sarah. It's in my hand."

"But it's a fluke. It doesn't set any precedents."

"Maybe this guy'll tell all his eccentric friends what a good deal he got. Let's hope so. Check's in the mail. Have some fun with it. I'm raising your prices. Bye, now."

Raising her prices! She'd probably never sell anything again, thanks to Connor Ryan. Sarah stared down at the assortment of colors on her palette, at odds with herself. She should have been happy about the sale. She wanted to be; she had waited long enough for one like this. But this wasn't the way it was supposed to work. The buyer was supposed to be convinced he'd found the next Picasso. It wasn't supposed to be conscience money. And what was she doing on Connor Ryan's conscience, anyway? Dannie wasn't his child.

But Dannie talked about him all the time, and Sarah thought about him more than she wanted to. He crept into her dreams at night and haunted her during the day. She could have excused these feelings if she could honestly have believed it was because he'd brought Kevin back, but she knew it wasn't the memory of that. Her mind was filled with Connor.

You and me and the river, babe,
Makin' misty morning love.

"Sarah, it's Connor."

"Connor." The name was caressed in soft surprise.

"The paintings are beautiful."

"They should be. You paid handsomely for them."

"Not enough. Not nearly. The colors are perfect here— warm and muted. I have a thing about color, and I like the way you use it."

"I'm glad you like them, but I wish you'd just paid what they were worth. Then I might believe you weren't just patronizing me."

She bristled at his soft laugh. It seemed indulgent. "Sarah, all the great artists were patronized. Michelangelo had a patron, didn't he? You shouldn't be scrubbing floors when you could be doing what you do so beautifully."

"Maybe I like scrubbing floors." She knew that sounded like a juvenile retort, but he had no business making judgments about her livelihood.

"Yeah. Maybe I liked pumping gas and busing tables. You're talking to someone who knows all about it, kid. I like to make music, and you like to paint, and it's great to get paid for doing what you like to do. How's Dannie?"

"Dannie's fine. She likes having a new uncle. She recognizes your songs when they play them on the radio. I bought her a record the other day, and she plays it all the time."

"On what?"

"On her little record player."

"I bet we sound less than great on a kiddie-time record player. You girls need a decent stereo. I'll see that—"

"No, Connor. Please. We're not your special charity. Your brother wasn't using your ID when he met me."

"My ID? Oh...yeah." He remembered making some remark about people coming after him for favors. "That was a joke, Sarah. You've more than convinced me that you weren't looking for anything. In fact, I'm beginning to wonder if I'm to be allowed *any* privileges. I want to be..." He couldn't say what he wanted to be. He didn't know yet. He knew he wanted to be in the same room with her right now instead of at the other end of a telephone cable. "I want to help."

"You have. You've almost convinced me that one of my paintings could be worth three thousand dollars."

There was a smile in her voice, and it put one in his. "I have them hanging up, and they've already appreciated in value. I've already gotten my money's worth. They give the place a whole different feeling."

"I'm glad. *Apple Pickers* is one of my favorites, and I'm glad it went to someone who'll enjoy it. And it *will* be worth a great deal more someday, I promise."

"I do have a problem with them, though." The suggestion was delicately scented bait for his hook.

"What's that?"

"They make the rest of the stuff I've got hanging around here look like dime-store junk. I took down that thing I had over the fireplace. Couldn't stand it anymore. What have you got that's about four feet by five feet?"

"My kitchen table."

He laughed again, and this time she tingled at the sound. "Come on, Sarah, I'm in trouble here. I'm doing my own thing, and I want to do it right. When it's all done, I plan to invite that decorator lady over and give her a taste of real class."

Sarah tried not to wonder anything about this "decorator lady." "Really, Connor, I have nothing that big. I don't think I've ever stretched a canvas that size."

"You could, though."

"Yes, I could, but I haven't any plans for anything that large. Maybe your broker should..."

"What you could do is come out and look the place over. Kind of get an idea of where it would go, what the setting's like."

"Go out to California?" The idea was absurd.

"Sure. Bring Dannie. She'll love it here. I hope she hasn't learned to swim yet because I want to be the one to teach her. And she can—"

"Hold it! Hold it right there, Connor." Sarah quickly swallowed any wistfulness that might betray regret and declared a firm, "We can't do that."

"Why not? Don't give me any nonsense about the price of gas. I'll send plane tickets."

"I can't just pick up and leave any time I want, Connor. I have obligations."

"Anytime you *want*," he repeated, examining the words. "That means you want to come, but the people of Amherst can't clean their own houses for a week or so."

"It means," she clarified, "that I plan our vacations months in advance, that I put money aside for them and that I buy my own tickets. I'm wary of eccentric musicians who spread their money around so freely, Mr. Ryan."

"Good God, you're methodical." He sighed. "Whatever happened to eccentric artists?"

"They learned from Michelangelo's example. Patrons have

a way of coming up with the most unreasonable demands," Sarah explained.

"And you're thinking if I ask you to spend some time lying on your back, it won't be to paint the ceiling of any chapel," he assumed in a humorless tone of voice.

Sarah felt her face grow hot. "I'm not thinking that at all," she said quietly.

"I'm not thinking that way, either. I'm thinking I like your work, and I'd like to own more of it. I'm thinking…" He took a deep breath. "I'm thinking I want to see you and Dannie again, but if I tell you that and you turn me down… I'm thinking maybe you should think it over, Sarah. I'm not looking for favors from you any more than you want favors from me. Let's put that illusion to rest and see what's left, okay? You give it some thought."

Sarah replaced the receiver in its cradle with deliberate care. This man confused her as no man ever had before. He lived a fast-paced, glamorous life. Men like that were supposed to be interested in fast, glamorous women, certainly not in a mother and child.

Since Kevin, Sarah had dated only occasionally. She had a child to consider. There were times when Sarah worried about Dannie growing up without a father, times when she felt the burden of her many roles, and she thought that burdens were meant to be shared. There were many times when Sarah reasoned that a comfortable, dependable, secure relationship with a man might not be a bad idea.

But Sarah's thoughts had taken a new tack lately. There were times when she felt terribly alone, and she needed to be close, to touch, to share herself. Those were the times when there was no logic or reason or decision. There was only an uncontrollable longing of the heart and an image of Connor. This man attracted her as no man ever had before.

For pure and unlimited exasperation power, no man could beat Sarah's brother. He'd been hanging around the house for three days and showed no sign of leaving. Sarah had planned to keep the news of her big sale a secret, but the cat was out of the bag when he took a follow-up call from Barbara at the gallery. The news gave Jerry a sudden spurt of energy, which he directed to a relentless pursuit of happiness in Sarah's be-half.

"You know, I've never felt quite right about moving out of here and leaving you and Dannie all alone. You need a man around here, Sarah."

Sarah eyed Jerry's clumsy attempt to trim carrots and won-dered how soon he'd cut himself. "I take it Pepper hasn't forgiven you yet."

"In her heart, she probably has. She just hasn't got the words out yet." Jerry tipped his head back thoughtfully, al-lowing himself a brief mental workout. The look that followed was meant to forewarn her that he'd arrived at a weighty con-clusion. "I think it's time I came home, Sarah. I've been shirk-ing my duties where you and Dannie are concerned. Pepper is just—" he shrugged, turning his mouth down in casual dis-missal "—just a passing fling. You and Dannie are family."

What had she done to deserve this? Sold some paintings? Cooked his favorite dinner? Either one would have done it for Jerry. "You're family, too, Jerry. We love you. You can stay one more night. Tomorrow you're going to call Pepper and let her get the words out."

"No, I mean it Sarah."

"Of course, you could get an apartment of your own." She cocked him a sweet smile.

"You're not as nice as you used to be, Sarah. Spinsterhood is making a mean old lady out of you. You're going to have warts on your nose and start cackling pretty soon." With the end of a carrot he indicated a likely spot at the tip of her nose. "Do yourself a favor. Take a trip out to California."

"I should never have told you. I can't imagine why he'd even suggest it."

"The man's crazy about you. He must be. Why else would he pay nine thousand dollars for three little pictures?"

"Obviously he knows good art. Cut those into sticks,

please." Sarah slid a roasting pan from the oven, inhaling the sweet, cured aroma as the drippings from the ham popped their last. "Then you can slice this."

"Ouch! Damn. Cut myself. Take over for me here, would you? I'm bleeding." The look on Jerry's face asked for pity, and she gave it as she would to any wounded, helpless thing.

It was easy to feel sorry for him. Their mother always had, and with her death just three years ago, the care and feeding of Jerry had been left to the women in his life who had a soft spot for wounded, helpless things. Their father, it seemed, had been gone forever. He'd left them for the lure of a more glamorous life as an actor and now and then turned up on a soap opera.

"I'm not good for much, am I, Sarah?"

Here it came. Jerry was going to hand her a little self-pity along with the knife and cutting board. Sarah returned a raised brow and no comment.

"No, I mean it. I never seem to be in the right place at the right time with the right idea." He smiled, and Sarah knew it was that smile that got him all he wanted. "I did write a damned good letter, though. And it turned out even better than I thought. He's a nice guy, Sarah." He laid a brotherly hand on Sarah's shoulder. "Take that trip. Don't think about it. Just do it."

Our love's a melancholy used-to-be
My cellar full of faded memories
The dusty echoes of a lie
A lonely, hollow, aching sigh
A room where nothing stands but me.

The idea came to him all in one piece when Connor paid his obligatory visit to his parents. He wondered, almost idly, what they'd say to news of a grandchild—a child of Kevin's flesh. Curiosity got the best of him, and he tried it out on them. They loved it. They wanted to meet her. He knew they meant to bring Kevin back through his child, and that was natural. He'd wanted that himself in a way; he knew that now.

Then he'd met Sarah and her daughter, and things had changed. She wasn't "Kevin's kid" anymore; she was Dannie. She was the princess who could wrap her arms around his neck, call him "Uncle Connor" and make his heart swell. And the woman in the picture he'd carried in his pocket had become Sarah—delicate and shy and warm. If she wanted to, she could split his heart wide open.

The idea was to get them here.

"Sarah, it's Connor."

"Hello, Connor." She really hadn't expected him to call again.

"I have a proposition for you."

No preliminaries. This was definitely not Kevin. Sarah cradled the receiver against her ear and tightened her other hand around the mouthpiece. "An offer I can't refuse?"

"I'm sure you can, knowing you. Here it is anyway: Dannie's grandparents want to meet her. They live in San Francisco. I don't know whether I told you, but Kevin was kind of larger than life for them. I told them about Dannie because...well, I thought they had a right to know."

Kevin was larger than life? What was Connor, then? "Of course they did. Were they shocked?"

Connor considered for a moment. "I guess they went through a range of reactions. They're saddened by the tragedy that Kevin died before he knew about his child—before he was able to marry you. But they're glad to have a grandchild. They figure I won't come through for them."

"Of course, a man in your position has to be careful."

"Of course." Was she actually teasing him? "They really want to meet her, Sarah. They deserve that much, don't you think? Let me send the tickets."

"San Francisco?"

"Yes."

"When?"

"Whenever you say."

A moment's deliberation, and then a sigh. "All right. Dannie deserves that much, too."

Connor smiled at the soft-colored painting that hung on the wall above him. Stroke of genius, Ryan. Whoever said you weren't that bright?

Chapter Five

Sarah had never flown first-class. It was an experience in luxury and decadence, she decided, looking over the luncheon menu. No hamburgers and fries. What was a four-year-old supposed to eat? *Boeuf Bourguignonne?* A glance at Dannie's wonder-lit face told Sarah that whatever this plane had to offer would suit her just fine. Sarah soon found herself sipping at a perpetually full glass of champagne and deciding that luxury and decadence had their good points. The pilot suggested they prepare for landing before Sarah fully realized she was flying.

She was feeling a bit foolish when she walked into the terminal, flight bag on one shoulder, Dannie's hand firmly clutched in her other hand. Her heart fluttered in her throat as she scanned the canvas of faces. She attributed her anxiety strictly to schoolgirl silliness.

Where was he? Did he send someone to pick them up, someone she wouldn't recognize? Did he remember the time, the flight number, or did he have a secretary to take care of all the worrisome little details in his life? Did some strange woman make the reservations, buy the—

"There he is, Mommy! Uncle Connor! See?"

Sarah lost control of her face's inane grin, and suddenly the absurdity she felt didn't matter anymore. He was smiling, too, behind a pair of dark glasses. There were barriers—people, a railing, a cart full of luggage—but some means of propulsion totally unconnected to her body carried her to him quickly. At a distance of three feet she stopped short and caught her breath, still beaming. She wanted to walk right into him, but she caught herself in time. Instead, she stared at the honey-tan face and tousled blond hair. Could he have been in a hurry to get here?

He wanted to hold her, but his arms stiffened awkwardly at his sides. He knew he was grinning like a Cheshire cat, and he couldn't help that. The instructions he'd given himself when he heard them announce her flight number—stay cool, look casual, sort of like, "Oh, you're here already?"—had been useless. She looked every bit as good as he remembered. He'd been planning to get her out in the sun, but maybe he shouldn't. That porcelain face was so translucent, so refined that it demanded to be pampered. Her hair hung soft and loose, and her brown eyes glistened. She didn't look like a woman who'd had her arm twisted over the phone.

"Great to see you, Sarah," he offered, and wished immediately it had sounded different.

Broadening her grin, she reached for the sunglasses and removed them from his face. He didn't flinch. "Great to see you, too, Connor." The low purr was not something she recognized as her own sound. She slipped the glasses in the front pocket of his blue blazer.

"Just one of the trappings," he explained.

"Trappings," she mused. "Yes, you seem to be an expert. The prey is even pleased to be here."

"Prey?" His smile become cocky. "I invited you here, polite as you please. You accepted."

"Yes, I did. And you didn't even have to mention the champagne."

"You started without me?"

"Started what?"

The smile melted, and the answer came first through his eyes. "The celebration, Sarah." They reached for each other in slow motion, and he repeated, "The celebration."

Dannie wasn't sure what to make of all this. She had the feeling she'd almost been forgotten, but the looks her mother and her uncle were giving each other felt warm, even from her perspective. It didn't surprise her when they stopped grinning and gabbing at each other and finally kissed. It sure seemed like a long kiss, though, and Dannie wondered if she'd get one, too.

"Uncle Connor?"

The little voice rapped at the perimeter of Connor's brain, which was bubbling with the taste of champagne. It took a supreme effort to drag his lips away from Sarah's, and his "Hmm" was more groan than question.

"I want a kiss, too."

The cherubic face smiled up at him, and he remembered himself. Without completely relinquishing his hold on Sarah, he scooped Dannie up in one arm, bringing their three faces within a nose length of one another. He gave Dannie a quick, hard, noisy kiss that left her frowning with confusion. "How come you kissed Mommy bigger than you kissed me?"

He laughed and bussed her once more on the cheek. "Because that's the way it's supposed to be, Princess. A big girl like your mom just gets one big kiss." The arm around Sarah's waist tightened in a reassuring squeeze as he pecked Dannie again, this time on her nose. "Little girls get a bunch of little kisses." Another peck had her giggling with delight. "You can have all you want," he promised with a firm kiss on her forehead. "You say when. I'm really glad to see you, you know."

Sarah watched them smile at each other. The resemblance between the two profiles was remarkable. He was good for

Dannie, she thought. She'd done the right thing in bringing her here.

"I guess Uncle Jerry doesn't know about different kisses," Dannie said. "He kisses me and Mommy both the same."

Connor dropped a glance at Sarah before pursuing. "Really?"

"He kisses little kisses," Sarah explained. "One each."

"Ah." Connor nodded, his eyes dancing from one face to the other and back again. "That's probably because Jerry doesn't understand the code of chivalry. He isn't a true knight."

"Are you a knight, Uncle Connor?"

"I'm a Georgia Night," he confided secretively. "We spell it a little differently, but then I never had much respect for spelling. I know a real princess when I see one. Ready to meet your grandparents?"

"Will they know a real princess when they see one?" Sarah asked.

"They can't wait. I've told them how you feel about spoiling her, but I don't think it did much good. They're crazy about her already." There was a kind of longing in Connor's eyes, a need that Sarah couldn't identify. "Thanks for letting me give them this, Sarah." Then it was as though he caught himself being too serious, and he shrugged it off with half a laugh. "It's your doing, of course, but I'm a hell of a facilitator. Don't you agree?"

Sarah gave him the warm smile she thought he needed. "You're a true knight, Connor Ryan."

Connor's parents lived in a stylish San Francisco apartment that boasted a lovely view of the city. The family resemblance was so strong that Sarah believed she'd have recognized his father if she'd met him on the street. If his hair had been allowed to grow, it would have been full and thick and completely white, but he wore it in a crew cut, as she imagined he had when it was the same straw color he'd given his sons. Even in retirement, the man was regulation army. His stature his dress, the very expression on his face was commanding. He offered Sarah a hearty handshake.

"Connor has told us the whole story. We're pleased, Miss Benedict. We're very pleased."

Connor's mother's voice was too melodious ever to be an intrusion. Its softness held the memory of a Southern upbringing, and the hug she greeted Sarah with was regulation would-be mother-in-law. "It should have been Mrs. Ryan, and if Kevin had lived—" Sarah was held at arm's length now, the woman's soft blue eyes intense with sincerity "—if Kevin had lived, he would have made it so."

Sarah could see this was not the time to suggest alternatives. "I know. But I'd still be Sarah." She smiled that assurance at them both.

Roberta Ryan nodded and squeezed Sarah's arms before she released her and turned to Connor, who held the prize in his arms. "Where's the little girl who's going to call me Grandma? Where's my little...oooh, Dwight, look. She's the image of Kevin." She held eager hands up to Dannie, who took a firmer hold on Connor's neck while she sized the woman up. "Will you come to see your grandma, Danielle? I've been waiting a long time to give you a hug."

Dannie looked first to her mother, then to Connor, who explained, "This is your grandmother, Dannie. Remember, I told you before that she was your dad's mother, and she's my mother. That makes her your grandmother."

Dannie checked the woman out again. She had no experience with grandmothers, and the grandma who talked about cookies on TV looked a lot different.

"Your daddy was my little boy, honey, my baby."

"You're my Uncle Connor's mommy?"

The woman nodded, smiling anxiously. She had gray hair like a grandma, but she didn't have too many wrinkles, and she didn't have glasses, and she was almost as thin as Dannie's own mother. Dannie liked almost everything about her, except she had long red fingernails. Dannie didn't like those at all. She decided to stay right where she was.

"Give her a little time, Mom," Connor suggested, reassu[ring] Dannie with a pat on the back. "She'll let you know whe[n] she's ready for that hug. Right, Princess?"

Dannie agreed with a nod, and Roberta backed off, turni[ng] to her husband. "I can't get over how much she looks li[ke] Kevin. Doesn't she look just like Kevin?"

"She does," Dwight Ryan confirmed. Dannie's curiou[s] look prompted him to offer, "I'm your grandfather, your[g] lady."

"And he's not as mean as he looks," Roberta put in, reac[h]ing for Sarah's hand. "He'll always be a soldier—all spit an[d] polish on the first meeting. You know how they are, Sarah. [I] thought we'd have dinner a little early, since your stomac[h] are probably still on Eastern time. Connor will put your ba[g] in the guest room. You just get comfortable, now, and we'[ll] give Danielle time to warm up to us." Roberta led the way [to] the living room, where Connor joined her in his preferred sp[ot] beside her on the couch. Dannie crawled over to her mother[s] lap.

"Would you like a drink, Sarah?" Dwight asked, his ton[e] losing its formal edge. When Sarah declined, he made Conno[r] the same offer.

"Not unless you have a beer, Dad."

"When are you going to start drinking a *man's* drink[?] Whiskey and water is a man's drink."

"When are you going to put a beer in the refrigerator fo[r] me when you know I'm coming over?"

"One of these days I'll remember. Put that on your shop[ping] list next time, Bobbie," Dwight ordered, sliding open [the] door on the liquor cabinet.

Sarah glanced at Connor in time to see his eyes glaze ove[r,] and she remembered that whiskey and water was Kevin['s] drink.

It was Dannie who smoothed over the evening's awkwar[d] edges. Within a few minutes, she ventured away from th[e] couch, which became home base, and she began prowling th[e] room. The room's decor had an Oriental flavor, and Danni[e] found lots of pretty things to examine. She'd been in Sarah's clients' living rooms often enough to know that you had to be careful with other people's things. A lacquered Japanese music box caught her attention, and Roberta happily showed her its workings. They smiled at each other as the box played "China Nights," and the pretty woman with the fashionably short gray haircut and the crystal-blue eyes became Dannie's grandma.

Throughout the evening, there was talk of the army. Dwight Ryan reveled in it. Roberta put in her reminiscences of faraway places and people who'd been stationed with them here and had turned up again there. Sarah listened, offering a memory or two of Wiesbaden, which was about all she knew of the army.

Connor found himself reverting to an old tactic. After turning off the lights in his brain and pulling down all the shades, he was able to nod or offer a word or two occasionally without allowing the insignificance of his presence to bother him. The talk was of the army and of Kevin and the old man. The focus was on Kevin's child and the woman whom Kevin had loved. Why had Connor expected anything different? He'd only brought them here.

As dinner wound down to apple pie and coffee, Dwight wondered aloud whether Sarah had seen Kevin's "chopper" up close.

"Yes, I did once," she said. "Kevin took me to an open house once—Armed Forces Day, I believe."

"What did you think of it?" Dwight asked.

"I loved the parade. The band and all the uniforms and the close-order marching."

"I mean the big bird," Dwight clarified. "What did you think of that?"

Sarah's stomach tightened. What did she think of the machine that had taken Kevin to his death? "It was…very big. Much bigger than I had imagined." She didn't care to remember any more than that.

Unexpectedly, Dwight chuckled. "Big. Damn right, it was big. I used to kid him about being a fly-boy instead of a *real* soldier, but we both knew what kind of soldier he was. And he went down like a soldier. You didn't know anything about his mission, did you, Sarah?''

''No,'' Sarah said quietly.

''Of course not. He was a soldier.''

Connor's brain activated, his jaw tightening as he focused on Sarah's discomfort. ''They wouldn't tell us anything, either, Dad.''

''He was shot down by enemy fire,'' Dwight said.

''We don't know that.''

''I know it. He was a soldier.'' Father's eyes caught son's, and there was an unmistakable judgment in them. ''Like his father. All man, one hundred percent. *A soldier*.''

The words had been thrown back and forth so often that they had become unnecessary. The space surrounding the stare-down was electric with the old dispute. The army had sent Dwight Ryan the honored remains of a heroic son. To Connor it had returned a dead brother.

''My father's name was Kevin, and he was killed in the war.''

Eye contact between the two men snapped almost audibly as each turned toward the little voice. ''You see? The child knows. Instinctively, she knows,'' Dwight insisted.

''She knows he's not here,'' Connor said gently. ''She knows she's never...''

Dannie flashed a grin at her grandfather. ''Mommy painted a picture of him, and it looks just like Uncle Connor. And I look like Uncle Connor, too. Uncle Connor sings on the radio. I just turn the radio on, and after a while he sings.''

Connor felt his heart grow inside his chest.

''We went to see his show, too,'' Dannie announced, turning to her mother for support. ''Didn't we, Mommy?''

''Yes, we did,'' Sarah confirmed, silently marveling at her daughter's diplomatic timing. ''We sat in the front row.'' Looking to Roberta for a contribution, she offered, ''It must be so exciting for you to watch your son perform before a huge crowd. He has quite a following.''

"Actually, we don't…the loud music and the wild crowds can be so unnerving, and Dwight doesn't…"

"Teenagers," Dwight mumbled. "Screaming idiots, most of them."

"We went to one," Roberta amended quickly. "But it was so nerve-racking. I was afraid they might tear his clothes off before the night was over. Of course, we have all the records."

"I know very little about music," Sarah admitted, "popular or otherwise. And crowds make me uncomfortable, too. But it's easy to understand why the crowd gets a little rowdy at a Georgia Nights concert." Turning to Connor, Sarah indicated that her comments to his mother were really for him now. "I've been listening to their music, paying more attention to the medium and the message. The medium is different from mine, but the message…the message isn't so different."

Connor smiled across the table at her and let the rest of the room drift out of focus. "No, it's not so different. But your statements are much softer."

"There's more excitement in yours," she countered. "Your colors are bolder."

"But there's quiet excitement in yours, Sarah. That softness creates a yearning for…for softness." The tinkle of "China Nights" pulled Connor's attention back into the room, and he offered his mother part of the smile he'd given Sarah, part of the good feeling her compliments had stirred. "My music may not be your style, Mom, but you'd like Sarah's paintings, I'm sure. See for yourself next time you come down. I intend to have a much bigger collection by then."

"It seems there's a sudden big-name demand for my work," Sarah reminded him. "Prices have skyrocketed."

"I'm planning to beat the run on Sarah Benedicts by commissioning a couple of pieces. So you know what you're getting for Christmas, Mom."

"How nice!" Roberta exclaimed. "I'm sure I'd love…"

"You really would, Mom. Sarah's work is quiet, understated—sort of like some of this Japanese stuff, only it's…"

Connor leaned toward his mother as his conviction grew in intensity. She'd like this gift.

"Did you really do a portrait of Kevin, Sarah?" Roberta asked.

"Yes, I did. It really isn't very..."

"I don't suppose you'd want to part with it. But maybe you could do another—a copy. I'd love a copy of Kevin's portrait."

Connor settled back on the couch, ignoring Sarah's response to his mother's request. It was no longer his gift. It was Sarah's and Kevin's. Connor had hit the nail on the head when he'd termed himself "a hell of a facilitator." His attention wandered to the corner where Dannie had been playing with the music box, and he saw that she was stretched out beside it, sound asleep. Putting the rest of the room behind him, he went to her, carefully lifted her in his arms and carried her into the guest room.

Sarah waited a few minutes before she followed him. Something in the tenderness of his gesture had mesmerized her. He'd assumed this duty without discussion. Kevin was still here in the middle of those who remembered him, but Dannie did not remember. Dannie needed someone to put her to bed, and Connor was there.

Connor never stayed in his parents' home when he visited them. He preferred a hotel to the guest room. He surprised his mother with his announcement that he'd sleep on the couch in the den, and she let slip that this was certainly unusual for him. But Sarah had stood in the doorway and watched as Connor removed each shoe and sock from Dannie's feet. She'd handed him a little pink nightgown without comment, and he'd undressed the child and slipped the nightgown on her without disturbing her sleep at all, as though he'd done this every night for the last four-and-a-half years. Sarah knew why he'd stayed. And the thought of how he'd tucked Dannie under the puffed coverlet and kissed the top of her head before he'd slipped quietly from the room filled Sarah's head after everyone had gone to bed.

A sliver of light was visible beneath the den's closed door. Sarah tapped twice, very quietly.

"Come in," Connor's voice invited. She was still dressed in her slim tweed skirt and soft red blouse, but she'd shed the matching jacket, and her legs and feet were bare. He'd made himself comfortable, too, tossing off his tie and rolling up his shirt sleeves before lighting up a cigarette. "Is your room comfortable?" he asked. "I can probably find you another blanket if you need one."

"No, everything's fine." She moved toward him slowly, not sure why she'd come. She gestured toward the couch before she sat down, tucking one leg under her. "But this doesn't look long enough for you. I think I've taken the bed you should have."

"I don't stay here as a rule. I just didn't feel like looking for a room tonight. Should have seen to it earlier." He took a last drag on his cigarette and stubbed it out.

"Why don't you take the other bed in the guest room and let me have the couch? I'm shorter."

He considered the concerned look on her face for a moment, and it occurred to him that she was trying to make up for something someone else had done—something she'd stumbled into and didn't fully understand. He should have introduced her to Kevin's parents and left. He didn't want her thinking any of this bothered him. "I can sleep anywhere," he assured her. "Airports, buses, hotel-room floors. When you travel with a band, you become a flexible sleeper."

Sarah watched her hands smooth the taut wool fabric over her knees. "They haven't accepted Kevin's death, have they?"

He sighed. "They haven't accepted it as the total waste that it was—that *I* think it was. Time stopped the day Kevin died, and nothing's changed for them since then. Five years later, they don't even know who I am."

Sarah noticed a display of photographs on the wall of shelves behind them. Connor and Kevin. As youngsters, they looked like a pair of bookends, but as they grew older, there were marked differences in style and expression. Kevin continued to be bright and shiny faced, hair trimmed above his collar and shorter still in uniform. Connor's expression said that he'd been dragged to the photographer's studio. His hair became rebelliously long, and there were no pictures of him beyond the age of about eighteen. But there was a progression of poses of Kevin in uniform beside other pictures of a young Dwight also in uniform. The display told an interesting story. "Your father identified with Kevin's ambitions, but not with yours."

"There's more to it than that. Kevin was our bridge." Connor thought the image over and cocked half a smile at its appropriateness. "The army blew up our bridge. Left a hell of a mess."

"Is that what you hoped Dannie would be?" Sarah wondered gently. "Are you trying to rebuild?"

"No." Connor frowned a bit, and then he shook his head at the thought. "No, I'm not using Dannie. I only meant to bring them together."

"That's what Jerry said he was doing when he wrote to you," Sarah remembered. "He just wanted to get some people together."

"There's nothing wrong with that. I'm glad he did. Sarah..." He reached for her hand. It felt cool in his. "I'm really glad he did."

Sarah smiled. "I am, too."

He wanted to take her in his arms, but he couldn't do that here. There was too much of Kevin here.

Sarah went back to the guest room wondering why Connor hadn't given her the kiss she'd seen in his eyes.

The five of them spent the following day together touring San Francisco. Dannie loved the cable cars, and she squealed with delight over the hills. Connor watched his father warm up to the little girl and his mother fuss over her, and he felt good. He felt as though he'd accomplished something, and he was standing back to admire his work. He felt good, too, because Sarah seemed to have taken a place standing back beside him. Feeling this way, he could spare more patience than usual on his parents.

By the third day of their visit, Dannie had added Grandpa and Grandma to her growing family. Grandma's red fingernails didn't bother her anymore, and she found that she could get around Grandpa's stern facade with a certain kind of a smile. Grandma would fix her whatever she wanted for breakfast, but she stalled, waiting for Uncle Connor to come to the table before she committed herself.

"I'll have what Uncle Connor has," she decided, scrambling for the chair next to the one she knew he would take.

Sarah set placemats and silverware in front of each chair. Hesitating on a fork, she knew before she looked up that he was standing in the doorway and that she'd been waiting for him as surely as Dannie had.

"Good morning, ladies."

"Good morning."

"Uncle Connor, Grandma will fix us whatever we want for breakfast. What do we want? Do we want French toast?"

"As long as you've got Grandma right where we want her, I guess we should take advantage of it." Connor peeked around the island of cupboards. "Good morning, Mom. We want French toast."

"It's been a long time, honey, but I think I can manage."

On his way to the table, Connor picked up the coffeepot. "Coffee, Sarah?"

"Yes, please."

He poured for them both and then took the chair beside Dannie. "What would you two like to do today? I could tag along on a shopping trip if you'd like, or maybe..."

"Can we ride the trolley again?" Dannie asked.

"Again?" Connor and Sarah exclaimed simultaneously.

"Oh, yes! I love going up the hills and down the hills." Connor caught Sarah rolling her eyes, and he thought better of laughing. "It's just like the little train that kept thinking she could, and then she tried and then she did. Do you know that story, Uncle Connor?''

''I think I do—I think I do—I think I do.'' His chugging made her giggle, and he ruffled her curls in response. ''There are lots of other things I want to show you, Princess. With this great streak of weather we've been having, we can go beachcombing.''

''Beachcombing?'' Dannie looked puzzled. ''Do you have to have a special comb?''

Roberta walked in on the laughter with a newspaper in one hand and a tray of glasses of juice in the other. ''You're in the paper again, Connor. Who's the girl this time?''

Sarah's chin snapped up a little too quickly for her own liking as she watched Roberta hand her son the folded paper. He flipped it over to the front page and nodded at the tabloid's masthead.

''Why do you read this thing, Mom? It's written by monkeys playing with typewriters.''

''I read it to find out what my son is up to.'' She reached for the paper and flipped it back to the picture in question. ''Who's this Marlene?'' she asked, pointing to the picture.

Connor gave a quick glance and then shrugged as he claimed a glass of orange juice. ''It says she was at the concert in Buffalo last month. She must be Marlene from Buffalo.''

''You've got your arm around her in the picture. Did you read what else it says?'' Roberta took the paper. ''Just read what else it says. 'Connor Ryan, the ever-elusive bachelor of Georgia Nights fame, was more than attentive to Miss Buffalo, Marlene—'''

The paper was snatched from her hands as Connor rose abruptly from his chair. ''I can read, Mom,'' he said quietly. ''Anything I want to read, I'll read myself. Don't *ever* read to me.''

Roberta lowered her eyes. ''I'm sorry, Connor.''

He relaxed visibly, muscle by muscle, and finally handed the paper back to his mother. ''Me, too. Mostly because I smell something burning.''

"The French toast!" she exclaimed, and she made a beeline for the kitchen.

Connor returned to his coffee and when Roberta brought the French toast to the table, helped Dannie cut hers up. But the scene had left Sarah considerably more shaken than she wanted to admit. Whoever Marlene was, she was none of Sarah's business. She made a tight wad of her paper napkin. Miss Buffalo, was it?

Chapter Six

"I want to take you and Dannie to Santa Cruz for a few
days—to my place."

Sarah looked up from the ponytail she was making on the
side of Dannie's hair. Connor shouldered the doorjamb, hands
tucked in the front pockets of his jeans. He was the picture of
boredom.

"Can we go beachcombing, Uncle Connor?"

Grinning, Connor hunkered down to Dannie's level. She
was his natural ally. "We can go beachcombing and horseback
riding and anything else you want to do, Princess."

"Ride real horses?" Dannie bounced on the balls of her
feet, and Sarah lost a handful of hair. "Oh, boy, real horses!"

"Hold your real horses until I give this one its tails," Sarah
ordered.

Connor lifted his eyes to the face above Dannie's. "We can
go hiking in the woods, too," he promised. "And anything
else your mom wants to do. *Anything.* I've got a case of cabin
fever like you wouldn't believe."

"But Dannie's here to get to know her grandparents," Sarah reminded him, pulling the elastic hair tie to make a second loop.

Connor straightened slowly, and Sarah's eyes followed his until she was looking up. "I suppose you're going to tell me it isn't necessary for me to hang around any longer," he guessed. "Or you could take the more tactful approach—say you don't want to take up any more of my time."

"Actually, I was going to thank you for staying. Your being here has made this visit easier for me." Her eyes told him she knew it hadn't been easy for him. "Don't leave without us."

"Then you'll come?"

"We do want to see redwoods," Sarah said thoughtfully.

"Lots of 'em," he promised.

"And real horses," Dannie added.

"With real tails," he said, giving one of hers a little tug.

"You'll have to engineer a graceful exit." Sarah honestly had the feeling that Dwight and Roberta Ryan could probably use a rest from their energetic granddaughter, but they weren't likely to admit that yet.

"Exits are my speciality. Finish with a flourish." With a playful chuck under her chin, Connor gave Sarah another promise. "You'll love it, Sarah. It's your kind of place. Your kind of peace and quiet. And your best colors."

Connor's flourish was dinner on Fisherman's Wharf. He wrinkled his nose at Sarah's Oysters Rockefeller, but he enjoyed his shrimp, and he helped Dannie crack her crab legs. His disclosure of plans to take Sarah and Dannie on a side trip brought a moment of awkward surprise from his parents.

"But...where will they stay, Connor?"

"At my house, Mom. I have plenty of room for guests." He gave her an indulgent smile. "Don't worry. The accommodations will be perfectly respectable."

"I hope so. Sarah isn't one of your..."

Sarah stiffened against the back of her chair.

"Uncle Connor's going to let me ride a real horse," Dannie

put in, and Sarah silently thanked her for another timely interruption. "And we're going to comb the beach."

"Don't you let this child get too near that water, Connor. Those waves can be..."

"I'll see to Dannie's safety," Connor assured her with practiced patience.

Dwight reached across the corner of the table to give Dannie a fond pat on the head. "She'll make a fine horseman. Her dad was."

"Her uncle *is*," Connor said quietly. Let it go, he told himself. Say the things they want to hear. The competition was over long ago. "We had some great times when we lived in Texas, didn't we, Dad?"

"You boys chased each other from one end of the state to the other on those two Shetlands you had."

"If you can ride a Shetland, you can ride anything." Connor held a forkful of crab meat up to Dannie's mouth. "But I've got something better for you, Princess."

"Uncle Connor's a *true* knight."

"Aren't you Connor Ryan?" All five heads turned toward the bright-eyed blonde who'd suddenly appeared by the table. As she spoke, her face got steadily redder, her eyes even brighter. "Connor Ryan from Georgia Nights? You are, aren't you?"

Connor gave her an easy smile. "Yes, I am."

"Oh, I *love* your music. I saw you in L.A. You were wonderful! I can't believe I'm standing this close. Will you sign something for me?" She fumbled through the big macramé bag that hung from her shoulder.

Connor laughed. "Anything but a check, honey."

The girl glanced down at her restaurant bill and giggled. "Oh, no, not this. Here." She produced a small pad and a pen, which he accepted with a smile.

"Do me a favor?"

"Anything!"

Connor finished scrawling good wishes on the pad and handed it back to her, his engaging smile obviously turning her to putty. "Don't flash this around in here. Every tourist in the place will think he has to have one, too, even if he's never heard of Georgia Nights."

"Oh, I'm sorry." Bright red now, she clutched the pad to her breast and stammered, "You're eating...I wasn't thinking."

"No problem. It was nice meeting you." Connor's wink sent the girl off on a cloud.

"That was very smooth," Sarah noted.

"It doesn't happen often. When you're just one out of four, they don't usually recognize—"

"You're Connor Ryan, aren't you? I just heard that girl say..."

They left the restaurant with Dwight muttering something unflattering about teenagers, but the flash in Connor's eyes told Sarah that he'd enjoyed the recognition, probably all the more so because it irritated his father.

Connor negotiated the morning fog and traffic in a solemn mood. Roberta's parting comments had left a knot in his stomach, which he told himself was a sign of his old weaknesses. It was natural for his mother to refer to Dannie as Kevin's daughter. She *was* Kevin's daughter, though Connor himself had stopped thinking of her in those terms some time ago.

The knot was still there. What had really gotten to him was his mother's attitude toward Sarah. It was as though she expected Sarah to be Kevin's widow for the rest of her life when she hadn't even been Kevin's wife. "We want you to visit us often. We want Dannie to know who her father was, and, of course, we want to share our memories of him with you, too."

If they wanted to sit around fondling Kevin's memory, they could damn well do it without Connor around, and he could do without knots in his stomach.

"It's a good thing you aren't a family man, Connor."

"Why?"

"The Corvette suits you, but—" Sarah cast a pointed look

behind her, where Dannie and the luggage seemed a bit crowded "—it's not built for kids."

"How do you like my car, Princess?"

"It's pretty," Dannie returned.

Connor's look was as pointed as Sarah's had been.

"If you had a beat-up '56 Mercury, she'd say it was pretty," Sarah protested.

"When we get home, we break out the Jeep. Practicality on wheels. It's the only thing I have that my father approves of."

"I'm surprised he doesn't have one of his own." Turning slightly in her seat, Sarah looked at him, choosing her words carefully. "It's hard to reconcile yourself to the fact that some of the people you're supposed to love are impossible to live with. You have a great deal of patience, Connor."

Remembering Sarah's errant brother, Connor smiled. The knot was gone. "Coming from someone whose name should be Patience, that's a nice compliment. Dad's not a bad guy, really. It's just that we're mismatched. We've never been able to please each other." He lifted one shoulder, never taking his eyes off the road. "It was different with Kevin."

"You and Kevin were two very different men," she observed. "Each likable in his own way."

"Kevin's way was *lovable*. How about mine?"

A coy brow angled upward. "I think that's a loaded question."

Connor pumped the Corvette a shot of gas and grinned with confidence. "I didn't expect an answer, either...not yet. I like to establish a firm foundation of *likable* and then ease on over to *lovable*."

"Is that your way?"

"That's...'m-y-y w-a-ay.'" The singer's gesture to the windshield brought a giggle from Sarah. They had driven out of the fog and into the sunshine.

The view of the ocean from coast-hugging Highway 1 was not enough to keep Dannie from falling asleep in the back of the car. Sarah leaned back comfortably and enjoyed the ride through countryside that had everything—mountains and sea, orchards, pasture and towering trees. In keeping with his promise of redwoods, Connor headed inland, navigating the narrow, twisting mountain road through the jack-pine and madrone forest. Huge redwoods dwarfed the misty-silver Corvette as it wound its way deep in the forest of Big Basin State Park.

Connor parked the car near the round, log ranger station and gently shook Dannie awake. He laughed when her sleepy-eyed face brightened suddenly with her first glimpse of the trees around her. "Where are we?" she gasped. "Does a giant live here?"

"No, the Giant lives in another park." Connor pulled a soft suede jacket out of the car before shutting the door. "But Father of the Forest lives here, and so does the Mother Tree. Should we take a look?"

Dannie craned her neck to give Connor a quizzical look. Everything around her was up so high. "The trees have names?"

"They're special trees, so they have special names." As they walked, Connor drew Sarah next to him, his hand finding a comfortable hold at the base of her neck over the upturned collar of her lightweight jacket. "You girls warm enough?" he wondered. "It gets pretty cool down here in these woods."

She nodded, not because she was really warm enough, but because his hand felt so good where it was on her back, and it felt right to walk with him this way. It felt, for the moment, as though they belonged together, as though the little girl scampering up the path ahead belonged to both of them.

"This must be the forest primeval." Even the sound of her voice seemed small and insignificant. "It reminds me of a fairy-tale setting. *Hansel and Gretel* or something. Could we get lost?"

With half a smile, Connor teased, "Sure, if you want to."

"No, really."

"The trails are well marked," he said, "and I probably know them as well as any ranger. Trust me?"

"Of course." At his smile, she amended, "You don't have a gingerbread house at the end of the path, do you?"

His voice became an eerie whine. "Have I got sweets for you, my pretty!" Then he pulled her closer and whispered, "Sugar and spice and everything nice."

"That's what girls are made of," Sarah recited.

"I know. That's why I love to have them for dinner." He gave her a quick peck on the cheek and sang out with a rollicking cackle, which brought Dannie to heel.

"Uncle Connor, are you trying to scare us?"

"Of course not. I was just promising treats for later. See that, Princess?" He favored Sarah with a wink as he pointed to a large round burl growing out of the trunk near the base of one tree. "What does that look like to you?"

Dannie sized it up. "It looks like the tree is bouncing a beach ball."

Dannie's wide-eyed wonder was contagious. Connor felt it all anew as Sarah tipped her head back in amazement every few yards. He talked about the lumbering that was done in northern California in the last century, stripping acres of these ancient beauties, and of the successful replantings in some areas along with the struggle to save what was left of the prehistoric stands. Indeed, time seemed to stand still in this place, the sun's position in the sky becoming irrelevant in the depths of the forest. It was a private, quiet time, with only an occasional hiker to intrude.

Guiding them along the twig-and-needle carpet runner, Connor explained that there really were mother trees, whose young shoots grew around their root collars in "fairy circles," a term that delighted Dannie. Only the hardiest would survive, and eventually the mother tree would fall. That fact saddened her, but Connor explained quite matter-of-factly that it was nature's way. Within forty to sixty years, the mother's shoots could become two-hundred-foot redwood giants, and the forest would continue its timeless life cycle.

The drive to Connor's home continued through the redwood-blanketed Santa Cruz Mountains. Following the San

Lorenzo River, they drove through another state park, by-passed the town of Santa Cruz and traveled several miles on a narrow back road before reaching Connor's secluded home overlooking the ocean. The house, a ranch-style rambler, was tucked into a hill, its sand-colored facade refusing to compete with the landscape to make a visual impression.

Though its style was completely different from her own home, Sarah loved the house from the moment she stepped into the red-quarry-tile foyer. There was a soft tranquillity here, and when she turned to Connor with her compliments on the tip of her tongue, she saw the calmness reflected in his face. Connor Ryan was home.

He was home, and he had Sarah and Dannie with him, and though he'd have to take a trip to Nashville in a few days, he was going to keep them here as long as he could. He needed to know what about them made him feel so good. Maybe he'd find a way to make it last.

"I'll show you Dannie's room first," he said, and with a suitcase in each hand he led the way past a sunken area with a gorgeous view of the ocean. Sarah turned her head all the way back over her shoulder as she followed, turning her attention to the hallway only after the view was completely behind her. "Great, huh?" Connor said. "That window and two others sold me on the house."

"Connor, Dannie and I can share a room. I have a feeling you've gone to...too...much...trouble...Connor!" The room's walls and carpeting were white, but everything else in it was pink—ruffled bedspread on the big brass bed, curtains, accents, stuffed panther.

"This looks suspiciously like a little girl's room." Sarah turned up an accusing brow. "Hardly your style."

"That's what the decorator said. I think she thinks I'm getting kinky in my old age."

Sarah's jaw dropped. "You hired a *decorator*? You didn't even know I'd agree to come down here."

"*You* didn't know you'd agree to come down here," he corrected her, grinning a little sideways.

Sarah shook her head slowly as she surveyed the room. It was too sweet, too pretty and definitely too neat, but then no little girl had ever lived in it. "You hired a decorator," she repeated, "for a two- or three-day visit at most."

"I hope it'll get more use than that." He reached for Sarah's shoulders and turned her to face him. "This won't be the only time, Sarah. I care about...Dannie. I want to see her as often as I can."

"Is this my room, Uncle Connor?"

Together they looked down at the anxious little face. Sarah knew this was no time to discuss the logistics of an impossibly fragile relationship, and Connor took pleasure in answering the question. "I thought you might like to have two rooms—one on each side of the country."

"Like your uncle, who has two homes," Sarah muttered.

"I have an apartment in Nashville. This is my home." He gave Sarah a meaningful look. "This is my private life, Sarah. I bring few people here. For the most part, I'm a very private person, like you."

Sarah wanted to question his definition of terms. How did he measure "the most part," and how much privacy could there be for a man who was asked to sign autographs during dinner?

"Do you have a room for Mommy, too?"

"You haven't told me what you think of yours, Princess."

"Oh, I love it!" Connor bent down to receive the hug he saw coming. "But does it have a night-light?"

"Would I put you in a room without a night-light? It's in the base of that lamp." The lamp he indicated had a gracefully sculptured globe of pink glass. "And I do have a room for Mommy, too. She'll be relieved to know how little trouble I went to on her account." He cast Sarah an upward glance. "I changed the sheets."

"*You* changed the sheets?" Sarah wondered, a smile tickling the corners of her mouth.

"*Somebody* changed the sheets." Rolling to his feet, he lifted the bag he knew contained Sarah's clothes. "It's two doors down. Come on." As he passed the next door, he commented, "I'll be in this room, right next door, Princess. Your room has its own bathroom, but if you need anything, I'll know where to find it."

"She might need her mother," Sarah said quietly.

"I'll know where to find her, too." He pushed the last door open and set Sarah's bag inside. The touch of a button opened a bank of pale blue drapes, and there, again, was a view of the ocean. The entire room was cool blue, and Sarah recognized one of her paintings, *Girl by the Pond*, featured prominently on one wall.

"This looks suspiciously like a big boy's room," Sarah guessed. Connor shoved his hands in the pockets of his jacket and shrugged, looking very much the part of a little boy waiting for approval. Sarah was drawn to the window, and he followed. "Imagine having the Pacific Ocean sing you to sleep every night. How lovely! But it must be scary when it storms."

"You get used to it."

Sarah glanced around the room again and saw that Dannie was gone. "I don't want to take your bedroom, Connor, beautiful as it is. Please let me stay in the guest room."

The porcelain face she turned up to him was all softness—the innocent eyes of a fawn, her lower lip a tiny pink satin pillow. He saw himself laying his forehead, his eyelids, his mouth against that pillow, and he knew he wanted her in his bed even if he couldn't be there with her. He wanted to think of her sleeping where he'd slept.

"I've moved everything I need into the other room." He nodded toward the waves, now breaking gently before rolling in to wash the sand. "I see this view all the time. You enjoy it for a few days. If we get a storm—" he offered a slow grin "—we'll think of something."

"You'll have two of us to contend with."

"Sounds like fun." Putting an arm around her shoulders, he suggested, "Let me show you the rest of the house. What would you like for supper?"

"You do great omelets."

"I'm pretty good with steaks, too."

The center of the house was divided into three areas by single-step levels. The sunken living room was big enough to be impressive, small enough to be comfortable. Its style was light, airy and contemporary, its sandy colors warmed by muted red and brown tones. The kitchen was a step up from the living room, and the dining room, bright with skylights, was a level above that. Flanking the main rooms on the opposite side of the bedrooms was Connor's "play area." There was a den, a recreation room with weight machines, sauna and whirlpool, and finally, with another window to the sea, there was a music room. Sarah knew at once that it was a room for an artist's work. Another of her paintings hung here, and the third was in the living room.

"Nice little hideaway you've got here," Sarah remarked, following Connor into the kitchen. "How much time do you get to spend in it?"

"When I'm not on tour or recording, I'm here." Rummaging through the refrigerator, he found some milk. "Dannie probably needs something to eat right now. What does she like?"

"Peanut butter," Sarah announced, certain he wouldn't have it.

A single finger cocked in Sarah's direction registered the order, and a new jar was produced from the cupboard. "How about you? Peanut butter?"

"Nothing, thanks. So you come here to write your music?"

Connor turned to her, staring through her with disarming blue eyes. "I live here, Sarah. I'm not a Gypsy. I do all the things a person does in the place where he lives, and I also do my work here, my songwriting. This is not home base. This is *home*."

Again she wondered about definitions. Being here for a few months out of the year obviously made this home to him. "It's a beautiful place, Connor. A private paradise, perfect for an artist."

He smiled, wondering whether she could possibly mean herself. "Sure I can't interest you in any…peanut butter?"

The smile was returned. "I'm saving up for steak."

"Mommy! There's a TV in my room and a record player and…" Dannie pattered to a halt and eyed the jar in Connor's hand. She went from excited to sweet. "Can I have a peanut-butter sandwich, too, Uncle Connor?"

"Coming right up," he promised, putting a spin on the jar as he tossed it up in the air.

"You're determined to send me home with a spoiled brat," Sarah muttered.

Connor laughed, thinking better of telling her that he wasn't determined to send her home at all and he wasn't above spoiling Sarah herself.

Before supper, Connor showed Sarah and Dannie his horses—a pair of gray quarter-horse mares with rich black manes and tails. They were housed in a small barn tucked behind a stand of pines. Connor assured Dannie that they were taken care of even when he wasn't home, and he promised her a morning ride.

Connor's stretch of beach invited walking in the early twilight. Sarah bundled Dannie up against the chilly breeze, and the three followed the rocky path down the hill. Dannie asked Connor how to comb the beach, and then she held up a handful of seaweed. "Is this its hair? Mommy wouldn't let my hair get *this* tangled."

He led them to a cozy spot sheltered by the hill, where several heavy wooden deck chairs stood waiting in the sand. With Dannie in his lap, he insisted that Sarah join them in the same chair. Huddled together, they watched the waves shatter themselves against the long rock jetty and then limp peacefully to lap the shoreline with lolling tongues. Darkness came too quickly, but Connor promised more time with the ocean in the days to come.

Making supper was a joint project, with Connor grilling steaks outdoors while Sarah and Dannie worked on a magnificent salad and surprised him with a quick torte for dessert.

When dessert came around, Dannie was losing in the struggle to keep her eyes open. By the time Connor had a fire going in the living room fireplace, Dannie was asleep in a chair. As before, Connor coveted the job of carrying the child to bed, but he left Sarah to get her settled in while he returned to the kitchen to resume his duties as host.

Sarah found him quite relaxed in front of the fire. In jeans and soft blue sweater, his flaxen hair burnished by the firelight, he looked the part of a young college boy, ready to impress his girl with all the proper amenities of romance. Sure enough, there was wine on the big stone hearth in front of him, ready to be poured into two waiting long-stemmed glasses. Sarah gave him a knowing smile. "I won't do the dishes myself, but I'll help," she offered, knowing it was not the activity he had in mind for them.

"They're done. What do you think this is, a busman's holiday?"

Laughter bubbling in her throat, Sarah dropped beside him on the expansive curve of the couch. "I think it's a plot," she said, "and I know I should be angry with you for it, but I'm too comfortable, and it's all been too nice."

"If you're enjoying yourself, then I confess to having plotted it." He poured two glasses of wine and offered in his eerie witch's voice, "Have a glass of mulberry wine, my dear. It will help you sleep."

She accepted. "*Mulberry* wine?"

"California rosé," he admitted with a shrug, "but what the hell?"

"The plot thickens." Lifting her glass in salute, she smiled, and he responded in kind.

"Dannie likes it here," Connor said, wondering immediately why he couldn't be more subtle.

"Of course she does. What's not to like? Sun, surf, trees, horses…"

"Me."

"You especially. You aren't what I would have expected from…someone like you."

"What's *someone like me?*" Shifting into a Southern drawl, he protested, "I'm just a plain country boy, honey. I do a little pickin' an' singin', is all." She rolled her eyes and groaned, but his open-handed gesture asked her to reconsider. "Hey, listen, it's perfectly possible for someone you know to suddenly become someone everybody knows about. With us it just happened in reverse. Now you know I'm human."

"Just a regular guy." Over the rim of her glass, she cast him a look of doubt. "Who has teenagers hounding him in restaurants for autographs."

"They like what I do."

"They also like the way you look, the way you..."

He shrugged all that off. "Whatever. They don't like *me*. They don't know me. They know what they read, which is a bunch of fairy tales."

She set her glass down and found herself leaning closer to him. "They know your music, and that's part of you, Connor. I guess I assumed the lyrics to pop music were just part of the act, but since I met you, I've been listening. It's more than lyrics, it's..."

"Part of the act? Are your colors part of your act?"

"They're part of my vision, just as your lyrics, your composition are part of yours. The people who know your music know a great deal about you, Connor." The hand she laid on his shoulder was meant to be reassuring, but it became a two-way conductor of a charge that simultaneously pulsed through both bodies.

"Then it follows that—" his mouth had gone dry, and he had to swallow "—someone who's attracted to your paintings would be attracted to you, too."

Suddenly she was in his arms, meeting his kiss with the full measure of her need. Her tongue danced with his, wanting him, welcoming him, celebrating his desire for her. She wanted his passion, knowing instinctively that it would be tempered by his gentle nature. There was nothing to fear from this man...unless it was the fear of loving him.

He touched his lips to her eyelids, her temple, the softest

part of her neck. She was the softness, the serenity he needed in his life, and he wanted to bury himself in that now, to burrow in it, to cover himself with softness. Softness must be handled with great care, he told himself, and he tasted the pearlized shell of her ear with the tip of his tongue. The shiver that ran through her then was absorbed into his own body, and he wanted more.

He lifted her sweater by quarter inches, easing her down on the couch as he kissed each piece of skin he exposed. The front clasp on her bra came open quickly. His hands slowed to let his eyes feast first. She was small and firm and lovely, and her pink nipples were tight with anticipation. The grip she had on his shoulders and the bright excitement in her eyes said, *yes*, said, *kiss them, too, Connor*. And he did. She sighed his name and laced her fingers in his hair to keep him close. He made her throb for him, and he knew the throbbing, too.

"Only if it's what you want, Sarah," he whispered, then traced an aureole with his tongue to be sure she could want nothing else.

"Oh, Connor…"

"I would never hurt you," he promised. "I'll give you everything you need. Just tell me…"

"I can't." He froze for a moment, then raised his head to look into her face. Her eyes were bright with both pleasure and fear, and he felt his throat tighten. "Not yet." She caught his face between her hands and searched his eyes for the patience he'd shown so many times before. "I'm not impetuous anymore, Connor."

On a ragged sigh, he dropped his head to her chest, gathering her in his arms.

"Forgive me," she whispered.

His mind spun with the crazy thought that he would like nothing more than to make love, here and now. He knew it was unfair of him not to take her wants into consideration but it was part of a feeling he had for her. There was nothing fair about feelings.

"I was going to ask the same of you," he said. "I wasn't thinking. I wanted to make love to you."

"I...wanted to make love to you, too."

They held each other in silence then, sharing both disappointment for the present moment and promise for the times to come.

Chapter Seven

Having lain awake all night, Connor had mentally mapped every inch of the dim ceiling above him. He wondered what kind of nightgown Sarah wore. He pictured her in white silk, her mink-colored hair spilling over his blue pillows. In his mind she slept peacefully, dreaming of him.

The clock told him it was technically too early to get up, but it was certainly too late to go to sleep. Today's activities would start early, anyway. Morning was the best time for tide pools. Dressing in jeans and a fisherman-knit sweater, Connor crept into Dannie's room. She looked too pretty to disturb, but he knew if he started with Sarah, he'd be tempted to crawl in bed beside her.

When he sat beside Dannie on the bed, she curled toward him and shoved a thumb in her mouth without waking. He watched instinct at work as she sucked vigorously, and it struck him that, as little experience as he'd had with small children, there must be some instincts at work in him, too. He would love this child as fiercely as any natural father could.

"Are we going to ride horses today, Uncle Connor?" Like everything else about Dannie, her yawn was contagious.

"Among other things. I've got plans, kid, big plans. We don't want to waste a minute." Poking through her suitcase, he found what seemed close to a small version of what he was wearing.

When he handed her the clothes, she shielded her flat chest with the flannel nightgown she'd just taken off. Lips pursed, her blue eyes flashed him a harbinger of the proper lady she would one day be. "Turn around, Uncle Connor. I can get myself dressed."

"Excuse me," he said with a serious nod, and turned away smiling. With his back to her, he launched into the agenda for the day. They'd explore parks and beaches, stroll the board-walk and check out the shops in Santa Cruz, and, as promised, they'd ride the horses.

"Isn't today Saturday?" Dannie asked.

"It sure is."

"I'll miss cartoons." She gave that some seconds of con-sideration. "But I don't care. You can turn around now, Uncle Connor. Would you tie my shoes?"

Dannie was assigned to awaken her mother while Connor whipped up some scrambled eggs and coffee, but when she was certain Sarah was getting out of bed, she dashed back to the kitchen, where things were already happening. Gliding on crepe soles, Sarah followed her nose to the kitchen area, but she stopped before she was noticed and stood back for a mo-ment, swallowing at the prickling in her throat. With Connor's close direction, Dannie was setting the table while he poured coffee.

She'd never associated masculine with domestic, nor hand-some with patient and selfless. A child can be perfectly well adjusted with only her mother to rear her, Sarah reminded herself. Yet there was something lovely about this moment of closeness between the man and the child. Sarah hesitated to intrude. A woman can have her own life, her child and her career and be perfectly content without a man, she reminded herself again. Yet there was a heady sweetness about having this man around, and the scene at the table beckoned her to savor that sweetness.

"Look, Mommy, we made breakfast. Uncle Connor says we need a good breakfast this morning."

"Oh?" Sarah accepted a steaming mug of coffee from Connor's hand. "Are we planning something strenuous?"

"We're planning lots of things," Dannie reported, obviously pleased with her role as planner's assistant.

"Long day ahead, ladies. Eat hearty. Oh, did I say good morning yet?" Leaning across the chair that stood between them, Connor slipped a hand behind Sarah's neck and gave her a quick kiss. "Hope you got a good night's sleep."

With a look, she told him she'd had the same sort of night he'd had. He smiled, gratified.

"Uncle Connor, that's the same way you kissed me this morning. You're supposed to give Mommy the big-girl kiss." Dannie folded her arms in expectation.

"The kid's got a good point." The longer kiss was warm morning sunshine, a welcome to today. "Good morning," he repeated softly.

"It is a good morning," she agreed, wondering at the fluttering in her stomach. "Thanks for the coffee. Anything left for me to do?"

"Eat."

Sarah filled her nose with the aroma once more and took a chair. "That I can handle. From the smell of it, I'd say you two are pretty good cooks."

"We make a great team." Connor tossed Dannie a partner's wink.

Natural Bridges State Park was one of Connor's favorite spots. The drive took them past the eroded rock arches that gave the park its name. At Sarah's request, they stopped while she made a quick sketch of a congregation of gulls and cormorants that were using one arch as a base. Then Connor parked the car and led them to a high area of the rocky beach. Sarah settled in to sketch, while Connor and Dannie poked around from tide pool to tide pool, the man squatting on his haunches almost as the child did and exhibiting no less fascination.

In the bright light of morning, Sarah watched at a distance for a while. This was Dannie at her best. She never tired of watching ants or following butterflies, though the activity often tried Sarah's patience, as undoubtedly it would Connor's. But Sarah continued to sketch, and her companions continued to poke, both heads glinting gold in the sun as they bent together over some tiny find. Connor's interest, apparently genuine, showed no signs of flagging, and Sarah realized that Dannie wasn't running to her with every little discovery. Finally, Sarah tucked her sketch pad under her arm and decided to see what they had under such close scrutiny.

"Look, Mommy! Periwinkles!" Dannie pointed to a cluster of small snails clinging to a rock. Tugging at Sarah's hand, she dragged her back a few steps. "And here's a black turban snail. Uncle Connor, he came out again. Oh-oh, there he goes, back in his shell. We scared him." Dannie dug down deep in her jacket and came up with a small shell, which she held out to Sarah on a chubby palm. "This is a hermit crab inside here. Uncle Connor says I can only hold him for a little while, but I have to leave him. We can only keep shells that nobody lives in, and we can't take the ones on this beach because the hermit crabs need them."

Dannie's eyes were bright with excitement, and Connor's, certainly bigger, were even brighter, if that was possible. Negotiating the rocks with the agile grace of a tightrope walker, he motioned to them. "Over here! I found a bigger crab."

He gave Sarah a hand up to his perch on a small ledge, but Dannie scrambled up beside him on her own. Rolling back a small rock, he exposed a small clawed creature that reared up indignantly, brandishing pinchers in a demand to be left alone. Connor identified it as a lined shore crab. He had names for all the seaweed, too—sea palms, sea lettuce, surf grass.

"How would you like to wear this one in the boudoir?" he

asked Sarah, swinging a long piece of wet weed in her direction. "It's a feather boa."

"Perhaps if I were a mermaid," she suggested gaily, acting out her fantasy as she told it. "I'd lunch on sea lettuce and lie in the surf grass, my feather boa flung about my neck for a touch of glamour."

"If you were a mermaid, I think I wouldn't mind being a sailor or a fisherman."

"My shoreline crabs would pinch you if you tried to catch me," she warned, and punctuated the word with a playful pinch on his thigh.

The gesture stimulated him unexpectedly, and the flash in his eyes became a flashing smile. He grabbed her wrist and twisted her arm behind her back, throwing an arm across the front of her shoulders to immobilize her against him. "They're *lined shore* crabs, and I think I'd like that," he growled in her ear. "Wanna try it again?"

Sarah giggled, shaking her head.

"What should I do with her, Princess? She's upsetting all the wildlife."

Dannie liked seeing her mommy play with Uncle Connor. When they laughed together, it made her want to laugh, too, even if she didn't know what they were laughing about. "Maybe you should send her to bed without supper."

"Don't you think she deserves a spanking?"

From her perch several yards from the wrestling match, Dannie shook her head. "Not unless she just won't stop being bad."

"So that's how it works," he called out, and then in Sarah's ear he whispered, "I'll let you go if you promise not to stop being bad."

"Oh!" she squealed as he gave her a warning squeeze. His play delighted her, but she knew how readily her skin bruised. "I promise!"

Their trek brought them to a sandier area where there were fewer live specimens to watch, but they found sand dollars, which Connor said could be taken home. Before leaving the park he took them to a grove of eucalyptus trees, where clusters of orange-and-black monarch butterflies hung from the branches. Connor explained that they were still tired from their October migration of three thousand miles and wished that Dannie and Sarah had been there for Welcome Back Monarchs Day.

The beautiful weather brought a good crowd out to the Santa Cruz boardwalk, which was open only on weekends in the off-season. Sarah agreed to ride in the bumper cars, and she found the old carousel with its classic wooden horses and calliope music irresistible. But she stood on the ground and watched in sympathetic terror as Connor and Dannie arced high over the crowd in their swaying ferris-wheel chair.

They ate lunch by a view of the harbor and then strolled the Pacific Avenue Garden Mall downtown. After shopping for the few items she needed, Sarah enjoyed browsing through small specialty stores. Dannie found a jumpsuit with appliquéd dolphins that reminded her of her "pink-elephant pants," and Connor insisted that since Uncle Jerry had bought the elephant pants, Uncle Connor would buy the dolphin pants. He also bought a conch shell that caught Dannie's fancy and a glass horse and a stuffed crab. Sarah realized after the fourth gift that protesting his extravagance was useless.

A group of street musicians was drawing a crowd in front of an antique shop, and Connor and Sarah joined the crowd at Dannie's request. Between songs, one bearded guitarist came over to Connor and offered a handshake.

"How's it going, man?"

"Real smooth, Randy," Connor responded, and nodded toward the group. "You've got a good sound here. What are you doing with it?"

"Playing some of the old spots. Sit in on one with us?" Connor accepted the proffered guitar, looping the strap over his head and testing out the strings with a chord. "Take the lead on 'Misty River Morning,'" Randy urged.

Connor glanced at the crowd. It looked small and harmless. There were so many copyists these days that he could usually

get away with pretending to be one of them. He glanced bac
at his old friend and smiled. "Just one."

The group swung into the song as though they'd practice
it together, but Connor carried it. With his voice he carried
to the crowd, offering it for their pleasure just as he did fo
any paying audience. With his eyes, he carried it to Sarah, lai
it in her lap like a treasured gift. It touched her soul and fille
her eyes with shimmery gratitude.

> It's a misty river morning, babe
> The world's just gettin' out of bed
> You lie sleepin' soft beside a happy man
> Whose mind's on all the sweet, sweet love
> we made.

That's how it would be with this man, Sarah thought. H
was a man who longed to give, and his lovemaking would b
a gift—gentle as his song promised. Her skin felt tight fro
head to foot, and her whole body became a pulse point as sh
listened to the last words of the song. You and me and th
river, babe, makin' misty morning love.

He left them stunned. Then he had them clapping, pitchin
handfuls of change and bills into an open guitar case, and th
hazy spell was broken.

"Sure sounds like the record to me," one young man de
clared. "You oughta try out for Georgia Nights, fella. You'
every bit as good as any of them."

"Thanks," Connor said with a nod toward the voice in th
crowd. "Would you put that in writing? I'll take it with m
when I take the bus to Nashville."

"Sure thing," the voice promised on the end of a goo
natured laugh.

Randy thanked Connor with a hearty handshake and a sla
on the back. Each musician took his turn shaking Connor
hand and wishing him well. The man in the crowd hung bac

watching the proceedings and asking finally, "Hey, man, you really going to Nashville?"

"Sure am," Connor said.

The man stuck out a hand. "Hey, good luck. I wasn't kidding. In fact, I think you're even *better* than the record. You're gonna do great, man, just great."

"I hope so. Thanks for the encouragement. It's really a long shot, but what the hell, right?"

"Right. Go for it, man. I'm telling you, you could be with Georgia Nights. I'm a big fan of theirs. You go for it." With a wave and another nod of reassurance, the man took his leave.

Connor and his friends enjoyed the moment when the man was out of earshot, but Connor's parting advice echoed his young fan's. "You guys are good. You go for it!"

"Did you know them?" Sarah asked as they walked along.

"Randy and I used to be part of a group a few years back."

"You were a street musician, too, then?"

"I've played my music in the street, in back-street bars, high-school gyms, you name it."

"Randy's good," Sarah observed. "Why is he still playing street corners?"

Connor shoved his hands in his pockets and shrugged. "He wasn't willing to take too many risks. He doesn't do too badly here, and at least he knows what he's got."

Sarah could understand that. Of the myriad people who dreamed of fame, there were probably many who had the talent, but only a few were really cut out to endure the rocky road that must be traveled. "Why did you take the risks?" she wondered.

"I had nothing to lose." He caught her arm and pointed to a building claiming to be the Artists' Co-op. "You'll enjoy this place," he promised, changing the focus of conversation.

"I thought you said this wasn't a busman's holiday."

"Can you walk on by?" he challenged.

Sarah grinned. "Of course not."

Crafts for sale at the co-op were of admirable quality, and Sarah examined pieces of handmade glassware and pottery that struck her fancy. She particularly liked a small wood carving, a child with a duck, that reminded her of the quality she'd seen in Munich. Connor stood to the side with Dannie, who saw little that interested her. But Connor took quiet consideration of everything Sarah touched, every comment she made, anything that reflected her taste. He watched while a weaver persuaded Sarah to try a handmade serape, woven in shades of emerald and white that looked lovely with Sarah's coloring. She wouldn't buy it for herself, of course.

They stopped for a late lunch at a sidewalk café, and while Sarah and Dannie munched on batter-fried shrimp and listened to a swinging jazz band, Connor excused himself for a few moments. It wasn't long before he was threading his way back among the strollers at an easy jog, a package under his arm.

"Where did you go?" Sarah wondered, eyeing the package.

Connor dropped into a chair and hoisted his soft drink for a healthy swallow. "Went back to the co-op. I asked them to send all the things you suggested out to the house."

"All the things *I* suggested?"

"Yeah, the stuff you liked—the pots, that glass gull, the wood carving—everything you picked out for me."

Aghast, Sarah sputtered, "Picked out for...Connor, I didn't...those things were..."

"They were great, every one of them." He leaned toward her with a conspiratory grin. "That decorator's a nice enough lady, but she makes the place feel uncomfortable. The furniture's okay, but she comes up with the most awful...art pieces, she calls them. I like your stuff. I like what you picked out today."

"I didn't suggest that you *buy* them," Sarah insisted, her eyes still wide with disbelief.

"The things you said were good...they really *were* good, weren't they?"

"Of course."

He craned his neck to give her an unexpected peck on the cheek. "I knew you wouldn't let me down."

"You could have picked them out yourself if that's the kind of thing you like."

"There was too much stuff in there. You went right to certain things, and each time I said to myself, 'Hey, yeah, that's the one.'" He laughed at himself and chomped on a cold shrimp. "I'm the guy who put horse feed in a handmade pot. Now I've got it sitting in the living room filled with cattails and marsh grasses. Looks pretty good."

"I noticed," Sarah said, remembering. "Scotch has a nice touch with clay."

Connor felt a twinge of jealousy, and he decided then and there he was going to show her what a nice touch *he* had. Catching himself, he smiled, telling himself he meant *artistic* touch, as in keyboard, synthesizer, songwriting…not in getting his hands on the soft body he longed to touch.

"What are you smiling about?" Sarah wondered.

On a chuckle, Connor chose his response. "Scotch. He must've ground his back teeth when he saw that pot full of horse feed. Can't blame him, either. Oh, here." He reached for the package as though he'd just remembered it, though that wasn't the case. He'd been anxious to give it to her. "This is something no one but you should wear."

Sarah took the package and unwrapped it carefully, knowing full well what it was and trying to decide whether to let her excitement show. On the fringe of her awareness, she heard Dannie's comments approving of the fact that Mommy was getting a present and Connor's response that Mommy deserved one, since Dannie had gotten so many. Sarah held up the serape. "Connor…"

"I know the weaver isn't a personal friend of yours like the guy who made your skirt, but still…it looks great on you, Sarah."

She clutched it to her and smiled at him. There was no point in protesting the cost of it. She wanted it, and he knew that. "The weaver is a friend now," she said. "And so are you. Thank you, Connor."

She'd accepted without protest. He was amazed, and when

he spoke, he found a strange hoarseness in his voice. "It...the colors seem right...with your hair and eyes."

"How did you know that the person who made my skirt was a guy?" she wondered.

"Just a hunch," he returned with a shrug.

"Just a friend," she found herself telling him. "A fellow artist."

"Like me?"

"No. Not like you." With her eyes she told him that there was no one like him.

By the time they returned home, Connor's purchases had arrived, and Sarah enjoyed the role of adviser as they decided where each piece should go. Trying one piece of pottery out on a high shelf, Sarah discovered dust, and she informed Connor that his housekeeper was overpaid.

He imagined telling that to fiery-eyed Carmel and laughed. "Scratch one decorator and one housekeeper. You wouldn't be looking for a job, would you?" Hands at her waist, he lifted her down from a small step stool. "I could fly you out, say, twice a month?"

Sliding her hands from his shoulders to his chest, she waited to be released. "That's a long time between cleanings. What will you do in the meantime?"

"Languish in my own clutter."

They stood that way for a moment, touching only with arms and hands. It was like lingering to enjoy the aroma of a pie fresh from the oven and still too hot to eat. Even the anticipation felt good.

"Your niece is waiting for her horseback ride," Sarah reminded him. "If you don't keep your promise, you'll witness tiny-tot rebellion, and your image of her will be shattered."

"I intend to keep all my promises." He held her gaze for a moment before asking, "Shall we saddle up and catch the last of the daylight?"

"I have a feeling I'm going to be sore tomorrow."

"Then we'll stay home tomorrow," he promised quietly into her hair. "And I'll minister to all your needs."

A shiver ran the length and breadth of Sarah's body—invisibly, she hoped. She was not a blushing maiden, and yet she felt seven kinds of anxiety all at once. Turning out of his arms without raising her eyes to meet his, she muttered something about getting Dannie ready for her ride.

A totally romantic notion prodded Sarah to wear her new serape. She laughed at the image she conjured of herself riding barefoot, a colorful gathered skirt billowing against her legs, hair flying in the wind as she galloped over the hills carrying a message for Zapata. Really, Sarah, she thought. You with all the courage of a mouse. She wore her most practical shoes, but she did leave her hair unbound.

Connor watched Sarah mount the gentler of the two mares and settle herself in the western saddle. Satisfied that she knew what she was doing, he put Dannie in his saddle and hoisted himself up behind her. When he figured everyone was broken in at a walk, he picked up the pace. Dannie giggled as she bobbled in front of him, but Sarah's horse was smooth gaited, and she sat the trot without difficulty. On a stretch of white beach he let Sarah lead them in an easy canter, and he pulled off to her side, the better to watch her serape flutter in the breeze and her dark hair ripple behind her. Her porcelain beauty was no fantasy. Connor conjured nothing but the prospect of having her in his arms.

But it wasn't as easy as he'd thought. When Dannie was sleeping contentedly in her bed, and the woman he'd wanted since the first moment he'd seen her was seated beside him in front of a crackling fire, he couldn't think of one glib line. He sat there for what felt like an eternity, staring into the fire, not completely comfortable with the slow burn he had going in the pit of his stomach. She probably thought he was some kind of tomcat on the prowl.

Sarah supposed he didn't find her much different from any other female groupie. Maybe she'd taken a little longer than most, but by the size of the tight wad of nerves in her stomach, she knew he'd worked his magic on her. She'd stopped kidding herself about having any resistance to him whenever he touched her, and she told herself to be realistic about what this was—a brief romantic encounter with a man whose world was much too big for her. *Right now, the thing to do is not ask yourself to accept that. Leave that for later, when it's too late.*

"Did you notice the way Dannie was walking after we took that ride?" Sarah asked, tentatively breaking the silence.

"Cute little swagger on her, wasn't it?" Connor's chuckle faded into another few moments of silence, and then he took his turn. "Can I get you anything? A glass of wine?"

Sarah shook her head. "No, thanks. I'm fine."

You're fine? You look as nervous as I feel. "Tell me about your parents," he suggested quickly, and at her skeptical glance he added, "or...or anything else you feel like talking about."

Their eyes met again, and they both laughed. It seemed natural to reach for her hand, and so he did. The contact brought them both a sigh of relief.

"My mother was a very hardworking lady who hoped that her son would become a successful businessman and her daughter would find a good husband. We both disappointed her, but she never complained. She died a little more than three years ago. Dannie doesn't remember her at all."

"But you haven't stopped missing her," Connor offered quietly. Sarah shook her head. "And your father?"

"He left my mother in pursuit of his theatrical dreams. He's a television actor of sorts." The bitterness was in her voice, much as she tried to deny it in her mind.

"Of sorts?"

"Well, he's been in a lot of soap operas. They usually kill him off within a year. Once in a while he'll show up in a commercial, and then he'll get another soap." She hastened to add, "Of course, I never watch them myself."

"You don't have time." He gave her a knowing look.

"Well...once in a while."

"Once in a while when you want to get a glimpse of your dad. He never came around much after he split with your mom?"

"He never came around at all, which is just as well. His influence might have made Jerry worse than he is."

"One of those crazy theatrical people, huh?" She nodded without looking up at him. "Kind of footloose and fancy-free? Totally unreliable?"

"I'm sure they're not *all*..." She met his gaze now, and he saw the fear just before she masked it with what she considered to be a mature outlook. "I'm sure they're not all that way. My mother simply married the wrong man. She was the first to admit it."

"Do you think they'll ever come up with a new kind of divorce?" Connor wondered. "A kid realizes things just aren't working out, and he says, 'I got the wrong father. I'm going to divorce him and look for a more suitable one.'"

"Would you divorce yours?"

He thought about it and shook his head, finally voicing his "No." And then he laughed at the news he'd just handed himself. "I'd go right on hoping for things to change. You?"

She thought if understanding were a color, it would be the blue of his eyes. "The same, I guess."

"Of course the same, Sarah Benedict. You're loyal. All he gave you was his name, but you've got a stockpile of love for him, though it's all hardened over with a shell of disappointment." He cupped his free hand around her cheek, almost beseechingly. "I could put some of that loyalty to good use, Sarah Benedict. Have you got any you could spare for another crazy theatrical person?"

She closed her eyes, summoning strength. Could she parcel it out in small doses? Was it possible for her to give a man one or two nights' worth of loyalty, just a small piece of her heart? She'd gone so long without giving any, and she wanted to give, longed to give to *this* man.

Her silence was his answer. He drew away from her. "I have some work to do," he announced in a stranger's voice. "You're probably very tired."

When Sarah opened her eyes, he was gone.

He did, indeed, have work to do. He had to earn her trust.

After two cigarettes, he toyed with some lyrics he'd been working on, synthesized some background, experimented with some chord progressions on the guitar and finally decided he'd worn himself out. He could probably fall asleep. Well, maybe after a glass of wine. He'd take the tomcat in him, the theatrical crazy person and the new part, which was behaving suspiciously like a lovesick calf, and he'd anesthetize them all with a glass of good wine before putting them to bed.

He felt pretty confident after half a glass. Everything was cool. All systems were shutting down nicely. But when he headed down the hall, he realized that he'd forgotten to address one stubborn aspect of his nature. The latent rebel. The damned nuisance walked him right past the guest room and tapped at his own bedroom door. True to form, when the misty white vision appeared at the door, the rebel had nothing to say. He just stood there, waiting.

Sarah tried without success to swallow the pulsing in her throat. She took his hand, letting him know that her silence hadn't been a refusal. He closed the door behind him and took her in his arms, his mouth finding hers on instinct. His hand slid tightly along the length of her back and took firm hold of her buttocks, pulling her against his body so there could be no mistaking what he wanted. She whimpered and drew his tongue deeper into her mouth in acceptance. His heart soared. He filled both hands with her and pressed her tighter, rotating against her until she was breathless.

He took her to his bed and lay her against the cool sheets. The blue room was moonlit, and her face was the color of a blue-white star. Strong arms propped him above her, bent for a kiss, straightened for another look and then bent to allow him to dip his head again.

"I need you, Sarah," he confessed against her temple.

"I wanted you to come to me, Connor. I willed it."

"I came because I couldn't *not* come. I wanted to give you more time...all you needed...but I don't know how much time you'll give me."

She locked her hands behind his neck and pulled his ear to

her mouth, whispering. "What I have to give you has nothing to do with time." Her tongue traced the curve of his ear, and he shivered. She pushed his sweater up and pulled handfuls of shirttail free from his pants while he breathed a line of kisses along the plunge her nightgown took to her breasts. Lacking patience with it, he peeled his sweater over his head, and she helped him undo the buttons on his shirt so that she could touch the pads of muscle over his chest.

His eager mouth found those small firm breasts and nuzzled them beneath the silky fabric before nosing her nightgown aside for a taste of nourishing sweetness. Her nipple was a firm berry in his mouth, and he was a hungry man, but he would only nibble excruciatingly gently, until she writhed and arched beneath him.

"I've only just started, sweet Sarah," he whispered, his breath hot against her breast. "This is only the beginning."

He was quick to remove the rest of his clothes but, oh, so slow to remove hers. He wanted to kiss and touch and taste each inch as he uncovered her. Her skin grew tight, and the blood flowed through her body like fire, pooling and pulsating beneath the parts of her skin his hands found most enticing.

"Connor, Connor, your hands are heavenly torture."

"I want to know you, love. I learn best by touch." He nipped at the hollow under her pelvic bone. "I have to take what I want to learn in my hands, roll it between my fingers, discover its texture." He dipped his tongue into the hollow of her navel, and she shuddered. "I remember by taste and by touch and by smell. I'm very primitive that way."

"Do you always...learn with such...agonizingly slow deliberation?" she panted.

"Yes," he groaned, his hand finding the hot, moist place he wanted for his own. "I'm a slow learner." He felt her hands clutch his hair, and he moved to taunt her breast while his hand worked elevating magic. When she shuddered against him uncontrollably, he soothed her, holding her close, and whispered, "But once I learn something, it's mine. It belongs to all my senses, and it never gets away from me. Are you prepared for that, Sarah? Are you ready for me?''

Her own hand fluttered and found him, touched him and drew him home. "Come learn one more part of me," she entreated. "This is the deeper part of me, the part that will make you mine."

Driving deeply, he knew he'd found his perfect fit, the piece of life's puzzle that he'd been cut to match.

Chapter Eight

There was little sleeping in Connor's big bed that night, but there was much learning. Indeed, Sarah found Connor's method to be very effective, and she put it to practice on him. They dozed in each other's arms, but Connor woke just as the sky began to lighten. He shifted slightly, and Sarah stirred with a soft, pleasured moan.

"Here comes the morning, Sarah."

His voice caressed her half-conscious brain, and she saw him bringing her the sun in a chariot just before she opened her eyes to his sleepy smile. "Did you bring it with you?" she asked.

"What?"

"The morning." She snuggled against his chest and closed her eyes again. "You brought me everything else I needed."

He chuckled. "Are you angling for breakfast in bed, sweet Sarah?"

"Mmm. I think there's a toll-free number you can call."

"Really? Got it handy?"

"I think you have to give them twenty-four hours' notice."

"What good is that? How do you know you're going to want breakfast in bed twenty-four hours ahead of time?" Cradling her in one arm, he leaned forward to shift several pillows behind them. "Scoot up just a little," he instructed. "The show's about to start."

They cuddled, kissing each other wherever was handy, but when the horizon reddened, they gave it their full attention. Morning rose from the ocean's depths, spreading light across the waters, splashing up on the beach and streaming through Connor Ryan's bedroom window. "So you found each other," it seemed to say. "That's good."

"Oh, Connor..." Sarah breathed, throwing back the covers and moving toward the huge window as though magnetized. "Connor, look how beautiful...*feel* how beautiful." Connor followed, but he stood by the foot of the bed, watching.

Naked, she stood before the sun, raising her arms above her head and stretching on her toes. She was Venus, closer to the sun than anything earthly, and the light painted the front of her body gold in celebration. Connor was awed, afraid to touch her, struck for an instant by the notion that if he did, he would burst into flame. When she turned to him and held out both her hands, he couldn't move. Then she smiled, and she was Sarah again. He took her hands in his, shaking his head at his foolishness.

"I must look a sight," she said with a laugh, "but I don't care."

"You're a lovely sight, and I *do* care. What's this?" He released her left arm as he drew her other arm closer, gingerly touching the marks he'd found on its soft underside. "What happened here?"

"You twisted my arm, remember?" she said lightly. "It's not..."

"But I was just playing," he protested, his eyes wide with disbelief. "I couldn't have..."

"It's nothing," she assured him. "I bruise too easily."

"But I must've hurt you."

"Not at all. I often get bruises without even knowing where they came from." He was still staring at her arm, mortified. "Really," she offered with conviction.

"Did I hurt you last night when I..."

"No." His eyes met hers, and she shook her head. Still, he dipped his head to touch his lips to the pale purple mark on her arm, and something tugged at her heart. Winding her arms around his neck, she stepped between his feet and held herself close to him. "You could never hurt me, gentle Connor. Last night...you gave me something I've never had before."

"You mean...never? Not even with..."

Dropping her head back, she lay one finger over his lips, shaking her head. "Never. Not with anyone else."

He tightened his arms around her, wishing he could surround her with a wall of himself. "Then I'm your first lover, my sweet Sarah."

"Yes, you are," she whispered against his shoulder, and her voice constricted around the bittersweet note of it.

"I'll be a good one. Always. I promise. I'll never leave you wanting." He ran the heel of his hand down the length of her spine and then massaged her with the circular movement of his palms. "I'll never bruise you again."

"Don't promise that," she pleaded. "You'd have to wrap me in cotton, which would leave me wanting."

"I want to wrap you in me, and myself in you. You know what happens when you rub up against me like this in an undressed state?" He pressed her hips into his.

"Umm, yes, I think I get your point."

"I think you're about to," he growled, lowering her to the carpet.

"Connor, the door..."

"Locked," he breathed over her breast.

"But..."

"It's all right," he assured her. "It's very... very...early. This is our time, Sarah."

"Oh..."

"That's right, sweet Sarah. Want me."

"I do."

"Tell me."

"I want you, Connor. I want…Connor. Oh, Connor, yes."

"You have Connor, Sarah," he whispered, rocking slowly inside her. "Be good to him. He'll never leave you wanting."

They couldn't keep this up much longer, Sarah realized, giving the arm that cushioned her head a parting kiss. "This is where I tear myself away and head for the shower," she announced. "And where you split the scene altogether."

"In the altogether?" He reached for her ankle, but missed as she skipped out of reach.

"In your pants, mister." They landed across his legs, followed by his shirt and sweater.

"Thrown out of my own bedroom," he groaned.

"These arrangements were your idea," she reminded him, and just before she closed the bathroom door, she tossed, "See you at breakfast," over her shoulder.

Many moments later, Sarah stepped from the shower, her head wrapped in a towel, and was handed a cup of coffee. She frowned, setting the mug aside. "Breakfast in the bathroom?"

"Just coffee." He mounted two tiled steps, set his own mug down and lifted a large round lid, which Sarah had already mentally dubbed King Kong's privy, having no idea what else it could be. At the flip of a switch, something in the privy started whirling. "But you might want breakfast here, too, once you get used to it."

"We can't keep the door locked all morning."

"Here." He tossed her her swimming suit, and she noticed, at second glance, that he wore one, too, though it was a rather skimpy model. "Dannie's still sound asleep, but I've left the door unlocked."

"We're going swimming in the bathtub?"

"Hot tub, my pretty little pilgrim."

Still wet from the shower, Sarah squirmed into her suit and stepped up to the platform to peer into the tub. "Cauldron, more like," she judged.

Connor laughed. "Nothing of the sort, my dear. It's just a pot of soup. Test it with your sweet little finger, and tell me whether it's hot yet."

Picking up her end of the game, she narrowed her eyes at him. "I get it. You can't test it yourself because water will melt the likes of you." Dipping her foot into the bubbling water, she kicked him a spray. "Take that!"

"Ungrateful wench!" he cried. "I'll teach you." He reached for her arms, but she held her hands up in surrender.

"At the risk of getting any more bruises, I'll go peacefully." She lowered herself into the water, and Connor retrieved her coffee and followed her.

"I forgot. A *real* princess gets bruised by a pea twenty mattresses beneath her."

"I think you've read all my favorite fairy tales."

"My brother...my *mother* read them all to us, like all good...mothers," he said awkwardly.

Sarah sank into the warm, gently whirling water, comfortable enough to let Connor's uneasy moment slide over her head. "Kids love fairy tales—the scarier, the better. You say you left the bedroom door open?"

"Mmm-hmm. She'll find us."

Dannie let them have fifteen minutes of peaceful soaking, and then she wandered in, sleepy-eyed, calling, "Mommy?"

"In the bathroom, sweetheart."

She padded to the doorway, blinked, yawned and then blinked again. "Uncle Connor, why are you in the bathtub with Mommy?"

"This isn't a bathtub, Princess. It's kind of a little swimming pool." He motioned to her with a dripping hand. "Come up here and see."

A peek in the tub made her smile. "It's like my Tommy Turtle pool. But you're too big to swim in here."

"It's just for sitting and soaking," Sarah explained. "Take off your nightgown and jump in."

Dannie crossed her arms over her chest, protesting that panties would not be enough. "Go put your swimming suit on,

Princess,'' Connor suggested. "This is just a big family bubble bath.''

His choice of words put an end to Dannie's doubts, but for Sarah, the doubts resumed their niggling.

Connor spent much of the morning playing with Dannie, taking great pleasure in producing toys from the closet and pretending not to have known they were there. Sarah and Dannie set up a sandwich bar for lunch while Connor worked out in his private gym. He insisted the key to his fitness program was planned irregularity. With the promise of another horseback ride, Dannie agreed to take her nap, a practice she had begun to think she might have outgrown in just the last week.

"I need some inspiration, Sarah, love.''

Sarah found herself being scooped along under Connor's arm toward the music-room door. "Oh, nice. Do I get a private concert?''

"Worse. You get to listen to me struggle through some new music.''

Struggle seemed an apt description. It would certainly have been a struggle for her if she had to manage all that equipment. Sarah sat quietly on the couch and listened while Connor took his place at the beautiful baby-grand piano and played through several songs. He used no sheet music, but, of course, some of the songs were his own. Then he turned on a tape recorder and worked with a melody that was obviously in the making. There were many false starts, subtle changes, replays, all recorded on tape. When he'd played the same melody through several times, he turned to her. "What do you think?''

"I think it's lovely.''

"Aw, come on." He hooked a hand over his thigh and leaned on his arm. "What does it sound like?''

"It reminds me of a summer night's breeze and a white porch swing, and oars dipping in and out of calm water, silver moonlight slithering bank to bank.''

He raised his brow, turning his mouth down slightly as he nodded. "You're right. That's what it sounds like.'' He saluted her appraisal with a single finger. "There might even be lyrics in what you just said."

"Really? What *I* said?" She beamed. "Write it down before you forget."

"I never forget," he said, touching his temple. "Besides, it's all on tape. Here's the part I don't like." He played several bars from the melody, played them again and shook his head. "It isn't right."

"That's the part with the oars," she said thoughtfully. "Maybe they need to drip a little bit."

He grinned, played with several changes in the notes and finally pronounced, "That's it! They just needed to drip a little bit."

"You work with imagery, too, don't you?"

He shrugged, swinging his knees in her direction. "I guess so. I can't *tell* anybody how it works. I've been asked, and when I can't explain it in words, people get very impatient and start asking easier questions, like, 'How's your love life?' All I can do is *show* somebody how it works, and either they tune in or they don't." He gave her a warm smile. "You, sweet Sarah, are a kindred spirit."

"I'm an artist, Connor. So are you."

He liked that. She was not a popular artist; she'd had little recognition in the art world. But she was serious about her work, she was good at it and she'd put him in her class—the class of serious artists. He reached behind the piano for a twelve-string that stood waiting in its stand. "This is something I've been working on, too. I want you to hear it," he said, chording softly before he sang:

Hey, lady with the paint and the brushes
Pretty lady with the warm brown eyes
What color do you use to make your music?
Oh, lady, can you paint me a song?
Does your soft pink kiss brighten with your
passion?
Will you touch me with cool blue

Like the ocean waters do?
My lady, can you paint me a song?
Give me red from your palette, I'll make fire
Give me gold, give me silver, I'll make love
Paint me what you feel, and I'll make you a deal
I'll sing you a picture while you paint me a song.

He watched his hands play the chorus through again, post-poning the quiet for just a moment. But then it came, the silence echoing in his ears. He stared at his hands and heard no applause, no approving words. Finally, he took a deep breath and looked over at the couch. He saw tears.

"That bad?" he ventured gently.

She shook her head vigorously. "That good. That beautiful, Connor. Tell me I really gave you that idea."

"Of course you did." He returned the guitar to its stand and went to her, stooping down in front of her and dropping one knee to the floor. The fingers of his left hand brushed wetness from her face, and she felt the calluses of his finger pads. "Tell me this means I really touched you with my song."

"Of course you did," she whispered.

Leaning forward, he kissed first one eyelid, then the other. "Sweet, sweet Sarah," he chided tenderly. "You're supposed to applaud at the end. You're not supposed to cry."

She laughed through the tears. That's what she'd planned to do at the end—a little applause, a graceful exit, certainly no tears. Obviously it wasn't going to work that way. Wiping her eyes quickly, she pointed to an instrument on the far side of the room. "What's that?" she asked with forced enthusiasm.

"What?" He pivoted on the balls of his feet. "Oh, that. That's a synthesizer. Here, I'll show you how it works."

With one ear Sarah listened to the machine that had a mynah bird's capacity for imitating the sounds of a whole range of instruments—strings, reeds, brass, percussion. Seated in front of the keyboard, Connor demonstrated it for her like a kid putting his model train through its paces.

Her attentive ear made note of his explanation as well as his enthusiasm. Her other ear listened to her heart, which warned her that it was leaving her for this man. Impossible! Don't you realize who he is? Don't you realize what he is? Well, it didn't matter. There was no reasoning with the heart. It knew only the flesh-and-blood man, not the eight-by-ten glossy.

"I'm having a computer system put in," he was telling her. "They've come up with this outfit that stores the music, plays it back for you, even prints everything out on staff paper. Some people like to see everything on paper." The look over his shoulder told her he knew she was one of those. "It'll probably take me a while to get the hang of it, but the sales-lady said she'd come out and give me lessons."

Unbidden, an image of the "saleslady" popped into Sarah's mind—a voluptuous computer whiz, California blond and tan. She joined the ranks of the "decorator lady," the housekeeper and the lovely Miss Buffalo in Sarah's mind. She turned up a very un-Sarahlike, narrow-eyed smile. "How considerate. How many lessons does she suppose you'll need?"

Connor's eyes danced. "She said she'd spend as much time with me as it took. Those manuals are useless, as far as I'm concerned."

"And so impersonal."

Grinning, he stood before her and studied her closely. "I think your eyes are turning green, Sarah. Yes, I do believe they're...and look! Your skin's taking on a greenish cast. Good Lord, woman, what have you been eating?"

He had her. She pursed her lips and then allowed a genu-inely sheepish smile. "Witch's brew."

"Eye of newt and toe of frog?" he teased. "Powerful stuff. Know what the antidote is?"

"I'm sure *you* do."

"Of course." He slid his arms around her with a satisfied smile. "It's true love's kiss." His lips were firm, reassuring, slightly moist as he gave her just a single kiss. "True love invites no jealousy, sweet Sarah. And it harbors none."

"Mmm, very quotable. I'll remember that." And the kiss, she thought, savoring the taste of it—I'll remember that, too.

With his finger, he traced a line around her chin, preparing his proposal in his mind. "Let's take Dannie back to her grandparents and let them spoil her for a couple more days while we take a jaunt out to Nashville."

"Nashville?"

"Very short recording session. There are some people I want you to meet there, too, and some great places to—"

"No, Connor. That won't work."

"Why not?"

She pushed her hands against his chest, needing room to think, but he wouldn't give it to her. "First, because Dannie doesn't know her grandparents that well yet, and I'm not sure they're ready for any more of her just now, either."

"And second?"

"Second—" she shook her head, pulling firmly away from him now and moving toward the window across the room "—secondly, I don't fit in. I didn't at the hotel in Springfield, and I won't in Nashville. I won't fit in with that scene anywhere, Connor."

"That was a road party, Sarah. I don't blame you for walking out on that. I don't fit in most of the time at those things, either."

"That's ridiculous. How can the cornerstone not fit in? That's your life, Connor, your career. It's part of you." Fixing her attention on the ocean, she tried to sound matter-of-fact. "This is just an interlude. Pleasant as it's been, we have to be realistic and call it that."

"An interlude?" he repeated slowly, making the word sound like something he didn't want to touch.

She turned to face him, but she put the piano between them. "An interlude with your brother's...with your *dead* brother's..." There was no putting a name to it. "No matter what the Biblical injunctions are, you have no responsibility for me, Connor. I don't belong in your world."

He followed her around the piano, and when she tried to back away, she backed into the guitar stand. She reached to steady it, and he snatched the opportunity to grab her shoulders and pull her up to face him, nose to nose.

"You and I were alone together last night, Sarah, in *my* house, in *my* bed. You are not my brother's anything. If what you told me this morning was true, you never really were."

She flushed, and her eyes darted away from him. "I bore his child," she reminded him.

"He never knew his child. He never loved her. But I do." Her eyes flashed his way again. "Yes, *I* do, Sarah. Dannie's never had a father. She wants one—needs one. She needs *me*."

"Is it really...Dannie you want?"

His eyes became ice-blue crystal. "You could ask me that?" He loosened his grip on her, and her shoulders sagged. "Yes, I guess you could if you could choose a word like 'interlude.'"

"Connor...you're a man who belongs to a lot of people, and I'm a woman who belongs to very few. It's not just the concerts and the parties and the bright lights. It's...it's Spider Woman and Decorator Lady and all the swooning Gidgets...and Marlene."

He gave her a dark frown. "Who's Marlene?"

"The woman in the picture in your mother's tabloid."

Marlene was dismissed with a gesture of disgust. "I don't even remember that woman."

"You see what I mean?"

"No, I don't see what you mean. Do you know why? Because you don't even see what you mean." He reached for her shoulders, more gently this time. "I'm not the 'interlude' type, Sarah. You do know that. You're having trouble looking me in the eye because you know that."

A sigh told him he was right. "And I'm not the jealous type, Connor, but knowing that beautiful women throw themselves in your path every day...I'm just being realistic."

He pulled her into his arms and touched her hair, letting his fingers trail the length of it. "I think I know what you're afraid of, and it isn't Spider Woman. It certainly isn't Marlene. Just give me a little more time with you. Let me show you there's nothing to be afraid of."

"I'm not afraid, Connor. I'm just extremely practical."

He lifted her face in his hands and gave her half a smile. "You're lying to me, sweet Sarah. I know what it means to be afraid, and you're scared to death. If you won't go to Nashville with me *this time*, will you wait for me? I'll only be gone a couple of days. Three at the most."

"I have work to do at home," she reminded him.

"You can work here. Santa Cruz is a regular haven for artists. We can find anything you need there."

"I have a housekeeping business that won't be around anymore unless I…"

"Oh, forget that," he urged, squeezing the tops of her shoulders. "Your real work is your painting. You're wasting your time and talent pushing a vacuum cleaner around other people's carpets." He knew instantly, by the cold look she gave him, that he'd said the wrong thing. "Listen, Sarah, I admire your ingenuity, but I also admire your talent, and I…will you wait for me?"

"Connor, I can't stay that much—"

"I'll make it two days. I swear." He planted a hard kiss on her mouth, assuming, in typical male fashion, that he'd sealed a bargain. "I need more time with you. I want to show you how it can be." He kissed her again, and she concentrated on how it was.

The night air hung thick and heavy over Sarah, but standing in the dark at the bedroom window, Connor pronounced it remarkably clear and calm. He'd offered her gentle lovemaking, but she'd responded with an urgency that had ignited them both and threatened to set the bed ablaze. She wanted nothing to do with rest or sleep—no part of anything that would steal this time.

"Come to the window, Sarah. I want you to see something."

Sarah slipped into a filmy peignoir before she joined him. Stepping behind her, he gathered her shoulders between his hands and pointed her toward the north, past the twinkling lights of Santa Cruz toward a light blinking in the distance. "You can't always see it from here," he said. "Only on beautifully clear nights."

"A lighthouse?"

"Yes. It marks the point where the ocean meets Monterey Bay. Sometimes I stand here at night and watch it for hours, especially when I feel like taking perverse pleasure in being sorry for myself."

"Sorry about what?"

He draped his arms around her like a shawl, and she hugged them to her. "I get lonely, and that gives me an excuse to feel sorry for myself."

"That light blinking out there in the night..." she observed. "That's the image of loneliness."

"It is when you want it to be. It was built by grieving parents in memory of a son who'd drowned."

"It's an appropriate warning, then."

"Watch it closely, Sarah. What does it warn against?"

The light blinked several times before she answered. "To be careful. Not to get in over your head."

"Ah, Sarah," he chided. "That's just what a lonely person sees, and it's a sure bet that he'll stay lonely if that's the way he chooses to interpret the message. When I interpret it that way, the lighthouse mocks me. It says, 'Wallow in it, then, Ryan. You think you're drowning in your sorrows. Stand up, man! You're only up to your ankles. You don't need me.' And then it goes away."

"It goes away?"

"The next night. Damned if it doesn't shroud itself in clouds the next night." He chuckled at the incredible truth.

"Look!" Sarah pointed to another light blinking offshore. "A boat."

"Coast guard, probably."

"It looks like they're talking to each other."

"I'm sure they are. I'm sure that lighthouse is a welcome sight to any sailor about to put in for the night."

She lowered her cheek and rubbed it against his arm, wishing he could be a sailor or a lighthouse keeper or almost anything but what he was. A performer. A *theatrical person*. "What's the lighthouse's true message, then?" she asked.

"It's a reminder," he told her. "Its beacon spears through the darkness and reaches out to the living. It doesn't say, 'Be careful.' It says, 'Take care.'" He turned her in his arms. "Take care of me, Sarah." Bending to her, he whispered close to her mouth. "Let me take care of you."

He took her to his bed, and she took him deeper inside herself than she had thought possible. She had never been in touch with herself as he was. She had never let herself know the softness she kept locked away in a spiritual package. But Connor knew it. He found it, and he opened it up and kissed it with the hard part of himself—the part of a man that must complete itself with woman's softness. He made Sarah whole in a way she knew that she would never be whole again without him.

The following day he left for Nashville, and Sarah knew that if she waited for him to come back, she'd never be able to leave him.

Chapter Nine

Moving from Connor's world back to her own was predictably depressing. Sarah told herself it was obviously because she'd broken the cardinal rule for maintaining contentment among the common folk. Ordinary people should never fraternize with the rich and famous. She found that she was lecturing herself aloud, trying to banish from her brain all thoughts of bedrooms with hot tubs and views of the ocean. She wasn't a California girl, and she never would be. She needed that good, solid New England...composure. Yes, that was it, and Massachusetts reliability and fierce Yankee independence. Those were sterling traits, tried and true. She was in tune with those things, and she wouldn't have the machinations of the entertainment industry fouling up good metabolism.

But when the phone rang ninety-six hours to the minute after she'd stepped on New England soil again, she had a premonition. It seemed unlikely that the heart could stop and the pulse race simultaneously, but Sarah's did.

"Sarah? Connor. You left Dannie's pants with the dolphins on them."

"Oh." Deep breath. Steady. "Yes, she's been asking for them. Maybe you could…"

"I knew you'd taken off. I called home from Nashville a couple of times. Let the phone ring off the hook."

"I'm sorry. I thought it was best…I tried to explain before you left, but… We did have a wonderful time. I wanted you to know that."

"Oh, yeah? A wonderful time? Sounds like a postcard."

Sarah bit her lip and squeezed her eyes shut. She was botching this. "Anything I say will sound inadequate. That's why I left without saying anything."

"I swore I wasn't going to call, but I decided that was foolish. No team has room for more than one grandstander, and you've laid claim to that position."

"That's hardly a fair description. I told you I couldn't stay. You wouldn't accept that, and I just…well, I didn't want to argue with you."

She heard him expel an impatient breath, and she imagined a cigarette in his hand. "I guess I misread you," he said. He sounded hard and unemotional. "When you described what we had as an 'interlude,' I thought you meant that as an accusation, not a confession."

Her voice tightened. "What are you saying?"

"I'm saying you made it an interlude by taking off like that. I had every intention of making it much more."

"What more could it be?" she asked quietly.

"Unless you're very good at faking it, you know the answer to that."

Of course. They'd had good sex. "I'm sorry, Connor, but the answer eludes me. Perhaps I have a limited vocabulary in that respect. I'm not sure what the word is for prolonging an interlude. Would you call it an affair?"

"An affair?" he rejoined with disgust.

"Whatever the arrangement might be called, it wouldn't

work. I have a four-year-old daughter. For most men, that's excess baggage.''

"But we both know I'm not most men.''

She sighed. "Yes, we do. You've been good to Dannie every minute you've spent with her, and if you can...find more time to spend with her, I think...''

"*Find more time!* That's what I asked you to do, Sarah. I asked you to find more time for me—for us. I'm not interested in an affair. If I wanted an affair, I'd call Maureen, or whatever her name is.'' He'd let an urgency creep into his voice that he didn't like. He paused for control. "I was thinking we could call the arrangement 'marriage.' Does that term give you any trouble?''

Marriage to Connor Ryan. Oh, God. The man she loved was proposing marriage. She'd expected almost any other possibility, but not this one. It didn't fit with what he was. With *who* he was, yes, but not with what he was.

"Apparently I just told a bad joke,'' he said quietly. "I'm getting no response.''

"It...it couldn't work, Connor,'' Sarah managed, the tears burning in her throat.

"You've said that before. It makes me wonder whether you have a crystal ball up your sleeve.'' She knew he was dragging on that cigarette again, and she felt the smoke crowding her own chest. "Okay, read the tea leaves for me. Why wouldn't it work?''

"Because you're Connor Ryan.''

"And you don't want to be married to Connor Ryan,'' he presumed, knowing somewhere in his gut that wasn't true.

"I don't want to be married to a life-style that terrifies me,'' she said.

"I'm not asking you to marry my life-style. I want you to marry *me*. My life-style right now is that of a bachelor. If we were married, that would change. Your life-style would change. We'd come up with a new one that suited both of us.''

Sarah pressed her hand back and forth across her forehead,

which was beginning to throb with the effort of holding back her tears. The pictures that flashed behind her eyelids were of a man she wanted very much to be with, a man who sang his heart out in a crowded auditorium and in a quiet room—a man who gave one child a seashell and another his autograph. And then, God forbid, there was a man selling detergent on TV, and she was angry and heartbroken both, but the truth was, she'd wanted to be with him, too.

"There's more to your life-style than that, Connor. There are things you cannot change as long as you are what you are."

"Look, Sarah, my private life is my own. I don't belong to my career like...like Kevin belonged to the army. My music isn't a life-style; it's a life force, and it has been since I was a kid. That's part of me, part of who I am and who I was long before Georgia Nights. I know you understand that. You understand it better than anyone I know."

"Yes," she whispered, "I do understand."

"Then why do you have trouble accepting me as I am?"

"I don't. I love you as you are."

"Marry me, then," he entreated quietly.

"I can't, Connor. You're a star. You can't come down to earth for me, and I'm afraid of heights."

"That's crazy talk, Sarah, and I won't accept it. But I won't prolong the argument, either. I'll be in touch."

He hung up the phone thinking he'd be in touch after he'd given her some time to be without him. She belonged with him, and he'd give her a few months to realize that. She'd miss him. Within four weeks, she'd gladly live in Grand Central Station with him if he asked her to. He'd give her an extra month or two just to make sure she felt exactly the way he was feeling right now. Damned miserable.

It worked. No one could have been more miserable in the weeks to come than Sarah was—unless, of course, it was Connor. Sarah's housekeeping business thrived, partly because of the holiday season and partly because she took to cleaning with frustrated furor. Her painting was another story. She wasted a lot of canvas. One fruitless afternoon ended with neat pats of blue and yellow paint splattered on the wall, where she'd dashed her pallet pad, and with one previously neatly stretched canvas lying on the floor, its frame broken over the radiator. New England composure had bitten the dust.

Connor, on the other hand, did some of his best writing when he was miserable. Sadness had always given him a different kind of voice, one that the dyed-in-the-wool country-music fans identified with. Since he was feeling sorry for himself, his lighthouse wouldn't talk to him, so he holed up with his piano and nursed his loneliness. It made for good melancholy music.

While Connor nursed melancholia, Sarah brought her instinctive mother's nursing skills to bear on Dannie, who had come down with a cold when they returned to California. It simply wouldn't go away. Sarah blanketed it and misted it, doused it with vitamin C and baby aspirin, but the cold hung on while the coughing got worse. California seemed to have taken its sunny toll, draining the hardiness and composure right out of both of them.

When Connor called again, it was because he'd seen a Christmas tree with a Raggedy Ann doll sitting underneath it in a department-store window. He'd stood in front of the window for a long time, and then he'd bought a bottle of whiskey. He never drank whiskey, but Raggedy Ann had that effect on him. Whiskey and water was a man's drink, or so he'd heard. He laughed out loud and toasted the image of his father, who stood off in the corner of his mind, nodding approval. Had he given her enough time? Would just the sound of his voice make her shiver inside her flannel painter's shirt? Hell, he wasn't about to grovel. He just wanted to talk.

"Sarah? Connor. How's it goin'?"

"Connor? It's...I...it's good to hear your voice."

He shivered inside his sweatshirt and fortified himself with another bitter swallow. Keep it casual, he reminded himself.

"Is it? Same here. So how's it goin'? You ready for Christmas?"

"Christmas?" His voice sounded as though it was listing a little to one side.

"Yeah. Have you decked the halls yet?"

"No. Not yet. Connor, are you drunk?"

"Gettin' there. I was...just out with some friends," he lied. He wanted her to think there was good reason for his condition, and he didn't want her to think she had anything to do with it.

"I see. You start your Christmas parties early out there."

"We've gotta do something. We don't get much snow." Another sip, and he set the glass down. It tasted like sewer water. "I called to ask you...what are you wearing?"

"What am I...a T-shirt and jeans."

"And a huge flannel shirt with paint all over it?"

She looked down. "Yes."

His laughter was warm and rich. "I thought so, but I had to make sure."

"Why?" she asked, too enraptured by the sound of his voice to worry about him making any sense.

"Because that's what you were wearing the first time I saw you, and I was just thinking how that outfit impressed me. Do you know, I can't remember what Miss Buffalo wore with her crown, but that big flannel shirt was great on you."

"And how is...Marlene?"

He chuckled. "Cold if she's in Buffalo. They're getting snow. It's supposed to miss you, but you may get some flurries tonight." The fog he'd tried to surround himself with wasn't thick enough. He was seeing her face. "Are you...cold, Sarah?"

"Yes," she said quietly.

"I am, too." He let the silence give him some breathing space before he picked up a conversational tone. "How's my Princess?"

"She's in bed with...she isn't feeling well."

"Not feeling well? What's the matter?"

As if on cue, Dannie called for Sarah from her room. "She's had a cold. Connor, I have to go. She's…"

"Put her on the phone. Just let me say hello."

"I really don't…I hate to get her up just now," Sarah hedged.

"Sarah, what's wrong?"

There was no trace of drink in his voice now. She'd alarmed him. "Nothing, really. She's calling for me, so I really have to…"

"Go on upstairs. I'll hold on."

"But it may be—"

"I said I'll wait." He could just as easily call her back, but somehow he couldn't bring himself to break the connection.

When she returned to the phone, she sounded distressed. "She wanted water. I've told her not to get out of bed. I'm sure it's one of those things that has to run its course, but that cough has me worried."

"Has she seen a doctor?" he wondered.

"I have an appointment for tomorrow morning." The racking cough started again upstairs. "Oh, Connor, she's having another coughing spasm. I have to go."

"I'll call you tomorrow," he promised. He hung up and lit a cigarette. Inexplicably, the lungful of smoke pinched his chest inside. Reaching past his unfinished drink, he snuffed out the cigarette. Late morning tomorrow? Noon tomorrow? When would she know something? Late morning there would be early morning here, but he couldn't wait that long. He made one more phone call and then heaved himself out of the chair and headed for the bedroom.

Chapter Ten

Connor remembered the feeling he'd had the first time he'd pulled up in this driveway. He'd been suspicious, true, but something had told him that what lay behind that door would change his life, and that thought had scared him. He hadn't minded the prospect of sitting on the hot seat in Kevin's behalf. How many times had Kevin done just that for him? What had scared him, even as it attracted him, was the image of that porcelain face and the feeling that what started out in Kevin's behalf might soon be in his own. Kevin had nothing to do with this now. It was Connor's little girl who was sick, and it was Connor's woman who needed his help, even if she was too damned stubborn to admit it.

The house looked like a forbidding sentry, its dark upper-story windows staring emotionlessly at the snow-covered front yard. Connor mounted the porch steps and tipped his head back for a look overhead. Gray-white clouds moved swiftly past the gray shingles of the gable above him. He shouldn't have called her three sheets to the wind. But if he hadn't, he might not have called at all, and then he wouldn't have known. She'd never have called him. Sarah was used to taking care of everything herself. That was something he'd come here to change if he could. She was going to start seeing him differently. The door knocker clattered under his fist.

"Hey, Connor, Sarah didn't say anything about you coming out. Come in, come in." Grinning and bright eyed, Jerry swung the door open wide and gestured for Connor's entry. "He-e-ey, great to see you. Dannie's been talking about California nonstop since they got back, and Sarah sure had a good time. Is Sarah in for a surprise, or was she just keeping me in the dark about you coming?"

Connor stripped off his leather gloves and offered a quick handshake. "She's in for a surprise. How's Dannie?"

Jerry's face settled immediately into an expression of concern. "I really don't know, man. Sarah just called. She says the doctor suspects pneumonia. They're admitting her into the hospital, I guess."

"What hospital?"

"Oh, geez, I forgot to ask. She'll probably be calling back later, though. We'll get the whole story then. Poor kid's been pretty sick." The solemnity on Jerry's face brightened with his next thought. "Say, how about a beer? Sarah said she might not be home for a couple of days, and she wanted me to watch the house, so I stocked up."

"No, thanks." An impatient wave of the hand dismissed the offer. Why hadn't this boy made it his business to find out a little more? "How long has she been pretty sick?"

"Well, she's had this cold, see. You know how kids get in the winter—nonstop runny noses, always coughing and sneezing." Jerry shoved his hands in his pockets and edged toward the living room. He figured if Connor didn't want a beer, he wouldn't have one, either. "Anyway, it's been hanging on. Sarah said she was up all night with her last night."

"Who's her doctor?"

Jerry wrinkled up his face and thought a moment. "Gee, I don't know that I've ever heard her mention a doctor. Dannie's not a sickly kid—nothing ever that serious. Sarah takes real good care—"

"All kids go to the doctor once in a while," Connor informed him as he pulled a soft plaid muffler like a bell cord, sliding it off his neck and tossing it on a chair in passing. "Sick or not. Where would Sarah keep a list of important phone numbers?"

"I don't know. Probably—" Connor was already rifling through the small drawer under the telephone table "—in that drawer," Jerry finished, shrugging.

Connor found the list he was looking for inside the front cover of the phone book. A call to the pediatrician's office turned up the name of the hospital.

"You're going to show me how to get there, Jerry. We're driving over together." The little drawer swallowed up the phone book as the receiver whacked into place under Connor's hand.

"Sure thing. It's only a few miles." Jerry returned to the front entry and took his nylon parka down from the coat tree. "Did you rent a car?"

"Yeah. Listen, Jerry." Connor took pains to lay a friendly hand on Jerry's shoulder, and Jerry was all ears. "I want you to go with me to the hospital and wait around there for a while until we have some idea what's going on."

"Oh, yeah. Sure thing."

"Sarah's probably exhausted, and I'm going to try to talk her into coming home with you later. I want her to let me stay with Dannie while she gets some rest. Will you do that for me?" Jerry nodded. He liked the idea of doing Connor a personal favor. He could see himself taking on other jobs, acting in some official capacity in behalf of Connor Ryan. He could probably become his personal adviser or bodyguard.

"It may take a while," Connor warned. "She'll think she has to do it all herself. But you'll hang in there with me, won't you?"

Nodding again, Jerry grinned. "'Course, she'll probably say she can drive herself." But nobody could say Jerry hadn't *tried.* Driving his sister around was a far cry from being a bodyguard. Willingness was what the man was looking for, obviously.

"Undoubtedly. But we're going to take care of *her* for a change. We're going to persuade her that she doesn't have to carry the whole world on her own little shoulders."

Jerry agreed. He liked the sound of that. It sounded pretty tough. He'd *insist* on driving Sarah home. Then he'd personally see to it that she got some rest.

Northampton Hospital was not far from Sarah's home in Amherst. Connor bypassed the directory on the wall and went straight to the reception desk for directions. The receptionist ran her finger through a list and shook her head. Dannie had apparently not been admitted yet.

He found Sarah in a waiting area holding her little girl in her arms. Wrapped as she was in a pink-and-blue blanket, Dannie seemed much smaller than Connor remembered. They both looked as though they should have been in bed, but Sarah brightened visibly when she saw him, whispering something to Dannie as he approached.

Sarah had thought of him often since he'd called, thinking he wouldn't be able to get hold of her at home and she'd have to try to call him as soon as she knew something. She hadn't allowed herself the hope of seeing him. He looked like heaven. He wore a camel topcoat, which hung open over a camel blazer and rust slacks. Only once before had she seen him in a dress shirt and tie, and she'd thought that effort had been made for his parents.

Wisps of hair the color of winter wheat dipped over his forehead, and he ran a hand through them quickly before he crouched next to Sarah's knees, offering both his girls his most winning smile. "I took the first flight I could get. I brought Dannie's pants, too."

Dannie offered the best smile she could muster, though her usual exuberance wasn't there. Sarah watched as Connor touched Dannie's wild blond curls, remembering how he'd done that so tentatively the first time he'd seen her. He cupped the child's cheek in his hand and kissed her forehead, his tenderness taking a tight hold in Sarah's own heart. When he lifted his eyes to hers, she couldn't speak. Her chest hurt with the effort of holding back the words, "Thank God you're here."

The words were in her eyes, and Connor read them. "You look tired," he said gently.

Sarah closed her eyes and nodded.

"I'm sick, Uncle Connor. The doctor says they can make me well if I stay here a little while."

Connor shifted his gaze to Dannie and smiled. "They've got all kinds of great stuff here, Princess. They've got medicine and pretty nurses to give it to you so you'll get better."

"Mommy gives me medicine," Dannie insisted. She looked much too pale, and her lips seemed dry and chalky.

"I know, and she's just as pretty as any nurse." He offered Sarah a reassuring wink. "Prettier, even. But she's not a nurse. And here in the hospital, the nice doctors tell the pretty nurses what kind of medicine to give and how much. They've got it all worked out."

"Is that lady over there a nurse?" Connor followed Dannie's finger to a white-uniformed woman behind the desk. Her cap identified her as a nurse, and Connor nodded. "Well, she isn't pretty," Dannie judged.

"No, she isn't," he agreed. "But I'm sure she's nice."

"She isn't nice, either. She won't let me in here."

Connor glanced up at Sarah, frowning slightly. "I don't know what they're doing back there. Probably checking our credit. I told them I had enough money to pay them, but they want insurance," Sarah explained, trying to make it sound like a minor inconvenience. The "minor inconvenience" had left her sitting here with a sick child in her arms for almost an hour.

"You don't have health insurance?"

"No. I know I should have, but I've managed to…I've been putting it off," she confessed.

"Has the doctor sent the order to admit her?"

"Yes. They said it would be just a matter of...getting a little more information or something. They needed some different forms and somebody else's signature."

"I don't want to stay here, Uncle Connor," Dannie whined pathetically. "I want to go home."

Connor patted her little hand before he rose to his feet. "Your mommy and I will stay with you, honey. I'll see if things can't be—"

"Connor," Sarah began, "There's no need for you to..."

He smiled encouragingly. "Where else am I going to stay? I came to visit you, and here you are. Besides, I *love* hospitals. They're so...clean. Who do you suppose does their housekeeping?" He couldn't resist taking Sarah's chin in his hand and bending to kiss her, briefly but firmly. "Let me take care of the nice lady at the desk, and then we'll call for the bellman."

Jerry joined the group, having parked Connor's rental car with special care. He handed Connor the keys just as Connor headed for the admitting desk. Then Jerry gave Sarah and Dannie each a loving pat on the shoulder and settled into a chair with two well-thumbed copies of *Road and Track*.

Connor's charm had a way of speeding things up behind the admitting desk. He'd learned long ago that he could get quicker action by lubricating the human cogs in any wheel with a little honey. He used his name, his identification and, on the very pragmatic head nurse, his assurance of payment of all expenses, a responsibility that he assumed gladly and in writing. It was gratifying and handy to find that people who were screaming fans of his by night were actually very dignified hospital personnel by day.

Sarah and Dannie were suddenly whisked to a private room in the pediatrics wing. One minute they'd been set aside in the waiting room, and the next they were being escorted by three nurses and two orderlies, one pushing Dannie's wheelchair, the other buzzing with one of the nurses about "Connor Ryan" and "Georgia Nights."

"Very effective bit of name dropping," Sarah muttered as

she and Connor stood out of the way while the nurses fussed over Dannie, provided her with a hospital gown and a plastic bracelet and took her vital signs.

"It's *my* name," Connor reminded her, matching her mutter with a deeper one of his own. "I'm allowed to drop it."

"What else did you drop? A little under-the-table cash?"

Connor shook his head. "I tried that, but Mrs. Morgan would have no part of it. She took my signature, though."

"For what?"

He shrugged. "For posterity."

"Connor, you're not going to pay any…"

"Let's not argue in front of the k-i-d. She's got enough trouble."

"All right," Sarah agreed with a sigh. "We'll argue later."

One of the nurses approached Sarah with an attitude that said she sympathized with Sarah simply because she was the mother of a sick child, which Sarah found somewhat reassuring. She'd begun to wonder whether this was turning into a fan-club meeting. "Dr. Rochard has ordered more tests and another set of X rays, Miss Benedict. We'll want to get those done and then let Dannie get some rest, which is what she needs most right now."

"I intend to stay…"

"One of us will be here as long as Dannie is here," Connor said. He glanced at Sarah. "Whichever one isn't dead on his feet."

"That's fine," the nurse told them. "You might want to find the cafeteria and have something to eat once we have everything taken care of. This little girl is too tired to keep her eyes open, and you look like you could use a break." Her sympathy was again directed at Sarah, who was unaware that the dark smudges under her eyes were a dead giveaway for exhaustion. She did know that she felt like an overwound watch.

Once Dannie was asleep, Sarah agreed to a break. There were a few customers scattered about the tables in the hospital's cafeteria, mostly people dressed in white, reading the evening paper over a cup of coffee. Connor ordered soup and sandwiches for both of them despite Sarah's protests. When they sat down at a corner table, which offered a measure of privacy, she was still protesting. Connor ignored her, setting the food in front of her. She ate, almost as a reflex, and he watched, satisfied. She looked as though she hadn't had a decent meal in weeks. He'd see that she had one soon, but he knew this was the most he'd get into her now.

"I heard one of the orderlies call her 'the Ryan girl,'" Sarah was saying. "I don't know what you told them, but I can't approve of the way you've just…"

"I think they assume she's my child," Connor explained, adding quickly, "I didn't tell them she was. I just…didn't say she wasn't."

Sarah rolled her eyes ceilingward and sighed. "And she calls you 'Uncle Connor.' They must think she's one of those children with all kinds of 'uncles.'"

Connor's lopsided smile was almost apologetic. "More likely, they think I'm one of those Hollywood creeps who isn't married to any of the mothers of any of his children."

"But they appear to be fans, and they adore you despite your little indiscretions." Sarah stared at him a moment. "They can't…you don't think they'd gossip loudly enough for one of those newspapers to get hold of it, do you?"

He shook his head. "Hospital records are out of bounds."

"But speculation…"

"Relax, Sarah." He reached for her hand. "No one knows I'm here. If the press shows up, I'll see that some heads roll. Hospital staff members are generally pretty discreet when it comes to the media. I'm not here for a concert, so no one's looking for me."

She fixed her eyes on the black face of the watch that peeked out from under the cuff of his shirt sleeve. "I read in one of those papers last week that you'd been rude to a waiter but that you were to be forgiven because you were trying to quit smoking. The writer saw you at a party two days later with a cigarette in your hand."

He squeezed her hand, tickling her palm with his fingertips. "Are you reading that stuff for the same reason my mother does? If you want to know what I've been doing, just ask me, Sarah. I've been out a few times since you left." She glanced from their hands to his eyes, betraying her reaction to that news. "With friends. Not with women," he assured her.

"It's none of my business."

"Then don't look for information in the tabloids. Don't read them at all. That's rule number one."

She pulled her hand away from his. "That would be the problem, wouldn't it, Connor? I'd have rules to go by, but there'd be none for you."

"I'd go by the same rules you would, Sarah. Haven't you noticed by now that I'm pretty damned straight? Why do you think they print stories about me trying to quit smoking?" She raised a brow at the question. "Because I don't give them much to write about. The pictures with Miss Buffalo were hard to avoid. The girl wanted some publicity." He lifted one shoulder, admitting, "I let somebody take our picture. No harm done."

"Are you really trying to quit smoking?" she asked. She realized she didn't want to think about Miss Buffalo.

"Isn't everybody?" He managed to take her hand and get half a smile out of her before he swore solemnly, "I would never let them hurt Dannie...or you. You'll be part of my private life, and I never let them touch that."

The concern in his eyes made her want to let go so badly. "I'm sorry, Connor. I don't know why I'm giving you such a bad time. I should be thanking you for getting us out of that waiting room. I should be thanking you for coming. It's just that...you've taken everything out of my hands, and I'm not sure I like that."

He opened her hand and smoothed his palm over hers, then cupped his hand under hers. "I haven't taken anything out of your hands, Sarah. I've just put my hands under yours, just to give you a little support."

The touch of his lips to her fingertips brought the tears she'd been trying so hard to dam up. She heard the scrape of a chair and felt him slide up next to her. Without another thought, she turned to him, burying her face against his neck. He rubbed her back while she wept silently. It didn't matter where they were just then or who else might be there. Connor shielded her from the world, and she was free to cry. She believed for the moment that he wouldn't let anything touch her.

Moments later she lifted her head from his shoulder, and he recognized the cue. He handed her a handkerchief. Wiping and sniffling, she eyed the mascara smudge she'd left on his collar. "Oh, look what I've done now. I'm sorry," she said, squaring her shoulders in search of the composure she'd lost.

"Don't apologize for tears," he said quietly, taking the handkerchief from her hand to dab away the dark, wet smudge she'd left under one eye. "Tears are my stock-in-trade. I've written my share of sad songs. I think people should cry more often."

She closed her eyes, and her sigh was quivery. "I'm just tired."

"I know."

"And I'm tired of being tired. Sometimes I hate Kevin for leaving me with all the responsibility. It's supposed to be..." Sarah opened her eyes, surprised by what she'd heard herself say. "Of course, it is my responsibility, and Kevin can't be blamed. He can never be blamed."

"Of course he can. He had no business making you pregnant, Sarah."

Sarah looked up at him, wondering if she'd heard him right. They were both spouting nonsense. "If he hadn't, I wouldn't have Dannie," she reminded him. "He didn't plan on dying within a few months."

"He didn't plan on becoming a father within a few months, either. You know, I don't think it's blasphemous to admit that you hate somebody for dying on you. I think it's normal. I hated him for checking out on me, too."

His arm was still draped behind her chair, and he was rubbing circles around the top of her shoulder with this thumb.

Everything he did felt good to her, and everything he said sounded sensible—even what he was saying now, which had to be utter nonsense. "I don't really hate him," she said. "And I'm grateful to him for giving me Dannie."

"I'm grateful for Dannie, too, but I'm honestly not grateful to Kevin for the role he played."

Sarah frowned, tilting her head slightly to the side as though she needed a different perspective. "You're not jealous of him...now. Are you?"

Lifting a shoulder in response, Connor sighed. "I don't know. I spent a lot of years envying Kevin. I figured to unload all that the day I proved to him that I was just as good at what I did as he was at what he did." He smiled a little sheepishly. "That was a tall order because Kevin did everything well. But I was just on the verge." His eyes became distant with the memory, his hand poised in the air as though at the edge of something. "Things were just about to happen for me. I wanted Kevin to be there, to see that I really was good and that none of that other stuff mattered because I could make good music."

"What other stuff?" she asked.

He glanced at her, and then glanced away, shrugging again. "Nothing, really. I was never much of a student or anything like that. Kevin was the whiz kid in school. Anyway, he was killed just before Georgia Nights really made it big."

Sarah laid her hand on his thigh. "Kevin told me his brother was a musical genius. He said you could pick up any instrument and play it without a lesson. He said you didn't even need a book."

Connor leaned back into a sardonic laugh. "Didn't even need a book. That's a good one, Kev."

"I'm serious, Connor. Kevin said...once when he was complimenting a sketch I'd done, he said he admired anyone who had artistic talent, and then he said it reminded him of his brother. He would've given anything to be able to play the piano the way you did, he said."

Sobering, Connor raised a brow in her direction. "He said

that?'' A nod confirmed what he already knew was a likeli-
hood. ''He would. He should've been there for one concert.
Just one. I could've given it all back to him with just one
performance.''

''Given what back to him?'' she wondered.

''The fruits of his labors.'' He reached past her and snatched
the remaining sandwich half from her plate, and she knew he
wouldn't explain further.

''I'm not going to make you finish your soup,'' he promised, waving the sandwich in front of her nose, ''because it's
full of salt water now. But you're going to finish this sandwich
before I send you home to bed.''

She accepted the sandwich but shook her head at the rest.
''I'm staying. Dannie's liable to have another night like the
last, and she'll be frightened if I'm not here.''

''I'll be here. She'll ask for you, and she'll get me. She
won't be frightened.''

Sarah knew it was true. Connor's presence would give Dannie almost the same sense of security her own would bring.
In a short time, he had become almost a… Oh, no, you don't,
Sarah. That's a dangerous thought. ''You can come back in
the morning, Connor. After you've had…''

''A good night's rest? That's what *you* need. You've been
at it long enough. Besides, I…'' He rolled his eyes with a
sudden thought. ''Damn, I forgot about Jerry. I asked him to
wait around and drive you home. I think I've just put his
loyalty to the test.''

''I can drive myself,'' Sarah protested. ''That is, I *could* if
I were…''

Connor smiled. She was weakening. He pushed his chair
back and handed her purse to her. ''But you don't have to,
sweetheart. Your loving brother is standing by. And good ol'
Uncle Connor claims the first shift at Dannie's bedside.''

''You *are* trying to take over here, Connor, and I won't let
you get away with it.''

With a firm hand at her waist, he guided her toward the
exit. ''You're a bit short-tempered right now, Sarah, really not

fit company for anyone. But that's only because you're tired. You'll be a brand-new woman tomorrow, one the rest of us won't mind being around.''

Sputtering, she allowed herself to be conducted to the waiting room, where Jerry was, sure enough, still waiting to take her home.

Connor sat in near darkness drinking coffee from a foam cup. The night-light by the bed cast Dannie's face, turned toward him as she slept, in soft relief. Her small features were more pronounced by contrast with the shadows. She looked like Kevin, and Kevin, of course, looked like Connor.

Kevin had been the younger of the two brothers by a year and a half, so it was fair to claim that it was Kevin who looked like Connor. Connor used to wonder why God had made them so alike on the outside and so different under the skin. He remembered thinking once that God had made a mistake with Connor, so He'd made Kevin to see if He could do better the second time.

They'd even sounded so much alike that they were able to fool their mother over the phone. Of course, Kevin couldn't carry a tune in a tin bucket. Connor smiled at the memory of Kevin shouting songs in the shower. It was awful. Their father had laughed whenever he heard it and said that Kevin had a voice "just like his old man—one you could scare a bear with." He never said much about Connor's voice, but his mother had always volunteered him for the boys' choir at every post's chapel.

Connor had started school two years ahead of Kevin, but by the time Connor was eight years old, Kevin was in his class. Kevin had skipped the first grade, and Connor had repeated it. To say that Connor hadn't been much of a student was being generous. His teachers couldn't imagine what the problem was. Connor had a good vocabulary, and he remembered everything that was discussed in class, whipped through his math facts faster than anyone else. But he couldn't read.

One teacher finally announced to his mother that Connor simply refused to read, that it was just pure laziness.

Connor wasn't lazy. He wanted to read, but he got mixed up. He hated the way his face would get hot and his throat would burn. There were sounds that were supposed to go with letters, but he couldn't put them together right, and he didn't know why. Then one day at recess he overheard the reason.

In class that morning he'd stumbled through a reading lesson, obediently taking his turn reading aloud, even though it always made his stomach hurt. It had gone pretty much the way it always did. The teacher never made him read very much of the story. He was glad of that because he always understood what the other kids read, but when he took his turn, he never could make any sense out of it. By the time he would struggle to the end of a sentence, the teacher prompting him all the way, he'd lost the meaning. Still, he tried because he didn't want anyone to tell his mother he was lazy again. Dad had spanked him for that.

He kept trying until that one day at recess, when he heard one of the boys in his reading group tell Kevin that his brother was stupid. Connor could still hear the words. "I may be a slow reader, but at least I ain't *stupid* like that big dummy brother of yours."

Connor had never seen Kevin fight with anybody before, but he did that day. Kevin lowered his head like a big-horned sheep and rammed the other boy right in the gut. It was Connor who broke them up. Connor was a head taller than any of the rest of them, and nobody messed with him. He remembered the look in Kevin's eyes when he hauled Kevin off the other boy's chest. It was a look of pity.

Being stupid was different from being lazy. You didn't get whipped for being stupid. You didn't get called on in class, and you never had to read out loud. The bigger Connor got, the less anxious the teachers were to hold him back a grade. After a while, he wasn't even expected to listen in class as long as he didn't disturb anyone. He'd sit in the back of the room, where the tall kids always sat, and he'd examine his latest collection of things he'd found—rocks, leaves, shells, beach glass, even bugs. He never bothered anyone, and no one bothered him. Everyone accepted him as he was—everyone except Kevin.

"You're not dumb, Connor. You're smarter about a lot of things than anybody, even Dad." Even Dad? That was quite a compliment, coming from Kevin. "I don't want you getting any more bad grades." Connor had laughed. "I mean it. I don't want people saying you aren't smart. I'm gonna read all the lessons to you, and you're gonna listen."

Their mother had stopped reading to them after Kevin had learned to read, and by the fourth grade, the teachers weren't reading to them much anymore. At first Connor would have nothing to do with Kevin's plan because Connor was no baby to be read to anymore. But there were things he wanted to know. He wanted to know about rocks, and that led to fossils, and that led to dinosaurs. He wanted to know about shells, and that led to marine life, which led to tides, which led to the moon, which meant the sky was the limit.

Tirelessly, Kevin read to Connor, and Connor watched as Kevin followed the words on the page with his finger. And then something curious happened. Connor began to whisper the words as Kevin read them. One day Connor took over and read a whole paragraph for himself, straight through, and it made sense. Kevin just sat there grinning at him. He'd known all along his big brother was no dummy.

Connor hadn't been quite so convinced as Kevin was, but the world began to look a little different to him. His grades improved. He experimented and found that there were some things he did very well when he put his mind to it. He remembered everything he heard and found that he had a real knack for memorizing whole passages. He was good in math, and whenever there were science experiments or social-studies projects to do, he excelled. He never became a good reader, as Kevin was, but he could get by. Connor preferred to learn about things by handling them. When he was introduced to the piano, it was love at first touch. At that moment, he became a musician.

Kevin's kid. That was why he'd come at first—because Dannie was Kevin's kid. He'd thought he owed it to Kevin. He'd thought that way so many times in the past. But here in the darkness, with only the sound of Dannie's breathing filling his ears, he used Kevin's memory to help him recall the lesson he had the most trouble remembering—Connor owed it to himself.

Connor took a room in a nearby hotel, and when Sarah came to the hospital the following morning, he had breakfast and went to bed. Dr. Rochard examined Dannie that morning and explained that the infection had settled deep in Dannie's lungs, which was giving them something of a problem in determining which pneumonia-causing organism was at fault. During the next three days, Sarah took days, and Connor took nights, but they shared late afternoons and had supper together.

"It's good to have someone to share the burden with," Sarah confessed over hospital-cafeteria coffee.

"It's good to be granted my share without feeling like I have to try out for the debating team."

"It isn't as though I couldn't handle it," she hastened to add. "But it's nice to have someone else feel the same way I do—worry about her the same way. *Almost* the same way."

Connor accepted the amendment graciously. "Almost. I think procreation's designer gave mothers a special province, especially when a child is hungry or tired or sick."

"But when a child is afraid, it's nice to have someone stronger there." Sarah studied her coffee cup. "Dannie said she had a nightmare last night, and she was glad you were around. You make the goblins disappear. It seems I can only chase them back."

"I just held her until she went back to sleep. Sang to her a little."

"Yes, she told me. You sing better than I do, you know."

"I've never heard you sing." He smiled at the thought.

"You don't want to."

"Yes, I do. I want to hear you sing in the shower and whistle while you work." She glanced up, and he caught her eyes with his. "I want to hear you hum while you rock Dannie to sleep. Dannie...or another baby." She caught her lower lip between her teeth, but she couldn't look away. "That same designer of procreation made raising kids a two-person job. It's a lot harder when you try to manage it with one."

"I know." But better with just one for sure than with a second who's never there, she thought. He's here now, a small voice said. But he'll be gone tomorrow or the next day, or the day after for sure, and it gets harder each time to let him go.

"I'm not pushing," he told her. "Not now, anyway. I just want you to know what's on my mind."

Dannie's recovery picked up speed once the troublesome bacteria was identified and the antibiotics began to do their work. Connor took her for rides in a wheelchair, taught her the rudiments of checkers and watched more TV than he'd ever hoped to have the time for. They were both becoming restless.

"I can't go to sleep, Uncle Connor. I'm not tired."

"Miss Mackie said, 'lights out,'" he reminded her, pushing the button on her bed to lay her down.

"Miss Mackie, Miss Mackie." She jackknifed to a sitting position, hands out in front of her. "Let's do 'Miss Mary Mack, Mack, Mack.'"

Connor chuckled, pushing her shoulders back to the bed. "I don't know that one."

"Can I draw one more picture?"

"Tomorrow."

"Then you have to read me a story. Mommy always reads me a story before bed. You never do."

Connor swallowed hard and felt a funny twinge in his stomach. "How about if I sing you a story song?"

Dannie popped up again, grinning. "Yes, a song!"

Thank God. His stomach muscles relaxed as he pulled his chair closer to the bed. He started with "There Was an Old

Lady Who Swallowed a Fly." By the end of that one, she was giggling so hard he knew he'd have to come up with another to settle her down. He pulled a quiet ballad from his repertoire and noticed that Miss Mackie peeked in three times, lingering on the second and smiling by the third.

An orderly appeared at the door with a boy in a wheelchair, and Connor motioned them in. With the third ballad, he had an audience of seven and a very wide-awake Dannie. He figured if Miss Mackie didn't care, he sure as hell didn't. Poor kid had been sleeping for days. Mrs. Morgan showed up, and Connor thought the party was over until she asked, more timidly than he'd have thought she had in her, for "Misty River Morning." Miss Mackie finally had to call a halt to the show, not because of Connor's singing but because the applause was getting out of hand.

"But it was wonderful," she told Connor after she'd cleared the room. She stayed to help straighten Dannie's bedding and put her books and toys on the shelf. "My, you're a good little artist for a four-year-old," the nurse said, admiring a drawing she'd picked up along with a couple of books.

"Four-and-a-half almost five," Dannie recited. "See? It's the same toy store as that book is about. See all the toys in the windows?"

Gray-haired Nurse Mackie held up the drawing and the book, comparing the two. The child had a good hand. "Yes, I see. But you put the door here, and the boat here, and the..." The woman smiled, handing the drawing to Connor. "It's almost a mirror image. Isn't that clever? Good night, Mr. Ryan. Sleep well, Dannie."

Connor felt the crispness of the paper between his fingers, but he was transfixed for a moment by the empty doorway. *Mirror image.* He lowered his eyes slowly to the page in his hand.

"I made that for you, Uncle Connor. Do you like it?"

The figures blurred in front of his eyes. "I like it very much, Princess. You draw beautifully."

Chapter Eleven

The threat of snow hung heavy just above the rooftops the day Connor and Sarah brought Dannie home. She fussed when Sarah draped her with an extra blanket, complaining she couldn't breathe, but Sarah flipped the corners of the double wrappings over Dannie's face and muffled further protests. Connor wasn't sure he had the correct end of the bundle upright until it started squirming.

"I don't know what you've got in this package, Sarah, but I hope it isn't supper," he teased, letting Sarah get the door. "It fights back."

"It'll be subdued soon enough." She closed the door behind her and added for Dannie's benefit, "It's going straight to bed."

"No, I'm not!" Connor flipped the blankets back to give Dannie's best mad face a breather. "I'm not going to bed anymore. I'm staying up."

"The doctor thought you could use one more day in the

hospital, young lady. I promised you'd go directly to bed without even letting your feet touch the floor.''

"And your dainty feet shall not touch the floor, my lady,'' Connor promised. Having a seat at the foot of the stairs, he proceeded to unwrap his charge, glancing Sarah's way in search of approval as he worked. "But maybe we could compromise on the location of the bed.''

"I think I detect a conspiracy afoot.'' Sarah hung up her coat and turned, straightening her blouse under the waistband of her skirt and wrinkling her nose in a rabbitlike sniff. "And I think I smell something strangely...piney.''

Connor winked at Dannie as Sarah edged past them into the living room.

"What...in the world...is all this?''

"Your mother must not get out much,'' Connor said, raising his voice toward the living room as he hoisted Dannie, caught up the blankets, and followed. "She doesn't even recognize a tree when she sees one. Wasn't she with us when we drove down to Santa Cruz?'' Dannie nodded anxiously. "And didn't she see those big green things sticking up from the ground all over the place?''

"A Christmas tree?'' Dannie squealed as she was carried through the living-room doorway. "Oh, boy!''

"I want you to be absolutely calm about this, Princess,'' Connor warned. "Anything that looks like overexcitement is going to get you a ticket upstairs.''

"Are we going to decorate it? Can I help? Can I put the angel on top?''

"I take it you have decorations,'' he guessed, looking to Sarah for approval.

She was holding back all but the gleam in her eyes. "We do have decorations.''

"Handmade stuff?'' he guessed again. "All very artistic?''

"Mostly. It's still early, Connor. I planned to get a tree next week. You're not dealing with Mrs. Scrooge here.''

"I'm one of those kids who can't wait,'' he explained, his boyish smile giving proof to his claim. "And you've been preoccupied, so I just thought I'd get things going. I have a good eye for trees.''

She turned to admire the tree, already standing in a pot and waiting for the festive touches. "It's beautiful," she admitted, "but what's all the rest of this stuff?"

There was a huge wreath, a coil of fresh garland, pinecones, candles, boxes of lights and Sarah wasn't sure what else. "It's just some stuff I ordered for decking the halls," he said.

"Ordered?" Sarah echoed. Connor had obviously been there before he came to pick them up at the hospital. The couch was arranged for Dannie's comfort with pillows and a coverlet. Dannie seemed content to let Connor situate her there, carefully covering her to her chin with blankets.

"I told them it all had to be pretty traditional and that we'd put it up ourselves." He tucked the blankets beneath the cushions, adding, "I didn't think you'd go for an aluminum light show. They did my place in green-and-white paper sculptures last year. Very clean lines, I was told."

"Who's *they*?" Sarah wondered, opening a box of candles and inhaling the bayberry scent.

"The decorator ladies."

"More than one this time?"

"They multiply at Christmastime. But this isn't department-store style, Sarah. This is authentic, old-fashioned New England greenery." He pivoted in her direction, rising to his feet. "I was going to get a tree myself—go out and chop it down with an ax—but they kicked me off the golf course."

Sarah laughed, pulling the box to her chest. "I love bayberry." Her eyes sought his across the room, telling him she loved what he'd done and loved him for *all* he'd done. The sweater he wore was the same shade of blue as his eyes, which shone as brightly as her own. He stood near the fireplace, hands in his pockets, the gift giver awaiting her approval. She wanted to go to him and show him how he'd filled her heart, but instead she clutched the box of candles and offered tentatively, "Will you...stay for Christmas?"

He shook his head. "I can't. I have to be in Austin. We're

doing a benefit concert that they're televising live on the twenty-seventh."

"Oh, yes. I think you told me that before." She looked down at the box in her hands. This was the way it would be with Connor—the uncle who visited between engagements. It couldn't be any other way. "We'll be able to see you on TV, then."

"Or in person...if you want to."

Laying the box back with the others, she took a step back from the evergreen array and from Connor. "No. We'll have our holiday at home. Perhaps another year you'll be able to join us."

He raised a helpless brow. "Christmas is pretty..."

"Why can't we have Christmas now?"

Dannie looked pleased with herself. She'd gotten their attention with a good idea.

"Because it isn't Christmas yet," Sarah pointed out. "And in two weeks, when it is Christmas, you'll want to have it again."

"Well, in two weeks Santa Claus will come because he can't leave the North Pole any sooner than that," Dannie acknowledged. She knew by now how this all worked. "But I think we could have some of it now, before Uncle Connor has to go. We could have Christmas dinner."

"We can certainly have decorations now," Connor suggested. "And if somebody opens the boxes behind the couch, I think we can have a little music." Dannie scooted up to take a peek. "Down, girl," Connor warned. "You're not to raise your head off those pillows." He brought several huge boxes to the middle of the floor, all wrapped in red-and-green paper, and then he retreated to get a fire going in the fireplace.

Sarah opened the boxes carefully, certain that each component part of the stereo system was eggshell fragile. With the fire blazing, Connor joined her in the middle of the floor, ripping into the boxes and setting the parts aside for assembly.

"Someone'll be out in a couple of days to wire this in for you and do a little cabinetwork. We'll have to decide where we want the speakers." He was putting things together in the corner of the room, attaching wires and plugging in cords. "Open that other green box, Sarah. We'll put some music on and see how it sounds."

The green box contained an assortment of records and tapes by a variety of artists, including Georgia Nights. "Doesn't your group have a Christmas album?" Sarah wondered as she read title after title on the album covers.

"I'm told we're going to do one next summer, which doesn't excite me too much, but they say it's a real 'down-home' thing to do. They're thinking of calling it 'Silent Georgia Nights.' Can you believe it?" She groaned, and he sent her a grin in agreement. "I think there's a Streisand Christmas album in there."

"What's in that big box?" Dannie wanted to know.

"Put it this way—when you watch the Christmas special, it won't be flickering in black-and-white. Some people are quite taken by the color of my eyes."

"Some people would be quite taken by the color of all the money you flash around," Sarah said. She knew there was no stopping him, but as she handed him a record album she added, "Personally, I think you've gone too far."

Taking the hand that held out the record, he murmured, "I've gone all the way, love. So have you." She looked up at him, and he smiled at the pink tint that rose quickly in her cheeks. "You know how I mean that. There's no hope for either one of us." He slid the record from her hand and touched her lips briefly with an unexpected kiss. Sarah watched him move away from her and told herself it was only the blaze in the fireplace that made the room suddenly feel too warm.

Music soon filled in for conversation while Connor followed Sarah's and Dannie's directions in stringing lights and mountain-scented garland. Sarah brought out a collection of candle-holders and bits of wire and cloth, and soon the dining room and the foyer as well as the living room were festooned with gaily trimmed greenery. They made a party of it, snacking on sandwiches, popcorn and eggnog. With candles and colored lights aglow, Connor lifted Dannie to top the tree with a hand-crocheted white angel, and the effect was complete. There was a three-way toast to early Christmases.

Later Sarah and Connor put a sleeping child in her bed and returned to the warm glow of a waning fire and red wine. Connor made a pile of Sarah's sofa pillows on the floor in front of the fireplace, sat down and gave Sarah a distinctly come-hither look, patting the spot on the floor beside him.

Sarah stood her ground. "Ahh...I think the atmosphere in here is a bit overwhelming, Mr. Ryan, and if I were a mind reader, I'd say you were thinking I'd be an easy mark about now."

Connor chuckled. "Easy is one thing you've never been, lady. The only thing on my mind right now is talk."

The single brow she raised in response put him in mind of a tempting little vamp, and he wanted to growl and spring. "Okay, so maybe there are two or three other things on my mind, but talk first." Reaching toward her, he entreated her with an outstretched palm, and she came to him, taking his hand and settling beside him in front of the fire.

"Just a friendly talk?" she asked.

"A serious talk. I think it's time you got to know me better, sweet Sarah."

"But I think I know you quite well. As you so aptly put it, we've..."

He dismissed that with a wave of the hand. "You know me well, Sarah, but I want you to know me better than anyone else, living or dead, has ever known me. And then..." *And then, I want you to love me anyway.* "And then, we'll see." He reached back and pulled a folded piece of paper out of his pants pocket. "Here's what I want to talk about."

Sarah set her glass down while Connor sipped at his, watching her as she unfolded the paper and studied it for a moment. "Is this Dannie's work?"

Connor nodded. "She drew that for me from a picture in one of her books. Does it look strange to you in any way?"

Frowning slightly, she puzzled over the drawing. "It looks like Dannie. She always crowds lots of little things into her pictures, fills all the space with funny little figures. It's in pencil, though. She usually uses crayons. Uses color quite accurately, in fact." With a shrug, she concluded, "I've always thought she was sort of a precocious young artist, but then I have a mother's bias."

A mother's bias, he thought. A lovely sentiment and a terrible standard for a child to live up to. How should the question be phrased in order to sneak it past a mother's bias? No preliminaries, he decided, just ask straight out. "Does she often draw mirror images of her subject or put things upside down, inside out, maybe backward?"

The frown returned to her face as Sarah looked at the paper again, and when she spoke, it was with furrowed-brow impatience. "She's not quite five years old, Connor. If you were hoping to hang something of hers in your living room, I'd say you may have to give her a few years."

"You haven't answered my question. Does this look typical of the way Dannie expresses things when she draws?"

"Well, yes, she does have things a little topsy-turvy sometimes, but… What's this all about, Connor? I don't understand what you're getting at. Do you see a problem with Dannie's picture—some Freudian meaning hidden here somewhere?"

"I don't know about Freudian, but I think there might be a problem." Connor draped his forearm over an upraised knee and admired the color of the wine he swirled in his glass. It was something he never discussed with anyone, not since Kevin, and he wondered if he could find a matter-of-fact approach, like Dannie's doctor Dr. Rochard: Your child has pneumonia, but I can take care of it. God, how he wished he could make promises like that. "Have you ever heard of dyslexia?" he asked finally.

"I think so. Isn't it some kind of…brain disorder?"

"They call it a brain *dysfunction*," he corrected, though he knew it was called by even less flattering terms. "It's a learning disability. A person who has it often appears to see some things in reverse."

"You're not saying…you think Dannie's retarded or something?" All of Sarah's maternal instincts armed themselves and came to attention. "Connor, you see how bright she is. How can you think that?"

"I said nothing about retardation. I said learning disabled, and I said I thought it *could* be a problem."

"You're jumping to that conclusion based on one little drawing?" Sarah extended the paper near his face. "Based on *this*? Who are you to say my child's—"

"I'm Dannie's uncle, Sarah. And I'm dyslexic."

The hand holding the paper lowered by slow degrees. "But you're not…"

"No, I'm not." He gave her a knowing smile. "In fact, I'm pretty damned smart."

"I wasn't thinking…I mean I wasn't going to say…" What was she going to say? *Brain damaged.* "I don't need any more brain damage," he'd once told her.

"You *were* thinking 'dumb,' but you weren't going to say it because it isn't a polite word." A gentle laugh said he understood. "The day I knew for sure that I wasn't really stupid, I wanted to send out an announcement. 'We are pleased to announce that Connor Ryan isn't such a big dummy after all.' In fact, I had a mental mailing list."

"Connor, you're…you're a bloody genius, for heaven's sake!"

Again she made him laugh, and it occurred to him this wasn't as bad as he'd thought it would be. He wasn't a kid anymore. He knew who he was and what he could do. "I've been called a 'musical prodigy' and a 'gifted musician,' but never a 'bloody genius.' It has a theatrical ring to it." Another sip of wine fueled his need to tell her everything. "However, I am not a gifted reader. I'm not even a decent reader. I'm sort of a…crippled reader. As a young kid, I was a *non*reader, and that, let me tell you, makes for a very disabled student."

"What causes it?" Sarah asked, her concern for Connor settling in beside her concern for her daughter.

"I don't think they really know yet. They call it a dysfunction because apparently some of the connections in the brain—the synapses—don't function quite right, sort of like faulty wiring. In my case, some of the messages sent from the eye to the brain get reversed somehow, and the brain registers a reversed image. I don't see the same thing on a printed page that you see."

"But you say you can read."

"I can now, though not with the same fluency you have. What happened was that I learned to compensate. I can't really explain how I do it, but I can tell you that it was mostly Kevin's doing. Kevin helped me learn to read."

Sarah looked at the penciled figures on the paper again, and she felt an awful burning in her throat and around her eyes. She wasn't sure what all this meant, but she didn't like the suggestion that Dannie's brain was any less than perfect. "Kevin had no problem himself, did he?"

"Kevin's only problem was that he had to stick up for his brother all the time." Sarah looked up at him, and the glistening in her eyes made his chest tighten inside. "Kevin had no problem, Sarah, and Dannie may not, either. It's more common among boys than girls, and, as far as I know, there's no real evidence that it's hereditary."

"What should we do?"

He chose to include himself in that "we" and hoped she had meant for him to. "We should have her tested by the best educational psychologist we can find. If she needs help, we'll get it for her. When I was a kid, they didn't know much about this, but things have changed a lot since then. The law is on our side now. All school systems have to provide for learning-disabled kids."

"Your parents, did they…how did they deal with it?"

Connor turned to the fire, letting his mind slide back in time. "I guess they never did," he concluded. "I only know what I do about it after the fact. Moving around with the army from school to school didn't help matters. Kevin always took it in stride, while I fell farther behind. We ended up in the same grade even though I was more than a year older. I hated bringing home report cards. My mother always got this pathetic look on her face, like I'd really let her down, and my dad got disgusted. I don't know how many times I heard, 'Why can't you be more like Kevin?' I figured I was too stupid to be like Kevin and wished everybody would just accept that and leave me alone. After a while they all did, all except Kevin.''

Hoping for a glimpse of what he saw, Sarah leaned toward the fire, too. ''When did you discover music?''

''When I was about twelve. I was getting along better in reading by then, and I'd gained a little confidence. Music teachers always liked me because I could sing, and I had one music teacher…'' He smiled at the memory. ''Long dark hair, soft brown eyes. I had the most painful crush on that woman. She found me at the piano in the school music room one day. I was picking out the melody of a song she'd taught us in class. When I told her I'd never had a piano lesson, I thought she'd have a stroke right before my eyes.'' He glanced sideways at Sarah and chuckled. ''Then she sat right next to me on the piano bench, and I thought *I'd* have a stroke. I did everything she showed me. I think I'd have played Chopin on the first try, just to keep Miss Raymond on that piano bench.''

''So you've had a lot of practice plying the ladies with your music.'' Sarah imagined the beautiful boy he must have been, responding to a teacher who finally offered something besides pity or criticism. Miss Raymond must have felt like the miracle worker.

''I didn't have much luck with Miss Raymond. She got married in June that year and broke my heart. But she did persuade my mother that I should have piano lessons. Dad thought it was a waste of time, but Mom stood her ground that time. I picked up the guitar, too. It was such a relief to find something I was good at, and I gave it everything I had. In junior high I picked up drums, trumpet, sax. I made so much noise Dad was ready to throw me out of the house. I ran track and cross-country to keep him off my back.''

"In high school, Kevin and I went separate ways. He wore his letter man's jacket, and I wore faded denim. He took up body building, and I took up smoking. I played in a rock band, and he danced to the music. Dad displayed all of Kevin's trophies in prominent places and stopped talking to me altogether.''

"When did you start writing music?'' Sarah wondered.

"When I was in high school.'' He drained his glass and turned to her again, relieved to find that the glistening in her eyes was gone. He searched for pity for himself in those eyes and felt good when he found none. She needed to understand, for herself and for Dannie and maybe even for him.

"I don't *write* music. I compose and record, but I'm inhibited by pencil and paper. My handwriting looks like bird tracks, and I don't even like to think about having to spell words.''

She smiled. "You can spell k-i-d pretty well.''

"I know the letters, but they never look right on paper. I've found other ways that work for me. From what I understand, there are as many manifestations of dyslexia as there are dyslexics. If Dannie has a problem, she'll find ways that work for her, too.''

Stretching out on his side, Connor propped his arm over a plump pillow. "I didn't mean to scare you with this, Sarah,'' he said. "I would never have told you about myself unless I thought you needed to know.''

"Did you think I would think less of you?''

His eyes met hers. "No. Not you.''

"If there's a problem…with Dannie…I want you to help me.''

It was the first time she'd asked him for anything. "I will.''

"Not for Kevin's sake,'' she added. "I'm not asking you to take over for Kevin.''

His spine grew rigid. "She's more mine than she is Kevin's. Don't you see that yet, Sarah?''

Sarah wanted to agree. She thought of Connor and Dannie exploring the beach for rocks and shells, of them making breakfast together and of Connor putting her to bed. Sometimes Dannie seemed to be more Connor's even than Sarah's. But that was impossible. In practice, he could never become...

"Kevin would have loved her, too," Sarah said.

"Kevin isn't here, Sarah. I am. We both have to stop feeling guilty about that fact." He sighed and consciously relaxed his back, muscle by muscle. "We have to stop stiffening up with guilt every time his name is mentioned."

She was sitting on one hip, her legs tucked to one side, her skirt pulled properly over her knees. He needed to claim her, declare his place with her. He spread his hand over the sleek, rounded part of her calf, rubbing his fingers over the silkiness of her stocking. "You're more mine than you ever were Kevin's," he said quietly. "Does that make you feel guilty, too?"

"It makes me feel foolish," she whispered, shivering under his touch. "I could no more marry you than I could marry the Prince of Wales."

"Don't be ridiculous, Sarah. He's already married."

"And all the king's horses and all the king's men can't keep the press out of his wife's closet."

"They were both born for that," he reminded her. His hand strayed under her skirt and found a silky thigh.

"I wasn't."

"Neither was I. There's nobody in my closet. My house has been empty since you left it." She closed her eyes and enjoyed the warm surge inside her stomach as his fingers crept along their chosen path. "Come back to me, Sarah. I'm not a prince. I'm not a pauper. I'm not even a 'bloody genius.' I'm just a man, and that's the best and the worst of it."

Just a man. Dear Lord, he could turn her inside out, and *that* was the best and the worst of it.

"I need a place to sleep," he told her. Her skirt had become his sleeve as he slid his hand around her hip. "I turned in my key at the hotel. I need a place—" he laid his head in her lap and snaked his free arm around her waist "—to lay my head. Oh, God, if you don't put your hands on me soon…"

On a sharp breath she curled her body around his head and buried her face in his hair. Groaning, he burrowed his head against her belly, hugging her hips with both arms. It was the desperate embrace of lovers whose only certainty was the present.

He released her only to roll on his back and reach for her again. Stretching herself along his side like a cat, Sarah braced herself up on her arms, one planted on either side of his face. Her hair hung over the right side of her neck like dark sheeting, giving them a curtain of privacy as she lowered her mouth to taste the pleasures of his. He responded to her as a man driven by hunger, working his tongue past her lips for a better taste of her. She was warm red wine, and he would drink his fill, enjoying one sweet sip at a time.

Taking her hips in his hands, he moved her over him, pressed his fingers into the roundness of her buttocks and rocked against her until she pulled away from his kiss and arched her neck, gasping his name. The sound of his name in her throat was intoxicating, and he drifted higher on the tension she created in him. He feathered kisses along the pale curve of her neck as he pulsed against her with the slow, steady rhythm of his heartbeat.

"This is…really hard," he whispered.

"Yes." Her voice echoed the soft hiss of the antique radiator. "I'll…soften it for you."

"Mmm." His smile traced her jawline. "I meant the floor, but I'm not complaining."

"You just said you needed a place to sleep. I suppose you'll be wanting a bed," she teased, dipping her chin for a nip at his ear. She wanted to tease him and increase her power over him, and then she wanted to use her power to give him infinite pleasure, pleasure that he would remember.

"I'll be wanting a variety of things, and they all start with Sarah." Whispered against her ear, her name sounded distant and exotic.

"The guest room is closest," she told him.

"What's wrong with your room?"

She pushed herself up and locked her elbows, giving her tighter contact with his hips. Connor rolled his eyes at the increased pressure while Sarah smiled down on him. "My room doesn't have a view."

"Give me thirty seconds, honey; it'll have a hell of a view."

"Besides, I went to a great deal of trouble to prepare the guest room for you."

"Oh? Did you put in mirrors?"

"No, but I changed the sheets."

Actually, she had prepared for him. A vase of sweet-scented carnations stood on the dresser and a large, unframed canvas hung above the bed. The painting was a lovely montage of small things, the shells and rocks, fossils and seaweed, driftwood and beach glass that fascinated Connor, all done in soft seaside colors. Connor was transfixed by it.

"It's for you, of course."

He turned to her, his eyes brimming with his love for her. She knew him better than anyone, living or dead, and she was there for him.

"I have this to give you, too," she said, stepping into his arms. She held her breath on the end of that confession. There was no helping it. Whatever the word was for this, she knew that whenever he could come to her and touch her as he did now, she would welcome him.

"Your beautiful body belongs to you, Sarah, always. But share it with me." He took her face in his hands and began covering it with gentle kisses, murmuring, "Give me the pleasure of sharing your body."

"I want to drive you wild with pleasure."

He smiled, letting one hand slip along her breastbone, thumbing her buttons open. "How wild?"

"How wild can you be?"

"That depends," he said, pushing the blouse off her shoulders, "on how long you can postpone getting me there."

She tossed her hair back, laughing wickedly as she began

bunching his sweater along his ribs. "A challenge," she said. "I love a challenge."

Once she had his sweater off, she worked on his buttons. Undressing each other became a game, but as they neared the finish, the play grew serious. His chest, with its sprinkling of curling gold hair, was still California-sun burnished, while hers, offset by her ice-blue slip, was New England snow. He let her explore the contours of his torso until she discovered she could make his nipples tighten with the light prodding of her fingertips, and he growled and fell back to the bed, taking her with him.

"The light," she said.

"Leave it. Let me see you."

"I'll turn it down," she decided, reaching for the key on the hurricane lamp by the bed. The small light in the base was a suitable compromise.

Connor tucked her under him and began making casual forays along her shoulders and chest with his mouth. He slipped her straps down and released the hook that freed her breasts. It was his wanton tongue that quickened the pace, making her breasts ache deliciously before he suckled them. With the flat of his hands, he rolled her remaining clothes down her body, kissing powder-soft skin as he exposed it, inch by inch. He slid lower, rolling his thumbs over the proud protrusions of her pelvic bones. He felt her stiffen against him.

"Relax, sweet Sarah," he urged, his voice low and soothing. "Share this with me, too. Let me show you how much I love you."

His voice came to Sarah through a haze of heat, intensifying as his mouth moved over her thighs, her abdomen, and into the hidden reaches of her womanhood, sending shock waves throughout her body. She called his name, and he rose above her on the strong pillars of his arms, dropping his head to answer near her ear, "I'm with you, Sarah."

"Be with me more," she pleaded. "Be with me now. Be part of me." He needed her. She felt the proof of his need and shifted her hips to welcome him, but he only lowered himself to his elbows and undulated against her.

"I will," he promised. "I'll be part of you even after I'm gone."

"I know."

"And you'll be part of me."

"I want you, Connor," she whispered desperately.

"I want you to love me," he insisted, his voice hoarse with the effort.

"I do. Oh, I do."

"Then say it. Say it now, while you need me more than the air you breathe."

"I love you, Connor. I love you." He slipped inside her, and she repeated the words as the pace of his thrusting escalated. With firm hands he rotated her hips toward himself, reaching to touch the deepest part of her. Her words became one soft, driven cry as she rose to meet him in shuddering mindless release.

Trembling, Connor rolled to his back. The power of his passion scared him. She'd said she would drive him wild, and she nearly had. But he'd managed to pace himself, and she'd trusted him and let herself go completely in his arms. If she could trust him in that, he had to believe she would trust him with her life someday—hers and Dannie's.

She stirred in his arms and rubbed her cheek against his shoulder. "Are you with me still?" he asked quietly.

"I don't want to fall asleep, not tonight." Her sigh echoed her contentment. "I want to stay awake and keep feeling this wonderful feeling."

"How do you feel?"

"Totally tranquilized. What did you give me?"

"Good loving."

"Mmm. If you could bottle it, you could make a fortune."

He drew her hair back from her forehead to find a spot for his kiss. "'I'm givin' my woman all I got,'" he whispered, quoting his own song.

"I wanted to work my wiles on you," she said. With one

eye she watched her forefinger tunnel through the tufts of golden hair on his chest. "I wanted you to be senseless with passion, but somewhere along the line I sort of...lost the nerve."

His chest rumbled with his throaty chuckle. "You kept up the volley pretty well, though. You work your wiles on me every time you flash me that soulful, brown-eyed look of yours."

"I should have worn something black and filmy," she decided.

"Your big flannel shirt with paint in the plaid drives me crazy," he confided. "Especially when you wear it with those shapeless jeans. Ouch!" Her tug on his hair left his chest smarting.

"I never pretended to be glamorous," she pouted.

"I never asked for glamorous. I asked for Sarah."

"I love you, Connor. If you'll be patient with me, I want to make love to you the same way you make love to me."

He wanted that, too. He ached for it in every corner of his heart, but he shook his head regretfully. "First you have to love me the same way I love you. You have to be willing to take all the risks, Sarah."

Sarah's hand stilled. "Don't you believe I love you?"

"Not enough," he said, his voice nearly toneless.

Chapter Twelve

Sarah did fall asleep in Connor's arms, but he lay awake long after he'd made love to her a second time. He loved the feeling of having her close while she slept. It was an intimacy, and he wanted every one he could have with her. She was fast becoming an obsession with him.

He was beginning to feel that he was the more vulnerable of the two of them, and he'd decided long ago that such a predicament was too costly. He'd shored up his defenses beautifully. He could handle his parents, his friends, his fans in groups of five or five thousand, but he knew he'd met his match in the woman who lay in his arms. Strange as it seemed for such a delicate, feminine creature, she epitomized the strong, silent type. If there were such a thing as emotional football, she'd make a hell of a defensive end.

He had a yen for a cigarette, and he decided to indulge himself. Without making a sound, he put on his pants and closed the bedroom door behind him.

The living room was bright with light reflected off the snow outside. Only the click of his lighter offended the night's quiet. He went to the window. He loved the warmth of this house, the comfortable feeling of home, but he hated curtains. He wanted to be able to see out. Shoving the sheer fabric aside, he braced his bare shoulder against the window frame and sent a stream of smoke toward the ceiling.

There was a fresh blanket of snow on the lawn, and it looked as though there would be more before morning. But for now, all was still and white. It was one of those nights when winter wound a cocoon around the earth, and everything slept peacefully inside the white shell. This was one of the things he missed about having winter—this kind of night. There was a coziness that you couldn't have inside unless it was cold outside.

Coziness was a woman's word, he thought. It was the kind of thing women made. It was the pillows and the slipcovers and the wicker basket that held the mail. It was the way he felt when he looked at a painting Sarah had done. The professional decorator couldn't give his home that feeling, but Sarah could. Her very presence could bring that feeling. She was his white cocoon.

Sarah was a clear, placid pool in a Japanese garden. She was the peaceful place he craved, and he wanted desperately for her to let him in. She was afraid of him, though. She was afraid he'd bring the loudness, the bright lights, the fast pace of his world with him and spoil hers. And then, he knew, she saw him leaving her after some time and maybe some words had passed between them. She wasn't able to trust him beyond the present.

Sarah crept into the living room on noiseless feet. Connor's shirt was her nightgown, and an afghan from the closet was her robe. She'd come looking for him without thinking about it first, and when she saw him standing there against the window frame, her breath caught in her chest. He was beautiful. The long, tapering V of his back made a leisurely descent into the beltless pants that rode low on his hips. The night bathed his shoulders and the crown of his head in soft white light. He was magnificently sculpted and well displayed in the subtlety of night light.

She had to remember that by tomorrow night he would be gone. She was glad he'd gotten up. Even in her sleep she'd missed him, and she'd awakened when her body realized he was no longer next to her. She didn't want to waste this time sleeping. Sarah wanted to crystallize this moment, save it under her pillow and relive it whenever she missed him unbearably. After he was gone, she wouldn't think of where he was or what he was doing or whether he was ever reminded of her under his hot lights and his reverberating amplifiers. She would think of him here, on this night, in the cool quiet of her living room.

Connor sensed her presence and turned toward her slowly. His hand came up, and the cigarette became a red glow in the darkness. "You caught me," he said, his voice low and husky. "Don't tell the press. They'll say you drove me to it."

"They'll say you did it out of spite because you know I have no ashtrays. It'll be quite the scandal."

The cigarette was deposited in the fireplace to become another dying ember. "It's starting to snow again. Come watch it with me," he said. When she did, he gathered her under his arm and turned to the window. It was a sparse, soft-sift snow, the kind that heralded the Christmas season.

"I want you to call me when you've arranged for Dannie's testing," he told her. "I want to be here. There are enough colleges in the area. I'm sure you'll be able to make some contacts through them. When you're ready, I'll be here. And I want all the bills."

"You're very difficult when it comes to money, Connor Ryan."

"I know. And I'm going to continue to be difficult, so brace yourself."

Sarah watched the falling snowflakes, but she saw the hot tears of frustration in the face of a small child. "What if it's true, Connor? What if she has this learning-disability thing? She isn't as strong as you are. Her feelings are easily hurt, and if she goes to school and can't learn..."

He had her shoulders in his hands before he knew it, and he had no idea how harsh his face looked in the shadows. "Don't ever say she can't learn," he said slowly, forcing absolute calm into his voice.

"I meant...normally."

He drew a long breath and kept his voice low and steady. "What's normal, Sarah? What the hell is normal? Is your brother, Jerry, normal? How about your parents, or mine? Was Kevin the normal one in my family, and are you the normal one in yours?" He paused and eyed her narrowly.

She grabbed his arms, bracing her hands just above his elbows. "Connor, I only meant..."

"Normal doesn't exist, Sarah. I have looked high and low, and I can't find it. Everybody's above the bell curve in some ways and below it in others. I thank God I found that out before I drove myself crazy trying to squeeze into it."

"Maybe normal isn't the word I wanted, Connor. I meant...usual, ordinary, run-of-the-mill. That's what I understand. I'm a very average woman, an average artist, and I guess I wasn't prepared for anything but an average child."

"None of that is true, Sarah." The intensity was still bright in his eyes, but there was no longer any harshness. In his heart, he felt every word he said. "You are the most beautiful of women. You're a gifted artist. But those judgments are made by my standards, my values. Another man might..." He stopped himself, shaking his head. "Another man would be crazy not to agree with me, but then I have a lover's bias. And as for Dannie, she's still the same child you rightfully called precocious. That hasn't changed."

Of course it hadn't changed. Dannie was still Dannie, and they didn't know anything for sure, and even if she had this problem, it wasn't... Sarah's face filled with tears. "Connor, help me. I'm afraid I'm not up to it. You said she was more yours than Kevin's, and that's true, and I'm afraid she's more yours than..."

"No, Sarah." He pulled her into his arms and held her close, giving his bare skin to her tears. "Shh. You're her mother, and that will never change."

"But you understand...everything..."

"Of course I do. It's been with me for a long time."

"It's not just that. It's the way you see the world—so much the way Dannie does. I've watched you together. You're so much alike, I could almost swear..."

"So could I. Do you doubt Dannie's love for you, Sarah?" he asked gently.

"N-no."

"Then why do you doubt mine? Why are you afraid to love me as you love her? You'll adjust for her; you'll compromise as she grows, as all the changes come. Why are you so afraid to do the same for me?"

She waited to answer until she thought she could hold her voice steady. It came out as a rasp. "I *have* compromised for you, Connor. More than you know."

"I think I know. You've decided to let me play the stud for you. It isn't what I want, but if it's all I can have, I'll take it."

She drew back to look at him, astonished. "Let you play the..."

He gave her half a smile. "Did I step on your toes there? Would you have had it the other way around? You're the one who refuses to marry me, Sarah."

"But you're the one who's..."

"Let me tell you who I'm not. I'm not your father, who ran out on your mother for the greater glory of television. I'm not Kevin Ryan, who went down with his helicopter and up in a cloud of smoke. And I'm not the college-professor type, who'd be home every night by five to give you your regular peck on the cheek." She lowered her eyes, and he shook her once. "Look at me, Sarah. I'm not a freak. I'm an entertainer, yes, but I'm not some Jekyll-and-Hyde crazy who gets lit with the groupies every night on the road and then spends a few weeks with his ladylove between tours. I want a home and a family, just like your *normal* men. I want you and Dannie, Sarah. And I want you for my *wife*, not my playmate.''

"Connor, you can't even be with us for Christmas," she reminded him.

"No man can promise he'll be there every Christmas. A man can only promise to do his best and ask the same of his family. You can't promise me forever, Sarah, but you can give me your love, starting now without exceptions."

"Oh, Connor, I do love you, but I can't..."

Groaning, he pulled her into his arms again. "Don't," he ground out. "Don't say, 'Connor, I love you, *but*.'"

"Connor, I love you," she whispered, holding him.

"Then will you marry me?"

He waited, but she said nothing more. He sighed, granting her the right to say no more for the moment. "Come sit with me for a while, then," he said, leading her to the couch. "Sit with me and hold me until morning. Tomorrow I'll have to go." The shuddering catch in her breathing was unmistakable. "But you'll make me one of those old-fashioned New England Christmas dinners first, won't you?"

"I was counting on it," she said in a small voice.

"So was I." He sat with her on the couch, and they held each other, sharing her afghan. "Dannie's going to be all right, Sarah. We'll take her lots of places, and we'll show her things. We'll let her learn with her hands, which we both know is the way she wants to come to know about the world. And it works. I think with my hands." She felt his fingers on her face and her breast at once, and she made a little gratified sound in her throat. "I think, 'My God, how lovely she is.'"

"Connor, could you...light some of the candles? I love candlelight."

He reached for the lighter he'd laid on the table and shifted it to his other hand. On the table behind them stood a squadron of candles, and he began lighting them, one by one. "Sarah," he began, hesitating on the name, "I've left something for you in an envelope under the tree. A gift for myself, really. I want you to come to Austin. I want you to be there in the audience for me."

"Connor..."

"I know Christmas is out of the question, but this is on the twenty-seventh. I want to look down front and see you there." She said nothing, and he knew she had not refused. *Understand what it means to me, Sarah. Understand what I'm asking you for.* "If you can't be there, then I want you to watch the show on TV. It's important to me."

He laid the lighter back on the table and looked at her in the candlelight. Filling their heads with the scent of bayberry, they closed the distance between them for a kiss.

Connor had seen to it that his presence would be felt on Christmas. Dannie had insisted on baking oatmeal cookies for Santa's reindeer. Her dollhouse was delivered to the house on Christmas Eve, and Sarah had less than an easy time getting her ready for church. The sleeve of her green dress had to be pulled over two fists full of small wooden chairs. They sat in the back pew of the wood-and-white New England-style church and listened to Christmas hymns, old favorites that generally brought Sarah a feeling of security and contentment. This Christmas, however, that feeling wouldn't come. The emptiness that was hammering at her inside drove the feeling out.

Red roses were delivered to Sarah, and she wondered how he'd gotten anyone to deliver flowers on Christmas Day. The card offered her his love, and for a moment she had that Christmas feeling. But she laid the card on the table and turned away, and the feeling was lost again.

On the twenty-sixth, Sarah cleaned Lavinia Porter's house, top to bottom. The only remaining disorder was a pile of boxes on the dining-room table, but Mrs. Porter had instructed Sarah to leave those there. They were gifts to be returned.

Gifts to be returned. The meaningless, obligatory exchange of merchandise at Christmastime had nothing to do with gift giving. One didn't return a gift from the heart of a loved one. Sarah smiled. Connor was such a wonderful gift giver. She saw the look he always had when he waited for a reaction to his gift, whether it be a serape or a song. He anticipated someone else's pleasure. He wanted to make people happy.

And then she remembered the envelope. Airline tickets were expensive, and she'd thought of returning it. She had to call him. As soon as she got home, she'd call and explain.

The envelope held two tickets, both dated December twenty-seventh. One was an airline ticket, and one was a concert ticket. There was nothing else. She tried the concert hall but was told, of course, that Connor Ryan was not available. That was that. No hotel, no way to reach him by phone. And he hadn't called her since he'd left. He'd left her only one way to reach him. She had to make a choice.

Sarah sat by the phone, lost in her thoughts. Dannie was watching the new television. Sarah had never been much for television, but she supposed, for Dannie, in limited doses... Eyes on the screen, Sarah did a double take. It was a beer commercial with a well-known baseball coach bantering over the bar with the boys. One of the "boys"—hardly a boy— was Tony Benedict, her father.

Sarah leaned forward, taking advantage of the few seconds she had to study him. It had been a long time since she'd seen him in color. He was almost as gray as the coach. In fact, Sarah probably knew that coach about as well as she knew the man with the amiable smile who slapped the coach on the back and offered him a beer. Her father? He was just a face on the screen.

Let me tell you who I'm not. I'm not your father.

Sarah had the phone in her hand before she had a plan in

her head. "Jerry, I need a favor. I have to be gone for a couple of days."

She went directly from the airport to the auditorium. She'd dressed for the concert before she left home, trying her best for chic with a simple, soft wool-jersey dress in emerald green. The dress's line flattered her trim figure, and the shade of green enhanced her coloring. She'd done her hair up with some artful French braiding, and she wore pure white pearl accents. She'd brought nothing but what she could carry in her purse. It was the most delightfully impulsive traveling she'd ever done.

If she'd expected to be outclassed by a glamorous audience, she was to be disappointed. People were dressed casually in jeans and western clothes. She was directed to her seat by a man in a cowboy hat. In fact, there were lots of cowboy hats around, most of them looking as though they'd actually ridden the range and been stepped on a time or two by the wearer's horse. There were rows of tables near the stage, and behind them were semicircular tiers of bleachers. People were drinking beer out of quart-size paper cups and generally gearing up for a rollicking good time, the kind Georgia Nights could provide.

A table near the stage had been saved for Sarah, and on it lay a single long-stemmed rose. She brought it to her nose and breathed its sweetness, thinking how sad it would have been for this rose to lie here at an empty table. She was glad she'd come. He must have known she would.

He watched her smooth her dress beneath her legs before she sat down, and his heart thumped like one of Scotch's wild drum solos. She picked up the rose, and he could smell it himself. All of his senses told him that she was really here.

"See any pretty faces in the front row, my friend?"

The hand on Connor's shoulder and the concerned voice that went with it belonged to Scotch Hagan. Connor hadn't told Scotch, but it hadn't been necessary to tell him. Scotch knew what Connor was waiting for. Without taking his eyes off Sarah, Connor reported quietly, "Just one. The right one."

"Hot damn!" Scotch exclaimed, slapping Connor on the back. "Let's go out there and make that woman some music, boy!"

"Didn't you get a beer, ma'am?" An older man in a western-cut three-piece suit leaned over toward Sarah from the next table. His Southern drawl and his friendly smile were both genuine. He was with an attractive brunette, who also offered Sarah a smile.

"No, I didn't."

"Would you like one? I'll get it for you."

"No, thank you."

"How far did you come for the show tonight?" the woman asked. No doubt Sarah sounded as out of place as she probably looked.

"Light-years," she said, and then added with a smile, "I'm from Massachusetts."

"You know someone?" the woman asked, tipping her head toward the stage. Sarah nodded, the pride showing in her eyes. "Connor Ryan?" the woman wondered.

"Yes. How did you know?"

"I'm Maggie Hagan, Scotch's wife. This is Scotch's daddy."

The man nodded, still smiling. "Wilbur Hagan," he offered.

"Come join us, Sarah," Maggie invited. "Scotch told me all about you. Connor should have told us you were coming instead of sitting you over there all by yourself. Of course, the minute I saw you, I knew who you were."

"He didn't really know himself, not for sure."

Maggie's eyes lit up with the prospect of witnessing Connor's surprise. "Then won't he be pleased!"

The warm-up was a flashy sister act, two whiskey-voiced

women with hair the color of cotton who were dressed in similar sequin-spangled black outfits. Their voices blended like a perfectly mixed Manhattan, and they went down smoothly with the audience, bringing the crowd up to a titillated pitch. The crowd was ready for Georgia Nights and Sarah was right with them. The stage was set, and the butterflies in Sarah's stomach were for Connor.

"Ladies and gentlemen—Georgia Nights!"

The crowd went wild as the four appeared on stage one after another—Scotch taking his place behind the drums, Kenny Rasmussen bounding to the far end to pick up his bass guitar, Connor taking his place on the side where Sarah sat and Mike Tanner coming on last to claim center stage.

Connor gave his eyes a moment to adjust to the light as the band launched right into its favorite opener, "Summer Nights in Georgia." The tempo was upbeat, and Connor felt it slither along his spine and down to his knees as he rolled with it. The minute he saw faces down the front, he looked for Sarah. The table was empty, and the rose was gone. He tucked his chin to the left and watched his fingers dance over the guitar neck's frets as though absolutely nothing was wrong. She'd been there. Maybe someone had offended her—spilled beer on her dress or something. He glanced back out and found Maggie's table, and his stomach somersaulted as he swung into the chorus.

Sarah knew the moment he saw her. He didn't miss a beat, but his blue eyes lit up like Roman candles, and she felt her face burn with the heat they gave off. She was radiant. He soared.

Connor was a professional, and he played to the audience, but he played for Sarah. On a bluegrass number he made a banjo come alive and chatter nonstop at the dependable guitars. His fiddle brought the Smoky Mountains to Texas, and the bleachers clattered with foot stomping. Even Mike Tanner was amazed as the crowd roared its approval.

"Y'all kinda like that fiddle?" Applause was the enthusiastic reply. "How long can you keep 'em stompin' like that, Connor?"

"Till the roof caves in," Connor promised, swinging into an encore on the fiddle.

Sarah became part of the crowd. She clapped and tapped and even shouted her approval once or twice. Every time she caught his eye, he grinned. He was on top of the world.

"Ladies and gentlemen," Mike said, wiping a sleeve across his glistening forehead. "Georgia Nights is proud to introduce a new song tonight, one that'll be featured on our next album. It's a song that Connor Ryan wrote, and one that only Connor can sing. He's about to show you why."

The stage lights were cut momentarily, and the white spotlight singled Connor out as he settled on a stool with a twelve-string guitar. He found Sarah in the darkness and announced huskily, as though only for her, "This is 'Sarah's Song.'" With backup from the rest of the band he sang:

You came to me in a whispered moment
When the crowd roared in my head
You gave me peace instead
And I knew love.

You came to me in the halo of the moon
When the sun had seared my eyes
You gave me no more lies
You gave me love.

You came to me on a wishful thought
In a palette of pastel
The face I love so well
And you saw me as I was
And you took me as I was
And gave your love.

Oh, Sarah, the touch of your hand, my Sarah
Just one kiss, my Sarah

And I can't let you go
Don't ask that of me, Sarah,
I can never let you go.

The stage went dark, and the audience was stunned. Sarah closed her eyes and let two tears roll down her cheeks. Applause thundered behind her, but the darkness gave her a few seconds' privacy. The song was hers, her gift from Connor's heart. Sensing sudden light, she took a quick swipe at the tears with trembling hands.

Connor took advantage of the dark seconds to hop down from the stage. He sidestepped a security guard and reached for Sarah just as the house lights came on. Pulling her from her seat, he saw her surprise, and he answered it with a quick, joy-filled kiss. There was a scattering of applause nearby, but the joyous roar in Sarah's ears blocked out all but Connor.

"It was beautiful," she whispered.

"So are you." He kissed her again, gently, as befitted a thing of beauty.

"Way to go, cowboy!" someone shouted.

Sarah's eyes widened. "Connor, all these people..."

Grinning at her, Connor confided, "I'm from Waco tonight. They're just giving the hometown boy a little encouragement."

He was pulling her toward a curtain while the security guard, tossing Connor an appreciative wink, ran interference with a small group of fans. Sarah found herself tucked in a small, dimly lit corner, a wall at her back and folds of blue curtain on either side. "Is this a break?" she asked.

He couldn't stop grinning. "Yeah, and I'm dying of thirst." His hands snatched her at the waist and brought her hard against him. Sarah dropped her head back as his mouth descended, this time in blatant hunger. He kissed her again and again, and she rose on tiptoe, fastening her arms over his shoulders, feeling the dampness of his shirt through her dress.

Raising his head at last he sighed with relief. "God, you taste good." Then he dove in for another kiss.

Laughing, Sarah tipped her head back. "Connor, you're in the middle of a concert."

"We've got fifteen minutes," he growled, settling for a ripe spot on her neck. "Sally Bridger has a solo here, and then she does a number with Mike."

"Who's Sally Bridger?"

"An up-and-coming country star." His spreading hands pulled her hips tight against his, and he gave her a hot-eyed smile. "In case you haven't noticed, babe, so am I."

Sarah feigned shock. "On national television, Mr. Ryan?"

"This is where the guitar comes in real handy." She laughed at that, and he looked at her, shaking his head and smiling as though she'd just performed an incredible feat. "You're here, Sarah. I can't believe it."

"You knew I'd come."

"I've never done so much hoping and praying, lady. I was afraid I'd backed you into a corner and lost you because of it."

Sarah glanced first to one side, then the other. "You've got me in a corner now. I don't see an escape." Her hands tightened at the back of his neck. "I want to take the risks, Connor. I love you."

He kissed her again, deeply and possessively. She wanted to be his, and she was willing to be part of his life, the best and the worst of it. His kiss reassured her that he was worth the risks. When he drew back, they heard applause. Their eyes met, and they laughed together.

"Let's go to the hotel," he urged in a husky voice.

"But the show must go on." Sarah's eyes danced as Connor rolled his skyward.

"I can see you're going to be one of those pushy stage wives. Tell you what. I'll go back out and give 'em 'Misty River Morning,' and they'll have to be satisfied."

Sarah shook her head. "I wouldn't be satisfied. I'd want my money back."

"That's why the encore's just for you." He slid his hands up her back and tightened his hold.

"Really?"

"I'm taking you back to the hotel..." He was nuzzling her ear.

"Mmm-hmm?"

"As soon as this is over..."

She felt a little nip at her earlobe, and she giggled. "And?"

"And I'm gonna do one hell of a job with 'Givin' My Woman All I Got.'"

Sarah smiled and whispered, "Let's hurry up and get to the encore."

* * * * *

Dear Reader,

Whenever I think about fathers, I always think about the nearly twenty years I spent as a public health nurse. Many, if not most, of the ones I encountered during that time were fathers only in the strictest biological sense of the word, the uncaring ones—for whatever reason—who make the newspapers or the evening news or the "deadbeat dad" lists because of their relentless indifference and sometimes cruelty to their own children. The experience for those of us whose job it was to help pick up the pieces was discouraging at best.

But every now and then, in among all those so-called fathers, I had the honor and the privilege of meeting some *real* ones. Sometimes they were hardly more than babies themselves. Sometimes they were grandfathers, or even great-grandfathers, who, because of some serious family crisis, suddenly found themselves in the situation of having to parent a small child again. Many of them were alone, and all of them were struggling to endure very difficult circumstances. But, to them, being a good father was clearly more than some vague hypothesis. No matter how tired or disheartened or inconvenienced they might have been, they were always, *always* willing to try to do whatever was best for their children, often at the risk of their own personal happiness. For them, the "father factor" was very strong indeed. They were—in short—magnificent. Even as I write this, I can still see their loving faces. I suspect that I am a better person for having known them. I *know* that the children are. It is this kind of selfless man, the kind who understands what being a father truly means, that inspired me to write about Adam Sauder in *A Crime of the Heart*.

Sincerely,

Cheryl Reavis

A CRIME OF THE HEART

Cheryl Reavis

For Linda Buechting and Dawn Poore,
who supported this book in
thought and deed: Many thanks.

For M.C., my Mennonite friend,
whom I remember fondly.

And for D.B., who shared with me
the Pennsylvania Experience: Be strong.

Acknowledgments

Thanks to Richard W. Reavis, who baby-sat a printer
and tore pages into the wee hours.

And to the gentlemen of MBI Business Centers in
Charlotte, North Carolina, who take great pains to
treat a writer with malfunctioning software kindly.

Author's Note

I was nineteen years old when I first heard about the Plain People. It was a snowy afternoon, and I was attending a lecture on coping mechanisms. At one point the lecturer cited Amish girls as an example. Since they were forbidden makeup and jewelry of any kind, young Amish girls, he maintained, sometimes satisfied their basic human need for adornment by wearing eyeglasses—whether they needed them or not. Fascinating! And what a tribute to the indomitable spirit of women.

Thus began my long interest in this remarkable group of people, who, by their own choice, remain firmly entrenched in another century. Finally, nearly twenty-five years later, I was ready to begin that wonderful writer's game of "What if..."

Chapter One

He hadn't thought it would hurt so much to see her again. He had expected, at the very most, anger. He had never really believed she would come back here, he hadn't *wanted* her to come back here, and yet here she stood, the long dark hair he remembered cropped off short in a way he supposed was fashionable.

"Adam Sauder," she said quietly, extending her hand to him as if they were old friends and not old lovers.

He hesitated a moment, then took it, because he thought it hadn't occurred to her that she might find him in the shambles of what was once her mother's kitchen on her first day back, and because he thought she wasn't quite well. She was very pale, and her hand—the same small hand he remembered—felt cold and trembly in his. He stared into her eyes, lovely hazel eyes that wanted to dart away but didn't.

He gave a small shrug and let go of her hand. "I don't know what to call you."

She smiled. "Quinn," she said dryly, teasing him as if she had the right to do that.

He didn't return the smile. "I heard you were married." He sensed Holland Wakefield, the contractor she'd hired to undo the damage the previous owner of the house had done, shuffling nervously in the background.

Holland, like everyone else, knew the old scandal about Quinn Tyler and the Amishman, Adam Sauder—or thought he did. But it had been a long time ago, and Holland had needed a good, dependable carpenter to work part-time on the interior of this house. A family as big as old Jacob Sauder's could always use the extra money, and, until this minute, Holland had obviously forgotten Quinn's connection to this particular carpenter. Adam had realized that the afternoon Holland had come to the Sauder farm to hire him. He had left his father and brothers in the midst of their spring planting and taken the job anyway.

"No," Quinn said. "We...we didn't have the wedding."

"The 'English' have strange customs," he said, not meeting her eyes now. He picked up a hammer and went back to his work.

Quinn heard quite plainly what he didn't say: *Like almost getting married. Like giving away my son.*

So that was how it was going to be, she thought. He was unforgiving—as unforgiving as old Jacob himself.

She gave a soft sigh. No doubt she was being unfair to Adam's father. Jacob Sauder had only wanted Adam to remain in the way of life he loved and believed in. In the end, she had wanted that, as well. And yet Adam was clean shaven. He was wearing the usual Amish clothes—black "barn door" trousers with suspenders and a blue shirt that gave more color to his pale blue eyes. His hair, light brown and sun streaked from the time he spent outdoors, was cut in the acceptable Amish fashion—a bit long, with bangs that wanted to fall into a center part. Yet he didn't have the untrimmed whiskers that were, among other things, the symbol of a married man.

She hadn't considered that he wouldn't have married, and

she tried to ignore the fact that, selfish or not, it gave her a definite sense of relief. She had hoped to have some time to get used to being home again before she faced him; she certainly hadn't wanted to come back and immediately hear about what a good wife he had. Or about his children. His *other* children.

But you wanted him to be happy, Quinn. It takes that to make an Amishman happy—a good wife and children.

"I'm sorry, Holland, what?" she said, belatedly realizing that the man was addressing her. She tried to drag her eyes away from Adam's strong back as he pulled nails out of damaged boards in the far wall. Adam was tall and rawboned like his father and, at the moment, just as reproachful. She remembered only too well Jacob Sauder's reproach. No matter how much she tried to forget it or how painful it was, the memory still came to her: old Jacob, standing on the porch in the dark with her.

"Don't take away my son, Quinn Tyler."

"I said, how much in a hurry are you to move in?" Holland repositioned his green ball cap with the Hurst and Hahn Lumber Company emblem on it, clearly recognizing an awkward situation once he was knee-deep in it.

"I'm moving in today."

"Honey, you can't do that. It's not near ready to—"

"The plumbing works?"

"Well, yes, but—"

"The fireplace in the front bedroom upstairs?"

"I had the boy sweep all the chimneys last week."

"The electricity's on, and I've got a hot plate. That's all I need." She looked around the big kitchen, remembering what it had looked like when she was growing up, when her mother was alive. It was unbelievable what selfish, careless strangers could do. The room had been stripped of everything that could be taken—cabinet doors, light fixtures, molding, built-in appliances, and, in some instances, the cabinets themselves. She had lost this house once herself, yet she hadn't wanted to destroy it upon leaving. It was going to take a lot of work to set this place right again.

She glanced back at Adam, but he worked on in that quiet yet condemning way he had. But for that, she might have thought he believed himself to be alone. She walked outside with Holland, who was visibly trying to work up to something.

"Holland, what?" she asked to help him along. She had always been straightforward, and she hated to see anyone suffer as much as he was in trying to decide whether or not he should speak his mind.

"Quinn, I forgot about Adam and…things. If you don't want him here, I can—"

"Holland, it's all right. I don't mind him being here."

She had never seen a man look so relieved.

"You sure? I mean, I know you've been sick and all."

"I'm sure." She made herself smile. "I don't mind."

"Well, good, then. You know you'll get honest work from him. He's a fine carpenter. He won't do anything halfway. I'll be by tomorrow, and we'll see about some of the work upstairs."

She nodded and watched him get into his truck and go. Business must be good, she thought idly, waving as he backed around. The truck was new. She stood for a while on the porch steps, staring at the meticulously cultivated field that led to a line of budding trees in the distance. The field had once belonged to her father. Eighty acres of fine farmland, and she'd only been able to get back the house and ten by paying considerably more than the market value. The rest of land had been auctioned off piecemeal, bought up by her Amish and Mennonite neighbors from the man who had acquired her father's farm and run the entire place into wrack and ruin. She walked down the rickety steps and out into the yard, turning back to look at the now neglected farmhouse she'd been born in.

She was glad her father hadn't lived to see the broken windowpanes, the desperate need for paint. The porch was rotting, and the four-in-one apple tree her mother had planted in the backyard had been chopped down to make room to park a car or a truck. She could still see the spots where the oil had leaked, and the grass no longer grew in the ruts. There were dozens of other places to park a vehicle that would not have required savaging such a grand and practical old tree. It had been quite a wonder, blooming in sections and bearing four different kinds of apples in a growing season. The man couldn't have been much of a farmer not to have seen its worth, nor to have followed the practice here of putting back whatever one took away. Adam, his father, her father—all would have replanted a cut tree.

She looked out across the fields again. This was her favorite season, spring, the time of new life and tender green. The sun was warm, and the wind gently lifted her hair.

Please...she thought, without really knowing what it was she wanted. A quiet life? To make peace with Adam?

She took a deep breath and turned to go back into the house. She hadn't eaten, and she resisted the urge to place her hand against the small circle of not-quite pain in her midsection. She had convinced herself that she had to come back to rural living for her health, to finally rid herself of the curse of the upwardly mobile—an old-fashioned, stress-induced stomach ulcer that had come with her job as head accountant for a brokerage firm in Philadelphia. And here was Adam Sauder, working silently in her kitchen.

"Adam, how much longer will you be here?" she asked as she opened the back door.

If he heard her, he gave no indication.

"Adam?"

He continued pulling nails, his broad back turned toward her, still unforgiving, unapproachable.

"What is this, the *Meidung*?" she asked, and he looked around sharply. "I didn't think you ever bothered shunning outsiders."

He pulled another nail. "You haven't changed, Quinn. You still make fun of us."

"That's not true. I've never done that."

He glanced over his shoulder at her. She was frowning, and she was still Quinn, regardless of their years apart, regardless of her "worldly" haircut. It was an old argument, one they'd begun when he was eight and she was six, and one they'd been destined to repeat over the years whenever he'd tried to make her understand the unbreachable differences between her life and his. He'd felt sorry for her then, when they were children and she couldn't comprehend that, no matter how hard she tried, no matter how good she was or how much she wanted it, she couldn't be Amish. She had loved his way of life, and she'd thought that he could somehow give her Amishness. But he couldn't make her Amish like him, and he'd had but one defense against her wanting and her disappointment. He had but one defense now—to deliberately make her angry.

"No?" he asked without looking at her. "That isn't what I remember."

"No," she said firmly. "And you know it."

He went on pulling nails. He hadn't fooled her. He'd never been able to fool her. She had always been able to tell what he was thinking. When he was sixteen and forced to quit school like all Amish children, when he was a barefoot boy plowing with a team of mules, she'd come to him in the fields time after time, secretly bringing him the books he wasn't supposed to want or need. He'd been unkind to her then, pretending that he had no interest in the "English" or their books, never expressing the gratitude that had filled his heart to bursting. But she had understood, and she'd lent him her books anyway, staying for a while to talk to him, walking with him as he cajoled the mules along, because she knew that he had to keep plowing, knew that he couldn't be idle.

But she hadn't known how upsetting her presence had been. He had loved her even then—he couldn't remember when he *hadn't* loved her. He had wanted only two things in his life. He'd wanted to know about the world, and he'd wanted Quinn Tyler, and his father had looked into his eyes and seen the longing for them both.

"What will your father say if he sees you out here with

me?'' he'd complained to her once, knowing it wasn't *her* father that worried him.

"He'd say, Adam, 'There's Quinn walking along with Adam while he plows.' *Your* father would think I was trying lead you into 'worldy wisdom and high-mindedness.'''

"Don't, Quinn! You always make fun of us!"

He'd hurt her with that accusation then, just as he'd hurt her with it now. She had never been any good at hiding whatever she was feeling from him, either. Even now he could see her struggle to keep her anger in check.

"Look, Adam. I'm going into town to buy some groceries. I don't know when the moving people are coming. If I'm not back before you go, just leave the door open for them, all right?"

He didn't answer.

"Fine," she said, snatching up her purse. "Lord!" she said under her breath on the way out. She pressed the circle in her midsection that was now a burning ache. She'd gone too long without eating, and she shouldn't have let herself get so angry. No, that wasn't right, either. According to her instructor in stress management, she should have done just that. She should have gotten angry and gotten it over with. She should have told Adam Sauder exactly what a jackass she thought he was being, so that she wouldn't be saddled with all this repressed emotion, and supposedly she'd feel better.

Except that whatever rudeness Adam Sauder showed her, she deserved. She sat behind the wheel of her car for a moment, then searched her purse for antacid tablets, popping two of them into her mouth and resting her head on the steering wheel. Her hands were shaking. She had to do better than this. She didn't know why Adam was here anyway. He'd known she was coming. She could tell the minute she walked into the kitchen that he hadn't been in the least surprised.

Adam. Her first lover. The father of her only child, a child she'd given away in adoption because he couldn't marry her without losing everything. Another memory surfaced, one of being sated from their lovemaking and wet with dew, and trying to creep into this very house. Her father—and his—had been waiting for her on the dark porch.

"I love Adam!" she'd told them defiantly.

"Yes," old Jacob had agreed, his voice tired and sad. "I see that from the time you are children. I see when you are a little girl that you love him as your brother because you don't have one of your own. I see you make him your hero and your friend. Now you would make him a husband you cannot have—"

"No! I *can* have him. We *can* be together!"

"Yes. You can be together—if he will never see his family again. If he will leave us, his home, the land that is to be his. Tell me this, Quinn Tyler. Our Adam is headstrong. He wants the books and the schooling. He wants to know, always to know worldly things. But is he unhappy to be what he is? Does he hate the land? Does he hate us?"

"No, of course not. He loves all of you. He loves being Amish."

"Yes! He loves that, and he thinks he loves you. But he can't have both. He will stay with us or he will leave—whatever *you* ask of him. Our children are raised up in the way they should go, Quinn Tyler, so that they should never depart from it. The shunning is a terrible thing for us. You know that, and you must be the one to decide which of these loves of his will hurt him more."

"I can't do that."

"You can, Quinn Tyler. You and you alone. I ask you now. Don't take my son! You say you love him. Do you love him enough to let him go?"

In the end, the answer to that had been yes. She had loved Adam Sauder with all her heart, but he was an Amishman, and he cared about his way of life as much as he cared about her. She hadn't known about the baby then, and by the time she did, her father was dying.

Like all farmers, John Tyler had been in debt, and his medical bills cost him the farm and everything else he owned. They had had to sell everything and take a small apartment near the hospital in Philadelphia so that her father could get the treatments he needed without the exorbitant expense of trips into the city and a hospital stay. It was there that Quinn learned the true meaning of the cliché, "mercifully quick." Her mother's death had been that, a stroke one quiet Saturday evening while she hemmed dish towels for the church bazaar; she hadn't lasted the night. But Quinn's father—she would never forget his bravery upon being plunged so abruptly into a disease whose cure was all but deadly, and, when he was still so bewildered by the loss of his wife.

He had been too ill to attend the auction of the property, too ashamed of having precipitated the sale, regardless of whether or not it was his fault. Quinn had taken care of it, stoically witnessing the final loss of purpose in her father's life. But, through it all, she had let herself be comforted by the knowledge that Adam Sauder loved her.

Then her father died; in a span of eighteen months she had lost both parents. She had been nineteen years old, not out of college, bankrupt—and pregnant. She could have let Adam choose between her and living Amish, but she didn't. There was the fact of her pregnancy, and his knowing about that would have left him no choice at all. He would have taken care of her—she knew that—and he would have lost everything else he loved. And not because he had made the decision himself, but because her circumstances had forced him into it. He would have been shunned, excommunicated from his family, his faith, forever. She hadn't trailed along after him for most of her life without knowing what pain that would cause him. Regardless of his passion for books and his insatiable curiosity about "worldly" things, he was Amish. It was one of the things she'd admired so about him, his reverence for this simple way of life and for the land, a reverence she herself had had. She had known in her heart which love would hurt him more, even without old Jacob's admonishments, and she had made the choice for him.

She hadn't kept their baby; she hadn't intended that he should ever know about him. And she had stayed away from here, because she had had to take away from Adam all possibility of a choice. She had known as no one else could that he would never have stayed Amish if she had kept his child. Dear God, the price she'd paid to give Adam Sauder a chance for a happy life—and he hadn't taken it. He wasn't happy; he hadn't married and had children....

"Quinn?" Adam said at the car window, and she jumped.

"You are...all right?" The eyes she turned to his were so filled with pain that he nearly reached out to her.

But then she looked away.

"I'm fine," she said coldly. And she started the car and drove off.

Chapter Two

The short trip into town took longer than she expected. She was caught in a string of vehicles behind an Amish horse and buggy, and it was a long time before she could pass, a long time to creep along and think about Adam Sauder. She went around the buggy carefully when she had the chance, unable to keep from smiling and waving at the small face that grinned at her out the back window. Life here hadn't changed, only she had.

She bought groceries first, then a cooler and some ice to keep the few perishables she had purchased from spoiling in case the moving van came late. In every store she searched the faces around her for someone she knew. She saw no one, and it occurred to her that she was truly a stranger here now. There was almost no one left whom she could approach and say, "It's me, Quinn."

Her parents were dead. She had no siblings, no relatives. Yes, she did have a relative. She had a child, a son who was ten years old now. She had gone to great pains to see that he would have a good life, handling his adoption privately through Edison Clark, a local lawyer she'd known all her life. She had reviewed the statistics of the nameless couples he gave her with the same relentless intensity with which she approached anything that mattered to her. She hadn't known their names, but she had known everything else about them. She made sure of that, sending Edison back to the couples with additional questions before she finally made up her mind.

She had known exactly what she wanted for her baby: she wanted her son or daughter to grow up, not necessarily rich or successful by today's standards, but a decent human being. Recognizing the kind of man and woman she thought could provide that, even with Edison's kind advice, had been no easy task.

She sighed and turned into the Dairy Queen for a milk shake to soothe her burning stomach. Edison was helping her now, too. She would do accounting for his office, and she would be able to stay at home to do it. Surely that would help, being able to do something she was good at, in her own time, instead of being embroiled in the killingly hectic world of high finance. She hoped to add other small businesses to her list of clients, enough to keep her busy and solvent. Perhaps she might even be able to buy back more of the Tyler land.

She watched a group of little boys pile out of a van and rush inside the Dairy Queen while she waited for her milk shake. What do ten-year-old boys do? she wondered. Little League? Cub Scouts? She knew what ten-year-old Amish boys did. They worked. A child as young as five had his 'job' to do. But it was a good thing for children, she believed, to be responsible for something necessary for the welfare of the whole family, even at so young an age. Adam Sauder was proof of that.

The Adam she remembered was hardworking and honorable and kind, strong and yet gentle. She had never, in all her years away, really met a man she admired more, not even the man she'd almost married. Marriage would have been a mistake, because she had hopelessly confused her dreams with reality.

She had wanted to be happy with another man, needed to be happy, but she had loved Adam Sauder.

On the drive back, she passed the one-room Amish school-house, a white wooden building with an open steeple and a front porch, where her mother had taught for so many years. On impulse she backed up, stopped the car and got out to walk around the school yard under the trees. It still had a hand water pump in the yard, and outhouses with symbols cut in the doors—a crescent for girls, a star for boys. Her mother had been "worldly" but an acceptable teacher because the Amish had no educated teachers of their own and because she had been their neighbor John Tyler's wife.

Quinn could still remember how hard her mother had worked to instill as much knowledge as she could in the short time an Amish child was allowed to attend school, rising to the challenge of many different learning levels in one class-room and the barriers of culture and language. Most of the young children spoke only their "at home" German dialect when they started school, and she remembered well her mother returning home, exhausted from a day of pantomiming class-room instructions.

Quinn had wanted so desperately to go to school here—but to be with Adam, not because her mother was the reverently titled "Teacher." Even then he'd been a focal point in her life. She couldn't remember *not* feeling the warmth of know-ing that they somehow belonged together, regardless of his being Amish and her, "English."

It was still there, that thread of belonging. She had felt it the moment she looked at him today. And he had felt it, as well. His silence, his aloofness told her that. She had always known him so well—still knew him so well.

Oh, Adam, somehow we're going to have to talk.

"You'd better get yourself together, Quinn," she said out loud, getting back into her car. She couldn't talk to Adam. What she had done was irrevocable, and to his mind, clearly unforgivable. There was nothing she could say, and there was no point in talking now.

She met another horse and buggy on the way home, one driven by an Amishman she thought was Adam's father. Their eyes met briefly as they passed, but he gave no sign of recognition. She didn't look the same, of course, but he did. Her heart began to pound as she drove past, even though she had no reason to be afraid of him now; she had done exactly what he'd wanted her to do that last summer night on the porch.

She hadn't been afraid the first time he had come to the farm to talk to her about Adam. She had been innocent then. She and Adam were only friends, not lovers, and perhaps they would have stayed friends, but for him. She had lived with the Amish community at her doorstep all her life, and she had understood Jacob Sauder's fear, understood that he believed she was willfully taking away his son. But understanding didn't prepare her for the beating he'd inflicted on Adam. She had known that the Amish were strict disciplinarians. Her mother taught in their school. There were never any problems with rowdiness or disrespect.

But Adam had been old enough to be beyond corporal punishment—she'd thought. Her heart contracted with the memory of that night he'd come to her, ashamed of what had happened to him but needing her desperately. She hadn't realized at first that he'd been hurt physically, seeing only the emotional pain, only him, standing in the rain on her back doorstep. He wouldn't come inside, and he wouldn't answer her questions. And when she reached out to touch him, he had pushed her hand away.

"What is it?" she kept saying, her alarm growing. And when he abruptly turned to go, she went out into the rain after him, hanging on to his arm to slow him down, finally throwing herself bodily at him to make him stop. He'd held her so tightly, the rain beating down on them both.

"I shouldn't have come here," he whispered. "I have to go, Quinn. If I don't, it'll be too late for us both...."

She remembered. The wet, green, damp earth smell of spring rain, the fierceness of her need to take away whatever it was that was hurting him so. They had never kissed before, but now her mouth sought his, knowing he wouldn't resist her. It was she who had led the way into the dry darkness of the barn. Their bed had been a rough army blanket her father kept in his truck, spread on a pile of hay in the loft. And there, in the torment of the impossibility of their love, they had bound themselves to each other forever.

"Get yourself together, Quinn!" she admonished herself again. "And keep your mind on your driving." It served no purpose to remember, to feel the pain of her loss again. If she'd learned nothing else in the years of her exile, she'd learned that. She drove the rest of the way, hoping that Adam had chores at home he needed to do and would no longer be here.

He was still working in the kitchen, and whatever had made him express concern about her earlier, he now had firmly in check. She made no further attempts to talk to him, filling the cooler with ice and the milk and cheese and cold cuts she'd bought and leaving it on the screened-in back porch. She made several trips to the car, lugging in a vacuum cleaner she'd brought with her, and a radio. She took them both upstairs, turning the radio on loud so she could hear it while she vacuumed the bedroom—her old bedroom, the one with the window that faced the Sauder farm. When she looked out, she could see the rooftops glistening in the sun, just as she had when she was young.

Don't! she chided herself. *Keep working. Don't think about it.*

This room was in much better shape than the kitchen. She vacuumed everything, then mopped the floor and washed the windows. She'd be all right here. She had to be all right here. But she was so aware of Adam's presence in the house she could hardly bear it.

The movers came, and she had no choice but to go downstairs again. She didn't have that much to move, thankfully, just enough for one small truck. She'd been able to salvage only a few pieces of her parents' furniture when the farm was sold—family antiques, a bed with a five-foot headboard and carved oak leaves, a few random tables and an armoire. And she'd lived in a Philadelphia apartment small enough for her not to have acquired much more—a refrigerator, a chintz sofa, a big oak library table, which she planned to use as a computer desk for her accounting work, and an elegantly carved and upholstered rocking chair.

She could sense Adam's covert watchfulness, his interest in the things she was bringing home with her, but she kept working, supervising the placement of her belongings. She wasn't able to get the refrigerator into the kitchen, and the boxes of dishes and small appliances had to be stacked in the wide front hall, as well, until the carpentry work was finished. The movers, clearly not used to Plain People, stared at Adam and his Amish clothes with a curiosity that bordered on rudeness. But they—and she, for that matter—might as well have not been there for all the notice he gave.

By late afternoon she was technically moved in, and she was once again alone in the house with Adam. Or so she thought. She looked up from unpacking her clothes and bed linens to see a young Amish boy standing in the doorway. It had always been difficult to guess who was actually related to whom among the Amish, but this boy was definitely a Sauder. He had darker hair and eyes than Adam's, but the same basic nose, eyebrows and chin.

"Hello," she said. She knew he was here for a purpose, and she knew also that he would be typically curious about this "English" house.

He gave her a shy smile, then looked carefully around the room, his gaze falling on a long purple satin evening dress hanging on the closet door. The dress was expensive, a designer original; it was one of the few times she'd ever indulged herself. The boy seemed to find the sequined bodice and sleeves most interesting, but after a moment he remembered the reason for his trip upstairs.

"Adam says the sky wants rain. And your car is...opened," he said, his English sounding as if it were a literal translation of German. She had almost forgotten that peculiarity of the dialect, and she tried not to smile.

"I guess I'd better close it then, hadn't I?"

He was staring at the purple dress again. "What for dress do you have?"

"That? That's an evening dress. English girls wear dresses like that sometimes when they go to a special party. I used to wear it when I lived in Philadelphia. It's…" She tried to think of the way he might phrase it. "It's just for fancy," she decided.

He gave a small sigh. "Not plain," he said to underscore her definition, but it was merely an observation, not a recrimination.

"Do you want to see what makes it sparkle?"

He looked up at her and grinned.

She took the dress down from the closet door and unzipped the protective plastic bag. "See? The little round things here— those are sequins. They sew them on close together, and then when the light shines—"

"Daniel!" Adam said from the doorway, making them both jump. "Did you do what I told you?"

The boy nodded, looking from one adult to the other.

"Then come away from here. You know better."

"I was only showing him the sequins on the dress, Adam," Quinn said, knowing better herself but trying to intervene anyway.

"The less he knows of the English, the better off he will be."

"Dear God, you've grown up to be just like Jacob."

"What I am," he said sarcastically, "*Jacob* had no hand in." He turned to go, stopping at the head of the stairs. "I won't be back here. You will have to get Holland to find another carpenter."

"No, I didn't think you would," she answered, following him into the upstairs hallway. "Adam!" she called when he reached the bottom of the stairs. He looked up at her. "I saw Jacob on the road when I went into town today."

He didn't reply. The only response she got from him was the slamming of the front door.

"English girls wear shiny dresses to parties," Daniel said as they walked home over the damp, fertile earth in the plowed north field. The sky was growing darker, and Adam could smell the coming rain. He kept walking, knowing that Daniel was having to take big steps over the furrows to keep up, knowing how impressed his little brother was with his first encounter with Quinn Tyler and how badly he wanted to talk about her.

"The English—what is her name, Adam?"

"What her name is or anything else about her, you don't need to know," Adam snapped, walking faster to stay ahead of any more questions.

"Adam! Adam, wait," Daniel called behind him. "Anymore, I won't be a bad boy, Adam. I'll be quiet for you."

"I'll be quiet for you." When had he learned that he had to make concessions to be allowed to stay in Adam's company? He had no right to take his foul mood out on Daniel, yet how many times had he done it without even realizing it?

"Daniel, come on," he said, waiting for him to catch up. The boy could hardly be accused of being too boisterous, of being anything but persistent. Compared to some of the others of the Sauder clan—to Eli and Mary and Anna—one hardly knew Daniel was around at all. He had always been the quiet one, and, if Adam admitted it, his favorite of all his brothers and sisters. Daniel watched and listened and loved without reservation—everything, everyone. He had such a gentle way about him, with animals, with people. Adam gave a sharp sigh and began walking again, more slowly this time. "Her name is Quinn," he said after a while. "Quinn Tyler."

"Quinn," Daniel repeated, as if testing the feel of it. "Quinn! She...smells like pretty flowers. Like clover and like...roses. Will Quinn wear her shiny dress here, Adam? It's just for fancy, not just for so."

"Daniel, I don't know. If she does, you won't see it."

"You could take me to her house there and I could see it,'' he said hopefully. ''In the buggy,'' he added, because he truly loved a buggy ride.

"No. I couldn't. And anyplace she'd wear a dress like that, we wouldn't want to go.''

''Philadelphia.''

''What?''

''She wears her shiny dress in Philadelphia. Could we go to Philadelphia again? On the train?''

''Sometime we will go to Philadelphia—to the zoo, not to see any shiny purple dresses.'' With that, he scooped Daniel up under his arm, striding along with his box of carpenter's tools and a dangling, giggling little brother. He had no reason to be in such a bad mood. He had seen Quinn again, and his curiosity was satisfied. She *had* changed, as he'd expected. She was different now.

And yet she was the same.

He pushed the thought away. It didn't matter that she was the same, that she looked and talked and smelled like Quinn, or that he remembered everything.

Everything.

He knew the feel of her body, how she would taste, what it was like to lie with her in the dark and hear her say his name. He closed his eyes with the pain of it.

''She wants to cry,'' Daniel said from his nearly upside-down position.

''What?''

''She wants to cry,'' he repeated as Adam put him down.

''Who wants to cry?''

''Quinn Tyler wants to cry.''

''Daniel...'' Adam said in exasperation. He didn't want to talk about Quinn anymore.

''But she can't. Why can't she?''

''Daniel, you talk too much. Get along now. You have chores to do before we eat. Go!'' He watched his youngest brother run ahead, his brother who was the same age as his own lost son. He smiled a bit as Daniel turned and waved. If he said Quinn wanted to cry, then she did. Daniel would know that about her without her telling him, just because he was Daniel.

He looked back over his shoulder at the Tyler house. He still believed something was wrong with her, something that caused her to look so pale and tired, something that caused Daniel's conclusion. But it was no business of his. None. He regretted his foolish trip out to her car to see if she was all right. She had made it clear that whether she was or not, she wanted no help from him. And he regretted the petulance that had made him say he wouldn't be back. He'd given Holland Wakefield his word; he had to go back. He had no choice about it.

"Stupid," he said under his breath.

The wind was picking up, and the first drops of the spring shower began to fall. In his mind's eye he saw her suddenly in that upstairs bedroom. The house would grow cold with the coming of the rain, and she'd need to make a fire. He could see her in that room with the firelight, and the rain against the windows, and the big bed. He'd never shared a bed with her, not in all the times they were together.

He looked around at the honking of unsettled geese. His father was bringing in the mules from the field.

"Adam!" he yelled. "You have nothing better to do than to stand in the rain and let your grandfather's tools rust?"

The truth of the matter was that he'd hardly noticed the rain at all. He gave his father a wave of acknowledgment and walked toward the barn, relieved that the old man had the mules and wouldn't be able to catch up with him immediately. He had planned to tell him that Quinn was back here. It would have been better if he'd been able to do it before Jacob saw her on the road. He had no fear of his father; he was thirty-two years old. It was just that he wasn't prepared to be questioned. Not when he had no answers, not even for himself.

He looked back. His father had stopped Daniel and was now gesturing in the direction of the Tyler farm. Adam made his way through the dark barn to the small workshop on the far side facing the house, savoring as he always did the smells of hay and dusty grain, new sawdust and warm animals, and the sweet smell of aged and weathered wood. He set the carpenter's helper on the rough table in the workshop, taking each tool out and drying it carefully with one of the neatly folded rags kept for that purpose. He was the third generation of Sauder men to use these tools, and he always wiped them carefully after he'd finished with them, even when he hadn't been caught standing out in the rain like a fool.

The wind changed, and the rain drummed against the windowpane. He could hear his brothers' voices in the animal stalls on the other side of the wall—Eli's and Aaron's and David's. And his father's. He waited. For his brothers to go into the house, for his father to stay.

Daniel's calico cat jumped onto the workbench, rubbing against his hand and arm for his attention.

"Daniel's looking for you, old lady," he said softly. "Shame on you, hiding your babies from him." As he stroked the cat's head, he knew that his father had come into the workshop. But he went back to drying the tools, putting each one away in its proper place. He had such a sense of déjà vu suddenly, of another confrontation in this barn. He'd been twenty-one then, the oldest son, new to manhood, expected to marry one of his own kind, and hopelessly in love with Quinn Tyler.

"I haven't done anything!"

"Not yet, Adam! Not yet!"

"Did you get the corn in, Pop?" he asked, pushing the memory aside. They stood eye to eye, alike in physique and totally different in opinion. Jacob Sauder was a hard man, though no harder on his sons than he was on himself. He was an elder in the church, and when Adam was a child, he had been certain that God himself must look like Jacob Sauder. He was well aware of the fact that he had disappointed the old man deeply, just as he was well aware that it couldn't be helped. His father had had great expectations, and he had never taken into account his son's humanness.

"I don't come in here to talk about the corn," Jacob Sauder said. "You go to *her* house, Adam. You don't say she is back. You know she is there, and still you go?"

"Yes," he said quietly. "If it's Quinn you're asking about." The rain beat against the window, and the cat meticulously washed her fur. He set the empty carpenter's helper to one side.

"Ach! Adam! What are you doing there?"

"Kitchen cabinets."

"You make jokes? This woman—this *English* who will lead you astray is here again, and it is something for joking?"

"Quinn never led me anywhere I didn't want to go."

"Is that something to make you proud? To make *me* proud—this sin of yours?"

"I don't want to talk about this, Pop. I have paid for what you call my 'sin.' I am a good son."

"You aren't one of us, Adam! You don't marry! You stay here, but you don't do your duty!"

"I've told you. There is no one here I want to marry."

"There are other places for you to look."

"No," he said, moving toward the door. He stopped in the doorway and looked back. "You're my father. I'm here, and I do everything I can for you, for the family. The one thing I can do for myself, I don't do unless *I* want it." He stepped out into the rain.

"Adam! You don't go back there!" Jacob Sauder yelled after him. "You don't go back into the English woman's house!"

He kept walking, ignoring the rain, ignoring the man he was supposed to honor. He fought to keep his resentment at bay, but his father wasn't going to leave it alone. He wasn't a boy now. He was a man, a man who'd let go of Quinn, let go of everything that mattered to him, to stay Amish.

Actually, it was Quinn who'd done the letting go. She'd left him here with nothing but his anger, an anger he'd lived with for years yet couldn't find when he saw her again today. He hadn't married because of her; he was spending his life alone because of her, and still, *still* he'd wanted to see her.

No. No, it wasn't just because of Quinn's leaving that he was alone. It was because his people didn't recognize the need for love in making a marriage. For them, marriage was based on mutual respect and a common goal: children—children to raise strong in the faith and in their love of living Plain. He hadn't married, because he had known something special with Quinn, and not just some recalcitrant emotion that happened because of his budding manhood and her proximity. She had been a part of him for all of his life; they were not separate entities. They were, and always had been, two halves of a whole. But for the accident of her birth, she would have been more Amish than he. She would have been a good wife, a good mother; she would have been a joy to their children and to him. His father, his family, all of them had to know that no one could take her place. No one. He had loved her when they were four and six and standing at their fathers' knees at the livestock auctions. He had loved her when he was twenty-one and had given her a child.

And he loved her now.

Oh, Quinn!

His father caught up with him on the slate walkway that led to the house. "Do you hear me, Adam? You don't shame this family again!"

"I have given Holland Wakefield my handshake that I will do the job for him," he said without stopping. "Is there less shame in breaking my word than in your suspicions about what I *might* do?"

"My suspicions? Am I wrong to be suspicious when you don't say she is here again? When you know she is back, and I have to see her on the road?"

"Enough, Pop!" Adam cried, jerking his arm free when his father would have detained him.

"Adam!"

He kept going, running the last few steps to the house to get in out of the rain. He hung his straw hat on one of the pegs by the back door. The kitchen was warm and filled with good smells. It should have been filled with conversation and laughter, as well, but there was only silence as the family waited to take their seats at the table. He could feel all of them looking at him. Eli, who was always sickly and who would marry soon and bring another woman into the family. Thirteen-year-old Aaron, who had saved his money and bought a set of "English" clothes he kept hidden in the attic just to try on from time to time, as if the clothes would somehow make clear to him a way of life he couldn't begin to understand. And David. Adam should have been closer to David—there were only ten months between them—but there was nothing similar in their appearance or their dispositions. David was dark-haired and short and stocky, taking after their mother's side of the family, and he was deeply serious about everything, like Jacob. He took his glasses off and wiped the lenses with his handkerchief in an effort at preoccupation. David had worn glasses as long as Adam could remember, but they did nothing to hide the accusation he could see in his eyes now.

He glanced at the women in his family, at his still-unmarried sisters Anna and Mary, at David's pregnant wife, Sarah, and at his mother, all of them dressed in their Plain clothes and their prayer caps, and all of them wearing the same fearful, worried expression as they hurried to get the food on the table ahead of Jacob's arrival. Daniel was the only one in the room who dared to give him a smile.

Adam had no idea how much of the argument they'd heard—clearly, enough to leave them strained and silent. He looked again at his mother, but she said nothing. She was a small woman, not beautiful by worldly standards, but beautiful to him. He was her first child, and he had always felt a special bond between them, just as he had always felt that she, more than anyone else, understood about Quinn.

Quinn had given him a book once—a shameful book, his father would have thought—about war and slavery and people so real they seemed to leap off the pages. *Gone with the Wind*, it was called. The woman Ellen in that book had always reminded him of his mother—quiet, hardworking, keeping everything running smoothly in Jacob Sauder's house without him having the slightest notion of how it came about or that she was entirely responsible for it.

"Mom," he said as he went to stand by his usual place. "You aren't feeding us 'pigeons' *again*?"

Lena Sauder smiled at his teasing and patted his shoulder. It was his favorite dish, turnovers made of raw potato, boiled egg, onions and parsley, and then steamed. He would have gladly eaten them three times a day, and she knew it.

"I give yours to the pigs, you don't want it," she said, setting the last of the steaming bowls around the table. No one sat until Jacob Sauder was in his seat at the head of the table. At his lead, they all bowed their heads. The prayer was silent and unusually long—the reason for which escaped no one, except perhaps Daniel. Adam glanced up once to frown at the boy's fidgeting.

"Adam," Jacob Sauder said as soon as he had lifted his head. He accepted the bowl of lima beans his wife offered him. "You will plant the corn with David tomorrow. Do you hear me, Adam?" He avoided Adam's eyes.

"I have another job, Pop."

"Do you hear me, Adam?" Jacob Sauder repeated.

"I hear you, Pop." He slid his chair back and slowly stood. "I have another job. I intend to finish it. I...I want to take Daniel with me, since you seem to think it's a good idea to send him after me at the Tyler house. If you don't trust me, surely you trust Daniel." His mother caught his sleeve as he passed her chair on the way out, but he gently removed her fingers and left the room.

"Adam?" David said behind him.

"What?" He had been standing on the porch out of the rain, listening to the sound of the evening meal as it continued inside and trying not to stare at the lights of the Tyler house.

"I want to say that I don't think you mean to do the things you do."

"And what things are those, David? I haven't read a book in years."

"You're not still—" David began, then stopped, and Adam moved to sit on the swing. The boards were damp from the rain, but he sat down anyway, letting the swing slowly move back and forth.

"Still what? What is it exactly you want to know?" He stared into his brother's eyes, refusing to behave as if he'd done anything wrong when he hadn't.

Not yet.

His father's old accusation suddenly presented itself in his mind, but he pushed it aside.

"I want to know what you are going to do about Quinn. We all do. If you go against Pop, they'll shun you this time, Adam. Will you put the girls through that, and Mom and Daniel?"

Adam gave a tired sigh. "And what will they shun me for? For doing carpentry work in her kitchen?"

"You always make jokes!"

"So our father tells me."

"Go ahead, Adam. Keep on with the jokes. I am your brother. I remember what it was like in this house before. I have a wife with a baby coming. I have a right to know what it is you plan."

Adam looked away, scanning the quiet spring night, fighting hard not to lose his temper. "I plan, David, to finish the work Holland Wakefield hired me to do," he said, looking back at his brother's troubled face. "I plan to take Daniel with me to set your minds at rest—or do you think I'd fornicate with Quinn on the kitchen floor with Daniel there?"

"You have a dirty mouth!"

"Not my mouth so much as your mind."

"There is no talking to you! Our father is right to think what he does of you."

"And what is that? What does he tell you he thinks of me?" It galled Adam to think that they had discussed his shortcomings, but he baited his brother anyway.

"You have no discipline. No self-control!"

No discipline. No self-control. He wanted to laugh. By his own choice he lived celibate, alone. He stood up from the swing and walked toward the back door. "Then how is it you think I've stayed *here* for the last eleven years?" he said.

He let the door slam behind him, and he didn't stop once he was inside the house. He could hear the clocks ticking in the kitchen and in the sitting room, and the hiss of the gas lantern in the room where his mother worked on her quilts long after the others in the household had gone to bed. He met no one on the enclosed, winding staircase to the second floor, and he continued through the dark hallway to his room at the front of the house.

The room was large and sparsely furnished, with only an oak bed and dresser and one chair; he had no difficulty maneuvering in the darkness. He took off his clothes, hanging them blindly on a row of pegs on the wall. But he didn't go to bed. There were no curtains at the windows, and he intended to pull the dark green shade before he lit the lamp. Instead, he sat down in the straight chair his grandfather had made for him when, as a young man, he'd first moved into this room. He was so tired, and he sat alone in the dark, staring across the fields at the lights in the Tyler farmhouse.

Chapter Three

Quinn was down on her hands and knees. She had believed Adam when he said he wouldn't be back this morning, and she hadn't expected him. But she looked up to find him standing in the front hallway, his carpentry tools in the box he'd carried with him yesterday and the same young boy at his side.

"What are you doing?" he asked, surprising her further. She hadn't expected him to talk to her, either. He was frowning enough to indicate that he certainly didn't want to, but his eyes moved over her, finally stopping at the empty white china teacup she had in her right hand.

"I might ask you the same thing," she said, crawling a bit to the left of a stack of boxes. "I thought you weren't coming back." She was wearing gray sweatpants, a grey Mickey Mouse T-shirt, and running shoes, suitable attire for what she was doing, regardless of his obvious disapproval. "Don't you ever knock?" she added irritably. She suddenly felt that he was appraising more than her peculiar worldly clothes, and, for some reason, she wasn't comfortable with the possibility that Adam, in spite of himself, still found her attractive as a woman—even with Mickey Mouse on her chest.

"I did knock—at the back door. No one came."

"Yes, well, I was busy." She kept crawling, then abruptly stopped and sat back on her heels. "Hello, Daniel Sauder," she said to the boy with him.

"Hello, Quinn Tyler," the boy said shyly, glancing up at Adam for what Quinn felt was permission to have done so.

"Quinn, what are you doing?" Adam said. He didn't like towering over her, and he didn't like trying not to notice how her breasts moved under the shirt with the mouse on it.

"Looking for a spider," she said, crawling around some more boxes. "It's here someplace. Want to help me, Daniel? The kitchen's that way," she added to Adam. "You are here to work on the kitchen, aren't you?"

"I gave Holland my word."

She looked up at him. And an Amishman's word was everything; he'd keep it, even if it meant coming here. "Right," she said, going back to her search. Daniel knelt down beside her.

"There it is!" he cried as the spider suddenly crawled across the floor toward the toe of Adam's shoe. She headed it off, dropping the cup gently over it halfway there.

"Now what?" Daniel whispered, again coming to kneel beside her.

"Good question," Quinn whispered back, and he smiled. He reached out to gently touch the cup, then look into her eyes.

"Do you want to kill the spider, Quinn?" he asked solemnly.

"No, Daniel. I'm going to relocate him—outside. I don't like spiders much, but you can't go around squashing something just because you think it's ugly, can you?" She gave a wink and a short nod toward Adam. "I mean, where would your big, frowning brother be if people went around doing things like that?"

"Squashed?" Daniel said, giggling at her heavy-handed joke.

She grinned. It was the kind of thing she would have said eleven years ago if she'd found Adam as out of sorts as he was now.

But Adam clearly didn't share her amusement; he stalked into the kitchen without a backward glance. Her grin faded. She would do well to remember that whatever made Adam Sauder smile these days, it wouldn't be prompted by her.

"Whatever I am now, Jacob had no hand in."

Oh, God.

"Now what?" Daniel said again, and she smiled at him. She had to stop worrying about Adam.

"Well..." She reached into a nearby box, searching until she found an envelope. "I'm going to lift the cup just a little and slide this in. And when the spider crawls onto the envelope, I'll let the cup down again and we'll have him. What do you think?"

"Good!" Daniel said.

"Then let's do it."

But she wasn't as ready to take on a spider as she thought.

"Go on!" Daniel prompted, clearly delighted with this adventure.

"Yes. Right," Quinn promised. The distinct possibility that anything as fuzzy and multi-legged as that particular spider might end up crawling over her fingers was a real consideration, and she continued to sit there by the cup until Daniel held out both hands, palms up, and raised his eyebrows.

"What?" Quinn asked innocently.

"You're not doing," he advised her.

No, she certainly wasn't. She crooked her finger, motioning for him to come closer. "Did I ever tell you," she whispered, as if she didn't want the creature under the cup to hear, "that I'm afraid of spiders?"

"The spider's afraid, too, Quinn Tyler."

"Is he?" she asked, smiling a bit because he sounded so wise.

"Yes. Spiders always run away."

"Always?"

"Always."

"All right," Quinn said, rubbing her hands together. "I'm ready. Here we go. Oh, I can't do it!" she said the minute her fingers touched the cup. "Daniel, I'm a big sissy."

"You can do it, Quinn," he said encouragingly.

"Can I?"

"Yes, but you have to be brave."

"I have to be brave. Brave..." she repeated to talk herself into it. She carefully lifted the cup.

Everything went as planned, except that the spider made a break for it, causing both of them to scramble—Daniel, after him, and Quinn, away from him.

"The cup, Quinn! The cup!"

She fumbled the cup, nearly dropping it, all but throwing it into Daniel's hands. "Daniel— Oh! Catch it!"

He did—it *and* the spider, quietly taking the envelope from her and trapping the spider inside the cup without difficulty.

"My hero," Quinn said, and he smiled his bashful smile.

"Where can he live, Quinn?"

"Any place you think is all right, except the woodpile. I don't want to bring him right back in." She sat back on her heels, watching Daniel march outside with his important catch, thinking how much he reminded her of Adam at that age. She looked up to find Adam watching her from the kitchen, and their eyes held. He wasn't frowning anymore.

Don't let me see it, she told him silently. *If I'm hurting you, don't let me see it.*

He abruptly turned away and began hammering nails out of one of the boards he'd pulled down yesterday, each blow delivered with more force than was needed.

Quinn gave a soft sigh and got up from the floor, fighting a wave of dizziness that almost always plagued her these days when she made any extreme changes in position. She was still slightly anemic from the latest flare-up of her ulcer, but the dizziness quickly passed. She really was feeling much better physically, if she discounted the sleepless night she'd just had. And she *was* going to look after herself. She was going to eat regularly and take her medication and rest. She was also going to worry, but that couldn't be helped—three out of four wasn't bad.

She could hear Adam dragging boards around in the kitchen, and Daniel had come back in.

"Where to put the cup, Quinn?" he asked.

"I'll take it. Did you find a new home for the spider?"

"In the barn—a good place in the corner."

"Wonderful. I thank you for your help, Daniel Sauder."

"You are welcome, Quinn Tyler."

They both grinned, until Adam called Daniel sharply from the kitchen.

"We are here to work," he said from the doorway. He was very careful of where he looked. He had at least a week of carpentry work in this house if he was to do what Holland wanted. And in order to stand it, he had to stay away from Quinn. He'd been deliberately vulgar in answering David last night, because he had been annoyed, and, if he was truthful, more than a little guilty of wanting exactly what David and his father suspected. Quinn was still beautiful to him, body and mind. And he was more certain than ever that she was still Quinn. He tried not to smile. Quinn and her spider. Quinn—kind to creatures, cruel to men. She was supposed to have loved him, and he would never understand.

He set Daniel to hammering nails out of the stack of pine boards that had been pulled off the back wall. He would salvage as many of the originals as he could, perhaps piece some behind the cabinets, to make the kitchen look as it had before. He wanted to do that for her, and he didn't dwell on the reason, other than the fact that he sensed her need to restore this part of her past. He could hear her unpacking boxes in the front hall, and, in spite of his resolve, he looked in that direction. He could just see her through the doorway, down on her knees again.

Quinn felt his eyes on her and glanced up just in time to

see him move away. Perhaps they needed to sit down and talk, after all. Anything was better than the covert stealth they were both using to hide their mutual curiosity. She went on with the unpacking, leaving the computer until last, and trying to tune out the two sets of hammering noises that echoed through the still-empty house. She sighed. What was she going to do in this big place but rattle around? She was too much of a loner to take in boarders. Poor Quinn Tyler, people would say, nothing but that big old house and her computer.

She slid the carefully packed boxes of computer equipment into the living room, setting up her work area on the oak library table as she'd planned and noting that, with Daniel, Adam seemed more himself—or at least more the person she remembered. After a time she could hear a running conversation between them in their "at home" German. Riddles, she thought, because she recognized some of the words and the form, and because they laughed from time to time. She got the computer unpacked and working with minimal difficulty, and someone knocked on the front door.

"Quinn Tyler, someone is knocking," Daniel called from the kitchen. She smiled. He was such a dear little thing.

Edison Clark stood on the front porch, cardboard box filled with client files in his hands. He was what one might tactfully describe as portly. And he was balding. To make up for it, he wore a thick, drooping mustache that rather reminded Quinn of a turn-of-the-century tenor in a barbershop quartet. He had been her father's fishing buddy long before she had given him cause to become the family lawyer, and he usually looked as if he were about to do just that—go fishing. He favored a pocket watch with a gold watch fob and Pennsylvania Dutch cooking and helping people, and he was probably the best friend she'd ever had.

"I've brought you your bread and butter," he said, grinning. His grin promptly fled at the sight of Adam working in the kitchen. "Is that a good idea?" he whispered, eyebrows raised.

"I don't know," she said truthfully, "and don't start on me."

"You look like hell," he said, starting on her anyway. "What's happened to you?"

"Nothing," she said, wishing he'd lower his voice. But he was used to courtroom theatrics, and no juror ever dozed through one of his speeches.

"Nothing? Quinn, I saw you only a week ago, and you looked great. Now you're pale and—"

"I...I didn't sleep well."

He glanced into the kitchen. "No, I don't suppose you did. How are things with him?"

She shook her head without answering.

"Can't say I'm surprised. He took it hard, Quinn. I told you that ten years ago. Your being here again is the last thing he ever expected to have to deal with."

"Edison, could we not talk about this?" she said pointedly.

He grinned under his mustache. "All right. A house doesn't have to fall on me—at least I don't think it does." He handed her the box. "Now, what I'm going to need on these are regular reports on who owes what, who's got what and how much. I'll keep giving you updates on some of the earnings and expenditures and stuff like that. Can you handle that?"

"Sure," she said, carrying the box into the living room. "I thought I'd stagger it. I'll send you printouts on some the first of the month and the rest on the fifteenth."

"That'll work fine. Quinn?"

"What!" she said testily, recognizing the tone of voice.

He grinned again. "You're not going to like this, either."

"No, I didn't think I would," she said dryly. "What is it?"

"Jake called me."

She didn't say anything.

"You know Jake," he elaborated. "Jake Burroughs. Man you used to be engaged to. I took the two of you out to dinner once. I was even invited to the wedding, and—"

"What did he want?" she interrupted because she couldn't see a way out of it. She and Jake had parted by mutual consent and on good terms, if there was such a thing in a broken engagement. She had no doubt that he still cared about her, that in a platonic, altruistic sort of way, she was now rather like his favorite charity. But he was a bit irrepressible at times, and he'd been loud and long in voicing his opinion about her coming back here.

"So you do remember him!" Edison teased.

"Edison…"

"Aw, I know I'm annoying you, Quinn, but you look so damn solemn."

"Are you going to tell me what Jake wanted or not?"

"He wanted reassurance. He's worried about you—and you didn't tell me how bad the ulcer thing was the last time, Quinn. He's afraid you're going to isolate yourself out here and not take care of yourself, and next time you won't make it to a hospital soon enough. I thought he was being overly cautious, until I saw you today."

"I'm all right!"

"Are you?" he asked, his eyes probing hers for the truth.

She bowed her head for a moment before she answered. "I will be," she said, looking up at him. "I just have some things to…get used to."

"Quinn, Quinn," he said, sighing. "I don't know what to tell you. Or Jake."

"You don't have to tell him anything."

"No, I don't—if you want him to come out here to see for himself."

She frowned. That was entirely possible. Jake Burroughs was one of the best stockbrokers on the East Coast, and he hadn't gotten there by not finding out what he wanted to know.

"You can tell Jake that I'm feeling better. Now, wait," she said when Edison raised his eyebrows. "I *am* feeling better. I simply don't have a lot of stamina yet. When I'm tired, I'm tired, and it shows. I'm tired today because of the move and because I didn't sleep very well, and that's the truth."

"All that doesn't concern me nearly as much as the *reason* for the move, which is likely the same reason you're not sleep-

ing. You know how potentially harmful this arrangement is?"
he asked, nodding toward the kitchen. "His people remember,
Quinn. It was a source of great shame for them. He's still not
one of them the way he should be, and he's still sitting right
on the edge of being shunned all the time, even if he is a good
man. The Amish are a gentle folk, but they won't put up with
flagrant disregard for their beliefs."

"Edison, it was his choice to come work on the house. He
was here when I got here—Holland had already hired him.
And he didn't have to stay. It's going to be all right. Really."

"Well, you'll have a hard time convincing me of that—and
old Jacob Sauder. I'd hate to be in that household when he
finds out you're back here."

"I...think he already knows. I saw him on the road yesterday."

"And Adam's here working this morning? Damn! The old
man must be mellowing." Edison checked his pocket watch.
"Well, I've got to be in court at one. You take care of yourself
out here."

"I will. I'm not suicidal, you know. If I were, I would have
stayed at the brokerage firm in Philadelphia."

He smiled and patted her cheek. "I can find my own way
out. I'll speak to Adam before I go."

"Edison..."

"Quinn, I've known him since he was born—longer than
I've known you. I'm just going to say hello."

It was what he might say *after* that that troubled her. She
gave a resigned sigh and looked at the box of files she was
still holding. She put them down on the desk by the computer;
she might as well get started. It would take her mind off Edison's chat with Adam. Except she was too intent on eaves-
dropping.

But even that was hopeless. Edison had lapsed into the dialect German he'd taken pains to learn when he first came to
practice in this area. Probably all the Amish here let him handle their legal work—transfers of parcels of land to older sons
and the like. At least Adam was talking to *him*, Quinn thought,

opening a file and trying to concentrate. But she could only think of the past, of Edison coming to her in Philadelphia shortly after the baby was born, when she was trying so desperately to get on with her life.

"You're a strong person, Quinn. I admire you," he'd said, and she had smiled, in spite of her fear that the other shoe was about to drop. "It's my job to give you legal advice. It's not my job to meddle in your personal life."

"And?" she had asked quietly.

"And I wouldn't presume to tell you what to do, but I think I ought to make sure you're apprised of the situation." He waited for her reaction, and, when she didn't say anything, he went on. "I've seen Adam, Quinn."

"What do you mean you've seen him?" she said sharply. She knew that Adam had looked for her, that he'd hired one of the Mennonite boys who had a car to drive him to Philadelphia—Edison had already told her that. If anything could have made her lose her resolve, it would have been knowing that Adam was still here, aimlessly searching for her on the streets of Philadelphia.

"Quinn, this is killing him."

"It's killing me, too, Edison."

"Everything is done now, Quinn. It can't be undone. It would be a kindness to let me tell him—"

"No! I thought you weren't going to tell me what to do!"

"I'm telling you what *I'd* like to do."

"He'll hate me more than he already does, Edison."

"No. No, I don't think that's true, honey. But if it is, at least he'll know what's happened, and he can get on with his life. That's the reason for all this, isn't it? You didn't want to take his good life away from him? It's the *not* knowing that's so hard for him, Quinn."

"Edison, I—"

"Quinn, Quinn," he had said gently, patting her shoulder. "You've given your baby a wonderful chance. You were in an impossible situation, and you did the best you could with it."

"Did I?"

"Yes. You did. You did a good and loving thing for your child."

"Edison, I wanted him so badly...."

"I know, honey. I know."

"And Adam—"

"I know that, too." He smiled. "I remember when you were a little girl—how you cried when you found out the Amish weren't accepting membership applications."

She gave him a tremulous smile in return. "I thought it was something like the Auto Club, I guess. All I needed was the membership fee and someone to sponsor me."

"I'll tell him gently, Quinn."

But there had been no "gentle" way to tell him, and if he was the better for having been told, she couldn't discern it by looking at him now. She had known that, while he might understand intellectually that she was alone and afraid and in debt, he would never understand in his heart. Children were the most important thing in the world to the Amish, and she'd given his away.

The back door slammed finally, and Adam and Daniel were hammering again, much to her relief. She worked steadily at the computer until nearly noon, entering page after page of financial data she found refreshingly tame without some hot-shot broker breathing down her neck every second to get the latest tally on his commissions. She paused for a moment, thinking she'd heard someone knock. She finally decided she hadn't, only to hear the timid knocking again.

"Now what?" she murmured on her way to answer it. There wasn't enough authority in the knock for it to be Holland. Or, God forbid, Jake.

Two young Amish girls stood on the front porch, one of them carrying a basket. They were both wearing eyeglasses, and they covertly inspected the red-framed ones Quinn took off and let dangle on a cord around her neck. She knew that Amish girls were forbidden adornment, and she knew that, like all females, they made do with whatever they could—in this case, glasses. There was a good chance that neither one of them really needed spectacles, but wore them in the belief that it enhanced their physical appearance. Her translucent red frames were clearly worth noting.

"Yes?" Quinn said, trying not to smile.

"For Adam and Daniel," the older of the two said, holding up the basket of food for the *Mittagessen*, the noon meal.

"Out in the kitchen," Quinn said, standing back to let them come in. They both hesitated, and their somewhat startled expressions made her wonder what these girls had been told about her. The truth, she imagined, watching the girls dart glances around as much of her "English" house as they could see from the porch. "That way," she said, still holding the door open. They reluctantly came into the front hall, and Quinn pointed out the direction again on her way back into the living room to the computer. She tried to place which of Adam's sisters these two were, but nothing came to her except that the names would be German or biblical. How had she forgotten the names of Adam's sisters?

She glanced up at the conversation that suddenly came from the kitchen. German again—*loud* German. If Adam expected a meal hand delivered today, he certainly didn't sound like it. Quinn needed to eat, too, and she waited until the commotion died down and Adam and the others went out onto the back steps.

Why was he so annoyed? she wondered. His day had likely started before sunup; surely he was hungry, and his mother's cooking was famous in the area.

Chaperons, she thought suddenly as she opened the refrigerator door. Jacob Sauder knew she was back, and Daniel and the other two were here to keep Adam safe. Quinn could see Adam through the kitchen window. He was still angry, and the girls sat and fidgeted on the porch steps while he spoke to them in a low, harsh voice, the basket all but abandoned. Edison had been right. This wasn't a good idea.

She took out some cheese and cold cuts and made herself a sandwich, shaking her head because old Jacob had little to worry about. Adam either snapped at her or ignored her. He didn't need two sisters and a brother to chaperon that.

She carried the sandwich and a glass of milk back into the living room. The morning had grown increasingly gray, and, though it hadn't yet begun to rain, the room seemed damp and cold now. On impulse, she decided to light the fire she had laid in the fireplace last night. Carrying firewood had been the only constructive thing she could think of to do after Adam left.

She was more lonesome than she wanted to admit. Would a fire in the fireplace help loneliness? She felt like the woman in one of Edna St. Vincent Millays' poems, the one who kept a kettle boiling for company. *Poor Quinn Tyler, with her empty house and her computer,* and *her fires.*

She smiled to herself. "Can't hurt," she whispered, lighting the kindling.

She sat down close to the hearth to eat her lunch, realizing after a few moments that someone had come into the room. It was the older of Adam's sisters. The girl stood awkwardly just inside the doorway, and Quinn waited as she had with Daniel, realizing that this girl must see her as some kind of hussy, an English *Windfliegel,* at best.

"My father asks if you will need a hired girl," the girl said finally, and Quinn nearly laughed. When Jacob Sauder wanted someone chaperoned, he didn't do it by halves, even if it meant exposing another child to the "English."

"No, I don't think so," Quinn said. Then she changed her mind almost immediately. She knew how suspicious Jacob Sauder could be, and she could use some help with the unpacking. Perhaps she could hire a maid-chaperon to get the house settled and make life a little easier for Adam at the same time. "No, wait," she said as the girl turned to go. "What I need is someone to help me get these things unpacked and put away. What's your name?"

"Anna Sauder."

"And the other girl?"

"Mary Sauder."

"Well, I want to hire both of you. To clean up and to put all the things in these boxes away. Could you do that?"

The girl nodded.

"Both of you?"

"I will ask."

"Good. How much do you charge?"

She took a piece of paper out of her pocket and handed it to Quinn. It was a painstakingly written notice of Anna Sauder's hourly wage.

"This will be fine," Quinn said, handing it back to her. "I'll pay this to each of you. You find out if that is agreeable to your father. Tell him that I want both of you to come when Adam comes and leave when he leaves, and I'd like you to start as soon as possible." She realized suddenly that she was sounding very much like the head of the brokerage firm accounting department and probably scaring this girl half to death. "And one other thing, Anna."

"What?" Anna said timidly.

"I like your glasses."

The girl gave a shy smile, reaching up to touch them before she backed out of the room. Quinn could hear her calling her sister, then caught a glimpse of both of them running across the plowed field toward the Sauder farm.

She sighed and sat down by the fire again, idly rummaging through a box marked Glass and Brass while she finished her lunch. True, there were brass candlesticks inside, and a number of glass vases and bric-a-brac. But there was also wood— primitive art, she supposed it would be called. She lifted the wooden figure of a cow standing knee-deep in flowers, painstakingly cut out and hand painted in bright colors. Adam had made it and given it to her on her ninth birthday. She had loved it—still loved it—and she had kept it in plain view on various mantels or open shelves ever since he'd given it to her. She unwrapped it carefully now, her fingers running lightly over the wood.

"Quinn," Adam said from the doorway, the fine edge of annoyance still in his voice.

Lord, she thought. She was so tired of this, his anger, her guilt.

"What?" she said sharply, letting his scowl put her on the defensive in a way that could only make matters worse.

"What have you said to Anna and Mary?"

"Anna asked if I needed a hired girl," she said, putting the wooden barnyard figure down. "I said I did. I'm hiring both of them." She picked up her glass of milk and drank some of it to have something to do. It was hard for her to get used to his being so...unhappy, when she'd expected him to have a wife and children of his own now, expected him to be settled and content with his life. She remembered one of her father's appraisals of Adam Sauder when she and Adam were still children: *"God made him merry."* It had been an apt description—once.

"Why would you hire my sisters?"

"Because I think Jacob wants us to be chaperoned, and I'm obliging him," she said truthfully.

"We don't need chaperons."

"I know that, but I don't think he does. I can use some help unpacking, and I think having your sisters here will make things...easier."

"I don't need you to make things easier for me."

She looked up at him. She had always felt that his eyes were able to look directly into her soul, and she felt that now. He was still so handsome to her, handsome and strong—but not strong enough to have endured the trouble she would have brought him, she reminded herself. "I didn't do it for you. I did it for me. Quite frankly, I don't need the aggravation. I've had enough encounters with irate Amish fathers to last me a lifetime."

Now. Now you can accuse me of making fun of you.

She looked away. "Where's Daniel?" she asked, because it suddenly occurred to her that Jacob's well-laid plan had already gone awry.

"In the barn. Checking on the spider."

"Oh." The glass of milk was empty, and she tried to find

something else to do, someplace else to look. There was no other place, and she raised her eyes to his.

I can do this, she thought a bit desperately. I can look at him and talk to him, and the past doesn't matter.

They both looked away.

"You've been sick," he said abruptly. She could feel him making comparisons, Quinn now with the Quinn he once knew.

"Edison was a little overexcited."

"I knew before I heard what Edison said to you, Quinn. With what were you sick?"

She glanced up at him but found his gaze too disconcerting. "Too much urban living, I think," she said, reaching into the box again.

"I don't know what that means."

"It means I have an ulcer, a stomach ulcer. They tell me mine comes from working too hard and caring too much."

"That doesn't make people sick."

"It does when you don't like what you're doing and you keep on doing it just because you're good at it and the pay's good. It's not the same as the hard work you do farming. You've always liked it so much it isn't work to you."

"You don't know what it's like to stay in a hot field from sunup to sundown. It feels like work, Quinn." To her surprise, he almost smiled.

"I haven't forgotten. I used to tag along after you in that hot field as long as I could get away with it. I haven't forgotten what Dad used to say about you, either. 'For Adam Sauder, to plow is to pray.'"

He did smile then, and he sat down on the raised hearth, his forearms resting on his knees, his work-roughened hands in plain view. She had always thought he had beautiful hands, and she tried not to remember the feel of them on her face, on her breasts.

"You didn't like Philadelphia so much, then?" he asked. He had caught her looking at his hands, and he folded his arms as if to keep them out of sight.

"Oh, I liked Philadelphia. I liked having people tell me what a good job I was doing, how important to the firm I was. But I'm a farm girl at heart, I guess. Always have been. I never got used to living and working with people who scramble to make money twenty-four hours a day. I missed—'' She broke off. She wasn't going to tell him how painful her exile had been. "You know what I had forgotten? Birds. I didn't hear anything but sparrows where I lived. I keep catching myself listening now—robins, cardinals, mockingbirds. I even like the blue jays and the crows."

Her eyes collided with his, eyes that were pale blue and sad and holding hers again whether she wanted it or not. He was sitting too close to her, much too close.

"Tell me," he said quietly. She couldn't have looked away if her life had depended on it. "Where is your husband?" The fire crackled and burned, and she was growing too warm, but she couldn't move.

"Where is your wife?" she countered, realizing that they both could have given the same answer: *I don't have one— because of you.*

He looked away, his gaze falling on the wooden figure. "What is this?" he asked, picking it up.

"You know what that is. You gave it to me."

"I gave it to you," he repeated.

"Adam, you know you did. For my birthday, when I was nine."

"And you kept it?"

"Yes," she answered, bewildered by the incredulity in his voice.

He abruptly stood up, and she rose with him. "Why?" he asked, his hand clenching the figure tightly. "Why did you keep this?"

"Because..." She faltered.

"Tell me, Quinn. I want to know. It's ugly. You said this morning you don't keep things around you that are ugly—not spiders, and not this."

"It isn't ugly." She reached for it, but he wouldn't let her have it.

"Why do you keep it?" he asked again.

She took a small breath and looked up at him. "Because you gave it to me," she said evenly.

"Mein Gott!" he said with such pain that she took a step toward him.

But he didn't want her comfort. He moved sharply away from her. "Because *I* gave it to you? How can you say that to me?"

"Adam—"

"What do you want from me now, Quinn, when I have nothing left? Do you think I can't feel it—your *wanting*?"

"Adam, please—"

He grabbed her by her wrist with his free hand. "Tell me what you want!"

"Nothing!"

He abruptly let go of her, and again she tried to take the wooden figure from him. He was too quick for her. He tossed it into the fire.

"Adam, don't!"

He grabbed her when she would have retrieved it from the flames, making her look at him.

"I gave you a baby, too, Quinn. Where is he? You keep the wood and you give away the child? What kind of woman does that!" He turned her around toward the fire, holding her tightly against him when she struggled to get free, his arms locked over her breasts, his face pressed against hers as they watched the wooden figure burn. "There is nothing between us now. Not even wood. Do you understand?"

She didn't think her legs would hold her, and she sagged against him, feeling his breath warm and quick against her face. His touch, even in anger, was nearly more than she could bear. She didn't want him to see her cry—she *couldn't* let him see her cry.

"Answer me!"

"I understand!" she cried, trying to free herself again. "I understand! I've *always* understood!"

"What does that mean?"

"It means that I did what I had to do. It means that you won't make me feel guilty for it now. Let me go and get out. Get out!"

He didn't let go. He could feel her trembling. He didn't want to hurt her. He just wanted to—

"Quinn!" he whispered harshly against her ear, holding her until she stopped struggling. He wanted her to know that he understood, too. He wanted her to know that he knew she would have come to him—*if* he had been man enough to take care of her. "Quinn, forgive me!"

Forgive him? She turned her head to see Adam's face. Daniel was standing in the doorway.

Chapter Four

"Daniel," Quinn whispered, and Adam let her go, stepping sharply away from her. Daniel stood just inside the room, his mouth pursed and trembling, his eyes huge and afraid.

"Daniel, come," Adam said. He reached out to turn Daniel around and point him toward the kitchen, and he thought for a moment that the boy was going to shrink away from him. My God, what had he done? He'd forgotten all about him. Daniel had no part in this misery with Quinn.

"It's all right," he said. "Let's go. We have work to do."

"Do you fight with Quinn?" Daniel asked, looking up at him.

"No," Adam said, hurrying him along into the wide front hall.

"She wants to cry, Adam," he insisted. He looked back over his shoulder into the living room. "The cow is burned. She wants—"

"It is not our business!" Adam said, maneuvering both of them among the boxes in the hall.

Oh, Quinn!

Daniel dropped his head, and Adam knelt down beside him
so they would be at eye level. He took a deep breath, trying
to calm himself, trying to regain some control, trying to think
of what to say.

"Daniel?"

The boy kept his head bowed.

"Daniel, look at me."

He waited, and finally Daniel raised his eyes to his.

"You are my brother. I will tell you the truth. Quinn...
Quinn has been my friend since we were both little like you.
My friend, Daniel. Do you understand?"

"Like Aaron Lapp?" he asked, his eyes probing Adam's.
"Smiling Aaron," he qualified in case Adam might not know
which among all the Aaron Lapps in the area, young and old,
he might mean.

"Yes. Like Smiling Aaron," he agreed. Aaron Lapp was a
likable young man who lived on a farm nearer to town. He,
too, was the oldest son in a family with too many mouths to
feed solely by farming. He had become an apprentice in a local
cabinet shop to help make ends meet, and he frequently came
to the Sauders to ask Adam's advice on carpentry.

"Even if she is English?"

"Yes." He watched as Daniel thought this over.

"Is she your friend now?"

"I...I don't know, Daniel."

"Is that why you want to hurt Quinn now?" he asked solemnly.

Adam grabbed him by the shoulders. "Daniel, no! I don't
want to hurt Quinn. I would never hurt Quinn." *I love her!*
he almost said. "It's just that sometimes people get angry, and
they say things, do things they don't mean. Quinn and I were
angry. That's all."

"About what? About the cow?"

"No. About...something that happened a long time ago."

"When you were little like me?"

Adam smiled. "Well, not quite that long ago. But it still makes us angry to talk about it, you see."

"You and Quinn—don't talk about it anymore, Adam," Daniel said, flinging himself into Adam's arms. "Please!"

Adam held Daniel tightly, feeling the ache in his throat, the stinging behind his eyelids. He was a grown man, and it had been a long time since he, too, had wanted to cry. He held Daniel away from him so that he could see his face. "It's nothing for you to worry about."

"I feel worried," Daniel confessed.

"Don't feel worried, little brother. I am your big brother, and I say so."

"What will Pop say?"

What indeed? Adam thought. Once again, Daniel's eyes probed his for the truth. He hadn't thought that Daniel understood much about the friction between their father and him, but he obviously knew it existed. "I don't know. He will decide when he asks you what you've seen here in Quinn's house."

"He will ask," Daniel said, clearly resigned to the ordeal.

"Yes, and you can tell him. He is our father, and we honor him. We tell him the truth."

Daniel nodded, then gave a big sigh of relief. "I bent a nail," he said, suddenly remembering now why he'd sought Adam out in the first place.

"Did you? Can't you get it out?"

"No, it's too hard. Will I get big like you, Adam, or will I be a runt?"

Adam laughed in spite of his inner turmoil. "A runt," he said, knowing his depreciation of Daniel's size would precipitate one of their bouts of teasing and wrestling and tickling. "Enough!" he cried after a moment. "Runt or not, you'll soon be too strong for me. Show me this bent nail of yours."

Quinn stood by the hearth, watching the last remnants of the wooden figure Adam had made for her as it burned. She turned her head sharply at the sound of laughter in the kitchen. She wanted Adam out of this house. She'd told him so, yet he was laughing in the kitchen. She whirled around, striding across the hallway with every intention of throwing him out. She didn't care if the carpentry work was never finished. She would *not* put up with his being here.

She stopped at the kitchen doorway. Adam and Daniel were kneeling on the floor, their heads together as Adam showed him how to straighten a bent nail.

"No, no. Turn the hammer the other way," he was saying. He was so patient with Daniel and his hit-and-miss hammer. He would have made a good and caring father. "Now, push down. Hard! There, you see? It's not so hard. You did it."

"Adam," Quinn said, and he hesitated before he acknowledged her, his face closed and tight. "What did you mean?" she asked when he finally looked up. She had fully intended to tell him to leave, but, looking into his eyes, that suddenly seemed not to matter.

"About what?" he asked, his eyes shifting away from hers. He stood up slowly, as if to give himself time to prepare for coping with her questions. She glanced at Daniel. The boy was wearing his worried look again, but that didn't matter to her, either.

"You know about what. About my...forgiving you. What did you mean?"

"This isn't the time, Quinn." He turned and said something in German to Daniel, who immediately began to gather up the hammers and put them into the carpenter's helper.

"It is the time, Adam. I want to know what you meant."

"Daniel and I are going now," he said, taking the toolbox from Daniel's hands and knocking his brother's hat crooked in the process.

"Adam..."

"No, Quinn! I've told you. There is nothing between us now. We don't talk about this ever again. The time for talking is long past. Daniel, let's go."

He straightened Daniel's hat for him and went out the back door so that he wouldn't have to come any closer to her. He couldn't bear it anymore, her nearness, not when he'd just had his arms around her, felt her warm and trembling against him. Not when he could feel her questions now, her *wanting* something he couldn't give. He heard her call him as he stepped off the back porch, but he kept walking.

He could feel Daniel's eyes on him from time to time as they cut across the field to Sauder land. The sun was shining now, and he thought that if he stopped and turned around, he would see Quinn, standing on the porch steps, eyes shaded, watching him go.

But the sun went behind the clouds, and he didn't turn around. It was going to rain again, and his father and brothers would be coming in from the fields. Daniel said nothing, walking forlornly along beside him. He should say something to make the boy feel better, but there was nothing he could say. He had other things on his mind—his father, for one. The old man would ask Daniel everything, and he would have to explain whatever Daniel told him. But he couldn't explain, and that was something Jacob Sauder had never understood. Whatever existed between Quinn Tyler and Adam Sauder had always been there, and it was unexplainable.

He sent Daniel to search for the newest batch of kittens and headed straight for the house, stepping on the randomly shaped pieces of slate that led to the back door. The slate was shiny and wet, and he tried not to remember another time, a time when he was little and holding Quinn by the hand as they jumped from one flagstone to another in the rain. He wanted to talk to his mother before the old man came up from the field, so he set the carpenter's helper on the back porch by the door instead of taking it directly to the barn. His grandfather would have to forgive him this one delay in taking care of his tools.

"Adam," Jacob Sauder said from the kitchen. "The rain comes too hard for planting today. It washes the seeds away. Does it come too hard for carpentry at the house of the English woman, as well?"

Adam braced himself before going inside. A pot of cabbage

simmered on the stove, filling the house with its aroma. He didn't see his mother about.

"Are you making trouble for us, Adam?" Jacob asked quietly.

Adam ignored the question, going to the water bucket on a small table by the back door. He took the dipper off a peg on the wall and plunged it into the bucket, drinking deeply, savoring the familiar metallic taste of the cool water.

"You have no answer for me, I see," Jacob said.

He faced his father squarely. "No, Pop. I don't." He hung the dipper back on the peg. "If I go there, you are unhappy. If I come back, you are the same."

The old man looked away, staring out the kitchen windows across the yard to the barn. "Where is Daniel?"

"In the barn looking for his kittens."

"I can feel the trouble coming to this house. Perhaps he will tell me why it is you make such a fuss to go to the English woman's house to work and why you come home too soon."

Adam fought down an angry reply. He would not be threatened by anything Daniel might say, and he didn't want to argue. He wanted to talk to his mother. He went into the front of the house, but she wasn't there.

"Mom?" he called at the foot of the stairs.

He heard her answer him from somewhere on the second floor.

"Mom?" he called again when he reached the second-story landing. She was in the big room at the front of the house, a room used for storing out-of-season clothes and making quilts and putting up unexpected guests. He found her and Mary going through a stack of shirts and undergarments on the floor, winter things that would be carefully mended before they were put away.

"It's not time to eat," his mother said, smiling.

"I'm not hungry," he replied.

"Then you are not my Adam," she said matter-of-factly, making him return her smile when he felt nothing like smiling.

He stood awkwardly, not knowing what to say now that he was here, particularly with Mary listening.

"Mary," his mother said after a moment, "take these things down to the kitchen."

"But we are not done."

"Take them on. I'll be bringing the rest. Or I'll make Adam carry them."

"Adam doesn't carry underdrawers, Mom," Mary said, picking up the pile and taking them out.

"You used to," his mother said to him. "When you were little. Do you remember that? How you would carry the things in from the clothesline to help me?"

"I remember." He looked around the room, remembering, too, the times he'd played up here with his brothers and sisters when the work was done, hide-and-seek, blindman's bluff.

"You had better tell me what it is," his mother said quietly. "I can't bear to look at so sad a face."

He sat down on one of the trunks that lined the walls, and he was silent. He had wanted to speak to her, but now that he was here, now that she had given him the opening, he was suddenly tongue-tied. It was as if he were a boy again with a problem or a pain, and he wanted his mother to fix it.

"Do you fight with your father again?" she asked.

"No—no, not a fight. I worry him, and—" he looked into his mother's eyes "—I can't help him with this. This time I have to help myself."

"Yes" was all she said. She went back to folding winter clothes.

"Quinn is…" He faltered.

"Quinn is back," his mother said for him. "After so long a time. And you can't stay away from her. You think I don't understand you, Adam, but I do. You are my son. My first baby. And Quinn has always been in your heart. I have seen how much you try to make yourself believe something else— that she is English, that she has no business being there, always so close to you. But she *is* there. From the time you are little."

"I don't want to hurt the family. I don't want to hurt you. I don't want to make you ashamed of me."

"Suffering comes from God to make us strong, Adam. I have seen *you* suffer. All this time, and it is not better for you. Maybe there is less hurt for me to see you better than you are now, even if you—" She stood up suddenly and began gathering the remaining pile of clothes, but then she put them down again. She walked to a cedar chest that sat under the front windows, opened it and took out a quilt wrapped in tissue paper. "This is the quilt the women made for Quinn."

"For Quinn?"

"When her mother died. Her father gave us the dresses her mother wore to the school, and we used them for the quilt pieces—to honor her, to make a remembrance for Quinn. She left before it was finished. I have kept it here for her."

The quilt was red and blue and black, with an intricate center star pattern that was typically Plain. He reached out to touch it, knowing the hours of work the women would have put into it. He could smell its cedar scent from the chest, and in his mind he could see Quinn's face, the reverence it would hold at receiving such a gift.

But she hadn't received it. She'd run away with his son inside her, and she'd come back alone.

"She will have the quilt now," his mother said.

"She won't take it," Adam said. "There's too much trouble between us."

"She will take it from *me*. Your trouble has nothing to do with this," his mother answered. She wrapped it back into the tissue paper. "Carry the clothing downstairs and give it to Mary, please, Adam."

He grabbed the pile of clothes and followed his mother downstairs. "Mom, don't—"

"I will give Quinn the quilt," his mother said firmly. "It is hers."

"Mom..." he began again. But this was a household matter—the dispensing of quilts. It was her domain, and even

Jacob himself would not interfere. "Are you going now with it?"

"Yes. The rain has stopped," she said as they entered the kitchen. "Mary, you watch the cabbage pot until I get back."

His sister was there, but Jacob was nowhere in sight. No doubt he'd already gone after Daniel.

"Quinn is...upset now," Adam offered as a stumbling block in lieu of the rainy weather.

His mother looked up at him. "Your doing?"

He did not want his mother talking to Quinn. "Not all mine," he said a bit testily.

She made no reply to that, and there was nothing he could do but watch her go. He picked up the carpenter's helper he'd left by the door and headed for the barn. Jacob and Daniel were making their way toward the house.

"Where is Mom going?" Mary called after him, but he wasn't about to get into that with his sister, not with Jacob so close at hand.

"Adam!" Jacob called, and Adam steeled himself for yet another confrontation. Daniel bounded up the walk and on into the house, out of the way.

"What is this thing that happened at the English woman's house?" Jacob demanded.

"Quinn!" Adam shouted, the anger he'd had earlier for Quinn spilling over at his father. "Her name is Quinn!"

"I know what she is called. What I want to know is what happened there."

"Daniel told you," he said, moving to get by his father.

"Daniel! Daniel says there is a burning of the cow!" Jacob said, not letting him pass. "What foolishness is that to tell the boy to say? Now you make your little brother lie for you?"

"I haven't told him to say anything. Daniel tells the truth. You know that." He walked toward the barn, willing himself to say no more. He was angry, but he didn't want to argue with anyone else today. He just wanted to be left alone. He had no idea what Quinn would say to his mother. Nothing?

Everything? He looked toward the Tyler farm, seeing his mother disappear just over the rise at the edge of the fields.

Quinn wandered aimlessly through the empty house. She had long since given up working at the computer. She needed to get out for a while, away from this place with so many memories, but she had nowhere else she wanted to go. She moved some boxes about, regretting her impulsive hiring of Adam's sisters. What on earth was the matter with her? She needed to keep Adam and everything that reminded her of him out of her life, not make it impossible to think of nothing *but* him.

Yet trying not to think about him had never worked, not in all those years away, where she never saw him or anything remotely Amish.

Someone knocked at the front door, and she closed her eyes. She didn't want to deal with anyone or anything else today. She moved quietly into the front hallway, immediately recognizing the woman who waited on the front porch.

"Mrs. Sauder," she said, opening the door wide for her. She couldn't have been more surprised if old Jacob himself had been standing at the door.

"Lena," Adam's mother corrected, reminding Quinn of what she already knew, that the Amish did not hold with such formalities. Titles were but an indicator of false pride. Even their children called adults by their first names.

"Lena," Quinn repeated, trying to mask her surprise. "Come in, come in. What have you got there?" she asked, though she really wanted to know about Adam. Was he still angry? Was he fighting with old Jacob. She stood back to let Lena Sauder come inside. She wished that the house were in better order. She never would have had it up to Lena Sauder's standard of housekeeping, but things could have been slightly less chaotic than this.

Heaven help me, she thought. All this time, and I still want Adam's mother to think I'm good enough to be Amish.

"I have brought you the quilt, Quinn. The remembrance

quilt for your mother. I have been keeping it for you, for when you came home again.''

She said it so matter-of-factly, Quinn thought. Not *if*, but *when*. She looked down at the tissue-wrapped quilt, and Lena Sauder placed it into her arms. Quinn carried it into the living room and sat down on the sofa, putting the bundle carefully in her lap so she could unwrap it. She recognized the quilt pieces immediately, the blues of the dresses her mother had worn to the Amish school.

Mama, she thought, the pain of her mother's dying more real than it had been in years. She looked up into Lena Sauder's eyes.

''I—it's—'' She broke off, dropping her head because the tears were so close. She stared at the quilt, rubbing her hands lovingly over it, admiring the fine stitching, the hours of painstaking work, while she bit her lip and tried not to cry. She hadn't known, hadn't even considered that Lena and the women would have done this on her behalf. She hadn't thought that Lena would keep it for her, bring it to her now— especially now. ''It's so beautiful,'' she said, her voice husky and low. ''Thank you. I'll cherish it always.'' She tried to meet Lena's eyes again but couldn't.

Lena's hand came to rest on her shoulder. The hand was gentle and warm, and the fact that it belonged to Adam's mother was nearly more than Quinn could bear. Lena Sauder had always been kind to her, but she didn't deserve her kindness. A tear spilled out of her eye and rolled down her cheek, and Lena sat down beside her, her arm sliding easily around her shoulders. Quinn savored her comfort. She had once thought of Lena Sauder as her second mother.

''Just yesterday, I was thinking about you,'' Lena said. ''Remembering. When I stand at the kitchen window, I can see the fence on the ridge. Do you know the one?''

Quinn nodded, not trusting herself to speak.

''One winter I am looking out that same window, at the same fence. Adam was just a boy—ten years old, or eleven maybe. He had to put in the new fence posts—carry them up the slope and fit them into the holes and put the rocks and the earth around them. It is so cold that day—fine snow coming— and I look out the window now and again because I am a mother and I want to see he is working all right. But one time when I look, I don't see my one boy—I see two boys, one bundled in a red wool cap and red mittens. Two boys, working and working to get done ahead of the dark and the snow. But no. It isn't a boy at all who is working so hard to help my Adam. It is Quinn Tyler—my little English.''

"You gave us fried apple pies and hot cinnamon milk when we were done," Quinn said, resting easily in Lena Sauder' embrace.

"To make your noses run so you don't catch the grippe."

Quinn laughed softly, and Lena gave her a hard squeeze.

"Quinn, I have something I want to say to you. About Adam."

Quinn took a deep breath and forced herself to sit up. "What?" She managed to look into Lena's eyes.

"I know what a hard thing you did for him so he is not lost from us. You went away and—"

"He hates me, Lena," Quinn interrupted, her face crumpling as she finally voiced the fear she'd carried so long. She hadn't been able to say it to anyone. She hadn't had anyone who would have understood, no one who knew how much she'd cared for Adam Sauder.

Lena patted her gently, putting her arms around her again to soothe her as if she were a child.

"No, Quinn. Adam is hurt and he's angry. But he doesn't hate."

"He wants his son. He knows that I loved him, but he can't forgive me for that."

She felt Lena stiffen. "His son?" The comforting arm dropped from around her.

Oh, dear God! Quinn thought. Adam hadn't told her. It never occurred to her that he hadn't told his mother and Jacob. She stood up, putting the quilt aside and wiping at her eyes.

"Quinn!" Lena said sharply, and Quinn turned around to face her.

"You will tell me this thing! You had a baby with my Adam?"

"Yes," she said evenly.

"And Adam knows this?"

"Yes."

"And where is the baby now?"

"Lena, I don't want to talk about this."

"Nor would I, Quinn Tyler. What have you done to him, my poor son!"

"Lena…"

"I will go now."

"Lena, *please*!"

"And I will not see you, Quinn Tyler, until I can find the forgiveness in my own heart."

Quinn followed Lena to the front door, knowing there was nothing she could say or do. Then she went back into the living room and stood by the front window to watch Lena Sauder until she was gone.

Why didn't he tell her?

The question repeated and repeated itself in her mind. Did none of them know, then? In her mind, miles away in Philadelphia, she had faced the ordeal of Jacob and Lena finding out. It had been real; she had thought they knew. She had thought they *all* knew. She wouldn't have come back here if she'd suspected for one minute that she would be the one to tell them. Dear God.

Old Jacob.

Her father was dead. If she had to face Jacob again, she would have no one to stand by her now.

You can do it, Quinn, she told herself.

She wasn't a child anymore. She could deal with Jacob Sauder if she had to.

There is nothing anyone can do, she reminded herself. It's

done. It can't be undone. How many times had she said that since she'd last lived here? A hundred? A thousand?

Adam. She wanted to see him, talk to him.

She sat for a long time in the dark, holding the quilt made from her mother's dresses.

Quinn awoke shortly before dawn. The house was cold, and she toyed with the idea of building another fire. Instead she opted for a sweat suit and a walk over the remaining Tyler land, standing for a time on the back porch and watching the morning mist rise from the low ground and hollows as the sun came up. She closed her eyes and listened. She had missed this, too, the damp freshness of the morning quiet broken only by bird song. No, not only bird song. There was more. She could feel the breeze rustling the new leaves and the tall grass, and somewhere, not far off, she could hear the rattle and clank of chain and tack in the still morning air, and the peaceful monotony of a cajoling human voice. Someone—a Sauder— was plowing. It was a good morning for it. The ground would be soft and wet from the rain. In her mind she could smell it, the newly turned earth, could imagine it cool and soft between her bare toes.

She stepped off the porch and walked around the yard, look- ing at the house and the lay of what little land she had left as if she'd never seen it before. She had enough acreage to plant *some*thing, and it was hard to tolerate a fallow field. She'd speak to Edison about it. He could find someone to plow it for her. She could manage a small garden herself—tomatoes, squash, cucumbers. Lord, she'd missed homegrown vegetables. The thought of such delicacies made her stomach rumble, reminding her that she hadn't eaten.

She walked back to the house, uncomfortably aware of her state of mind. She was waiting. Hoping. Praying Adam would come to the house today. She had no idea how Lena would handle the news of Quinn Tyler's having had a Sauder child. She would speak to old Jacob surely, and then...

Her mind refused to surmise about that. Jacob was not a violent man, but he was devout, and evidently Adam hadn't told him the worst of his sin. She wanted desperately to know what was happening at the Sauder place, but she had no way to find out. She certainly couldn't go there. She sighed heavily, stopping for a moment to grieve once again for the old apple tree. She reached out with the toe of her running shoe to poke the dead stump.

"You can't bring it to life again," Adam said from the porch, making her jump. The lilac bushes had concealed him; she had no idea how long he'd been waiting. His hair was damp under his hat, freshly combed. If she got close enough, she knew how he would smell—skin that was soap-and-water clean, clothes that had dried out in the sun. Apparently he intended to stay and work. A basket and his carpenter's box sat beside him on the porch.

"No, I can't bring it to life again," she said, knowing it wasn't necessarily the apple tree that she spoke of. She stood with her arms folded over her breasts and didn't get any closer.

"I thought you were still sleeping."

"No," she said again, taking a few steps in his direction. He didn't seem angry. Lena must not have said anything. If she had, he wouldn't be speaking to her so civilly. If she had, he wouldn't be here at all.

He reached out to pull a leaf off one of the lilac bushes.

"You're going to have to do something about these bushes, Quinn. They've got the black spot."

She said nothing to that, and he let the leaf fall.

"Well, do you tell me I can go inside to work, or do you leave me standing here on the porch?"

She frowned. The remark should have been sarcastic. It wasn't. He wasn't teasing her exactly, but almost. Almost.

"Yes, of course," she said, climbing the porch steps too quickly. She'd forgotten that they were so rickety, and she was off balance when she reached the top. Adam stretched to steady her, his hand firm and warm on her elbow. She looked into his eyes, her mouth pursed to say that she didn't need any help, but she didn't get the words out. She stood there, her eyes locked with his. Hers, she was certain, were wary and filled with questions; his... For once, they were unfathomable. She had no idea what he was thinking, feeling. She knew only his closeness, his hand still firmly clasping her arm.

"There's Quinn Tyler!" Daniel called suddenly from behind them, and Adam let go of her arm. "We knocked and knocked on the front door. Were you sleeping?"

Quinn smiled. The "we" included Anna and Mary, one dressed in a plain green dress, the other in a deep-blue one, and both wearing their white prayer caps with the strings dangling and their typical aprons. Somehow, when she'd really expected no one today, the whole clan had arrived. "No. Not sleeping. Just walking around."

Her smile broadened. She could tell by the girls' expressions that they considered the activity typically English and entirely trifling. "Let's get to work," she said, leading the way into the house and only vaguely concerned about whether or not they'd noticed Adam's touching her.

She left Adam and Daniel in the kitchen and took Mary and Anna to the stacks of boxes in the hallway, starting them on the linens first. The cartons were heavy, and she and the girls were struggling to get the necessary ones up the stairs when Adam intruded with his greater strength and carried the boxes to the second floor as if they weighed nothing.

"Anything else?" he asked, clearly annoyed at having to interrupt his carpentry.

"No, nothing, thank you," Quinn said coolly.

Anna looked perplexed. "What?" Quinn asked her.

"The boxes were heavy, Quinn Tyler. Didn't you want Adam to help us?"

"Of course, I wanted him to help us," Quinn said loudly enough for him to hear her. "I just didn't want him to be so arrogant about it. There are only two ways to be strong, girls—mentally and physically. And each of us has only one of those. It's not *our* fault God put all our strength between our ears."

To her surprise, she heard Adam laugh, really laugh, when he reached the kitchen. She set the girls to cleaning out the linen closet, then lining the shelves with flowered paper.

"Will you tell us where you want the towels and sheets to go, Quinn?" Anna asked, clearly worried at the responsibility of the task.

"Put the sheets and pillowcases on the higher shelves. The rest you can do however you think is best."

She went back downstairs to Adam and Daniel's vigorous hammering in the kitchen. She had to find something for her breakfast. She was determined not to ask Adam anything about Lena. If he didn't know she'd told Lena about their child, she wasn't about to bring it up. He'd know soon enough, and, if she were truthful with herself, this sudden and uneasy truce of his was not unpleasant.

She rummaged around until she found a can of cream of chicken soup. She heated it on the hot plate and made toast in the toaster—not standard breakfast fare, but more than soothing. She ate with relish—it was quite good, actually—and she stayed out of Adam's way, casting glances in his direction from time to time from her perch on a bar stool in the corner.

He ignored her, his mind on pulling boards off the wall and his conversation only for Daniel.

When she had finished eating, she washed the pot and the one bowl she'd used, then went into the living room to work on Edison's financial records. She found that in spite of Lena Sauder's visit and her subsequent sleepless night, in spite of Adam's being in the house, she could concentrate—for a time. But with the fifth folder of financial data, her mind began to wander.

The house was alive this morning, not deadly quiet the way it was when only she was there. Anna and Mary laughed together upstairs—the Amish strived to teach their children to be happy in their work. And Adam and Daniel told their riddles.

How she'd always longed to be part of a big family like this, a part of *his* family. And yet, she couldn't deny that she'd tried to make him "worldly." She'd fostered Adam's desire for learning. She'd brought him books, told him about the movies she'd seen, let him listen to her "English" music. Once, they'd danced together in the moonlight on a creek bank. She even remembered the song, "I Love How You Love Me," by the Paris Sisters. It had been considered an oldie, even then. They hadn't yet become lovers, but she and Adam slipped away to talk, to listen to the music that was forbidden to him, to simply be together. He was always so filled with questions about the things she saw and heard in her world, and the song had come on the small transistor radio she'd brought along. Adam, non-dancing Adam, had held out his hands. They'd stepped into each other's arms, the way he knew English couples did, and awkwardly they had moved together to the music. She had never forgotten. The feel of his body against hers, his heady masculine smell, his breath soft and warm against her ear as they danced so innocently.

"Quinn," Adam said behind her, and she jumped.

"What's wrong with you?" he asked, his voice taking on the sharp edge she dreaded.

"Nothing's wrong."

"Then why do you jump out of your skin every time I speak to you?"

"Adam, I didn't know you were there. You startled me, that's all."

He stared at her, and she could feel him deciding whether or not he believed her. "Are you afraid of me?" His eyes probed hers.

"No, I'm not afraid of you."

"You're just...nervous, then?"

"I guess so," she acknowledged. "City living and all that. What did you want?"

"I need you to help me."

"Me?" she said, unable to keep from sounding incredulous. Somehow that was the last thing she'd considered, that Adam Sauder would ask for *her* help.

"Yes, you. You are too much of a big shot to help?"

"No, I'm not too much of a big shot." She got up from the computer and followed him into the kitchen. "What is it?"

"There's a piece of molding that's fallen down into the wall. The hole is too small for me to get my hand in, and Daniel's arm is too short to reach it. I think you can do it. Reach up in there," he said, showing her the hole. "The piece is diagonal between the studs, I think."

She looked at the hole, then at him. "Adam, you know there could be spiders in there."

"Yes, I know that," he assured her. "Daniel, here, knows it, too. Don't you, Daniel?"

"Yes," Daniel said.

Quinn needed more incentive than she was getting. "How do you know the molding is in there?"

"Because I dropped it in there. See that hole higher up? For some reason, somebody put it in that hole. Just the tip was showing. I knocked it the rest of the way in trying to pull it out."

"Couldn't we just leave it?"

"Yes, we could do that, but I think it's part of the fancy original ceiling molding—one of the pieces your father made. I thought you'd want to keep it. I don't want to have to pull off any more boards to get it if you can reach it."

She looked at the hole again. She did want to keep the molding. She just didn't want to stick her hand in there.

"And you want me to put my hand in that hole with the spiders," she said.

"That's what we want," Adam said. "Don't we, Daniel?"

"Yes," Daniel said again. They were both trying not to grin. It was becoming obvious to her that her aversion to spiders had been discussed at length before she'd ever been summoned.

"You two are just too cute for words," she said.

"We are," Adam agreed.

"I'll be right back."

She went into the hallway to rummage through the boxes, coming back with one red-and-blue-striped knee sock. She put the sock on over her hand, pulling it all the way to her shoulder. She stuck her well-covered hand and arm into the hole and located the molding easily enough. Dislodging it was something else again, but after a few minutes of blind maneuvering, she was finally able to get it free.

"Good job," Adam said when she brought it out.

"Thank you. Do you see this here?" she asked, pointing to the sock. "Spiderwebs. All over my arm."

"You were very brave," Adam said to pacify her.

"Just don't let this happen again," she admonished them.

"No, we won't. Will we, Daniel?"

Daniel grinned, and Quinn left on the heels of their laughter, laughing herself once she was out of the kitchen. But her smile quickly faded. It was so easy—too easy—to put aside all the hurt and the pain and the sorrow. She was behaving as if nothing had happened between her and Adam Sauder, and she couldn't afford to do that.

She went back into the living room, determined to work at the computer. She needed to get the financial data entered, and she needed not to resurrect any more old feelings.

"Quinn?" one of Adam's sisters called from upstairs. Quinn wasn't familiar enough with their voices to tell which.

"Yes?" she called up the stairs.

"Come see, Quinn."

She climbed the stairs, feeling the strain of the past two

days in the last few steps. She was tired—too tired in light of her promise to Jake and Edison to take care of herself. She hesitated for a moment on the landing to catch her breath.

"It's done, Quinn," called Anna, who seemed to do all the talking. Mary, the younger of the two, was dutifully subordinate, staying quietly in the background.

"It looks fine," Quinn said truthfully as she inspected the stacks of carefully placed linens. She couldn't have done better herself.

She turned them loose in the bathroom next with various spray cans they seemed delighted to try. She went back downstairs, deciding to set up the refrigerator, even if she had to leave it in the hall outside the kitchen door for a while.

The cord wouldn't reach the wall plug. She tried moving the refrigerator, but it was an older model without wheels, and she could barely budge it. She caught a glimpse of Adam out of the corner of her eye, and this time she didn't jump.

He put his hammer down. "Where do you want it?"

"Closer to the wall socket so I can plug it in."

"Come, Daniel, you, too," he said, not, Quinn suspected, because he needed Daniel's help, but because he wanted Daniel to feel that he did.

Such a good father, she thought yet another time and promptly pushed the thought aside.

Together the three of them moved the refrigerator close enough for the plug to reach.

"Anything else you want the mentally weak to do?" he asked, and again she was struck by his lack of vindictiveness. She looked up into his eyes.

What are you doing? she demanded silently.

His eyes slid away from hers, and he reached across her to retrieve his hammer from the top of a box where he'd laid it. He was too close again, too close and too obliging.

"I'm going into town," she said abruptly. "I have to get some groceries."

"I'll come with you."

"You'll come?"

"I need nails. Unless you're afraid to have me ride into town with you."

"I'm not afraid of you!" she snapped, but she was. She'd never been so afraid in her life.

"Then there is no problem, is there?"

Yes, there's a problem, and you know it! she wanted to say. It took everything she had to stop herself.

"I have to find my purse."

She walked away from him, ostensibly looking for her purse and her keys but in actuality seeing nothing. What was the matter with him? He couldn't be seen riding around town with her!

"It's in the kitchen," Adam said. "On the counter by the hot plate."

She went to get it, and he called upstairs in German to his sisters, and then to Daniel, who was watching her search through her purse for the car keys. He wasn't taking Daniel with them. She could tell immediately from the boy's crestfallen look.

But she said nothing. She could be alone with Adam Sauder. She wouldn't be afraid of him. She would show him that she could be alone with him. He followed her out to the car, getting in and trying to keep his knees from pressing against the dash. He was much too tall to be comfortable.

"There's a lever under the seat in front. Push it to the side if you want to move the seat back."

"No," he answered, staring straight ahead, as if such a flagrant concession to personal discomfort was a road that would lead straight to his destruction.

Fine, she thought. He could suit himself.

She drove into town quickly, meeting no Amish horse and buggies to slow her down. She attempted no conversation with Adam, nor he with her. They simply rode in silence, each acutely aware of the other's presence.

"Turn in there," he said shortly after she'd pulled onto Highway 340. "At the flea market."

"Adam, you don't want to go in there," she protested.

"Why not?"

"Because..." *You're with me,* she almost said. But she bit down on it, deterred by the challenge she saw in his eyes. She pressed her hand against the burning ache in her stomach. "You won't find nails *here,* will you?"

"I will if Abe Zook is here today. He sells them cheaper than in town. Park the car over there. It won't take long to see."

She parked where he indicated.

"Aren't you coming?" he asked as he got out of the car. "Come on, Quinn. You may see something you want for your house." He opened the door on her side and stood waiting. "Are you afraid of the flea market, too?" he asked. Although he didn't speak the words, his voice challenged her, *There is nothing between us Quinn. Why can't you act like it?* "What else are you afraid of? How did you live in so big a place as Philadelphia when everything scares you?"

"Everything doesn't scare me," she said as she got out. If he didn't care, there was no reason she should, she told herself, knowing it wasn't true. *She* had nothing to lose in being seen with him. She trailed after him, trying to stay far enough behind so that no one would think they were together. He waited until she caught up. Together, they walked down an aisle of vendors, Amish women and girls with their hand-lettered, often misspelled signs. HONY FOR SALE. APPLESAUS FOR SALE. She bumped into an Amishman coming in the opposite direction. He was barefoot and dirty, his feet tough and nearly black from going without shoes. He had two small boys with him, equally dirty, and the combined stench that rose from their three unwashed bodies nearly took her breath away.

She stepped away from him as if she'd been burned, only to find Adam watching.

"Philadelphia has made you too good for us," he commented.

"It hasn't made me too good," she snapped. "For some reason that man and his children weren't following your cleanliness-is-next-to-Godliness rule. He was dirty and stank!"

He walked on ahead of her, and this time he didn't wait for her to catch up. She followed at a safe distance, pretending to be interested in the nearest booth—jars of bean chow-chow and pickled cauliflower and celery. She watched out of the corner of her eye as Adam conducted his business with another Amishman who kept showing him boxes of nails. Adam came back empty-handed.

"Now what's the matter?" Quinn said.

"Too short," he answered succinctly, walking past her toward the parked car.

"What is an Amishman doing with all that hardware anyway?" she asked from behind him.

"A store was going out of business. He didn't want the store, but he did want the inventory. He bought it to sell here. Low overhead, you see. And good prices to get the people to come and to come back. He's making extra money for his family without having to send his children out among the English to work."

"Clever man," Quinn said as she caught up with him.

"Yes," Adam agreed, finally looking at her. "A clever man."

Quinn's car was boxed in by two others when they reached it, no major problem for a woman used to city living. Quinn pulled forward and backed up, maneuvering inch by inch until she could get the car out.

"Good job," Adam said when she cut the steering sharply for the last time. She glanced at him. He meant it, and she smiled, getting them onto the road again and heading toward town.

"Let me out here," he said when they were still several blocks from the second place he wanted to try for nails.

"I can take you the rest of the way," she insisted. It was crazy for him to walk with her right through half of Amish Lancaster County, and then not let her take him to where they'd likely see no one.

"No. The tourist buses are in town. I can walk there easier than you can drive. I'll wait for you here on the corner."

She let him out, watching for a moment as he strode down the street. He was a beautiful man, strong and gentle and kind, and, once again, this time simply by being seen with him, she'd likely ruined him.

A car horn blew sharply behind her, and she drove on. Down the main street, lines of tour buses with logos from all over the eastern United States were creeping into town, backing up traffic at the stoplights and intersections. The entire downtown smelled of diesel exhaust fumes. She was finally able to get out of the press and into a grocery store parking lot, but it, too, was crowded. She didn't linger over her shopping. She'd be glad to get out of this and back home.

"Is it always this busy?" she asked the girl at the checkout counter.

"It is during the tourist season," she said without looking up. "Five million tourists last year—and they all came in here at least once. There's something about traveling on a tour bus that makes people think the next place they're going to stop to eat will be out of everything."

"Miss! Excuse me!" a large woman wearing a straw hat and white heart-shaped sunglasses interrupted. "Quick! Where's the candy aisle!"

The chekcout girl pointed. "See what I mean?" she said to Quinn.

Traffic was still congested as Quinn drove back through town, and Adam was waiting on the corner where he'd gotten out. She could see him plainly; she just couldn't get to him. Two tour buses had stopped on the street, and he was now standing stoically in the center of a rush of disembarked passengers with cameras. They either didn't know that the Amish did not like having their pictures taken or felt that their tight itinerary excused them from courteous behavior.

She rolled down the car window. "Adam!" she called, but he couldn't hear her over the bus engines. "Adam!" she yelled again, without success. She leaned on the car horn, causing him and most of the tourists to look in her direction.

'Hurry!'' she called, because she had stopped dead in the
treet with yet another tour bus all but in her trunk.

Adam disengaged his arm from the grasp of a young red-
ead in a halter top and skimpy shorts who was trying to get
im to stand beside her for a picture. Quinn flung the car door
pen for him.

"Drive!" he said before he was all the way inside.

"Did you get your nails?" Quinn inquired when they'd
;one less than a block. He was more rattled than she'd
hought, seeing him from a distance, and she couldn't keep
rom teasing him.

"Yes, I got the nails." He showed her the crumpled paper
•ag in his hand, then sighed heavily. "I thought I was going
o have to run for it." He glanced back over his shoulder as
f he thought the girl in the shorts might be hanging on to the
•ack of the car. "And it's not funny."

"I'm not laughing," she assured him.

He looked at her, and she kept her face carefully neutral.
'See?"

He shook his finger at her. "The *outside* is not laughing,"
ie said suspiciously. He sighed heavily. "There may be some-
hing to this never wearing shoes and never taking a bath,"
ie observed. He glanced at her, and they both laughed.

They came out of one snarl of traffic and right into another.
'When did it get like this?" she asked. "It wasn't so crowded
he other day."

"The last few years or so. When the weather gets warm,
iere they come in their buses and their vans. Open season on
he Plain People. Every year it gets worse."

"For you. Not for the ones who make a living off the tourist
rade."

A small red car pulled out in front of her, and she slammed
>n the brakes. "This is worse than Philadelphia. I'm sorry,"
.he said, realizing she'd nearly thrown him into the wind-
.hield.

"So am I," he answered. Their eyes met and held, and

suddenly they weren't talking about the influx of tourists any more.

Quinn looked away, trying to keep her eyes on the road her mind on her driving. The car suddenly felt too hot and stuffy for her, and she rolled down the window, bracing herself for whatever his look suggested he was about to do. But he remained silent, staring straight ahead again in the start-and stop journey out of town. The heat and the noise of idling engines, car horns and irritated voices surrounded them, making conversation impractical, had either of them wanted to talk. Quinn certainly didn't, and she was thankful that, for the moment, Adam seemed lost in his own thoughts. She only wanted to get back home, except that Adam would be there too. Lord, how she needed some peace in her life! She had merely exchanged one grief for another, her loneliness in Philadelphia for a renewed guilt about Adam Sauder here.

But her relief at Adam's silence was short-lived. He waited until they were back at the Tyler house, until she'd pulled the car into the yard and was ready to get out, until Daniel was jumping down the back porch steps to meet them.

Then he reached out and put his hand on her arm. "Quinn," he said quietly. "What did our baby look like?"

Chapter Six

Adam knew she wouldn't answer. Daniel was bounding up to the car, and she wouldn't have the time, but he still asked. The question was there between them; it had been since the first day, and he couldn't *not* ask it. Her eyes blinked with the pain he'd given her, just as he knew they would, but he'd still asked. She shook his hand off her arm and flung open the car door, remembering only when she'd gone a few steps that she had groceries to bring in. He tried to help her with the bags, but she wouldn't let him. Clearly, his question had reminded her of the time she'd had to make do without his help.

"We *will* talk about this, Quinn," he said out of Daniel's hearing, but she gave no indication that she heard him.

"Is it eating time, Adam?" Daniel wanted to know. "Is it?"

"Not yet," Adam said in German, watching all the while as Quinn hurried into the house. It struck him again that she wasn't well. She was too thin, even in her strange, baggy, men's-looking clothes. Perhaps she didn't wear dresses any-more.

He followed her into the house. She was on her knees, put-ting things into the refrigerator, when he came in. Mary and Anna watched both of them from the kitchen doorway, Mary fiddling with her glasses in her nervousness about keeping him apart from Quinn the way their father wanted.

"What did you say, Adam?" Daniel called as he ran up behind him.

"I said, not yet!"

"Not yet? This is a hungry time, Adam!" Daniel pulled on his brother's arm to get him to go in the direction of the food basket they'd brought and left sitting in a window in the kitchen. Adam suddenly smiled, because he could see the tell-tale smudges of strawberry jam on the corners of Daniel's mouth.

"What is this on your mouth then? I will be lucky if there is anything in Mom's basket left."

He let Daniel urge him toward the basket, then took it and him out of the house and onto the back porch to eat, leaving Anna and Mary to marvel over Quinn's refrigerator now that he was far enough away for them to relax their vigilance. He sat down on the steps in the warm sun, taking his hat off and putting it aside, trying not to smile as Daniel mimicked him exactly. He noted again that the lilac bushes needed to be sprayed, and he reached to pull at the wobbly top step. He would fix it before he left here. The step was dangerous, and he didn't want Quinn to fall.

He sighed heavily and glanced at Daniel. He was tired sud-denly, and the boy was waiting as patiently as he could man-age for his portion from the basket.

"Anna! Mary!" Adam called abruptly. They had lingered long enough with Quinn and her English refrigerator.

They came quickly, crowding around the basket and waiting while he bowed his head over the cheese, frizzed beef, bread, fried apple pies and biscuits and jam his mother had packed for them. He raised his head, aware that his sisters were more interested in him than in his offering thanks for their dinner. They were supposed to watch him, and he'd gone off into town with Quinn alone. Now they were looking for some sign of whatever it was they were supposed to monitor in him. He carefully lifted the four jars of lemon tea out of the basket and passed them around. There was an extra jar in the basket, cabbage juice his mother had sent to Quinn for her stomach troubles. He'd forgotten to give it to her. He could hear Quinn in the kitchen now, and he got up with it, leaving his chaperons uncertain and worried again as he took the jar inside.

Quinn looked around sharply as he came in the back door, her eyes wary. She had a pot of something in her hand, and she stirred it vigorously before she put it on the hot plate.

He set the jar on the counter. "Mom sent you this to help your stomach. It's cabbage juice. Drink some every day, she says. Three times a day. She will send you more when it's gone—" He broke off because she was looking at the jar so strangely.

"When did Lena give you this?"

"When? This morning. Why?"

"I just…wondered," she said.

"It isn't spoiled, Quinn."

"No, I didn't mean that," she said quickly, picking it up as if he'd just given her some rare and precious gift. "I was just…surprised." He thought for a moment that she was going to cry.

"Tell Lena that I—I thank her very much." She put the jar down again. "You won't forget to tell her?"

"I won't forget. Quinn?"

She turned away from him to stir the pot on the hot plate. "What?"

"I'm waiting for you to answer me."

She didn't pretend that she didn't know what he meant. "This isn't the time, Adam."

"It will have to do. Daniel and my sisters will be here as long as I am. I would have said what was on my mind in the car, but I didn't—"

She turned to look at him. "Didn't what?"

He stared at her, for once feeling detached, separated from her by his need to know about their baby. He struggled to stay that way. Yet all the while, some part of his mind insisted that he see how beautiful she still was. More beautiful than he remembered. She'd been a girl when he last saw her, and now, for all her thinness and her strangely cropped hair, she was a lovely woman. "I didn't want to give you any more pain. But I need to know this. I *need* to know. Do you understand?"

"I understand," she said quietly.

I always understand, she had said before, and that is what he saw when he looked into her sad eyes now. Did she?

He waited. She glanced toward Daniel and the girls outside on the porch. Daniel had the giggles, the kind that little boys invariably get over nothing and the kind that unfailingly annoys their older sisters.

"He...was very small," Quinn said, looking back at him. "Only five pounds. He came a few weeks early, but he was healthy. His hair—he had a lot of hair. It was dark like mine. The nurse in the nursery told me that he liked to be bundled up in a blanket, liked to be wrapped up tight and touching the side of the bassinet. He was too young for us to know what color his eyes would—"

"Didn't you know how important a child would be to me!" he interrupted, surprised at his sudden rise of anger. "How could you not know that? Children are everything to us. There is no purpose in our lives—not for a man or a woman—without children."

"I knew, Adam. Probably better than anyone who isn't one of you. Your way of life was mine as long as I could get away with it."

"And you still gave my child away!"

"Yes. I did what I thought was best."

"What *you* thought. You had no time, no need to ask the baby's father."

"My baby's father was lost to me."

"Your baby's father was in *hell*!" he hissed at her. He

made a sweeping motion with his arm, sending the jar of cabbage juice onto the floor. It spun and rolled, but it didn't break, and the giggling stopped abruptly on the back porch. Quinn stooped to pick up the jar. He stared down at the top of her head, wanting to reach out, to touch her shiny dark hair, to put his arms around her. He turned on his heel and went back outside.

He stayed on the porch as long as he could, until Quinn had gone back to her computer, but he gave no explanations to Anna and Mary and Daniel. What they had overheard and what they would tell Jacob, he had no idea. He didn't care.

Quinn stayed well out of his way. He didn't blame her for that, but he still listened to her activity, hoping she would come into the kitchen again. He sent Daniel out to the porch with a stack of boards that needed the nails hammered out, but he could do nothing about Anna and Mary. Quinn put them to work unpacking boxes of books in the hallway while she worked on the things Edison had brought her. He couldn't get to her without Anna and Mary knowing, and he couldn't tell anything about her state of mind; he could only hear her clicking on the keys of the computer.

He worked on, pulling off boards, patching up the damage to the walls with the clean, reusable boards Daniel brought him from his project on the porch. The work was not difficult, but he intended to do it well. He would restore as much of the original wood as he could—for her—because he knew she wanted it, needed something around her from her past, or at least the part of her past when she was happy. He didn't think she was happy now, he knew his questions weren't helping her to overcome it.

He raised his head. Anna and Mary were singing a hymn, not a hymn in the English sense, but an Amish one that was usually sung at weddings. It was called *Guter Geselle*, ''Good Friend.'' Quinn sang along with them; she had learned it when she was a little girl. Her voice was pure and disciplined, her execution of the erratic, chanting notes faultless. He could see her suddenly, standing in his backyard, earnestly singing that same song for him in the German she didn't understand.

My good friend, he thought in spite of himself.

Quinn, don't!

She had been that to him always, his good friend, and he closed his eyes against the pain of remembering. Everything happened for a reason. He'd been taught that all his life. But what was the reason behind this? What good did it do in God's overall plan for both of them to suffer so?

Quinn suddenly stopped singing, and he could hear her talking to Anna and Mary in the hallway, then going up the stairs.

He went to the kitchen doorway. "What did she say?" he asked in German.

Mary glanced at Anna before she answered. "She said she had to rest sometimes, and she'll be upstairs if we need to ask anything."

"She said I can run the vacuum cleaner," Anna put in, clearly pleased with the opportunity to use such a powerful forbidden convenience.

"If she has to rest, you don't run the vacuum cleaner until she comes down again," Adam said.

"But she said—"

"*I* said," he snapped. He cast a glance up the stairs, then retreated to the kitchen. For a brief moment he heard Quinn walking around overhead. He gave a short sigh and went back to work.

"You're hammering," Anna ventured through the doorway after a time. "She can't rest with you hammering."

"I'm getting paid to hammer," Adam said.

"I get paid to vacuum," she countered.

"You get paid to put away the things in the boxes and to clean the house. You have other things you can do until Quinn comes down again. I don't."

Anna pursed her lips to say more but didn't. She turned around and went back into the hallway. He could hear her voicing her complaints to Mary, who, not chosen for vacuuming, apparently was not impressed.

A man from the telephone company came shortly after Quinn had gone upstairs, and Adam intervened when Anna would have gone to tell her. He went himself, leaving the three of them standing in the front hall. He suspected from the lights he'd seen on Quinn's first night back that she'd taken her old bedroom, the room with windows he could see from his own room at home. The comfort and the anguish it had given him when their love was new, knowing that he could look out across the moonlit fields and see the place where she lay, as sleepless with longing as he was. And the comfort and the anguish it had given him when he'd crossed those same fields in the dark and hidden in the yard below, knowing that when he shined a forbidden flashlight on her window screen, she would come to him.

He walked quietly along the upstairs hall; she was in her old bedroom, as he'd thought. He reached up to knock lightly on the half-open door but didn't. He could see her plainly on the old-fashioned bed, curled up and sleeping under the quilt his mother had just given her, her shoes dropped carelessly on their sides on the floor. He could call her, knock as he'd intended, and she would wake, but he didn't do either. He stood watching her quiet breathing, realizing how much he'd once wanted this, to be in the same house with her, living, belonging together in all things, to legitimately have this privilege he was taking now, that of watching her in unguarded sleep.

She stirred, and he did knock, after all. She came awake immediately, and he worried for a moment that she might have been aware of how long he'd been standing there.

"There is a man from the telephone company who wants to know where to put the telephone," he said, and she sat up.

"I'll be right there."

"I can tell him where if you need to rest longer."

She worked hurriedly to get her feet into her shoes. "No. No, I'll do it."

Left with nothing else to offer her, he turned to go. But he stopped just outside the doorway.

"Quinn?" he said quietly because he knew that Anna and

Mary would be trying to listen. "Our...the baby. Don't you ever want to see him?"

She had her shoes on now, and she stood up. Her eyes met his calmly. "Every day of my life, Adam."

"*Have* you seen him? Since he was born?"

"No."

"Why not?"

"I can't."

"Can't or won't?"

"Adam, I—I don't know where he is." It wasn't entirely the truth, but it would have to do for now. She tried to get by him, but he caught her arm.

"You could find out."

"I don't want to find out."

"How could you do this thing, Quinn?"

Again she looked him unwaveringly in the eyes. "It's the price I had to pay."

His fingers tightened on her arm. "For what you did with me, you mean?" He couldn't call their loving a sin, even now. She had been so much a part of him that, in the years since he'd been with her, no lawful wife could take her place.

She didn't answer him, reaching to pull his fingers off her arm, her touch nervous and cold to him. She walked on toward the head of the stairs.

"Quinn," he called, and she looked back, her face pale and grave, her eyes still deadly calm. Whatever her reasons for doing what she'd done, he realized that she had come to terms with it. Far from being comforted by her acceptance, he felt more abandoned and alone than ever, and totally of no consequence. Why was it that *he* hadn't mattered in any of this? He suddenly didn't want her to be calm and accepting. He wanted her to be as anguished as he was. Then he could understand. Then he would know that he and his blind devotion had meant *something* to her.

Didn't she see what had happened to him? He wasn't Amish anymore. He had tried so hard, but he *wasn't Amish anymore!* He still lived by the rules, by the *Ordnung*, simply because he'd had no alternative. But their goals in life weren't his. Jacob had told him over and over. *"You must stay one of us."* He had stayed, but he had brought them only his indifference, his apathy in the guise of obedience. He had loved this woman, and he'd refused to pretend that it wasn't so, regardless of the pain and embarrassment it had caused his family. And yet, standing here now, he deliberately meant to hurt her. "I think you would have done better to let God give his own punishments. He would not have been so hard on us as you have been."

He regretted the remark instantly. "Quinn, I—"

"No," she said, holding her hands up as if to physically keep him away from her if she had to.

"Quinn, wait—"

But she didn't wait. She left him standing in the upstairs hallway. Alone. Always alone. He followed her to the head of the stairs, watching as she descended into the hallway. He hadn't wanted to make her run away from him. He had wanted things to stay easy between them, like this morning when he'd gotten her to retrieve the lost molding. He wasn't like her; he hadn't *always* understood. He hadn't understood at all, and that was all he wanted—to understand. Perhaps if he did, he could get on with his life.

He went down the stairs. He could hear Quinn and the telephone man talking in the kitchen, and a new emotion surfaced. Jealousy.

"I didn't think you'd remember me," the telephone man said.

"For heaven's sake, why not? We had classes together all through high school."

"Yeah, well, you've been gone a long time, Quinn. Welcome back, by the way."

"Thank you, Bobby. It's good to be home."

"So the great Thomas Wolfe wasn't right after all?"

Quinn laughed. "Not that I can tell," she said.

Adam stood in the hallway trying to follow the conversation. Thomas Wolfe. Thomas Wolfe. The name was familiar, but he couldn't remember why. He was so—*ignorant*, for all the work Quinn had done years ago to enlighten him, bringing him the books about her world, explaining things to him, teaching him. He still hated it, the not knowing what other people, "English" people, took for granted. It surprised him how much he hated it. No. It surprised him how much his ignorance mattered to him now that Quinn was back.

He forced himself to walk into the kitchen, and he immediately began hammering, careful not to look at Quinn, or Daniel and the girls, or this telephone man. He was glad to note—covertly—that if Quinn was impressed with the telephone man's expertise in worldly devices, in the installation of the modern convenience, it didn't show.

"Daniel," he said finally, "we don't get paid for you to stare at this telephone."

He set Daniel to working again, not missing the fact that Bobby grinned and winked at Quinn, as if what Adam had said was immensely funny and they had just shared a private joke at Adam's expense. He turned his back on the pair of them, working hard, intently, as he always did when he needed to shut the world out. But it wasn't really the world that he needed to escape. It was the people in it. The English with their telephones and their Kodak cameras and their amusement at people who chose to live Plain.

"Daniel!" he said sharply, because the boy was intent on watching the telephone man again.

"I think we'd better get out of the way," Quinn said, taking the girls away with her into another part of the house.

In a moment Adam could hear the vacuum cleaner start with enough roar and force to make Anna happy. He kept working. Hard. If he had no interruptions, he'd be finished in this house this afternoon. The patching of the walls would be done, and he'd have no reason to return until the new cabinets were made. Perhaps he would tell Holland Wakefield to send another man.

It was what he wanted, he decided. To be free of his obligation to Holland Wakefield so that he wouldn't have to see

Quinn again. He worked harder, pushing Daniel to get the boards he needed ready faster. By late afternoon there was nothing left to do but replace that found piece of molding Quinn's father had made. As he hammered it into place, he was suddenly aware of Quinn watching him. He hesitated a moment before he climbed down from the ladder, bracing himself for whatever he would see in her eyes.

He turned around. No anger, he thought in surprise. She was carefully inspecting the work he'd done, her face almost wistful.

"It looks fine, Adam," she said, moving around the room. "With a coat of paint, it'll look the way it used to." She finally gazed at him. "Do you know when I can expect the new cabinets?"

"Holland has already started one of the carpenters on them. They should be ready in a week or so."

She nodded and glanced around the room again. "It'll be nice to get the stove in."

"Quinn—" he began, unable to continue with inane conversation.

"Don't," she whispered, her eyes pleading. "Let's just be done with this, can't we?"

He wasn't certain precisely what she meant, and she moved to the counter to pick up her purse, glancing up once as the girls came into the kitchen.

"You've done a very good job for me," she said to them. "Both of you. If you need references for another job, you can give my name, all right? If your father asks, you can tell him that I'm well pleased."

She counted out the money to both of them, and Adam could feel how careful she was being not to look at him. He moved closer.

"Take Daniel and wait for me outside," he said to Anna in German, but she refused to do it, stubbornly standing her ground. He had escaped their surveillance once today, and she wasn't going to let it happen again. Jacob Sauder's was clearly the higher law. He pressed his lips together and began gathering up his tools.

"Anymore, if you have another spider, Quinn, I'll help you," Daniel told her.

She smiled. "Thank you, Daniel. You're just the person I'll call. Adam?"

He looked around at her, trying to keep his face neutral, his emotions detached, yet fully aware of the response her voice saying his name evoked in him.

"Tell your mother that I thank her for the cabbage juice."

"I've said that I will, Quinn," he responded more sharply than he had intended.

"Yes. So you did. I just…didn't want you to forget." She took a deep breath and looked at each of them. "Thank you all. I'd better get busy with Edison's files. You know the way out."

She turned and moved toward the front hall. Adam was standing between her and the doorway, and he didn't move. She came very close to him as she passed. He could smell her scent—soap and the sweet woman smell that was hers alone. He could almost but not quite feel the brush of her strange English clothes as she went by.

I want to touch you, he thought, and she glanced up into his eyes. For a moment he was afraid that he'd said it out loud.

"Should I pay you?" she asked. "Or will Holland do it? He didn't tell me."

"Holland pays me. Not you."

"Oh. Well." She gave a small shrug, her lips pursed as if she was about to say something else. Whatever it was, she didn't say it, escaping into the hallway. He could hear her going up the stairs instead of to her computer, and he finished gathering up his tools, checking the room one more time before he left to make sure everything was in order. There was no mess. No sawdust. No forgotten bent nails. He had no reason to say here. The job was finished.

Finished.

He picked up the carpenter's helper and led the way outside. There *was* still the wobbly step. He'd forgotten it until now, and he set the toolbox down. He inspected the step closely. It wasn't rotted, only loose. He carefully selected the nail he wanted and drove it through the top board and into the frame. Then another. And another. He tested the step to see if it was secure, letting Daniel bounce on it as a double check. Then he gathered up his tools and the carpenter's helper again and started out across the backyard, breathing in the fresh spring air, feeling the late sun still warm on his face. He looked around him. This was good land here, land that wanted to be cultivated and planted.

"Did you get the basket?" he suddenly asked his sisters.

"Yes, we got it," Anna said. "*You* have your mind too much elsewhere to remember things like baskets."

He walked on, oblivious to the insinuation in Anna's remark, savoring the late afternoon, the satisfying tiredness of a job well done. He glanced back once at the house. Quinn was standing in the upstairs window.

Chapter Seven

Quinn heard him before she saw him. He was whistling, and more to the point, he was whistling *alone*. There was no Daniel with him, no Anna or Mary. Illogically she'd been waiting all day for him to come back to the house. But, as the day wore on, she had finally given up. She had come to believe that she wouldn't see him again except at a distance, at some chance meeting in town or along the highway. She had even decided that that was for the best. He would never understand what she had done, and he would never forgive. And she had known that. She had come back here for no other reason than to get on with her life—with or without the burden of her guilt about Adam Sauder. She'd had the chance to talk with him, and they'd gotten nowhere. His feelings, and hers, were still unresolved, but there was nothing more she could do.

But now, here he was, strolling jauntily toward the house, and carrying a sapling tree with the roots wrapped tightly in a cloth sack. She moved to the kitchen window to watch him proceed along the narrow road that cut between her fallow field and his carefully planted one. Walking out onto the back porch as he came into the yard, she stood on the top step he'd repaired for her.

"Where is your shovel, Quinn?" he asked without prelude, his eyes flicking over her in a way that told her he appreciated the fact that she was a woman.

"I don't have a shovel."

He looked back in the direction from which he'd come, then set the tree down at his feet. "I'll have to go get one then."

"No, wait," she called after him. She went back into the house to get her car keys. "I've got an entrenching tool in the trunk. Maybe that will do."

"Entrenching tool?"

"It's like a shovel. I keep it in the trunk to shovel snow. It folds up. Soldiers carry them in their backpacks to dig foxholes and things like that—I got it at the army surplus store—I—" She broke off and tried not to smile. Adam was wearing that ask-a-simple-question look she'd seen thousands of times before whenever she'd bombarded him with "English" information he didn't particularly want. "Where are you going with that tree anyway?"

"I'm not going anywhere," he said, following her. "I'm here."

"Did I order a tree?"

"No. But you get a tree, even so."

"Oh," she said, unlocking the trunk. "Even so." She got the tool out. Adam took it out of her hands before she could unfold it.

"I can do it," he said. And he did so without difficulty. "Where do you want the tree?"

"Do I get to know what kind it is?"

"Apple."

"Apple," she repeated, looking into his solemn blue-gray eyes. She used to look into his eyes and see *her* there. Now she saw only the sorrow she'd given him.

"Four-in-one apple. I think you need a new one."

The look lengthened until finally they both glanced away.

"Yes," she said brightly—too brightly. "Mine seems to be gone. Well, if it's really mine, I'd like it planted close to where the other one stood. I know they grow well there."

He nodded and walked in that direction.

"This is a good place here," he said, pointing out a spot in the general vicinity of the old tree.

"Did you graft this one?" Quinn asked as he began to dig. The ground was soft from the rain, and he had no difficulty even with so small a shovel. She watched his blue shirt pull tightly across his back, his muscles bunching as he strained to move the dirt.

"Yes," he said, not looking at her. "Grandfather Beiler taught me," he added unnecessarily, as if he'd forgotten—no, as if he refused to acknowledge that she had had any part in his past.

"I remember," she said. Just as he remembered how much she had loved that tree. "Adam, you don't have to do this."

"Yes, I do. Grandfather Beiler grafted the other one. Your father bought it from him. We guarantee our trees." A simple and innocent explanation for so tender a gesture.

She smiled. "This is some guarantee. The old one was chain-sawed."

"Even so," he said again, still shoveling dirt.

"I'll get a bucket of water," she offered.

"Good. Do you have a folding bucket, too?"

"Very funny," she said, heading toward the house.

"I thought so," she thought he said. She looked back over her shoulder. He was still shoveling, and he was smiling.

She came back carrying a white enamel bucket full of water, walking carefully so as not to slosh the water on her shoes. She set the bucket down, waiting until he had the hole dug deep enough to suit him. He loosened the sack but didn't remove it, setting the tree gently into the hole so as not to disturb the dirt on the roots.

"Now," he said to Quinn, indicating that she should pour the water. She poured carefully around the tree so as not to collapse the sides of the hole, until Adam said "Enough."

She knelt down and began to help fill in the hole, using both hands to scoop the damp earth.

"You'll get dirty," Adam said, careful to keep his eyes away from hers.

"I don't care about that. I want to—"

He caught her wrist. "I'll do it."

She felt his touch as if it were an electrical current that passed between them.

"You don't want to be digging in the dirt." He still had her wrist, and he still tried to avoid her eyes. He finally took the chance, giving her a quick glance. Her eyes were waiting.

"Don't I?" she asked.

He smiled, but he didn't look away. "Always you ask too many questions."

She pressed her lips together, fighting down the need to ask him the thing she really wanted to know. *Why didn't you tell your family about the baby?* And why hadn't Lena and Jacob said anything to him yet about his earlier omission? Surely he wouldn't be back here if they had. Her eyes searched his for the answers, and he abruptly let go of her wrist. He didn't like that, she thought. He could feel her "wanting" again, and he didn't like it at all.

She stood up, moving back a few steps to give him room to work. She looked around her. The shadows were growing long, the air cool with the coming dusk. She heard the dinner bell ringing at the Sauder house, calling the family to their evening meal.

"I can finish that," she said. "Lena won't want you to come to supper late."

"I'm not going to supper," he said, standing up to gently tread on the soft mound of earth around the tree. "Keep this watered, Quinn. Especially when the weather turns hot and—"

"Why aren't you going to supper?" she interrupted.

He turned his head to look at her. This close to him she could see plainly the weathered lines in his face that weren't there when she'd left here so many years ago. "Because I'm here to talk to you."

She didn't ask about what. She said nothing, feeling her anxiety rise. So. It wasn't finished after all. And sooner or later he would ask *his* question.

Where is our baby, Quinn? Where is our baby?

"You're scared of me again," he observed, bending down to pick up the shovel. He folded it and reached to take her car keys out of her hand. "Round is for the trunk," he said, holding up the correct key, and she nodded.

"I'm not...afraid of you, Adam," she said. She followed him to the car to show him that she wasn't. "It's just..."

"Just what?" he asked when she didn't go on. "You can say whatever you think you have to say, Quinn, but I feel it—this fear in you. It makes me wonder what it is that scares you. And it makes me feel sorry to know that I put it there." He unlocked the trunk, brushed off the shovel and laid it inside.

"You didn't—I mean, it isn't there. I'm *not* afraid," she said as he slammed the trunk lid down.

"Then are you worried that you'll feel embarrassed if people see us together? Are you worried about them seeing me with you and knowing that I'm the one you ran around with? I make you ashamed, as if I was like the man at the flea market who didn't take a bath? If I do, I can go. I don't ever want to make you sorry to know me."

"Adam, no. I'm not ashamed to be seen with you."

"Then what are you, Quinn?"

She didn't answer him. She didn't know herself what she was.

"I *am* worried," she admitted finally.

"About what?"

"About you."

"Why?"

"Because...*because*, Adam! You know why! You can't work on my house and bring me trees. You can't let them think you've started up with me again."

"They will think what they think no matter what I do."

There was such resignation in his voice that she bowed her head rather than see it in his eyes, as well.

"Are you still my friend?" he asked quietly, and her eyes flew to his face. It was the last question in the world she expected.

"Are you?" he asked again when she didn't answer, his eyes searching hers.

"I am."

He smiled. "I am your friend, too."

"Adam, I don't want to do anything that will hurt you—" she began, but he wouldn't let her finish, holding up his hand to cut her off.

"Then don't," he said blithely. "You worry too much, Quinn. I'm not a boy now. I'm a man. And even when I was a boy, I was much stronger than you thought. I wasn't weak."

"I never thought you were."

"Didn't you?" he said evenly.

"No. I didn't."

"I would have taken care of you—and the baby—if you had given me a chance."

"I know that."

"You know that, and still it was you who would pick and choose for me. You still do it. Yesterday at the flea market you did it. I know what I want and what I don't want. I know what I can live with and what I can't. My sins are *mine*, Quinn, and you don't try to save me from them or from the consequences. Not anymore. Do you understand? Not ever."

With that, he walked off in the direction of the Sauder farm.

"Adam," she called after him. "Let me pay you for the tree." She wasn't sure he heard her, but then he waved his hand in refusal.

"It's nothing, Quinn," he said without looking around. She stood staring at his retreating back.

"Yes, it is," she whispered. "And you know it."

She went to bed early, and for all her agitation, she slept well. She woke up with the sunlight streaming in the bedroom window and with a feeling of dread, knowing that what she dreaded was *not* seeing Adam again. She showered and dressed quickly, then went about her work, trying not to listen for his step on the porch, his merry whistling across the yard. But she couldn't keep from it. She was waiting for him, just as she always had. As the sun set, she gave up again, only to have him knock at the back door. She should have been ashamed of how happy she was to see him.

"No tree?" she asked, and he smiled. How is it, she thought, looking at him now, that he's always so new to me? How is it that I look for every smile as if I'd never seen him smile before? She had never tired of seeing him or being with him. How could it still be like that after all that had happened? She had no answers, only questions, questions that he must surely see in her eyes.

But he wasn't the one who looked away, the one who'd grown so furtive. Today he was relentless about looking into her eyes. "Come outside," he said. "It's nice this evening. You're not busy with Edison's things, are you?"

"Yes—no—I'm almost finished—" She was rattling, and she knew it, because she wanted to be with him, and she shouldn't, and she was going to do it anyway.

"Then come out here. I would like to sit on your swing. Do you have lemonade made, Quinn?"

"Do I—?" she said incredulously. When she'd let herself imagine his coming to the house again, she hadn't imagined this particular inquiry. "Yes, I have lemonade made. I bought lemons yesterday."

He smiled again—not much, just a little bit of the old, teasing kind she recognized. "I saw them. That is why I asked. I thought if you were still the same, you wouldn't let them sit long."

"And if I didn't have lemonade and you were still the same, I suppose you'd ask me to make it," she said, coming out onto the porch just as he wanted.

"Yes," he said agreeably. He moved to sit on the swing, which faced the fallow field, taking his summer hat—straw with a black band—off and setting it aside. "You make better lemonade than Mom."

"That'll be the day," Quinn said.

"No, it's true. Mom wants to save sugar. You don't."

She looked at him doubtfully, not sure if she could accept that as a compliment or not. Somehow, it made her sound flagrantly thriftless. He raised both eyebrows in polite but mischievous solicitation. She couldn't keep from smiling in return.

"I'll be back in a minute."

She went inside and got two glasses down from the one usable cabinet in the kitchen, taking them to the refrigerator in the front hall to fill them with lemonade. How long had it been since she'd done this, shared lemonade and a porch swing with Adam Sauder?

She could hear the swing squeaking now and again as Adam idly let it move back and forth.

"The apple tree looks good," he said as she came back outside, his eyes lingering over her in a way that left her feeling flustered and unsure and intensely aware of herself. The look, as if everything about her pleased him, made her feel desirable and no less than beautiful and afraid that he'd suddenly see her flaws and realize that it wasn't true at all—all at the same time. "Lemonade doesn't bother your stomach?"

"No."

"Are you drinking the cabbage juice?"

She reached to hand him one of the glasses of lemonade, standing well away from him. She felt certain that he knew exactly the discomfiture he was causing. He knew, and he was going to do it anyway.

"Three times a day before meals. It's pretty good," she said.

"I have more instructions for you. You are to eat molasses mixed with peanut butter. It's supposed to build up your blood. If you do that, Mom promises you will be well soon."

"It's done me a lot of good just being here," Quinn said,

hoping it was true, hoping she hadn't simply swapped one misery for another.

He smiled again, then drank deeply from the glass, tilting his head back so that she could see the strong, muscular lines of his chin and neck. He really had been thirsty, and she took advantage of the opportunity to gaze at him. Until yesterday, she would have thought that she knew everything about his face, every line, every scar, but she didn't. He was changed, older, and yet he was still the same, enough so to make her remember all the things she shouldn't be remembering. Such a well-loved face, one she had held between her hands and shyly kissed, passionately kissed. He looked tired to her, tired of body and of soul, and she had the sudden urge to put her arms around him and tell him that everything would be all right.

"Do you want some more lemonade?" she asked instead.

"No," he said, turning the now almost-empty glass around and around in his hands, regarding it thoughtfully. He reached and moved his straw hat off the seat and dropped it onto the porch. "The lemonade—it's good, the way I thought." He held up the glass. "Sweet. And really cold." His eyes suddenly found hers, holding them with no hint of uneasiness. "Sometimes things aren't as good as what you remember. You will sit down?"

She hesitated. If she didn't sit with him, they would surely get into that same discussion about whether or not she was afraid of him. And she wasn't afraid! Not of him, at any rate, she'd decided. If she was afraid of anything, it was of herself, of some bad judgment on her part that would make things worse for him.

"They will think what they think no matter what I do," he'd said.

"The question is so hard?" he asked quietly.

"No, it's not hard." She had no difficulty with the question at all. It was the answer that was the problem: Yes, *yes*, she wanted to sit by him.

She sat down. She was still holding her own glass of lemonade, and she sipped from it awkwardly. There was no sense in trying to make herself believe this was only a casual visit between old childhood friends, and that she did not recognize him as anything else, that he was not a beautiful man to her. He *was* a beautiful man, not just his body, but his spirit, as well. Gentle. Kind and loving. And he had been her lover. Her first lover. She had known with him what she had never known with anyone else. And she'd refused to marry Jake because of it.

Their bodies were not touching, but for her, his proximity was nearly as potent as actual contact. She suddenly could find no place to look. If she glanced anywhere in his direction, she was aware only of his acute masculinity, of a body made strong by hard, physical work, a body once beloved by her beyond the point of reason. And if she let her eyes meet his, he would…everything. She stared out toward the fallow field.

"Tell me about Philadelphia," he said after a while.

"There's not much to tell. Everybody's in a hurry there. It's crowded. Nobody sends a neighbor cabbage juice."

"But you stayed a long time anyway." There was no challenge in his voice. It was a statement of fact, and she took it as such, one that required no comment from her. She hoped.

"It's a pretty dress you have on today," Adam offered. He still seemed to be completely at ease, as if he did this sort of thing every day. It suddenly occurred to her that perhaps he did. He was handsome, eligible; it was his duty to court someone, to sit on the porch swing with her and drink her lemonade.

But he hadn't married. Not yet.

She pushed the thought aside. "Thank you," she said, knowing that such a response was not necessary. Adam and his people didn't subscribe to what the "English" thought were the social graces. He said her dress was pretty because, to him, it was.

"I thought you had given up dresses and were always going to wear the mouse with the big feet on your shirts."

He was teasing her, and she laughed softly, amazed that he felt kindly enough toward her to do that. "No. The mouse is just...comfortable." She glanced at him. He was staring at her, his eyes traveling over her face.

How sweet it would be...she thought.

But she didn't let the idea complete itself. Nothing she did with him would be sweet, not really; it would cause more trouble, and she cared about him too much to give him any more grief than she already had.

"Sometimes you wore the purple dress, the one Daniel likes, in Philadelphia. To parties, he said."

"Yes."

"There were many...parties?"

"No, not many. Business gatherings mostly. I was never one for the party circuit."

"When you did go, did *he* take you?"

She forced her eyes to meet his. She could feel the tension in him, feel how close they were to another confrontation, and almost in spite of herself, she was deliberately obtuse. "Who?"

"This man you didn't marry."

She looked away. "Sometimes."

"He liked parties."

"What he liked was to make money. Parties, for him, were a way to do it."

"He made a lot of money then?"

"Yes. He enjoyed that—the way you enjoy carpentry."

He was looking out across the yard now, and he suddenly turned to her. "Will he soon come here after you?"

"No. Why would you think he'd do that?"

He folded his arms across his chest and set the swing to moving again. "I don't think it. I was only wondering."

"Wondering about what?" she asked, digging her heels into the porch to keep the swing still.

"About him. About why a man smart enough to make a lot of money at parties is stupid enough to let you go away from him."

"I...think we'd better talk about something else," she said, forcing a smile. "Tell me about the family."

"There's not much to tell. David is married. He and his wife have a baby coming. Eli will marry the first Thursday in November. Nobody seems to want to marry Anna. And Mary and Aaron and Daniel are too young to get married. It's all we Amish think about," he added. "Getting married." He was deliberately trying to annoy her now, and he was entirely successful at it.

"Then tell me about you," she said, determined not to let her annoyance show.

"Was there somebody I *didn't* marry, you mean?"

She smiled again, but it wasn't sincere. "Was there?" she said lightly. She regretted the question the moment she'd asked it.

"Yes," he said without hesitation. "Her name was Sarah. She was very...gentle. We would have had a fine farm and fine children."

"You should have married her."

"Don't tell me what I should have done, Quinn. No one can judge that but Sarah and me."

She sat there, staring straight ahead. Then, although she knew better, she allowed her eyes to graze his. Such beautiful eyes, pale blue-gray and filled with quiet sorrow. She would always feel his sadness, because his sadness was also hers. She shifted her position on the swing, and their knees touched. She had no strength, no desire to move away from him, but she did. She looked down, finding nothing to look at but his hand resting on his thigh.

"Quinn," he said quietly, and she looked up at him. His eyes were sad still, but she saw something else there, something intense and burning, something that made her knees weak and her belly warm. "I don't mean to be...unkind to you."

"You haven't been. You haven't been anything that I don't deserve." She tried to look away and couldn't.

"Yes, I have. Quinn, you are so beautiful still." His eyes

probed hers, looking for things she knew she didn't have. His voice had gone soft, loving, surrounding her, caressing her as surely as if he were actually touching her. It was the voice of the Adam she remembered.

She tried to get up off the swing, but he reached out to make her stay, his fingers strong and warm on the underside of her arm. He didn't seem to mind doing that, touching her, but it was nearly more than she could bear.

"I have things to do," she managed, her voice steady only because she willed it to be.

"No. I'm sorry, Quinn. I had no right to say that. It's true, but I won't make you uncomfortable. Don't go." He released her arm.

She gave a short sigh—and stayed where she was.

"Where are Daniel and your sisters?" she asked for something to say, something neutral that would get them on to safer ground, because she wanted to stay on the swing with him.

"At home."

"Aren't they supposed to come with you here?"

"Are you *still* worrying, Quinn?"

She sighed again. She wasn't doing well at all at establishing any kind of neutrality. "I guess so."

"Don't. Rest easy. Look around you. The sun is nearly gone. The evening is quiet and beautiful. You said it had done you good to come back here, but it won't last if you don't settle down and find peace."

She looked out over the yard. She could see the first star of the evening just above the horizon. "I wish I could do that. Find peace," she murmured wistfully. "Adam?"

"What?"

The swing rocked slowly back and forth, and she could feel him staring at her again, studying her in the shadows. She decided there was no point in trying to be neutral, no matter how painful the alternative. "Why didn't you tell Lena about the baby?"

He waited a long time before he answered, and for a moment she thought he wouldn't. "It was *my* sorrow, Quinn. And my joy. And it was your...shame. I didn't want to make it worse for you."

"It wouldn't have made things worse."

"Yes. It would. If you ever came back here—like now. To the family, you are worldly. What happened between you and me would have always been your fault."

"I didn't realize that you hadn't told Lena."

"I know that."

"Was she—is she very upset?" She wanted desperately to take Lena's gift of the cabbage juice as a sign of forgiveness, but she still had to ask, knowing that Lena would be kind to her regardless of her personal feelings. She met his eyes again, knowing, too, that he would tell her the truth but that she would see it in his eyes first.

"Yes, Quinn."

Her heart sank. "She must be very upset...now."

He made no reply to that, clearly understanding what she didn't say—that his mother would be upset because he was here with her. He suddenly drank the last of his lemonade and stood up.

"I can see you'll get no peace with me here," he said, setting the glass down on the porch railing. "Good night, Quinn. The lemonade was good."

She nearly called out to him when he stepped off the porch and crossed the backyard. She didn't want him to go.

Don't! Don't! she kept telling herself. *It's better this way.*

"Will you come back again?" she finally called, but he didn't hear her, and he didn't look back. She watched him until he was swallowed up by the twilight, finally putting her hands to her face in exhaustion. Her weariness was more mental than physical, and she knew that what Adam had said was true. She'd get no peace with him here. But she felt no peace with him gone, either.

If only she could...

If only. The lament of all unhappy humans. If only what? If only she hadn't come back here. If only she hadn't let Adam stay to work on the kitchen. If only she hadn't once loved him in the first place. And now there was nothing to do but wait, and for what, she had no idea. For the time to come when she'd wake up one fine morning and Adam Sauder wouldn't matter to her anymore?

But the waiting became excruciating. She could never quite suppress the intense feeling of anticipation she had, and every day it got worse. She kept expecting Adam to turn up in the evenings when his chores were done. But he didn't. And there was nothing she could do about it. Nothing she *should* do about it, except be both relieved and disappointed. She passed the time by getting the house into shape and supervising various workmen—the one who hooked up the washing machine and dryer, the one who installed the new range top in the kitchen, the one who painted the kitchen the soft yellow she wanted. She had the refrigerator moved from the front hallway to the kitchen, and Holland Wakefield came, with bad news about the rest of her cabinets. The cabinetmaker's wife was having surgery, and he wouldn't be working on them for several weeks. Unperturbed by the delay, Quinn asked Holland to recommend someone with a tractor she could hire to plow her field.

"Now, Quinn, you're not thinking of taking up farming, too, are you?" Holland teased.

"Just enough to get me a tomato or two," Quinn said. "Come July, I want a ripe, red tomato that's just picked and still hot from the sun. And a big fresh buttermilk biscuit with the butter oozing out the sides."

"Sounds good to me," Holland said. "There's an old man on the other side of town who'll do it. He can't farm much anymore, but he sure can plow. His wife can't hardly get him off that tractor of his. I think he makes just enough side money to keep her from selling it out from under him. I'm going right by there. Want me to tell him to come see you?"

"If you don't mind, Holland. He won't charge me an arm and a leg, will he?"

"Oh, hell, no, Quinn. He knew your dad. He wouldn't charge you anything that wasn't fair."

Holland was as good as his word. The old man came to see her—tractor, bib overalls and all—and his plowing rates were definitely reasonable. She put him to work on the fallow field, listening to the sound of his plowing from time to time as she worked at the computer, remembering when her father was alive and readying that same field for planting.

When she heard the tractor stop, she got up from the library desk to look out the window, but the old man hadn't finished. He'd merely paused to have a word with someone—Adam Sauder. She had no idea what they were talking about; she could tell only that the conversation was friendly because they both laughed. The old man went back to plowing, and Adam came toward the house.

She stopped at the mirror she'd hung over the living room mantel, brushing her hair into place with her fingers, shamelessly pinching her cheeks to put some color in them before she met Adam at the door.

He was all smiles when she answered his knock. His shirt-sleeves were rolled up, and he was more tanned than when he'd been there last. "It's good!" he said, looking back at the old man and the tractor.

"What's good?"

"You're getting the land plowed again. The ground is rich there. What will you plant?"

"Nothing," she said, coming out onto the porch. He looked so scandalized at that revelation that she nearly laughed.

"You have to plant *something*, Quinn. It's not too late yet for corn, tobacco seedlings—"

"Now what would I do with corn and tobacco?" she asked, teasing him shamelessly. He was a true farmer. It was incredible to him that she wouldn't do something with such good land. "I don't smoke, and I don't have any pigs or chickens."

"You will lease the land, then?"

She hadn't considered that. "You think anybody would want it?"

"It's late in the season, but yes, I think so."

"For what?"

"For what?" He shrugged. "I would have to look at it."

"Then look, and tell me. If I'm going to lease it, I'd like to say what it's good for."

"Come with me," he said, suddenly turning back to her when he was halfway down the steps. "You'll want to see up close, how the soil holds the rain and such. Come on," he insisted, but she stood there thinking how crazy their relationship had been since her return. They vacillated from the comfortable oneness they'd enjoyed all those years ago to outright animosity, and she was constantly off balance because she never knew which situation she'd find herself in.

The old man was just finishing the plowing, and she went back into the house to get him his money.

"You got some fine farmland there, missy," he yelled to her over the noise of the tractor. She nodded and handed him a check for the amount she owed him. She stepped back from the tractor, giving him a small wave as he rode out of the yard.

Adam was waiting for her at the edge of the field. "Come on," he called again. "This is good! You have to see!"

She smiled and walked in his direction.

"Are you sure this land can be leased?" she asked when she reached him. "It hasn't been prepared. It hasn't been limed and harrowed."

He sat down on the ground and began taking off his shoes. "It's still good to play with."

"To play with?"

"If he can spare the time, a man sometimes likes to see how good a farmer he is. Not with the land he needs to survive, but with something extra like this. Just to see. It's like...a little showing off. Just enough to make him feel good, to make the others talk about what a good man he is at growing things, but not enough to offend. You see?"

"I see. You want to make the troops go 'Ah.'"

He glanced at her, and she realized he didn't understand her analogy. She let it go.

"You come with me now," he said. "Take off your shoes."

"No, thank you," she demurred. "You walk the field barefoot. I'll wait here."

"You used to like walking in new plowing without your shoes. But I forget how English you are now—a big city woman who keeps her shoes *on*."

"I don't happen to like walking barefoot in the mud," she insisted.

"Don't you?" There was the barest hint of a smile at the corners of his mouth.

"No, I don't. I was always afraid of stepping on earthworms."

"Then why did you do it so many times?"

To be with you, she thought, but she didn't say it.

"Come walk with me, Quinn. Who will see you? Your friends from Philadelphia? If they come, I will tell them you can't know about land with your shoes on. The Amish are famous for farming, so your city friends would believe me."

"I'm sure they would," she said, gazing at the newly turned ground. She tried not to smile; she wanted to pretend she was young and happy, earthworms or not.

"Come on, then. Before it gets dark."

She looked up at the sun and laughed. It was barely past noon. She slipped off the red canvas espadrilles she was wearing and wiggled her toes, stepping boldly onto the raw ground. The earth between her toes was soft and damp and wonderful and without earthworms as yet; the sun was warm on the top of her head. She took a few experimental steps. "Ah, Scarlett O'Hara, eat your heart out."

Adam was grinning from ear to ear.

"What?" she asked.

He shook his head.

"*What?*" she insisted.

"Well, for once I know what you're talking about. You gave me that book to read. *Gone with the Wind*. Scarlett

O'Hara loved the red soil of Georgia—but not more tha[n]
Quinn Tyler loves *this*. Come on,'' he said, holding his han[d]
out. She took it without hesitation, her small hand lost in his
his fingers rough and warm around hers. Barefoot, they walke[d]
the plowed ground together, the way they would have whe[n]
they were children, lost in the joy of such a simple pleasur[e]
and lost in the joy of being with each other.

A noisy flock of crows flew overhead. ''You remembe[r]
Gone with the Wind after all this time?'' she asked, lookin[g]
to watch the birds disappear into the treetops on the far sid[e]
of the field.

He glanced at her. ''It's not hard. My head is not so full o[f]
books as yours.''

''Well, you've got a lot more up there besides Englis[h]
books—all the things you know about living and working th[e]
land, for instance.'' She paused. ''I...I probably shouldn'[t]
have done that—brought you those books to read.''

''Why not?'' he asked, stopping to look her directly in th[e]
eyes.

''It only made you unhappy.'' She held his gaze for a mo[-]
ment, then started walking again.

''Not unhappy, Quinn. For me, the books were bread to [a]
man dying of hunger. I needed to know about things ther[e,]
about places and history and the stories in books. I was won[-]
dering, who is the Thomas Wolfe you and the telephone ma[n]
talked about?''

''A writer. He said you can't go home again, or somethin[g]
like that.'' She could feel him digesting this information a[s]
they walked. He had always had such a fine, quick mind, an[d]
rightly or wrongly, it had always given her pleasure to tell hi[m]
about whatever he'd wanted to know.

''That depends, I think,'' he said. He looked into her eye[s]
again, and this time she held his gaze.

''On what?''

''On if you're looking for yesterday or tomorrow.'' Cha[r-]
acteristically, he made his profound announcement an[d]
jumped to another subject. ''This is good land,'' he sai[d]

clearly pleased with what the walk was telling him. "You can grow anything here. But for now, this late, corn will be best. The ground will have to be sterilized with steam for tobacco."

"It wouldn't be worth the trouble this late, would it?"

"It depends on how much the farmer wants it. Tobacco is money."

Quinn suddenly remembered herself. She was standing in the middle of a field, hand in hand with Adam Sauder. True, he seemed much more in control of his feelings than she, and their being together was not nearly so distracting for him, but if someone should see them here...

They were no longer innocent children, regardless of how much she wished it. She couldn't turn back time any more than she could be Amish.

He stood beside her, quiet and still, but he knew. She could feel the anger in him. "Now what is it?" he asked.

"You know what—"

"Yes. I know what. Nobody knows better than me!"

She tried to pull her hand free of his, but he wouldn't let go, his strong fingers clamping down hard on hers as he tried to keep her close to him.

"Don't. Don't run away from me, Quinn. Not if you—"

He suddenly let go and stepped back from her. "I am being a fool."

"Adam," she said, but he walked away from her. "Adam!"

She'd hurt his feelings, and she hadn't meant to do that. She was *not* ashamed of him or anything that had happened with him, but she couldn't seem to convince him of that. She hurried to catch up, grabbing him by the arm to make him stop. He shook her hand off with such vehemence that she recoiled as if he'd struck her.

"Adam, I didn't mean anything—"

"That's the trouble with you, Quinn. You don't *mean* anything."

"I don't deserve that!"

"And I don't deserve—" He broke off and turned away from her, looking out toward his own land. "Sometimes, when

I'm here, it's like it used to be. And I keep forgetting that you don't want anything that has to do with us.'' He looked back at her. ''Can't you see this is killing me?''

''Then why do you keep coming back?'' she cried. ''Why don't you stay away? For both our sakes?''

He gave a short laugh, shaking his head as if he couldn't believe her stupidity. He started walking again, then abruptly turned back to her. ''You want to know why I come here? I'll tell you then. I'll give you the same answer I would have given you when I was twenty-one. Or sixteen. Or ten. I'll give you the answer that will make you laugh.'' He paused, seeming to gather up his courage to say it. ''I love you, Quinn Tyler. And you know that.'' He stared at her, as if he expected some response, and when none came, he stalked away toward where he'd left his high top farmer's shoes sitting in the grass.

Stunned, she followed him. He was putting on his shoes, and she tried to make him look at her. ''Adam, please.''

''It's funny, isn't it?'' he said, but he kept putting on his shoes and avoiding her eyes. ''*I* laugh, all the time. My mother, my father—they laugh. Even now they stay up late in the night talking, it's so funny to them. Now you can laugh, too. You and your damned English friends.''

''Adam!'' she cried, flinging herself on him when he got up, her arms wrapped tightly around his shoulders. ''Don't! Don't!'' She pressed her face into the side of his neck, trying to take his pain away by sheer force of will. He was hurting so, and she couldn't bear it.

He stood as if he were made of stone, rigid and separate from her. She wanted him to put his arms around her. She was crying; she could feel the tears she never wanted him to see streaming from her eyes, taste them as they ran down over her lips. She wanted him to press her close to him, to hold her the way he used to. It was true. It was the same between them. Nothing had changed. She still belonged to him, and she was glad, so shamefully glad, that he hadn't married.

His hands reached up and clamped down hard on her shoulders. She thought that he would kiss her; she knew how badly he wanted to. He was trembling, and she leaned into him, her mouth close to his, her lips parting. But he held her roughly away from him.

"I want you, Quinn," he said, his breathing rapid and harsh. "Can you feel how much I want you? You don't understand at all, do you? There is more to us than *this*!" He let her go then, leaving her on the ground on her knees, leaving her with nothing but the growing realization that eleven years ago she had made the best decision she could for him—and it had been wrong.

Chapter Eight

The spring rains came in earnest. Quinn stood by the upstairs bedroom window, staring at the wet countryside, trying to remember a line of poetry. It was something about the sound of rain, coming as gently, as quietly, as a woman's voice. But this was a farmer's rain, steady and warm and soaking, the kind that made tender seedlings take root and grow. Her gaze shifted to the small garden plot she'd marked off close to the house, to the two rows of tomato plants drenched and drooping in the afternoon drizzle. She had planted each one the way her father had taught her, working the ground until the dirt was soft and fine and free of weeds, digging each hole and mixing the fertilizer into the soil with her bare hands before she set the plant. She held her hands out in front of her now. Her fingernails were ragged and broken, nothing like an accountant's hands—which was just as well. She was nothing like an accountant.

She looked out across the field toward the Sauder place, her eye catching some movement along the fencing nearest her property. She strained to see but could tell only that the walker in this wet weather was Amish.

She didn't hesitate, hurrying downstairs to get her yellow rain poncho off the peg by the kitchen door. She put it on, on her way out, knowing that, wearing it, she was nothing if not conspicuous. Her mind was already at work looking for some excuse—she was going the long way to the mailbox, she was out for a walk—anything to explain her presence on the edge of Sauder land if the person happened not to be Adam.

But she had no need for explanations. Whoever was on the other side of the fence saw her well in advance and bolted—Daniel, she suddenly realized.

"Daniel!" she called after him. She knew he heard her, but he didn't answer, stopping only once to turn and look at her before he disappeared into a grove of willows.

She stood staring in the direction he'd gone. Why had he run from her? Daniel had no reason to, or none she could imagine. If she expected anyone to run at the sight of her, it was Adam. He had said he still loved her, and now, clearly, he must be ashamed he'd said it. She hadn't seen him since. She'd kept a lonely vigil at the windows that faced the Sauder farm, and she'd seen no one near her property until today.

And Daniel had run away from her.

She needed groceries; she was feeling better physically, and she was going to heed Lena's advice about the peanut butter and molasses. She went back into the house to get her car keys and purse.

She didn't want to go into town, knowing that, rain or not, the tourist trade would likely be booming. Instead she headed for a little Amish community store a few miles away.

She met a number of Amish buggies on the road, all of them moving slowly on the rain-slick pavement. She peeked at each driver as she passed, and she knew perfectly well that she wasn't looking merely for someone familiar. She was looking for Adam Sauder.

Something was wrong. It had to be. If Adam still loved her, he'd want to see her, if for nothing more than to make sure she was all right. She knew that; after all her chief concern was, was *he* all right? She was never going to forget the look on his face when he'd told her he still loved her, and she'd only stood there.

Oh, Adam.

The grocery store was rimmed only by Amish buggies, the horses standing forlornly in the rain. She parked as close as she could without crowding any of the vehicles, smiling a bit at one of the buggies that clearly belonged to a teenage boy, one who was in his wild time of "running around" before he joined the church and became a staid member of the Amish community. The buggy had more rearview mirrors than its driver could possibly use and a bunch of vivid blue-green peacock feathers dangling just inside the door. She was a bit startled to read the bumper sticker that had been carefully placed in the middle of the big triangular reflector on the back. Feel The Thrill Again and Again and Again, it proclaimed. Only when she was closer did she realize that it had to do with fishing. I Support Catch and Release, it further declared in smaller letters. She laughed and ran the rest of the distance from her car to the porch to get in out of the rain.

The porch, which boasted soft drink and ice machines, was crowded with families waiting for a break in the weather, the women patient, the children eating bags of corn and potato snacks, the men talking and laughing as men caught with a little time on their hands always did. Quinn could pick up a few words of the local German dialect—*rain, weather, horses*—but then the conversation abruptly stopped. She was suddenly ringed in stares and silence. She went into the store, hearing the silence change to a quiet murmuring behind her. The man who ran the store regarded her with the same silence—not with hostility or malice precisely, but with an attitude Quinn would have described, for lack of a better word, as incredulous. The man's wife, who had been sweeping the aisles between the shelves when Quinn entered, stopped to stare, as well. Enduring their scrutiny, it occurred to Quinn that she must be experiencing something akin to what Adam felt that day on the street corner while he waited for her to pick him up. She tried to effect the same dignity he had displayed, selecting the items she wanted as quickly as she could without having to ask where anything was. The things she couldn't immediately find, she let go. She knew that "English" people came in here all the time, and whatever had precipitated the situation she now found herself in, it wasn't her non-Amishness.

The proprietor had a long gray beard, but his hair was still dark and thinning on top. He said nothing as he counted up what she owed, and Quinn met his eyes without reticence when she handed him the money. The front door opened, and a few of the men who had been standing on the porch came back inside. She took her change and the box the proprietor had put her groceries into and moved carefully among them to get outside, feeling their complete attention all the way to the door. Before she could get to her car, she had to wait for a young bearded Amishman to turn his horse and buggy around, his small children peeping at her out the side window as the buggy went by.

She didn't go home. She drove into town after all, straight to Edison Clark's office. His receptionist was new to her, a quietly efficient older woman, who advised Quinn that Edison would be in court until three. But Quinn didn't leave. She waited, sitting in a leather wing chair by the front window and turning the pages of magazines she never really saw. And all the while, she could feel the receptionist's quiet concern for one of Edison's potential clients, one who was so obviously in distress.

Shortly after three, the receptionist excused herself to go to the post office, discreetly locking Edison's inner-office door in the event Quinn turned out to be some sort of pilferer. Quinn continued to wait, relieved to be alone for the moment. She caught sight of Edison coming from across the street, and she suddenly had misgivings about what she wanted from him, misgivings that lasted until he came in.

"Well! This is a surprise," he boomed. "Didn't I bring you enough work to keep you busy? Where's Margaret?"

She smiled, or tried to. "If that's your receptionist, she's gone to the post office. Edison, I—" She broke off and pressed her lips together, certain she was going to make a fool of herself and cry. Not that she hadn't cried in front of Edison before. But she had no real reason for feeling the way she was feeling now, and she didn't want to try to explain it.

"What's wrong?" he asked, cutting short the pleasantries.

"I don't know. I want you to find out for me."

He looked at her thoughtfully. "Go on."

"It's—it's Adam."

"Quinn, Quinn," he said, shaking his head in concern.

"I want to know if he's all right, Edison."

"Is there any reason he shouldn't be?"

"No."

"Then is there any reason you think he isn't?"

She didn't answer immediately. She looked into Edison's eyes and decided how much she wanted to tell him. "He's...been coming to the house."

"To work on the kitchen," Edison supplied.

"Since the work on the kitchen," Quinn corrected, refusing to look away from her friend's intent stare.

"I see. And?"

"And nothing, really. He came by a few times. He brought me a new apple tree, I gave him lemonade, and I walked a plowed field with him. But if somebody saw us, they might have gotten the wrong idea about...things."

"Yes, they might. *If* they saw you. And *if* the 'they' you're worried about happened to be old Jacob or a bishop or somebody like that. Is that what happened?"

"I don't know."

"Then what did happen?"

"I haven't seen him for days, and—"

"You were expecting to, I take it."

"Yes—no."

"Now, an answer like that, Quinn, can't mean anything but

trouble," he said, poking the air in her direction with his fore-finger.

"Maybe so, but it's the only answer I've got."

Edison sat down on the edge of Margaret's desk, his arms folded over his chest. "And?" he said again.

"I went to the Amish grocery store to get some things. Everyone there was so...quiet. The place was crowded, and everyone just stopped talking when I came in. It wasn't be-cause I was English, Edison. It was because I was *me*. I want you to find out if something's happened."

"I told you how close Adam's been to getting himself shunned."

"I know you did. I want to know if it's happened."

"Well, I guess I can find out for you. I've got to go out to see one of the bishops tomorrow about some deeds. I think he'll tell me if I ask."

"Good," Quinn said, giving a brief sigh.

"Quinn. Is there a reason for Adam to be shunned?"

Again she met Edison's eyes. "No," she said evenly. The desire, the passion that had risen between them had been more hers than his. Surely Adam couldn't be blamed for her behav-ior.

"Then it'll be all the harder for him."

"What do you mean?"

"The frame of mind Adam Sauder's been in, all it's going to take is somebody accusing him of something he hasn't done."

"I don't understand," Quinn said when he didn't go on.

"I don't think he's Amish anymore, Quinn. He hasn't been for years, really. He's stayed, and he's gone through the mo-tions, but out of respect for old Jacob, I think, not because he still believes."

"No," Quinn protested. She had suspected that possibility herself, but it was completely unacceptable to her. "He has to believe, Edison. He *has* to."

"Honey, I know you sacrificed a lot for him to stay Amish, but you did it without asking him. I told you what I thought about it then, and I haven't changed my mind. Unless you're sitting on the bench, you've got no business trying to be the judge of what's best for somebody else—and even then it's iffy. I've learned that in thirty-some years of practicing the law if I haven't learned anything else. But I can see this thing's worrying you, and I'll do what I can to find out."

"You'll call me as soon as you know?"

"Yes, I'll call you. Or I'll come by. Whatever I find out, I'm not going to sit on it."

"Edison, thank you."

"Don't thank me yet, Quinn. I may be bringing you more information than you want to know."

She gave him a small smile and left the office, stepping once again into the rain. Perhaps the information Edison brought her would be painful, but whatever was happening in the Amish community, knowing was far better than imagining. She sighed as she walked to her car, realizing for the first time what her disappearance eleven years ago and the subsequent *not* knowing must have done to Adam.

He'd been in hell—his own words—and she'd put him there, when she'd wanted only to protect him. You can't judge what's best for somebody else, Edison had said. Certainly, it was a lesson neither she nor old Jacob had learned.

When she arrived home, Holland Wakefield was just backing his truck out of the driveway. Quinn rolled down her car window to talk to him.

"You going to be home the rest of the afternoon, Quinn?"

"Yes, I'll be here."

"Good. We got your kitchen cabinets ready. Some of my boys got rained out today, and I thought I'd have them come on out here and get as much done as they could. Ain't no use in having them sit around with time on their hands. That okay?"

"Fine, Holland." She was almost certain Adam wasn't one of the "boys," but she didn't ask.

"They'll be here in a little while then." He gave her a wave and backed the rest of the way out.

Quinn carried her groceries inside, taking the time to put them away and eat, appetite or not, before the workmen came. If the truth be told, she was glad to have someone in the house for the afternoon. She had too much she *didn't* want to think about, and she didn't want to be alone.

However, she soon realized that solitude would have been better. The sound of hammering in the kitchen only served to remind her of Adam, and one of Holland's men considered himself a country-western singer. His voice wasn't bad, really, but his choice of sad, hurting songs left Quinn ready to scream. She didn't want to hear about love that still burned no matter what happened or how much time passed. When she couldn't sit staring at the computer screen any longer, she went upstairs to stand by the windows that faced the Sauder farm. In the distance she saw three Amish buggies coming down the secondary road. All three of them turned in at the Sauders'.

The telephone rang downstairs, and she ran to answer it. It was a timid-sounding young woman who wanted to sell a photograph package that would include Quinn and her entire family with a special rate for children under three.

"No, thank you," Quinn said, abruptly hanging up the receiver. She glanced briefly around the kitchen. The men were hard at work, including the singer. They would easily finish the work today, she thought. And if nothing else worthwhile came out of her return home, this part of the house would be in good shape again. She looked back at the telephone.

Call me, Edison! she thought. Logically, she didn't expect him to drop everything and go find out about Adam, but her persistent feeling that something was wrong had little to do with logic.

She suddenly realized that Edison wouldn't be calling her today. He had said he'd see the bishop tomorrow. She was agonizing for nothing. She might even be worrying for nothing. Everything *could* be all right with Adam—except for the fist of anxiety she had in the pit of her stomach. She simply couldn't get rid of it, no matter what she tried. And she tried everything—a long walk after the workmen left, evening television, a book she'd been meaning to read. Nothing she did broke through her worry. It was simply there, real and nearly tangible, she felt it so acutely.

She stayed up until nearly midnight, finally going to bed with a glass of warm milk and the grim determination not to anticipate the worst. She lay for a time in the darkness. Then, unaccountably, she got up from her bed to turn on a lamp, sleeping the rest of the night with it on in case Adam needed to see her lights from across the field, needed to know she was there.

Edison came by the house early, finding her sitting on the back steps watching the sunrise and drinking coffee, which she shouldn't have been drinking with the stress she'd been putting on her delicate stomach. The morning was clear and fresh and breezy, and, as usual, Edison looked like anything but a lawyer. He was wearing "brier pants" with long leather patches from thigh to ankle that hunters wore to protect their legs in the underbrush. The porch was still damp from yesterday's rain, but he sat down beside her anyway.

"You're going to get your rump wet," she said.

"So are you."

"I'm sitting on the *Intelligencer-Journal*."

"I'm wearing my L.L. Bean waterproof hunting britches," he countered.

She smiled, and he gave her a fatherly pat on the head. He was being kind, and she braced herself for whatever he would tell her.

"I thought I'd find you up. You got any more of that?" he asked, motioning toward her cup.

"Yes," she said. She made an attempt to get up, but he held up his hands.

"Sit still. I can get it. I'd rather talk out here anyway. I don't get much chance to see the sun come up."

In a moment Quinn could hear him rattling cups in the kitchen.

"Do you need any help?" she called.

"No, I've got it." He returned and sat down beside her. He nodded toward the vivid orange and red and gold in the eastern sky.

"You know, if there's a sin in the world, it's not taking the time to appreciate beauty like that."

"Yes," Quinn said. Now that he was finally here, she didn't press him. Aside from his kindness, the fact that he'd come out this early suggested that something was indeed happening with Adam. "I finished your financial reports. You can take them back with you."

He nodded, then sipped his coffee. "You think we've beaten around the bush long enough now?"

She managed a small smile. "Yes. I do. Have you seen the bishop, or is it too early?"

"Well, you've got to get up early if you want to see a bishop when he's an Amish farmer. You've got to catch him between the milking and his breakfast, so you get invited to breakfast, too. You know what I had to eat? Eggs. Cornmeal mush. Liverwurst. Ham. Oatmeal. Fried potatoes. Biscuits with apple butter. That's what I need the coffee for. I made a pig of myself, and now I need to wash it all down."

"I thought we weren't going to beat around the bush anymore," Quinn said before he could go on rhapsodizing about food. "What did the bishop say?"

"It's what you thought, Quinn." Edison looked out toward her small garden. "You planting tomatoes?"

"Edison!" she said in exasperation. "I'm scared enough of what you're going to tell me. Will you just get on with it?"

"All right, take it easy, honey. It's this. Adam was refused communion at their last Sunday worship. If he'd repented and made a public confession before the church, it would have been all over. You know the Amish believe in forgiveness, in accepting anyone who's strayed, back into the flock if they show they want it. But he walked out. He wouldn't do it."

"He's being shunned, then," Quinn said, surprised to find that she'd been holding her breath.

"Yes."

"What is he accused of?"

"Being...involved with you."

"How involved?"

"You know how involved, Quinn."

"He's not my lover, Edison." She abruptly stood up. "He can't confess to something he hasn't done. I'm going to have to see Jacob."

"I wouldn't do that, Quinn."

"I told you, Edison, Adam isn't guilty of anything!"

"Then it's up to him to say so, not you. Now, if you think you're going to set Jacob Sauder and a bunch of Amish bishops straight about anything, then you've either been away too long or you're not as savvy about living Amish as I thought. You *cannot* interfere, you understand me?"

"Edison—"

"Not if you care about Adam Sauder. This is his problem. Not yours. And you keep out of it."

"They're shunning him, Edison!"

"Quinn, he knew what he was doing in coming to this house. And he knows what to do to get unshunned—if he wants to do it. He can confess to having the *will* to sin. He can repent of that. As it is, the bishop tells me he won't say anything one way or the other. Not a word."

"He said no matter what he did, they'd believe whatever they wanted to believe."

"My feeling is, he didn't give them much choice."

"He'll lose everything. All his property will be sold," she said, unable to keep from enumerating what would happen to him.

"Yes."

"No one Amish will talk to him, sell him anything, eat with him. Jacob won't have to do anything for him he'd do for David and his other sons—no land, no inheritance. He'll live in the house, but he'll be dead to them. They'll all turn away from him. Even little Daniel can't have anything to do with him."

"Yes. That's the way it'll be."

"How will he stand it, Edison?"

Edison looked at her for a moment before he answered. "The truth is, honey, I think he's been through worse."

Had he?

"My sins are my sins."

The phrase echoed through her head. She suddenly realized that Adam had known even then that he would precipitate this.

Adam, Adam, what are you doing!

"Quinn, I mean what I say. If you care about Adam, you'll stay out of it. If you interfere, believe me, he won't thank you for it."

She believed him. Adam had said as much himself.

"You don't try to save me—not anymore. Not ever."

"Edison?"

He looked at her over the rim of his coffee cup.

"It was all for nothing, wasn't it?"

He sighed. "Quinn, I don't know. I'm pretty much of a fatalist myself. Things happen the way they happen, and we mortals just have to do the best we can."

The best we can. She thought about that after Edison had gone. She had no "best" anymore. She'd used it all up eleven years ago.

"Are you worrying again, Quinn?"

Yes, she was worrying. Adam had given her no alternative. In her mind's eye she saw the Sauder farm. Where would Adam be? In the fields? No, that wouldn't be likely. His father and brothers wouldn't be allowed to accept his help in running the farm. Perhaps he wasn't even there anymore. Perhaps he'd moved out rather than suffer the ostracism of shunning. In any case, he'd have to get a job somewhere, perhaps as a hired hand with one of the Mennonite farmers or with Holland Wakefield. That thought made her feel a little better. Adam was a good carpenter. Holland would be glad to have him on a permanent basis.

Adam!

She made herself work. Work was the cure for everything. She braved the trip into town, fighting the tour buses to get to the hardware store to buy a hand cultivator for her small garden and the spray she needed for the blight on the lilac bushes. She worked outside for the rest of the day, and, when it was dark, she showered and had her supper in the almost new kitchen. Then she began working on a new stack of financial reports Edison had left for her. Edison had lived in this area long enough to believe in the work cure, too.

The evening was warm. She had left the house open, and she could hear the peaceful night sounds of crickets and frogs and an occasional passing car. Once she heard a number of Amish buggies, but she didn't get up from the computer to see where they were going. She knew where they were going—the Sauder farm. She turned on the radio, finding a station that played the old fifties and sixties hits.

Shortly after nine, someone knocked on the front door. She stood up and walked into the hallway, knowing she was visible to whoever waited on the porch. She could see the silhouette of a man through the screen, and she hesitated.

"Quinn Tyler," the man said.

"Yes?" She took a few steps closer.

"It's David Sauder."

She walked rapidly to the door, unlatched the hook and held the screen open. "Come in," she said, standing back to give him room.

He stood stubbornly where he was. "No. I will not come into your house."

"Suit yourself," she said. She remembered him well, and he could stand anywhere he pleased. She only wanted to know what had brought him here. "What's wrong?"

He wasn't a tall man, and they stood nearly eye to eye. He had always seen her as a danger to Adam, and in that, perhaps he had been right. He stared back at her now, his eyes hidden behind the thick lenses of his glasses, his lips pressed into a hard line. Clearly, being here was distasteful to him.

"David, what's wrong?"

"I don't come of my own choosing," he said finally.

"Fine. I can see that. You don't like me, but you need something. Are you going to tell me, or do I have to guess?"

"It's not *me* who needs anything from you, Quinn Tyler. My mother has sent me. I come for her—"

"Why?" Quinn interrupted.

"She wants you to come to the house."

"You mean now?"

He turned away and stepped off the porch.

"David? Is something wrong with Lena?"

"Not with her," he said, walking rapidly away toward the Sauder farm. Quinn rushed out the door and followed him, trying not to stumble in the dark. David, like Adam, was in prime physical condition, and it was all she could do to keep up.

"With Adam? David, is something wrong with Adam?"

"Don't ask me these questions, Quinn Tyler. I came here because my mother asked. That is *all* I will do."

Chapter Nine

The stars were out, but there was no moon. She followed David Sauder along the dirt road between the cornfields, and she didn't try to keep up any longer. He was more accustomed to getting about in the dark than she was, and she had a stitch in her side from hurrying. She was sure, too, that David wouldn't let her come any closer to him than she already was, and that, whatever had happened, he held her entirely to blame.

She stepped into a hole in the dark, and she stumbled briefly, but she didn't fall. David strode on ahead of her. She had been right about the Amish buggies she'd heard earlier being en route to the Sauder house. As she got closer, she could make out a row of them parked at the edge of the field. But she could see no one around, hear nothing but the crickets and frogs and a quiet whirring sound she identified as the windmill behind the barn. There were no lights in any of the windows on this side of the house.

"Wait here," David said over his shoulder when they

reached the main yard. She waited, standing under the trees at the edge of the slate path to the back door. The wind rattled the new leaves overhead, and she shivered, not with coldness so much as with anticipation. One of the dogs, a short-haired mongrel, approached her warily. She didn't think David would have left her to the mercy of some vicious canine protector of the Sauder property, but she was by no means certain.

"Well, come here," she said softly, extending her fist for the dog to sniff. "And stop worrying." The dog immediately began to fawn around her legs, and she reached to scratch it behind the ears. The dog had had a bath today; she could smell the strong scent of brown laundry soap in its fur. "Hasn't been a good day for you, either, has it?" she whispered, letting the animal lick her fingers. "What with baths and strangers in the dark."

The dog's enthusiasm grew, and she knelt down to keep it from jumping up on her. She looked up sharply at the sound of the screen door opening, and the dog bounded off toward the house, giving excited barks along the way.

Quinn expected Lena, but it wasn't Adam's mother who had come out of the house. It was Jacob who quieted the dog with one sharp command. Her heart fell. She remembered Adam telling her once that, when he was little, he had been certain that God himself looked like Jacob Sauder. Watching Jacob approach, she could identify with Adam's feelings completely, and she felt as she always had whenever she met him face-to-face—inappropriate and unacceptable. It suddenly occurred to her that perhaps he didn't know that Lena had asked David to bring her here. Perhaps he was coming now to send her away again.

She glanced at the windows behind him. She could see a woman—not Lena, because she was obviously in the latter stages of pregnancy—carrying a gas lantern into the kitchen. The woman—David's wife, she guessed—set the lantern on the table and waited for the group of men who followed her to be seated. Church elders, Quinn thought. What was happening now? If Edison's information was correct, they'd already decided on Adam's excommunication. She had no idea what else they could be doing.

"So, Quinn Tyler," Jacob said, drawing her attention away from the activities in the house. "You have come."

"Yes," she said. She willed her voice and her knees to hold steady. She couldn't see his face in the darkness, but she could sense the tension in him. She braced herself for his anger, but she refused to let the threat of it make her meek. "But I don't know why—"

"You are here because *she* asks it," he interrupted.

Quinn understood immediately the "she" Jacob meant. Amish marriages were built on respect, not passion or love as the worldly knew it. There were no open displays of affection between a husband and wife, and she was not surprised that Lena was not referred to by name. But Jacob Sauder's simple statement, and his apparent permission for Quinn to come here, spoke volumes about his regard for the woman he'd married.

"Her heart is not strong, and she cannot find the rest she needs otherwise," he said. He looked back toward the house. "Now you are here, and I can do no more for her. The other elders will have to say if it is good to let you stay." He looked back at her in the darkness, and Quinn waited, her heart beginning to pound. "They are deciding now," he went on. "We will wait here until they tell us."

"I want to see Adam," she said, feeling the fear rise. She was afraid to ask where Adam was in all this, and she was afraid not to.

"Even so. We will wait here."

Even so! Quinn thought in exasperation. "Why did you send for me if I can't see him?"

"It was a hard thing, asking you to come here," he said sharply. "I think now I shouldn't have done it. You are headstrong like Adam. It will take time for them in there to know what is the best thing to do. In this, I ask that you respect our ways."

"I have always tried to do that," she said quietly. But she

was angry. If he only knew how much she'd respected his ways. She didn't want to offend him, yet she had no doubt that her very existence was likely offensive to him, and nothing she did now would change that. She walked a few steps away from him, looking around at the neat, orderly house and yard. Everything was trimmed, raked, weeded. Typically Amish. No clutter in their homes, no clutter in their lives. The place hadn't changed—even in the darkness, she could tell that—and neither had Jacob Sauder. The dog fawned at her feet again, and she reached down absently to pat its head. She looked toward the kitchen windows. The elders still sat en masse at the table.

"It may be Adam will not want to see you," Jacob said after what seemed a long time.

Was he pleased at that possibility? She couldn't tell. "Jacob, please. Where is he? Tell me what's wrong."

"You are an outsider."

"Please! Don't send for me and then tell me I'm an outsider!"

"Adam has shut himself away. We cannot talk to him because of the shunning. Do you understand?"

"No, I don't understand!" Quinn said, becoming alarmed now. "What do you mean he's shut himself away?"

"He is out there in the barn. In his grandfather's workshop. He goes in yesterday, but he doesn't come out again. My wife is afraid of this long silence—Quinn, where are you going!"

"I'm going to find Adam. How do you know he's not hurt?"

"I have heard him working. Even now he is working."

The back door suddenly opened, and the elders descended into the yard.

"Wait here," Jacob commanded, going to where they gathered on the slate path. Quinn watched the black-clothed Amishmen come together, heard their soft murmuring of German as they conferred with Jacob. She stood with her arms folded, ready to scream with impatience at these doings. She wanted to see about Adam, and she wanted to see now, whether the elders sanctioned her visit or not. But she forced herself to wait. If Adam was working, doing some kind of carpentry, then he must be all right.

She took a deep breath, her eyes turning toward the western sky and the distant rumbling of thunder. It was going to rain again. She could already smell it on the wind. She strained to hear some sound from the barn, but she heard nothing, only the night sounds and the windmill and the muted voices of solemn Amishmen.

"I will show you where Adam is," Jacob said behind her, making her jump.

"I know where the workshop is," she replied, already heading toward the barn. "I've been there before."

"Wait!" Jacob called. "You will need a light."

He walked with her to the lower barn doors, reaching inside and feeling along the wall until he found the lantern hanging on a peg. He lit it carefully and adjusted the wick. "Take this," he said, but he didn't give it to her immediately. He held the lantern higher, as if he wanted to see her face.

"Let me go to him, Jacob," Quinn said impatiently, waiting for him to stand aside.

He handed her the lantern. "I have done you great wrong."

"Me? You haven't done anything to me."

"I have thought ill of you. I have thought you were a selfish English woman who didn't understand us for all the times you were a child here in this house—an evil woman who enticed my son into evil ways. My wife has told me how you had the...right to take Adam from us. You could have taken him with only a word. That word you did not say. I think that you didn't say it because you knew in your heart that, for him, living Plain was more than—" He suddenly broke off.

How careful he was not to mention the baby, Quinn thought. Perhaps that sin was too unspeakable. "Yes," she agreed. "I knew what living Plain meant to him." And she *had* known, just as she had known that she and Adam Sauder were separate halves of the same whole. She had known both those things, and she had made her choice. "None of that matters now."

"It matters to me. I am an old man. I don't want to face God with such ill feelings in my heart. I ask your forgiveness."

"Jacob, I don't—"

"Bitte!"

She stared at him in the darkness. *I gave away my baby,* she thought. *Don't you understand? I gave away my baby!* Everything else was of no consequence.

But she said nothing, particularly the words he needed to hear. She was suddenly too aware of her irrevocable loss, too aware that Adam was excommunicated after all and it had all been for nothing. She could forgive no one until she could forgive herself. She tried to move by him, but Jacob reached out and caught her hand, holding it tightly in his two rough ones. "You must tell me I have done you no harm in this."

"It doesn't matter!" she said, and he abruptly released her hand. "I—we both did the best we could, Jacob. I see no need for forgiveness for that."

"You have no reason to feel charity for me, that I understand. But you can find out what is in my son's mind, Quinn Tyler. Talk to him. Tell him he knows what he must do—for himself, for this family."

"He isn't going to listen to me, Jacob. He'll do whatever *he* thinks is right. That's why I left here the way I did eleven years ago—because I knew I couldn't keep him from—" She abruptly stopped. She didn't want to talk about that with Jacob.

The old man looked up at the night sky for a moment, then back at her. "Before, I have told you this, Quinn Tyler. We bring up our children in the way they should go so that they will never depart from it. Adam will be lost out there in the world. They, the ones who leave us, are always lost out there among the English."

"And has he been happy here?"

"We are not put on this earth to be happy."

"And we're not here to choose what is happiness for somebody else!"

She abruptly turned away, remembering that night on the porch so long ago.

"Do you love him enough?" Jacob had asked her then. If she let him, he'd ask her that again. Did she love Adam enough to do what *he* wanted? For all his talk of forgiveness, Jacob hadn't changed. Once again he wanted to make her his ally.

But Adam was beyond her influence now, because he knew his child was lost to him and because she had been away for so long. She couldn't press him about anything, whether he still cared for her or not.

"Are you still my friend?" he'd asked.

Yes, she was still that, regardless of what had happened between them. She didn't want to tell him anything on Jacob's behalf; she only wanted to know that he was all right. Jacob would have to take up his own case.

She held the lantern carefully as she stepped into the barn. It was dark and quiet, smelling of dust and horse, leather and aged wood. She moved silently past an open "courting" buggy and a row of horse collars hanging on pegs, hesitating to listen to the faint sounds coming from the carpentry workshop. Adam was indeed working. She could see the lantern light through the chinks in the wall up ahead. She walked on, looking around sharply at a noise behind her—Jacob and the elders, gathered now at the outside door to wait. They were not about to permit her to see Adam Sauder alone. Her toe caught on the uneven flooring, and she gave a soft cry as she tried to right herself. The noises in the workshop abruptly stopped.

She stood very still, listening, sensing that behind the door of his grandfather's carpentry shop, Adam was doing the same. She took a deep breath and moved on, setting the lantern down on the floor and going the rest of the way without it. She could see several years' worth of almanac farm-and-garden calendars on the walls as she approached, and the lantern cast her shadow long and thin onto their pages.

When she reached the workshop door, she rested the flat of

her hand against the rough boards for a moment before she tried it. She had no idea what she would say and no right to say it if she had. She pushed on the door, but it was braced from the inside and didn't budge. She tried again, but it didn't open. Clearly, Adam had heard her, and he had barred the door against her. Because of the shunning, he would have no need to bar it against anyone else.

She leaned her forehead against the wood, trying to remember. Had he always wanted to be alone like this when he was troubled? Yes, she decided, but he'd wanted to be alone with *her*, to talk to *her* about whatever bothered him. She remembered when he'd had to quit school, and when Jacob had tried to make him see that he couldn't keep associating with the English girl. She had sat with him on a creek bank well away from both their houses and felt his pain as if it were her own.

"There is nothing in you that would harm me," he'd said then, and they'd both believed it. They had been so innocent.

"Adam?" she said. She could hear him moving around, but he didn't answer her. She waited, her head still resting against the rough wood. There was a small square opening cut in the lower corner of the door, and a calico cat poked its head out to peer at her. She made no move to touch it, but it suddenly withdrew as if she had.

"Adam?" she said again. She caught a glimpse of movement behind her. Jacob and the elders had moved closer. She turned her face away from them.

"I just want to know if you're all right," she said, feeling her desperation rise. "Do you hear me?"

The silence lengthened.

"Edison told me what happened. Adam, can't you—"

"Are you alone, Quinn?" he suddenly broke in.

She looked back over her shoulder at Jacob and the men, wondering why he wanted to know. "No. The elders from the church are here. And your father. Adam—"

"Go away from me," he interrupted. "Now."

He was close to the door; she could feel him there on the other side.

"Adam, listen! All those times I brought you books to read... Sometimes, when everything was so hard for you, when you missed going to school so much, you pretended you didn't want them. But I knew you did. I could tell when I looked at you. I could tell how badly you needed them—it didn't matter what you said. How can I know what you want now if I can't look at you?" Her voice quavered, and she closed her eyes, trying to regain her composure. "Adam, let me see you," she whispered. "Let me—"

He heard her quite plainly, and that softly whispered plea on the other side of the door nearly tore him in two. It was all he could do to resist it. How had she come to be here? Quinn!

He couldn't let her in, no matter how much she pleaded, no matter how much he wanted to see her. He was so tired, and he had to be alone. If he let her in, they—his father and whoever else was out there—would always think that *she* had persuaded him to do what he knew he had to do. Worse, the day might come when he would think that himself. This was his final chance to make some sense of his life, and he was going to be very careful with it. The only way to do that was to stay separate from Quinn, entirely, so that Jacob and the others would know she was without blame, that he'd come to this himself, when he had no hope at all of a life with her.

"Adam? You know if you need anything, I'll help," Quinn said, keeping her voice low to avoid being overheard.

"I don't need anything, Quinn. I only want to be left alone. If I have any need, it's that."

The *Meidung*—the shunning. Eleven years ago, for the sake of the family, he had buckled under the threat of that punishment because he had thought Quinn lost to him and there was nothing else out among the English that mattered. Such a solemn and terrible ritual, like attending one's own funeral. He had grown up with the fear, of someone doing something that would bring the *Meidung* into the house. And how strange it seemed that it had finally happened. He had sat among the weeping women and the stern-faced men and listened to the account of his supposed sin, and to the announcement that he was a threat to others and had to be cast off from everything he knew and loved. And yet, the alienation, the aloneness he'd felt since the shunning began was somehow no worse than it had always been. True, no one spoke to him now, not even Daniel or his mother, for whom, if he could, he would have spared this trouble. He ate his meals alone after everyone else had eaten, and he was no longer given the status he'd always known as the oldest son. The days passed without the constant "Ask Adam" from the rest of the family. It was hard to suddenly behave as if he were not needed, when the needs of this family had been what had kept him here after Quinn had gone.

But he didn't delude himself. The real difference now was that he was irrevocably at the crossroads in his life where he must decide precisely what it was he wanted—to "repent" and continue his marginal compliance as an Amishman or to leave. He couldn't make the decision lightly, and he refused to be swayed by the terribleness of the *Meidung* or by his longing for Quinn. In time, he knew that the strain of his not belonging would become too much for all of them, and he would be asked to leave the Sauder house rather than divide family and community loyalties. He knew he had his mother's sympathies, and Sarah's, and all of his brothers' except for David.

Poor David. The shame was nearly more than he could bear, and there was nothing Adam could do about it. David believed there was no excuse for Adam's behavior with Quinn Tyler. Adam was a man now, not some infatuated boy who'd let his pretty childhood friend seduce him.

"Adam, can I tell Lena anything? She's—"

He closed his eyes against the need to give in. "What you can do is go away from me!"

He could hear the fear in her voice. And worry. And caring. He had no doubt that she still cared about him. He'd felt that from the first day she'd come back. But did she love him? Or did she hold for him the same charity she held for encroaching spiders, something to be moved out of her sight, albeit kindly, but moved nevertheless?

That, he didn't know. He knew the passion was still there; it had leaped up wild and strong between them the day they'd walked barefoot over the plowed field. Even now, the memory of it left him restless and aching. He still loved her with all his heart, and his desire for her had nearly overwhelmed him. How angry it had made him to have *that* within his reach again. It would have given him such joy to make love with her, but he'd wanted so much more.

He had but one certainty, and that was that he would never be satisfied with illicit meetings in the dark again. This time he would have every part of Quinn Tyler, every hope, every dream, every weakness and fear. He would have every part of her—or he would have nothing.

"It never bothered you to leave me before," he said finally, knowing it would hurt her.

She stepped back from the door, then pounded it once hard with her fist. "All right! All right! If that's all you want, then it's the least I can do for you." She turned away, grabbing up the lantern as she went.

"He wants to be left alone," she said to Jacob. "That's all he'll say. I'm sorry."

She made her way through the group of men, remembering at the last moment to give back the lantern.

"You will need this to light your way, Quinn Tyler."

"No, thank you. I'll go home the long way by the paved road." She headed across the Sauders' backyard toward the macadamized road that bordered both farms. The mongrel joined her as she passed the vegetable garden and the grape arbors. Suddenly something moved in the vines behind her.

"Anymore don't hurry, Quinn Tyler!"

"Daniel! You scared me. You'd better go back inside."

But he didn't go back inside. He flung his arms around her waist instead. "I want to cry, Quinn Tyler," he said, his voice muffled against her. The wind was picking up. A flash of lightning illuminated the house and yard, and a crack of thunder rolled across the night sky.

She held him tightly. "Oh, Daniel, I know." She felt like crying herself. "Go inside now. It's going to storm."

"No. I can't talk to Adam. Quinn Tyler, is he going away from this house?"

"He didn't tell me. He only said he wants to be by himself for now."

Daniel leaned back to look at her, his features a blur in the dark. "Can you make him stay with us? Can you ask him? I can't talk to him." He let go of her and rubbed both eyes hard with his fists. "So bad I want to cry." He took his hands down, and the wind rattled the grape arbor behind them. Quinn reached out to touch his hair, but this time he fended her off. Clearly, like his brother, he needed answers more than he needed comfort. "I'm too big for crying. What will he do, Quinn Tyler? What will he do?"

"Daniel, I don't know that. I think he has to decide. And we just have to wait."

"Anymore I don't want to wait."

"Daniel!" David said sharply behind them. "Get into the house!"

"Can Adam stay at your house, Quinn Tyler?" Daniel asked desperately, pulling on her hands to keep her attention before David got any closer. "Can he? You wouldn't have the shunning there."

David came forward as if to cuff him on the ear. "Daniel! Get inside!"

The boy let go of her hands and disappeared around the corner of the house.

"He's afraid, David," Quinn couldn't keep from saying.

"We are *all* afraid, Quinn. All of us. Does it make you happy, this thing you've done?"

"No, I'm not happy! And I haven't *done* anything!"

"You came back here. Already you've led my brother into—"

"I love your brother!" she said vehemently.

He made a derisive sound. "And what good does it do him, this love of yours? You ruin him. You ruin this family. You see how Daniel is, how we all are. We have the *Meidung* in this house because of you!"

"David," a woman said worriedly, the woman Quinn had seen through the window. Neither Quinn nor David had heard her approach, and he looked sharply around at her. It was clear that he was not ready to forgo having his say, and he lapsed into the German dialect to speak to her, spewing angry words too rapid for Quinn to follow. There were only two words she understood—her own name and that of the woman. Sarah.

The gentle Sarah Adam had almost married? she wondered briefly as she stood there, temporarily forgotten. Whatever Sarah said displeased David even more. That was all Quinn could tell, and, whatever the words were about, she didn't care. She wasn't waiting any longer. She was going home.

"Wait, Quinn," Sarah called after her.

"It's going to rain. I have to go," Quinn said without looking back. She walked on toward the road, the playful dog pouncing at her heels.

"But Lena wants to see you!"

Quinn hesitated. Lena. She'd forgotten about Lena.

But she didn't want to cause any more trouble. David and Jacob were upset enough by her presence. "The elders will be coming back to the house. I shouldn't be there."

"Please, Quinn. She wants it," Sarah persisted. Clearly, she was a dutiful daughter-in-law. What her husband's mother wished, she would try to do.

Another flash of lightning lit up the yard, but Quinn wasn't able to see Sarah's face well enough to read her expression. She didn't exude the same animosity as her husband, but there was something there.

"All right," Quinn said finally. All the elders together couldn't be any more intimidating than Jacob alone. "Your name is Sarah?" she asked as she walked back toward the house. She didn't want to feed her jealousy at the possibility that this Sarah could be the one Adam had courted, but she needed to know if Adam had any allies at all. If this was the Sarah who had once planned to marry him, surely she must feel some kindness for him.

But Quinn was forgetting. Even if that were so, Sarah was David's wife now, and his feelings in the matter were likely to be hers.

"Yes. Sarah," the woman said. "Lena is waiting in the kitchen. She's not feeling well today. Last night she doesn't sleep much. Quinn," she added as they reached the back door, "I...never thought you wanted to hurt Adam."

They looked into each other's eyes, and, whether this was Adam's gentle Sarah or not, in that moment they seemed to understand each other perfectly. Quinn could feel the sting of tears behind her eyes, and she nodded, reaching blindly for the handle on the screen door. Sarah didn't come inside with her, but she had no difficulty finding her way; nothing had changed since the last time she had been in this house. She followed the hiss of the gas lantern into the large kitchen.

Lena was sitting at the table. Quinn stood in the doorway for a moment, not knowing quite what to do or say, remembering their last meeting.

"I will not see you, Quinn Tyler, until I can find the forgiveness in my own heart."

Had Lena found that forgiveness? Or at least some measure of understanding? In the eyes of the Amish, she had led Adam into sin. In the eyes of Adam's mother, she had also hurt him deeply, and it must have seemed a coldly deliberate act. Her sinning with Adam and then staying away from him all these years had been one thing; taking his son from him was quite another. Lena was Adam's mother, and no one deserved to be hurt the way he had been, not even in the name of love.

Tell me you understand, Quinn almost said, but she bit down on it, forcing herself to be still. Lena Sauder was a kind woman, a good woman. It was better not knowing whether she had her forgiveness, because if Lena couldn't forgive her, then what she had done was truly unforgivable.

"You have seen Adam?" Lena asked finally.

"Yes, but I can't tell you anything, Lena. He wouldn't talk to me."

The older woman sighed and pulled out the chair next to her for Quinn to sit in. It struck Quinn that Lena was not in the least surprised. Apparently she hadn't expected Quinn to accomplish anything, even though she had insisted that she come here.

"It isn't the talking so much as the knowing," Lena said as Quinn sat down.

Quinn propped her elbows on the table and rested her head in her hands for a moment. "I don't know what that means, Lena," she said tiredly. "I don't know what anything means anymore."

Surprisingly Lena reached out to her, and Quinn clasped her hand as if she were in danger of drowning.

"It means that Adam has put himself in a wilderness of his own making, and he can't see your lights across the way. But still, he needs to know that they are there."

Quinn looked away so that Lena couldn't see her face. Leaving her lights on all night had been a desperate, childish gesture, and she was embarrassed that Lena was so perceptive. She was sure now that, forgiven or not, it was for Adam that Lena had wanted her to come tonight, not for herself. But she didn't believe Lena's assessment of Adam's need of her.

"He didn't want me there. He locked the door."

"If he did, he locked the door *for* you, not against you."

Quinn shook her head, still not willing to accept it. "I don't—"

"I know my son, Quinn. I think he doesn't want you blamed, whatever he decides. He must think what to do now, what it is he really wants, and he wants no one to say Quinn Tyler talked to him tonight and made him go."

"Or stay?" Quinn asked softly.

Lena made no reply to that, looking at the windows as the first drops of rain splattered against the glass. "You must wait with us until the rain is over."

"No. No, Lena, I can't. I'll go home now."

"Quinn…"

She stood up. "No, I don't belong here. I have to go home."

She meant to squeeze Lena's hand one last time, but Lena stood up with her, hugging her tightly for a moment before releasing her to run out into the rainy darkness.

Chapter Ten

The telephone was ringing. She had left the house open in her haste to follow David, and she could hear it the minute she reached the front yard. But she made no attempt to answer it. She stood in the rain, looking at the tree Adam had planted and trying not to cry.

"It never bothered you to leave me before."

He didn't understand. Or if he did, he couldn't accept what she had done. She had to face that and stop punishing herself.

"This is killing me, too," she said aloud, the sound of her voice lost in the pouring rain. She had known full well how it might be when she came back here to live, and she'd had no surprises. Now she had but two choices, the same ones Adam faced: to go or to stay.

She took a deep breath and reached out to touch the leaves on the apple tree. It was thriving, and so should she. She just had to—

Had to what? That was the difficulty. She didn't know what to do to make the situation better. She didn't even know if it *could* be made better. Perhaps that was a solution in itself. Perhaps she should simply accept the fact that the part of her life that involved Adam Sauder couldn't be mended, that she was like someone with a serious physical injury, one that had left terrible scars that she would have to learn to live with.

She was drenched and shivering by the time she went inside. She went straight upstairs to a hot shower and dry clothes, thinking all the while of her mother. Taking a shower during a thunderstorm was breaking one of her mother's cardinal rules. But then, she'd broken more than one of them in her life. What would her mother say about Adam?

What should I do? she thought again and again as she stood under the hot water, and the answer was always the same. Nothing. Edison had told her that. There was nothing she could do for Adam Sauder. She tried not to think about him, about the aloneness he must be feeling that was so much worse than hers.

She couldn't wash the worry away, but the gods of lightning were kind this time, leaving her unstruck but with a longing for someone who would understand the turns her life had taken. She was exhausted but wide-awake, and she knew there was no sense in trying to sleep. Her throat ached, and her eyes burned with unshed tears for Adam. And for herself. And for their baby.

She wanted to believe Lena Sauder. She wanted to believe that Adam had asked her to go because he didn't want her blamed for whatever decision he was making now, not because he wanted nothing more to do with her. But, like it or not, she had to consider the latter possibility.

The rain had stopped. She put on jeans and a T-shirt, intending to risk working at the computer in spite of the now-distant rumblings of thunder, until she felt sleepy enough to go to bed. Impulsively she lit a fire in the fireplace to rid the room of dampness, and she concentrated on Edison's account figures, somewhat comforted by the precision of dealing with numbers. In this part of her life at least, there were no unaccountable variations. One and one were always two.

The fire burned into embers, and another thunderstorm came out of the west. She shut down the computer, and the telephone rang again. She went into the kitchen and reluctantly picked up the receiver. There was no one in the world she wanted to talk to.

"Quinn?" a man's voice said.

"Yes," she said into the receiver. She couldn't keep her voice from wavering.

"What's wrong?"

"Jake?" She closed her eyes and forced herself to sound calm. "Jake! How are you?"

"Don't dodge the question. What's wrong? I've been trying all evening to call you."

"Nothing's wrong. I—I was out for a while. I got caught in the rain." She wasn't making any sense, and she knew it. She tried to concentrate.

"What the hell were you doing out in the rain at this time of night?"

"Visiting."

A noise on the front porch caught her attention, and she stepped into the hallway so that she could see the front door, forgetting that she'd closed it. The old-fashioned door had a large oval window of beveled glass, and she hadn't had the time or the inclination to find a curtain for it yet. Since the hall light was on, she knew that anyone on the porch could see in better than she could see out.

"So," Jake said in her ear, "how are you doing?"

She walked down the hallway as far as the phone cord would reach, half expecting David Sauder to be out there again with the rest of what he'd wanted to say to her. But the porch looked empty. Just the wind, she thought. "Fine. I'm fine. What about you?"

"Oh, I'm better than ever. Now here's where you're supposed to be impressed—I made ten thousand bucks in commissions Thursday. What do you think of that?"

She cringed at a loud crack of thunder. Taking a shower in a thunderstorm was one thing; using the telephone was something else again. "That's nice. Jake, listen, there's a storm here, so I'll have to—"

The front door opened.

Adam came into the hallway. He stood for a moment, then walked toward her, leaving wet footsteps on the bare wood floor. He wasn't wearing a hat, and his clothes were drenched, his hair plastered down by the rain. He said nothing, but, oh, the pain in his eyes.

His name formed on her lips, but she, too, said nothing.

"Nice? *Nice*, Tyler?" Jake protested. "You're damned right ten thousand bucks is nice. The market's been a bitch— or haven't you been reading the papers?"

"No, I—Jake, I have to go. I'll call you tomorrow or—"

"No, wait, Quinn. I want to know how you're really doing. You sound like hell."

"Jake, I told you, everything's fine." Fine, she thought, staring into Adam Sauder's eyes.

"When are you coming to Philadelphia?"

Adam stood silently, waiting, dripping rain on the floor.

Dear God, she thought. *He's done it. He's broken with Jacob.*

"What?" she said to Jake because she'd all but forgotten him.

"I said, when are you coming to Philadelphia. I want to see you, Quinn."

"I can't come to Philadelphia. Jake, goodbye. I have to go."

"Quinn!" he called, but she wasn't listening anymore. She stood clutching the telephone receiver tightly against her chest.

"I don't think you told him the truth, Quinn," Adam said. "I don't think everything is fine." His eyes traveled over her face. She looked so forlorn to him. So little. And so sad. Her eyes were bright with unshed tears, although the mouse with the big feet smiled bravely on her chest.

Quinn. My beautiful Quinn.

"Why are you here?" she asked.

"I came of my own choice. I wasn't driven out or—"

"What happened with Jacob?" she interrupted. Something must have happened. He'd refused to see her only hours ago.

"I am no longer his son." He was so calm, so matter-of-fact. "He understands, Quinn."

"How could he understand? You're his first son. Adam, what are you doing here? I never wanted to take that away from you." *Too*, she'd almost said.

"He understands because I've told him. I can't live Amish anymore."

Quinn pressed her lips together, not trusting herself to speak. She was like Daniel, she thought crazily. She wanted desperately to cry, and there was nothing she could do to hold it back anymore. Her eyes filled with tears, which spilled over and ran silently down her cheeks. She hated for him to see her cry, and she turned away, going back into the kitchen to hang up the phone.

"This man who called you, he's not so stupid as I thought," Adam said from behind her. "He wants you to come back to him."

She stood in the middle of the kitchen, not knowing where to go next or what to do. Adam moved around her to see her face, but she bowed her head. She has always been like this, he thought. Always wanting to hide her tears from him. But there were tears he should have seen, the ones when she knew she was having his baby, the ones when she knew she was leaving him.

"Will you do what he asks, Quinn? Will you go to Philadelphia?"

She looked up at him. "No," she said, her voice barely a whisper.

His heart began a slow pounding in his chest. No. So easily she said it. As if it were never a possibility. Again he was determined to look into her eyes. They were the same in that respect. He couldn't know what she was feeling if he couldn't see her eyes. She looked so wounded, so cornered, like a rabbit in a trap, but still he had to know.

"Why won't you go to Philadelphia?" he said, and she looked away.

"Adam, you shouldn't be here," she said, attempting a composure she didn't feel.

"Where else should I be then? I promised myself I would never do this again, Quinn. I wouldn't come to you in the dark like when I was a boy. I'm a man now, but I'm here. Because I can't *not* be here. That's how it is with me. I...I want you to say how it is with you."

"There is still so much wrong between us," she began.

"Just tell me!" he said impatiently. "We can't settle anything if you won't tell me what you feel."

"I don't know what I feel."

"Then let me help you. Do you want me to go? This other man, this Jake, do we just leave you alone here? Is that what you want?"

"Adam, I can't—"

"Do you want me to go!"

"No!"

"Then what do you want?"

She took a few steps toward the back door. He went with her. "I want you to be happy," she said, turning around to face him.

"And this time will you ask *me* what it takes for my happiness? Or will you and my father decide and leave me out of it?"

"Adam, I—"

"Ask me what will make me happy, Quinn! Never mind— I'll tell you. It would make me happy to know at last what is in your heart. You're right that there is still much that's wrong between us. Maybe we're both too hurt, too battered to deal with the why of how we came to this. But we have to start somewhere. You have to tell me if there is anything between us now. I ask you again. What do you want?"

She tried to get away from him, but he caught her arm.

"Say it! Once and for all if you want me out of your life, then tell me. Tell me so I can believe it. You kill me with what I see in your eyes, the need you have. You *need*, Quinn, and I don't know what I have to give you."

"It's not just what *I* want!" she cried.

"No? Then who else is there? I have told you I love you. I have no pride when it comes to that. I didn't stop loving you while you were gone. But I tried, Quinn. I tried! So tell me, who else is in this? Jake?"

"No, not Jake. You're Amish, Adam," she said desperately.

"Yes. *I* am Amish. Me. Not you. I will decide what I want to do about it." He brought her around to face him. "Now, you look at me. You look at me, and you tell me. You have my word I will believe you. If you can give me nothing else, then give me the peace I need. Say it! Say, 'Adam, I don't want you. Adam, I don't love you.' Say it! 'I never wanted you or your son!'" His fingers dug into her arm, hurting her, but they didn't hurt nearly as much as what he wanted her to do.

"Please!" she cried, and he abruptly let go of her. She was trembling, and she couldn't stop. She tried to hold her body rigid so that she wouldn't sob out loud.

"It's not true," she whispered. "I wanted you—and our boy. I wanted you so much!"

"Quinn. Quinn..." he said, but she didn't understand the rest because he'd lapsed into German.

She looked up at him. She wanted to go to him so badly, but she only shook her head because she didn't understand.

"I said, don't cry," he translated. "Don't, Quinn. We've had enough tears, you and I."

"Oh, Adam." She reached out her hand to him, and, amazingly, he took it, his fingers interlacing with hers. He drew her to him, and she gave a soft moan as she sagged against him. She had had her reasons for separating them, good reasons, and they suddenly counted for nothing. He put his arms around her without hesitation, reaching up to rest his hand against her tear-stained cheek. He was wet from the rain, but his touch was warm, so warm. She held him tightly, her fists clutching the back of his shirt. He felt so good to her. She needed his strength, and she despaired at the possibility that he might withdraw it.

"Don't leave," she whispered urgently. "Please, don't leave."

"Why?" he asked quietly. One way or the other, he was going to make her say it.

"Because—I—Adam, I didn't know what to do! I didn't! I loved you so!"

Loved. Past tense.

He closed his eyes, holding her tightly. *And now?* he wanted to ask her. *What about now?*

But he didn't ask. He had lost his nerve, and she was too distraught. She seemed so fragile to him. So fragile, and yet she was so strong. He knew what she had done for him. She had tried to give the one thing he couldn't give her—his Amishness—and she'd sacrificed their child to do it.

"Quinn!" he whispered against her ear, all the love, all the pain he was feeling riding on the sound of her name.

She clung to him, her face pressed against his. His face was smooth, just shaven, she realized. She could smell the scent of soap on his skin. She suddenly understood his sending her away earlier, his being here now. He hadn't come to her the way he'd always done as a troubled boy, and he hadn't wanted to see her while he was unkempt and unfocused. It was even more than not having her blamed for his decision to leave the Amish. He had wanted to come to her as a man, a man who was in control of his life and who had made his choices deliberately, just as she had done.

"What was I to you?" he persisted, keeping the promise he'd made to himself. He had to know, even if the knowing ended it.

"Everything," she said without hesitation.

"Was I?"

"Yes! You still are."

Still?

He held her away from him, cupping her face in his hands. The softness of her cheeks was sweet against his rough and callused palms. He was afraid to hope, but he was driven by the years of not knowing. He asked anyway, his eyes searching hers for the truth. "And what am I now?"

Time stood still. There was nothing but the rain coming down and the sound of their breathing.

"My friend," she said quietly. "My lover. My...husband."

His heart soared. "Yes!" he affirmed, his mouth coming down hard on hers, the taste of her already in his mind. He was all those things. Always.

Always.

He intended to be gentle, to make the kiss sweet and lasting. But he was too hungry, too starved, too long without her. He tore his mouth away from hers, pressing another kiss against her jaw and then into the delicate fragrance of her neck. He was trembling. His hands shook with desire. His mouth found hers again, and she parted her lips, accepting the probing of his tongue as if she, too, were starved. He lifted her up off the floor, and her arms went around his neck. She weighed nothing, he thought as he carried her into the hallway.

"There is more to us than this" she remembered as he carried her up the stairs. There was more to their relationship than their physical attraction. And it was because there was more that *this* was so consuming. She had been in such pain for so long, alone for so long, and so had he. And it was *this* that they both needed to heal them.

He set her on the edge of the bed and let her turn on the small lamp by the bed. He kneeled down beside her, putting his head into her lap for a moment before he began to undress her. Her fingers entwined in his hair as he pressed a warm kiss against her belly, a kiss she could feel deep into the soft, secret, womanly part of her. She loved his touch, a touch that was both reverent and demanding. She loved his damp, sun-streaked hair, his pale eyes that shaded with his moods from blue to gray. She loved his taste, familiar and distinctive, and she wanted more.

"Adam..." she whispered.

He lifted his head to look into her eyes, the beautiful hazel eyes he'd always found so easy to become lost in. His passion was strong; he trusted himself to leave only the briefest of kisses on her mouth. And he wouldn't let her help remove her clothing or his. He wanted to do that himself, to peel away every vestige of her Englishness and his Amishness until they were only a man and a woman.

How beautiful! he thought. Her high, firm breasts that were neither large nor small but just fit the palms of his hands. Her hips and thighs and legs, with their silky, woman-soft curves. Her body was so smooth beneath his hands. Warm. Smooth. Soft. And willing. She leaned back on the bed, resting on her elbows while she watched him with half-closed eyes, accepted his worship with a soft sigh as he caressed every part of her. In that look, he could feel her wanting the touch of his hands, and the look alone was enough to make him catch his breath. He pulled down the quilt and the sheet on the bed, lifting her and placing her gently in the middle of it. He felt no shyness at having her see him remove his own clothing, no shyness that she should see how much he wanted her.

How beautiful! she thought as she watched his clothes drop away. He was neither awkward nor hurried. She loved his body. She had always loved it. He was trim and muscular from the hard, physical work he'd done all his life. She lay back against the pillows, languid with anticipation. Only the tremor of his hands, and his eyes grown needy and dark, and then his final nakedness gave away his rising desire. His bold desire. His unsatisfied desire.

He stood before her without shame, and she held out her arms to him. How many times had he imagined this? A bed with cool, crisp sheets, and Quinn, warm and pressing against him. And privacy. And time. All the time in the world to be with her. That it was really happening was incredible to him, that she was covering his shoulder and neck with warm, wet kisses, that her belly strained against his, and the twin hard peaks of her breasts flattened against his chest. The male part of him lay swollen and hard against her thigh, and when she reached down to touch him, her hand encircling, stroking, he heard himself grunt with unabashed pleasure.

It was no longer enough to be the recipient. He wanted to touch, to kiss, to taste. He held her to him with both arms and legs as they tumbled together on the bed. The sweet woman smell of her, the sweet woman taste, drove him on. His hands slid into her dark, cropped-off hair. Strange, when he remembered her hair being long, braided sometimes, and the braids coming undone. But he loved the sleek, crisp feel of her hair now. And it smelled so good. Like flowers, Daniel had said. She smelled like flowers. He stroked her body, cupped her breasts, probed the delicate, petallike folds of her womanness until she arched against his clever fingers. When he kissed her breasts, when his mouth gently suckled and his teeth gently bit, she writhed in pleasure, sliding her fingers into his hair to keep him there. Such a joy it was to please her, to make her whimper at his ministrations, to make her cry out his name.

"Adam!"

Who else had done this for her?

The thought rose unbidden, and he pushed it aside. That didn't matter to him. There was only the now and the need he had for her. Quinn, who had given him such joy and such misery and pain.

"My beautiful Quinn," he said, holding his body above hers, staring into her eyes. He could see everything she wanted to tell him there, the things he was afraid to hear, the things she was afraid to say. She reached to bring him down to her, but he abruptly scooped her up, kneeling in the middle of the bed and holding her so that she had to lock her legs around his hips to keep from falling. He was a man, and he was strong and virile and delighted, and he wanted her to feel it. He held her as if she were no burden to him at all, and he kissed her, devoured her, her lips and shoulders and breasts. Every place he could reach, he covered with kisses, nipped with his teeth. He could feel that most female part of her, dewy and warm and straining against him. Then he tipped her backward, lowering her slowly, so slowly, back onto the bed. He was kneeling between her thighs, and his hands cupped her hips, sliding her closer to him.

Again her arms reached up; he smiled into her eyes as she embraced him. He kissed her lips, her nose, her eyes, then her lips again, letting his tongue explore the sweet taste of her mouth, savoring, remembering, experiencing it all anew, letting his hardness press urgently against the threshold of the place he was so desperate to be.

"Love me, Adam!" she whispered against his ear, and he felt the words, burning, all the way to the heart of his desire.

And then he was inside her, thrusting deep, his moan of pleasure lost in hers. She was so hot and tight and wet around him. So good. It felt so good. Nothing had ever felt so good. He tried to remember to be gentle—she was so small, and she'd been ill. He wanted to love her slowly, completely; he wanted to make her belong to him again, to make it last. He braced his weight with his hands, and the muscles in his arms trembled with the strain of holding back.

But he had been her first lover, and he knew. She had learned this most ancient of rituals between a man and woman with him. Virgins both, they had learned to pleasure each other together, and he had known her body as well as he knew his own. That hadn't changed. She didn't want his restraint. She wanted him, all of him, and she thrust her hips into his.

"Quinn, Quinn," he whispered, his body answering hers in a primitive rhythm he was powerless to stop. "It's so... good—you feel so good around me."

"You feel good," she murmured against his mouth. "I—love you—Adam."

From somewhere far away, he was aware of the thunder, of the rain beating against the roof, but he was lost now in a storm of his own. And Quinn was the center of it. He was drowning in the meaning of her words, in the exquisite joy of her body. Such pleasure. He had never known such pleasure, and the pleasure was not his alone. Her soft cries filled his heart to bursting. That he could do this for her, that she should want him so—like this—deep inside her—

And then the pleasure sharpened, and sharpened still more, and rushed through him to splinter into a fiery path of a thousand white-hot shards. He wanted to hold back; he thought he would die if he couldn't reach the end of it.

"I love you, Quinn!" he cried, feeling himself empty into her. "I love you," he murmured again and again. In English? In German? He didn't know.

She was listening to the rain, a quiet pattering sound now against the front windows and on the gutters. The lamp was still on, and she lay quietly at Adam's side, watching him sleep. He was lying on his back, the sheet only minimally covering his body, one knee bent, one hard, muscular thigh clearly exposed. When she was young, just on the threshold of being a woman, she'd dreamed of this, of having Adam in this house, in this bed. He would be her husband, and they'd sleep together, make babies together, grow old, be happy.

She loved him so!

Always.

Still.

Adam suddenly turned to her, taking her into his arms so that they were lying face-to-face. He pressed her close to him, and he gently kissed her eyes. "Is it all right?" he asked.

"Yes," she answered, resting her head against his, knowing that he was using one of his Amish idioms. He didn't mean "it." He meant her. Was she all right. Since their lovemaking. And before whatever in their lives was coming next. She felt that they were both dwelling on the now of their situation, not the past and not the future, and it was so good to be in limbo like this, she thought. And so...precarious.

"I want us to marry," he said quietly, dragging them both into reality. He put his fingertips against her lips to head off any protest she might make. "I want us to marry," he repeated. "I don't want to wait. I don't want to think it over. I want you. The wrong between us can't be fixed while we're apart. I want us together. Now."

She looked into his eyes and saw no trace of uncertainty,

only his quiet strength and his love. He knew all her arguments, so she made none. She had but one question.

"Are you sure?"

"Do you love me?" he countered.

"Yes," she said firmly.

"Then I'm sure."

She hugged him tightly, burying her face in his neck as if she could hide them both from the difficulties to come.

"It's going to be harder for you," he whispered.

"No, it isn't."

"I…can't give you anything, Quinn. I have nothing but myself and what I can do with my own two hands."

She leaned back to look at him. "I don't want anything but you."

"You know I'll work for you, for us. Holland will hire me, I think. It shouldn't be too bad." He smiled, but his smile quickly faded.

"What?" she asked, her eyes searching his.

"We never did this before. All those times we were together, we never really talked about making a life together."

"No," she said sadly. "We didn't."

"Quinn, I never thought of marrying anyone but you. I should have said that. I should have made sure you knew. But your father was so ill then, and I young and stupid, and you suffered for it. Somehow I thought everything would just go on the way it was and—"

"Don't. Don't. No *if only*s. All right? For my sake. Promise me that."

"Quinn—"

"I wouldn't have let you talk about it. I didn't want you to lose everything because of me. Now, please, for my sake…"

He seemed about to say more, but he didn't, smiling instead. "Tell me. Why were you looking at me so?"

"When?" she asked innocently, trying not to smile in return.

"When you thought I was asleep."

She kissed him softly on the chin. "Oh. Then."

"Yes, then. Why were you looking at me?"

"You're very beautiful?" she suggested, and this time he grinned.

"Me? Beautiful?"

"Very beautiful," she corrected.

"Ah. *Very* beautiful. And what else am I?" he asked, clearly at ease with her earlier inspection of his body and clearly fishing.

"What else? Well, you're—" she let her fingers trail over his chest and abdomen, watched his eyes flutter closed "—kind."

He opened his eyes again. "I see. Kind. And who am I kind to?"

She pressed the smallest of kisses on his chest. Then another. "To your family." And another. "To Jacob and Lena, and Daniel, and your sisters, and—"

"I'm not always kind to my sisters," he interrupted, letting out the breath he was holding.

"Yes, you are. You made them all marriage chests—Anna told me when we were unpacking dishes," she added when he was about to interrupt again. "She said no one had a brother as good as you."

"Anna said that?"

"She did."

"She must have had her hair twisted too tight—don't stop," he added because she'd found yet another place she wanted to kiss.

She obliged him. "She did not—have her hair—twisted too—tight."

"Then she was out in the sun too long—oh!"

"No, she was in the house with me. She said all her girl-friends in the—I've forgotten what you call them—the groups that meet at each other's houses on Sunday evenings…" She outlined his hard male nipples with her tongue.

"Supper gangs," he managed. "Quinn—"

She lifted her head. "Yes. In her supper gang. They all have crushes on you because you're so smart and handsome."

"I thought I was beautiful."

"Oh, well, that's only my opinion," she said, lowering her head again.

"I like your opinion," he said, lifting her chin so that his mouth could find hers. "I like everything." The kiss was soft and friendly, but it quickly escalated in degree and purpose. "I want you again, Quinn," he whispered, his mouth moving hungrily over hers. "I want you." His mouth left hers to suckle her breasts, and she closed her eyes at the hot, wet, exquisite pleasure it gave her. His hands, his urgent, knowing hands brought her leg up, stroked and teased and explored her most sensitive places until she moaned with the pure sensuality of it.

"I love to hear you," he whispered. "I love to hear you want me."

And then he was inside her, deep, so deep. His urgency compounded her own. She did want him. She wanted him very badly.

"Quinn...you are..."

But he didn't tell her what she was, and she didn't wonder. She had but one hope. That he would understand and that he would be kind to her, too.

Chapter Eleven

Adam woke with a start at the abrupt trilling of a mocking-bird outside the window. He should have been disoriented, unsure about where he was, but he wasn't. He knew instantly, even before the soft body lying in his arms fully registered.

Quinn.

He closed his eyes again, savoring the memory of the night they'd just had. Unbelievable, he thought for the thousandth time. He was here. And Quinn Tyler loved him. She was so beautiful lying there, and he pressed a soft kiss against her temple before he eased out of bed.

"Adam?" she murmured sleepily.

"Go back to sleep," he whispered, gently stroking her hair. The morning was cool, and he pulled the sheet up around her shoulders.

He quietly dressed—in his plain Amish clothes. He wanted to get rid of them; they were only a reminder to him and to Quinn, but for now he had no choice. He was hungry, and he went downstairs to hunt through the kitchen for something to eat. He found cheese and bread and milk and a pear.

He walked out onto the porch, eating. The sun was just coming up, and the buildings of his father's farm—the silos, the barn, the house, the windmill—were silhouetted in a brilliant orange predawn glow. He could see the mists rising from the fields, and he knew that his father and brothers had already been at work for hours.

You can't go home again, he thought, remembering his walk in the plowed field with Quinn. In this instance, the writer Thomas Wolfe was right. He couldn't go back to the farm—but then, that hadn't been his home for a long time. His home, his true home, was wherever Quinn was. He walked the length of the porch, savoring the morning stillness, hesitating as he felt the give of rotted porch planking at the far end. He trod on it again, and suddenly nothing became more important to him than to fix it. He smiled. Happy or sad, he needed to work, needed the satisfaction of a job well done.

He walked out to the barn to look for something he could use to piece into the rotted places on the porch, but the barn had been stripped clean—there was nothing there except perhaps Quinn's transplanted spider. He walked back to the house. Voices carried in the early-morning air, and in the distance he could hear his father calling his brothers to some task. He stood listening, assessing his feelings about his estrangement at the same time. Nothing had changed. He was sad, yes, but he loved Quinn Tyler.

He went into the house, finding a hammer in the kitchen, and Quinn's car keys.

It had been a long time since he'd driven. That particular sin, that of having acquired a working knowledge of the automobile, no one could blame Quinn for. He'd learned when he'd been too old for school and too young for a salaried job, and he'd become a hired boy for one of the Mennonite farmers across the valley. He had liked driving, and it pleased him that he still remembered how. Quinn's small car was easier than the tractors and trucks he'd used before.

He remembered Quinn's instructions about the lever under the seat to slide it back, and he accomplished that without difficulty. He'd been so stupidly angry that day, angry enough to sit with his legs cramped all the way into town and back again. But he had been more angry at himself than at her, because he'd been squarely faced with the fact of how much he still wanted her. He thought of her now, sleeping, so soft and warm in the big bed upstairs. It he went to her, awakened her, what would she do?

He smiled again. When he came back, he'd find out.

He drove to Holland Wakefield's with minimal difficulty, worrying a bit that some law officer might want to see his driver's license along the way and he'd have to call Quinn to come get him out of jail. How *that* news would fly around the Amish community. *Adam Sauder, one day left—in jail he is the next.*

But no one stopped him, and he found Holland on the brink of leaving for a job in the next county. He tried not to grin as Holland recognized him, then realized that he had arrived in a car—alone.

"Well!" Holland said, clearly dying to ask but trying not to intrude into something that was none of his business. His eyes flicked over the car, and Adam could pinpoint the exact moment of Holland's second realization: this was Quinn Tyler's car. "Well," Holland said again.

Adam forced the grin to subside. "I've come asking for work, Holland. Do you have any carpentry for me?"

But Holland was still puzzling over the Adam-Sauder-in-Quinn-Tyler's-car situation, and Adam wasn't certain his friend had heard him. "Holland?"

"What? Oh! Yeah, Adam. I'm glad you asked. I got— Adam, are you legal in this car?"

"I didn't steal it, Holland."

"I know *that*. But have you got a license?"

"No."

"No? Well." Holland frowned. "Ought to be some way we can work this…"

"Work what?"

"I got a nephew that runs a bed-and-breakfast in Gettysburg. He's got some things he wants done—inside work mostly. If I take you down there, maybe he can put you up till the job's done. Take about ten days, maybe two weeks. You interested in something like that?"

"I need the money, Holland," Adam said simply.

"Well, then, let me see what I can do. I think the nephew'll be glad to get you. Otherwise, it'll be a long time till I can free up another carpenter to do it."

"I need something else, Holland. A favor."

"What is it?" Holland asked.

"An advance on my wage. I need to fix a rotted porch. I need some boards and nails."

"Go on out there in the shop," Holland said without hesitation. "Give me a list later of what you take. Anything else you want?"

"If you could lend me a saw and a square, just for today."

"The shop's full of them. Take what you need."

Holland was clearly puzzling again. "Okay, okay," he said with a sheepish grin. "I want to know what the hell you're doing in Quinn's car, but I ain't going to ask. I'll see you later—after I know what to tell you about going to Gettysburg."

Quinn was still sleeping when Adam returned, and he didn't wake her after all. He'd given her precious little rest during the night, and it was good for her to sleep now.

He rummaged in the trunk of the car, finding a tire tool he could use to pry up rotted boards. It worked almost as well as a crowbar, and the job progressed steadily. He glanced up once to see a car turning into the driveway, a sleek, new model of some kind that was low to the ground and silver in color. The man who got out wore sunglasses and clothes that were, to Adam, somewhat baggy looking—tan pants, a blue-and-white checked shirt, and a white pullover sweater. He thought it odd that each sleeve of the shirt and each sleeve of the sweater were rolled up together in one big roll just below the elbow, which must hinder bending the arms, but he'd seen enough tourists to know that there was no accounting for English modes of dress. They either wore too much, like this man, or nothing, like the girl in the shorts and halter who kept badgering him the day he'd gone into town with Quinn. He grinned to himself. Quinn to the rescue. He'd never been so glad to see anyone in his life.

But this man didn't look like a tourist. He looked like someone from the city. From Philadelphia perhaps.

He came up onto the porch, and Adam thought he was going to ignore him, but then he seemed to think better of it, stopping just short of knocking at the door. He lifted his sunglasses and shoved them to the top of his head. "I'm looking for Quinn Tyler," he said. "This is her place, right?" He eyed Adam warily, as if he couldn't quite decide what his function was here. Was he a hired man or what?

Adam pried up another board. It was too early for any kind of business call, for insurance salesman and the like. "Yes," he said succinctly. "But she's asleep," he added when the man was about to knock on the door.

The man frowned. "And how would you know that?" There was just enough annoyance in his voice to confirm Adam's suspicions.

"I know," Adam said obscurely, prying up yet another board. "Will you hand me that hammer there?"

He passed Adam the hammer. "Look, I'm here because—"

"You love Quinn," Adam finished for him, hammering the nails out of the board he'd just removed. He thought some of it was salvageable, a good three-foot length. He glanced up. The man was clearly taken aback.

"Who the hell are you?"

"Adam Sauder. You're Jake, right? Quinn didn't tell me your last name."

"Oh, she didn't," he said, the annoyance replaced now by the sharp edge of sarcasm.

"But then, I didn't ask," Adam said mildly.

"Look," the man said again, "I came to see Quinn."

"I understand."

"I don't give a damn if you understand or not, Sawyer!"

"Sauder," Adam corrected. "You came to see Quinn because you love her. Probably you still want to marry her. I want to marry her, too. But right now, she's asleep. She'll be awake soon, and you can talk to her then. In the meantime, Jake, do you know anything about porches?"

Quinn woke up shortly after nine, to the sound of hammering, and when she ventured to the head of the stairs, men's voices. She dressed quickly, arriving in the kitchen in time to see Jake Burroughs hammering and to hear his next typically Jake question.

"So how much does land run around here?"

"An acre?" Adam said. "For prime farmland, maybe ten thousand."

"Ten thousand!"

"Maybe more."

"Jeez. You have any idea how much Quinn could get for this place?"

"I wouldn't want to sell it," she interrupted. "Good morning, Jake. What brings you out here?"

He grinned his perfect, all-American, I-can-sell-them-anything grin. "I heard your porch needed fixing."

She laughed. "Among other things. How about some breakfast?" She spoke to Jake, but she was looking at Adam. He gave her a short nod, the best he could do in front of a stranger, and she smiled.

"Breakfast would be good, Quinn," Jake told her. "You know what I like," he added for Adam's benefit.

"Okay," she said, glancing at Adam again. Lord, he was handsome this morning. "Coming up, and it's potluck, Jake. There are no menu selections. Oh, I take it you two have met."

"You might say that," Jake said, going back to hammering.

She cooked what she had—eggs, bacon, toast and coffee, knowing that Adam was accustomed to a great deal more. His usual fare at home would be something like what Edison had described when he went to see the bishop.

But Adam seemed not to mind, eating heartily and keeping up a running conversation with Jake. Quinn said little basking in the quiet smile she saw in Adam's eyes whenever he looked at her. They might have been completely alone.

"I've got blisters on my hands," Jake grumbled at one point.

"Don't worry," Adam told him. "It's what happens when you work hard. You are a good apprentice carpenter, Jake. You should learn more—something for you to do when you get tired of making money."

"I'm not likely to do that, am I, Quinn?"

"I doubt it. So, did you come to tell me my stocks are wiped out or what?"

"No, I came to see why you hung up on me last night."

Quinn glanced at Adam, who abruptly stood up.

"I'll be outside, Quinn," he said, giving Jake a brief nod on the way out.

"Tactful to a fault, isn't he?" Jake said as the back door slammed.

Quinn looked at him across the table. He was an attractive man, dark haired, blue eyed. He was funny and irreverent, fashionable, rich and getting richer. But he wasn't Adam Sauder.

"So is he the one?" Jake asked bluntly.

"The one what?" Quinn said, meeting his eyes head-on.

"The one who went to bed with us every time—"

"Jake!" she interrupted.

"Yeah, I know. I'm being crude. I'm not as gracious as he is. You want to know what's funny? I *like* the son of a bitch. He's had me hauling and hammering boards half the morming, he's had the gall to tell me he wants to marry you, and I *still* like him!"

"I'm glad."

"You're glad," he repeated. "Does that mean you're going to marry him?"

"I...want to."

"You want to. He wants to. That sounds pretty definite, except for the look on your face."

"There are problems," she said obscurely.

"You mean his being Old Order Amish—yeah, he told me," he said when she frowned. "He said your mother taught at the Amish school he went to—something about the state being all bent out of shape about their teachers not having a teaching certificate, so his people hired her to meet state requirements."

"How in the world did you get around to that?"

"How the hell do I know? We exchanged life histories, I guess. Rivals like to check up on each other. I make a lot of money; he goes back a long way. Do you know there is nothing you can tell an Old Order Amishman about how you acquired your first Porsche that will impress him? So, how long have you known Quinn, I asked him. 'I've never *not* known Quinn,' he said. Funny you never mentioned him."

"There was no reason to mention him."

"I could probably differ with you on that. I think it's damned likely he's the reason we didn't get married."

"Jake, I don't want to talk about this."

"Well, I do, kid. I'll say this for you: you were honest with me all the way about what you were feeling before, during and after my grand marriage proposal. It's just that I think maybe I could have made you forget about him if you'd let me."

Quinn didn't want to hurt him any more than she already had, but he wasn't giving her much choice. "Jake, it's like Adam said. We go back a long way."

His eyes searched her face. "You know, last night I thought all kinds of things might have happened to you, besides a rainstorm. You didn't sound like yourself, Quinn. At the very least, I thought the ulcer had kicked up again or you'd had some kind of financial crisis. I thought you were too proud to tell me you needed looking after since we weren't...together anymore. So here I come to say I told you so and to save you, and you look better than you've ever looked."

She smiled. "I'm sorry. I feel fine. What can I say, except that I think it's the cabbage juice I've been drinking."

"You could say you're not going to marry him. You could say you'll forget all this rustic stuff you're into and come back to Philadelphia—"

"Jake..."

"Yeah, yeah, I get the picture. I saw the hot looks you two were giving each other over the buttered toast." He sighed. "Well, where does that leave us?"

She shrugged and smiled again. "Friends?" she suggested.

"No, hell, Quinn. I don't want to be your *friend*. I want to be...something sexual," he decided, trying to be flippant. But he couldn't maintain his teasing air. He reached to touch her cheek with his fingertips. "I don't suppose that's all there is between you and Sauder?" he said hopefully. "Something sexual? You know I could wait around if that's all it is."

She took his hand in hers and shook her head no.

He sighed again. "That's what I thought. Well, I'd better get out of here before Sauder has me giving the bride away."

He kissed her gently on the cheek, and Quinn walked outside with him. Adam was still working on the porch, and he didn't look up as they came out.

"I feel responsible for this, you know," Jake said as they stood on the porch steps. "I'm the hotshot consultant who wheeled and dealed your money into enough to buy this place."

"I would have come back anyway," Quinn said, knowing it to be true.

"Yes, you probably would have," Jake admitted. He looked up at the blue sky. "It's nice out here, you know?"

"I know."

"Well, Sauder," he said to Adam, "thanks for the blisters."

"You are welcome for that," Adam said, looking up from his work and giving a slight smile. "It's good to have a chance to learn things. For both of us."

Quinn walked Jake toward the car. "There's only one thing I wonder about," he said.

"What's that?"

He looked into her eyes. "Why you're still so damn unhappy. No, don't explain to me," he said when she would have protested his observation. He nodded toward Adam. "Explain it to him." Then he turned away and got into the car. Quinn stood watching him jerk the expensive sunglasses into place and back the silver Porsche out of the yard. She could hear the whine of the motor long after he'd disappeared from view.

"Is it like he said?" Adam asked from behind her. "Are you so unhappy?"

Quinn looked up at him. "I love you," she said simply.

"Which answers nothing," Adam said. "I can see, Quinn. I can see the same thing Jake Burroughs sees." He turned away and walked back to the porch, setting some nails into a length of the replacement flooring and hammering them into place. "You know what you get with me," he said, not looking at her.

She caught his arm when he was about to hammer another nail in, sliding around so that she was between him and the porch. "Tell me what I get," she challenged him, because she knew he was unsettled by Jake's visit, regardless of his superb handling of the situation, and because she knew that, except for her, he was alone.

"No parties and no purple satin dresses," he said, trying to get around her.

"That's what I *won't* get. Try again."

"Me!" he said angrily. "You get me! And that's all, Quinn. That's all!"

"Good enough!" she said. She was still in his way, and he moved her aside.

"Maybe you'll get tired of me," he said, hammering again.

"Maybe you'll get tired of living English," she countered, swapping worry for worry, if that's what he wanted to do.

"I have no property. No money. No silver car. Maybe you'll be ashamed of me."

"I can't cook and run a house like Lena. Maybe you'll have dirty underwear and starve."

He threw the hammer down. "You know what I think?" he shouted, jabbing the air with his forefinger.

"No! Tell me!" she shouted back.

But he didn't go on. He sighed, his face grave suddenly. "You haven't said you'll marry me, Quinn."

"You haven't really asked, Adam. You've only said what you wanted."

He thought about that for a moment, then nodded. "I keep making the same mistake, don't I? Thinking that I don't have to *say* what needs to be said. So I ask you. Will you marry me? In spite of everything, will you put your life with mine?"

His face was still grave, and she looked into his eyes, his beautiful eyes that made her forget all past and potential pain.

In spite of everything.

She didn't voice her reservations. Adam was waiting, and he was so dear to her. In her mind's eye, she saw him at the different stages of their lives. Adam, the boy. Adam, the man. It was true: the wrong between them couldn't be settled if they were apart. She was still afraid, but she pushed the fear aside.

"Yes," she said evenly. "I'll marry you."

He reached for her, and suddenly it seemed like a very long time since she'd been in his arms. He held her tightly, and she could feel the tension in him.

"I was afraid you'd go with Jake," he said after a moment.

"You heard what I told him last night. I told him I wasn't coming to Philadelphia."

He leaned back to look at her. "Telling the voice is different from telling the man." He reached up to smooth her hair back. "Your face is still sad."

"It's only because—" She stopped. Would they ever get away from it? Sadness. Distrust. The legacy of their youthful passion.

"Go on," he said, his eyes probing hers as they always did.

"I just didn't want you to lose—everything."

He pulled her to him. "Don't you understand by now?" he said fiercely. "*You* are everything. *You*. Even those years when I never saw you, we were together."

Yes, she thought. That was exactly how it was. If they'd never seen each other again, they'd still be together.

He nuzzled her cheek, then gave her a gentle kiss. Then another one at the corner of her mouth. And with a soft moan, his mouth covered hers. His touch was warm, and it scrambled her senses. She closed her eyes, giving herself up to the sensations his touch elicited, to the warmth of his lips and to the warmth of his body against hers, feeling him respond in return. His hands slid over her, one to find her breast, one to press her even closer.

"Quinn," he said, and she opened her eyes. He was smiling, his eyes filled with mischief. "I can't fix the porch now."

She smiled in return. "I'd be very disappointed if you could."

He laughed. "No, that's not what I mean. Well, yes, I mean that, too."

"Make up your mind, Sauder."

"Holland Wakefield's coming," he said to explain his dilemma.

She looked around as Holland's truck pulled into the drive.

"Hello, Holland," she called as he got out of the truck, wondering a bit that he seemed not in the least surprised that he'd just seen her with her arms around Adam Sauder.

"Quinn," he said, tipping his lumber company ball cap. "I see you got back in one piece," he said to Adam.

"Yes," Adam said, and Quinn thought he looked a bit sheepish. He rubbed the side of his nose with one finger, then grinned. "I was out driving," he advised her, trying unsuccessfully to keep the grin under control.

And pretty darn pleased about it, too, she thought. "Driving what?" she asked pointedly. She didn't miss the looks he and Holland exchanged.

The grin broadened. "Your car."

"*My* car?"

"It was the only car I had the keys to," he advised her further.

"Oh. Well, that makes sense. No use stealing one," she said dryly, wondering what else he'd done while she slept.

"How did you think I got the boards for the porch?" he asked reasonably.

"I don't know, but I can tell you I didn't think you drove off someplace in my car to get them," she assured him.

"Aw, he did a good job, Quinn. Didn't jump more than two or three ditches the whole time, and that was just because a constable was after him."

"All right!" Quinn laughed. "Don't tell me any more!"

"Well, son," Holland said, still grinning, "we're okay on the job. My nephew will put you up and feed you. But don't let him work you longer than eight hours unless you want to. I'll pick you up about five or so and take you on down there." He nodded toward the porch. "You might have time to finish the work you're doing there before you go."

"I don't think it'll take me five hours to finish it, Holland."

"No, that's not what I mean, son. I saw your old man in town this morning. He said if I saw you to tell you to come to the farm and get your clothes. I figure you'll want to go see him before you leave. Well, I got to get out of here. Quinn, honey, take care of yourself. And if I was you, I'd hide my car keys."

Quinn smiled a goodbye, but she didn't feel it. Adam went back to work on the porch, and she sat down on the steps close to him, watching him work but saying nothing.

"The job is in Gettysburg," Adam said after a time. "I need the money for our marriage."

She nodded, still watching him closely.

"It's good that it came up, this job," he went on. "It's at one of those tourist places, a bed-and-breakfast. Holland's nephew owns it. He needs some work done on the inside. It'll take about ten days, two weeks, maybe. Will it be too soon for you if we get married the Saturday afternoon two weeks from today?"

"No," she answered. She reached out to touch his arm so that he wouldn't start hammering again. "Tell me what you're feeling."

"About getting married?"

"No, about getting your clothes."

"I've left there, Quinn. It doesn't come as any surprise that Pop wants me to get my belongings."

"Don't patronize me, Adam."

He made an impatient gesture. "Quinn, I don't even know what that means!"

"It means that I want you to say to me, out loud, what you're feeling. Your sins may be your sins, if you insist, but your pain is mine. I don't want you to spare me."

He took a deep breath. "Quinn," he began, but he didn't go on. He came and sat down on the steps with her. "I feel you worrying, Quinn. And yes, I will miss my family. I told you Eli will marry the first Thursday in November. You remember Eli? He was about Daniel's age when you left. He was born too early, and he's always been sickly. But he's going to marry anyway. I admire Eli. I would have liked to be there for his wedding. I'll miss him, and Aaron and my sisters. And my mother. I'll even miss David and Pop. I'll especially miss Daniel. But my missing them takes nothing away from the love I feel for you."

She turned sharply away from him. "Dear God, Adam, I wasn't trying to make you say that. I wasn't trying to force you to give me reassurances."

"Quinn, Quinn, what am I going to do with you?" he said, taking her by the shoulders and making her look at him. "You can't make me say what I don't feel. Are we always going to go around and around like this?"

"I don't know," she said, resting her head on his shoulder.

"Don't make it harder than it is for us," he whispered against her ear.

"Adam—"

"I'm not the first Amishman to leave, Quinn. I won't be the last."

She took a deep breath. "All right," she said, straightening and looking into his eyes. "I'm going to do better. I promise."

He smiled and patted her cheek. "Now I have to ask you a favor."

"What is it?"

"I would like for us to be married in the meadow over there under the trees, where your property joins the farm. So I can invite the family."

"Adam, I don't think they'll come."

"Even so. If it's outside, they won't be breaking the *Ordnung* about entering other churches. And even if I'm being shunned, that doesn't extend to you. I want to ask them, and I want to make it possible for them to be there if they want to. If they don't come, that's their choice. I will understand."

She reached up to touch his face. "All right. I think it's the right thing to do."

He smiled. "Saturday two weeks?"

"Saturday two weeks," she affirmed. "What if the job isn't finished?"

"You don't worry," he said, giving her a bear hug. "It will be finished!" Laughing together, they tumbled back onto the porch. She reached up to touch his face, to run her hands into his hair, her lips parting as she saw the passion in his eyes.

"You make me forget everything," he said, his mouth brushing lightly over hers.

"Do you think this is a good place for this?" she whispered, and he grinned.

"I think if I don't get to work on the porch, I won't care if it's a good place or not." He kissed her soundly and let her up, pulling her to her feet so he could finish the job at hand.

Quinn went into the house, cleaned up the kitchen and worked for a while on Edison's accounting records.

"Adam, take off your clothes!" she called when she heard him come inside. She got up from the computer to find him.

David Sauder stood in the front hallway, his face as rigid

as if it had been carved in stone. There was only the red blush on each cheek to tell her he'd heard what she said.

"I was going to wash his clothes for him," she said inanely, as if she could make him believe it, and hating herself for explaining yet unable to stop. "He's coming to see Jacob."

"You don't answer my knock on the door," David said stiffly. "So I came inside. I have brought his things here, where people say he is living now." His eyes flicked over the house. "I don't want to leave them outside and have him say we mistreat him."

"He wouldn't do—"

"You tell him, Quinn Tyler," he interrupted. "You tell him there is no need for him to come to our house. He is not to come on our land again." He pushed the box containing Adam's clothes at her.

"David," she said as he walked toward the door, but he turned on her with such anger that she took a step backward.

"You!" he said, pointing a finger in her direction. "I have nothing to do with a whore like you!"

"What did you say?" Adam said quietly from the kitchen doorway. He took a step closer, and David tried to get by him. "What did you say to her!" Adam demanded, grabbing him by the shirtfront and slamming him against the wall.

The answer was in German, and Adam lashed out at his brother with his fist. But David anticipated the effect his remark would have, and the blow only grazed his head.

"Stop it!" Quinn cried, following them into the kitchen as they dragged each other around. She was still holding the box, and she dropped it as they crashed into the kitchen table. "Stop it!"

Neither of them heard her, and she tried to get between them.

"Adam! Adam, please!" She was holding on to his arm with all her strength, and it gave David the chance he needed. He hit Adam hard, splitting the skin above his eye, and Adam lunged at him, causing them both to fall. He had David down, his fist raised.

"Adam!" Quinn screamed at him. "Don't! My God, don't!"

He looked at her then, and after a moment he let his hand fall, his chest heaving from the exertion, his face bloody. He still had David by the throat, and he seemed dazed, as if he had no idea how all this came to be. He moved away from his brother, sitting in the middle of the floor, his head bowed.

Quinn grabbed a towel and knelt beside him, trying to hold it over the cut.

"Please," she said to David, "just go."

"Adam, I didn't—" he started to say, but he suddenly stopped, going out the back door and letting it bang shut behind him.

"Don't fuss over me, Quinn," Adam said, getting up from the floor.

"Adam, wait. You're bleeding."

He didn't answer her; he went out the back door.

"Adam, where are you going? Adam—"

"I'll be back later," he said without stopping. "I have to settle this once and for all."

Chapter Twelve

Adam saw his father as soon as he entered the yard. The old man was working intently on a buggy wheel in the shade of trees, dragging it off the axle and setting it aside. He was wearing his straw hat and his usual black vest, the sleeves of his shirt rolled up above the elbows. His hands and the front of his trouser legs were greasy from the wheel.

Barefoot and humming to herself, Anna was pushing a hand cultivator through the rows of pepper plants in the vegetable garden nearby, shooing the flies away from her face as she walked. He heard the cultivator fall when she caught sight of him, and his father looked around sharply. Anna was already running for the house, as if Adam were some unclean thing she had to escape.

"Anna!" his father bellowed. "You work the garden! You do not worry the others with this!"

Anna hesitated, torn between having to obey Jacob and wanting to get inside. She turned back to the garden, picked up the cultivator again and pushed it raggedly down the row, casting furtive looks at Adam as she went.

Jacob waited until Adam came closer, his eyes immediately going to Adam's face and his torn shirt. "You come here like this? You let your mother see you like this?" he began, but there was the *Meidung*. He pressed his lips together to silence himself, but evidently there was too much he needed to say. "Come away in here!" he hissed at him. "Do not let your mother see you all bloody. Fighting yet! Who are you fighting with?"

"It doesn't matter," Adam said, following his father into the dark coolness of the barn. "It's not as bad as it looks."

"Did you stand in front of the mirror to decide that before you came? Why are you here, Adam? David took you your belongings. You know I can't talk to you."

"You don't have to talk, Pop. I want to do the talking. I don't want to argue with you. I only want you to listen."

"No!" his father said impatiently. "It's over, the time for talking and listening!"

"Pop," Adam said quietly, trying to hold on to his temper. The memory of Quinn's face at David's insult was still raw in him. He was only too aware that he had never *said* what he was feeling, what he wanted, either to his family or to Quinn. He was going to say it now. "You will hear this. If I have to sit on your chest, I'm going to say it. The only way you can keep me from saying it to you is to call David and the rest of them to throw me off the place. Do you want my mother to see that?"

His father made an impatient gesture with his hand and moved to sit down on a bale of hay near the doorway. He took off his hat and reached into his pocket, pulling out a blue bandanna and wiping his brow and then his hands. "I'm listening," he said finally, but in keeping with the *Meidung*, he said it to no one.

Adam came closer and sat down on another bale. He had both loved and hated this man who was his father, but he had always respected him. Jacob Sauder was strong in the *Unserem Weg*, the Amish way, and he meant for his sons to be strong with him. Now that Adam had Jacob's attention, he didn't know where to start. He had so much he wanted to say, and only this one chance to say it. The day was hot already, and a cool breeze wafted through the barn. The sparrows chirped and quarreled overhead, flitting from their perches along the eaves. He looked at Jacob closely, surprised somehow at how old he seemed today, and he leaned forward with the need to make him finally understand.

"I want to tell you the thing that has been so hard for me, Pop," he began. "Listen to me!" he cried when Jacob was about to get up again. "It's that you and David always behaved as if Quinn was some kind of—of crazy notion I had." He gestured with his hand. "Like wanting fresh strawberries in the dead of winter. That even if she had spent a great part of being a child *here*, she was a stranger to us and not real. You behaved as if you thought she was something I'd get over if I only tried hard enough. Or maybe I'd wake up one morning and what I felt about her would be gone. I did try, Pop, and you know that. It wasn't just for you and the family that I tried, but for myself, because after I knew about the baby, I didn't think anything was possible between us."

He paused, then went on. "But nothing helped. Not the lectures from you and the elders. Not going out to the Ohio relatives. Not trying to make myself think I wanted to marry Sarah. I still cared about Quinn. I always have. Even when we were children, it seemed my life was bound up with hers. I don't believe that will ever change, no matter where I go or what I do or where she is. It was wrong, what we did, having a child together when we couldn't marry. It's a sadness I'll carry all my life. But I don't want to carry the sadness of not being with her, too. I lost my son. I don't want to lose her.

"I know you think you failed. I know you think you're not a good father because of me, because I can't do what I'm *supposed* to do. It's not true. All the things you taught me, I still have. All the things you made me, I still am. Even if I'm away from here, I'll still love the land, and I'll still believe that it's my calling to care for it, to replenish whatever I take. No matter what I do, I'll still try to be fair, I'll try to behave honorably. And if I fail, it will be my failure, my weakness, not yours. You need never be ashamed.

"'Be gentle unto all men,' you taught me. From the looks of me, I need to try hardest of all with that. But, Pop, I believe it. I *believe* that's the way a man should live, with all my heart, and I thank you for teaching it to me.

"I know you think that I should do my duty. So do I. It's only on what that duty is that we differ. I believe my duty is to Quinn. I *am* going to marry her, Pop."

His father moved restlessly on the bale of hay, then stood up.

"Why can't I make you understand?" Adam cried, grabbing at his father's arm to keep him from leaving. "I'm only telling you what you see—what you've seen for the last eleven years of my life!"

But Jacob held up his hands. "Sit down, Adam. The place over your eye needs tending. Your face is not so unhurt as you think."

"I don't care about my face, Pop!"

"Sit down! Will you do nothing I ask of you?"

Adam bit down on an angry reply. *Were eleven years nothing?* he wanted to ask, but he didn't. Nor did he sit down. He stayed where he was, pacing, watching as his father went outside to the watering trough and searched in his pockets again for the blue bandanna. He wet it from the trickle of water that ran constantly by gravity from a pipe at the trough, and then he brought it back into the barn.

"Sit down," he said.

"It's nothing," Adam said, reaching up to touch the place that hurt so over his eye. His hand came away bloody.

"Did you think I was not telling you the truth? Sit."

Adam sat down again, and Jacob adjusted his spectacles and

found a clean corner of the bandanna. With that, he quietly began to wash the blood from Adam's face. It hurt when his father wiped the place over his eye, and he winced.

"Sit still," Jacob said gruffly. "Even as a little boy, you couldn't sit still."

"Pop, you don't have to do this."

"You are still my son!" he said sharply, and Adam let it go. It was not his place to worry about whether or not Jacob was upholding the strict rules of the *Meidung*.

"I have never known why you are like this, why you decide what you decide and never change it. Adam, Adam, it aches me to see you like this!"

"Don't hate seeing me happy, Pop," Adam said quietly.

Jacob moved away to a small cabinet on the wall, bringing back a jar of the *Zeek Schmer* he kept there. How many times had Jacob done this for him? Adam wondered, soothed his wounds with the homemade salve his mother cooked all day on the kitchen stove and put into baby food jars?

"I didn't say the truth just now," Jacob said. "I do know why you are the way you are. It's because, of all my sons, you are the one I see myself in most. It's a man's vanity to want a son to be like him, but you are the son I will lose because of it."

"I can't be what you want, Pop," Adam began, but Jacob made a hissing noise of protest to stop him.

The old man fumbled at removing the lid on the jar of ointment, and Adam took it away from him, opening it and handing it back again. Jacob gave a quiet sigh and reached into the jar, taking a bit of the salve onto his fingertips. His fingers were gnarled and weatherbeaten from a lifetime of working the land, and Adam closed his eyes as his father gently rubbed the salve into the cut. The camphor and turpentine smell of it rose between them, and with it, the memories of his childhood and all the scraped elbows and cut fingers that had come to him while he worked at Jacob's side.

He had tried hard to learn to become a man, a man who

could farm the land as well as Jacob Sauder did, and feed his family, and be firm or be gentle with his children. Strange, Adam thought. He had never considered it, but perhaps it was true. He and his father were alike. He had always understood him, even during their worst arguments about Quinn. Even when Jacob had punished him, he'd never doubted that his father loved him.

He looked into Jacob's face. There were tears gathering at the corners of his father's eyes, and they suddenly brimmed over and slid unheeded down his cheeks and into his beard.

"I haven't failed you, Pop. Not the way you think," Adam began, but he didn't go on. This was the last time they would be father and son together, and they both knew it.

"Pop," he said as his father turned to go. "Pop, I'll be getting married in two weeks, on Saturday afternoon, in the meadow down there by the willows. I would like it if you and the family would come. Quinn doesn't have any family but this one. It would please us both if you could be there."

Jacob stood silently for a moment, but he made no reply. He walked out of the barn to the broken wheel he'd been working on, and he didn't look back.

It's over, Adam thought, staring after him. It's really, finally over.

And he felt nothing. Not happiness, certainly, but not sadness, either, except in a detached way, as if it were all happening to someone else. He wished he could have spared his family the upheaval and the shame, but he had always known that he belonged with Quinn, just as he had always known that it would take his leaving here for them to be together. He looked across the field toward the Tyler place. Quinn was waiting there, thinking the worst, and he had to get back to her. In the end, his father had been right. The time for talking and listening was over.

He saw David as he cut across the backyard. His brother was standing near the grape arbor where Jacob wouldn't see him, waiting for Adam to pass. But Adam wasn't hiding anything ever again. If David wanted to say something to him, he would have to come out into the open to say it.

After a moment of struggling with his conscience, David approached.

"What is it?" Adam asked him. "You want to call *me* names, too?"

"I want to see if you're hurt."

"Quinn is the one who is hurt."

"I didn't meant what I said to her. I—I'm sorry. I want you to tell her that."

"No. You tell her, David. If you want her to know that, you'll have to make the apology yourself. I won't do it for you."

"It hasn't been easy here! I have a lot of responsibilities!"

"And you have a lot of jealousy because I might have married Sarah."

David flushed crimson. They had never spoken of Adam's courtship of Sarah Stolzfus, and he expected David to deny his resentment now.

"You had no reason to say what you did to Quinn," Adam said. "I hate to think that you would hurt her so because you still think you're being stuck with my hand-me-downs."

"You told Pop all about it, I guess."

"No. I didn't tell him. This is between you and me. It has nothing to do with him, except that he didn't bring you up to call any woman, regardless of what you think of her, a whore."

"I told you I didn't mean it!"

"And I told you I'm not the one who needs to hear it!"

Adam walked on, but then he turned back. "David," he called, waiting until his brother looked up at him. "You have a good wife, the one you wanted. And she's married to the man *she* wanted. She's going to have your baby. The two of you will have a happy life together. Don't begrudge me the same chance with Quinn."

When he reached the edge of the field, he heard a chorus of voices in the house calling his name. Anna and Mary.

"Adam!" Anna called again. "Wait for us!"

His two sisters bounded out the door, but there was still the *Meidung*, and they grew embarrassed when they reached him, standing awkwardly.

"We're not afraid to talk to you," Anna finally announced, more for her own benefit than his. She was clearly afraid— they both were—and the fact that they'd come to him anyway made it all the more precious to him.

"I'm glad," he said, not trusting his voice. "I wanted to say goodbye to you."

"Are you going to marry Quinn?" Mary asked.

"Yes."

"You won't ever be back here then?"

"No." He held out his arms and hugged them both soundly. "Go on back inside now. Are Eli and Aaron here?"

"No, they went to help old Mr. Zook with his milking. His hired boy is sick."

"Then will you tell them I'll miss them?"

"I'll tell them," Anna said.

They started for the house, but Mary turned back to him. "Adam, I'm glad you and Quinn are getting married," she said in a rush before she lost her nerve.

"So am I. Go on now."

His mother was coming out the back door, and he walked toward her to save her the exertion of catching up with him. He was about to minimize the cut on his face and the dried blood on his shirt, but she didn't give him the opportunity, meeting him at the end of the stone path and hugging him tightly before he could say anything.

"Don't cry, Mom," was all he could manage.

"I don't cry for your going. You've been gone a long time—ever since Quinn left, all those years ago. I just don't want you to leave with bad feelings between you and David."

"Mom, I don't have any bad feelings. David knows what to do if he wants to make it right between us."

She leaned back to look at him, to satisfy herself that what he said was so. "Look at your face. Come inside, let me fix it."

"No, Mom, Pop's already taken care of it."

If that surprised her, she didn't show it. "Don't forget us, Adam."

"No, Mom. I won't forget."

"And you and Quinn—you be careful out there in the world."

"We'll be careful, Mom. Isn't Daniel here?"

"He's here, but he's afraid to see you, Adam. He's afraid of the shunning."

Adam looked away, out across the fields. Poor Daniel.

"I'll go and talk to him."

"No," his mother said. "Not yet. I'll tell him you wanted to. And I'll tell him that you still love him, no matter what happens."

He nodded, acquiescing to his mother's handling of the situation.

"Don't forget us!" his mother said again, but she didn't wait for him to reply. She managed a wavering smile, then she turned abruptly away, leaving him much the way Jacob had.

He looked back once as he walked on the dirt road between the cornfields, hoping to catch a glimpse of Daniel. He saw no one. He took a shortcut across the stepping stones over the creek instead of going the long way to the bridge. He had but one thought now: Quinn. His fight with David had done nothing to reassure her that he was doing what he wanted to do, and he watched the house anxiously as he approached, half expecting her to be waiting on the porch.

But she wasn't there. He was relieved to see that at least her car was parked where he'd left it.

He could smell something cooking when he reached the

backyard, and she met him at the door with a wooden spoon in her hand and flour on her nose. He smiled, and the worried look she was wearing wavered.

"What are you cooking?" he asked as he stepped inside, as if nothing out of the ordinary had happened, as if he weren't standing there with his face cut and swollen and blood all over his shirt.

"Adam!" she said, throwing her arms around him. He lifted her off the floor, leaning back, savoring the feel of her against him. How good it was to hold her! His body responded instantly, and his hands slid over her to press her closer. Once again, he marveled at the miracle of it—Quinn glad to see him, Quinn lifting her mouth to his.

He moved her bodily to one of the kitchen chairs, pulled it out from the table and sat down with her in his lap. She curled against him, and he cradled her close, for in comforting her, he comforted himself.

And what a relief it was to know that, while his anger at David had been painful for her, she had understood.

"Everything's all right," he whispered to her, knowing how much she wanted to ask him and that she wouldn't.

"Is it?"

"Yes."

"Are you sure?"

Her hand clutched the front of his shirt, and he placed his hand over hers. "I'm sure. I'm sorry about what David said to you."

"You didn't fight with David any more, did you? I don't think he meant it."

"No, I didn't fight with David. I talked to Pop. I invited him and the family to the wedding."

She sat up to comment, but he pressed his fingers against her lips.

"We won't worry about whether or not they'll come. I've asked them. That's all I can do."

She gave a heavy sigh and closed her eyes. "I wish—"

He didn't let her go on, pulling her against him and holding her fast. "Don't. Don't, Quinn," he said roughly. "There's no point in wishing."

But she sat up again, reaching up to rest her hands on his shoulders, her eyes searching his face, assessing his injuries up close. "*Zeek Schmer*," she said abruptly, wrinkling her nose, and he smiled a smile he didn't quite feel.

"Pop thinks *Zeek Schmer* cures everything."

"Even wayward sons?" she asked quietly.

"Quinn…"

"I'm sorry, I'm sorry. I told you I'd do better, and I will."

She sighed heavily. "Adam," she whispered, leaning against him again, "we're orphans in the storm, you and I."

"It never storms forever," he whispered back, and she smiled.

"It can feel like forever. Oh, no!" she cried, jumping off his lap. "The pie!"

He laughed in spite of the trials of the day. "What pie?"

"The pie I'm burning for your dinner. Corn Pie," she said as she threw open the oven door. She showed it to him, only slightly overbaked.

"Looks good," he said, but his mind was already on the two weeks he was committed to work in Gettysburg.

"What enthusiasm," she commented.

His eyes met and held hers. "I'm not very hungry."

"Neither am I," she said, setting the pie down heavily on the counter. "I just made it to have something to do while you were gone. I knew I couldn't help you, and I didn't seem to be able to add and subtract—well, what the heck. I probably used sugar instead of salt, or salt instead of flour, or something."

She still had her back to him, and he got up from the chair, putting his arms around her and holding her tightly. He buried his face in her neck, and she reached up to touch his hair.

"You don't listen to me, do you?" he said. "I told you everything's all right."

She sighed heavily and turned to him. "I'm afraid," she said candidly, her eyes searching his.

"Don't be. The worst is done. It's only going to get better now." Did she believe him? He couldn't tell.

"I hope so," she said after a moment. "Do you want to eat now?"

"No. I want to go to bed with you."

It wasn't the answer she'd expected. It wasn't the answer he'd intended. It was simply the truth. They were orphans in the storm, and he needed her. She said nothing, reaching around him to turn off the oven, and then taking him by the hand.

He followed her lead. Wherever she wanted to go, he would follow. Always.

"You've got flour on your nose," he told her when he kissed her on the stairs.

"You don't look so hot yourself, Sauder," she responded, making him smile. "Don't worry. I'm going to fix us both."

It had never occurred to him that one might make love in a shower, but it was his exquisite pleasure to have her show him the possibilities. To stand naked with her under the steaming hot water, to soap her fine body, to have her do the same for him. Such intimacy with another person. Such pleasure. He could die from such pleasure.

And yet he didn't want to consummate his passion there. He stepped out of the shower, pulling her with him, lifting her up to carry her to the bed. He didn't care that they were both dripping; she didn't care. There was only the need, only the body that ached with desire, only the knowledge that his love for her was returned. With the full force of his passion, he plunged into her, and she responded, met each thrust, until they both lay spent and sated and no longer so alone.

I didn't know, he thought. *I didn't know it could ever be like this.*

What if Quinn had never come back here and he'd spent the rest of his life alone? Before, when they'd been lovers, the physical relationship had been exciting, primed by the danger of it and by the lustiness of youth. It had been like forbidden fruit for them both. But now, when his love for her had been tested by time and by their long separation, there was no comparison. It was beyond anything he'd ever experienced, this oneness of body and mind.

We are the same person, he thought, turning over to look at her.

She was dozing. He stared at her face, at the dark lashes that lay against her pale skin, at the curving lines of her mouth. She was so beautiful to him.

He gave a quiet sigh. He was tired, and he was restless with something he couldn't name. He listened to the wind in the maple trees outside, a warm spring breeze that dried the ground so that a man would work in the fields. A patch of sunlight fell across the bed, dappled sunlight that moved with the wind in the trees.

He drew a deep breath and slowly released it, letting his eyes close. He *could* name the restlessness in him, and there was no use to pretend otherwise. It was caused by the need to know. He leaned forward to kiss Quinn softly on the shoulder. Her skin was still damp from the shower they'd shared, still fragrant from the soap.

He reached up to touch her hair.

Quinn, he wanted to say. *Quinn, where is our son?*

But he didn't, and that was the restlessness in him. He needed so desperately to tell her that they had to find their child, and he was afraid everything with her would end if he did. She had said she didn't know where the boy was, and he'd believed her—except that that had been *before,* when she'd just come back and he'd been so wary and suspicious and he'd tried so hard to pretend that he didn't love her.

He opened his eyes to find her looking at him.

It was still there in her eyes, he thought. The fear he'd seen her first day back.

Why are you afraid, Quinn?

"Your face looks terrible," she said, and he smiled. He smiled, but she knew. He could feel it. She knew there was some wrongness between them, something they both knew existed, and something they both could identify—if they dared.

I'm afraid, too. He wanted to tell her this. But he didn't.

He sat up on the side of the bed. "I have to finish the porch," he said, rummaging through the clean clothes David had brought until he found something to put on. The rest of his everyday clothes he rolled together and stuffed into a duffel bag Quinn had put into the box for him. He felt something between one of the shirts. An envelope. He took it out and opened it. It was his birth certificate, the one his mother had kept in the big Bible on the shelf in the sitting room. He handed it to Quinn.

"I'll need this to get married. Do you think you could bring it up to Gettysburg one afternoon next week? We could go get the license and—" He broke off because of the look on her face. "What is it?" he asked quietly. "Is this too fast for you?" He tried to smile. "I'm not going to have to go tell my father he's uninvited to a wedding, am I?"

She reached for him, and he took her into his arms. She kissed him gently, careful of his injured face. "No, no. I know what I want. I want a life with you. I just—you've been so quiet. I know it's a sad time for you. I just didn't know if you still—"

"I have no regrets, Quinn. Well, one," he said candidly. "Daniel. He wouldn't talk to me today. He's afraid of the *Meidung.*"

"He asked me to take you to live with me," Quinn said, and Adam smiled, feeling infinitely better suddenly. Daniel, child or not, was in tune with everything. If he didn't have Jacob's blessing, he had Daniel's.

"When did my little brother do that?"

"When I came to your grandfather's carpentry shop to talk

to you. He was very worried. If I couldn't make you stay, then he wanted me to take you with me.''

He kissed her softly. ''I told him once that I'd known you since before we were his age. I told him you were my friend.'' He looked into her eyes.

Now. Tell her now you want to find our son.

She hugged him tightly. ''That's right! Now. Let me feed you before Holland gets here,'' she said, getting up.

He let the opportunity slip by. It had hurt her so before when he'd asked. He didn't want to hurt her anymore.

''If you're going to walk around like that, I'm not going to be interested in food *or* Holland.''

She smiled at him, looking young and carefree the way he remembered her. ''I wish you weren't going.''

''I don't want to come to you with nothing, Quinn. The money I make will help us get started.''

''I know. It's just that two weeks is a long time.''

''Not compared to eleven years,'' he said, and her smile faded, the specter of their son between them again. She looked as if she were about to say something, but she didn't, pulling a T-shirt on over her head instead.

''Come help me with the porch,'' he said, because he wanted to be close to her as long as he could.

She was smiling again as her head emerged from the shirt, as if his request pleased her. ''Be right there.''

He went downstairs, and they worked on the porch nearly an hour, finishing it in time to share the corn pie before Holland came.

This is what he wanted, he told himself. To just *be* with her. To work and to laugh. To feel the love and the warmth and the undercurrent of sexual desire running strong between them. And he told himself that there was no reason to worry.

He took several helpings of the pie, because it was as good as his mother had ever baked, and he told her so.

''She taught me to make it,'' Quinn said. ''One summer when I was always underfoot. Holland's coming.''

"Come here then," he said, holding out his arms to her. He kissed her deeply, feeling his need of her as he always did. He lowered his head to press his face against her breasts for a moment, the love he felt for her nearly a physical pain. "Want to come with me?"

"Yes!" she said emphatically, and he laughed.

He gave a resigned sigh. "Saturday afternoon, two weeks, all right? And you'll come to Gettysburg before so we can get the license?"

"My pleasure, Mr. Sauder," she said, smiling up at him.

"I'll call you," he added.

"You will?" she said, as if that possibility hadn't occurred to her.

"It's all right for me to use the telephone now, Quinn," he reminded her. He made himself let her go, swatting her on the behind and walking outside, because Holland was already on the porch. He dreaded this initial encounter with Holland. Quinn had been tactful at best; his face did look awful.

"What the hell happened to you?" Holland demanded on sight, and Adam sighed again. He took the duffel bag he'd forgotten from Quinn's hands, letting his eyes linger on hers for a moment so that she would know the things he couldn't say with Holland watching. He put his hand firmly on Holland's shoulder to steer him away from questioning Quinn and back toward the truck.

"Holland, you've been good all day today about not asking about things that are none of your business. Don't push your luck now."

"Don't push my luck?" Holland asked, grinning.

"That's right. Now get into the truck."

"I'm not to push my luck," he advised Quinn over his shoulder. "I'm to get into the truck. You didn't do this, did you, Quinn?" he asked, pointing to Adam's face. "I was married to a woman one time who was that touchy about who drove her car."

"You want to come to a wedding?" Adam asked him, interceding before she had to answer.

"Whose wedding?" Holland said suspiciously.

"Mine and Quinn's."

"Well, if she did that to you and you still want to marry her, it must be love, is all I got to say."

"Do you want to come to the wedding, or don't you?" Adam repeated, glancing at Quinn and trying not to grin.

"Hell, yes, son. Me and mine'll be there with bells on."

Chapter Thirteen

With bells on, Quinn thought. Unfortunately, it wouldn't be that kind of wedding. She had no family, and Adam's wouldn't come. But she was happy anyway. Almost.

The house was so empty. She had thought it empty before, when she'd first come back, but devoid now of Adam's presence, it was nearly unbearable. On Sunday afternoon she worked on Edison's financial reports—when she could put Adam out of her mind enough to do it—and on Monday she made herself available for the possibility of his telephone call, never straying out of earshot of the phone and breaking up the time by finishing the financial reports and admiring the repair work on the porch. Adam didn't call, but she didn't worry; telephone calls were expensive. She continued to work around the house, eating on time and even napping, all the while with the same thought echoing happily in her mind: *Adam and I are getting married.*

On Tuesday she drove into town to take Edison's reports to him. Her good mood had persisted, and she greeted his receptionist, Margaret, warmly as she entered the office. Perhaps too warmly, she decided; she could feel Margaret making the comparison between this meeting and their last.

She was ushered in immediately to see Edison, and she waited until he was nearly through looking over the files she'd brought before she mentioned anything to him.

"I was wondering if you'd be busy—"

"Want to invite me to a wedding?." he interrupted, trying to keep a straight face.

"What makes you think that?" Quinn asked, trying to give as good as she got. "And how did you know about it anyway?" she asked testily when he grinned. She couldn't surprise him with anything.

"It's out in the Amish community," Edison said. "The proverbial grapevine. Jacob Sauder's Adam is marrying English—you're the English. Saturday, two weeks, I'm told. Ah, three in the afternoon. It's to be an outside wedding out of deference to Adam's family. Oh, and Margaret and I are invited already."

"You are?"

"Mmm," Edison said, thumbing through a few more papers. He looked up at her over his reading glasses. "Unless you object?"

"Oh, no," she assured him. "Do I get to know who invited you?"

"The bridegroom himself. Talked to him this morning. Margaret and I are handling the reception. Close your mouth, Quinn, before a fly flies in."

"You talked to Adam?"

"Honey, now you know when the Amish get married, the bridegroom handles the invitations. This is going to be one bang-up wedding. I'm looking forward to it. Margaret, too. You got anything in particular in the way of food you want served?"

"What? No," she said, a bit bewildered.

"Good. Margaret and I were hoping you'd just let us run wild."

"Well, don't run too wild. I don't want to have to sell what's left of the farm to pay for a wedding reception."

He grinned. "You won't. It's all taken care of."

"What do you mean it's all taken care of?"

"Never mind what I mean. Now, I've got to get to court. Anything else I can do for you?"

"No, no," Quinn said, still bewildered.

"Good! Go buy your wedding dress or something."

She didn't buy a dress. She went to buy groceries, finding along the way that the wedding guests also included two hardware salesmen, a veterinarian and the entire staff of the Amish Country visitors' center. The latter invitation troubled her a bit; she didn't want to get married surrounded by tour buses.

She came home to find Margaret waiting on the porch—with six ladies from the Mennonite Church who did Pennsylvania Dutch catering as a service project for the church missions fund.

"They want to do the cooking here, Quinn," Margaret explained as Quinn unlocked the back door.

"Margaret, I don't even know how many are coming."

"That's all right. Adam said to plan for about a hundred."

"A hundred!"

"That's what he said. Do you mind if we see what dishes you have?"

"I don't even know a hundred people," Quinn said under her breath. And she knew she didn't have enough dishes.

But she stayed out of the way while Margaret and the Mennonite ladies worked that out. The kitchen was large, and that pleased them—that and the fact that Quinn didn't have much in the way of furniture.

"Plenty of room for the tables," they assured her.

They gave Quinn a menu for her approval: roast chicken with bread, herb-and-giblet stuffing, mashed potatoes with gravy, cold ham, celery in sweet-and-sour sauce, coleslaw, canned peaches, bread and butter, pickles—three kinds— strawberry jam, apple pie, cherry pie, whipped cream, chocolate cake, mints.

"Do you think that will be enough, Quinn?" one of the women asked her in all seriousness.

"Yes," Quinn assured her. Particularly since she'd envisioned ten guests at most. "Margaret," she whispered, taking her aside, "how much is this going to cost?"

"It's already paid for."

"By whom?"

"Your husband to be."

"He doesn't have any money."

"Well, he had enough for this. Anything else, ladies?"

Margaret left with her cooks, and Quinn paced around the kitchen, not seeing the men on the back porch until they knocked. They were not Old Order Amish—she could tell that by their hats—but they were still Amish. Beachy or Church Amish, she thought.

"Yes?"

"This is the house where Adam Sauder will marry Quinn Tyler?" one of them asked.

"Yes," she said, looking around the group.

The speaker took off his hat. "We come to give our gift for the wedding."

"I don't understand."

"We have the glass panes. We will put them in the windows now."

With that, he withdrew, leaving Quinn full of questions with no one to ask.

The telephone rang, and she went to answer it.

"I miss you," a beloved voice said in her ear, and her heart leaped.

"I miss *you* Adam, you won't believe—"

"Quinn, I need you to come to town—now—to the courthouse."

"They're fixing the windows—I didn't get their names—it's a wedding present—the courthouse? What courthouse?"

"This one. I got a ride here. Can you hurry?"

She hurried, remembering to ask the name of each of the men working on the windows so she could tell Adam, and remembering, when she was already backing out of the drive, that she had to have the birth certificates. She hurried back to get them, leaving the motor running and dashing through the yard, nearly bowling over one of the men who picked that moment to step down from the ladder.

"Oh, Mr. Zook, I'm sorry! Did I hurt you? I have to go get the marriage license—no, I have to get the birth certificates so I can go get the marriage license."

"Snickelfritz!" he said sternly to admonish her, but then he laughed, and she laughed with him. That was precisely what she felt like—a rowdy little kid.

She hurried as well as she could in a town full of tour buses. Adam was waiting on the courthouse steps, pacing anxiously. She ran the last few steps to him, wanting to throw her arms around him and hug the stuffing out of him, and knowing she couldn't do it. No public displays of affection. It was only officially that Adam was no longer Amish.

He looked so handsome to her. His face looked better, he was still wearing Amish clothes—a blue shirt and black trousers—and he was all business. He had no greeting for her other than a short nod, and he barely looked at her as they went inside. But when he opened the courthouse door for her, he said, "I love you, Quinn." He said it so quietly that no passerby could have heard it, and even she wasn't sure.

Until she looked into his eyes.

No one was ahead of them, and it took only a few minutes to fill out the forms and pay the fee, in spite of the obvious curiosity of the clerk. Clearly, while they might see the Amish come in for a license, they were not accustomed to "mixed marriages." She wanted to take Adam's arm as they walked out together into the bright sunlight, but she refrained. She knew the rules of proper behavior. But Adam's fingertips lightly brushed hers as he gave her the envelope with the license to keep.

"My ride is here," he said, looking over the top of her head. "He's helping me with the carpentry at the B & B. He's a good helper." He reached up as if he were going to touch her cheek, but then didn't. She could feel the warmth of his hand on her face as if he had.

"Can't you stay?" she asked hopefully. "I could take you back."

"No. I have to get some things I need for the job. He won't know what I want."

She gave a soft sigh. He was looking at her mouth.

"Well, I have to go." He walked off a few steps. "Quinn?" he said, turning back to her.

"What?" she murmured, letting his beautiful eyes probe hers. It was torture being this close to him and not being allowed to touch him.

"I can't wait to be your husband."

Her heart soared.

It was only later, when he called from Gettysburg, that she remembered she hadn't asked him about the expected hundred people at their wedding, or how they were going to afford it.

His answer was simple. "I have some money put by. I want to marry you the best I can, Quinn."

She didn't need a hundred wedding guests, but she understood his need to do the best he could. He didn't want anyone thinking that there was anything clandestine or shameful about his "marrying English."

"How's the work going?" she asked him, sensing something in his voice that made her want to get into her car right then and go find him.

"Good. The wife of Holland's nephew bought all the books at an estate sale—a whole library. It's going to take a lot of bookcases for them." He sighed. "The guests at the B & B get in the way. They think I'm part of the tourist attraction, like the battlefield. What do you call it? Living history. It surprises them that I don't know about the two armies and the generals and Pickett's charge.''

She waited for him to go on, but he didn't.

''Where are you now? At the B & B?'' she asked.

''Burger King.''

''Burger King?'' she repeated, her voice incredulous enough to make him laugh.

''It's something you don't know about me, Quinn. I have a bad weakness for french fries.''

''I knew that about you,'' she assured him, and he laughed again. But something was wrong. ''Adam, what is it?''

''Tell me—'' He broke off, and she could hear a car or truck going by.

''Adam?'' she said when the silence that followed lengthened.

''Tell me if you love me, Quinn. I need to hear it.''

The wedding gifts continued to arrive, from people who knew her father, from people Adam had done carpentry work for, and perhaps from people who were simply curious to see the woman who had set the Amish community on its ear— twice. Late Friday afternoon she was interrupted at her computer work by the UPS man with a huge box from Philadelphia.

It was from Jake and the staff at the accounting department—a microwave oven and a note saying they'd all be there for the wedding. She kept walking around the box, smiling. Adam. It wasn't only his friends that he'd invited; he'd taken care to invite hers, as well.

Late Saturday afternoon she had a visit from Daniel. She saw him crossing the fields, and she waited until he came up onto the porch, letting him knock loudly because she thought that little boys would probably like to do that—knock on a door loudly.

''Yes?'' she said solemnly, as if he were a stranger to her.

He looked up at her. "Daniel Sauder," she said, pretending to recognize him, and they both smiled.

"I came to see you, Quinn Tyler," he told her.

"So I see. I'm glad you did. Come in, please." She held the door open wide for him, and only then did she notice that he had something in his hand, something wrapped up in brown paper and tied with string.

"Come into the kitchen," she said, leading the way. "I need somebody to help me eat some chocolate chip cookies and drink some milk."

"I can do that," he said, and she smiled.

He took off his hat and sat down at the table, watching her as she got out the cookies and poured two glasses of milk.

"Adam isn't here," she told him, in case that was the reason he'd come, or if not, in case he was still afraid of the *Meidung*.

He took a bite of cookie. "He's in Gettysburg."

"That's right," Quinn said, eating a cookie of her own. "I forgot about the grapevine."

He sighed. "I don't know about any grapes. This is a good cookie," he advised her.

"I'm glad you like it." She pushed the plate in his direction. "Have another."

He took one, and he handed her the small parcel he was holding.

"What's this?"

"A marriage gift," he said with his mouth full. "Will you unwrap it now?" he asked solemnly.

"Yes, if you don't mind."

"Now I want you to see it. I made it," he told her as she began to pull off the string. "Eli helped me cut it out. And Anna helped me paint. Aaron said it was the wrong thing for a present. But I said you liked them—"

She had the paper off.

"—and you need one."

She held Daniel's gift in her hands. "It's beautiful," she

said, swallowing hard. She cleared her throat. "It's—it's the most beautiful thing I've ever seen."

"You like cows, Quinn Tyler, ain't? Cows like this, standing in the flowers."

"Very much." She took a deep breath to steady her voice. "It was so clever of you to make me one, especially when I—" she didn't want Daniel to think he'd made her cry "—need one the way I do."

He looked at her and nodded, then smiled. "One more cookie?"

She returned his smile, thinking how innocent and dear he was. Like Adam had been at his age. Like all Amish children.

"Take all of them," she told him, and his smile broadened into a grin.

"This is a good kind of cookie," he said again, filling both hands. "I have to go now. Will you put my hat on me, Quinn Tyler?"

"My pleasure." She picked up his hat and set it firmly on his head. She opened the door for him, as well. Then she went back to the kitchen table, sat down and picked up the wooden figure of a cow standing knee-deep in flowers.

There was a knock at the door almost immediately.

"Quinn Tyler," Daniel said when she opened the door again. "I forgot this telling." He was still eating cookies, and his mouth was full.

"What telling, Daniel?"

He swallowed hard. "Pop is coming to see you."

Oh, Lord, Quinn thought then and a hundred times a day afterward. And she began to look for him constantly, expecting every sound to herald the arrival of Jacob Sauder. But he didn't come. She had thought that she wouldn't mention it to Adam when he called, but she did. Almost immediately.

"Your father is coming to see me."

Adam said nothing.

"Adam? Did you hear me?"

"I heard you."

"Then *say* something."

"Better you than me?" he offered, teasing her.

"Adam, this is serious! What could he want?" She didn't mean to sound so distressed, but a visit with Jacob Sauder was nothing if not distressing.

"I don't know, Quinn. You'll just have to wait and see."

But Jacob was in no hurry. He waited until the early morning of the day of the wedding, when Quinn was trying to deal with the Mennonite ladies cooking and moving furniture all over the house and with Adam's sudden telephone announcement at the crack of dawn that he wasn't coming from Gettysburg until after noon. Basically, she was ready. She had her dress, a simple pastel-pink cotton dress with a dropped waist and a white lace collar. And she had a minister to perform the ceremony—Edison's brother, whom Adam already knew somehow. And several men had come, apparently at Adam's instruction, to mow the grass in the meadow. And Lord knows, she would have enough food for the reception, even if all hundred people came.

But she wasn't prepared for Jacob Sauder's visit, and she was just beginning to let herself hope that Daniel had been mistaken, or that Jacob had changed his mind, when she saw him come up on the back porch.

Oh, Lord.

She competed with one of the Mennonite women to open the door, but she didn't ask him inside. The kitchen was full of women cooking, and it was her wedding day. She didn't want her feelings hurt if he shared David's attitude toward entering her house. Bracing herself, she went out onto the porch to talk to him.

"Your father was a good neighbor," he said without prelude. "And your mother, when we had our trouble with the school board, was a good teacher in our school and careful of our ways. I have a marriage gift for you if you will accept it."

A marriage gift? Quinn thought, wondering if she'd heard

right. Jacob Sauder wanted to give her a marriage gift? She suddenly realized he was waiting.

"Yes, of course," she said quickly, but Jacob had nothing with him. Except the carpenter's helper sitting on the top step, the one Adam had carried when he worked on the kitchen, the one that had belonged to Adam's grandfather. He abruptly bent over to pick it up and thrust it into her hands, as if it had to be done before he changed his mind.

"This gift is for *you*, Quinn Tyler," Jacob admonished her. "You understnad that? Not for anyone else."

"Mine?" she said. She looked down at it. It was heavy with carpenter's tools, and it was all she could do to hold it. She looked up into Jacob's eyes, suddenly understanding. Jacob was trying not to break the rules of the *Meidung*.

She cleared her throat and hoisted the toolbox up a bit to get a better grip on it. "Thank you, Jacob. For *my* gift. This is exactly what I wanted." She stared into his eyes, and she had never been more truthful. She had no use for carpenter's tools—Adam did—but she had great use for the gesture that meant that Jacob Sauder, even if unable to condone Adam's decision, at least understood.

To her surprise, he almost smiled.

"Jacob," she said when he turned to go. "I know Adam asked you to come to the wedding. It's at three this afternoon in the meadow there, close to the willows. If you can't come, it would mean a lot to us both if you could just be close by. You wouldn't have to stand with us if it's too...wrong for you."

He refused to acknowledge her invitation. "You take care of those tools, Quinn Tyler" was all he said. He walked back across the yard toward his own place.

Edison called shortly before nine to tell her that Jake had arrived and that the two of them had some things to do before they came out. She thought the announcement a bit odd, but she had no time to worry about it.

At one, she made a last inspection tour of the house, It

needed painting. It needed repairs. But it had a semi-new porch, new windowpanes, and two thriving rows of tomato plants and a four-in-one apple tree, and she was proud of it.

Margaret brought flowers for the living room and pots of red geraniums for the front walk.

"You've been very kind," Quinn told her as she directed the last-minute setting up of tables.

"It's been my pleasure, Quinn," she said. "I know what you're going through. Of course, with me, it was the other way around."

"I don't understand."

"I thought Edison might have told you. I married English."

Quinn looked at her in surprise. She'd had no idea Margaret had been Amish.

"Old Order," she said. "Like Adam."

"Did it work, your English marriage?"

Margaret smiled. "It worked. It wasn't easy, but then, no marriage is."

"You don't regret it, then?" Quinn realized suddenly how desperately she wanted to hear her answer.

"Sometimes," Margaret said candidly. "I don't regret marrying Thomas. Things that are worth having come at a price, Quinn. And he's worth the price I had to pay. But I miss the simplicity of the Amish life. Living close to nature and letting the world take care of itself with no help from me. It was so...easy then. Would it rain or wouldn't it? Would the peach crop be good or wouldn't it? That's all I worried about."

"How did you meet Thomas?"

"Oh, he had a summer job with the vet. The cows got sick. And then I was running our roadside vegetable stand. That boy bought enough tomatoes to kill him."

They both laughed.

"Do you want to know what I really think?" Margaret asked. "From personal experience and from poring over the paperwork on all those divorce cases of Edison's?"

"Tell me."

"I think it doesn't matter how mismatched you are when it comes to money or religion or education or race or age or anything else you can think of—as long as you've got one thing. And it's not love, either. You can be as alike on the surface as two peas in a pod, but if you don't have the same philosophy of life, the love won't last. If you don't feel the same about the way you live in the world, and about the way you deal with the people in it and with each other, it counts for nothing. Thomas and I were kindred spirits. And so are you and Adam."

Quinn thought about this for a moment. "Margaret," she said finally, "thanks." And she didn't mean just for the flowers and the Mennonite ladies.

"You're welcome, Quinn. You've got some time before the wedding. Go on upstairs, take a nap, get ready in peace. I'll man the door and take care of things down here."

"If anybody comes," Quinn said.

"They'll come."

"I don't even have a bridegroom yet."

"Now he, I know, will be here."

Quinn went upstairs, dragging the carpenter's helper with her and stopping on the landing to look at the preparations below. The old house really did look fine, and the aroma of roast chicken and baking bread that wafted upstairs was heavenly.

I'm getting married today! she thought, smiling to herself.

She looked at her watch. She had plenty of time. She took a leisurely shower and laid out her dress, but she didn't put it on. She dried her hair and wrapped herself in her robe and lay down for a moment, not expecting to fall asleep, but she woke up with Adam sitting on the side of the bed.

"Hello," she said sleepily, holding her arms out to him. "I haven't slept through my wedding day, have I?"

He smiled and lay down beside her, pulling her close to him and holding her tightly. "Almost."

"I'm so glad to see you," she whispered as his mouth found

hers. His kiss was urgent from their two-week separation, but no more urgent than her response. He tasted so good, felt so good. And the soft sound he made as their lips met made her knees weak and her belly warm. He kissed her eyes and her neck, and when he found the delicate spot behind her ear, she gave a soft sigh of rising desire. His hand slid over her, finding its way inside her robe to a lace-covered breast and squeezing just enough to make her arch toward him.

"I'm glad to see *you*," he said as his mouth nibbled hers. "Oh, Quinn." He kissed her, hard this time, throwing his leg over hers. She could feel him, his maleness, hard and aroused, against her thigh.

But then he suddenly stopped, pressing his face between her breasts, his breathing heavy and ragged. "I have to stop," he said. "Or I won't be able to."

She ran her fingers into his hair, loving the crisp, clean feel of it. "I don't want you to stop."

He lifted his head to look at her, smiling broadly. "I'm not delaying our wedding for anything. Not even this." He sat up, pulling her up with him.

"Hurry. It's almost time. Let me help you get dressed."

She was ready except for putting on her dress, and she let him bring it to her, slip it on over her head and pull it down over her hips.

"You look beautiful."

"So do you," she suddenly realized. "Where have you been?" He was wearing "English" clothes—dress pants, a blue shirt and a maroon tie. He'd even had a haircut—no, more than simply a haircut. His hair was layered, styled, perfect for him, a haircut that didn't look like a haircut. She'd always thought him handsome. Now, incredibly, he was even more so.

"Everywhere. Jake and Edison took charge," he said, smiling again, obviously pleased that she approved. "I didn't want you to be ashamed of me."

She reached for him and hugged him hard. "Don't say

that!" She leaned back to look into his eyes. "Don't ever say that."

"This is your last chance to change your mind," he reminded her.

"Yours, too."

"I married you a long time ago, Quinn."

She went into his arms again, feeling his strength and his love. She'd always felt married to him, too. Today was merely the formality.

"I want you to see something," she said, pointing to the place by the windows where the carpenter's helper sat.

He walked over to it, reaching out to touch the top of the handle. "This is mine," he said, looking back at her.

"No, actually it's mine. Jacob brought it this morning. He was very stern, except once when he almost smiled, and he was very definite. All those tools are for me."

"And what did you say?"

"I said they were just what I wanted."

Adam smiled, and he reached out to touch the carpenter's helper again. "They're all here, and a few more besides. Everything I need to make a living for us. I can't believe he did it."

"And Daniel brought a gift."

"Daniel? Let me see." He was obviously pleased, and Quinn had a brief qualm about showing it to him. It would surely call to mind what had happened to the other wooden figure, and she wanted nothing to spoil their wedding day. But she went to the dresser to get it, bringing it lovingly back to him. She watched as Adam inspected it closely, turning it over and over in his hands. He looked up at her. "He did a good job, didn't he?" He looked down at the cow again and took a deep breath. "They're doing the best they can, Quinn. I don't ask any more than that. Well," he said, looking up at her. "Are you ready?"

"Ready," she assured him.

He put Daniel's cow carefully on the dresser again and

kissed her one last time. He took her hand as they went down the stairs, and the few people who remained in the house gave them a round of applause as they appeared. There were faces she recognized, and faces she didn't, but they all wished her and Adam well. She glanced around for Jake, but she didn't see him anywhere.

Edison came out of the kitchen eating a pickle. "Boy, these are good. Adam, you want one?"

"No, I'd rather get married," Adam said, making the onlookers laugh.

"Well, we got that covered, too. Quinn, honey, you are a beautiful bride!" He kissed her on the cheek and hugged her soundly. "My brother, the Reverend, is around here someplace. Ah, there he is!"

"Quinn, Adam, the hour is at hand," the Reverend Clark announced. To Quinn's mind, he was a tall, skinny version of Edison—comfortable and kindly and ready to get this show on the road. Still clinging to Adam's hand, Quinn let Edison lead the way. She caught his eye as they stepped out onto the front porch, and he smiled reassuringly. If he knew anything about whether Jacob and the rest of the Sauders would attend, it didn't show.

Please, she thought as he followed Edison down the porch steps and began the walk toward the meadow. *Please.*

The day was hot and hazy, with blue-tinged clouds that promised a thunderstorm by evening. A slight breeze rustled the leaves and the loose folds of Quinn's pink dress. Adam squeezed her hand as they walked, and she looked up at him.

"They may not be here, Quinn. Stop worrying," he said.

"I'm not worrying."

"Yes, you are."

"Yes, I am," she agreed, and he laughed.

"Are you happy with this?"

"Very happy with it," she answered, knowing he meant the numerous guests who sat in the shade in kitchen and folding yard chairs ahead of them, and the array of food being prepared in the kitchen. Margaret had been out here, too, with her pots of flowers, more huge red and pink and white geraniums.

"It was the only gift I could think of to give you—a good wedding."

She smiled up at him. "It's wonderful, Adam."

"Wait here," Edison said when they reached the edge of the meadow. "Brother is going to stand up there with the flowers, then he'll nod at you, and you walk up there to him. Got it?"

"I think we can handle that," Adam said.

"I don't know," Edison said. "I've seen couples so nervous they couldn't handle the time of day. I don't take any chances. Besides which, if we don't do it right, Margaret will kill me."

Quinn smiled, but she was looking over the guests. Holland Wakefield and the wife who didn't mind his driving her car were there, and some Amish from the more liberal sects. But not the Old Order Sauders. She could see Jake and three of her former co-workers sitting in the third row of mismatched chairs. All of them waved. Quinn gave them a discreet wave in return, but her mind was elsewhere.

"It's not going to ruin the day if Pop doesn't come, Quinn," Adam said quietly. "It's their loss if they stay away."

She nodded her agreement. She did agree, but, oh, she hurt for him.

The Reverend Clark had reached the array of potted geraniums, and he turned to face the guests. He nodded to Quinn and Adam, then raised both hands for the congregation to stand. Adam tucked her hand into the bend of his elbow, and together they walked forward.

They walked slowly, Adam sometimes stopping to shake someone's hand. Quinn felt surrounded by the good wishes of the people who had come. Jake winked as she passed, and Mr. Zook, who had helped replace the windowpanes, and his wife, were there with their brood of towheaded children of assorted size and gender sitting on the grass at their feet. Three girls, five boys, Quinn counted. He, too, shook Adam's hand.

When they reached the Reverend Clark, he smiled, then indicated that the guests were to be seated.

"We are gathered here today," he began, speaking comfortably to the guests without a book or written notes, "to share with Adam and Quinn the occasion of their marriage. We offer them now, as signified by our presence, our friendship and our support as we witness their pledge, before God, of their love and their commitment to each other." He paused as a calico cat and her kittens strolled into the assembly.

"Daniel's," Adam whispered, smiling. The cat rubbed against his legs, then moved on.

"Now if the two of you will join right hands. Adam, do you—"

The Reverend broke off again, and Quinn looked around. The murmuring among the guests was too insistent to be caused by a mother cat.

Coming quietly through the cornfield behind them she could see the tall form of Jacob Sauder. Lena followed, holding Daniel's hand. And then Aaron and Eli, and Anna and Mary. And finally, David and Sarah. Edison was already producing chairs for them, making another front row, and Quinn clung to Adam's hand. She stood dazed, feeling the tears sting the back of her eyes. They'd come. They'd really come!

"No crying," Adam whispered, and she struggled hard to contain it, giving him a tremulous smile.

"Adam Sauder," the Reverend Clark began again when everyone was seated. "Do you take Quinn Tyler to be your wedded wife?"

"I do," Adam said, looking into Quinn's eyes, his voice strong. She looked so beautiful to him, and he was so proud to be standing with her at his side.

"Do you promise her, before God and this gathering of family and friends, that you will never depart from her, that you will care for her and cherish her, in sickness and in health, in good times and in bad, and that you will be her good and constant friend and her husband until God will again separate you from each other?"

I love you, Quinn.

"I do."

"And Quinn Tyler. Do you take Adam Sauder to be your wedded husband..."

She continued to look deeply into Adam's eyes as she answered, letting nothing come between them. They might well have been alone as she made the same promises to him.

My good and constant friend and my husband, she thought. That was precisely what he was. *Adam, I love you. I love you with all my heart.*

"May God be with you and help you together through all your days. I now pronounce you husband and wife."

There was a soft sigh among the guests and yet another round of applause, led this time by Holland Wakefield. Quinn smiled up at Adam, knowing that kissing the bride was inappropriate for him but seeing the desire to do so burning in his eyes. Together, they turned to face the wedding guests, both of them beaming. They were immediately surrounded with congratulatory hugs and kisses and handshakes.

"Speak to my family, Quinn," Adam whispered urgently into her ear. "Tell them they must stay for the wedding dinner. Tell them I'll respect the *Meidung*—they won't be asked to sit down at the same table with me, and I won't speak to them."

Quinn made her way through the crowd to the Sauders, intercepting them as they were about to go.

"Jacob," she called, wanting to catch him by the sleeve to keep him from leaving but not daring to do so. He waited, but his impatience with whatever she might say was already clearly visible. She plunged on anyway, feeling David's eyes on her. "Jacob, you—all of you—are the only family I have." She looked quickly at each of them. "You've been very kind to Adam and me today, but I want to ask even more of you.

I ask you to stay for the wedding dinner. Adam says he will respect the *Meidung*—you need have no worry on that account. Please, Jacob," she said, glancing again at Lena. Lena said nothing, but both women looked toward Jacob, waiting. He glanced at his wife and then back at Quinn.

He made a small noise of exasperation. "I trust Adam to keep his word in this. To respect that we are bound by the *Meidung*. And I can't fight *two* pairs of eyes. We will stay."

"Thank you, Jacob."

"Quinn! Quinn!" Daniel said, catching her by the hand. She bent down so that he could whisper into her ear.

"I thought you'd wear the shiny purple dress, Quinn," he told her, obviously disappointed.

"Don't you remember? It's for parties."

He gave a sigh of exasperation, and she ruffled his hair.

"Be sure to eat everything you want," she whispered.

"Can I look for the spider?"

"If you leave him out there where he belongs." She laughed. "Daniel," she called when he was about to dash off. She bent down again to speak to him. "Adam says you did a wonderful job making the cow."

He gave her a shy smile that reminded her of Adam.

She walked back to Adam's side, collaring Edison on the way. "You have to be my substitute father," she whispered to him. "You have to seat the Sauders at the table and not break the *Meidung*."

"You got it. Damn, Quinn." He glanced in Jacob's direction. "He's a tough old bird. I never thought you'd get him this far."

Neither did I, Quinn thought.

"They're staying," Quinn said quietly to Adam, and she could feel his relief. Together they walked to the house. He held out his arm for her to take, pressing her hand firmly but discreetly against his side. She could feel his warmth through his shirt, and the memory of his hard, muscular body—without the shirt—immediately came to mind.

She looked up at him, and he grinned.

"Better not look at me like that, Mrs. Sauder, or we won't get through this dinner."

She chuckled. "I don't think the Mennonite ladies would let us *not* eat, after they've cooked all morning. But what did you have in mind?"

"You'll see."

"Oh, good," she whispered, and he pressed her hand more firmly against his side.

Tables had been set up in a U shape in the living room, Amish fashion, with the far corner, the *Eck*, reserved for the bride and groom, where they could see and be seen by everyone who came in. There were more tables in the kitchen and one in the front hall. Quinn could see Edison respectfully seating the Sauders there. It struck her how well Adam had planned this wedding for her, as if he were taking the best of the Amish version of the ceremony and giving it to her. She looked up and down the tables. There were candy dishes and small glass plates and pitchers and goblets, all filled with sweets or mints, and all meant to be served to the guests and the containers kept as gifts for her and Adam. There was even a kerosene lamp, tied with a pink ribbon, the chimney filled with M & M chocolates. And so many cakes! She leaned forward to read one of the fancily decorated ones: *Best Wishes Adam and Quinn*.

"David is coming to speak to you," Adam said to her as they took their places in the corner. She looked at him in alarm. Adam nodded in the direction of the hallway, and David was indeed making his way through the crowd of people who were trying to find seating.

"Quinn—" *Tyler*, David almost said when he reached her. "Quinn," he said, starting again. "I should not have said the rude things I said to you. I ask you to forgive my angry words." He glanced at Adam, and he seemed unaware of the people around them who were overtly listening.

"I've known you since we were children, David. You're

Adam's brother. I don't want there to be any bad feelings between us.''

He nodded and then, almost as an afterthought, offered her his hand. She shook it firmly and she thought for a moment he was going to speak to Adam in spite of the *Meidung*. But he turned away, going back to his place at the table in the hall.

She looked at Adam, who was watching his brother's retreating back.

"Did you ask him to do that?" she said.

He shook his head. "He apologized to me. I only told him I wasn't the one who needed his apology."

She reached out to touch his hand, and the wedding dinner proceeded flawlessly, thanks to the skill of the Mennonite ladies and those of Adam's friends who volunteered to keep the dishes washed and the places set as the guests waited their turns at the tables. The food lived up to its delicious aroma, and Quinn found it wonderful to be able to sit with Adam amid all the laughter and celebration.

Jake was in the second group of guests to be fed, and he made a point of coming to say goodbye and shaking Adam's hand. "Quinn," he said, turning to her. "Be happy."

"I will, Jake. Thank you for coming."

He suddenly bent across the table and gave her a quick kiss on the forehead. "And you treat her right," he admonished Adam.

"You don't have to worry about that, Jake," Adam said.

Jake gave an uncharacteristically awkward shrug and a lopsided grin. "Well, Philadelphia awaits." Then he turned and left, managing to saunter out with an attitude that was pure devil-may-care Jake Burroughs.

"He's a good man," Adam said as he watched him go.

"He said the same about you." She looked into his eyes and smiled.

"Come on," he said, standing and pulling her up with him. "Let's see if we can't make these people eat faster."

They moved among the guests, visiting together and separately, but always aware of the other's whereabouts. The Sauders ate and left quietly, with Lena turning back at the last moment to give Quinn a quick, tearful hug.

"You be happy, you and Adam," she whispered fiercely. For Adam, she had only a brave, long look. She had defied the *Meidung* in speaking to him before. She wouldn't do it again.

More people and more food and more visiting followed, until abruptly, when it was well after sundown, the wedding celebration was over. Everything was as it was before, the big tables gone, the furniture back in place. The only difference was that Quinn was no longer alone—not in this house she'd been born in, or in her life. She was pleasantly tired, and she could feel Adam's eyes on her as she moved about the kitchen.

But there was nothing more to do to it, and, when she turned to him, he was waiting.

"My wife," he whispered, sliding his arms around her and burying his face in her neck. "My wife."

She leaned back to look at him, and he kissed her gently on each eyelid, then her forehead, then her cheeks. And when his mouth sought hers, her lips parted, giving access to his sweetly probing tongue.

Her hands slid into his hair, and she pressed her body against his. *Adam.*

He broke away, needing to see her eyes, needing to see if the fear was still there.

It was.

"Quinn," he said desperately, lifting her up off the floor. He carried her upstairs and into the bedroom—their bedroom now—laying her gently in the middle of the bed. He stood up to take off his clothes, the still-strange English clothes he'd bought with Jake Burroughs's help today.

Quinn lay quietly, watching him as he knelt on the side of the bed and reached for the buttons on her dress. His fingers were trembling, and she helped him undo the row, helping him pull the dress up over her head.

He tossed it carelessly aside. His fingers caressed her smooth, warm skin and slid under the straps of her bra to bring them off her shoulders. He found the clasp—he was no longer bewildered by such fastenings—and when her breasts spilled forth from their lacy confinement, he thought he might die from the sheer pleasure of seeing her. She was so beautiful! It seemed to him that he always forgot just how incredibly beautiful she was.

He bent his head to take a taut nipple into his mouth, first one and then the other, loving the soft sounds she made as he teased her with his warm breath, then tasted her, then teased again with lips and teeth.

His suckling, sometimes gentle, sometimes not, made her whimper with desire. Her hands moved over him, as if she were savoring the feel of his body.

He moved away from her long enough to discard his briefs, coming back to her to take away her silk panties. His hands stroked the length of the silk stockings she wore, then his fingers hooked in the tops to free them of their garters and slide them down.

"Beautiful," he murmured in appreciation, giving each stocking a careless sling, and she smiled, not knowing if he meant her or the silk. He kissed her thighs, her belly, and all the while his hands knowingly caressed and caressed.

She could feel it, the love in his touch, love that had lasted all this time, love for her.

And then he was lying on top of her, his body covering hers. She reveled in the feel of him, of his weight pressing her down, of his maleness, hard and aroused between them, of the warm strength of his arms sliding over her as he reached up to cradle her face in his hands.

"I love you, Quinn," he whispered, his eyes holding hers.

"I love you," she answered without hesitation. "I've always loved you. I always will."

He shifted his position so that he could come inside her. Her eyes fluttered in response to the pleasure he elicited when he gently pushed forward.

"Look at me," he whispered urgently, and she opened her eyes. He thrust deeper. "Why are you so afraid, Quinn?" And deeper still. "*Why*, Quinn—oh!"

She heard the question clearly, but she was beyond answering. He filled her completely, and he felt so good, so good! She loved him past all reason. He was her husband, and tonight she wanted him to give her another child—not one to take the place of the boy they had lost, but because they had loved each other so long, a child would make that love complete.

I'm not afraid, she meant to tell him, but even in her need of him at that moment, she knew it wasn't true. The knowing made her cling to him all the harder. She needed something of him, to have and to keep no matter what. She loved him. And he had to feel that love. Now. Now!

If he knows how much I love him, he'll understand.

But logic born of passion and need was not logic at all. Coherence fled from her grasp, leaving nothing but exquisite pleasure.

They lay together, arms and legs entwined, the lamp still softly burning. The evening thunderstorm Quinn expected had arrived, and she watched the flashes of lightning from time to time. She listened to the distant roll of the thunder and to the pattering of the rain against the windows. And she listened to the steady beating of Adam's heart.

He wasn't asleep. She could feel his wakefulness as if it were a tangible, living thing in the room with them. And still she said nothing.

"It's not just you who is afraid," he said after a long time.

She didn't answer him, and he gave a sharp sigh.

"This, Quinn, is where you say, 'What are you afraid of, Adam?' Then I'd tell you I'm afraid of whatever it is in your eyes that makes you always look at me the way you do. I'd tell you that I was afraid enough *not* to ask you anything else about it until we were married, because, whatever it is, I think it can tear us apart.''

She abruptly sat up, and he grabbed her to keep her from getting out of bed.

''Quinn! Now. You have to tell me now.''

He had a firm grasp on her wrist, and she stared back at him, finally reaching up to touch his face.

My good and constant friend.

She could tell him this. She had to tell him this. She took a deep breath. ''All right,'' she said quietly. ''I'm afraid that you want to find our son, especially now that we're married.'' She could tell from the look in his eyes that that was exactly what he had been hoping.

''And?'' he prompted when she didn't go on.

''And we can't do that.''

''Why not? There's always a chance we—''

''There's no chance, Adam.''

She moved away from him, and this time he let her go. But she was trapped again. She had no place to go. She knew from bitter experience that being apart from him—even eleven years apart—was no solution. Still, if she was going to have to do this, she wasn't going to look into his eyes.

She stood up, switching the lamp off and plunging them into darkness. She moved to the window, feeling a rain-damp breeze on her skin as the curtains billowed outward. She stood naked for a moment, with her back to him, but then she fumbled on the foot of the bed for her robe, slinging it on and going back to the window. She stood looking out at nothing, her hands clasped together so that she wouldn't wring them like some distraught heroine in a silent movie.

''Quinn,'' Adam said. ''Will you come here?'' He held out his hand to her, but she didn't go.

''Is that why you wanted the marriage?'' she asked him quietly. ''So you could find your son?''

She turned around to face him, his features a blur in the dark.

"No," he said pointedly. "I wanted to get married because I love you. And you know it."

"Well, love me or not, we can't have our child."

He sat up on the side of the bed. "Why not?"

She stared at him.

"Answer me!" he shouted.

"I told you before. It's done. It can't be undone."

"You don't want to even try," he said. It was more an accusation than a question. "You don't want him."

"Yes, I want him! Every day of my life I want him! I want him more than anything on this earth! But it can't happen."

"Quinn—Quinn, maybe we can find him.

"No. We can't. I didn't loan him out, Adam. It's legal. It's permanent. He's been with his family for ten years."

But he wasn't listening to her. He had worked it all out in his mind, and he wasn't listening. He was Amish still; he was a loving, caring man. His son unaccounted for was more than he could bear. He wouldn't bear it. She knew that.

"I think we can get the information we need from Edison," he said.

"I don't have to get the information from Edison."

"Why not?" he persisted.

She took a deep, ragged breath. *This is where you undo it all.*

"Because I know where he is."

The room was deadly quiet, suspended in the silence of his incredulity. She was glad that she couldn't see his face. Crazily, she was aware of the sounds around her, of the rhythm of his breathing and the soft whisper of rain.

"You know," he repeated dully. "And when were you going to tell me, Quinn?"

She said nothing. She wanted to back away, not from him, but from the pain she had given him. She forced herself to stand still.

"I don't think I was," she said finally, realizing suddenly that it was true.

"Why not?"

She shook her head. "I don't know. Because it hurts too much. Because it was so…final. I was afraid—" She closed her eyes for a moment. "I didn't want to hurt you."

"And what is this now? Do you think I'm not hurt? It doesn't hurt me to have you lie to me, to have you not want us to be a family if we can? Quinn, sometimes children are returned to their real parents. Even I know that."

"Not this time!"

"Because you don't want it?"

"Because we have no choice."

He stood up from the edge of the bed, angrily looking for his pants and jerking them on. He was a million miles away from her.

"Adam," she said, and he turned his head to look at her.

"I don't believe you, Quinn. I don't believe there's no chance. And I don't understand why don't you want him. What if he needs us? What if he's mistreated?"

"He isn't mistreated, Adam."

"You can't know that. All this time you knew where he was. You had a good job in Philadelphia. You made a lot of money. How could you *not* try to get him back when you were able to take care of him? Why didn't you get him, Quinn?"

Because of you! she almost said. *Because of you!* She had only wanted him to be happy, both he and their son, and not by chance, but by design. *Her* design.

She suddenly couldn't bear any more. She walked toward the door, and he swiftly crossed the room, taking her by both arms before she reached it. "This is your house. If anyone will go, it will be me. Why are you afraid to talk to me about this?" He made her look at him.

"I told you—"

"It's what you *don't* tell me that's the problem between us!
Is something wrong with him? Is he dead?"

"No, Adam, no—" She faltered.

"Tell me! Do I have to get on my knees?"

But he didn't wait to hear. He was angry with her, but not
angry enough to take away his fear of knowing, his fear that
it was all coming undone around him. He had to think, and
he had to get away from her to do it. He slammed past her
out the door.

"Adam!" she called after him, but she didn't follow.
"Adam."

Dear God.

She kept expecting to hear a door slam downstairs, but there
was nothing. She had to talk to him. Now. They had gone too
far to just leave it.

She went down the stairs in the dark. He was sitting at the
bottom of them. She stood for a moment, unsure of what to
do, then she sat down beside him. His arms were resting on
his knees, his head bowed, and he looked up at her.

She wiped furiously at her eyes. She was going to tell him
and be done with it. And she wouldn't begin with how alone
and afraid she'd been then; that had been only a part of it.
That he already knew, or could guess.

She took a deep breath, trying to keep her voice steady.
"When I decided to...let the baby be adopted, Edison found
people for me, people who wanted a child, but none of them
seemed right. I had to be sure, Adam. I had to know he'd have
a good life. I wasn't getting anywhere. I kept sending Edison
back to them with more and more questions. But the more
questions I asked, the more dissatisfied I became. The more
they told me, the less I knew.

"And then he brought me the information on one last couple. The man was thirty. The woman was twenty-six. She
wrote me a letter—I still have it. There was no chance that
they could have a child of their own, ever. I knew if I chose
this couple, I could do something for our son that couldn't be

done any other way, something you and I couldn't do for him, even if we'd married. And I could be sure that he'd be all right."

And you would be safe, too.

She didn't say that. He hadn't been safe. He'd said it himself: he'd been in hell.

"I gave our baby to them. Knowing that he's with that couple is what's gotten me through all the years since. I haven't interfered in his life—we can't interfere now—because it would be too cruel. He's happy, Adam."

"Quinn, you can't know that."

"I do know it. I know firsthand what his life is like, and so do you. We don't ever have to worry that he isn't someone special in his parents' lives. Adam...he's Amish."

She waited, wanting so badly to reach for him, to at least touch his hand. But she didn't, and she knew the exact moment when he realized the full impact of what she had told him. Their son was lost to them forever, even more so than if she had put him out among the "English." If they truly loved him, they could never know him, and no one knew that any better than they. Their son was being brought up Amish, and he would be well loved, and he would be innocent. He would know nothing of "worldly" things. How could a little Amish boy be told that his mother was not his mother, and that his real mother was "English"? Or that his real father, even for the best of reasons, had been excommunicated from the Amish faith?

Adam stared at her; she could feel his eyes in the darkness, feel the question he didn't ask.

"I knew what I was doing," she said quietly, and he believed her. She was another part of himself, and he understood immediately. Eleven years ago she had deliberately removed all hope, all temptation, of their ever being a family, not just because she was alone and without money, but for him.

Why didn't you ask me, Quinn? he wanted to cry out, but he said nothing. He already knew the answer: *What she had done, she had done for me.* The only thing she could salvage in all of it had been his Amishness. She knew he never would have stayed away from her if she'd kept their child, and she had put their son in the very best place she could.

He took a ragged breath. "How—?" he began, but his voice broke.

"Edison must have realized what it would take to set my mind at rest. He went to the bishops. He knew about us, and he told them about the baby. The baby was your child, too, already Amish enough for them not to want to let him go to anyone else. So they had a lot of meetings. I don't know if they bent the rules or not, but they gave Edison the name of the couple who had no children. They told him they would approve the adoption if I agreed."

"The boy's...here."

"In the state, yes. But not here. I couldn't bear that, and I didn't think you would be able to if you knew. I said I knew where he was. I know he's in the state, but I don't know which community. I don't know his last name. I'm...afraid to know those things. Sometimes his mother still writes me letters. She sends them to Edison. She's...very kind. She understands that I—" She swallowed, then swallowed again to keep from crying. "She tells me what he's like, what he can do now. He's in the fifth grade, and he likes animals. All kinds. And he likes to grow things. He's had his own garden since he was eight. He likes cookies, and he doesn't like math. I think he must be very much like Daniel."

She was crying openly now, and she got up, turning abruptly and going back upstairs. Adam let her go, when there was nothing he wanted but to keep her near.

But his mind was reeling. His son was Amish! How incredible it seemed to him, and yet how logical somehow that Quinn would have done this thing. He had always worried about the harm that might come to the boy out in the world, just as he had worried about Quinn when she was in Philadelphia. He had been taught to be wary, and he couldn't change that part of his upbringing. But their son, for all intents and purposes, was safe.

Adam had known that the boy was likely beyond their reach. He was not so naive as to think that he and Quinn could undo the "English" adoption laws without good reason. But he had never been able to put aside the fear that there might *be* a good reason if their son was living somewhere among those rude people who intruded constantly in their tour buses.

He thought suddenly of his father, of how heavy Jacob's hand must have been in all this, and yet he felt no bitterness. Jacob was Jacob, the true believer, and both he and Jacob Sauder would know the painful absence of their first sons. But he knew, too, how much kindlier Jacob would think of Quinn once he knew that it was *she* who had contributed to the all-important Amish cycle of 'keeping the faith,' generation unto generation. Regardless of the *Meidung*, he would tell him. And if Quinn felt the need of Jacob and Lena's forgiveness, then she would have it, without reservation.

He got up from the bottom step and climbed the stairs slowly. Quinn was sitting in the dark by the front windows, staring out toward the Sauder house. She looked around sharply as he came into the room, and it was still there between them, her fear of his finally knowing what had happened to their son.

But Quinn was strong, and he could feel her bracing herself for this final confrontation. She said nothing as he came nearer.

"You will have to trust me more than this," he said quietly, and he heard her soft, ragged intake of breath. "You will have to trust me to know how you feel...how you felt then. Can you do that?"

"I think it's too much—" she began, her voice quavering.

"Don't!" he said sharply. "Don't do it again, Quinn. Don't decide for me. I understand, Quinn. Did you think that I couldn't?"

"I thought—knew—you'd have to go through the same

things I went through to accept that we can't see him—not now, not ever. If I'd let him go to an English family, when he was old enough, maybe he could have been told about us, but I—''

She suddenly bowed her head, and he was acutely aware of her sadness, of her sense of aloneness, of all the things he himself had felt so many times in the past. He reached out to gently stroke her hair, then touched the side of her face, feeling the dampness of her tears.

"I'm so sorry, Quinn," he whispered. "I'm so sorry!"

She looked up at him. "No, no, there's nothing for you to be sorry about. I love you, Adam."

And *he* loved *her*. They still had that, their love for each other. It was alive and strong, but it would need great care if it was to survive this. He reached for her then, overcoming her brief resistance, her disbelief that he would want her close. "Put your arms around me," he said. "No one can comfort me but you."

She held him fiercely, and he took a deep breath. It was so hard, hard for them both, not to have regrets.

But regrets were useless. He and Quinn had come through a long and unhappy time, but they had each other.

"I would do anything for you, Quinn, and you would do anything for me. That's the way it is with us," he said.

"I— Do you understand that I wanted him to be like you? Oh, God, Adam, Adam—I knew what I was doing! He's gone, and I'm to blame!"

"Quinn, don't cry anymore. Don't—I love you. It's going to be all right."

But they cried together, there in each other's arms.

He kept thinking about something she had said when she first came back.

"It's the price I had to pay."

Perhaps it was true, he thought. And they had both paid it— for being young and foolish, for loving too much. But it was not so bitter as it could have been. For the first time since

Quinn had left all those years ago, that dark emptiness in him was gone. Their son *would* have a good life, a life he himself would have chosen for him if he could. And they would have a good life, too. They were two halves of one whole, and neither would ever be alone again.

He gently kissed her lips, tasting her tears and his own.

"Don't cry," he whispered again. "We're going to be all right." And he believed it with all his heart. They would go on, stronger, surer—together.

*   *   *   *   *

Bibliography

Other reading:

Hostetler, John A., *Amish Society*. Baltimore, Maryland: Johns Hopkins Press, 1963

Good, Phyllis Pellman and Rachel Thomas Pellman, *From Amish and Mennonite Kitchens*. Intercourse, Pennsylvania: Good Books, 1984

Pellman, Rachel Thomas and Kenneth Pellman, *The World of Amish Quilts*. Intercourse, Pennsylvania: Good Books, 1984

McGrath, William R., *Amish Folk Remedies for Plain and Fancy Ailments*. Freeport, Ohio: Freeport Press, Inc., 1985

Seitz, Ruth Hoover and Blair Seitz, *Amish Country*. New York, New York: Crescent Books, 1987

Television Programming:

The Amish—Not To Be Modern. Produced by Victoria Larimore and Michael Taylor. PBS and The Arts and Entertainment Network

American Tongues. A videotape by Andrew Kolker and Louis Alvarez. The Center for New American Media. The Arts and Entertainment Network

Dear Reader,

When my editor asked me to write something about fathers for this publication, I told her, "Of course, no problem." But after sitting at my computer for thirty minutes with my mind as blank as the screen, I have only one clear thought: Fathers are a mystery!

Is it the same for other women? We can only be mothers, and men are so very different. We know the father of our children and the man *we* call "Dad." If you're old enough then you might know the father of your grandchildren.

Obviously I can speak only from my own experiences, so here goes. A father doesn't shudder when putting a worm on a fishing line, doesn't fall apart when a child takes a head-over-handlebar fall from his bicycle. He helps his sons tear down motors, and shows them how to put them back together. He teaches them *manly* things, then perpetuates that old double standard by pampering his daughters. He suffers agonies because they're too pretty at twelve years of age, knowing full well that the neighborhood boys have to be noticing.

A father is an important part of his children's lives, and he's an extremely fortunate man if he truly grasps and understands that simple fact. Most mothers know how important *they* are before their child is even born; it's something men have to learn.

Maybe the mystery of fatherhood is in my own mind. After all, a woman can only be an observer, can't she?

A few words about *Ramblin' Man*. I'm sure every author has personal favorites. *Ramblin' Man* is one of mine, and I am very pleased it was chosen for reissue. Yes, it's about a father. A family, really, and I think the problems between the hero and heroine, Jess Lonnigan and Casey Oliver, are very realistic.

I truly hope you enjoy reading it.

Jackie Merritt

RAMBLIN' MAN

Jackie Merritt

One

The grandstand, which was located on the west side of the rodeo arena, was packed, and crowds of people milled around at ground level. The hot sun hadn't kept anyone away, Casey Oliver Maddox noted. The entire Oliver clan was there. And so was practically everyone else she knew, braving the glare and the ninety-plus temperature with dark glasses and wide-brimmed cowboy hats.

Casey's hat was straw, as was her son, Bobby's. Like most everyone else in the throng, mother and son wore jeans, cotton shirts and boots, and sipped cool drinks while the rodeo events unfolded in the arena. Through the public address system, the announcer's voice relayed participants' names, data on their past performances, and anecdotes, forming a continuous background to the din of voices, applause and laughter from the audience.

The annual July rodeo was a big event in Blythe, Wyoming, and many of the locals took part, although equally as many outsiders descended on the small town to vie for the quite substantial cash prizes. Casey used to be very good in the women's barrel-racing event and had a trophy at home to prove it. But that was before she'd had Bobby. After he came along, she had dropped out of a lot of the activities she had once enjoyed.

Today she was cheering on her younger sister, Kelly, in the final round of the barrel-racing contest. Bobby was cheering for her, too. While Kelly rode her horse around the barrels in the arena without a falter and gave a very near-perfect performance, Bobby was standing and yelling, "Come on, Aunt Kelly! You can do it!"

Bobby, a wiry little boy with nearly black hair and vivid blue eyes, was going on six. Casey loved him to distraction, but she never failed to see his father in her son. Bobby was the picture of Jess Lonnigan, a tiny replica of the man who had fathered him.

Kelly had been the second finalist in the event, and after two more young women had done their best, she was announced as the winner. Bobby whooped and threw himself into his mother's arms. "She won, Mom! Now there'll be two barrel trophies on the shelf."

Laughing, Casey glanced at her mother, and Lucille Oliver smiled back. All of the Olivers were in the stands: Casey's father, Ben, her two brothers, Buck and Brady, and their families, and her older sister Dee-Dee and her family. Altogether, the Olivers numbered eighteen—a large group, especially when they congregated to eat together. Only Casey, Bobby and Kelly still lived on the family ranch with Ben and Lucille, but the others all lived within a twenty-mile radius. Holidays were loud, confusing...and wonderful.

"Can I have an ice-cream cone now, Mom?" Bobby asked.

"Sure, why not?" Casey stood up, took her son's hand and began the precarious journey to ground level. When friends called a hello as she passed, Casey responded with smiles and waves, and in a few minutes she and Bobby were away from the grandstand.

They wound through the crowd to the refreshment stand and

Casey ordered a chocolate ice-cream cone. "Don't you want one, Mom?" Bobby questioned.

"No, honey."

"How come?" Bobby's blue eyes contained total amazement that someone wouldn't eat ice cream at every opportunity.

Casey laughed and bent over to give her son a hug. "Because I'm already full of hot dogs and soda, that's how come. I don't know where a sprout the size of you puts it all."

"I'm just a growing boy," Bobby announced solemnly, parroting his grandmother's almost daily observation.

The crowd roared and clapped with approval. "What's happening, Mom?"

"The bull riding, honey. Someone must have had a good ride." Casey paid for the cone and passed it to her son. "Let's get back to our seats now."

"Yeah. I like the bull riding."

They hurriedly retraced their steps and settled down again. There were a dozen different bull riders to watch, and Bobby jumped around in glee over the colorful, agile clowns who were also in the arena. As comical as the gaily costumed clowns were, they weren't there simply to make people laugh. It was their job to draw the bulls' attention away from unseated riders.

Fifteen-year-old Kelly had joined the family and had been undergoing a lot of good-natured teasing. It was apparent every Oliver was proud of her performance and win, but it wasn't their way to gush over it. "When do you get your trophy, Aunt Kelly?" Bobby questioned.

"After the last event, Bobby."

"Will you get some money, too?"

Kelly grinned impishly. "Enough to buy some great new clothes, Bobbo!"

Lucille shook her head. "I hope you'll do a little more with your winnings than that, Kelly."

"Like what?" Kelly—with Casey and Bobby—was sitting

a tier down from her parents, and she glanced over her shoulder with an almost belligerent expression.

"Like saving it for something important," Lucille retorted.

"Oh, Mom," Kelly said disgustedly, and faced the arena again.

Casey looked back and exchanged an understanding smile with her mother. Kelly couldn't stand having a dollar in her purse or pocket, but she was a good kid all the same.

The announcer's voice battled with the crowd's noise: "...a little surprise for you today, folks...award the trophies...we're proud to have such a rodeo star..."

"What's he saying?" Kelly demanded.

"Something about the man who's going to pass out the trophies, I think," Casey answered.

"...over six years ago...ranch in Clear Creek Valley... really great...Jess Lonnigan..."

Casey froze. But even worse than the immediate stiffness in her limbs and body, was the feeling that the blood had just drained from her head. Her thoughts were suddenly as disjointed as the announcer's words had seemed to be. *It can't be... No, I misunderstood... It can't be!*

Then she felt her mother's hand on her shoulder, and she knew she hadn't misunderstood at all. Lucille Oliver had heard Jess's name, too. Casey turned slowly and looked at her mother with pain-filled eyes. She couldn't speak about what they were both thinking, because no one else in the family knew about it. Casey's eyes darted to her father, and he gave her a warm smile. For the smallest fraction of time she wondered if he did know. There was something in his eyes....

But no, Lucille would have told her if she had related the old story to anyone. Ben didn't know. He didn't!

Casey's heart was suddenly pumping adrenaline through her body at a furious rate, and she turned away from her parents to wildly search the crowd. Somewhere in this crowd, *somewhere*, was Bobby's father. But *he* didn't know he was Bobby's father. Only two people knew that: Casey and her mother. Everyone else believed a lie about Casey and a completely fabricated husband.

But would Jess know if he *saw* his son? Would he see in Bobby what I do? Casey agonized.

Sick at heart, Casey got up. "Come on, Bobby. We're going home." She grabbed the little boy's hand.

"Home?" Bobby was clearly stunned.

Half of the Oliver clan called, "Why are you going before the rodeo is over?"

She was behaving too much out of character, Casey realized. Taking a deep breath she faced her family. "My stomach is really upset all of a sudden. I must have eaten too much junk food."

"Well, leave Bobby with us," Brady, Casey's oldest brother, suggested.

"No...no! I...he's better off with me."

Lucille said nothing, but there was a sad look in her eyes. Ben said nothing and just watched. Bobby looked ready to cry over leaving before the awards were distributed, and again Brady urged, "Leave him, Casey. I'll take personal responsibility for him. I promise not to let him out of my sight."

"Brady, that's not the problem. Thanks for the offer, but I want him with me," Casey replied firmly. "I'll see you all later," she added lamely, and tugged Bobby along. "Come on, Bobby. Don't drag your feet."

By the time they reached the ground, Bobby's big blue eyes were spilling tears. It was rare that his mother didn't smile and give him a hug every few minutes, and the little boy sensed there was something very different about her strange expression.

They passed the refreshment stand. Casey was walking fast, as if the very devil himself were on her heels, and Bobby was practically running to keep up. The parking lot was congested with cars, pickups and horse trailers, and the proof of Casey's state of mind was her reaching the Olivers' four vehicles before she realized she hadn't asked anyone for a key.

None of the vehicles was locked, though, and Casey opened

the door of her father's car. "Get in, Bobby. I've got to go
back and get the keys from Grandpa. I'll only be a few
minutes." Guilt struck her as her son climbed into the car and
huddled against the seat with silent tears running down his
cheeks. "I'll bring you something from the refreshment stand,
honey," she said with more gentleness. "What would you
like?"

Bobby looked down. "Nothing, Mom."

"Come on, honey. Don't be like that. You know I wouldn't
make you leave if it wasn't important, don't you?"

"I guess so. Are you really sick?"

Casey bit her lip and looked away from the shining innocence of her son's eyes. "I'm deathly sick," she answered
dully, realizing how true the dire words were. But a five-year-
old couldn't handle that kind of answer, and she quickly
amended the admission. "I just need to lie down, honey. I'll
be fine. Now, what can I bring you?"

A small smile shone through the tears. "Another ice-cream
cone?"

"You've got it, honey. I'll hurry." Casey glanced around
then. There were strangers present, people she didn't know,
and her gaze returned to her precious son. She couldn't possibly leave him alone, and yet the prospect of taking him back
into the crowd and risking an encounter with Jess Lonnigan
chilled her.

Just then someone called "Hi, Casey."

Turning, Casey smiled. "Oh, Janice, hi. Listen, would you
do me a tremendous favor? Bobby and I were leaving, but we
got clear out to the car before I realized I didn't have Dad's
keys. Would you stay with Bobby for ten minutes?"

"Well, of course. No problem." Janice Miller, an old
school chum of Casey's, slid into the car with Bobby. "Hi,
Bobby. How you doing, pal?"

"Thanks loads, Janice." Casey took off running, and
dodged among the vehicles as she went. By the time she
reached the grandstand again, she was out of breath. But she
quickly climbed up to the level where the Olivers were sitting.

"I need somebody's keys," she announced, including the whole group in her plea.

Ben reached into his pocket. "I never even thought about keys, Casey. Where's Bobby?"

"In the car. Janice Miller's keeping an eye on him. I've got to hurry back. Bye, everyone. Catch you later."

She was back on the ground in seconds, dashing for the refreshment stand. There were three people ahead of her, and she got in line.

"Casey? Casey Oliver?"

The deep, masculine voice went right through her. Even after six years she recognized it. Jess Lonnigan. The situation didn't seem possible, it *wasn't* possible, and yet she was alternately hot and cold with indisputable shock.

Very slowly, Casey turned. "Hello, Jess," she replied coolly.

In a torrent of memories, the past came rushing back. For one week, six years ago, she'd made love with this man like there was no tomorrow. She'd been completely mesmerized by his rugged good looks and devil-may-care personality and drugged by the first adult passion of her life. It struck Casey that he looked the same—tall, dark and handsome—except for a few new lines at the corners of his outrageously blue eyes and maybe a few more well-distributed pounds.

He was studying her as boldly as the first time they'd met, and while she was as cold as ice inside, Casey felt heat in her face.

"I was *hoping* you were still around," Jess said softly.

Fury exploded within her, and she had to consciously remember where they were—in public, within hearing range of a dozen people. She kept her voice down, but it was no less venomous than what was in her heart. "Why? I'm not seventeen and stupid now."

"Seventeen!" Jess looked as if he'd just been slapped. "You weren't only seventeen."

Casey moved up a place in line, aware that Jess Lonnigan was watching her closely. She would have given her right arm to avoid this confrontation, but perversely, she was glad she looked good, glad that her jeans were tight and her bright red shirt was darted to fit just so. Her breasts were fuller than they'd been six years ago, but that was the only place she'd gained either inches or weight. Her hips and long legs were as lean and firm as always.

She was glad that her heavy dark hair was curled and fluffed below the straw hat, and that her boots were high-heeled and flattering. But most of all, she was glad that Bobby was in the car and out of sight.

"You weren't really only seventeen, were you?"

She gave Jess a disdainful look. "What are you doing back in Blythe? Besides passing out awards, that is."

Jess's frown added perplexity to his face. "You don't like me very much, do you?"

"Should I?"

"You seemed to like me just fine six years ago."

Casey took another step forward as one of the people ahead of her left with two handfuls of hot dogs. "Still a gentleman, I see," she hissed heatedly.

Jess's frown deepened. "I never pretended to be anything but what I was."

"A transient rodeo rider!" Casey sneered.

"That's not what I am now."

"Oh? Well, tell it to Superman. I'm not interested."

Jess kept staring. Casey Oliver was as pretty as he remembered—maybe prettier. She had big green eyes—which were presently well concealed behind dark glasses—a fabulous complexion and just about the sexiest mouth he'd ever witnessed on a woman. She'd knocked him for a loop six years ago, and as he'd told her, he'd been hoping she was still living in the area. He sure hadn't expected bitterness, though. Their week together during Blythe's big July rodeo six years ago had been one of the more memorable of his life. They'd danced, flirted, made love and had one helluva good time. At least *he*'d had a helluva good time. Was he that wrong about how she'd seen the whole thing?

And had she really been seventeen?

Impossible!

"If you were underage, why didn't you tell me?" he asked accusingly.

Casey looked disgusted. "Why didn't you ask?"

Jess's blue eyes darkened. "Because it never occurred to me that such a wise lady was really nothing but a kid," he answered in a lethally quiet voice.

Defensive anger sparked in Casey's eyes. "I was much wiser when you left, wasn't I?"

"Are you mad because I *left*? You knew the score. You knew damned well I was only in town for the rodeo."

"A one-night stand? Oh, pardon me. I meant a one-*week* stand."

"Stop being so nasty," Jess ground out tensely. "Obviously you'd prefer I disappear. Well, lady, you've got it. I've never had to beg crumbs from a woman, and I don't intend to start now!"

He spun on his heel and strode away, and Casey stared straight ahead, refusing to watch him go. *I hate you,* she thought passionately, mentally repeating it again and again. She did, too. There wasn't anything phony about the hot, burning hatred churning in her midsection.

"What'll you have, Casey?"

"What? Oh. One chocolate cone, Joe."

Casey drove home with exactly the upset stomach she'd invented only a short time ago. Bobby licked and ate his ice cream happily. Apparently he'd already forgotten being dragged away from the rodeo early. The blessed resiliency of childhood, Casey reflected, relieved that her beloved little son wasn't pouting.

Her hands clenched and unclenched on the steering wheel with every wave of new thought. *Why is Jess in Blythe? After six years, why is he back?*

And worse yet, *How long is he going to hang around?*

He knew how to find the Oliver ranch of course. It was only

ten miles out of Blythe and easily located. But it wasn't likely
Jess would drop in after the treatment she'd given him today.
So, what she had to do was keep Bobby away from town for
a few days. The rodeo was officially over this evening, and a
few more days was the longest Jess would stick around.

Casey didn't have even a wisp of guilt at keeping Bobby
from Jess Lonnigan. It wasn't Jess who'd been left behind,
crushed by the desertion of a man she'd imagined herself in
love with. Nor had it been Jess who'd nearly died of shame
having to tell her mother that she was pregnant by a rodeo
rider who'd been in the area one lousy week.

And when Jess had gone, that had been it—not a telephone
call, not so much as a card. Two months later, when Casey
had understood her condition, she had wept and pleaded with
her mother to keep her shame from the rest of the family.
"Dad would never forgive me. Mom, never."

"You underestimate your father, Casey."

*"I could never look him in the eye again. Please...
please..."*

Lucille had given in, and together, mother and daughter had
concocted an acceptable story. Casey went away to college
that September, and within a month called home with news of
an elopement that never really happened. She talked to her
father. *"I'm Mrs. Don Maddox now, Dad."*

*"Dammit, Casey! You've always been too impetuous. Why
didn't you bring your young man home before you got married?"*

*"School, Dad. Don's in school, too. Neither of us wanted
to cut classes."*

At Christmastime she came home, obviously pregnant, and
unhappy about a pretended divorce. *"I'm sorry, Dad. I made
a terrible mistake. I know that now. Don doesn't want anything to do with the baby. Could I stay with a man who doesn't
want his own child?"*

Lies, lies. During her pregnancy she'd lied so much it was
a wonder Bobby hadn't been born a congenital liar. She'd lied
not only to family, but to friends, as well. And oh, yes, she'd

seen doubt in some people's eyes. After all, no one, not even the Olivers, had met Don Maddox. With her family behind her, though, other people eventually forgot, and it had been years since Casey had sensed an odd stare from anyone. Bobby was Bobby Maddox, but he was one of the Oliver grandchildren, and in and around Blythe, the Oliver name merited respect.

But Jess's coming back could destroy everything she'd lied to protect. Casey knew her initial fear had been for herself, and in retrospect, from her present twenty-three-year-old viewpoint, she could see that she'd been scared silly at seventeen, willing to do almost anything to keep her predicament private. After Bobby came along, though, she'd stopped worrying about herself; her son was more important than anything or anyone else. But the lies were almost set in concrete now, and no one needed to learn at this late date that Bobby's real father was an itinerant cowboy who'd stopped in Blythe for a week, and that the little boy's mother had been the biggest fool of the century.

Gritting her teeth, Casey turned the car off the highway onto the half-mile driveway leading to the family home. The Oliver ranch was two thousand acres of prime Wyoming grassland, with a stately old two-story house that had sheltered three generations of Olivers, two massive barns, numerous other outbuildings and several thousand head of cattle grazing on its lush pastures. It was a productive, successful cattle operation and provided Buck, Brady and Dee-Dee's husband, Ray, with good jobs, even though the three families lived elsewhere.

It was home and, right at the moment, felt like a sanctuary to Casey. There were a dozen enormous elm and oak trees shading the house and yard, and after Casey and Bobby climbed out of the car, Casey collapsed on one of the front-porch chairs.

"Aren't you gonna go to bed, Mom?" Bobby questioned.

Casey smiled at her son. "I already feel a little better, honey. Maybe the sun was too hot at the rodeo grounds. I think I'll just sit here for a while."

"Are Julie and Mike coming over?"

Julie and Mike were Brady and Cindy's two children. Of Bobby's seven cousins, Julie and Mike were the closest to him in age and were his favorite playmates. "I'm not sure, Bobby," Casey replied.

"Well, gee, I hope they do," the little boy said, looking rather forlorn now that he was home and had remembered that all his cousins were still at the rodeo.

Casey leaned forward. "Why don't you run out and see how the puppies are doing?" One of the dogs, Pearlie, had just had puppies, and Bobby adored looking at them. "Don't pick them up, though," Casey cautioned as Bobby took off.

Sighing then, Casey sat back.

Jess Lonnigan. It still didn't seem possible that he was in Blythe again, even though she'd seen him with her own eyes. She'd come as close to fainting as she ever had when she heard his name. Her mother, too, probably. "Poor Mom," Casey murmured to herself. Lucille Oliver probably didn't know *what* she should be doing right now. Lies were even harder for Lucille than they were for her daughter, and Casey felt that her mother often wished she had insisted Casey tell her father the truth six years ago. It was probably the only secret between Ben and Lucille Oliver, and they'd been married for thirty-six years.

If for nothing else than that, Casey hated Jess. Some allowances for bad judgment might be made for a panicked seventeen-year-old; but Jess Lonnigan hadn't been only seventeen, and he'd given Casey every reason in the world to believe he'd meant everything he'd said.

"You're a special gal, honey."

"I love you, honey."

"You're the prettiest little thing these eyes have ever seen, honey."

Honey! Casey winced at the memories. How stupidly gullible she'd been. For one delirious week she'd worshiped Jess Lonnigan and followed wherever he'd led. She'd been putty in his hands—soft, pliable putty. She had thought him the handsomest, most wonderful man in the world. She had opened her lips, her heart and her legs for him, simply because she'd been so head-over-heels smitten, she hadn't even thought of saying no.

Then, his last night in town, he'd talked about leaving. Casey laughed bitterly now, when she thought of Jess's nonchalance. *"We've sure had a good time honey. It'll be a long while before I forget Blythe, Wyoming."*

"But I don't understand. You mean you're just going away? Why?"

Jess laughed. *"Why? What kind of question is that? You know I follow the rodeo circuit."*

"But I thought..."

"What would I do around here? Ask your old man for a job? No way, honey. I'm doing too good in rodeo to tie myself to a broomtail and ride fences for a few hundred bucks a month."

"Dad would pay you better wages than that. But you wouldn't have to work for him. There are dozens of other ranches where you could get a job."

"Sorry, honey. No can do. Come here and show me how much you'll miss me."

It disgusted Casey now to remember that she had done exactly as he'd asked: shown him how much she would miss him. In defense of her idiocy, she also remembered she'd actually thought that if she loved Jess passionately enough, he would change his mind and stay.

It hadn't worked, of course. The next day he was gone. And less than two months later, she'd realized she was pregnant.

It hurt so much to think of that terrible time that Casey couldn't stop the tears that filled her eyes, although it had been a long while since she'd cried over it. There had been months of tears that fall when she was supposed to be in school and wasn't, and sporadic bouts of crying sessions even after she was back home and safe again. After Bobby's birth, though, she'd cried very little. The wonder of her beautiful, perfect son had very effectively made her understand the old adage, "Every cloud has a silver lining."

Bobby had made her want to rejoin the human race and live again. It was caring for him and loving him that had matured her and turned the self-centered girl she'd been into a woman. She was no longer awed by masculine good looks and catchy, cocky phrases. Now, the rare times she dated were casual evenings with men who understood that she wasn't interested in anything beyond a movie or dinner.

She'd never been tempted, even once, to lose herself in a man the way she'd done with Jess. And that silly smugness over looking good to Jess today had only been a momentary regression, a never-to-be-repeated instance of femaleness that had unexpectedly struck her at the shock of seeing him. If she'd had a moment to think and compose herself, she'd have done much better at letting him know how much she despised him.

Well, he'd probably gotten the message, anyway—even if he had taken her by surprise. And it wouldn't hurt her a bit to stay on the ranch and out of Blythe for a few days. She did her work at home anyway, and any deliveries to be made could be handled by someone else.

Four years ago Casey had realized she couldn't keep living off her parents, even though they had both told her otherwise. She wanted to continue living on the ranch because she honestly felt it was the best place to raise Bobby. But she needed a little independence, and after thinking about what she might do to earn her own money, short of leaving Bobby in someone else's care and taking a full-time job, she hit on the idea of a secretarial service. Casey had been a whiz on the typewriter ever since completing her high-school typing course, and there hadn't been anything even remotely resembling such a service around Blythe.

She had placed an ad in the local twice-weekly newspaper, then called on the businesses in town. Casey knew all the shop owners, of course, and everyone was willing to display a small poster in their storefront windows. Word soon got round. Her first customer was an elderly man who wrote freelance hunting and fishing magazine articles. Casey began typing Lloyd Abbott's manuscripts from hand-scrawled yellow pads, and went on from there.

If she'd had to completely support herself and Bobby from her earnings, things would be rather tight. But she made enough money to buy their clothes and pay for extras. What's more, she'd been told many times that if she opened an office in town she would get a lot more business, even though she did pick up and deliver. Casey had been giving it a lot of thought. Bobby would start first grade in September, and she could coordinate her hours with his. Lucille and Ben—even Kelly, on occasion—were willing to baby-sit, but Bobby was a responsibility Casey didn't take lightly and she seldom imposed on her family to care for him.

Thinking of the past six years gave Casey's pretty face a melancholy expression. She never let herself think too much about happiness or fulfillment or what it might be like to really be married. She loved her parents and was grateful that they were the kind of generous, supportive people they were. They were wonderful to Bobby, as they were to all their grandchildren, and growing up on a ranch among people who loved him was a definite plus for any little boy. But Casey still couldn't help wondering, at odd moments, what it would be like to have a home of her own.

She still slept in the bedroom that had been hers as an infant, she ate at her parents' table, and she listened to and took part in conversations that were as familiar as the seasons. She had to admit, if only to herself, that if she didn't have a child, she would try her wings in some far-off place.

But she did have a child. And she wouldn't trade Bobby for anything in the world. More than that, she would *protect* him from anything in the world, and that included his own father!

Casey didn't get a chance to talk to her mother privately when Lucille and Ben returned from the rodeo. The entire family accompanied them home for a barbecued-rib dinner, and the large kitchen was chaotic with preparations for enough food for eighteen people. As usual, all the women helped, but it was Lucille's kitchen and she orchestrated the cooking and salad making with a symphony conductor's sense of timing.

They were a noisy bunch. The kitchen buzzed with six females talking at once, four men coming in and out to get beer from the refrigerator, and eight children vying for some kind of attention. Everyone appeared to accept Casey's story of feeling better once she got home, and she busied herself with a macaroni salad, the dish Lucille had asked her to prepare. No one seemed to notice that Casey's voice was the one least heard or that she gave the salad an inordinate amount of concentration.

But then Casey nearly choked when Kelly made a remark about the "handsome hunk" who'd awarded the trophies. "His name is Jess Lonnigan," she announced while chomping on a stalk of celery. "I wish I was five years older," the fifteen-year-old added with a sprightly grin.

"Stop talking so foolishly," Casey snapped.

"Well, what's wrong with you?" Kelly demanded testily. "You never even saw him. Honestly, I can't say anything around here without someone biting my head off."

"That's not true, Kelly," Lucille put in, with a warning glance at Casey.

She was overreacting again, Casey realized unhappily. If Kelly had made that kind of remark about a man Casey didn't know, she would probably have teased her baby sister rather than snap at her. "I'm sorry," Casey mumbled, and gave the macaroni salad a stir it didn't need.

The apology brightened Kelly's countenance. "Anyway, Lisa Mackey told me that he bought a ranch in Clear Creek Valley."

"*Who* bought a ranch in Clear Creek Valley?" Casey asked sharply.

"Jess Lonnigan," Kelly answered triumphantly. She was

obviously pleased to be the bearer of such good tidings. "He has three national rodeo championship belts. Three! It's really thrilling to have a genuine rodeo star living only a few miles away, don't you think?"

Two

Casey didn't know if she was going to laugh hysterically, burst into tears or faint dead away. The kitchen actually swam before her startled eyes for a few seconds, and within the confused clamor of her own stunned brain, she was positive everyone was staring at her.

They weren't, of course—not even her mother. Lucille was at the sink with her back to Casey, and probably no one else in the room even noticed the odd set of Lucille Oliver's shoulders. The conversation was ebbing no more or less than it had, Casey finally realized, and with trembling hands she ripped a length of plastic wrap from its box, molded it over the salad bowl and placed the bowl in the refrigerator. Then she quietly left the kitchen.

Once away from the room she began to run, and taking the stairs two at a time, she raced to her bedroom. She closed the door behind herself and started pacing. It can't be true, it can't! she kept thinking wildly.

Why Blythe? Why, of all the millions of places in the world, why Blythe? A few miles away! My God, how can I keep Bobby away from him if he only lives a few miles away?

Why?

A soft rap at the door stopped Casey's frantic pacing. The door opened and Lucille came in. The two women looked at each other, then Lucille went to her daughter and put her arms around her. Casey clung to her mother and burst into tears. "Try to calm down, honey," Lucille soothed, though she sounded close to tears herself.

Taking a step backward Casey wiped her eyes. "He'll never get Bobby, Mom, not as long as there's breath in my body."

"Of course, he won't. No one's ever going to take that little fellow away from you, Casey. Even the boy's father couldn't do that, not when you've been such a good mother."

"He might try," Casey said sharply.

Lucille sat on the edge of the bed and regarded her distraught daughter. The older woman had a few lines in her face, but she was still very attractive. All of the Olivers were slender, handsome people, with pronounced similarities in facial features.

Years ago, Lucille had recognized that of her three daughters, Casey was the closest to being a real beauty.

Although Dee-Dee and Kelly are very pretty, too, she never failed to add when her biased opinion came to mind. With a mother's loving eye, Lucille couldn't really find too many flaws in any of her children's physical appearance. But there had always been something very special about Casey's looks.

Which, Lucille now acknowledged with a sad sigh, were probably what had drawn Jess Lonnigan's notice in the first place.

"Sit down, honey, just for a few minutes. I've got to get back downstairs, but I noticed you leaving and figured you might need a kind word."

Casey had gone back to her pacing, but at her mother's bidding, she sank onto the dressing-table stool. "I had been planning to keep Bobby out of Blythe for a few days," she recited bitterly. "It never even occurred to me that Jess might be in the area permanently."

"Why would it?" Lucille agreed quietly.

"Maybe I'll just take Bobby and go away, Mom."

"And leave your family? Casey, this is your home. It's Bobby's home. Where would you go? Please don't consider running away as one of your options."

"Mom, if I keep Bobby here and do nothing, sooner or later Jess is bound to see him."

Lucille nodded. "I know. But what you're overlooking is the fact that Jess knows nothing about Bobby's parentage. More than likely he doesn't even know you have a son. When he does learn about Bobby, he'll hear the Maddox name. And people are funny, Casey. We seldom know how we really look to other people. Jess might never see the resemblance you say Bobby has to him."

Casey shook her head with agitation. "When you see Jess for yourself, you'll understand my fears better."

"Possibly. Frankly, I'm very anxious to get a look at Mr. Lonnigan. I wish I had met him six years ago." Lucille leaned forward a little. "Casey, maybe it's time to talk to your father about this. If Jess should decide to come around..."

"He won't," Casey interrupted dully. "I saw him today after I got the keys from Dad."

Lucille's eyes widened. "You saw him?"

"Yes. I stopped at the refreshment stand to get another cone for Bobby on the way back to the car. Jess came up."

"You spoke to him?"

Getting to her feet, Casey went to the window and looked down at the backyard. The kids were running and playing and the men were sitting on the patio while Ben watched the beef ribs on the barbecue. It was a peaceful scene, vastly different from the storm in her soul.

"I wasn't very kind," Casey intoned. "I'm sure he understands that I want no part of him."

Lucille frowned. "You mean he intimated otherwise? For Pete's sake, it's been six years. What did the man think you were doing all that time? You could be married. Did he think you'd been sitting around waiting for him to come back?''

Facing her mother, Casey raised a speculative eyebrow. ''Now that I think about it, you're right. At first he acted like he thought I'd be glad to see him. Can you even believe such an ego?''

Sighing with perplexity, Lucille stood up. ''Well, I'd better get back down to the kitchen. Are you coming?''

''Not yet. I'd like to be alone for a while.''

Lucille walked over to her daughter and gently brushed a lock of her hair back from her forehead. ''Don't let this get you down, Casey. You don't have to pay for one mistake the rest of your life, you know.''

''I'm not worried about me, Mom,'' Casey whispered brokenly.

''I know, honey. But think about something for me, all right? Think about talking to your father. I'm not saying I told you so, but I've never yet seen a case where lies didn't somehow come back to haunt a person.''

Casey's eyes were misty again. ''I'll think about it,''' she agreed, and studied her mother. ''He doesn't know, Mom? You never told him? Today, at the arena, I had the strangest sensation.''

Lucille's expression remained noncommittal. ''Someday you're going to have to talk to Dad about it.''

''I'm afraid to,'' Casey murmured.

''He'll understand, Casey. He loves you as much as I do.'' Lucille kissed her daughter, then started for the door. ''I'll tell the others that you're still not feeling very well.''

''Thanks, Mom,'' Casey answered raggedly.

Jess was puzzled, damned puzzled. On the drive back to his ranch in Clear Creek Valley at the close of the rodeo, he mulled over the strange meeting with Casey Oliver and what he'd learned about her later. She'd been married and divorced and had a little boy. Well, there wasn't anything so unusual about that information—certainly no reason for Casey to treat *him* like dirt. He sure hadn't done anything to hurt her. Hell, he'd shown her a great time six years ago.

Of course, he hadn't known she was only seventeen years old at the time. Who would have guessed?

Jess's brow creased with a frown. Had she been a virgin?

Damn, he couldn't even remember. There'd been so many women before and since Casey, it was hard to sort them out.

But he'd thought of her when he found himself seriously considering Wyoming as the place to raise the quarter horses he loved. And he'd also thought of Blythe, the pretty little town surrounded by the must beautiful rolling hills of grass he'd ever seen.

After twelve years of rodeo he was ready to settle down. He'd saved his earnings, which had amounted to a substantial sum once he'd started winning the bigger purses. Then, after taking the first national championship, there'd been endorsements and paid personal appearances. He'd done all right, and now he owned twelve hundred acres, with a nice house to boot. There were stables and a barn to build before winter, but he looked forward to getting into their construction. He'd already ordered the lumber and tools he would need.

That part of his life was planned and gratifying. But seeing Casey again—a prospect he'd been anticipating—had really given him a jolt. He'd considered the chance that she might be married now, although he'd sure been hoping she wasn't. But all his speculations about Casey Oliver hadn't even touched on the possibility of her just not wanting anything to do with him.

It made no sense, either—not when they'd had such a great time before.

Why, she'd acted as if she actually hated him. Whereas he thought of Casey with only the fondest of memories…and a few that were downright arousing, even six years later. She had made him very happy during that long-ago week, and he'd been under the impression that he'd made her happy, too.

Now he had to revise his thinking: and ever since he'd stalked off, leaving Casey in line at the refreshment stand, Jess had been trying to figure out the icy reception he'd gotten from her.

It made no sense at all. None. Not from any angle.

Well, he'd leave her alone for a few days, then either drop in at the Olivers' ranch or give her a call. Maybe she'd just been upset over something that had nothing to do with him. That made more sense than anything else. Casey had probably only been in a bad mood. She'd come around.

On Monday, as there was no longer any point to hiding on the ranch, Casey went about her business as usual. Ordinarily, when she made pickups or deliveries, she took Bobby with her. That was the only deviation from her regular routine this Monday; she left Bobby in her mother's care. Tuesday, she stayed on the ranch and typed Lloyd Abbott's latest article, plus six letters for a new customer—an attorney who'd just opened an office in Blythe and seemed to be procrastinating about hiring a secretary.

Wednesday morning, Casey got ready and drove into Blythe—alone again—to deliver the work she'd put out the day before. First she stopped at Lloyd Abbott's house, then she drove to the hardware store and parked on the street. Wesley Upton had rented three rooms above the store for his law offices, and when Casey had picked up the cassette for transcription, the attorney had been painting the drab walls.

He was still painting, Casey realized as she caught fumes of fresh paint while climbing the stairs. "Mr. Upton?" she called.

"In here." Wiping his hands on a paint-spattered towel, Wesley Upton came out of one of the rooms. "Hello, Casey."

He was a big man, stockily built, with thinning brown hair and glasses, probably around thirty-five. "Hi. Still hard at it, I see," Casey commented.

"Almost done. Come on in."

Casey followed the attorney into a room that had been efficiently transformed into an office. She looked around at the shelves of law books, the massive desk and the comfortable-looking chairs. "Very nice."

"Thanks. Got time for a cup of coffee?"

Casey laid the manila envelope she'd been carrying on the desk. She'd seen a glint of admiration in Wesley Upton's eyes at their first meeting, and if she wasn't tied in such knots today she might have accepted a cup of coffee. But not one minute had passed without worry since the last day of the rodeo, and she was too tense to participate in small talk or an attempt to further a brand-new relationship into something more than it was. Like everyone else around Blythe, she had heard that the new attorney in town was a divorced man. And while he wasn't really handsome, Wesley Upton was pleasant looking. If Jess Lonnigan wasn't hovering over her head like a threatening black cloud, Casey knew she would probably have welcomed the chance to get to know Wesley better.

"I'll take a rain check on that, if you don't mind. I've got to run today."

Wesley Upton nodded. "Anytime. I have another cassette ready."

"Great. I appreciate the business." Casey accepted the new cassette. "Thank you. I'll deliver the day after tomorrow, as usual."

She hurried away, already forgetting Wesley Upton. Casey felt that she was living on the brink of disaster.

She was driving one of the ranch's pickups today, and with her mind so overloaded, she didn't even notice someone sitting in the truck until she was only two steps away. Casey reeled with shock; Jess was smiling at her through the open window of her own vehicle!

She took one more step. "Get out of my truck," she demanded hotly.

Jess's smile disappeared. "Not until we talk. Get in."

A woman walking by slowed down. "Morning, Casey."

Casey's head jerked around. "Good morning, Stella."

Stella Patterson stopped, making Casey cringe inwardly. Stella was one of the biggest gossips in Blythe, and it was more than apparent that she was interested in the little scene unfolding in front of the hardware store. Her avid gaze was on Jess. "Aren't you Jess Lonnigan? I saw you at the rodeo on Saturday."

"Yes, ma'am," Jess replied with a look of amusement.

Stella stuck her hand in the window, inviting a handshake. "I'm Stella Patterson. I heard you bought a little ranch in Clear Creek Valley."

"Yes, ma'am."

Stella beamed. "Well, isn't that nice. You'll have to come to dinner some evening. Do you have a telephone?"

"Yes, ma'am."

"Wonderful. I'll give you a call. Casey, tell your mother hello for me."

"I will," Casey agreed stiffly. But when Stella was out of earshot, she muttered something unintelligible.

Jess had caught the gist of the comment, if not the words. "Afraid to be seen with me?" he asked quietly.

Casey's green eyes narrowed. "Get out of my truck," she repeated tersely.

"I want to talk to you."

"We have nothing to talk about."

"That's what's bothering me, honey. How come you and I don't have anything to talk about?"

Casey's jaw clenched. "Don't you dare call me honey."

Jess's dark blue eyes bored into hers. "Get in, Casey. You're going to tell me why you hate my guts."

"I'm telling you nothing!"

"Then I'm sitting right here. It sure doesn't bother me if every citizen in Blythe sees us fighting in front of the hardware store."

Casey was trembling with frustrated anger. "You arrogant jerk," she whispered.

"Make a scene, honey. Go ahead. Scenes don't bother me one little bit."

The bell on the hardware store door jangled, and behind her Casey heard two men talking. A quick glance backward lowered her spirits another notch; she knew both of them. "Hello, Casey." "Hi, Casey."

Responding with a weak "Hello," Casey marched around the front of the pickup, opened the door and climbed behind the steering wheel. She didn't say a word or glance at Jess as she started the motor and pulled away from the curb.

Jess was watching her closely. "Where you heading?"

Casey ignored him. Covering the main street of town took only a few minutes. At the edge of Blythe she turned the truck onto a dirt road, drove a silent half mile and stopped in a secluded wooded spot. Switching off the key, she stared straight ahead. "Say your piece and get it over with," she said coldly.

Jess was studying her with a frowning, questioning expression. "All I want to know is why you so obviously hate me."

"Why?"

"Why, what?"

"Why do you want to know? If my feelings are so obvious, why not let it go at that? Isn't a big rodeo star capable of accepting that every woman he meets isn't falling at his feet?"

"Why are you being so damned sarcastic? Can't you talk about this in a normal way?"

"No."

"Look at me."

"No."

Tension was in the air, heavy and thick. Jess felt anger in his gut. She might have a reason to despise him, but he had a right to know what it was. He slid across the seat. "Dammit, you *will* look at me," he muttered, and grabbed her.

They struggled, and there were several minutes of curses and grappling before Jess had Casey in a grip she couldn't escape from. "Big man," she taunted. "Does it make you feel good to subdue a woman?"

Jess was breathing hard. He stared down at livid green eyes and a beautiful face that contained nothing but hatred. "Just tell me why," he ground out angrily.

Her breasts were pushed into his chest, her arms held to her sides by his and their faces were no more than an inch apart. Irrationally, she registered the blue of his shirt as being the same color as his eyes, and his scent as something spicy and masculine.

"You don't just hate me, Casey. You'd like to see me squirm. I wouldn't be questioning your feelings if all I picked up from you was dislike. But there's a helluva lot more to your sarcasm and insults than dislike. Between the last time we saw each other and now, something happened. I can't even begin to imagine what it was, but—"

"Don't bother to try," Casey snapped. "I just grew up. Apparently you didn't. You still think you're the greatest thing since sliced bread."

"See? That's what I mean. You've handed out insults as though they were gifts both times we've seen each other. *That*'s what I can't understand, Casey. Dislike is one thing. But you act like you've got some kind of personal vendetta against me. Have you felt this way for six years?"

"Don't flatter yourself," she sneered. "I never even thought of you once!"

Their eyes met and held. Casey's face was flushed, her lips grim. Jess felt her the same way he had six years ago—somewhere deep inside himself. How had he forgotten Casey Oliver so easily? Holding her, even with anger between them, was bringing everything back. How many times had they made love during that week? Six times, eight, a dozen? "Are you really only twenty-three now?" he asked hoarsely, approaching the issue of her age six years ago from a safer direction.

"How long are you going to keep me in this disgusting position?" she returned tautly.

"At least you're looking at me now."

"I can hardly do anything else, can I?" she jeered.

"And you find being in my arms disgusting?"

"I'm not in your arms! I'm being held against my will!" To prove her point, Casey began to struggle again. "Take your hands off me," she yelled angrily. Her left arm eluded his hold, and she went for his face with her fingernails.

"Whoa, there," Jess growled, catching her wrist just in time. "You little hellion, what're you trying to do, scratch my eyes out?"

"It's a thought," Casey retorted, gulping a mouthful of air. Escape was impossible. He could hold her there all day if he chose. She was getting hot and sweaty, although the open windows allowed the passage of a warm, gentle breeze. Casey stiffened with a new fear and an immediate denial: she wasn't getting warmer because of Jess, she absolutely was not!

But why, after all the misery he'd caused her, was she so aware of the width of his shoulders and the hard bulk of his chest? And why did she keep looking at his mouth? She'd caught herself doing it several times. Oh, traitorous soul, she lamented in a bout of anguished self-castigation. How could she even notice that he'd only grown better-looking in six years? That the few silver hairs she could see mingled with all that black were dazzling, and that the crinkled corners of his eyes looked like perfect spots to plant tender kisses?

"I hate you," she whispered raggedly.

Jess stared directly into the centers of her tormented eyes. "I know you do. The big question is why? You loved me the week I was here before."

"I did not! I never loved you. No more than you loved me!"

"Well, honey, if that's the problem, rest assured. I loved you like crazy that week."

Casey's heart had already been beating hard, but now it raged in her breast. "You don't know the meaning of the word! Love isn't something you turn on for a week, then turn off again like you would a spigot!"

Jess was watching her with acute circumspection. He was beginning to understand Casey's scorn, or he thought he was. "Is that what happened to you? You couldn't turn it off?"

The implication of the conversation blasted Casey. "I *never* loved you!" she shouted.

"You don't have to yell. I'm not deaf."

"You're not only deaf, you're blind! What's it going to take for you to see that I wish you had never come back to Blythe? Nothing would make me happier than to hear you had disappeared from the face of the earth.''

Jess's face was suddenly dark with anger. "You sound like you need some lovin', Casey. How long has it been since you've had some real lovin'? How long have you been divorced?''

She was torn with two debilitating emotions: fury over his crude remarks and fearful astonishment that he'd already learned about her "marriage" and "divorce." Did he also know she had a son? "That's none of your business," she cried, struggling wildly again. "Let me go.''

"I will,'' Jess stormed. "But first...'' He grabbed the back of her head and brought his mouth down on hers, hard. Casey's gasp of surprise was muffled, nearly soundless. She twisted her head, trying to tear her mouth away, but Jess only kissed her harder and pressed his full weight against her. The door made ridges in her back, and the buttons on his shirt pressed tiny indentations in her breasts.

Her mind alternately raced and stood still. Jess's lips had quickly grown kinder, more sensual. She felt his tongue and her own stronger heartbeat, and vaguely realized one had caused the other. She might loathe and despise Jess Lonnigan, but he was still the sexiest man she'd ever known. Having had Jess as her first lover, was it any wonder she'd found little to respond to in other men?

She was kissing him back, she realized, opening her mouth for his tongue. His body weight relented a little, enough to allow room for his hand between them. It found a breast and closed around it, and she felt how agitated the contact was making him. His palm chafed her nipple through her blouse and bra, and the resulting sting of pleasure shooting through her system had the impact of a lightning bolt. Her responsive moan drifted on the July breeze filling the cab.

Jess's lips moved against hers, and he whispered, "You don't hate me, honey. You want me, just like I want you.''

Before she could agree to or deny the sensual accusation, Jess's mouth opened over hers again.

Breathing in short pants, Casey felt her fear growing in a direct ratio to her desire. She was getting lost again. Jess was commanding her senses again, just as he'd done six years ago. She had to stop this, she *had* to!

Working a hand upward, she slid it past the muscles of his chest and shoulder. Thinking she wanted to twine her arms around his neck, Jess adjusted, giving her more space. At last both her arms were free, and Casey grasped two handfuls of black hair and yanked his head up.

Jess looked down at her, surprise in his eyes. "What's wrong?"

Casey's irregular breathing made speaking normally difficult. "Do you intend to rape me?"

"Lord no!" Jess sat up and away from her. "Why would you think such a crazy thing?"

Flushed, Casey tried to smooth her disheveled hair. "I won't make love with you, Jess," she stated, her voice raspy and husky.

His eyes narrowed. "You want to. Or, you did. A man knows, Casey, and you wanted exactly what I did."

"Maybe for a minute or two. All that proves is what you accused me of—needing a man. If I do, he's not going to be you."

"Why not? Casey, you're the most dumbfounding woman I've ever been around. You kiss like no one else, and—"

"*You* kissed me." Wishing her hands were steadier, Casey reached for the ignition key. Before she could turn it, Jess covered her hand with his.

"Just a minute. I started out kissing you, but you kissed me back."

"It won't happen again, I can assure you." She felt his eyes on her, searching every angle and curve of her body. She was wearing a simple green knit sleeveless blouse and white cotton slacks, but she suddenly felt as if her clothing were evaporating. "Stop looking at me like that," she demanded heatedly.

"Like I'd like to undress you and make you whimper, sweetheart?"

She swallowed hard. "You're crude," she managed weakly.

"Not crude—truthful. We both know what happened a few minutes ago was no accident, honey. The same thing happened between us six years ago. One kiss was all it took, right?"

Casey shook his hand away and turned the ignition key. "I don't plan to relive old memories with you—not when I find them repugnant."

Jess snorted. "Repugnant? Hell! Who're you trying to kid? You loved every minute we spent together that week."

Shooting him a black look of resentment, Casey turned the pickup in a circle and started back to town.

He began to talk softly. "You know what's strange in all of this, honey? You've been protesting too much. I'm beginning to wonder who you've been trying to convince with all those bitter words. Me or you?"

"You're talking pure drivel."

"Am I?"

Casey was a seething mass of confusion. She had accomplished nothing beyond whetting Jess's curiosity even more than it had been. And pretending coolness over kissing him back when she despised herself for being so weak was making her furious, at herself as much as Jess. But she couldn't scream at herself.

She slammed on the brakes, slapped the gear lever into Park and turned on Jess. "This is the last time I ever want to see you. Are you capable of understanding that? If we meet on the street, I intend passing you by without so much as a blink. By way of an explanation, which you seem so bent on getting, I was seventeen years old when you were in Blythe six years ago. I'm not seventeen now. I'm—"

"Beautiful," Jess murmured.

She took a shaky breath, realizing deep inside herself that she was getting very close to hysteria. "Jess...you've got to leave me alone. I can't take much more of this."

His brow knit. "Much more of what? We've seen each other exactly twice since I've been back."

Casey dropped her gaze. "What do you want from me?" she asked in a ragged whisper.

Jess leaned closer and touched her hair. When she cringed back from his hand, he didn't press her. He withdrew his hand and said, "I think you know what I want."

Her eyes darted fitfully, evading the hot light she saw in his. "Why'd you come back here?"

"I always liked Wyoming."

"Wyoming's a big place. You could have bought a ranch hundreds of miles from Blythe."

"Yeah, I could have. Something drew me back here. Was it you? Maybe I never really forgot that week, honey."

Her expression grew colder. "You're lying."

Jess laughed easily. "Not lying, honey. But maybe exaggerating a little, huh? Truthfully, I was so busy the last six years, I never looked back at much of anything."

Sighing. Casey turned and slipped the lever back into Drive. In all honesty she respected Jess's "truthfulness" a lot more than she did his glibness. It didn't matter, anyway. She knew he hadn't thought about her all those years, so it wasn't news now. It didn't even hurt—not when she had another much more serious ache in her heart: Bobby. The little boy's big blue eyes were Jess's. Bobby's thick thatch of black hair was Jess's. Bobby's special half-smile, so endearing on his handsome little face, was Jess's.

Casey saw a dozen other similarities between the two—in expression, in movement. A child didn't have to grow up around a parent to imitate him: it was in the blood, a trick of genetics.

"Where do you want to get out?" Casey asked quietly, strangely coiled into numbness after the onslaught of emotions she'd undergone the past half hour.

"My truck's close to the hardware store. I was inside making a purchase when you drove up." Jess cocked his head in Casey's direction. "I understand you have a little boy."

"Yes," she replied through numbed lips.

"How old is he?"

"Five."

Jess frowned. "Then you must have gotten married right after I left."

"I did."

"To a local guy?"

"No. I met him in college that September."

"How long were you married?"

Casey shot him an angry look. "That's enough, Jess. I don't plan to give you a day-by-day update of the past six years." With tremendous relief, she steered the pickup into a parking space in the same block as the hardware store.

Jess didn't immediately jump out, though. He sat for another minute, then looked at her. "Would you go out with me some night?"

Her eyes widened. "You never give up, do you?"

"Not when I see something I want."

Casey took an impatient breath. "All right, I'll say it again. No, I will not go out with you. My most ardent wish is that it will eventually sink in that I want nothing to do with you— not today, not tomorrow, not next year. Just forget we even knew each other, because that's how I look at us: as total strangers."

The pupils of his eyes seemed to grow darker. "You're lying through your pretty teeth." Jess reached for the door handle. "One of these days I'll figure out why. See you around, honey."

Casey drove home, alternately crying and cursing.

Three

A week passed—an unholy week with Casey peering at ever
pickup she met on the road and constantly looking over he
own shoulder in town. She was positive Jess was lurkin
around every corner, just waiting for another chance to chal
lenge her. But she never saw a sign of him, and after a whil
she began to breathe a bit easier.

Casey had told her mother about Jess confronting her tha
day. She didn't mention Jess's personal advances, though, sim
ply because she could hardly bear even thinking about th
episode, let alone talking about it. But she did relay the fac
that Jess had already heard that she'd been married, divorce
and had a little boy.

Lucille's response was a seriously posed: "Did he seem t
doubt what he'd heard?"

"I don't think so," Casey replied honestly.

Lucille smiled with apparent relief. "There, you see? You
were worried about nothing. By the time he sees Bobby, *if* h
does, he'll be so used to the story he won't see anything bu
a very handsome little boy."

"I hope you're right, Mom." Casey still wasn't so sure of that, however. Whenever she looked at Bobby, she saw Jess—even more strongly now than she had before she'd gotten another look at Jess. Just to play it safe for a while longer, she continued to leave her son at the ranch when she made her trips to Blythe.

Wesley Upton had quickly gained a few clients, and his work was taking up more and more of Casey's time. The attorney offered her a cup of coffee whenever she made a delivery, and one afternoon Casey accepted. They sat in Wesley's office, Casey in one of the big chairs in front of the desk, the attorney seated behind the desk.

"Your offices turned out nicely," she remarked.

"Thank you. By the way, please call me Wes."

"If you like."

Wes smiled rather warmly, then put his cup down and leaned forward. "I'd like to ask you something, Casey."

"Go right ahead."

"Well, I've been wondering. I like your work very much, but I can see a time coming when I'm going to need a full-time secretary. Would you ever consider giving up your business and going to work for just one client?"

Casey hesitated. "I've been thinking of moving my business to town, Wes. Quite a few people have indicated I'd get a lot more work if I were closer. However, I really don't want to make any kind of change until Bobby is in school."

"And next summer, when he's out of school again?"

"I don't mind admitting that's been bothering me. My mother is very generous about taking care of Bobby, but I couldn't impose on her time for three months every year."

"Other mothers work, Casey. I would imagine pretty well all of them are faced with the problem of their children's summer vacations."

Casey nodded. "That's true. But I've never left Bobby with anyone but family. Anyway, as you can see, I haven't made a decision on the matter yet."

"Will you give my offer some consideration?"

Rising, Casey smiled. "Of course I will. I appreciate it, as a matter of fact."

Wes walked to the door with her. "Perhaps we could have dinner together some evening," he suggested.

"Perhaps," Casey agreed pleasantly. "Bye, Wes, I'll see you in a few days."

After three more deliveries, Casey started back to the ranch. She was driving with her eyes on the road, but her mind was on Jess Lonnigan. Maybe, as her mother had suggested, she had gone a little overboard about Jess's return. It was only because she didn't want Bobby's life disrupted with some kind of parental clashing, but it really wasn't very likely that Jess, being the type of man he was, would lay claim to his child, anyway—even if he should become suspicious. Rationally thinking, it wasn't even very likely that Jess would do more than catch a peek at Bobby now and then, possibly spot him from a distance in Blythe.

She felt a little better about it, Casey admitted to herself. The shock of hearing Jess's name, seeing him, then learning he was living only a few miles away, had caused her to panic. If she were going to be totally honest with herself, wasn't her own reaction to Jess much more dangerous than the slim possibility of him figuring out Bobby was his son?

The morning Jess had cornered her, for example, she, herself had made Jess suspect there was more to her animosity than mere dislike. *Dislike.* Casey smirked grimly. To her, the word denoted mild feelings of ill will. For six years she had *hated* Jess Lonnigan. Small wonder she couldn't stop herself from using sarcasm and insults around him. But she could see now that her open hostility had only aroused his curiosity. If— or more likely, when—she ran into Jess again, it would be much wiser to behave with less bitterness—if she could.

On the other hand, if he tried something personal again, she'd... She'd what? Frowning, Casey struggled with the obvious: Jess still had the power to turn her knees to jelly. She could despise him—and she did—and still, she couldn't halt a tide of desire when he kissed her. Why? Why was she able to handle every other relationship—granted, they'd been few—but have absolutely no control with Jess?

A horn behind her blasted her reverie, and Casey glanced into the rearview mirror. A black pickup was right on her bumper, and quickly Casey veered to the right to give the impatient driver more room to pass. The horn honked again.

"What's wrong with you?" she muttered. "How much room do you need?" The road had only two lanes, but there wasn't another car in sight. The honking continued.

Slowing way down, Casey frowned into the rearview mirror again. Only this time, she got a good look. Jess!

Automatically she speeded up, just wanting to escape. But the black pickup stayed right on her bumper, although the intolerable honking had stopped. Then Casey realized that Jess would follow her clear to the ranch, and her heart sank. She could convince herself all day that Jess wasn't the kind of man who would want his son, even if he knew about him, but she wasn't ready to take that chance. And the minute she drove up, Bobby would run out to greet her. He always did.

She let up on the gas pedal and pulled off the road.

In the rearview mirror, Casey watched Jess get out of his truck, toss his hat back in and start her way. She faced front and waited.

"Hi," she heard at the open window.

"What do you want?"

"Are you going to talk to me without looking at me again?"

Reluctantly Casey turned her head a fraction and gave him a cold stare. "Why are you following me?" *Do you have to be so damned good-looking?* In the bright sunlight, Jess's black hair, tanned face and vivid blue eyes were radiant.

Jess was seeing the same kind of thing in Casey: the purity of a flawless, creamy complexion, clear green eyes and a head full of thick, dark auburn curls. He cleared his throat. "I've been doing some thinking about us. We got off to a bad start."

Casey did nothing but raise one eyebrow slightly.

"I'm not the same guy I was six years ago, Casey."

"No? So far, I've seen nothing different," she said coolly.

"I know. But you riled me that day at the rodeo. I was glad to see you and I didn't expect what you dished out."

"So, what you're saying is that it's my fault you manhandled me last week in my own truck?"

Jess gave her a hard look. "Is that what I did, 'manhandle' you?"

"What would you call it?"

"Did I hurt you?"

Casey looked away. "I assume there's a point to this conversation?"

"Yeah, there is. I want to see you."

Her eyes flashed his way again. "No."

"Why not?"

Rolling her eyes in exasperation, Casey took a long breath. "Are we going to go through that again? How many times...?"

"As many as it takes."

"You think you're going to wear me down," Casey accused heatedly. "Well, you're not, Jess. Once was enough with you."

"What if I promise to keep my hands to myself? Would you see me, then?"

She laughed grimly. "I can't believe this. Why would you want to see a woman who so obviously doesn't want to see you?"

An approaching car drew Jess's attention, and he watched it speed toward them, then whiz on by. He turned troubled eyes and a frown back to Casey. "I honestly don't know," he confessed quietly, almost sadly. "There's some kind of pull...hell, I don't know what it is. I only know I keep thinking about you."

Something swirled within Casey. Resentment, maybe. She had thought of Jess a lot, too. At first. For months, after he left, she had cried herself to sleep every night thinking about him. If he suffered a hundred times more than she had, it wouldn't be enough. He'd been right about that personal vendetta. She would love hearing him say "I love you" with meaning instead of lust, so she could laugh in his face. And she'd push him into it, too, if it weren't for Bobby. With her son at stake, she couldn't risk revenge, as sweet as it would be.

But she had already decided to soft-pedal her hostility—for Bobby's sake—and remembering that decision, Casey kept her expression passive. "I'm sorry you don't understand me better. I rarely date, and I have no desire to renew a mistake I made at seventeen. That's all there is to my refusals. Don't try to read more into them than that."

A flush darkened his face. "I didn't know you were only seventeen, Casey. I never would have gotten so physically involved if I'd have known your age."

"I accept full responsibility," she answered sharply, then took a calming breath. "I should have told you. I knew you were older."

Shaking his head, Jess looked away for a moment. "I just grabbed at fun in those days. One town blurred into another. Women—"

"Blurred, too, I'm sure. Forget it. I have." *Grabbed at fun?* Casey's stomach was aching.

Jess gave her a direct look. "No, you haven't. You haven't forgotten at all. That's the problem. I know that now. You got emotionally involved, and when I left—"

"You're wrong!" Casey's mouth was suddenly dry and her heart pounding. "You're wrong, Jess. Look, I've got to go."

He put a hand on the window frame. "See me, Casey," he pleaded. "Go out with me. I promise I won't lay a hand on you. We'll take in a movie, or have a drink someplace. Dinner. Anything. You name it."

She shook her head sharply. "No. I can't. Please don't press me."

"Dammit, I *will* press you! You melted in my arms last week."

Casey met his eyes. "I'm the first to admit that I'm a fool sometimes. Please move back from the truck." She watched his eyes narrow.

"I'm not giving up, Casey."

She lifted her chin. "I guess that's your decision. Goodbye." Slipping the truck into gear, Casey eased it away. Looking in the rearview mirror again, she could see Jess, and he was standing in the same spot, just watching.

"Have you thought anymore about talking to your father about Jess?" Lucille asked.

They were sitting on the back patio. Casey had just told her mother about Jess stopping her on the road, and they had agreed that Jess's promise to "keep pushing" could present some problems.

Sighing over the question she hadn't really faced up to yet, Casey replied, "Yes. Whenever I think about it, I see Dad's face. It's cowardly, I know, but I'm just plain scared to tell him."

"Casey, there's no reason for you to be afraid to talk to your father about anything."

"I'll do it, Mom. Just give me a little more time."

Lucille nodded. "Just don't put it off too long."

Casey grimaced. "I've already done that, haven't I? I wish I had listened to you six years ago and told him then. Mom, what if Dad resents your part in it?"

Lucille looked away. "I don't think we should worry about that right now. Jess is back in your life, like it or not, and we have to think of Bobby."

"Yes, we do."

Lucille looked thoughtful. "Casey, I know what Jess did to you. I know you were devastated by what appeared to be desertion six years ago. What I'm getting at is, you've changed a great deal. Could Jess have changed too?"

"I don't understand."

"Well, every child needs a father and—"

"Mom! You're not suggesting I *tell* Jess!"

Lucille sighed. "I don't know what I'm suggesting. But it has occurred to me that Jess might have grown up, just as you did. He seems to have settled down, at any rate."

"He was grown-up six years ago," Casey argued. "He has to be ten years older than me."

"I meant emotionally, honey."

With her elbow on the arm of the chair and her chin in her hand, Casey stared morosely at her feet. "I won't share Bobby with a man who didn't have an ounce of concern over seducing a seventeen-year-old girl and then running off like it never happened."

"I thought you said he didn't know how old you were. Casey, you were pretty headstrong in those days. Try and remember yourself as you really were. No, Jess didn't do right. But neither did you, honey. Your father and I thought you were spending that entire week with a girlfriend in town."

Casey heaved a sigh. "I know. I gave you and Dad fits back then. When I see Kelly doing a lot of the same things I did, I feel like smacking her."

Lucille laughed. "It's just part of growing up, honey. After raising four other teenagers, I don't think Kelly's any better or any worse than the rest of you were."

"Dee-Dee never gave you any trouble."

"You're right. Dee-Dee was always pretty level headed. Buck and Brady were another story. Dad and I never knew what they were up to."

"None of them did what I did."

Lucille's blue-gray eyes softened. "It never made me love you any less, Casey. And there's a bright side to the whole thing—Bobby. Let's not forget that without Jess, we wouldn't have Bobby."

Casey smiled, though her eyes were misty. "He's my life, Mom."

"Yes, he is. But maybe it's time you expanded your life."

"With a man?"

"With a man," Lucille agreed solemnly, regarding her daughter with maternal concern and affection.

Stripped to the waist, Jess worked at unloading the first of the lumber he'd ordered for his new barn and stables from the back of his truck. The sun was hot, and his face and back glistened with perspiration. Hauling boards off a truck and stacking them near the proposed building site took little concentration, and as he did more often than he liked, Jess was thinking about Casey while he worked.

He knew she wasn't the same woman she'd been six years ago, even if that long-ago memory had a lot of fuzzy edges. Although he had easily recognized her at the rodeo that day, Jess realized. The changes in Casey just weren't apparent on the outside. She had the same beautiful face, glorious mane of hair and exciting body. Where she'd changed was inside. Instead of the soft, pliant girl he remembered, Casey was now guarded, caustic and hard. How come?

Had her marriage been bad enough to turn her into a man-hater? Maybe that was it. Maybe she treated *all* men the way she'd been treating him.

Jess knew she still lived on the family ranch, having picked up that detail at the same time he'd heard about her marriage, divorce and little boy. Well, whatever had caused her bitterness, she sure had been something six years ago.

Wiping his forehead with the back of his arm, Jess leaned on a board and looked off into his own past. Blythe. It had been full of people that week, just as it had been during rodeo week this year. The sleepy little town came alive during rodeo week, and the restaurants and bars had been overflowing with customers six years ago. Jess had had a few beers at one of the bars, then went back to the rodeo grounds to tend his horse.

A group of young women came along. Yes, now he was remembering. That's how he and Casey had met. She'd been strolling around the evening-quiet rodeo grounds with some friends. They'd stopped to talk—the whole group laughing and flirting. Then they'd wandered off.

Attracted by her startling green eyes and husky laugh, he'd picked Casey out. He hadn't once thought of how old she might be, even though now, he remembered that her girlfriends had seemed pretty young.

He'd found her again. It hadn't been a problem. People had been all over the streets. Somehow the two of them had ended up at a dance in the high-school gymnasium, and they'd danced a few dances, then left together. He had asked her to go for a beer, and she had said she didn't go into bars. Damn, that had been another hint she'd been too young! Why hadn't he taken it?

He'd been bowled over, hadn't he? That was his only excuse. She was beautiful and dazzling, and he'd known she was dazzled. He'd bought a six-pack and asked her where they could go to be alone. She'd shown him a place by a river about five miles out of Blythe.

Jess's jaw clenched. Now he was remembering a lot.

He'd spread a blanket on the grassy bank of the river. The moon had been big and bright. They'd sat down on the blanket and she had taken sips from his can of beer. He'd teased and flirted with her, and she had laughed and flirted back. He'd kissed her, tentatively at first, then with more passion. She'd surprised him with a wild response.

Jess wiped his forehead again. Oddly, his hands weren't very steady and his mouth was dry. Dropping the board he'd been leaning on to the stack on the ground, he strode to the house. Popping the top on a can of icy beer, he came back outside and plopped down on one of the chairs on the porch.

She *had* been a virgin. He remembered that evening very well now. He'd been stunned; she'd been consoling. The week had progressed from there.

Damn! Double damn! She hadn't been the kind of girl to make love with a man for a week, then forget him. What kind of horse's patoot had he been back then? His damned brain had been so full of rodeo and the next town, the next contest, that he'd gone off without a thought for what Casey might be feeling.

Was it any wonder she hated him now? He might have put that week and Casey behind him with the first sign of open road, but apparently she hadn't forgotten quite so easily.

Putting the other bits and pieces of her life together, Jess remembered her saying she'd met her husband that September in college. She hadn't wasted any time. Had she married on the rebound?

Then she had a son.

When?

How long had she been married before the boy was born?

Jess became as still as a statue. *How long had she been married before the boy was born?* "My God," he mumbled as the thought took form and grew to something almost unbearable. Had she had *his* child? Was that what she was hiding?

"How old is he?"

"Five."

Five. Five and what? Five and a half? Dates stormed Jess's mind. He'd been in Blythe in July. That would make a baby due the following April. Jess gulped a big swallow of the cold beer. If it was true, if Casey had gotten pregnant that July, then he had a son.

A son.

He put the beer down and covered his face with his hands while something hot and anguished flowed through his body. A son. He'd never had a family. He'd been kicked around as a kid, shunted off on one reluctant relative after another. His mother had run off with some guy: he'd never even known his father. At sixteen, he'd split, gone off on his own. It had been tough. He'd taken odd jobs to eat, then met an old cowboy named Ace Goodfield. Ace had sort of adopted him, giving him a roof over his head, even making him go back to school.

Ace was dead now, but if it hadn't been for him, Jess never would have gotten a high-school diploma. He never would have gotten into rodeo, either. Ace had introduced him to horses and the exhilaration of rodeo. The rest, he'd done on his own.

Jess raised his eyes wearily and stared across his land. A son. Damn Casey Oliver's selfish soul. She could have told him. The past was irrevocable. He couldn't go back and change inconsideration and thoughtlessness into something good. He'd been a jerk and there was no way around that. But keeping a man's son from him was just about as low as anyone could get. If it was true, the punishment far exceeded the crime.

He'd better find out if it was true. He'd never have a peaceful moment again until he knew for sure, one way or the other.

Casey was helping with the dinner dishes. While Lucille put leftovers away, Casey rinsed the dishes in the sink and stacked them in the dishwasher. Kelly came bounding in, her long, blond hair flying, her blue eyes excited. "He's here! Out on the porch with Dad."

"Who's here?" Lucille asked with only mild curiosity.

"Jess Lonnigan! He's sitting on the front porch with Dad. He is only the most gorgeous hunk that's ever been on our front porch."

"Don't overdramatize, dear," Lucille admonished softly with a worried look at Casey.

"Oh, honestly," Kelly groaned, and dashed out.

"Casey? Are you all right?"

She was facing the sink. The water was running and she was holding a plate, but she wasn't moving. Her shoulders rose as she stopped holding her breath. "Why would he come here?" she whispered, and turned to her mother.

"He told you he intended to press you, Casey."

"Yes. But, here? That takes a special kind of gall, Mom." Casey's eyes darted wildly for a moment. "Where's Bobby?" Grabbing a dish towel, she dried her hands hastily. "I've got to find Bobby," she tossed over her shoulder as she ran from the kitchen.

Lucille sighed sadly. She'd seen Bobby only a few minutes ago, playing in the front yard with the dogs. There was no way Jess could have missed seeing him.

Feeling choked, Casey dashed through the house, praying that Bobby was in front of the TV. The living room was empty. She reached the front screen door and saw Jess, her father and Kelly on the porch. Just beyond, rolling around on the grass with the dogs, was Bobby.

He was giggling, and looked so adorable she wanted to run out and hug him, then hide him. Her hands were itching to touch her son, and her heart was aching to protect him. She heard her father's laughter, Jess's voice. They were getting along very well.

Weakly, Casey slumped back against the foyer wall. Her mind raced. Hadn't her father and Kelly immediately seen the strong resemblance between Jess and Bobby? Why weren't they already in the house, questioning her, accusing her?

Had Jess noticed it?

She heard her father's voice. "I'm glad you stopped by, Jess. A man should meet his neighbors."

Then came Kelly's voice: "Everyone is so-o-o excited about you moving here, Mr. Lonnigan."

"Call me Jess, Kelly."

"Oh, thank you."

Casey's stomach turned over. Why hadn't she gathered her pitiful supply of courage and confessed the awful truth to her dad? It was going to be even harder to do now. *Dad, that man who dropped in last night—Jess Lonnigan? Well, he's really Bobby's father.*

Oh, God, what a mess she still was making of her life!

"Is Casey around?" she heard Jess ask.

"Do you know Casey?" That came from Kelly, sounding totally amazed.

Casey stiffened, anticipating Jess's answer with bated breath.

"We've met," was Jess's noncommittal reply.

Then came Ben's voice again. "Well, she's around here somewhere. Kelly, go see if you can find her."

Casey ducked into the foyer closet while her sister ran past. Then she opened the door to eavesdrop again.

"You've got a beautiful place here, Ben."

"Yeah, it is. It's home, Jess. Three generations of Olivers have lived here."

"I'm just starting out, but someday, maybe Lonnigans will be able to say that."

"Gonna raise quarter horses, I hear."

The men were soon in a technical discussion on the qualities and characteristics of the quarter horse. The conversation was so impersonal, Casey was feeling a little better—but only a little. Jess's nerve at just driving up and apparently introducing himself astonished her, even while it angered and frightened her.

"I'm starting construction on a barn and a stable within the next few days," Casey heard.

"A barn? Do you have any help lined up?"

"I hired a couple of guys to give me a hand."

"A barn's a pretty big project."

Bobby let out a whoop and Casey slipped from the closet to peek out the screen door again. The little boy was running as hard as he could, with the dogs yapping and chasing after him. Both Jess and Ben were watching the chase with big smiles.

"Oh, there you are."

"Kelly..." Casey began, on the verge of warning her sister to keep quiet.

"Casey? Come on out, honey." Ben had heard.

Taking a deep breath, Casey pushed the screen door open. Jess slowly stood up. "Hello, Casey."

The second she looked into his eyes, Casey wanted to flee. Jess knew. No one else knew, but Jess did. Ben hadn't seen the resemblance, it had escaped Kelly, but Jess knew.

Her voice was dull, her spirit dead. "Hello, Jess."

His gaze flicked over her. She was beautiful in white shorts and a green T-shirt, her long, tanned legs dark in the waning light and in contrast to the white fabric of her shorts. "I've been having a nice talk with your dad."

"Have you?"

"And your sister Kelly." Jess gave Kelly a glance that the teenager responded to with a bedazzled smile.

"I also enjoyed watching your son playing."

Casey's eyes darted to Bobby. "He...he's a wonderful little boy," she said hoarsely.

"I can see that." Jess turned to Ben. "Would you mind if I asked Casey to take a ride with me?" Kelly's eyes had grown as big as saucers.

Ben looked from Jess to Casey. "That's entirely up to her, Jess. I wouldn't presume to tell that little filly what to do."

It was a joke, but Casey wasn't laughing. "No...no," she stammered, then looked at Jess and wilted inside. It wasn't exactly a threat she saw in his dark, cold, blue eyes, but it was something that sent a chill up her spine all the same. "All right," she amended quickly.

Lucille stepped through the door. "Oh, honey, meet Jess Lonnigan," Ben piped up. He dropped an arm around his wife's shoulders. "Jess, this lovely lady is my wife, Lucille."

Casey watched this nightmare unfold as if she were a great distance away and looking down on the front porch. Her skin felt clammy and cold, and though the evening was warm, she wanted to heave a mighty shiver.

Lucille extended her hand. "I'm glad to meet you, Jess," she replied in a clear, controlled voice. "I've heard a lot about you."

Jess cocked an eyebrow over the handshake. "I hope it wasn't all bad, Mrs. Oliver."

"Well, I suppose that depends on what one considers bad, Jess."

Kelly looked ready to burst. "Casey's going for a ride with Jess, Mom."

Lucille looked at Casey. "I'll put Bobby down at his regular bedtime," she said quietly.

"Thanks, Mom." Casey bit her lip for a troubled moment, then gave her mother a kiss on the cheek. "I won't be long," she whispered.

Smiling, with her husband's arm still around her, Lucille stood on the porch and watched Casey and Jess walk out to his pickup. "He's very good-looking, isn't he?" she murmured softly.

Kelly gave her a sharp look. "He's only a dream, that's all," she retorted dryly. "Lucky Casey. I sure wish I was older."

Ben laughed. "Your time will come soon enough, little girl."

"Little girl!" In a huff, Kelly dramatically swept into the house.

Sighing, Lucille sat down. "What did you think of him, Ben?"

Ben took a minute, then nodded solemnly. "He seems like a real nice fellow, honey. A real nice fellow."

Four

Neither spoke. Jess stared straight ahead while he drove. Casey stared out the side window. They were miles away from the ranch before she realized where he was going—the river. She clamped her teeth together to keep from telling him not to go there. It was where they had gone again and again six years ago. She hadn't been back, and she didn't want to go now.

But there was so much tension in the truck. What they were both feeling was in the air, thick, heavy, as dense as pea soup. She couldn't determine clearly what was in Jess's mind, but she sensed how tightly coiled his emotions were.

He jerked on the knob for the headlights, though it was still twilight. Lucille would be bathing Bobby about now, hearing his prayers soon. Casey chewed her bottom lip, then a thumbnail. What did Jess intend to do? She would fight with every drop of blood in her body: he would never get Bobby away from her. Never!

Jess turned onto the bumpy, rutted road leading to the river. The pickup bounced and rolled for a mile, then Jess braked it to an abrupt stop and switched off the motor. The silence of a Wyoming evening permeated the cab of the truck.

"He's mine, isn't he?"

The words slashed the quiet, increasing Casey's pulse, breaking her heart. She felt hot, burning tears threatening. "No, he's mine," she whispered.

Jess swiveled in the seat and leaned forward. His eyes were hard, his face tense. "Did you think I wouldn't figure it out? Did you think I wouldn't know when I saw him?"

"I knew you'd know. That's why—"

"Why you tried to turn me off with insults," Jess interrupted harshly. "I want him, Casey."

"*No!* You can't do this, Jess. Think of him."

Jess remained cold. "What poor sap did you marry to give Bobby a name? What *is* your married name, by the way? That's one piece of information that eluded me."

"Maddox," she replied numbly. "But—"

"Forget it. I don't give a damn who the guy was. The only thing that's important right now is my son. *My son!* Lord, I can't believe you hate me so much you'd want to keep Bobby away from me."

Casey turned on him, fury erupting. "I have every right to hate you. Don't you dare make me the heavy in this. You're not the one who had to lie and sneak around, to leave Blythe and pretend to be in college, damn you! What do you even know about what I went through? Nothing! Did I have even the slightest idea how to find you? Did I have any reason to hope you might come back?"

Stunned, Jess absorbed her rage. "All right, all right. Don't come unglued. Maybe we can figure something out."

"Like what? Let me tell you something, Jess. The day you make trouble for Bobby will be the sorriest day of your life! He's a happy little boy. He lives among people and family who love him. He's got cousins and pets to play with, and he's got—"

"He doesn't have a father!" Jess's voice lashed the air. "What do you tell him when he asks? Does he think that other guy is his father?"

Casey swallowed. "I...told him..."

"Then he has asked?"

Hesitating, Casey realized she hated admitting that Bobby had asked. Of course, he'd noticed that his cousins all had fathers: *"Where's my daddy, Mommy?"*

"You have Grandpa, honey."

"Yes, he's asked," Casey said in a low voice.

"And what did you tell him?"

Enraged again, Casey stormed, "Could I tell him his real father ran off before he was born? He's only five years old."

Breathing hard, Jess retorted scornfully, "I didn't run off, and I never would have left at all if I'd known you were pregnant."

"Oh, sure," she scoffed flippantly. "You thought so much of me, didn't you? That's why I never got as much as a post-card from you."

Jess looked away, stung for an answer. Casey's anger was justified as far as his lack of consideration went. When he brought his eyes back to her, he released a heavy breath. "Look, fighting like this is getting us nowhere. All I want is a chance to get to know my son."

"No," Casey whispered, battling tears again.

"You can't stop me, Casey."

"I *will* stop you. I'll take Bobby and leave. You'll never know where we went, even if I have to completely break all ties with my family."

"You wouldn't do that."

"Oh, yes, I would. I've already thought of leaving, but my mother talked me out of it."

Jess was silent a moment. "Your mother knows, doesn't she? I'm not sure about your dad, but your mother knows."

"She knows," Casey admitted with misery in her voice. "Don't underestimate my threat, Jess. If you cause Bobby one moment's pain, you'll never see him again. I swear it."

Miserable too, Jess sat back. A long pause ensued, and the night silence descended around them.

"All right, you seem to have all the answers," Jess finally responded. "What do you propose we do?"

Another silence stretched while Casey fought with herself over the sadly limited alternatives.

Jess spoke again. "We could get married."

"*What?*" Her eyes practically glowed with righteous indignation.

"We've got a good reason to get married, Casey—a lot better than some couples have."

"Where do you get your conceit? Do you actually think I would even consider marrying you? Haven't you gotten the message yet? I loathe the ground you walk on. Is that clear enough?"

Jess's voice was thick with sarcasm. "Is that why you kissed me back, because you loathe me so much?" He moved quickly and grabbed her arm, pushing his face very close to hers. "Who do you think you're kidding, sweetheart? I could make you want me right now. Should I prove it?"

Casey cringed back against the door. "Just stop it! I won't be manhandled again. Not by you, not by anyone!"

He glared at her in the near darkness for a minute, then backed off. "You're right. I'm sorry."

Sitting upright again, Casey rolled her window up against the cooler air coming in. Her shorts and T-shirt were great during the day, but it always cooled down after sunset.

"Are you cold?"

"I'm fine," she answered stiffly.

"Look, there must be a compromise we could make."

"If I let you see Bobby on occasion, what would you do?" Jess's heart leaped. "See him how?"

Casey thought a moment. "At the ranch. You could come by once in a while."

"As what?"

"What do you mean, 'as what'? As a friend. As a neighbor."

"How's the boy going to get to know me if I can't tell him who I am?"

"Don't you dare tell him! Don't you dare tell anyone!" Groaning, Casey buried her face in her hands. "It will never work. Why don't you just disappear back to wherever you've been for six years?''

Jess looked at her, his heart in his throat, then opened the door of the truck and got out. He gave the door a slam and walked away, going closer to the river. Despair gripped him, and he stared at the dark water moving past, at the silvery touches of moonlight rippling across its surface. He was right, Casey was right, and the boy was in the middle. There was no solution to the dilemma.

For Bobby's sake he couldn't make trouble. Besides, he believed Casey's threat. She obviously loved their son and would do whatever she felt offered Bobby the best protection. And if that meant Jess was out of the picture, so what? So damned what? Who was Jess Lonnigan, anyway? Just a guy who had hurt her. A guy like that didn't have feelings, did he?

Cynically, Jess wished he didn't have them. It would be a lot easier to deal with this without emotion.

He'd almost died from feelings when he'd sat on the Olivers' porch and watched his son playing with the dogs. That handsome little fellow, that bright-eyed, sturdy little boy was his son. Jess Lonnigan's son. It didn't seem real.

Well, maybe it wasn't real. He'd had hope for a few hours...but what the hell? The boy was a lot more important than he was—any day.

Jess went back to the truck and climbed in. Casey was huddled against the seat and sniffing, obviously winding down from a good cry. "Stop worrying," he told her wearily. "I won't do anything."

"You won't? Oh, Jess..." Sobs shook her again, and she reached a hand out. "Do you have a handkerchief? I came away with nothing."

"Sure." Pulling out a white handkerchief, Jess pressed it into Casey's hand. She wiped her eyes and blew her nose. Her dry sobs sounded like hiccups, and she had to blow her nose again.

"I...don't know what to say," she said huskily. "But you have my thanks."

"I'll tell him when he's an adult, Casey."

Tears choked her again, and this time they were for Jess. She never thought she'd be crying for Jess Lonnigan, but she was. She felt his pain in her soul, the sorrow he had to be suffering over gaining and losing Bobby all in one evening. Casey tried to put herself in Jess's place and imagine how she would feel if she were him. "I can't bear this," she sobbed.

Sighing, Jess slid across the seat. "Com'ere," he muttered, and pulled her into his arms. He rested his chin on her hair and held her while she cried her heart out.

They were close, as much in spirit as body—both parents, both thinking of their child. It was a long time before Casey calmed down. She sat up and blew her nose again. "You can see him, Jess. Come by whenever you want. It might be good for him to—" She stopped and wiped her eyes. "I can't seem to stop crying."

"You've been a good mother, haven't you? I can tell, Casey."

"Yes," she whispered brokenly. "He's very easy to love."

Jess rubbed his eyes, as if he were worn out. "Lord, I wish I'd had more sense six years ago." He heaved a sad sigh. "Casey, for what it's worth, I'm damned sorry I treated you the way I did. How can I explain what kind of guy I was then? The only thing that meant anything was getting to the next rodeo. The fun and games along the way were only that: fun and games. I wish I could tell you that I intended coming back, that circumstances kept me away. But that's not the truth, and whatever else I am, I'm not a liar."

"I am," Casey said sadly. "I lied so much for a while it's a wonder my tongue didn't fall out. I even lied to my dad."

"But not to your mother."

"No. I had to tell her. I had to tell someone, and Mom's always been easy to talk to."

"And your brothers and sisters? None of them know?"

"Only Mom. After you came back, she asked me to tell Dad the truth."

"Are you going to?"

"I...don't know. If I do, it will be the hardest thing I've

ever done. Dad is the kind of person who sees mostly good
in others. Mom's more of a realist, although she does have a
stubborn streak about her own children."

"You've got a nice family. You're lucky, Casey. Really
lucky."

"I know I am." She looked at him. "What about you?
Don't you have any family?"

"No."

"None?"

"No one."

"Oh, Jess, I'm sorry." She sighed forlornly, then added,
"What a mess. I was such a fool at seventeen."

"Why were you?"

"A fool?"

"Yeah. Why were you so...?"

"Easy?"

"Cooperative. You were very nice to me, Casey."

Something began to tremble within her. "I had never met
anyone like you before, I guess."

"You were a virgin."

She gulped hard. "I'm surprised you remember."

"I remember a lot about that week," Jess said quietly.
"This is the place we came, isn't it?"

"Yes. Why did you pick it tonight?"

"I don't know. I just kept driving."

"Maybe it's appropriate." Casey sighed again.

"Yeah, maybe it is. Casey...?"

"Yes?"

Jess moved closer. "Casey, let's forget everything except
you and me and Bobby. We could be a family, honey, a real
family. My ranch is small, but it's going to be a winner. It's
got a nice house, not as big as your folks', but it's nice. You'd
like it."

"Jess, I can't," she groaned unhappily. "You don't understand. Too much has happened. I've been here for six
years..."

"Hating me."

"Yes. I can't turn my feelings around that fast."

"I wouldn't expect you to. I wouldn't push you. I swear wouldn't. We could even have separate bedrooms. Your family is great, Casey, but don't you wonder what it would be like to have you own home? Your own life? I've seen those posters in Blythe's store windows. I know you're trying to contribute to Bobby's care. Honey, let me take care of you both. I've got money in the bank. You wouldn't have to work—"

"I don't have to work now, Jess. Both Mom and Dad have told me that. I'm working because I want to. Please don't go on with this. We've made some headway tonight, but this kind of talk could ruin it."

He leaned closer, and his arm stretched along the seat behind her head. "Casey, listen to me. Please. Life's too short to dwell on the past. Bobby will shoot up. You'll only have him a few short years. Let me share those years. Give Bobby his father. What bigger or more precious gift could you give him?"

Casey's heart was pounding, and she wasn't sure it was from what Jess was saying or because he was so close. "Please, you're crowding me. Give me room to breathe, Jess."

He took her chin and held it, turning her face up to him. "Will you at least think about it?" His voice was ragged, hoarsely tense. "Casey, don't throw it out without some thought. You could lay down the rules. I'd sleep in another room. I wouldn't touch you."

Casey pulled his hand down from her chin. "Like you're not touching me now?"

"Aww, hell," he groaned, and fell back against the seat. "You're right. I'd touch you. How could I help it? You're a sexy, beautiful woman. Of course I'd touch you. I'd do it right now, if you'd let me."

Casey watched the river a moment, then faced Jess again. Her face and voice were sad. "You'd make love to any woman who came along, Jess. You might have changed some, but apparently not in that respect. Let me say something here. If and when I marry, it's going to be for love."

"Marry again, Casey. You forget the 'again.' And it's all well and good to hope for some kind of great love to come along, but don't you think that's kind of a foolish fantasy? What about the reality of what's happening right now? I'm offering something now, not five or ten years down the road. What would be so terrible about marrying me?"

"It's out of the question. I think we should go now."

"You're mad again."

"No, I'm not mad. But you're so insensitive I can't believe it. You've got some crazy picture in your mind of a happy little threesome—you, me and Bobby. Jess, you and I don't even know each other. We spent one week together six years ago and we've seen each other exactly four times since you've been back. Do you think I would uproot Bobby from the only home he's known and move him in with a complete stranger? That's what you are to him. In all honesty, that's what you are to me, too. A stranger."

Jess had listened and he was beginning to understand Casey's point of view. They *were* strangers. A week of flirting, dancing and making love six years ago sure wasn't a foundation for a relationship—any kind of relationship. He was willing to take the chance that they could work everything out after the ceremony, but Casey wasn't. She might have been impulsive six years ago, but it was all too obvious she was anything but that now—especially where Bobby was concerned.

"All right," Jess said quietly. "I think I see what we have to do."

"Oh?"

"Yeah. You and me have got to get to know each other better."

"Jess!" Dammit, that wasn't what she'd been trying to get across. She'd relented on Jess seeing Bobby because the alternative was taking her son and leaving Wyoming. She'd also been deeply moved by Jess's unselfish announcement that he wouldn't make trouble. But she had no intention or desire to further her and Jess's personal relationship. His marriage proposal was almost insulting. Live under the same roof with a man who had treated her so shabbily? It was unthinkable.

And "getting to know each other better" was almost as unthinkable.

Casey set her chin at a stubborn angle. "I don't want to know you better," she said, as emotionlessly as she could manage with the hope of maintaining the uneasy truce they'd somehow reached.

"You've got to give somewhere, too, Casey. So far, it looks to me like I'm doing all the giving."

"Are we adding up sides here? Does it matter who has the most points, you or me? Bobby's what's important—not that you might have given a bit more for his sake than I might have."

"You've had him for nearly five-and-a-half years," Jess accused softly.

Casey's pulse leaped with renewed fear. "You said you wouldn't do anything!"

"I won't. Neither Bobby nor anyone else will ever hear a word about this from me, not until he's an adult. You have my word on that. But it wouldn't hurt you to give a little, too."

Casey's voice wasn't quite steady. "I have given. Didn't I say you could see him?"

"Yes. And I appreciate it. But if there's a chance, the slimmest chance that the three of us could be a family, I think we should at least make the attempt."

He sounded so sincere, and as if his heart had been irreparably broken. Casey's innate kindness was responding. Only with Jess had she ever been so cold and waspish. It wasn't natural for her to play judge, jury and prosecutor. Yet, she couldn't even begin to forget the pain Jess had caused her. "You have no right to that argument," she whispered, frightened that her defenses were weakening. "You're using Bobby to make me feel guilty, and that's not fair. He's happy—"

"Are you?"

Her head jerked around so she could see him. "Would I be happier with you?" she snapped.

Jess raised a hand and gently touched her hair. "Maybe you would. I'd do my best, honey."

For a single moment a flash of the magic that Jess had dazed her with six years ago inundated Casey. Frightened by the strong, sensual feeling, Casey pulled away from his hand. "Don't try physical persuasion," she warned sharply. "I'm not a kid anymore, Jess. I've learned to think before I leap into something."

"Maybe you've become a little too cautious. Maybe you're afraid to take a chance now. Is that it? Are you afraid of getting hurt again? Or have you blamed and hated me for so long, you're afraid of losing the biggest part of yourself if you gave up despising me?"

"Don't be silly," she scoffed, but she knew he'd given her something to think about. Had she clung to hatred because she had no other emotions to hang on to?

Jess was silent a moment. "All I'm suggesting is seeing each other for a while. If we get along okay, then bring Bobby into the picture. We could do it gradually, Casey—spend a few evenings a week together."

"And do what?" she questioned suspiciously.

Jess sighed. "Nothing you don't want to do. Maybe just go for a ride so we could talk."

Did he deserve that? Did he deserve even a dram of her consideration? There was something sad about Jess's position in all of this, but hadn't he brought it on himself? Was it her fault that he used to live for nothing but rodeo and "fun and games"? She'd paid her dues during the terrible year following rodeo week six years ago; wasn't it time Jess paid his?

She was confused, ambivalent, sorry for him, protective of herself. "I just don't know," she admitted wearily, tired of the battle.

"Will you at least think about it?"

"Yes, I'll think about it. Please take me home now."

"So what did you tell him?" Lucille inquired quietly.

Sighing, Casey got up from the kitchen table and went to the window. Bobby was playing in the backyard. Dressed in blue shorts and a red T-shirt, his black hair glistening in the sun, he was a lovely picture of health and boyish enthusiasm. "I told him I'd think about it," Casey replied dully. "I wish he'd never come back," she added after a moment.

"But he did, honey." Lucille stood up. "Well, you've got quite a decision to make."

Casey turned, and every inch of her body conveyed unhappiness. "Tell me what to do, Mom," she pleaded.

Lucille shook her head sadly. "I can't do that, Casey."

"What would you do?"

With a thoughtful expression, Lucille sat down again. "What would I do?" she repeated, as if asking herself the question. "It's impossible to put myself in your shoes, Casey. I'm older and see things differently than you do."

"You think I should do it, don't you? Deep down, you think Jess should have a chance."

"I'm only thinking of Bobby," Lucille cautioned. "What Jess asked isn't that terrible." She paused. "Your father said he thought Jess was a pretty nice guy."

Casey rolled her eyes. "Dad saw him for five minutes. Besides, when's the last time Dad met anyone who *wasn't* a nice guy? He likes everyone."

"Honey, if Jess was just passing through again I'd be dead set against him disrupting Bobby's life in any way. But he bought a ranch here, he's making his home here. And," Lucille added softly, "he *is* Bobby's father. Everybody makes mistakes, Casey. Would there be any real harm in spending a little time with him to see if the two of you couldn't come to some kind of understanding?"

"He doesn't want an understanding. He wants marriage."

"I know, and I'm certainly not suggesting marriage is the best conclusion for the two of you. I'm in complete agreement with you that a marriage based on anything other than strong emotional ties doesn't stand much of a chance. In short, love— a very deep, abiding love. I don't expect you and Jess could ever reach that point. But there are other levels of communication that might be very important to Bobby. Apparently Jess is going to be a part of his son's life, with or without your blessing.''

"Not as a father," Casey reminded with strong conviction.

"Whatever the relationship evolves into, wouldn't it be easier for Bobby if you and Jess were on reasonably good terms?''

Casey looked crestfallen. "And how do I deal with my feelings for him? How do I forget what he did?''

Lucille smiled gently. "People don't forget, honey. They just learn to live with unhappy memories. Maybe once you get to know Jess, there'll be things about him that will make the past less meaningful.''

Casey was about to respond with doubt when Kelly swept in. "What's for lunch, Mom? I'm starving.'' She looked from her mother to her sister. "Did I interrupt something?'' Unconcerned despite the question, Kelly opened the refrigerator to check its contents. "How'd your date with the hunk go, Casey?''

"It wasn't a date," Casey retorted, and left the kitchen.

Wide-eyed, Kelly looked at her mother. "What's wrong with her?''

Lucille sighed and got up from the table. "Let's make some lunch, Kelly.''

Jess looked up from the blueprint he'd been studying. The print was a plan for a barn, and he'd recently purchased it, along with another for a stable, because he'd had little experience in construction. Now, with the print stretched open across the hood of his pickup, he was beginning to realize the complexity of his undertaking. Joints, joists, beams, window frames, flooring—it was hard to relate the stacks of various-sized lumber beside the pickup to the terms he'd been studying.

The truck kicking up dust on his driveway was a welcome reprieve from the print, and Jess rerolled the several large sheets and secured them with the broad rubber band that had come with them. He went to meet his visitor.

Surprised to see Ben Oliver getting out of the pickup, Jess

hurried over and offered his hand. "Nice of you to stop by, Ben."

Ben looked around. "Just wanted to see what you've got here, Jess. Looks like a good house."

"It is. You can see I'm short on outbuildings, though."

They walked toward the stack of lumber. "This is the barn site," Jess said. "I plan to get it built first, then the stable."

Ben grinned. He had a pleasant round face, hazel eyes and iron-gray hair. "How would you like a little help?"

"I've got a couple of men lined up—"

"I mean real help. The kind that will put that barn up in a weekend."

Jess flushed clear to the roots of his hair. No one, other than Ace, had ever offered to "help" Jess Lonnigan. "I'm not sure what to say, Ben."

"Say yes and tell me when you want us. That's what neighbors are for, Jess. A man doesn't build a barn alone around these parts."

"Tonight?" Casey echoed weakly. She clutched the phone with white knuckles, all of her strength seemingly having gone from her voice to her fingers.

"Around seven."

"Jess—I haven't made up my mind yet," she stammered.

"Do you have other plans for tonight?"

"No, but that's—"

"I'll see you at seven, Casey."

The line went dead. As she put the phone down, a spark of anger infiltrated Casey's numbness. She was being railroaded. Jess was completely ignoring her doubts, and even her mother was on his side!

When Jess arrived a few minutes before seven, Kelly was on the front porch, obviously determined to get another look at "that hunk." From her upstairs bedroom window Casey watched Jess get out of his pickup. He was wearing new-looking jeans, a fitted, Western-cut white shirt and highly-polished black boots. He looked fresh from the barber, with his normally unruly black hair smoothly in place. He was all "slicked up," and it made Casey madder than hell.

A sense of helplessness made her mad, too. Things were happening that she didn't want to happen. She didn't want to go out with Jess, not even for a ride. He was dangerous to her emotional health. She hated the silly, female reactions she felt whenever he touched her, and she didn't trust him not to take advantage of his sensual influence. Why couldn't he have been content to stop by now and again and spend an hour with Bobby? It was more than he deserved, if one were to get down to hard facts. She'd made one enormous concession in agreeing to him seeing Bobby at all; how many more was Jess going to demand?

Casey saw Bobby run around the corner of the house and heard Kelly call, "Bobby, come say hello to Mr. Lonnigan."

Through narrowed eyes, Casey watched her son cautiously approach Jess, who squatted to be on the same level with the little boy. They shook hands, with Bobby's small hand getting lost in Jess's.

Casey dropped the curtain as tears filled her eyes. She simply had to stop feeling sorry for Jess. He'd caused his own misery, and hers. He had no right to intrude on her life now. He especially had no right to try and push her into marriage.

Marriage. The mere thought was ludicrous. What would the reality of such an unlikely liaison be?

"Casey? Jess is here!" rang from the foot of the stairs. It was Kelly, yelling out what she thought was good news.

Casey called from the doorway, "I'll be down in a few minutes."

She went to the mirror, gave her hair a pat and checked her lipstick. She was wearing a faded denim skirt, a white eyelet sleeveless blouse and sandals—good enough attire for the totally wasted evening ahead. She would not be talked into anything, above all a marriage that repelled her.

With a sweater, in case she got chilly again later, and a small purse, Casey slowly descended the stairs. Everyone was on the front porch—her mother, her father, Kelly, Bobby and

Jess. Their laughter and friendly voices annoyed Casey no end, but when she stepped outside and saw Bobby sitting on Jess's lap, her annoyance turned to bitterness.

"Hi, Mommy."

"Hi, sweetheart." She wanted to snatch her son away from Jess, and it was all she could do to stop herself.

Jess was looking at her with wary eyes. "Hello, Casey."

"Jess," she allowed stiffly.

"Sit down, honey," Ben invited. "I think our Bobby's made a new friend."

"I see that," Casey replied coolly.

Lucille spoke. "Casey, your father and Jess were discussing the barn raising."

"What barn raising?"

Jess answered. "Your father was kind enough to offer help on my barn."

"Not just me." Ben laughed. "There'll be a hundred men there, Jess. I like your place, and—"

"You've been there?" Casey interrupted, astounded.

"Today, honey. Jess's got a nice place."

"Oh, great," Casey muttered, and turned to Jess. "If we're going somewhere, let's go."

"Casey!" Ben exclaimed over her rudeness, and his wife laid a restraining hand on his arm.

Jess stood up, with Bobby still in his arms. "Well, pardner, I'll see you again in a few days, okay?"

"Okay," Bobby agreed as he was lowered to the porch. Jess turned to Casey.

"Let's go."

Casey quickly kissed Bobby, then her mother and her father. "I'm sorry, Dad," she whispered.

And when she and Jess left the porch to go to his pickup, everyone had to hear Kelly declare, "Well, I never! If somebody doesn't tell me what's wrong with Casey these days, I'm positively going to explode!"

Five

Exactly like the night before, they drove away from the ranch in stony, cold silence. But Casey didn't wait for a destination tonight. After a few minutes she stormed, "What are you trying to do? Get my whole family on your side?"

Her gaze fell on Jess's hands gripping the steering wheel. She saw frustration in their hold, anger. She heard the same intense qualities in his voice when he growled, "Aren't you the one who said, just last night, that we shouldn't be adding up sides? Who's doing it now, Casey?"

"You're forcing *me* to, that's what's happening. I'm on to you, Jess. You think if you put on a nice-guy image, my family might try to influence me in your favor. That's dirty pool," Casey fumed.

Jess threw her a dark look. "Did it ever once occur to you that I might really *be* a nice guy? You're judging me by what happened six years ago. Would you like me to judge you based on that week? You were very—"

"Cooperative?" she drawled sarcastically, beating him to the punch.

"Easy," Jess retorted.

Casey gasped. "That's a cheap shot."

"What do you expect me to do? Keep taking your crap without fighting back? My good nature only goes so far, honey."

"Your good nature? Now, there's a laugh. And don't call me honey. I'm not now, nor ever was your 'honey.'"

Jess laughed humorlessly. "The hell you weren't. For one memorable week, that's exactly what you were. A travelling cowboy's 'honey.' Baby you were—"

"*Stop it!*" Casey covered her ears with her hands. When he gave her a surprised look, she dropped her hands to her lap. "Last night I actually felt sorry for you," she said disdainfully.

"Don't feel sorry for me, Casey. I don't need or want your pity."

"No, you want my son," she snapped, bitterness tinging the accusation.

"He's my son, too."

"A biological accident."

"Well, that's how you got him, too, *honey*. By accident."

"I loathe and despise you."

"Except when I kiss you. You don't loathe and despise me in a clinch, lady."

She was so wounded she couldn't speak for a moment. Maybe it hurt so much because it was true, but Jess's saying it made her feel totally degraded. "Turn this truck around and take me home!"

"No way. You'll cool down in a few minutes. Then maybe we can talk like two reasonably intelligent people."

This is it! Casey thought. *This is the last time I spend so much as five minutes with you! I'm taking Bobby and leaving.*

Her mind spun with the enormity of the decision. Where would she go? She'd never been entirely on her own. She didn't have much money.

She fell silent, brooding over the situation. Jess drove, keeping his eyes on the road ahead. They reached the outskirts of Blythe, and the pickup slowed down to the speed limit. The evening streets were quiet, almost deserted. Jess drove to the opposite end of town, then turned around and started back.

"Want a beer, or a soda?"

"No, thank you," she replied coldly.

Jess shook his head grimly. Casey saw his disgust, and all at once felt totally drained. She put her head back against the seat and closed her eyes. All this fighting and dissension were taking a toll. She wasn't a fighter; she never had been. She'd been keyed up ever since Jess's name had come over the PA system at the rodeo, and she wasn't used to running on nervous energy. She'd been rude to Jess tonight on the porch, startling her father; she'd been snapping at Kelly. Probably the only reason she'd been decent to her mother was because she needed at least one ally. Where was she headed? How could so much bitterness and antagonism end up any way but badly?

Her voice was low and indistinct: "I'm sorry."

Had he heard right? Frowning, questioning his own ears, Jess glanced away from the road. "Pardon?"

"I said, I'm sorry. I hate this sort of thing. I can't go on this way."

She looked small, forlorn, frightened. Something tugged at Jess's heartstrings. "You've been worried. I understand, Casey."

"I've been behaving like a shrew."

"Don't be so hard on yourself. By the same token, honey, don't be so hard on me. Don't you believe that I wouldn't do anything to hurt Bobby?" Jess's expression brightened. "Casey, he's really something. Do you know what he did tonight? He shook my hand like a little man."

Heaving a sigh, Casey opened her eyes and raised her head from the seat back. "I know. I saw you arrive."

"You were watching?"

"From my bedroom window." Casey realized what the real problem had been tonight. She'd turned inside out with jealously over Bobby warming up to Jess. My God, was she really so petty? she wondered. She didn't much like the person she was becoming.

"All right if we drive down to the river again?" Jess asked.

"I really don't know where else to go, Casey. Unless you wouldn't mind going to my place."

"Your place? No, the river's fine."

Jess gave a slight laugh. "I wouldn't suggest the river *or* my place if we were ready for a public appearance. But I don't think we are, do you?"

"This isn't a regular date," Casey agreed quietly. "Just go to the river. We'll talk a bit then go home."

"Right. That's what I was thinking, too."

When they were parked, Casey turned her face to the open window. The sun was low on the horizon, almost down, backlighting the trees and brush that grew along the river's meandering path. It was a pretty spot, full of greens and yellows and browns; and the river was many colors—here gray, there greenish blue, with crests of sparkling, foamed silver wherever the moving water met and splashed against some obstruction to its flow.

The silence reached Casey's personal disquietude and meshed with it to produce a strange feeling of lonely upheaval. Here, in this placid, isolated place, even with Jess within reach, she all of a sudden felt as though she were completely alone in the world. Her sigh contained pathos and a little self-pity. She felt emotionally bruised, and wondered with a faraway vagueness if Jess had really thought her "easy," or had only lashed out because of her own shrewishness.

She had been that, she admitted with a ponderous sadness. She had been foolish, immature and easy. Regardless of Jess's careless what-the-hell attitude then, she could have kept things cool between them. She'd kept things cool with other men— rather, with the boys she'd been dating.

But Jess hadn't been a boy. He'd been a man—a worldly, self-assured, full-of-gusto male—and his handsome face and cocky manner had literally swept her off her feet. Right in this very spot, on a blanket, with the riverbank for a bed and the gurgling river water as music, he had taught her the joys of making love, shown her the strength and beauty of a man's body.

"What are you thinking about?" Jess asked softly.

Casey kept watching the river's slow passage. "Us," she murmured quietly.

"As we are today?"

"No. As we were six years ago." She heard Jess suck in a quick breath.

"Casey, try not to dwell on the past," he urged.

"I wasn't thinking of what came after that week. I was thinking about what happened during your stay."

"Oh."

She turned her eyes to him, and Jess saw how raw and exposed her feelings were. "How old were you?" she asked.

Jess swallowed. "Casey..."

"How old, Jess?"

He looked down. "I'm thirty-two now."

"You were twenty-six, then. You were very smooth, Jess, very...ardent."

He shook his head. "I was a jerk," he said gruffly.

"No. You weren't a jerk. You were the kind of man a young girl dreams about. Not that young girls should be dreaming about men like you, but then, teenage girls are notoriously romantic." Casey sighed again. "At least, I was."

"You were sweet—"

"I was a fool!" she snapped. Then, sorry she'd become angry again, she tried to release the tension from her face.

Jess eyed her thoughtfully. "You can't forgive yourself, can you? How can I hope you'll ever forgive me when you can't even forgive yourself? Casey, we made a mistake. Mine was worse because I was old enough to know better. But it was a mistake with a wonderful result: Bobby. Would you turn back time if you could and undo that week?"

Startled, Casey looked into Jess's expressive blue eyes. "I love him more than anything in the world," she whispered raggedly.

"If you didn't, you'd be a heck of a lot less than you are." Despite promises to keep his hands to himself, Jess slid across the seat. And when he put his arms around Casey and brought her head to his chest, she let him, just sighing softly. The loneliness she'd been enduring melted away in Jess's arms.

She didn't want it to leave her because of Jess, but it did. His shirt was soft and heated by his body; his arms around her were a fortress of security.

He pressed his lips to her hair. "Stop punishing yourself, honey," he said softly. "I'm sorry I made that crack about you being easy. You were no easier than I was. I was as bowled over as you were. You were young and sweet and beautiful." Jess felt his body stirring and his blood heating from holding her. "You're still young and sweet and beautiful," he murmured.

He tipped her chin up and studied her face, and Casey stared back. There was a new tension in their locked gazes, and she knew where this was going, but she couldn't pull away. She wet her lips, and saw Jess watching. "I...can't get involved with you again," she said huskily.

"I want to kiss you."

"No." But she didn't move away, and Jess's face slowly descended. His mouth brushed hers. "Jess," she whispered in a weak stab at protesting. His lips grazed hers again. "Please," she begged, agonizing over the curling heat he was causing in her body.

His thumb caressed her cheek while his mouth teased hers with butterfly kisses. His eyes closed and opened, closed and opened again, giving her glimpses of the sensual nature of his feelings. His breath was minty, he was wearing that spicy scent again, and she absorbed the essence of Jess with every breath. Her head whirled with objections and old resolutions, and yet she sat still and let him go on teasing her.

But his nearness was bringing the past close enough to touch, too, and six-year-old sensations were beginning to cloud the present—not the hatred and vindictiveness she'd undergone after Jess left, Casey realized. What she was reliving were the feelings she had experienced in Jess Lonnigan's arms at seventeen. They shook her to the depths of her soul.

Jess was having no such crippling thoughts, however. His mouth was actively seeking hers. Casey turned her face, eluding his lips. "No, Jess," she pleaded, sounding strained.

"Honey..."

She made no reply. But when he continued to hold her, and
he couldn't bear his insistent, quizzical look any longer, Casey reached for the door handle. Slipping from his arms, she
got out of the truck. It was almost dark now, and the colors
he had noted earlier had grown muted, flavored with the
heavy grayness of late-evening light. Casey walked over to the
river, aware of Jess behind her.

Her eyes were sad and questioning as she watched the water. "Why do you affect me like that?" she asked in such a
quiet, unhappy voice that Jess frowned. "I don't want to want
you," she whispered.

Jess took a step closer. "What can I say, honey?" he returned softly. "There's something between us, want it or not."

"I feel like I'm not in control of my own life anymore. One
day, from out of the blue, here you are. You've changed everything, Jess. Why did you decide to come back here?" Casey turned with the question.

Digging his hands into his pockets, Jess faced the river. "I
don't know. There are a dozen other places I could have gone.
I love Wyoming, and I remembered Blythe as a nice little
town. But other than that, I just don't have a good answer,
Casey. Maybe it was fate," he added musingly.

She gave him a sidelong glance. "Do you believe in fate?"

"I never gave it much thought before. I'm beginning to
wonder, now. Something made this particular spot on the map
stand out." He turned to her and put his hands on her shoulders. "Anyway, I'm here. I thought of looking you up, Casey,
but not to make trouble for you."

She met his gaze evenly. "No, you thought we could pick
up where we left off six years ago, didn't you?"

He thought of lying, for her sake, then trashed the notion.
Whatever their relationship evolved into, it wasn't going to be
based on lies. "Yes. That's exactly what I thought," he admitted with a trace of bravado.

Her eyes flickered. "Do you remember telling me you loved
me?"

An invisible fist struck Jess in the gut. "No. Did I say
that?"

An almost imperceptible nod of her head made Jess wince
again. "And you believed me," he said with a profound sadness. His hands moved down to her upper arms. "Did you
love me, Casey? Is that why you hated me so much after I
left?"

At the feeling in his voice, Casey's knees got weak. She
heard wonder, hope, curiosity in his question. And she remembered him ridiculing love, calling it a "foolish fantasy." Had
he never been in love? She caught a sense of Jess's former
life-style—towns blurring, women blurring, nothing ever real
or solid to hang on to. *A different bed every few nights.* How
many women had he shared those beds with?

She'd been only one of many. And he had been and still
was the only man she had ever made love with. The inequity
seemed overwhelming, stunning. And yet, for the first time
she was beginning to understand the man she had met six years
ago. No family, the heady roar of the rodeo arena, a winner's
adulation, rushing to the next town, the next fair, the next
contest. My Lord, how would any man remember one seventeen-year-old girl in that confusing montage of everchanging
scenes?

But could she confess that she'd imagined herself truly in
love with him? No. A confession of that nature at this late
date would accomplish nothing. Not when she was only one
of the blurs in Jess's past. "I think my feelings at that time
are better described as a rather serious crush," she finally replied, and saw a tiny flame die in Jess's eyes. He'd been hoping for more, Casey realized, probably because of his marriage
proposal. Well, she might understand Jess a little better now
but she hadn't reached the point of saying yes to a loveless
marriage.

She remained silent, leaving Jess to unanswered speculation.
His hands flexed on her arms, and his gaze was relentless.
Their conversation had been personal enough to have raised
some provocative points. "Did you get married only to give
Bobby a name, or did you care for the guy?" he asked.

Jess didn't know! Casey had actually forgotten that he
didn't know about the farce of her pretended marriage. For a

moment she battled with an urge to blurt it out, then common sense prevailed and she only replied, "I'd rather not talk about that, Jess."

"Casey, you talked about love last night. Did you love your husband?" he persisted.

"What difference does that make now?" she hedged.

His gaze roamed her face, looking beyond her features, probing her evasiveness. "Maybe none. I don't know. It suddenly seems important."

She was getting uncomfortable beneath his scrutiny. And he was too close again. She could feel him penetrating her senses; she was afraid of his power. Lifting her hands to his wrists, she tried to pull them away from her arms. "Don't push me, Jess," she warned unsteadily. "You said you wouldn't touch me and you keep doing it."

"Don't you question the feelings between us?"

The sky was dark now except for the faint, pearly reflection on the western horizon. They were shadowy figures on the bank of the river, visible to each other by shape and form, becoming less distinct, communicating through a contact Casey was finding increasingly disturbing. They had made love here, more than once, more than twice. Even in the dark Casey could pick out the spot where Jess had laid the blanket. Why did they keep coming back here? Even Jess's house would be more impersonal than this place.

Casey shivered, chilly from the night air, chillier still from the emotional drubbing she'd taken lately. "I'm going back to the truck," she announced. It was more than a hint, but Jess didn't take it. His fingers clasped and caressed simultaneously, warming her bare arms with the heat of his hands.

She knew what was in his mind; she knew what he was going to do. Later, when she remembered this moment, she asked herself why she hadn't broken away and run. But she didn't break and run. She let him pull her forward, and when his mouth claimed hers, she only moaned over her lack of control and kissed him back. On tiptoe, with her breasts squashed into his chest and his arms inching her closer, she opened her mouth and kissed him back.

It was a complex kiss from the outset, involving old memories and new desires. The firmness of his mouth was like an old friend, welcome, familiar. After six years it was *familiar* Jess's way of holding her, one strong arm around her, positioned low on her back, lifting her up and to him was familiar too, although Casey knew it wasn't something she'd spent time thinking about. His right hand twined into her hair, amassing a handful of curls, then releasing it to find another. He touched her cheek, her throat, with gentle but inquisitive fingertips, and he explored the heated moistness of her mouth with his tongue.

To Jess she was soft and warm and female. Her lips moved beneath his with emotion far surpassing what he'd hoped for. His body had responded quickly, and his mind went back in time in an attempt to associate the achingly desirable woman he was holding with the girl he'd seduced. He wasn't quite able to make the connection, but he only dwelled on the puzzle for a few heartbeats.

Casey was no longer chilly. Her temperature was soaring. She felt flushed, giddy. Breathing hard, Jess raised his head. She saw the reflected light of the rising moon in his eyes, in the wetness of his mouth. She couldn't deny what kind of kiss it had been; her breath, too, was coming in short spurts.

"Don't...don't do this because you want Bobby," she rasped hoarsely.

"I want you both, Bobby *and* you." He meant it. He could imagine nothing better than his own family, his own son, his own beautiful, sexy wife. And he had no doubt that Casey was a sexy woman. She'd been sexy six years ago—he at least remembered that very well—and if anything, she was even more so now. What more could a man ask for? Oh, yes, he'd meant his proposal of marriage with heart and soul.

Casey knew how aroused he'd become. The proof burned into her abdomen and ignited more intimate memories—Jess naked on the blanket, without modesty, without the slightest embarrassment. He had a tiny little scar just over his left nipple, and another, high on his right thigh. She'd touched the scars, even kissed them. She'd done so much with this man...so much...all in the space of one week...all in the name of a love, a passion she hadn't been able to control.

She still couldn't. With Jess she was Silly Putty, with *silly* being the key word.

Casey placed her palms on his chest and pushed herself away. "I need time, Jess," she said as steadily as she could manage.

He held his hands up in a pleading gesture. His voice was ragged, gravelly. "How much time?"

"I don't know." She started back to the truck, but Jess caught her arm.

"Casey, we made a lot of headway tonight."

She stole a shaky breath. "Yes, but in what direction? What did we prove, other than how physical you are and how weak I am?"

Physical? Wasn't that what it was all about? Frowning, Jess followed on Casey's heels. He reached around her to open her door. "Maybe I'm dense, but what's wrong with physical?"

She paused to look at him. "Nothing, unless that's all there is."

"You're talking about love again."

"Yes, that's exactly what I'm talking about."

"Do you want me to tell you that I'm in love with you?"

Casey drew a shuddering breath. "My Lord, no. That's the last thing I want. I pray that no man ever says those words to me again unless he means them." She climbed up into the cab of the pickup. Jess stood by, one hand on the door.

"I think I'm finally getting the picture," he muttered, and gave the door a push to close it. When he got in the driver's side of the truck, he noticed that Casey had wrapped her sweater around her shoulders. "Would you like me to start the motor and run the heater?"

"I think we should just go," she demurred.

"In a few minutes. I want to explore something first. You're not going to marry me because we're not storybook in love, right? It just dawned on me when you made that remark about—"

"Jess." She sighed. "In the first place, getting married was and is entirely your idea. I never encouraged you in that direction."

"You said you'd think about it."

"It's only been a day," she reminded sharply.

Jess's eyes narrowed. "Yes. But I have a strong feeling your mind's already made up."

"Why is that such a surprise?" Casey questioned. "I told you last night how I feel about marriage."

His voice dropped several notches, becoming very serious. "Casey, I don't want just an affair with the mother of my son."

"Good Lord!" She sputtered out a stunned sound, something between a laugh and a scoff. "Where did you ever get *that* idea?"

Jess stirred uneasily. "Well, something's going to happen between us. There's too much chemistry to ignore it indefinitely."

Casey hid her eyes behind a weary palm in a this-is-too-much gesture. She had only herself to blame, she knew. Jess obviously listened more to actions than to words, and kissing him back and turning to mush in his arms apparently had made a much deeper impression on him than all her stabs at candor.

Dozens of interactions rushed through her brain, hers with Jess, Jess's with Bobby, her and Lucille's, Lucille and Ben's, even Ben and Jess's. The whole damned thing was getting mixed, co-mixed and intermixed, a tangle that threatened only deeper entanglement in the frightening future.

That she herself was at the heart of it, maybe even the cause of it with her ridiculous on-again, off-again feelings for Jess, only made Casey feel worse. An affair: that's what they'd had six years ago, a tasteless, thoughtless, *stupid* affair. And if she'd been old enough and experienced enough to sort it out, she would have recognized it for what it was. Instead, at seventeen, in her silly romanticism, she'd seen her feelings and Jess's lust as love.

At least now, even if nothing else positive ever came from Jess's return, she understood what had really happened during his first visit to Blythe. There hadn't been a speck of love between them—not *real* love. The man sitting beside her was till a stranger, albeit one who seemed in control of her baser urges. He was right about the chemistry between them, but that was all he was right about!

Dropping her hand, Casey prepared herself for a speech. She took a deep breath and found Jess in the dark with a relatively calm eye. "Your ultimate goal is Bobby, Jess. I have no problem with admitting I was terrified over the two of you even meeting. As little as we've talked, however, I feel that I understand you better now. Myself, too, I might add. I'm not afraid of what you might do about Bobby, at least. I think you have a lot of feeling for him already. But..."

"Like you said, he's easy to love," Jess put in.

"Yes, he is. That's not the point I'm trying to make, though. What's bothering me is you thinking in terms of 'us.' I don't want you counting on a future for the three of us. And I'm not saying that in anger, or with any thought of revenge, or with anything else the least bit vindictive. You and I are worlds apart. I can see now that even if you had stayed in Blythe six years ago it wouldn't have worked for us."

"How can you say that?" Jess intruded gruffly, and Casey heard a harsh note in his voice. "What do you mean, we're worlds apart?"

"Jess, you think the only relationship between a man and a woman is physical," Casey said with an odd gentleness. She had no desire to hurt Jess anymore, she realized. None at all. "I honestly believe that you don't have a romantic bone in your body. I'm not denigrating you for it, but I am saying it's not for me. I meant it when I told you I would never marry for any reason but love."

"Not even for Bobby, apparently," Jess replied sharply.

"Not even for Bobby," she echoed in choked agreement.

Jess took a breath that sounded painfully resigned. "Well, I guess you put me in my place, didn't you? In other words, Tess Lonnigan, forget everything except an occasional visit with your son."

"That's a rather cruel way to put it, but..."

"But it's all there is, right?" Now there was some of the

old cockiness in Jess's voice. "Tell me something, honey
How do you know so much about this love you keep talking
about? Have you experienced it? How many times? Was it far
far above the nasty old physical side of your nature? Who was
the guy, your ex-husband? Did you two have such a lofty
relationship, you never made love? And if it was so great, how
in hell come you're not still married?"

Stunned, Casey heard the cockiness in Jess's voice turn to
bitterness. The deluge of questions, coming one on top of the
other left no room to jump in with any kind of answer, and
barely gave her time to think. But they did accomplish one
thing: they made her realize she was far from an authority on
the subject of love.

But one didn't have to experience the emotion firsthand to
know its strength and power. She'd grown up in a home with
parents whose mutual love was a strong and abiding one. Her
brothers both had happy marriages, Dee-Dee, too. No, she
would never settle for less.

"Cynicism isn't going to change my mind," she declared.

"Yeah, and you're not going to answer my questions, ei
ther, are you? Just answer one for me, honey. Tell me how a
woman with your sex drive keeps it under control while she's
waiting for that great love to come along."

"My—! You're wrong about me, Jess. You're judging me
again by the way I misbehaved six years ago," she stammered

"I'm judging you on right now, sweetheart, on how you
come alive in my arms, how your body curls into mine, how
your mouth feels under mine. What do you want me to do
Pretend I didn't notice? Well, I did notice, and I know when
the woman I'm holding wants exactly what I do."

Gone was her brief spurt of aplomb. Her voice was trem
bling again. "I admitted it, didn't I? Didn't I say only a shor
time ago that I didn't *want* to want you?"

"And it galls the hell out of you that you do, anyway. Well
let me tell you something, Casey. You might consider whe
you were at seventeen a silly, romantic fool. But you were
one helluva lot more woman than you are now! At least then
you weren't afraid to *live!*"

Angrily, with jerky, erratic motions, Jess started the truck and slammed it into gear. He drove away from the river with a rock-hard profile and a straight-ahead stare that, after one brief glance and a shiver, Casey refused to look at again. She had no idea just what Jess might do in a temper, and it was more than obvious he was boiling mad.

Well, she wasn't in the best of moods, either. He'd said some rotten things to her tonight, like that last crack. Afraid to live? Just because she didn't cater to his every whim? And what about that other insult, the one about *him* not wanting an affair with the mother of his child? Now, there was a laugh!

They drove up to the ranch in the same cold silence they'd left it with. Jess didn't get out and he didn't turn the engine off. "Well, good night," Casey said after a moment, and reached for the door handle.

"I'll be by to see Bobby in a few days," Jess answered coldly.

"All right." Casey opened the door and slid to the ground. The minute the door was closed again, the pickup started moving, and when it was turned around it sped away, kicking up dirt.

Casey watched it go for a minute, then moved toward the house. It had been a difficult evening, she admitted wearily, and it had accomplished little beyond upsetting them both.

She knew she would think twice before going out with Jess again. They saw things too differently to ever do anything but fight, which she'd had quite enough of. He could see Bobby—simply because she suspected that Jess would make everyone miserable if she tried to stop him.

And she'd try to go on with her life as it had been before his return. She had her business to keep up and make future plans for, she had friends and family to spend time with, and if she wanted more, it wouldn't be hard to find a male friend. Wes Upton, for one. All she'd have to do was hint mildly, and Wes would jump at the chance to take her out.

She'd put Jess out of her thoughts once, and she could do it again. She *would* do it again.

Six

"Why, Lily! How nice. Come in." Lucille held the door for Lily Hastings and eyed the sizable box she carried. Lily owned and operated Blythe's one florist shop, and it was obvious she had driven out to the ranch to deliver some flowers.

"Hello, Lucille. Is Casey here? This is for her."

"She's out back with Bobby. Come in and have a cup of tea. I'll call her."

The two women went to the kitchen. Lily sat down at the kitchen table while Lucille called out the back door. "Casey? Could you come in for a minute, honey?"

"Sure, Mom." Casey had been playing catch with her son and she gave the soft rubber ball one last toss. "Good catch!" She laughed. "I'll go see what Grandma wants, Bobby."

"Will you come back and play some more, Mom?"

"If I can, honey." Casey hurried into the house. "Hello, Lily," she exclaimed, surprised to see the small, pudgy woman in the kitchen. Casey's gaze fell on the florist's box on the table.

"It's for you," Lily announced, and gave the box a little push forward.

"For me?" Puzzled, Casey looked to her mother. "Who would be sending me flowers?"

Lily smiled knowingly, but she only said, "Open them, Casey. There's a card inside."

A sudden premonition hit Casey, but it was one she didn't quite trust. Surely Jess would never think of sending flowers to a woman.

She pulled the ribbon off the box and lifted the lid. Long-stemmed white roses greeted her startled eyes, and she breathed, "White roses. Oh, they're gorgeous!" Removing one from the box, she sniffed it and smiled.

"Read the card," Lily urged.

Casey picked up a small envelope. "It's sealed," she murmured.

"He wrote and sealed it himself," Lily announced with pride in her own integrity. "I never even got a look at it, but I know who it's from," she teased.

Breaking the seal on the envelope, Casey extracted the card. She quickly scanned the masculine handwriting.

Casey,
This romance thing is new to me, but I hope you'll consider this a start.

Jess

It had been three days since that second night by the river, and Casey had just about decided Jess had given up on her. In one way, she was relieved; in another, strangely empty. Her ambivalence was showing again, Casey knew, but Jess had played too big a role in her past for her to just eliminate him now without some repercussions.

"They're from Jess," she told her mother in a strangely subdued voice.

"They're beautiful," Lucille remarked softly, then added briskly, "I'll get a vase."

Lily was chuckling. "Had to order these special, Casey. There's not much call in Blythe for white roses."

"No, I don't imagine there is," Casey agreed.

"That Jess is sure a handsome fella, Casey."

Casey smiled faintly. Lucille returned with a crystal vase, which Casey recognized as the best in the house. Smiling her thanks to her mother, she placed the rose she was still holding into the vase and reached for another.

When the flowers were arranged, Casey stepped back to admire them. "They must have cost a fortune," she murmured, more to herself than to either Lucille or Lily.

Lucille was pouring tea. "Would you like a cup, Casey?"

"No, thanks, Mom. Where should I put the vase?"

"Flowers that beautiful deserve a place of honor," Lucille declared. "Put them on the piano, honey."

"Good idea." Carefully balancing the lovely vase and roses, Casey smiled at Lily, then left the kitchen. After placing them just so on the piano in the living room, Casey sat down and pulled Jess's card from her pocket to read it again.

Was he going to court her? A funny little smile played on Casey's lips. Apparently, despite the black mood he'd been in when he dropped her off the other night, he'd given some thought to her arguments against a marriage of convenience. Even so, in spite of the vased evidence sitting on the piano, envisioning Jess as a romantic suitor was rather difficult. He was as physical as she'd pronounced him: earthy, rough around the edges, even crude at times. She could easily visualize him hopping in and out of bed with willing women, but romancing them?

Sighing, Casey sat back with her gaze on the almost pearlescent perfection of the roses. She had undergone quite a metamorphosis the past few days, she realized. She could think of Jess without hatred, without a knot in her stomach. Casey knew that understanding his old life-style had caused the change. Before Jess's return to Blythe, whenever he'd come to mind, she had seen him only in the context of their short-lived and heartbreaking relationship. Now she saw him in a broader sense. He'd been a man long before they met, and had lived a different kind of life than she could previously have imagined.

Her world had been confined to Blythe, the ranch and only a few forays beyond. Even after Bobby's birth she had relied on old habits and patterns. It had been more beneficial for her son to stay under Ben and Lucille Oliver's generous roof, and she'd willingly taken the easier route. Her small business provided the extras she would have hated asking her parents for, but would provide very slim support for herself and Bobby on their own. Staying on the family ranch had resulted in her living a rather insulated life.

Jess, apparently, had had no such buffers.

They were like night and day, black and white. Yet, because of an explosive passion between them six years ago, they had produced a child. There was an odd mystique about it, in retrospect. She might not have been in town that week; she might not have strolled down to the rodeo grounds with her friends that fateful first night. Jess might have bypassed Blythe. They might not ever have met. In which case, there would have been no Bobby.

A shudder of pure agony rocked Casey at the painful conclusion she had reached. No Bobby? Not even in her deepest depressions, once she'd held her son in her arms, had she ever wished he hadn't been born. Jess felt that way, too. *Would you go back in time, if you could, and undo that week?*

No! her inner spirit cried. Nothing could ever make her wish that Bobby wasn't a part of her life. He was the most important part of her life, and her love for him was like a living thing, an emotion that inhabited every cell of her body.

So, what about Jess's role in this? Would he do anything—even "romance" her—for the opportunity to openly claim his son?

It had surprised Casey that Jess hadn't come around for three days after he'd said he would—to see Bobby, of course—but the roses were now giving her some insight into Jess's absence. He must have been thinking, sorting things out. His apparent decision to "court" her made her feel strange, almost embarrassed, as though she had pushed him into something completely foreign to his personality. He'd obviously interpreted her stand against a loveless marriage as a bid for him to perform differently, when she hadn't meant that at all. It hadn't even occurred to her that Jess might attempt to change himself to fit what he'd labeled her "foolish fantasy."

He was obviously planning an all-out assault on her emotional defenses. What she *had* to do was keep her perspective. The roses were beautiful, but she didn't want to be courted simply to fulfill Jess's goal. She hadn't thought him devious, but now she was beginning to wonder. After all, as she'd told him, they didn't really know each other.

Female voices in the hallway broke up Casey's thoughts, and she got to her feet to thank Lily for the delivery. After goodbyes, Lucille closed the door, then gave her daughter a tentative smile. "Jess gave her a standing order, Casey. White roses each week for a month."

Getting another glimpse of Jess's determination created a frown on Casey's smooth forehead. Silently she pulled the card from her pocket and held it out. "Read it, Mom."

Lucille read the message quickly, then handed the card back and walked into the living room. Casey followed and stood by while her mother examined the bouquet again. "What do you think?" Casey asked uneasily.

Lucille smiled. "I think he intends to win your affection," she said calmly.

"It could be just a ploy to get Bobby," Casey warned, and met her mother's clear gaze with a troubled expression.

"One can fake feelings only so much, Casey. You'll know."

"Will I?" Casey replied uncertainly. She'd already been having a problem with the way Jess affected her physically. If he managed to do the same thing with her emotions, would she know anything?

Lucille patted her hand. "You'll know," she repeated— much too mysteriously, her daughter thought—and with another soft smile, left Casey alone with the roses.

Ben Oliver had confirmed the last weekend of July for the barn raising. In the meantime, Jess was to get the site prepared, and he'd been working on leveling the ground and constructing forms for the cement floor. As he wanted water in the barn, he also had to plan for water pipes and drains, a task that would have been a much bigger problem for an inexperienced builder without the aid and advice of another neighbor. Kelvin LeRoy understood plumbing and was generous with both his time and expertise.

Constantly amazed at the warmth and friendliness of his reception in the area, Jess had been working from sunup until dark every day to make sure everything would be ready for the actual raising of the barn. He had enjoyed the physical labor, and had found it therapeutic to the mental gyrations he'd been involved in since he'd last seen Casey. He'd been so deep-down stirred up and angry with her the other evening, he'd put in one helluva restless night and got up the following morning still angry.

Later, with a hot sun burning his bare back and shoulders while he shoveled and moved dirt from the building site, he'd thought it all out.

"So you think you want love," he'd muttered, and ferociously dumped a shovelful of dirt into the wheelbarrow. Then, another, and another. The physical exertion had felt good, had seemed to clear his head.

Finally, after dumping numerous overflowing wheelbarrow loads a safe distance from the construction area, Jess had mopped his sweaty forehead and admitted there wasn't any way on God's green earth that he was going to succeed in pushing Casey into marrying him, given her obstinate attitude on the matter.

It amazed him that she didn't see the issue as he did. What better reason could two people have for marriage than a great little kid like Bobby? It was so cut-and-dried for Jess. He had settled down with great plans for his horse ranch, and even if it took several years to really get it going, he had a nice sum in the bank—more than enough to support a family until the ranch began showing a profit. He couldn't figure out that obsession Casey had with finding a "great love"—not when she had the father of her son just begging for her hand.

By midafternoon he'd decided what he had to do: if Casey would only marry for love, love was what she'd get. He could be as romantic as the next guy, couldn't he?

Frowning, Jess had leaned on the shovel and thought about it. How did a guy in love act? Activities were limited around Blythe, but there were a few decent restaurants. At least the food was good. As for atmosphere, well, vinyl booths and neon lighting weren't very romantic in anyone's book. Scratch dinner out, Jess thought wryly.

Okay, what else was there? Flowers? Yes, there was a small florist shop on Main Street. Candy? Perfume? Jess had smiled smugly, positive he was getting the hang of it.

But, where would he take her? An occasional movie was fun—if the theater wasn't full of noisy kids, that is. What about a picnic? Or, yes, what about taking some horseback rides together? Riding off by themselves could present some interesting possibilities. They could go swimming, too, over at that nice little lake he recalled seeing about twenty miles to the south.

Besides, maybe it wasn't where they went that was as important as how he acted when they were together. He'd avoid arguments if he had to tape his mouth shut. He'd be polite and try not to cuss; and above all, he'd try not to pressure her.

That same afternoon he'd driven into Blythe to the florist shop, found out that the stock on hand was nice but ordinary, and made arrangements with the owner to order something special. After looking through a catalog, he'd chosen white roses, plunked down an outrageous sum of money and left instructions to make a delivery to the Oliver ranch each week for a month. He'd written a card giving Casey fair warning of his intentions, then waited the two days Mrs. Hastings said it would take for the flowers to be shipped in and delivered.

Now, today, he knew she would have received the flowers. And he had a plan in mind for the evening. At three o'clock he laid down his tools and went into the house to the telephone. Lucille Oliver answered his call, but Casey came on

the line soon after. He heard her voice, that sexy little huski-
ness in it, and felt a tightening in his gut. Whether Casey liked
it or not, she affected the hell out of him. "Hello, Jess."

"Hello, Casey. How've you been?"

"Fine. You?"

"I've been pretty busy." He proceeded to tell her what he'd
been so busy with—the preparation of the barn site. "Anyway," he concluded, "everything will be ready when your
dad and his friends show up."

"That's good. By the way, thank you for the flowers.
They're very beautiful."

"I'm glad you like them. Are you free tonight?"

"Tonight? Why, Jess?"

"I'd like to see you."

"I've been expecting you to drop in to see Bobby."

Jess gave a dry little laugh. "I needed a little time to cool
off. I was pretty hot under the collar the other night."

"Jess, I don't want to spend another evening fighting with
you."

"I couldn't agree more. No more fighting, Casey. I promise."

"Well…"

"What I'd like to do is show you my place. I could pick
you up around five and bring you over here. I've got a couple
of nice steaks to barbecue. No funny stuff, Casey. Just dinner
and a quiet evening together." He heard a sigh.

"Going to your house isn't wise, Jess."

"Casey, we're both adults. I'd suggest dinner in one of
Blythe's cafés, but they're always packed. What I'd really like
is an opportunity to talk, and we could do that a whole lot
easier here than in a restaurant."

"I see." Casey was walking around with the phone to her
ear, twisting the cord through her fingers. Since the flower
delivery a few hours ago, she'd done almost nothing but study
the situation. She had reached several conclusions. One, there
was no keeping Jess out of his son's life, not unless she took
Bobby and severed all connections with her home and family.
Just moving away without a total break would accomplish

nothing; Jess would follow her if he knew where she'd gone. Besides, running away would hurt Bobby. He was far too young to accept leaving his beloved grandparents, aunts, uncles and cousins without trauma. Even leaving the new puppies, who were beginning to open their eyes, wouldn't be understood by the little boy. He'd known only one home—the ranch—and uprooting him to the point of complete separation was too cruel to consider seriously.

Two, as a result of her first conclusion, Casey had realized she may as well cooperate with Jess on the matter of their son. She now believed that he wouldn't cause trouble, and she also believed he really thought marriage was the most sensible answer for the three of them. That was the point where she got bogged down each time she thought about it. She felt rather silly about inadvertently having pushed Jess into courting her, because he obviously thought he could win her affections with flowers and a more romantic approach.

People didn't fall in love that way, Casey strongly believed. They didn't set out to fall in love. It was something that happened or didn't happen, on its own. That Jess apparently felt differently about it only proved how little he knew, or had experienced, with the emotion. Not that she was any kind of authority on the subject, but at least she'd been exposed to solid, steady couples who *were* in love with each other.

Three, Casey recognized a strange void in herself. With the exhausting hatred she'd harbored for the Jess Lonnigan she'd met and made love with six years ago gone, there seemed to be a hole in her emotional makeup. She realized that she now had room for other relationships. For the first time in her adult life, she could see herself going out more, making more male friends, expanding her social activities. After Bobby's birth she had dropped out and dedicated herself almost entirely to her son. Now she felt freer, unburdened; and if Jess's return had caused that—despite the anger and fear she'd initially suffered over it—then perhaps she owed him the courtesy of friendship at least.

Still, going to his house for an intimate dinner for two was encouraging his romantic aspirations, wasn't it? Unless—

"How about me bringing Bobby along?" she suggested.

"Bobby? You'd do that?" Jess instantly got so excited he completely forgot about the advantage he might gain while wining and dining Casey alone. "Oh, honey, that would be great, just great! What does he like to eat? Does he like steak?"

Casey laughed. "He'd prefer a hamburger, I'm sure."

"What else? I could go to Blythe and get—"

"Jess, a hamburger is plenty. He's not a big eater. Oh, if you really want to impress him, he's a nut about chocolate pudding."

"Chocolate pudding. Well, I can probably figure out how to fix it, huh?"

Casey laughed again. "It's easy. The directions are right on the box. What time should we come over?"

"I could pick you up."

"No, that's not necessary, I'll drive us over."

"What time does he usually eat dinner?"

"Around five-thirty."

"Then that's when we'll eat. Casey, this is great of you. I'd like to ask why, but I'm afraid of starting another argument." Was it the flowers? Had they worked that fast? Jess wondered, puzzled about this romance thing. Maybe there *was* something to it.

"We'll be there around five," Casey said, and put the phone down with an astute smile. The enthusiasm in Jess's voice over having dinner with his son far outweighed what she'd heard when he'd posed the invitation just to her. She was very, very right about Jess courting her only to get closer to Bobby. Which she couldn't really fault, Casey admitted thoughtfully. But she would have to make Jess understand that no amount of "courting" was going to change her mind about marrying him.

Dinner went well—to a point. Jess and Bobby got along famously, with Jess definitely pleasing the child with bowls of chocolate-pudding dessert. But Casey felt Jess's blue, blue eyes—so like their son's—on her as much as on Bobby.

Of course, she had taken special care getting ready for the evening. And she had even noticed, while putting on her makeup, that she seemed to have lost the harried look she had come to expect every time she looked in a mirror. Casey actually felt as if she'd been running a long, long mile and somehow had made it past a hurdle that had once kept eluding her. It was a strange feeling to sit at Jess's table and realize she was free of hatred and bitterness. She wondered if that was what Jess was seeing, or if he was merely responding to having a woman in his house.

Actually, Jess was doing both—and indulging in a bit of fantasy at the same time, too. Casey was wearing a gauzy pink dress, and she looked softer, more feminine, than he'd ever seen her appear before. It wasn't at all difficult to understand why he'd been so taken with her six years ago, not when he saw her like this.

She was wonderful with Bobby, he noted, loving but mindful of manners. Bobby ate like a little gentleman, and Jess was so proud to have him at the table he felt like bursting. Having Casey there involved some explosive feelings, too, although they were very adult, very sensual, explosive feelings. The fantasy in Jess's mind incorporated Casey and Bobby living there, with dinner together every night, a pleasant few hours together before bedtime, then bedtime.

Bedtime. They would tuck Bobby in, both he and Casey, kiss the little guy good-night, then go to their own bedroom. He would peel that pretty pink dress away...kiss that pulsebeat he could see at the base of her throat above the rounded neckline of the dress...and wear both of them out making love until the wee hours. Yeah, there was no doubt he still found Casey Oliver maddeningly attractive even if she maintained a cool, hands-off expression on her beautiful face.

When everyone had finished eating, Casey got up to clear the table and felt Jess's restraining hand on her arm. His voice was low and persuasive. "Leave them for now. Let's take Bobby for a walk while it's still light out."

For a moment Casey looked deep into Jess's eyes, and she realized how judicious her decision to bring Bobby along had been. Without their small son present, Jess would make a move, and with her heart skittering just from recognizing his mood and recalling how easily he could get to her, Casey knew that coming over here alone could very well have ended up in a way she was dead set against.

But Bobby *was* here, and Jess could give her all those steamy looks he wanted to. Nothing could come of them. Casey nodded her approval. "All right. Want to take a walk, Bobby?"

"Have you got any puppies, Jess?" the little boy questioned hopefully.

"Afraid not, pardner. Maybe I will have by your next visit, though. What's a ranch without puppies, right?"

Outside, Bobby ran ahead while Jess and Casey walked along at a slower pace. The sun was low but still warming the earth, and the evening quiet was lovely. As Casey looked around, she decided she liked Jess's place. The house was roomy and comfortable, there were six or seven big, old trees scattered around the backyard, and ahead of them, beyond the yard, she could see where Jess planned to build the barn and stable. "Your place is nice," she told him.

Jess gave her a wistful smile. "What's nice is this, Casey: the three of us together."

"It's been a pleasant evening," she agreed quietly. "Bobby seems to like you."

"And you?" He stopped walking, and Casey took another step, then turned to face him.

"I think we like each other well enough," she allowed.

Something flickered to Jess's eyes. "You don't hate me anymore, do you?"

"No, I don't. I think there's every chance of us becoming friends."

He shook his head. "That's not enough, Casey." He looked off at Bobby, who had climbed up on the corral fence to pat one of the horses inside the enclosure. "Even if Bobby wasn't in the picture, I'd want more than your friendship."

Casey's eyes narrowed. "I know what you'd want, Jess."

His gaze returned to her face and seemed to be assessing each feature. Casey looked away, but she still felt the impact of Jess's slow study. "Is that so terrible?" he asked softly. "Honey, I vowed I wouldn't put any pressure on you, but you're so damned beautiful. Maybe I'm too human, or, like you said, too physical. But when I look at you, I want you. I can't help it, Casey."

She cleared her throat with sudden nervousness. "I had hoped this wouldn't happen with Bobby here. Maybe it would be best if we called the evening to an end."

Sighing, Jess tore his eyes away from her. "I'm sorry. Let's go down to the corral so I can tell Bobby about the horses."

Casey stood by while Jess took Bobby into the corral and introduced him to his horses. "Can I ride 'em, Jess?" the little boy asked eagerly.

"Not tonight, pardner. But if you get your mom to bring you back during the day, you sure can."

"He has a pony at home," Casey called over the corral fence.

"But it's still fun to ride other horses, isn't it, pardner?" Jess returned.

"You bet!" Bobby agreed enthusiastically. "Mom, can we come back tomorrow?"

Casey sent Jess a silent warning. "Not tomorrow, honey. Maybe some other day, all right?"

Jess caught the message. "Well, maybe we *could* take a little ride tonight," he said at the disappointment in Bobby's big eyes. With that, Jess swung up onto the bare back of one of the horses. Then he put an arm down to Bobby. "Grab hold, pardner. I'll swing you up."

Casey watched with an odd constriction in her chest. The sight of her son and his father on the same horse was doing some funny things to her. They were so alike, Jess and Bobby—one big and handsome, the other small and handsome; the same black hair, the same blue eyes. Jess directed the mare with his knees and a hold on its mane, and horse and riders slowly circled the corral.

Bobby chattered and Jess replied, and Casey listened to the blend of their voices. With the sinking sun the air was growing chilly, and she hugged herself and watched the man and boy, noting after a while that her legs were shaking. She was getting too emotional over the camaraderie within the corral, she realized, trembling with more than just the late-evening air. Bobby was in seventh heaven with a man's total attention. He adored his uncles and grandfather, but Buck, Brady and Dee-Dee's husband, Ray, had their own children. As for Ben Oliver, he was a wonderful grandparent, but he was older and, although he was attentive to Bobby, his mind was often on the ranch or the daily news.

The heart of the matter was, no one loved or paid attention to a child as thoroughly or as selflessly as a parent. It was perfectly obvious that Jess was enjoying the ride every bit as much as Bobby was, and a niggling guilt began to eat at Casey. Was she being selfish because she didn't want to marry her son's father? Who, in all the men she knew and was likely to meet in the area, would ever care about Bobby as much as Jess already did?

Worried again and not very thrilled about it, Casey glanced at the setting sun and called, "I think we'd better go back to the house now. It's getting cool out."

They were laughing like old pals as Jess slid to the ground and lifted Bobby down. The pair ducked between the corral's pole fencing and the three of them started for the house. Casey swallowed a lump in her throat when she saw Bobby slip his hand into Jess's and try to match him step for step.

"Do you like cartoons, pardner?" Jess asked. "I rented a cartoon video today so you could watch it while your mom and I do a little talking."

Casey felt her pulse give a wild leap. "It's almost Bobby's bedtime, Jess. I'll help with the dishes, then we better be on our way."

"Aw, Mom, please?" Bobby cajoled.

"You can watch it until the kitchen is in order, honey. Then we really have to go home."

Back at the house, Jess took Bobby to the living room. Casey looked around the kitchen, then got to work cleaning up. She was still clearing the table when Jess returned.

"How about some coffee?" he suggested.

"None for me, thank you."

"Well, I'd like a cup. I'll put a pot on."

Casey began rinsing dirty dishes at the sink. Jess was moving between one counter and another, and he reached over her head to a cabinet for the coffee filters and murmured "Excuse me" when he brushed against her. When he did it a second time, Casey shot him a dark look.

"This kitchen is large enough for two people, Jess. I don't think it's necessary to keep bumping into me."

"I said I was sorry, didn't I?"

"You're doing it on purpose."

Jess switched on the coffeepot, then looked at the woman who was giving him such fits. She was small and very female in that pink dress, her auburn hair a cloud of curls around her face. She was determined to keep him at arm's length for only one damned reason: her own unwelcome reaction to physical contact with him. She could come up with fifty different excuses, reasons, justifications or explanations why there couldn't be anything personal between them, but they all boiled down to one thing: she was scared silly of him.

She knew, as well as he did, just how close to the surface lurked some very powerful feelings. Maybe they were entirely physical. Jess wasn't sure that he could dispute that. But Casey kept trying to ignore them, and that seemed childish to him.

His decision to give her space and time suddenly mocked him. How could he be anything but what he was? The flowers were fine. That was something he should do in any case. But the rest? Dancing around the obvious? What he wanted to do was to pull her into his arms and kiss her until she admitted the strong, compelling magnetism between them.

Instinct told him to do what felt right, and kissing Casey was suddenly as right as anything he'd ever encountered. He took the one long step that separated them, clasped the back of Casey's neck and tilted her head back. He caught only one glimpse of startled green eyes before his mouth settled firmly on hers.

Seven

Jess had the advantage. Casey's hands were under running
water, a plate in one, a sponge in the other, her back to the
kitchen; Jess had taken her completely by surprise. Her
thoughts exploded in two different directions: Bobby's in the
next room! and, Damn you, you promised you wouldn't do
this!

Nevertheless, Jess *was* doing it. His mouth was firmly in
command of hers while his hand under her hair kept her head
still. Casey angrily refused to close her eyes or participate in
the kiss in any way. Then her own libido began noticing Jess's
scent. No man should smell that way—all spice and sex appeal, she thought wildly. His right arm boldly pressed into her
breasts when he lifted his hand to her face.

Dripping water or not, sexy scent or not, she dropped the
plate and sponge and grabbed at his arm, attempting to twist
out of his hold. Instead of release, she got turned around and
gathered up. His mouth never relaxed an iota either, and she
still couldn't unleash any of the venomous phrases searing her
brain.

His body and arms were unyieldingly taut, pinning her between the edge of the sink and him. Her brain devised savage revenge, to be heaped on this insufferable man when she was free again.

And then, in the midst of fury and the frustration of being the weaker sex, her own senses began to betray her. A choking, tight sensation in her chest, a pounding heart, a burning flame lapping at her insides—every trace of femaleness in her body began to respond.

I can't!

But she was. Desire hit her hard and fast. She wanted to lift her arms to his neck, to forget everything else and kiss him back, to fill her hands with his hair, to touch him and hold him and take him and have him. Six years and six million tears meant nothing in the heat of a kiss so sensual, so arousing. Tears glistened on the eyelashes that, only a few moments ago, she had been so determined to keep from covering her eyes.

Jess felt the change in her—the change he'd known would take place—and he relaxed his tight hold on her enough to explore the pink dress. His hands moved on her back, her waist, the curve of her hips, and she didn't pull away. Her breasts were plumped into his shirt, her lower body united with his. His lips relented to steal a quick, harsh breath, then took hers again. *And she didn't resist!*

One kiss demanded another. Casey's hands slid up his chest and around his neck. She was leaning into him, and her mouth was soft and open. His tongue moved into its velvety heat, and he emitted a quiet groan of intense pleasure. The hunger between them was growing, on the verge of an impossible intimacy, with Bobby in the next room. Yet they clung, their lips meeting again and again.

He was so hard and ready, he ached. But he kept torturing himself with more kisses, unable to refuse what she was offering now—soft lips, an ardent tongue, the pressure of her sweet body against his. In the background, from the living room, Bobby's youthful laughter mingled with typical cartoon honks, squeals and comical voices. While the innocent little boy giggled over the movie, his mother and father gasped and panted and groped in the kitchen.

There was something sensual even in that, Jess admitted behind the more urgent thoughts he was having about the woman he held. Their child, their flesh and blood, was proof of the passion they'd shared six years ago. And in that regard, nothing had changed.

Breathing hard, Jess raised his head and looked at Casey. "Marry me," he rasped. "Marry me and make us a family."

She couldn't speak for a moment. He'd sent flowers, he'd had them over for dinner, but he knew nothing of the real need in her heart, that part of her that longed for a normal relationship, with love as a strong foundation. Jess was impulsive and impatient, thinking he could have his son by kissing her senseless.

Well, not quite senseless. Even with her breasts rising and falling with overheated, rapid breaths, she was resenting Jess's presumption that an assault of wild kisses was going to dull her common sense. They stared into each other's eyes.

"I'm going home," she whispered raggedly.

Jess tasted the bitterness of defeat. "You're a coward, Casey." He dropped his hands and took a backward step.

"Don't start name-calling," she warned. "I don't want another fight, but I won't back down from one, either." She drew a deep, shaky breath. "Let me explain something to you. You've only recently discovered Bobby. I've loved and cared for him for nearly six years. Whatever I do with my life, it will never hurt my son."

Amazement entered Jess's eyes. "And you think marrying his father would hurt him?"

"I haven't finished. I won't do something to hurt Bobby, but neither will I hurt myself again. That's what I did with you six years ago, Jess. I didn't hurt you. I hurt *me*! It isn't selfish of me to want a good marriage. And I do know the difference between a good and bad marriage. Every member of my family has a good marriage, starting with my parents."

"Everyone but you, huh?" Jess drawled sardonically.

"What?" Startled, Casey caught herself. "Yes...yes, that's right. I...I don't want another mistake."

Folding his arms, Jess leaned his hips against the counter. "Tell me about your marriage. What went wrong?"

She dropped her eyes from his ruthless gaze, and as before when he'd asked about her "marriage," took refuge in "I don't want to talk about it." She moved back to the sink. "I'm going to finish the dishes and leave. When I came over here tonight, it was with the hope we might be friends. Apparently that's impossible."

"I told you friendship isn't enough."

She shot him a sharp glance. "It's all I have to give you."

"So take it or leave it? Is that what you're saying?"

Casey concentrated on a dirty plate, cleaning it under the stream of running water. "Don't court me, Jess. Cancel the flower order. Come and see Bobby when you want to, but leave me out of it," she said in a low voice.

He cursed under his breath. "This evening didn't turn out like I planned. You probably won't believe me now, but I didn't intend to make a pass. You affect me, Casey. I wish to hell you didn't but you do."

"No more than any other reasonably attractive woman, I'm sure."

He flushed. "There was a time when that was true. It's not true now." He moved closer again, his voice low. "Have you really forgotten what it was like for us?"

A rush of anger made Casey's voice caustic. "No, I haven't forgotten. But then I haven't slept with every available man across the U.S. either. Don't try to convince me now that that rodeo week six years ago made a lasting impression on you. You only remembered it *after* you returned to Blythe!"

"Aw, hell," Jess muttered, turning his back to her and raking his hair in frustration. She was right. The memories of Blythe and Casey Oliver had been only a vague pleasantness in a mind overloaded with similar memories.

The bottom line was that she wasn't going to be cajoled, persuaded or forced into anything. She was going to stay on

the Oliver ranch—with Bobby—and he could like it or lump
it.

Ignoring Casey's concern with the kitchen—at the moment
he couldn't care less if the damned dishes ever got washed—
Jess walked out and went to the living-room doorway. Leaning
against the frame, he looked at Bobby. The child was sitting
on the floor with his attention riveted on the television set.
Completely oblivious to the tall man watching him from the
door, Bobby laughed and bounced around periodically—a typically active, wonderful, adorable little boy.

Jess's mouth curled with bitterness. Why should his son
grow up without knowing who his real father was? Why
should he—Jess Lonnigan—live five miles away and pretend
to be only a friend?

Jess had never felt so trapped before. His rootless life-style
had given him hundreds of acquaintances, if few real friends;
and casual acquaintances didn't rip a man's heart out and fling
it back in his face. He'd played hard, but he'd worked hard,
too, and he hadn't squandered his earnings, always knowing
that someday he'd reach the point of wanting to settle down.
He could equally thank and curse whatever fate had brought
him back to Blythe. What a man didn't know didn't hurt him.

Jess's eyes closed for a moment, then jerked open. No, by
God, he wasn't giving up!

Whirling about, he returned to the kitchen. Casey had just
finished and was wiping down the countertops. "Thanks for
doing the dishes."

She eyed him with a distant expression. "You're welcome." After drying her hands, Casey folded the towel and
laid it on the counter. "We'll be going now."

"The movie's almost over. Let him finish watching it."

After a moment's thought, Casey relented. It wouldn't hurt
Bobby to stay up a few minutes past his regular bedtime this
once. "All right," she murmured, and bypassed Jess to go out
the back door.

The night air was cool but felt good to her in her present
state of feverishness. While she'd been alone, doing the dishes,
she hadn't been able to think very far beyond Jess's kisses.

No, that wasn't quite true. Her thoughts had progressed far beyond kisses. She had too many memories of passionate, fulfilling lovemaking with Jess to keep her mind only on kisses. She knew what his body was like beneath his snug jeans and white shirt, and how his skin had glistened in the moonlight six years ago. She had memories as hot as an erotically explicit movie, although at the time, she'd only seen Jess's expertise as beautifully romantic. He'd had no qualms at teaching her what he liked and wanted, nor in discovering what pleasured her.

Did he remember any of that? Did he remember laying her down and kissing her thighs and…

Biting her lip, Casey hugged herself against a chill and leaned against a porch post. She heard the screen door open and close, and she lifted her eyes to the stars overhead, feeling Jess's presence behind her. He stood silently, and she felt that he was staring at her back.

Then he spoke, low, distinctly, urgently. "I want him, Casey."

Her heart skipped a beat, and all thoughts of passion fled her mind. What Jess aroused in her was a separate issue from Bobby. She didn't turn around. "You said you wouldn't make trouble."

"For him."

She turned slowly. "And for me? Do you think trouble for me wouldn't touch Bobby? What are you planning to do?"

His form was backlighted by the house behind, making him a tall, dark silhouette. "I don't know. Right now I have no plans, but I'm not going to stand by and do nothing."

Casey's mouth had grown dry. "You don't believe I'll leave, do you?"

"Leave if you want to. I'll find you. I know this country a helluva lot better than you do, and I'll find you." He paused, but began again before Casey could drum up a reply. "Let me tell you a few things about myself. I never had a home. My mother took off when I was about Bobby's age, and I never even knew which one from the parade of men before that was my father. I was passed around from one distant, reluctant relative to another. Then came the foster homes. Do you have any idea what that kind of life does to a kid?''

He'd spoken forcefully but without passion. There was no bid for sympathy in his voice. He'd presented the facts of his life as if he were talking about someone else. And he wasn't accusing when he added, ''You couldn't begin to understand where I'm coming from. You have a great family—brothers, sisters, parents who are real parents. That's what I want for Bobby. You're a good mother. I know that. Watching you with Bobby, no one could doubt how close the two of you are. But a boy needs a father, too. And that boy inside *has* a father. Through my own stupidity I've already missed nearly five-and-a-half years of his life. I'm not going to miss any more of it.''

A minute later Casey was glad she'd been too stunned for a comeback and that a stretch of silence had prevailed on Jess's back porch. ''Mom?'' Bobby was standing at the screen door. ''The movie's all done, Mom.''

Though her head was spinning, Casey pulled herself together. ''All right, honey. Come out and say good-night to Jess while I get my purse.'' When Bobby came out, she went in. It took only a minute to retrieve the small purse she'd placed on a table earlier, so she was back at the screen door almost immediately.

Jess was on his knees and Bobby's boyish little arms were around his neck in a good-night hug. ''We had a great evening, didn't we, pardner?'' Jess was murmuring.

Bobby agreed with a nod of his head. Casey could see that her son wasn't questioning Jess's affection, and why would he? Hugs were commonplace and familiar to Bobby. Everyone in the Oliver clan hugged him frequently—even Kelly, who was at an age where affectionate displays were sometimes considered embarrassing. Bobby wasn't lacking in love, but watching him hugging Jess, and being hugged in return, touched Casey so deeply she felt tears in her eyes.

She blinked several times, then stepped outside. Jess rose slowly. ''Well, thank you for dinner,'' she said briskly, and took her son's hand. "Good night," she called as she led Bobby to the car.

Just before he got in, Bobby yelled, "I'll be back, Jess."

As young as he was, Bobby's call had contained a note of masculine communication, a man-to-man sound. Dismayed, Casey hurried the little boy into the car.

After hearing Bobby's prayers and tucking him in, Casey locked herself in the bathroom and turned the bathtub's spigots on full blast. Ben Oliver almost always went to bed early, but Lucille and Kelly were still up. Casey didn't want to talk to anyone, though, and taking a bath would not only soothe her frazzled nerves, it would limit conversation about the evening with Jess to the few exchanges that had occurred when she and Bobby had first come in.

Lying back in the big old tub, Casey closed her eyes. She felt terribly burdened and worried, questioning her stand with Jess. Did she have the right to keep father and son separated? Were her own hopes and dreams of someday having a good marriage more important than giving Bobby the advantages of living with his own father? Jess already loved the boy, and it was all too apparent that Bobby could very easily love Jess.

Tears spilled out of Casey's eyes and slid down her cheeks. This was a serious, totally adult situation, and one that superseded what she wanted for herself. She had to think of Bobby and what was best for him. What Jess wanted, and what she wanted, was heartbreaking but immaterial. What was best for Bobby? Staying on the Oliver ranch—a home that guaranteed security for the little boy—and knowing Jess only as a friend? Or having his very own daddy?

Casey covered her eyes with her hand and wept. Jess had made threats tonight, but she doubted he'd follow through. That's not what was tearing her apart. He wouldn't do anything that would result in Bobby being hurt, she felt, which all but eliminated any kind of dissension, other than a private bitterness between her and Jess. But she couldn't stop thinking of Jess and Bobby together on the horse, and Bobby slipping his hand into Jess's while they walked. And the good-night hug, and the awful childhood Jess had had.

Wiping her eyes with the washcloth, Casey thought of asking her mother's advice. But with the next heartbeat she realized that only she could make a decision about marrying Jess. She'd leaned so heavily on Lucille in the past, cajoling her even into keeping the truth from Ben.

Wasn't it time she stood on her own two feet and stopped involving her mother in every move she made? At seventeen it was understandable; at twenty-three and with a near six-year-old son it was unforgivable.

It was hours before Casey found the blessed peace of sleep that night.

Ben Oliver had stopped by to check the progress Jess had made on the barn site. The two of them walked around and inspected the wooden forms Jess had built for the cement floor of the barn. "Looks real good to me, Jess," Ben commented.

"Everything will be ready for the last weekend of the month," Jess replied. "I sure do appreciate so many people giving up their weekend to build a barn for me."

Ben grinned. "You'll do the same for someone else, Jess. It all evens out."

Jess lifted his hat and settled it a little lower on his forehead. He had the strongest urge to confide in Casey's father, one he could hardly suppress. Ben Oliver was a very special man, and Jess could almost see himself telling him everything. *Bobby's my son, Ben. I was in Blythe six years ago.*

No, he couldn't confess seducing a seventeen-year-old girl and then walking away as if she'd been one of the free-and-easy women who hung around rodeo cowboys. Casey was Ben's daughter. He'd be hurt, wounded, by such a confession. In fact, Jess was discovering, every idea he came up with to get closer to Bobby would hurt someone. In the long run, the hurting wouldn't stop until it affected Bobby.

As painful as it was, Jess knew that his hands were tied. He'd put in a bad night, sleeping little, wrestling with irrevocability. Inadvertently, unknowingly, he'd already hurt his son enough. Casey, too. He'd leave them alone, or at least leave Casey alone. He'd have to see Bobby, and with friendship blossoming with the little boy's grandfather, no one would see anything strange in Jess Lonnigan dropping in every so often.

It wasn't until Ben was driving away, with Jess looking after him thoughtfully, that Lucille came to mind. Jess's heart started pumping faster. He'd completely overlooked Lucille. She knew the whole story. Would any good come out of talking to her? Casey had said her mother was understanding and easy to talk to. Lucille would be biased in Casey's favor, of course, but it might not hurt to approach her, maybe get her blessing as far as visiting Bobby went.

It was something to think about, at least.

When the rest of the week passed with no further word from Jess, Casey's nerves began to settle down. On Friday afternoon she made a delivery to Wes Upton, and at his urging sat down and accepted a cup of coffee. The attorney was a pleasant man with a mild, unobtrusive way of speaking and moving. He was calming, Casey realized. Just as Jess created a storm in her soul, Wes's personality calmed her.

They chatted about a number of topics—Wes's increasing practice, the possible potential of Casey's secretarial service if she rented office space in town, and several events around Blythe. Then, smiling pensively, Wes brought up his divorce and the fact that he'd been married for fourteen years. "The life of a bachelor isn't all it's cracked up to be, Casey."

She smiled, putting an understanding into the gesture she really didn't have. "No, I'm sure it's not. Do you have children, Wes?"

"Two boys. Brian is twelve and Tommy is nine. They live in Cheyenne with their mother."

"But you get to see them."

"Yes, of course. Not enough, though." Wes sighed then, giving Casey a glimpse of some profound unhappiness. "After the divorce I just wanted to get away from the whole mess. I'm not sure now that it was the wisest move to make. I don't see the boys often enough, and I'm beginning to realize that I gave up a lot more than a lucrative law practice. It's not the money. I can see that in a year or so this will be a busy office. But my ex-wife wouldn't be caught dead camping out overnight. Boys need their father, Casey, or a darned good substitute. They need someone to be boys with, to camp and fish and hunt for frogs with, someone to cheer them on during a Little League game, or to take them horseback riding in the mountains.''

Casey listened as if hypnotized. Bobby was only five and a half, still several years away from some of the activities Wes had mentioned. And she knew that her son would be welcome to go along anytime her brothers or brother-in-law took their own children on such outings. But would it be the same as having his very own father teaching him about camping and riding and fishing?

Maybe she was putting the cart before the horse, though. Would Jess even be that kind of interested father? Casey remembered very well all the time Ben had spent with her brothers. For that matter, Ben hadn't differentiated between his sons and daughters an iota. The girls were always invited on camping, hunting or fishing trips, the same as the boys. Only it was the boys who'd been giddy over such excursions, while Casey, Dee-Dee and now Kelly hadn't been all that thrilled with them.

It was another facet of the complex problem she was living with, Casey realized sadly. She felt bad for Wes, but Wes was more in Jess's position than hers. Like Wes's ex-wife with his sons, Casey had Bobby twenty-four hours a day. She was the recipient of his kisses and hugs and boyish humor. She was the one who shared those special few minutes at bedtime each evening, when all signs of little-boy toughness vanished and Bobby snuggled his favorite stuffed animal, a raggedy, disreputable tiger, under the covers with him. It was Casey who almost melted with tenderness and love during those beautiful moments, not Jess. Jess had never experienced them—not even when *he*'d been the little boy saying good-night.

Suddenly choked, Casey stood up. Her voice was huskier than normal. ''I have to run, Wes. Thanks for the coffee.''

Wes got up, too. "Casey, there's a dance tomorrow night at the Eagles' Lodge. Do you like to dance?"

She stopped and drew a shaky breath, pulling her emotional thoughts together. "Yes, I like to dance."

"Would you go with me?"

She could see that Wes wasn't very confident of an acceptance. He was such a nice man, and terribly lonely. In her present state of mind she was relating to his unhappiness a whole lot more than she might have a few weeks back. She hesitated, but only briefly. "Sure, why not?" she responded with a smile.

Wes heaved a relieved breath. "Great. What time should I pick you up?"

"I put Bobby to bed at eight-thirty."

"Nine, then?"

"Make it nine-thirty, all right?"

On the drive back to the ranch Casey thought about the date. She wasn't uncomfortable about spending an evening with Wes, but a niggling worry gnawed at her just the same. It had to do with Jess, and it annoyed her to realize she was concerned about how Jess might take her going out with another man. Not that it was any of his business. Jess Lonnigan had no claim on her whatsoever, on neither her time nor her affections. But she wondered if maybe he didn't think he did, which could possibly cause more problems than if she really were committed to him.

Jess was a part of the Blythe area and her life now, Casey admitted with a long sigh. Would he be in her thoughts forever, no matter what she did with her and Bobby's future?

Casey knew nearly everyone at the Eagles' Lodge and gladly introduced Wes to people he hadn't yet met. The attorney made a small joke during one dance. "I really didn't ask you out to make new contacts, Casey."

She laughed and glanced over Wes's broad shoulder. Wes wasn't a great dancer, but he was easy to follow and Casey had been enjoying herself. Seeing Jess standing at the wide doorway between the dance floor and bar instantly altered her mood, however. Her smile faded and she stumbled. "Sorry," she murmured absently, still watching Jess.

It was impossible not to notice his good looks and lean body. Jess had a way of wearing clothes that made them seem a part of him. His jeans and white shirt weren't a bit too tight, but the fabrics seemed to flow over his form.

His dark Stetson shadowed his eyes, but Casey knew where they were focused, all the same—directly at her and Wes.

"Another friend?"

A little embarrassed that Wes had caught her staring, Casey nodded. "Jess Lonnigan."

"Oh, really?" Wes turned his head to give Jess another look. "I heard he'd moved to the area. I'd like to meet him Casey. Would you mind one more introduction?" At the questioning look on her face, Wes added, "I understand he has some excellent quarter horses. My oldest boy, Brian, wants a quarter horse in the worst way, and his birthday is coming up."

"No, I wouldn't mind," Casey said quietly, wondering if Jess would have come to the dance if he hadn't somehow discovered she would be there. "We can go over right now, if you'd like."

With his hand on the small of Casey's back, Wes steered her through the couples on the dance floor and over to Jess, who watched them coming with an emotionless expression.

Casey looked great in a colorful floral-patterned sundress with narrow straps that showed off her smooth tanned shoulders, and a full skirt. She wore multicolored high-heeled sandals, and jewelry—bright pink earrings, and matching bangle bracelets on her left wrist. The man with her was big and stocky, a stranger to Jess.

"Hello, Casey."

"Jess. This gentleman would like to meet you. Wes Upton, Jess Lonnigan." The two men shook hands and made the usual polite comments about being glad to meet each other. "Wes is interested in your horses, Jess, so if you both will excuse me, I'll make myself scarce for a few minutes."

It wasn't until Casey was safely in the ladies' powder room

that she acknowledged her feelings of the last few minutes. Maybe those feelings had been building from the moment she'd heard Jess's name at the rodeo grounds that day, but it made her almost ill to realize that whatever she'd felt for Jess Lonnigan six years ago, she felt now. She'd appeared calm during the brief introduction between the two men, but only through supreme effort. Now she felt the quaking of her interior spreading to her hands and her knees, and she wilted onto one of the chairs in the lounge area. How could she feel so much for a man who had caused her such unhappiness? And why now? Why tonight?

Casey put her head in her trembling hands, not at all happy with her discovery. Jess would marry her, but only to get his son. Oh, he'd make love to her; he'd already attempted that several times. But *love* her, as in falling in love? As in caring, for better or worse, for a lifetime? No. Hoping for anything resembling that kind of relationship was wasted effort. Jess was who he was—a rootless man—despite the ranch he'd settled on.

What was she going to do?

Filled with confusion, Casey sighed and got up. She knew she wasn't going to find an answer in this little room, possibly nowhere else, either. Maybe there was no solution to the dilemma she felt herself in—not one that would satisfy everybody concerned.

Casey was surprised to see Wes back at their table, sitting alone, when she walked out of the powder room. "Where's Jess?" she asked as she sat down.

"He said he had to leave," Wes replied. "I made an appointment to take a look at his stock tomorrow afternoon."

The evening progressed, but Casey functioned on two levels. Beneath her laughter and conversation were questions. Why had Jess dropped in at all, if not to see her? And why had he left again without so much as asking her to dance? She remembered them dancing in the high-school gym six years ago, and she could still feel the dizzying sensation of moving to music in his arms.

Maybe he *hadn't* known she was at Eagles' Lodge, and maybe he'd been upset to unexpectedly see her with Wes.

And then again, maybe he was only doing what she'd asked—leaving her out of his and Bobby's relationship. It was a surprisingly chilling thought.

When Wes stopped his car beside the Oliver ranch house shortly after midnight, Casey thanked him for a pleasant evening. He agreed it had been very enjoyable and asked to see her again socially. Casey looked straight ahead for a long moment, then faced the attorney.

"I won't be anything but honest with you, Wes. I'm…involved with someone." It was true. Until she made a final declaration about Jess, all her emotions were wrapped around him. The decision was still hers, Casey felt, even if Jess's determination to get his son by marrying her was flagging.

"Your ex-husband?"

"My…?" Casey was dumbfounded.

Wes laughed uneasily. "It happens, Casey."

"No," she said softly. "He's not my…ex-husband."

"Well, whoever he is, he's a lucky guy. You're a nice woman, Casey."

"Thank you. You're a nice man, too. I probably shouldn't have accepted your invitation for tonight, but…"

"I'm glad you did. Are you and your…friend having problems? I'm not trying to pry, Casey, so if you don't want to answer that, just tell me to mind my own business."

Tears burned her eyes at the empathy she heard in Wes's voice, and Casey had all she could do to keep from shedding them. She had no intention of blurting out the details of her private life, but there was something about the attorney that invited confidence. "Very serious problems," she admitted in a low and husky voice.

"I'm sorry," responded Wes with a forlorn-sounding sigh. "If there's anything I can do, if you ever need someone to talk to, don't be reluctant to let me know, Casey."

She cleared her clogged throat. "Thanks, Wes. I'll say good-night now."

Wes walked her to the door. "Don't doubt the power of love," he said quietly. "If two people are truly in love, they can work most problems out." He looked away with an unhappy expression. "It's only when there isn't enough love that there's very little chance, Casey."

He was talking about himself, Casey realized sadly. But it fit her situation quite accurately. She knew Jess didn't love her and she certainly had no illusions about the wildly unsettling feelings she had for him. What she and Jess had was chemistry. Without Bobby in the picture, would she and Jess give each other even a moment of serious consideration?

Or was it possible that the flame that had ignited between them six years ago would be burning even brighter now, without her concern over Bobby's future restraining her impulses?

Eight

In the following week Casey saw Jess only twice, when he stopped in after supper on Tuesday and Thursday evenings, presumably for a few words with Ben. The two men sat on the front porch and discussed the construction plans for Jess's barn, with Bobby hovering close by.

Lucille and Casey knew the real reason Jess was dropping in, but Kelly was quite obviously perplexed. "I thought he was interested in you," she said to her older sister with all the finesse of a bull in a china shop. "Now you don't even show your face on the porch and he just sits and talks to Dad and Bobby. What's going on?"

"Kelly, it's none of your affair," Lucille chided.

"It's all right, Mom," Casey soothed. But it wasn't all right, and she'd been asking herself the same question. What *was* going on? Jess didn't ask for her or about her. He drove up, got out of his pickup and spent about a half hour on the porch with Ben and Bobby. After barely speaking to her at the dance, now he acted like she wasn't even on the ranch during his visits. Had he completely given up on any sort of a relationship with her? She'd told him to do just that, but, with a great deal of emotional dissemination, Casey began to realize it wasn't an acceptable solution to the situation.

Another disturbing aspect of the visits were Bobby's enthusiastic greetings. At the first sight of Jess's pickup, the little boy would run out to the edge of the driveway and wait for Jess to get out. Then he'd grin and say a deep-voiced "Hi, Jess" as if addressing a peer.

Casey's heart nearly stopped the first time she watched him do it from a living-room window. But when her son reacted the same way on Jess's next visit, she knew that something very real was developing between father and son. She watched them cross the lawn together, Bobby's small hand enfolded in Jess's, and with her heart in her throat, she saw that the little boy was even emulating Jess's walk.

On the second visit Lucille came up behind her. "I marvel that no one else seems to see the resemblance," she said in a very low voice.

Casey turned away from the window, with nervous tension on her face. Lucille's eyes searched her daughter's. "I haven't pressed you about talking to your father, but I think it's time, don't you?"

"Yes," Casey whispered meekly, ashamed of her procrastination. "I'll talk to him, Mom."

"When?"

Casey sucked in a startled breath. Lucille wasn't going to let her delay any longer. "I...I think I should talk to Jess first." The idea had come out of nowhere, but it seemed only sensible—and considerate—to let Jess know what had to be done. Friendship between him and Ben was growing, and this was a delicate matter. "Is that all right with you?" Casey asked anxiously.

Lucille nodded. "I think it's wise, yes. Talk to Jess first." She glanced at the door to the hall, which led to the front porch. "Tonight?"

"Not here, Mom!" Casey returned with a touch of panic.

Lucille sighed. "I know none of this is easy, Casey. But it simply cannot be put off any longer."

Casey brushed away a tear. "Dad's going to be hurt when I tell him how I lied."

"As I said before, don't underestimate your father's love for you."

"He…he might turn against Jess," Casey speculated with a strange twist of her heartstrings. It seemed odd to want to protect Jess in this, but she really didn't want a breach between the two men.

"Your father's a fair man. I'm sure he'll think before he does anything rash."

After Jess left, Casey went about her evening chores—seeing to Bobby's bath, reading him a story, tucking him into bed—with a divided mind. She was still a little girl where her father was concerned, she realized, and confessing her transgressions to him was a frightening prospect. It couldn't be put off any longer, though. When Lucille made up her mind that adamantly about something, there was no changing it. Casey knew that if she didn't tell her father, her mother would. And while she might still suffer pangs of immaturity with Ben, she was a grown woman and preferred that the story came from her. Besides, Lucille's role in the episode needed explanation, and Casey wanted to make sure her father understood that his beloved wife had only kept the secret because of Casey's impassioned pleas.

When all was quiet in Bobby's room, Casey took her purse and went downstairs. Lucille and Ben were in the living room, but Ben was in his stocking feet, his normal prelude to going to bed. "I'm going for a drive," Casey announced, and saw understanding in Lucille's eyes and surprise in Ben's. Casey never went out alone at that time of night, and her breaking a longtime habit was clearly making Ben uncomfortable.

As luck would have it, Kelly came bounding in. "Where you going, Casey?"

"Just for a drive."

"Great! I'll come along."

Casey's heart sank. "No, Kelly. Not tonight."

Ben frowned while Kelly's mouth dropped open. But before either could respond vocally, Lucille said firmly, "Run along,

Casey. You don't have to have company if you don't want it. Kelly, stop looking like the last rose of summer. Your sister has a right to some privacy once in a while.''

Casey quickly made an escape, tuning out both Kelly's and Ben's objections to her driving around alone after dark. She was going to see Jess, and it was with a serious enough mission that she was in no mood to worry about Kelly's pouts. Ben's concern was strictly parental, which was understandable when she still lived under his roof.

While she drove the five miles, Casey began to see her life differently than she had before Jess's untimely return to the area. Was it any wonder she still felt like a child in some respects? She'd never lived on her own, never fully supported herself, never assumed complete responsibility for herself, or her son. Why wouldn't Ben be worried about something as innocuous as her going somewhere alone after dark?

In all honesty, the time to get out of her parents' hair was long overdue. They shouldn't have to worry about a twenty-three-year-old daughter. They still had Kelly at home, which was enough after raising a big family.

All of which meant leaving the ranch.

Why hadn't she seen before how complacently she'd burdened her parents? Not that either Lucille or Ben would ever admit to such a thing. They'd never once so much as hinted that Casey and Bobby weren't welcome to spend the rest of their lives with them.

Well, she had some serious thinking to do. She would only move to Blythe, of course. Casey knew now that her threats to Jess had been only angry blusters. Leaving the ranch would be traumatic enough for Bobby without taking him very far away from all the people he loved. She could expand her business, or go to work full-time for Wes Upton. It would take some planning, but the thought of self-sufficiency was satisfying.

Jess's house was a good quarter mile off the highway, and right at the turn Casey could see that there were no lights on. Frowning, she proceeded toward it. It was nine, maybe a bit late for an unannounced call. Then, too, maybe Jess hadn't come home after he'd left the Olivers' front porch.

But no, his pickup was parked up ahead. Casey could see it beside the house. Was he in bed already?

She stopped behind the truck, without turning off the motor, and debated whether she should knock on Jess's door. A dog came around the house then, a big, shaggy, cream-colored dog with a wagging tail and a friendly "Woof!"

On closer inspection, Casey could see that the dog was pregnant, and she remembered Jess's comment to Bobby that a ranch wasn't much of a place without puppies. Her heart softened dramatically, and she turned the ignition off. This call was for Bobby and Ben, and maybe the first step in straightening out the convoluted mess she'd made of her own life. If she woke Jess, he would understand why after she'd told him the reason she'd come.

Casey opened the car door and stepped out. The big dog all but turned inside out welcoming her. "Some watchdog you are." Casey laughed softly, reaching down to pat the friendly animal.

"She's not a watchdog."

Casey looked toward the voice and found Jess standing with the front screen door partially open. Even in the dark she could see the delineation of skin and clothing, and it looked to her as if Jess had been to bed and only yanked on jeans when he'd heard the car. "I'm sorry to bother you this late. I didn't think you'd be in bed already," she said, putting a foot on the porch stairs.

"It's not that late. I wasn't sleeping, anyway. Come on in."

Casey slipped past him, avoiding contact. "When did you get the dog?"

"The other day." Jess snapped on a light, which revealed his bare torso and feet and a pair of jeans. "Her name's Sunny. A guy I met in town couldn't keep her because of the puppies due any day. Bobby will like her."

"Bobby will be delighted about the puppies," Casey agreed.

Jess gestured to a chair. "Sit down."

"Thank you." She wished Jess had more clothes on. His skin was as brown as toast, and her eyes kept going to the mat of hair on his chest. She cleared her throat and tried to appear calm, although her interior was quaking—because of her mission, because of Jess's half-naked good looks. Jess Lonnigan was as much of a flame today, tonight, as he'd been the first time she'd set eyes on him. There was a weakness in Casey Oliver Maddox, and this man, the father of her son, was at the heart of it.

Jess plopped into another chair and threw one long leg over its arm, stretching the fit of his jeans just a little too snugly for Casey's comfort. "What are you doing here?" he asked without a dram of tact.

"I need to talk to you about something."

"I was at your house earlier tonight," he bluntly pointed out.

"I know. But it's not something I wanted to discuss with an audience."

"Private subject?" he drawled with a suggestively raised eyebrow.

Casey colored. "It's not about us, Jess. Well…it is, but—"

"But not about marriage," he finished dryly. "For a moment I'd hoped you'd changed your mind. No such luck, huh?"

Casey sat back and looked at him. Why was she so against marriage with Jess? Almost every day something else happened to undermine her determination——thoughts of personal selfishness, recognition of what Bobby would gain from the union, the brand-new acknowledgement tonight that she couldn't continue living off her parents indefinitely. What on earth made her think that some great, profound, epic love awaited her? Jess was as close to love as she'd probably ever come. And he wanted to marry her, even if his reason was less than the romantic fantasy she carried in the back of her mind.

No! She couldn't marry a man who didn't love her. She just couldn't, no matter how many sensible other reasons she unearthed!

Giving her head a quick, sharp shake to clear it, Casey saw that Jess took it as a negative reply to his comments. She didn't alter his opinion. "I'm planning on telling Dad that you're Bobby's father," she announced, keeping her tone reasonably level and with very little inflection.

Jess's reaction was physical—a leap out of the chair. He walked around with a heavy, very serious-looking frown. Casey watched him pacing, then asked, "Do you object?"

He turned. "No. I think he should know. I almost told him myself the other day. Casey, I want to be there."

"When I tell him?" she asked, taken aback. She hadn't anticipated Jess's wanting to participate in the confession, and she immediately suspected it would make the ordeal more difficult. "I'm not sure that's a good idea," she said slowly. "Dad could be very upset."

Jess's mouth twisted grimly. "I wouldn't expect him to be anything else." His eyes, containing a hard light, landed on Casey. "Actually, I think he should know that I've offered to do the honorable thing."

She stiffened. "Don't you dare! No, I don't want you there. I only came to tell you about it because you and Dad are becoming friends." Besides, there was an aspect of the story that was none of Jess's business, her manufactured ex-husband. Ben had a right to hear the complete truth, but there was no reason for Jess or anyone else to know that Don Maddox was only a fabrication.

Lies were such a burden! This whole thing wouldn't have been necessary if she hadn't lied and forced her mother to lie. Yes, there might have been hell to pay when Jess showed up again, but it would have been an honest furor. Now Ben liked Jess, and Jess liked Ben; and who knew just what would happen between the two men when the deep, dark past came to light?

And none of them dared forget Bobby. The little guy was the focal point around which some very adult events were about to take place, and heaven help the one of them who hurt Bobby!

Folding his arms across his naked chest, Jess leaned against a section of wall with a determined expression. "Once Ben knows who Bobby's father really is, do you think I'm going to stay out of it? Forget that notion, if you have it. You bet I'm going to tell him I offered marriage when I found out I had a son. I might have made a bad mistake six years ago, but I'm willing to do just about anything to rectify it."

Casey gave him a cold look. "Even marry me. How noble and self-sacrificing. And of course, when Dad learns that I refused your proposal, I'll be the heavy, won't I?"

"Do you think that's how Ben will look at it?" Jess couldn't help the elation in his voice. If the Olivers lined up in his favor, wouldn't that influence Casey?

Well, strangely enough, he had some influence with Casey, too. So far she'd been fighting it, but Jess knew very well how strong the chemistry was between them. It suddenly occurred to him that they were completely alone—alone in his house. Casey looked beautiful, as she always did. Tonight she was wearing a red cotton skirt and a white blouse with a scoop neck and no sleeves. A lightweight white sweater was thrown over her shoulders, and the white blouse had minute red dots and red buttons almost as tiny.

Studying her, Jess relived last Saturday night when he'd walked into the Eagles' Lodge and seen Casey dancing. A wash of possessiveness, and especially a sting of jealousy, had nearly made him do something foolish—like walking out on the dance floor and hauling her out of that guy's arms. Jess had seen red, and only with supreme effort had he forced himself to stay at the doorway.

He'd been surprised to see Casey bringing the guy over, and his first impulse had been to ask her what the hell she was doing out with another man. When they'd been walking his way and he'd watched her skirt swaying with her movements and seen how incredibly sexy she looked in high heels, he'd actually wanted to punch the guy and drag Casey out of there. Again, common sense had prevailed, which, once Jess had talked to Wes Upton, he'd been darned glad of. Upton was a nice guy, and if he admired Casey, Jess could hardly blame him.

Since that night, Jess had asked himself a dozen times why seeing Casey with a date had affected him so adversely. He figured he had the best reason in the world for wanting her for his wife: Bobby. Along with that, Casey was an arousing, beautiful woman. Few men wouldn't get a few hankerings around her. But—and it was a damned big but—were the feelings he was noticing and trying to understand something more than a desire to experience her body again?

Something deep and masculine stirred in Jess. Right now Casey's pretty face contained the tension of worry and anger. But he knew he could soothe that away—very easily. She couldn't help responding to him, any more than he could help wanting her. That was the one area of their relationship where they were on the same wavelength, whether she wanted to admit it or not.

Moving almost lazily, Jess pushed away from the wall. Casey darted him a nervous glance but was still preoccupied with the horror of Jess announcing marital intentions to her father. Just how would Ben look at the situation if Jess butted in with that information? Casey knew that as kind and generous-minded as her father was, he was still a God-fearing, family-oriented man. He was also inclined toward that old saying, "If you dance to the music, you have to pay the piper."

Well, she'd danced—six years ago. And paying the piper, in Ben's eyes, could very well mean a marriage she wasn't ready for.

When Jess stopped right in front of her, Casey's gaze lifted to his face, and a sudden jolt shook her. She hadn't come here for a shot of Jess's physical persuasion, but the look on his face conveyed his intentions to be very different from hers. Casey's mouth went dry. "No, Jess," she warned.

He bent over, putting his hands on the arms of her chair. He was close enough to smell, and she caught a drift of mint, probably from toothpaste. His eyes contained a touch of laughter, giving him a boyish appearance. "You look good enough to eat," he told her in a voice that sounded both suggestive and admiring.

Casey's pulse had gone wild, but she tried to maintain a

forbidding expression. "This isn't fair, Jess. I came here to tell you something that I consider very important. Please don't try to turn it into something else."

"I consider it very important, too. And I appreciate your coming by to let me know about it." The amusement left his eyes. "But we're all alone here tonight. Doesn't that do something to you?"

Apparently it did "something" to him. He was giving off sexually charged vibes, and she was picking them up, *soaking* them up, as if her flesh had suddenly turned porous and thirsty.

He raised a hand and touched her hair, following Casey's head back when she tried to avoid it. "So pretty," he whispered. "My son has the prettiest mama in the whole state."

"Jess..."

His eyes were darker and exuded a hot light, and he lazily wound a burnished curl around his forefinger. "Hair like silk, skin like satin, eyes like warm jade. But your mouth—ah, your mouth. There aren't words, Casey, none that I know of, to describe your mouth. It makes me feel, it makes me remember, it makes me want."

She drew a long, quivering breath. "I'm not...I won't..."

"You won't what?" He bent lower and brushed his lips along her hairline, tracing it down to her ear. "What won't you do, sweetheart?"

His voice was as much of a caress as his mouth. Casey's heart was pounding at a furious rate. She struggled against herself, against a liquefying weakness in her bones, against a curling heat in her stomach. She must remember how glib Jess had been six years ago, too, and not be overly impressed with flowery phrases.

But her senses were betraying her. She'd never wanted any other man. She'd never felt soft and liquid and so utterly female for any other man. This man, with his shock of shimmering, dark, unruly hair and sky-blue eyes, was the only man who had ever reached and stirred and tormented the woman in her.

Her hands were fluttering, afraid to light anywhere. The bronze sheen of supple skin over rippling, sinewy muscles, the dark mat of hair on his chest—she didn't dare touch him, not anywhere. He wasn't wearing a belt, and his jeans rode low on his hips, below his navel. He was half naked, and the half that was covered was straining against faded denim, reminding her of soft-summer nights beside a gurgling river.

"Leave me alone," she whispered raggedly.

His lips moved in her hair, heating her ear. "I can't leave you alone. I'm burning to death from wanting you."

"Any woman would do."

"No, any woman *wouldn't* do." Jess raised his head, tipped her chin and looked directly into her eyes. "I haven't so much as kidded around with another woman since I got here. I don't want any other woman. And even if I did, I wouldn't dishonor you or my son with some cheap affair."

Casey's eyes widened. "Since when have you become so scrupulously moral?"

He studied her. "Good question, isn't it?"

Casey's insides did a strange flip-flop. Even Jess looked surprised by what hung in the air, his own intimation that some kind of incomprehensible transition was taking place.

Well, she didn't understand it, either, and she was certainly too cautious to trust it. Just because Jess Lonnigan, rodeo star and first-class Casanova, had bought a ranch and settled down didn't mean he'd changed his philandering ways. By his own admission he'd played at life and love. The discovery of a son might have cooled his ardor temporarily, but leopards didn't change spots overnight.

Casey took his hand and brought it away from her chin. "I think I'd better be going."

That slow, heartrending smile of his appeared again. "Why?"

"I don't have to explain myself to you, Jess."

His hands cupped the arms of the chair again. "No, but maybe you want to. Maybe if you had the courage you'd say, 'Jess, if I stay I'm going to end up in your bed.' Maybe you'd like to say, 'I need you, Jess, I need you to kiss me and love me, like you did six years ago.'"

Casey turned her face away, eluding the compelling look in his eyes. "Don't be absurd."

He lowered his head until his lips were against the side of her throat. "Prove to me you don't want me," he murmured.

"I think that's exactly what I've been trying to do. You don't pay the slightest bit of attention to—"

"To lies?" Jess's hands moved from the chair to Casey's upper arms, and he straightened his long back then, pulling her up with him. His eyes bored into hers. "Stop being a coward, Casey. Stop pretending you don't feel what I do. Be your real self. Let yourself go."

Casey's knees were rubbery. *Let yourself go!* She closed her eyes and was immediately bombarded with emotions. *Be your real self!* Oh, Lord what was her *real* self? *Coward... coward...coward...*

Jess didn't hurry. His hands slowly moved around her and down her back. The white sweater slipped and he let it slide to the floor. He pressed his lips to her forehead, gradually drawing her closer. Her scent careened through his system like a speeding ball in a pinball-machine game, knocking against nerves, setting off bells and flashing lights. "Casey...baby..."

He caught her hands then and brought them up to his neck. His skin was warm and dry and vibrant with life. Casey felt his hands lock behind her, just below her waist, and she stared up into his blue, slightly hooded eyes. "Don't push me, Jess," she whispered.

"I can see in your eyes what you want."

"There's more at stake than..."

"You're too cautious these days."

"I have a son to think of."

"So do I, but making love isn't going to take anything away from Bobby."

Casey was desperately trying to cling to sanity. She knew she was at some sort of crossroad and that Jess had forced her there. It almost seemed like a battle for maturity; she was, after all, twenty-three and living a celibate life. By choice, of course. But it had always been so easy to do. Since that one week six years ago, she'd never been faced with the overwhelming desire for a man's body that Jess had provoked every time he touched her, until now. Yet, getting that involved with Jess seemed so traitorous to her situation.

And then Jess put into words some of the questions that had been hounding her. "Why do we have these feelings if they're so wrong, Casey? Why do we burn for each other? Why do I want you, and why do you want me?"

"Oh, Jess, I wish I knew," she lied, deeply shaken over her inner conflict.

His lips moved over her face. "There's nothing wrong with two people wanting each other. In fact, honey, there's something very right about it." His mouth rested on hers, and Casey sighed—deeply, emotionally—and parted her lips.

A sound resembling a growl came from deep in his throat and his mouth opened and possessed hers. His tongue slid between her lips and teeth, and his body molded around hers. Every dip and curve of Jess's form was hotly influencing. It was as if his chest were shaped to accept the configuration of her breasts, and there was no denying how perfectly their lower bodies melded. Even with the difference in their heights, they fit together as nature intended a man and a woman to fit.

Casey gave up on sensibility. She'd fought Jess since that day at the rodeo, and maybe more devastating to her, she'd fought herself. Perhaps she was completely wrong in everything she'd been feeling lately, or, at least, concerning the worries she'd had about Jess, himself. Maybe she *should* marry him. Maybe she should say goodbye to a dream and take what was available.

It was a subject that was easier to contemplate in Jess's arms than out of them.

She felt herself being lifted, swung up off the floor as though she weighed nothing, and she experienced only a small echo of remorse. Her heart was beating a wild cadence, and a strange joy that she was again going to experience Jess Lonnigan's magic filled her mind.

During the short walk down a hallway, Casey let her hands wander. His skin was smooth, hotter than before, and she

turned her face into the hair on his chest and inhaled the male
scent of him.

His bedroom was dark except for the pale, silvery moonlight. "Don't turn it on," she objected huskily when Jess
stopped at the light switch by the door.

"Anything you say," he agreed softly. "This time," he
added, and let her feet slide down to the floor. He straightened
and reached for the tiny red buttons on her blouse.

Casey watched his face in the moonlight. It was shadowed
and mysterious. She'd never made love as a woman, she realized. At seventeen she'd been eager but ignorant. Of course,
by the time Jess left Blythe, she hadn't been at all ignorant.
Yet, the sum total of her sexual experience was with this man,
although he didn't know that. Jess still thought she'd been
married, and he'd never asked about other men. For all he
knew, she could be very experienced, very polished and so-
phisticated in bed.

The thought made her bolder—bold enough to caress and
touch and run her fingertips over the planes of his bare torso.
She could feel his heartbeat, a powerful, steady thumping under her fingers. His muscles were tight and firm, and he
seemed quite controlled until she bent forward and licked at
one tiny male nipple.

"Oh, baby," he groaned thickly, and twining his fingers in
her hair, he tipped her head back and took her mouth in a
hungry, devouring kiss. His tongue was insistent now, and
within the dazzling effects of his increased desire, Casey felt
his free hand working the rest of her buttons free.

With their mouths still united, Jess slid the blouse from her
shoulders and arms. Casey was wearing a white teddy, and
when he realized that, he undid the button on the waistband
of her skirt and let it drop around her ankles.

Then he stood back a little to look at her. "You're so beautiful," he breathed hoarsely as he took in the long, tanned legs
beneath the white satin of the sexy undergarment. Her nipples
were visible bumps in the cups beneath two slender straps over
her shoulders.

Jess opened his jeans—first the brass button at his waist,

then the zipper on his fly. But he didn't push the pants down. Casey's startled gaze dropped to what she could see of maleness within the veed opening. Surprisingly enchanted with her curiosity, Jess slipped the teddy's straps down over her shoulders, and exposed the tops of lushly full breasts, then their pouty, dark nipples.

"Oh, Casey," he whispered raggedly, and bent his head to take one in his mouth.

"Jess," she moaned, and instinctively reached for that compelling vee in his jeans. He wasn't wearing underwear, which she'd already guessed, and his body was hot and rigid and velvety in her hands. She had touched him like this six years ago; he'd taught her, he'd shown her what to do. She'd been mesmerized by the intimacy then and, she realized, she was mesmerized by it now.

His tongue moved on her nipple, wetting it, while he gently sucked. She felt as if a live flame were loose within her, searing her breasts and leaping downward to a point of almost intolerable aching between her legs, only to crackle and shoot upward again.

Perspiring, Casey was having trouble breathing. A band had tightened around her chest. She wanted what she remembered from six years ago with an urgency that was becoming unbearable. After Jess had left Blythe and Casey had finally faced her predicament, she'd done a lot of reading. Several times, in novels, she'd encountered a female character who was considered frigid. It was one disadvantage she knew she would never have to deal with. She was far from frigid; not with the right man, she wasn't.

The right man! Casey's heart skipped a beat when the thought ran wild and encompassed the fact that Jess was the only man she'd ever really responded to.

The teddy was sliding down over her hips, and when it reached her ankles, Casey kicked it away. She pushed Jess's jeans down then, and he got rid of them just as easily as she'd disposed of her undergarment.

They fell to the bed and tangled into a sensual embrace, their mouths and hands searching. She felt Jess's hot breath on her ear. "It's been too long. I can't wait any longer," he whispered. "Are you on the Pill?"

"The Pill? No...no..."

Dazed, Casey watched him open the drawer of the night-stand and take out a small foil-wrapped packet, and when she understood what he was doing, she whispered, "Why didn't you do that six years ago?"

Jess shook his head. "We'll talk later."

She could see how agitated he was, how deeply aroused and excited he was. But so was she. Her breasts were rising and falling with harsh, labored breaths, and the fire in her loins was painfully insistent. He returned to her, laying himself within the cradle of her thighs, and sought her mouth for an-other soul-searching kiss that lasted until neither could breathe at all.

Casey's hands restlessly roamed his back. When her mouth was free she gasped for air and moaned. "Do it. Make love to me. Do it."

His penetration was swift and hot, and Casey whimpered with utter abandonment. Her hips rose, pressing him deeper. He was masterful, leading them both, and for the first time Casey really understood why, at seventeen, she'd mistaken this wild, mind-bending rush of feeling and emotion for love.

But she knew what it was now, and she could even label it. There wasn't anything wrong with recognizing one's sexual appetite, and as Jess had stated, there might even be something very right in it. She was years away from being a teenager, and sex was a very important part of adulthood.

The only thing slightly wrong with this was that she was awakening again for the same man who had hurt her so badly the first time around.

Casey didn't have to push the thought away; it quite easily dissolved on its own within the much stronger sensations of pleasure and desire controlling her mind and body.

It wasn't until it was over, until her skin and Jess's were both wet with sweat and her blood had stopped racing and her heart had settled down, that Casey realized she'd whispered words of love at the end. With Jess weighting her down, she tried to remember exactly what she'd said.

He raised his head and smoothed the damp curls back from her forehead. "That was perfect," he told her in a low, husky voice.

Her head bobbed once, a silent agreement. For pure physicality, nothing could ever be more perfect. But what about emotions? Hers were in a terrible snarl. How could she be in Jess Lonnigan's bed like this? She'd come to his house to discuss a serious topic, and that had been only her first mistake. How could things look so different in the space of a few minutes?

"Damn you," she whispered on a dry sob.

Jess stiffened. "Now you're mad at me?"

"Not just at you. I should have known better than to come here alone."

"Casey, whatever you do, please don't regret this. It was beautiful and right."

"It was as sordid as it was six years ago! Only I don't have the excuse of naiveté this time. Let me get up."

Jess tried to laugh, but it came out sharp and bitter. "I don't believe this." He moved away, freeing Casey, and watched as she got off the bed and searched in the near darkness for her clothes.

Nine

When they were both dressed and in the living room again, Jess tried to talk some sense into Casey. "You're wrong to take this attitude. We didn't do a damn thing we didn't have a right to do. Are you attached to anyone? Am I? We're consenting adults, and there's a lot of feeling between us, Casey."

He was right on that point. She had way too many feelings, which was part of the problem. But if genuine feelings were all there was to it, she might not be so upset. What hurt was that she knew all about Jess's feelings, and they were centered in one particular portion of his anatomy. She, stupid woman that she was, had succumbed again to Jess Lonnigan's fatal charm!

Casey retrieved her white sweater from the floor and gave it a shake. "I'll be speaking to Dad in the next day or so, whenever there's a good opportunity."

"Talk to me about this, Casey. Don't act like it didn't happen."

She swung angry eyes to him. "Oh, it happened, all right. But don't expect me to turn handsprings because I just proved again what a fool I am where you're concerned." Casey advanced a step, eyes burning. "I'm weak with you, Jess. I was weak six years ago and I'm still weak. It infuriates me, so don't *you* act all hurt and put-upon because I'm not thrilled about tonight."

His eyes narrowed. "Think what kind of marriage we could have."

"One based on sex?"

"What would be so terrible about that? There isn't a married couple on earth who wouldn't be lucky to have what you and I have in bed. And don't forget Bobby. We'd be a family, and there's not a whole lot wrong with a family where the mother and dad can't keep their hands off each other. We could even have other kids. I'd like that, Casey. I'd like to fill this house with kids."

Casey's memory had just gotten a nudge, and she wondered if she should ask Jess again why he hadn't used condoms six years ago.

"Casey, you'd be the most well-loved woman in the state."

She almost made a very crude retort, because she was positive that Jess's affections had nothing to do with love. Instead, Casey drove both the question and retort from her mind and started for the door. "I'll let you know how Dad takes it, if you want me to."

Jess followed her. "I'd still like to be there when you talk to Ben."

"No."

"Just like that, a flat-out no. You're not a very generous woman, Casey."

"Just drop it, Jess. He's *my* father and you have no right to interfere."

Casey was halfway through the doorway when Jess caught her arm. "Maybe tonight gives me a few rights."

She whirled on him. "*Tonight gives you nothing!* Don't you dare try to make something out of what happened. I fully admit to being a fool, and I certainly don't need any pressure from you about it."

Jess stared down at her with a hard expression. "A half

hour ago you were kissing me back and wanting more. I didn't force myself on you, Casey. You willingly opened your legs.'' She sucked in a startled breath, but he wasn't through. ''It's going to happen again, too. This kind of fire isn't extinguished with one glass of water, honey. I think you know that as well as I do.''

Casey tore her arm loose and lunged away. She knew Jess had come out of the house behind her, but she didn't look back. Her hands were trembling as she started her car, and then she glanced at the porch and saw him standing in a patch of light reflected from the living room. Casey drove away with tears running down her cheeks.

Casey put in a strange night. Oddly, as upsetting as it was, the evening with Jess also made her feel somewhat stronger. Her life was taking a new direction, one with a decidedly more adult perspective. While she showered and dressed the next morning, she visualized her future, both immediate and longer-range. She would talk to Ben first thing, then tell both parents about her decision to move to Blythe with Bobby. It was time she stood on her own two feet, and she couldn't do that under her parents' roof.

As for Jess, Casey's thoughts about him had gone around in circles. She could look on their lovemaking in two ways, she finally concluded: either Jess had just been, to put it crudely, horny and she'd been the only woman handy, or he'd deliberately tried sexual persuasion to get her to marry him— only because of Bobby, of course. No matter which, she'd be an even bigger fool than she already was to let it happen again, despite Jess's dire prediction.

Ben had already gone when Casey finally went downstairs. ''Where's Dad working today?'' she asked her mother who was the only person in the kitchen.

''He and the boys are moving some steers from one pasture to another. I doubt if you'll be able to talk to him until lunch, Casey.''

''All right. I've got some typing to get out, so I guess I'll get that done. When Bobby comes down, have him come to the den.''

Casey had fixed up one corner of the den for her work. It had a desk, a typewriter and a small cupboard for supplies. With a cup of coffee, she went to the desk and sat down. Lucille hadn't asked how the meeting with Jess had gone, and Casey was glad she hadn't had to talk about it. But she couldn't stop thinking about it.

Making love with Jess was like nothing else Casey had ever experienced. Of course, she had no other sexual encounters to compare it with, but how could anything be better? It was total immersion into sexuality, both hers and Jess's. He had the ability to draw her to a whole different level of emotion, one that was far distanced from the mundane aspects of life. In his arms she became beautiful, soft, a fantasy creature, and in retrospect, the memory was framed with sparkles of light and wind-chime tinkles.

Casey gave her head a shake. The reality of what she'd done was far from a star-speckled, musical dream. The reality was that Jess brought out her baser instincts, and what they felt for each other was only lust.

And he wanted to build a marriage on lust?

Disgusted with herself as well as Jess, Casey set her coffee mug down and opened a file folder. She had at least two hours of typing ahead of her, and then, later in the day, she would make her deliveries in Blythe. It would be a good opportunity to begin making inquiries about a rental house.

''I'll walk out with you, Dad,'' Casey announced when Ben had finished lunch and was preparing to go back to work.

''All right.''

''Me, too, Mom?'' Bobby enthused.

''No, honey. You stay with Grandma. I need to talk to Grandpa alone.'' Casey saw the pure, unmitigated nosiness on Kelly's face, but followed her father out the back-door without alleviating it.

They walked along in silence for a minute, then Ben gave his daughter a glance. ''Something on your mind, Casey?''

"Yes."

Ben veered from a direct path to his pickup to a fence line and the shade of three massive oak trees. "Warm today."

Casey put her hands on the top rail of the white wood fence and looked at the horses that were contentedly grazing within the enclosure. "This is something I should have talked to you about years ago, Dad," she said quietly.

"Yes, I think you should have. It's about Bobby, isn't it?"

Casey's head jerked around. She searched Ben's eyes and saw that there never had been a secret! For a moment she was flustered. "You know?" she whispered.

"Most of it, yes."

"But, how…"

"Casey—" Ben sighed "—children have been asking their parents that question since time began. How do you know when Bobby does something you'd have preferred him not doing? You sense it, don't you? You know your own child so well that the slightest change in him alerts you."

"Dad…"

Ben smiled then. "Besides, your mother told me about it six years ago. You see, Casey, we don't keep secrets from each other."

Casey's mind was in a muddle. "But all this time Mom kept telling me I should tell…" Her expression cleared. "No, that's not true. She never said to *tell* you, she said I should talk to you." Casey's hand moved from the fence to Ben's arm. "I don't understand, Dad. I thought I had the secret, and all this time it was you."

Ben nodded. "Let's go back a ways, honey. When you were going through your trouble and confiding in your mother, you were very young and very hurt. Mom told me how you begged her to keep it from everyone in the family, including me."

"Especially you," Casey whispered brokenly. "I knew you'd be disappointed in me, and I couldn't bear it. Dad, it was wrong of me to ask Mom to lie, but I was so ashamed."

"Casey, everyone makes mistakes. Disappointed? Yes. I suppose I was, to a degree. But I was a lot more concerned with your and the baby's welfare than I was with my disappointment. At any rate, I decided to remain silent on the matter. You had enough heartache to deal with, and your mother was doing everything anyone could to get you through it. With circumstances being what they were at the time, I agreed that a manufactured husband was best.

"Honey, I knew that someday you'd talk to me about it." Ben slipped his arm around Casey's shoulders and hugged her. "When you grew up," he added quietly.

He hadn't mentioned Jess, and Casey's heart was doing flips in her chest. "There's more," she admitted weakly.

Ben cleared his throat and moved away. "You know, before Bobby was born and your mother and I talked about the baby's father, the man's name was mentioned only a few times. You were apparently convinced that there was no chance of locating him, and I gathered, from your mother, that you were in such a state, any attempt on my part to do so would only upset you more."

Casey was staring at her father in stunned silence. He'd known all along—everything.

"Besides, you were so young, and a forced marriage didn't seem like the best course to either your mother or me. That day at the rodeo grounds, when Jess's name was announced it rang a bell. But I didn't put two and two together until I saw your and your mother's reactions to it. Then, when I met Jess—and liked him, by the way—I decided again to stay out of it. The two of you are adults, Casey. It's for you two to work out—not me or your mother or anyone else."

Ben turned and faced his daughter. "Now, tell me what you feel about all of this."

"Oh, Dad," she whispered tearily. "I thought this was going to be so terrible. When I was younger I was deathly afraid of telling you, and then it became a humiliation I couldn't bear facing. I've been such a fool, in so many ways."

"Well," Ben mused philosophically, "foolishness is a human frailty. You don't have a monopoly on it, believe me. I doubt if there are too many people around who haven't done something in their lifetime that they don't regret."

Casey shook her head adamantly. "Not you, Dad. Or

Mother. No one could ever convince me that either of you ever did anything even close to my mistakes."

Ben chuckled softly, as if remembering some long-ago indiscretion. Then he sobered. "I guess what's important is what you do from here on in, Casey. Jess and Bobby are developing quite a relationship, and I'd guess that dealing with that is your most pressing problem right now, wouldn't you?"

"They look so much alike. You've seen it, haven't you, Dad?"

"Yes, I suppose there's a resemblance. But Bobby looks a lot like your brother Brady, too."

Casey's eyes widened. "Do you really think so? Mom sees his likeness to Jess very clearly. Well, that's neither here nor there, is it? Dad, you really do like Jess?"

Ben nodded and replied firmly. "Yes, I do."

He wants to marry me! Casey tried, but she couldn't quite get the words out. Although, now that she thought about it, Ben probably knew about Jess's proposal, too. There really were no secrets between her parents, she was relieved to discover.

Still, if Ben knew about the proposal he also knew about her reluctance. And at this point she didn't want to even talk about it—not after last night. Instead she said, "I was afraid that once you found out, you might change your opinion of him. You seem to like most people, and the possibility of a breach between the two of you made me uncomfortable. He's just getting established here, and I know how much he values your friendship."

Ben gave her a long, in-depth scrutiny. "Do you still have special feelings for him, Casey? I know you must have had six years ago. You were an impulsive teenager, but you were never... Well, what's the word I want here?"

"Promiscuous? You're right, Dad. Jess is the only man I...." Casey stopped and looked away. She'd always been able to talk relatively freely with her mother, but there were some subjects that had never come up between her father and her. "I did have special feelings for Jess six years ago," she said softly, introspectively. "I imagined myself in love with him."

"Imagined? Why do you say 'imagined'? Weren't you capable of feeling love back then? Casey, don't denigrate what you felt. Subsequent events might have tarnished your feelings, or even destroyed them, but initially they were real. You have a right to remember that and to admit that Bobby's conception was a result of love."

Tears blurred Casey's vision. She *had* loved Jess. She had loved him so much she'd wanted to die when he left. And then the love had turned to hatred, to an obsessive, impossible wish for revenge. Now she didn't hate him, but she still wanted him physically; and what did one call that?

"Here, dry your eyes." Casey took the large red handkerchief Ben held out. "I'm glad it's finally out in the open, Casey."

"I am, too, Dad. What...what about the rest of the family? Do you think they should know?"

Ben frowned while he mulled it over. "I think that's something for you and Jess to decide. Apparently you've come to an agreement on him seeing Bobby, which I feel is wise."

Sniffling, Casey handed back the handkerchief. "Dad, there's something else I might as well say now, too. I've lived off you and Mom long enough. I don't completely understand it, but Jess coming back brought about an awful lot of change in me."

"You grew up, honey," Ben commented reassuringly.

Casey sighed. "Yes, I think I did. Anyway, I think it's time that I accepted responsibility for myself and my son. I'm planning to move to town. Wesley Upton has asked me to come to work for him full-time, and I can't see any reason why I can't handle that job and still keep up my business."

"Have you discussed this with your mother?"

"Not yet. But I will." Casey put her arms around her father's middle and hugged him. "Oh, Dad, why was I so worried about talking to you?"

"I don't know, honey. I never thought I was that tough to talk to, but maybe I was wrong. Listen, do you intend to tell Jess that I know the truth?"

Casey backed away. "I already told him I was going to talk to you."

"Yes, last night. Your mother told me about it after you left. How did Jess react?"

"He was glad. He said he almost told you himself one day. He wanted to be with me during this talk, but I preferred doing it alone."

"I would imagine Jess would like to openly claim his son?"

"Very much. I...I'm very undecided on that, Dad. What's best for Bobby? There would be so much talk if it got around. I don't know. It's a point I'm very confused about."

"Well, I'm sure you'll work it out."

Casey smiled faintly. "I'm going to do my best, Dad."

"That's all anyone can ask, honey."

"You're really not going to the barn raising?" Kelly asked in complete astonishment the Friday evening before the big event.

"No, I'm not," Casey replied.

"But, everyone's going! The whole family and most of our friends will be there. Mom, why isn't Casey going?"

"I'll tell you myself." Casey sighed. "I have a ten o'clock appointment tomorrow morning with Mrs. Loomis to look at that little rental house she owns on Third Street in Blythe. I'm moving to town, Kelly."

Kelly looked shell-shocked. "Moving to town! Why? What for?"

"Simply because it's time I took care of myself," Casey said quietly.

"Mom?" Kelly wailed.

Lucille walked over and hugged her youngest daughter. "It's your sister's decision, Kelly. We must respect it."

Casey and Lucille had had a long discussion on both the "secret" and the matter of Casey's proposed move. At first Lucille had been adamantly opposed to the idea, but she'd finally seen that Casey was right.

But Casey hadn't expected Kelly to be so unhappy about

it. "It's only to Blythe, Kelly," she said gently. "You can spend time in town with me and I'll be back and forth a lot."

Kelly wiped at a tear. "I just don't see why you have to move. I'm not just being a kid about this, Casey. I honestly don't understand."

Casey looked at her baby sister and felt a deep tug of empathy for the teenager. "No, of course you don't. Take a ride with me and we'll talk about it. Mom, Bobby's sound asleep for the night."

"You two go right ahead. Bobby's just fine."

"Thank you. Coming, Kelly?"

"Yes...and thanks, Casey."

Casey took Bobby with her to look at Mrs. Loomis's house on Saturday morning, while the rest of the family departed for Jess's ranch and the barn raising. The little boy was full of questions. "Is this where we're gonna live now, Mom?" "Why?" "How come?" "Can I have a dog?" "Can I bring one of Pearlie's puppies with me?" "When are we gonna move, Mom?"

"Hush, son," she finally told him, then said to Mrs. Loomis, "You mentioned something about a deposit."

"I always get a cleaning deposit, Casey." The older woman hesitated, then smiled. "But I know your family so well, I'm sure I could waive the deposit in your case."

"That's very kind of you. I would never move out and leave the place dirty, Mrs. Loomis."

"I'm sure you wouldn't. Well, what do you think?"

The house was small, with two tiny bedrooms, a living room, a bathroom, a kitchen, which also did double duty as a dining room, and a storage room, which was plumbed and wired for a washer and dryer. What had caught Casey's eye about the little place was its large fenced yard. Also, Third Street was strictly residential and the traffic was minimal.

"Do you allow pets, Mrs. Loomis?"

"Oh, my, yes. I have two dogs and a cat, myself. Certainly this young fellow can have his puppy, Casey. Just watch that it doesn't chew holes in the carpet."

Casey had to smile to herself. The carpet was clean but had certainly seen better days. In all honesty, the house wasn't much. But it was a start at independence, and Casey could see herself and Bobby being quite comfortable in it after she fixed it up a little. Lucille had told her not to worry about furniture, as the Oliver ranch house had more than it needed and there were even some good pieces in the basement, only gathering dust.

After Casey had agreed to take the house, she put Bobby in the car and drove to downtown Blythe. The little boy chattered gaily during the short ride, and Casey wondered if he really understood what "moving" meant. He'd had no practical experience with it, because not even any of his aunts and uncles had moved within the realm of his memory.

Casey had promised her son a hamburger for lunch, and she parked in front of Summers' Café, which was across the street and down two doors from the hardware store. Getting out of the car, Bobby startled his mother by shouting, "Jess! Hey, Jess!"

"Bobby!"

Casey watched Jess lope across the street. She'd taken the coward's way out when she'd told Jess about the talk with Ben, using the telephone rather than chancing a face-to-face with him.

"Hello," she said, managing a semblance of calmness, which was nothing short of remarkable considering the way her insides had begun acting up.

"Hello, Casey." Jess knelt down and gave Bobby a hug. "How you doing, pardner?"

"We're gonna move, Jess."

Casey blanched when Jess gave her a cynically startled look. "Where to?" he asked, rising and letting Bobby slip his hand into his.

"To a house here in town." Casey answered. She could see that the topic infuriated Jess. "It's none of your business," she added tartly.

"The hell it isn't," he returned angrily, then glanced at

Bobby and forcibly swallowed his temper. "I need to talk to you," he said to Casey.

"We have nothing to talk about." Casey took Bobby's free hand. "Come on, honey. Let's go get that hamburger."

Jess's lips were set in a grim line. "Tell me where and when, Casey, or I'll come to the ranch tonight and say everything I have to say in front of your whole family."

"What are you doing in town, anyway?" Casey hurled back.

"I came to pick up another keg of nails from the hardware store."

Bobby yanked on Jess's hand to get his attention. "I get to bring one of Pearlie's puppies to our new house, Jess."

Jess glared at Casey for a beat, then smiled down at his son. "That's great, pardner. Did your mom tell you about my new dog? Her name is Sunny and she had seven puppies last night."

"Seven?" Bobby's blue eyes were shining like new pennies. "Gee, I'd sure like to see them."

Jess looked directly into Casey's green eyes. "Have your mom bring you to my place this afternoon, pardner. You should be there, anyway, and so should she. No one should miss a barn raising. It's a very special event."

"Bobby's been to a barn raising before, and so have I," Casey replied coldly.

"Have I, Mom?" Bobby asked, his little face mystified.

"Last summer, son. Don't you remember that big picnic table with all that good food and running and playing with dozens of children? You talked about it for weeks afterwards."

"Oh, yeah, now I remember." Bobby's blue eyes turned to Jess. "Are you having a big picnic at your house, Jess? Are there lots of kids there?"

Casey was clinging to one of Bobby's hands, Jess to the other. Clearly the little boy was in the middle and neither Casey nor Jess wanted to let go. Two pairs of adult eyes locked and silently battled. Anger and determination and memories rode the paths of their gazes. "Bring him to the barn raising, Casey." Jess told her in a lethally quiet undertone. "I want him there."

"It's not your decision."

"I talked to your dad this morning."

"Drop it, Jess. I'm not going to discuss that now."

"I only said it to give you a preview of what's coming when we get a chance to really talk. Let's make it tonight, and since I've decided on the time, you get to name the place."

"You're the most exasperating…"

"Mom?" Bobby interjected, "Can we go to the picnic? Then I could see Jess's new puppies, too."

Casey glared a hole right between Jess's eyes. "I thought you wanted a hamburger," she reminded waspishly, then sighed and looked down at her son. His handsome little face was animated with eagerness, and what he was asking wasn't that terrible. "All right. We'll go to the barn raising," she finally agreed, but with obvious reluctance.

Bobby began hopping up and down. "Can I ride with Jess, huh, Mom? Can I, Jess? Can I ride with you?"

"If it's all right with your mother," Jess said quietly, giving his son a smile, then turning a hopeful look to Casey. "I'd take real good care of him, Casey."

A lump of solid tears clogged Casey's throat. She'd never been the sole recipient of her son's affections, although there'd never been a doubt that he loved her best of all the people who loved him. But the boy was turning to Jess in ways that would pinch any mother's heart. How did Bobby sense Jess's feelings for him so keenly? Casey knew he did. It was as her father had said: a parent recognized changes in her own child that no one else would ever notice.

There was camaraderie and boyish adulation in the look Bobby was bestowing on Jess, and Casey had to consciously swallow the sob that insisted on welling up. She cleared her throat and blinked at the hot tears threatening her last hope of maintaining her poise in this confrontation.

Jess frowned. "Casey…"

"No, it's all right. Bobby may ride with you. I'll follow in my car." Quickly she stooped over and hugged her son. "Don't forget to buckle your seat belt."

Then, with a brave smile, she turned and walked away, heading for her car. "Casey, I've got to pick up the nails before we leave," Jess called.

"Fine," she yelled over her shoulder, and climbed behind the wheel of her car, giving the door a hasty slam. The sight of Bobby and Jess carefully crossing the street, Bobby's hand in Jess's, the two of them talking together, brought fresh tears to her eyes.

While they were in the hardware store, Casey found a tissue and blew her nose. She was being silly, she told herself. She wasn't losing Bobby to Jess, and she *had* to adjust to the friendship between them. As Bobby grew older, Jess would probably request more and more of his son's time.

In a few minutes they came out of the store. Jess was carrying a keg of nails on his right shoulder and holding Bobby's hand with his left one. He dropped the keg in the back of his pickup, then got Bobby settled in the cab. Casey waited to start her car until Jess got into the truck, but she saw him say something to Bobby through the open window, then bound across the street again.

He came up beside her car and bent down to see her. "I just wanted to say thanks, Casey." His deep blue eyes contained a compassion she had never seen in them before.

"You're welcome. Make sure he buckles his seat belt. He forgets sometimes." Casey heard the raspy quality in her voice, evidence of the emotion she was still battling.

"I will. Casey..."

She bit her lip. "Please don't."

"I just want to say one more thing. Bobby's a happy, well-adjusted little boy because of you. I love you for that."

Casey sucked in a stunned breath, but before she could make a response, Jess was jogging back across the street.

Ten

The activity at Jess's ranch was just as Casey had anticipated. After a mammoth lunch the men returned to the barn construction, the women cleaned up and gossiped, and the children ran and played themselves into exhaustion. By the time darkness threatened, everyone was worn out, but the barn was up—walls, roof, windows and doors. So many men had shown up to help out, it had taken only one long day. The interior work was up to Jess, but the hard part was finished.

As families got into their vehicles to leave, Jess shook hands and expressed deeply felt thanks. Casey gathered up Bobby, preferring to leave while Jess was too occupied to notice. He looked as tired as the other men, but she suspected he would still want that talk he'd insisted on earlier, tired or not, and she would just as soon avoid it.

When she led Bobby to her car, however, Jess spotted her. "Casey! Just a minute."

"Get in, Bobby," she told her son. "I'll speak to Jess and then we'll leave." The little boy scrambled into the front seat and sat back without a word, and Casey smiled and shook her head. He'd had a wonderful afternoon and his eyelids were already drooping. He'd probably fall asleep during the short drive home.

Jess walked up. "I'd like you to wait until I say good-night to these good people."

"I can't, Jess. Bobby's completely done in." It was true, but it sounded like an excuse, even to Casey. "Some other time, all right?"

"When?"

Casey bristled a little. "What's this all about, anyway?"

Jess put his hands on his hips and looked away. Then his eyes refocused on her, a little more intently than before. "I talked to your dad this morning. You weren't completely candid in your discussion with him."

"I was as candid as I wanted to be. I certainly hope you didn't start something by talking about..." Casey glanced to the car. The windows were down and Bobby was probably listening. "I don't want to discuss this now."

Jess's expression didn't relent. "Then come back. Take Bobby home and come back." He saw another car pulling out. "I've got to thank those people, Casey. Either come back or I'm coming to you. Take your choice. We're going to talk here or at your folks' house." He bent over at the car window. "Good night, pardner. See you soon, okay?" Then he turned and walked away.

"You arrogant—" Casey whispered, stopping herself just short of a curse word. "It can wait until tomorrow," she shouted.

Jess kept walking, but he looked back. "No, it can't! One hour, Casey."

"One hour," she repeated under her breath. "Just who do you think you are?"

"Mom?"

Frustrated and angry, Casey climbed into her car. As she was driving away she saw her parents' car stop beside Jess. He bent over and shook hands with Ben, and it was obvious from his smile that everything was just great between the two men.

Heaving a disgusted sigh, Casey turned her attention to the road.

After Bobby was tucked in, Casey went downstairs. Lucille was in the kitchen putting away the leftover food she'd brought home. Every family had taken scads of food to the event, and while the hungry carpenters had definitely put a dent in it, it would have taken an army to eat everything. "Where's Dad, Mom?"

"Taking a shower, honey. Why?"

"Jess said they talked this morning and I'd like to know just what was said. Jess is insisting I go back to his house to discuss it, whatever *it* is. Do you know anything about it?"

"Yes, I do," Lucille said, and closed the refrigerator door. "Jess told your father that he'd asked you to marry him."

"I knew it!" Casey fumed. "Damn him! I told him to keep his big mouth shut about that."

"Casey, anger isn't going to help your situation. Your father already knew it, anyway, and he and I have discussed it. No one is going to pressure you into anything."

"No one but Jess," Casey retorted.

"Are you going back to his place?"

"He said if I didn't, he'd come here."

"Well, suit yourself about that. You can talk here as well as there."

That wasn't quite true, Casey acknowledged with an inward wince. There were things between her and Jess that she preferred to keep a secret from her family, such as her being dumb enough to go to bed with him again. "It's probably best if I go there," she decided aloud, and then asked, "Dad doesn't think I should marry Jess?"

Lucille had just rinsed her hands at the kitchen sink. She picked up a towel to dry them. "I didn't say that, Casey. Your father…"

"You're going to marry Jess?"

Kelly was standing in the doorway, and her eyes were as big as saucers. Casey groaned. The talk she'd had with her younger sister hadn't touched on Jess in the slightest. She had merely given Kelly the sound reasons she had for moving out on her own, which Kelly had seemed to finally understand. Or at least accept. But this had to be a surprise for the teenager, and with Kelly still so admiring of Jess Lonnigan, Casey didn't have the slightest notion how to explain what was going on.

She was about to appeal to her mother when she saw the weary expression on Lucille's face. Not only was Lucille exhausted from the long day, she had to be just plain tired of problems, Casey realized. That was one of the reasons she was moving to Blythe; she'd burdened her parents long enough.

"Kelly, it's like this. Jess has asked me to marry him, but I've told him no. My reasons are personal, although Mom and Dad know what they are. But I'm not going to discuss them with you or anyone else, and I'd appreciate your keeping this to yourself."

Kelly looked startled, but her sister's adult tone was more of a compliment than anything else. "Well, sure, Casey. It's your business. I understand."

Casey's features softened into a smile. "Thank you." She glanced at her mother. "Looks like I'm not the only one growing up around here."

Lucille hugged Kelly, then Casey. "You're both good girls, and I love you very much."

Casey used the drive to Jess's place to organize her thoughts. She was pretty confident of what was coming. Now that everything was more or less in the open with her folks, Jess was really going to press hard. The remark he'd made about loving her for being such a good mother to Bobby made Casey a little more tense every time it came to mind, and petty or not, she didn't like him playing the "wonderful father" role. Jess had only discovered his parenthood a short time ago, and she didn't want to hear his judgment, either good or bad, on the quality of her care of their son. The one point she intended to get across very clearly was, once she was settled in Blythe, Jess's visits would be highly regulated. She wasn't going to have him just dropping in and disrupting her and Bobby's schedule whenever the spirit moved him.

It was very dark when Casey arrived, and it didn't surprise her to see a light on in the new barn. Jess must have strung in an extension cord, she decided, because he couldn't possibly have completed the electrical work. Casey bypassed the house and stopped her car close to the newly erected structure.

She got out and saw Jess coming through one of the barn doors. His long, lean form was backlit, and that jab of intense awareness she was getting so accustomed to in his presence invaded her senses. But she didn't say hello; she wasn't there for polite conversation.

"Thanks for coming," Jess said, approaching her.

"You didn't give me much choice."

Jess jerked his head toward the barn. "Want to take a look inside?"

"I came because you demanded some sort of discussion, not to look at your barn."

"I know, but it's the prettiest barn any man's ever had, Casey." She had to smile, but Jess barely noticed. "I owe my neighbors more than I could ever repay," he continued softly, introspectively. "I was never in one spot long enough to make the kind of friends I have now. I've found a lot more here than I even knew existed—real friends, a son, you."

Casey's smile had slowly faded while Jess spoke. He was strongly and emotionally affected by the generosity of his neighbors, and his mood was reaching her. Yet she didn't want to be lumped with Jess's other newly recognized acquisitions. "Not me, Jess," she told him quietly.

His eyes lost their reflective cast and became laser sharp. "Tell me what to do and I'll do it. Tell me what you want and you'll have it. I want you for my wife. I want you in my bed at night. I want—"

Casey's anger suddenly blazed forth. "*You* want? What about what I want?"

"I just asked you what you want. Name it. If it's humanly possible, I'll give it to you."

Appalled, Casey took a backward step. "You're actually trying to *bargain* me into marriage! Do you think I'm looking for something material? Jess, I told you what I want out of marriage.''

"Love," Jess said flatly.

"Yes. Love, dammit!''

He stepped closer. "Well, I love you.''

Casey flushed three shades of hot red. "Like hell you do! Jess, just stop it. I like you a lot better when you're honest with me. I believe you want to marry me, and yes, I believe you want me in your bed. But, love? No. You didn't love me six years ago, and you don't love me now. You *love* Bobby, Jess, and I just happen to be his mother.''

"That's not true! Casey, there was something between us six years ago, and there still is. Just because I was too damned thickheaded to know what it was didn't mean it wasn't there.''

"The only thing between us was sex!'' she snapped. "I've faced it. Why can't you?'' Casey whirled and walked away, with Jess right behind her. "I asked you not to tell Dad about your proposal, and you did it anyway. Thanks a lot,'' she said sarcastically. She was at her car door, but Jess's hand on the handle stopped her from opening it.

"I felt he should know.''

"Well, it didn't do you any good. For your information, he already knew, and Mom told me tonight that she and Dad aren't going to pressure me one way or the other. The decision is mine, Jess.''

"Yeah, some great decisions *you* make,'' Jess jeered. "Moving Bobby to town—now there's a real winner. Just what will he be doing while you work every day in Upton's law office?''

"Oh, I see the grapevine is alive and thriving,'' Casey drawled. "Like it or not, Jess, I *am* moving to Blythe. And don't worry about Bobby. I have a very reliable sitter lined up. I think you know me well enough to know that I'd never neglect my son.''

"*Our* son. I think you might be having a little trouble remembering that he's also *my* son.''

"Don't kid yourself. It never leaves my mind for a second.''

"You still wish I'd never come back to Wyoming, don't you?"

The accusation jarred Casey. In some ways Jess's return was a blessing. It had rid her of the immobility of hatred and given her life new direction. No, she wasn't wasting her time now wishing Jess hadn't come back.

The anger suddenly drained out of Casey's system, and she leaned against the side of the car with an unhappy sigh. "Oh, Jess, let's stop this. I'm so tired of fighting and bickering. All I want to do is get on with my life. I want to make a decent home for Bobby and myself."

Jess was staring at her with a stubborn expression. "I want you to move here, not to Blythe."

Casey drew a long, hopeless-sounding breath. "You never give up, do you?"

"Did you watch Bobby today? Did you see how excited he was to be with all those other kids? And the freedom he had? Is he going to have that in town?"

"No," Casey admitted uneasily. "No, he won't have the freedom he's used to, but..."

"Casey, you're doing this for you, not for Bobby. From where I stand, it looks like you're being damned selfish. You already had one chance at making that 'decent' home and it didn't work. Why don't you give me that same chance now?"

"What chance? Just what are you talking about? I've never lived anywhere but with my—" Flustered, as Jess's meaning struck her, Casey's words floundered. "Oh...I meant..."

But it was too late. All of the strange little omissions and mistakes Casey had made in the past weeks had rushed Jess in an explosive understanding. "You never were married, were you? That was another lie."

He sounded positively amazed, and his reaction infuriated Casey. "Don't you dare judge me," she raged. "While you were off enjoying your fun and games, I was seventeen and pregnant! Can you possibly understand what that's like for a young girl? That's why I thought my dad didn't know anything about it. I begged my mother to lie for me, to help me plan a marriage, a husband that didn't exist."

"Casey..." Jess's stomach was turning over. He couldn't have imagined Casey going through it alone. He'd thought, he'd *believed*, she'd fallen in love with a man willing to take her baby. He'd wondered why it hadn't lasted—hell, he'd even asked Casey why it hadn't—but he'd still believed she'd been married to a man named Maddox.

Casey heaved a dry sob. "Mom did tell Dad, but he's such a wise man, and he knew I would have been more upset than I was if I thought he knew the truth. I would have been, too. I felt safe thinking that no one knew but Mom—less ashamed. It took a while, even at that, but I eventually learned to hold my head up again. As a divorcee, my son wasn't considered a bastard, at least."

Jess sucked in a harsh breath. "He's not a..."

"It's not a pretty word, is it? Especially when it's applied to your own son."

For the first time Jess was getting a true sense of what Casey must have lived through, and he felt sick to his stomach with remorse and shame. Because of him, the Oliver family had gone through hell, with Casey bearing the brunt of it. It was a miracle that Ben would even speak to him, let alone give him his blessing as he'd done that morning.

These were good people. In fact everyone he'd met in Wyoming had been nice, and Ben Oliver was the best of the lot. And he, Jess Lonnigan, was the biggest jerk that had ever walked around on two legs. No wonder Casey didn't want to marry him. How could she ever forget what he'd put her through?

"I wish you had told me this before," he said in a low, anguished voice. "I didn't know, nor could I have guessed, what you went through. I visualized a man behind you, with you, caring about you, during those months. I'm not even going to say I'm sorry. There aren't words to express what I'm feeling. But I will say this, Casey: I'll leave you alone. I understand now why you could never marry me. As for Bobby, I'd still like to see him as much as possible, if you agree."

It was Casey's turn for amazement. "You mean you won't talk about marriage again?"

"Never. Everything that's happened between us makes sense now...the anger, the battles." Jess hesitated a moment. "Almost everything," he murmured, and Casey knew he was thinking about the night they'd made love in his bed. He sighed then. "Go on home, Casey. I've got a lot of thinking to do."

He walked off, and Casey felt almost glued to the spot. She watched him go around the back of his new barn, and then she heard a peculiar sound. Her thoughts tripped over one another. Surely Jess wasn't crying!

She moistened her dry lips, uncertain what to do. Jess's obvious sorrow wasn't something she'd wanted, not since she'd started understanding him. Before that, she would have relished this moment, she realized unhappily.

Moving slowly, Casey finally opened her car door and slid behind the wheel.

"You can take that sofa from the den, and there's a perfectly good dinette set in the basement." Lucille was making a written list while she talked. "Bobby's bed, of course, and dresser, and the bed in your room..."

Kelly suggested an end table from another bedroom, and lamps. The list was filling out nicely. "Oh, the mail's here, Mom. The truck just went by. I'll go out and get it."

"Thanks, honey. Casey, what about that bookcase in the upstairs hall? Is there room in your living room for it? And you've got to have a television set. We never use that small one in the kitchen. You can have that."

Casey was staring out the window. "Casey?"

"Oh, sorry. Yes, the small set in the kitchen will be fine, Mom. But just as soon as I can replace everything, I'll return all of your furniture."

"Nonsense. This house is overstuffed. It will be good to unload it a little." Lucille smiled at her daughter. "Well, by tomorrow night you'll be in your own place."

"Yes." Casey sighed.

Lucille's smile evolved into a frown. "Casey, you don't

have to do this, you know. You and Bobby are welcome to stay here forever.''

''I know, Mom. No, it's best if I...''

Kelly burst in with the mail. ''Casey, you got a letter from Jess!''

''From Jess?'' Casey accepted the envelope. ''Why on earth would he write a letter when he lives only five miles away?'' She started to open it, then glanced at Kelly's avidly interested face. ''I think I'll read this upstairs,'' she said, and got up from the table.

Kelly's disappointment was almost tangible, but Casey left the kitchen and hurried up to her room. She closed the door and sat in the bedroom's one upholstered chair.

The first thing she did was study Jess's handwriting on the envelope. She'd never seen it before, and his masculine scrawl somehow touched her heart. Since Sunday night Casey hadn't been able to get rid of the idea that Jess had gone behind the barn to weep in private. If he'd been that emotionally worked up, Casey knew he would seek privacy. He was exactly the sort of man who would think crying was effeminate and a sign of weakness.

To her, it denoted a sensitivity she found extremely moving. Jess's comments about the good friends he'd found in Wyoming were also meaningful. It seemed to Casey that Jess was doing some growing, too.

She tore the sealed flap loose and pulled out a folded piece of paper. Then her mouth dropped open, because when she opened the letter, a check fell into her lap. It was for three hundred dollars.

Quickly, then, Casey read the letter.

Casey,

Please don't tear up this check. He's my son and I want to help with his support. I know your reason for hating me now, and you've been more than good about me seeing Bobby. It would mean the world to me to know that I was contributing to his care. Once you're settled in Blythe, I would appreciate a call so we can make arrange-

ments for me to stop by. I meant what I said about not
bothering you again, but I want to see Bobby. Please
understand. I will send you a check every month.

Jess

Casey lowered the letter and stared across the room. She
blinked at the tears in her eyes for a moment, then put her
head in her hands and just let them flow. Emotions roiled and
fed her unhappiness, and she wept until her eyes felt seared.

Then she sat back and admitted what she'd been fighting
against for weeks now. She loved Jess. She would always love
Jess. She hadn't merely been infatuated six years ago; she'd
fallen deeply, irrevocably in love. No wonder no other man
had ever moved her. No wonder she burned when Jess touched
her.

She wiped her eyes. Was there the tiniest speck of honest
affection developing in Jess Lonnigan for the mother of his
son? They were becoming closer, even if it was caused by
dissension. His arguments were changing. Hers, too, for that
matter. Anger was becoming influenced by that infernal physical attraction neither of them seemed able to ignore. And he
truly admired how well she'd raised Bobby. How, really, was
she to read the signs?

Sighing, Casey refolded the letter and returned it and the
check to the envelope. Then she got up and tucked it into her
purse. She didn't know if she was going to keep the money
and, in fact, didn't even want to think about it right now. She
would make that decision later, when her mind wasn't so
bogged down with frustration and, yes, self-pity. It wasn't fair
that she'd been destined to love a man who didn't love her
the same way—not fair at all.

The move was going smoothly. Buck, Brady and Ray were
carrying the furniture Lucille had donated from the house to
one of the ranch pickups, and Ben was overseeing its placement on the truck bed. Lucille was still digging out dishes,
pans and cutlery for Casey's use. Kelly was filling a box with

bedding, and Casey was packing up her clothing. Bobby had been given the task of putting his toys into two large cartons in his bedroom.

Casey folded another pair of slacks, then realized she wasn't hearing sounds from Bobby's room. She left her room and crossed the hall to Bobby's, intending to tell him to stop dawdling. "Son..."

She stopped. The little boy was sitting on the floor by one of the cartons, and crocodile tears were slithering down his face. Casey's heart turned over, and she quickly went to her son, dropping to the floor beside him. "Why are you crying?" she asked softly.

His big blue eyes, swimming in tears, lifted, and Casey saw what had happened. Bobby had finally understood what "moving" meant. Instinctively, Casey pulled him onto her lap and hugged him. "We must look at this as an adventure, honey," she said gently.

"But we won't be living with Grandpa and Grandma and Aunt Kelly anymore."

"That's true. But do your cousins live with Grandpa and Grandma? They come to visit, don't they? Well, that's what we'll do, too. Whenever you want to, we'll just get in our car and zip right back to the ranch. Think how glad Pearlie and the other dogs will be when we come driving up."

Bobby smiled. "Can I bring Rusty with me?"

Rusty was one of Pearlie's puppies. It had been a hard decision for the little boy to make when he loved each and every one of the litter, but Bobby had finally settled on a chubby little rust-colored pup.

"Of course you can. We wouldn't dream of leaving Rusty behind when we visit the ranch, would we? Now, let's both work on your toys. The men will be ready to load the boxes on the truck very soon."

Bobby slipped to the floor again and began scooping up toy cars and trucks, dropping them into the carton. "Mom?"

"Yes, honey."

"Does Jess know where our new house is?"

Casey's swift activity slowed. "He knows it's in Blythe, Bobby. I promised I would call him when we're settled."

"Maybe...maybe you should call him now. What if he wants to come and see me?"

Casey looked into her son's deep blue eyes. They were so like Jess's. Maybe she was the only one who really recognized the similarity, but when she looked at Bobby, she saw Jess. Her heart ached for this small boy, and for his father, too. How could she continue to keep them apart? They were becoming closer every day, regardless of anything she might do or feel about it.

Tears stung her eyes as she thought about the love developing between Jess and his son. Bobby sensed that he was special with Jess; he felt it and responded to it as a blossom reaches for the rays of the sun.

"I'll call him," she said huskily, and got to her feet, "Finish your toys, honey, and I'll go and call him right now. He'll know exactly how to find you in Blythe."

Jess didn't answer his phone, however, and Casey returned to Bobby's bedroom with an ardent promise to keep trying until she reached him.

That night was the first night Casey had spent away from her parents' home since she'd returned from "college" pregnant and supposedly divorced. Her bed was the same, but the tiny bedroom smelled and felt much different from her large room on the ranch. She'd left a small nightlight on in the hall in case Bobby should awaken and be frightened in the strange surroundings, and that little light gave Casey, too, a surprising comfort.

She wasn't afraid, but there were different noises to become accustomed to. The street was quiet, but still an occasional car passed by. Dogs barked, a cat screeched, someone banged a garbage-can lid, the little house creaked unfamiliarly.

There was so much newness to get used to. She would start working for Wes Upton on Monday, which gave her four days to get settled. It wouldn't take the entire four days, for she had scrubbed the house through and through before moving in. Her most important task, she felt, was to get Bobby oriented, and she planned to spend plenty of time with him. When he started school in September, he wouldn't be riding the school bus as he would have if they'd stayed on the ranch, and Casey wanted to walk the few blocks to the grade school several times with her son, making sure he understood the route and the danger of crossing streets carelessly.

She'd tried calling Jess several times throughout the day, but he'd never answered, and Casey had concluded that he was probably out working on his barn. Bobby had mentioned him again while he was getting into his pajamas, and Casey had again promised to keep trying until she got to inform Jess of their new address.

Now, while she lay in the feeble glow from the nightlight in the hallway, Casey felt a trickle of tears from the corners of her eyes. They were for her son, and she knew she couldn't go on battling forces that were growing stronger daily. Perhaps she had enough love for both her and Jess, she pondered emotionally. Maybe she was looking for the impossible, anyway. She wasn't apt to fall *out* of love with Jess, and even if she met a man who would really love her, how would she love him?

Casey let her mind take her into a future that included Jess as her husband. Her insides roiled at the image, but she tried hard to see him as a full-time father and mate. Jess had said, "Well, I love you," but she didn't feel it was true. She felt his desire and his determination, but not his love—although she very easily recognized that he loved Bobby.

Her thoughts turned to the more personal: to their lovemaking, to Jess's hard body, to his kisses. For purely physical love, she could ask for no more. Jess's sexual appetite was unquestionable. A touch, a look, a word, and he was ready to make love. He would be an ardent mate.

As for emotional love...?

Casey turned over in bed and quietly wept into her pillow. She was still romantic enough to want that special communion with the man she married. She'd seen her father and mother exchange thoughts without a word. She'd witnessed her broth-

ers and sister and their respective spouses together, and while
the air around them zinged with sexual exhilaration at times,
there was also a quiet, secure aura about their communication.
That's what she wanted with whomever she married. That's
what she would give almost anything to have with Jess.

But maybe she should forget all that and settle for giving
Bobby the best home possible. Casey flopped onto her back
again and stared at the dimly lit ceiling. Perhaps she should
let Jess know she was considering his proposal. She wouldn't
rush into it, of course, but in a few weeks...?

One thing she knew for certain: she wasn't going to be mean
about Jess's visits. He could see Bobby on his own schedule,
not hers. She simply didn't have the heart for any more battles
and ultimatums.

Casey fell asleep wrangling with it all.

"Jess! Jess!"

Casey went to the window and saw Bobby running to the
front gate. Jess was climbing out of his pickup, which was
parked right at the curb, with a broad smile. "Hi, there, pardner!" He came through the gate and swung Bobby up. The
little boy wrapped his arms around Jess's neck and squeezed
so tightly Jess yelped and laughed.

It was late Saturday afternoon and Jess's first visit. Rusty,
Bobby's puppy, began yipping excitedly, and Casey smiled at
the heartwarming scene. Then she went to the front door.
"Hello, Jess."

He let Bobby slide to the ground, and his smile faded to
somberness. "Hello, Casey."

Bobby was tugging on Jess's hand. "Come and see my
swing, Jess. Grandpa put it in the big tree out back for me."

"Sure, pardner." Jess's eyes lingered on Casey for a moment, then he let Bobby lead him away. She watched them
disappear around the corner of the house, then closed the door
and went back to the dinner she was preparing.

The kitchen window was open and she could hear Bobby's
excited chattering and Jess's replies. Bobby hauled Jess all
around the yard, pointing out his play areas, the sandy patch

of yard where he had a fleet of toy trucks and cars, the swing in the old oak tree, the plastic wading pool, where, he told Jess, "Mom lets me put water in it with the hose and I swim when I get too hot."

Casey's interest was more on what was going on outside than on the meat loaf she was putting together, and she stood close enough to the window to watch. Jess pulled something out of his shirt pocket and hunkered down beside his son, and Casey saw him press an object into the little boy's hands. She squinted to see what it was, but she couldn't make it out, although it obviously delighted Bobby.

"For me?"

"Yes, for you."

"Gee, thanks, Jess. I've gotta show Mom." Bobby ran to the kitchen door and burst through it. "Mom, look what Jess gave me."

Casey took the object and looked at it. It was a trophy belt-buckle, one that Jess had won in rodeo, intricately designed and engraved. "It's beautiful, Bobby. You'll have to take very good care of it."

"I will, Mom," he declared.

Jess stood at the door. "Come in, if you'd like to," Casey told him.

"Thanks." Stepping in, Jess smiled rather uneasily, "I thought Bobby might like the buckle. I hope you don't mind."

"No, I don't mind." When Casey had finally reached Jess by phone and given him their new address, she hadn't mentioned the check. It was still in her purse, and she was still undecided about accepting it. Oddly, if she hadn't admitted her feelings for Jess, she would have found it much easier to take his money. As it was, loving the man and knowing that she must keep it a private matter, she wasn't comfortable spending his money.

"Can you stay for supper, Jess?" Bobby asked eagerly.

Jess's eyes met Casey's, then slid away. "No, not tonight, pardner. Some other time, okay?"

Casey didn't encourage him to stay. She was finding her way, she felt, and soon she would talk to Jess on a different level. For tonight, it was best if he spent an hour or so with Bobby and then left.

Eleven

It was Jess's third visit—an after-dinner call—before Casey mentioned the check. Jess had stayed, at her invitation, to tuck Bobby in for the night, and he'd been grateful for the opportunity to share that special bedtime warmth with his son. As they left Bobby's room and walked into the living room, Casey said. "Would you like a beer or a soda? I need to talk to you about something."

Jess nodded. "Thanks. A beer would be great."

Casey went to the kitchen and returned with two bottles of beer. She handed one to Jess, then sat on the couch. Jess sank into a chair. "You've got the house fixed up nice, Casey."

"Thank you. It's small, but it's not bad little place."

"How's the job going?"

"Fine, really. I'm not fond of leaving Bobby all day, but we're both adjusting."

Jess's gaze held hers. "Are you?"

"Yes, Jess, we are," she replied evenly. Earlier, Casey had put Jess's check in her skirt pocket, and now she pulled it out. "This is what I want to talk to you about."

"You haven't cashed it."

"I've been undecided about keeping it."

"I'm sure you can use the money."

"That's not the point."

Jess took a long draft from his bottle, then gave her a hard look. "What is the point? I want to contribute to Bobby's care. Maybe it's not enough. Is that it?"

Casey's expression chilled. "I think you know me better than that. It's a very generous sum. It's the idea of taking your money, Jess."

"Is there something wrong with my money?"

He'd spoken cynically, and it struck Casey that since the night she'd thought she heard him crying, he seemed to have developed a rather hard shell. They were both going through a troubling period, she realized, which gentled her voice some. "Jess, there's nothing wrong with your money. But there could be something wrong with me taking it. You're playing the role of a friend, not a parent, and why should you—"

Casey didn't get to finish. Jess interrupted with a harsh "Playing a role? Yes, I guess that is what I'm doing." He drained his bottle and stood up. "Good night, Casey. Cash the check or tear it up. Do any damned thing you want with it."

With wide, startled eyes, Casey watched him go to the door. She rose then. "Jess, I'm sorry."

He turned, and never before had Casey seen him move so listlessly. His eyes looked older, tired, dull. "I'm sorry, too. I think this whole thing is getting me down. I don't like you and Bobby living here. I don't like you leaving him all day with a stranger. I don't like anything that's happening, but there's not a damned thing I can do about any of it."

"Dora Martin, the lady watching Bobby, is not a stranger. Come and meet her sometime. I've known her all my life. And please don't act like a working mother is some kind of misfit. Bobby is not neglected in any way."

Jess hadn't really touched Casey since the night they'd made love. But he moved to her and touched her now, and she didn't back away. His fingertips traced the curve of her cheek, and then her jaw, ending up on the side of her throat.

"I know you don't neglect Bobby," he said quietly. "I just wish things were different."

So do I. Oh, so do I. Casey felt Jess in every cell of her body in a rush of radiating warmth that caused a lump in her throat and an ache in her stomach. She wondered if this was the time to tell him that she'd been doing a lot of thinking about his marriage proposal.

But he withdrew his hand suddenly and backed away. "Sorry."

She accepted the apology with a slight nod of her head.

"Good night. I'll drop by next Tuesday or Wednesday, if that's all right."

"Tuesday or Wednesday is fine."

After Jess left, Casey locked the door, turned out the living-room lights and sat on the couch in the dark. The only time she'd ever been unhappier was during the months she'd been pregnant. It looked to her now as if she'd handled Jess's return to Blythe as badly as anything she'd ever done.

To add to her misery, she was lonely. Was Jess going directly home? It was a Saturday night, after all, and there were places around the Blythe area where a single man could find anything he might be looking for. The thought of Jess with another woman was like a knife blade in Casey's heart, but she knew she had no right to object. He was a virile, healthy man, and he wasn't going to go without female companionship indefinitely, despite his remarks about not dishonoring her or Bobby by having some cheap affair.

Besides, there were plenty of decent women available, and not every affair would be cheap. And a lot of women in the area would jump through hoops to go out with Jess Lonnigan.

In the dark, sipping from the bottle of beer, Casey again visualized marriage to Jess. Maybe he would fall in love with her after they were married for a while, she mused. Was that possible? Or would she spend her life yearning for something he could never give her if she married him?

Sighing, Casey set the bottle on the end table and put her head back. Her job was going well. Wes Upton was a pleasant man to work for, which she'd anticipated. His law practice was gaining ground, but there were hours when Casey wasn't busy, and Wes had no objections whatsoever to her using the time to keep up her freelance secretarial service. She still typed Lloyd Abbott's manuscripts and did letters for several other clients. Her combined salary and fees wouldn't provide a princely income, but with sensible management, Casey knew she could support herself and Bobby.

Of course, there was the future to think of—Bobby's future. She would love to be in a position to assist her son financially, should he wish to attend college when the time came. Casey thought about it for a few moments, then took the check from her skirt pocket again. Yes. Now she knew exactly what to do with it. Three hundred dollars was an impressive amount for starting a savings account for Bobby's education.

Casey and Bobby spent Sunday at the Oliver ranch. The whole family was present, and the day passed normally, with noise, laughter and good food. The highlight for Bobby was an invitation from his Uncle Brady to go on a camping trip. It was Brady's son's birthday, and the youngster had requested an overnight camp-out as his gift. Bobby was thrilled to be invited along, and Casey agreed to have him ready to leave the following Tuesday afternoon.

At one point during the hectic day Casey found herself alone on the front porch with her father. They talked about her job and living in town, and then Ben asked, "How are you and Jess getting along?"

"Reasonably well. Do you see him very often, Dad?"

"Oh, now and again. I stopped by his place a few days ago, and he's just about got the interior of the barn completed. He's got plans for a twenty-stall stable, too, you know. He's a hard worker, Casey. His place is shaping up really well. His quarter horses are splendid animals, and buyers and other breeders are already coming to him. I firmly believe he's going to be successful with his operation."

Casey's expression was seriously reflective as her gaze absently rested on the children playing on the grass. "He comes by about twice a week to see Bobby."

"Only Bobby?" Ben inquired gently.

"I've been giving his marriage proposal a lot of thought," Casey said in a low voice. "Dad, Jess doesn't love me, but..." It was too painful to put into words.

"But you love him."

"I...I'm afraid I do," she whispered, then turned worried eyes on her father. "Please don't tell him."

Ben reached out and patted her hand. "I won't. So you're thinking of marrying him, even though you feel he doesn't love you?"

"I've weighed it from every angle, Dad. Bobby needs his father, more every day. Look how excited he got over the invitation to go camping with Brady. Jess adores his son, and what Bobby feels for him is becoming stronger by the day. As for me, I don't see myself falling in love with anyone else." She smiled weakly. "It's a big mess, Dad."

"Are you that sure of Jess's feelings? Or maybe I should say, lack of feelings?"

Casey hesitated. "Actually, I'm sure of very little. I can only go by what I feel from him. Jess would probably be...well, an affectionate husband, but I don't think it would be out of love." Casey's cheeks had gotten pink with that admission.

"Don't be embarrassed, Casey. There's nothing shameful about physical love between a man and women who are in love with each other."

She dropped her eyes. She and Jess didn't quite fit that mold, did they?

"I tried to call you, Jess, but there was no answer."

"I've been working on the barn." Jess was standing on the small front porch of Casey's house. He'd come to see Bobby, but Bobby had gone camping with his uncle and cousins. "I'll come back tomorrow night."

He was so excitingly handsome, standing at her door, and Casey's insides were acting up something terrible. His shirt was a white-on-white pattern, and fit his long, lean torso like a made-to-order glove. His jeans, dark blue and quite new-looking, hugged his narrow hips and muscular thighs. His skin was that lovely toasty color she found so fascinating, and his thick dark hair was neatly arranged, unusually controlled, just daring someone to muss it up with a flippant caress.

She didn't want him to leave.

"Would...would you like to come in?"

Jess's gaze shot to hers with the precision and impact of a well-aimed, steel-shafted arrow. There was no logical reason for the invitation, not with Bobby gone. He probed the depths of her green eyes for an explanation and saw a strange sort of confusion. "Yes, I'd like to come in," he said quietly, but his heart had begun pumping his blood faster.

Casey stood back from the door, holding her breath while he passed by her. Her emotions were turbulent, her mind a whirlpool. She wasn't sure what she was doing, but she didn't want him to leave.

"Please sit down. I'll get us something to drink."

"Thanks." Jess perched uneasily on the edge of a chair, while Casey hurried to the kitchen. He heard the refrigerator door open and close, and then she was back with two ice-cold bottles of beer. She sat on the sofa, exactly as she had last Saturday night. Everything was like last Saturday night—where they each were sitting, the bottles in their hands—except for what was in the air. That was something new and incredibly exciting. Jess watched her while he tilted his bottle for a drink.

She stared back, then asked with studied nonchalance, "Are you dating anyone?"

Startled, Jess lowered his beer. "No, are you?" He was afraid to hope, but Casey had to be aware of the sexually charged atmosphere in the room.

"No."

"Are we having this conversation for a reason?"

Casey's heart was knocking against her rib cage. "I...I'm not sure. Do you object to it?"

Casey was wearing yellow shorts and a matching sleeveless, low-necked T-shirt. The day had been warm, and she must have changed clothes after work, Jess decided. Her feet were bare, but there was a pair of tan leather sandals in front of the couch. Her hair was tangled, as if it hadn't been brushed since morning, and her face was almost free of makeup. She hadn't planned this, Jess realized. Whatever was happening was spontaneous.

But...just what *was* happening?

"No, I don't object," Jess replied with less restraint in his voice. He'd been very careful with Casey ever since the night he'd learned that she'd never been married. He'd fully intended keeping his promise not to bother her again, and his visits to the house had been only to see Bobby. If he'd suffered at seeing Casey and knowing it was over between them, he'd kept it to himself. But this—her mood tonight—was an intriguing change of attitude. "I'll talk about anything you want to discuss."

"Well, I don't have a list of topics or anything," Casey said with sudden nervousness, which Jess didn't miss. "Actually, I was just making small talk, I guess," she added lamely.

Was he going to let her get away with it? Jess asked himself. It was a blatant lie. There was something on her mind. Or, on second thought, maybe it wasn't her mind she was having trouble with. Casey was a sensual woman. She'd been a sensual woman six years ago, although neither of them had had the sense to recognize her response for what it really was.

Old feelings swirled in Jess's brain. And memories of those nights by the river. He'd been a horse's patoot, maybe, but what man could have resisted the utter abandonment of this beautiful woman? Even then, she'd been completely female. It still amazed Jess that she'd been only seventeen.

Well, she hadn't been only seventeen the night she came to his house. And why was a woman with her drive and passion not dating someone? Why wasn't there a long line of men at her door?

He stretched his long legs out in front of him, adopting a deceptively lazy slouch. "All right. I'm game for a little small talk. In fact, I've got one question I wouldn't mind an answer to."

"Oh? What kind of question?"

"If it's too personal, just say so."

Casey's brief laugh sounded brittle, uncertain. "Of course."

"Fine. Other than the guy you're working for now, I haven't seen you with anyone. How come?"

Casey didn't answer right away. There were several different ways she could answer, and she needed to think about them. She was in a strange mood, she knew; a daring mood. It wasn't that she wanted to tease Jess or lead him on, but she hadn't wanted him to leave and then wonder where he'd gone. He knew almost everything there was to know about her now, and she suddenly realized she didn't want to kid him about her nonexistent love life.

Her gaze rose in a steady look. "Since Bobby was born, I've dated very little. An occasional movie, a dinner out, nothing even remotely serious."

Jess's system began a strange buzzing. He had to clear his throat to speak. "Are you saying what I think you're saying?"

Her eyes remained on him. "What do you think I'm saying?"

"That there hasn't been any other man."

Casey looked away for a beat, then returned her eyes to him. "There hasn't been. You're it, Jess."

"Why?" The word was sharp and piercing, then his voice dropped to a husky caress. "Why, Casey? Why hasn't there been someone else? You're an exciting woman. I can't be the only man who sees that, who feels it."

Her eyes were a steady green glow, warm and clear within the dark lashes surrounding them. Her voice was sensually husky. "Do *you* feel it, Jess?"

Jess stared. She was issuing an invitation. She was sitting on that couch, kitten soft and radiant in that bright yellow outfit, with her long legs bare and tanned, her toenails painted a pretty coral, the peaks of her breasts all too evident under cotton knit, and issuing an invitation!

The buzzing in his system expanded into a dull roar in his ears. He took a long swig from his bottle, then set it down on the floor by his chair. He got up, slowly, unhurriedly, and

watched her eyes follow his movements. She knew he was
coming to her, and her reaction was a deep intake of air and
a holding action, a waiting.

He crossed the room. It was only three steps on faded blue
carpet, and he sat down beside her, not leaning back but sitting
sideways, facing her. He took the bottle out of her hand and
reached across her to deposit it on the end table. Then he took
both her hands and brought them to his lips, watching her face
all the while.

He saw the light of response ignite in her eyes, and heard
the long release of the breath she'd been holding. "I feel it. I
always feel it, Casey. You know I want you. I always want
you."

She pulled her right hand loose from his grasp and reached
up to touch his hair. "I want you, too."

His eyes searched hers. "Just for tonight?"

"Would you be angry if I said I didn't know?"

"Do you still think you're weak where I'm concerned?"

A silent renunciation took place behind Casey's eyes. *No,
I'm not weak. I'm in love!* "You have something I've never
found in another man," she said simply. "If responding to it
is weakness, then I'm weak."

"My Lord," he mumbled, shaken to his soul. "Casey, I
don't want to hurt you again."

"Will you?"

"Not intentionally. But I didn't set out to hurt you before,
and look what happened." He'd promised never to mention
marriage to her again, but the word was scorching his brain.
If she wanted him so much, why not marry him? If she'd never
found what they had with another man, why not seal their
future with vows and wedding rings?

Casey had been staring at his mouth while he spoke. The
power of the look was wringing Jess out. "Do you know what
you're doing to me?" he whispered raggedly.

"I know what you're doing to me. Kiss me." She leaned
forward, bringing her mouth to within a fraction of his. "Kiss,
me, Jess. I'm burning for you."

Groaning, he wrapped his arms around her and kissed her

fiercely, hungrily, His tongue was in her mouth for long, breathless moments, and his hand moved on her breasts. "Oh, Jess," she whispered breathily against his lips.

"Casey, Casey..." He pressed her down on the couch and their kisses got hotter and wilder. He pushed her T-shirt up, and then lavished all of the desire tormenting him on the beauty of her bared breasts.

"The bedroom," she whispered.

"Yes, the bedroom." His head spinning dazedly, Jess scrambled up. He took her hand and brought her to her feet, and together, arm in arm, stopping to kiss and taste each other every few steps, they made their way to Casey's bedroom. She closed the door, symbolically blocking out the world. This moment was hers—hers and Jess's.

In a minute they were naked. Casey moved to him and wound her arms around him, pressing her hot skin to his. Her mouth moved over his chest, his throat. "You're so beautiful," she whispered. "So utterly beautiful."

Her lips traveled downward, and then she was on her knees and kissing him intimately. Her aggressiveness drew Jess deeper into the smoldering caldron of their desire, and his pleasure at her boldness was so acute it brought a rumbling growl from his chest.

"I love you, Casey," he whispered hoarsely.

She didn't contradict him, remembering that he'd always been free and generous with such sentiments during lovemaking.

Jess took her arms and lifted her to her feet so he could kiss her lips. They moved to the bed, and he leaned over her while his fingertips adored and explored the curves of her body. His mouth followed close behind. His breath heated her breasts, her waist, her inner thighs and finally the very center of her desire.

This was not the first time Jess had made love to her like that. Six years ago Jess had turned her innocence to passion, and their lovemaking had been totally uninhibited. With Jess there were no taboos. She had fallen wildly, irreversibly in love with his reckless lovemaking, and the emotion was so strong now, she felt smothered by it.

She heard the whimpering deep in her throat, and remembered Jess's comment that day about wanting to make her whimper. He knew he could do it, and she knew it, too.

But she could also make him whimper. They had some mysterious sexual power over each other, and it had started six long years ago. Her only trouble with it was that she'd also fallen in love.

Casey's hands slid over his back and shoulders. She twisted her fingers in his hair. She traced the contours of his rugged features. And her desire rose and gathered and exploded into white-hot spasms of pure ecstasy.

Jess moved up and held her while her emotions cooled. Their bodies were no longer dry. The room was warm, though the window was open, and their skin glistened with a fine layer of perspiration.

When she was breathing more normally, Jess looked into her eyes. "We belong together," he whispered.

Her lashes fell, fanning out on the soft skin just below her eyes.

"Casey?"

"Don't talk, please." She knew he was right. They *did* belong together, and they were going to be together, too. But some small part of her still held out. One stubborn area of her brain still hoped and ardently wished he would fall in love with her. The words he uttered in the throes of passion meant little. She'd heard them six years ago, too.

Jess's promise to remain silent on the subject of marriage taunted him. And it was all too apparent that Casey still didn't want to hear about it, anyway. He sighed, lowered his mouth to hers and kissed her into a second response. When he raised his head, her eyes were dreamy and soft, containing that light of desire he knew he'd see.

He stretched an arm down to his pants on the floor and found his wallet. Again Casey watched the sensible process of birth control. "You've become more cautious," she said quietly.

He moved between her thighs and looked down at her. "Didn't I do that six years ago?"

"No, you didn't."

Jess shook his head. "I was a jerk, Casey. That's my only excuse, which is pretty damned unacceptable, I know."

She sighed. "You weren't a jerk. You probably thought I was on the Pill."

"I wish I could say that was true, but I honestly don't remember."

"I know."

He touched her face, caressing her lower lip with his thumb. "I feel you, Casey. In here." His hand detoured to his chest, then returned to her mouth.

"In your heart?"

"In whatever's in there. I want you so much—not for just tonight. Is that love?"

A small thrill darted within her, but just until she remembered that he was still as aroused as he'd been when they started. Only *she* had reached a more serene plateau, although Jess's body pressing into hers was again creating internal demands.

He held her face and kissed her lips, his mouth opening and taking hers, possessing hers. And then, while his tongue roamed and tasted and teased, he claimed her body.

Casey released a long, soulful breath and closed her eyes for the joyous ride. She knew what it was like with Jess, and it was what she had needed badly enough to invite him into her house tonight. Her hips lifted in unison with his thrusts, and he reached that point of searing heat within her that even her initial release, as beautiful as it had been, hadn't been able to quench.

It was the ultimate pleasure. No matter what else they did— the kisses, the caresses, the touching and fondling—no matter how exciting every other phase of their lovemaking was, this was the best. She was beginning to see herself readily settling for a completely physical relationship and giving her son his father. No doubt some very good marriages had been built on less, and perhaps her deep, abiding love for both Jess and

Bobby would be enough to bond the three of them into a family.

Casey began to weep as sensation built and her emotions expanded. Jess was a masterful lover: strong, demanding, tireless. Casey's old bed rocked rhythmically with energies never before imposed upon it. Limbs intertwined and positions altered slightly, but the forces of nature never wavered. And gradually, excitingly, the explosion of completion drew nearer and nearer.

They climaxed only seconds apart, each crying out, each clinging to the other, taking gasping, needful kisses, whispering words and phrases of untamed, unthinking joy.

Then it was over. The bed was silent and still, the room was silent and still, the world was silent but spinning faster than normally. It took several minutes for Casey's racing pulse to relax. Her body was at peace—free from the feverish needs that had driven her to Jess's arms again. But it would happen again and again. Jess had said it aptly: one didn't extinguish this kind of blaze with one glass of water. In her case, Casey suspected the entire Pacific Ocean might not do the trick.

She stirred, moving her legs beneath the weight of his. Jess raised his head. His eyes were dark, his expression was sober. "We're not going to stay away from each other, are we?"

"Apparently not."

"An affair, then?"

The word *marriage* stuck in her throat. If he mentioned it now, asked her right now, she would say yes. But he had promised, and if it were to be discussed she would have to bring it up. She realized that she couldn't; the words simply would not come. Casey felt sick at the thought that if she couldn't talk about it at a time like this, when could she?

"Must we label it?" she whispered shakily.

"No, not if you don't want to." He pressed a gentle kiss to the corner of her mouth. "May I stay the night?"

Suddenly the world rushed into the room. She lived in town now; she had neighbors to think of, she had to get up early and go to work in the morning. "I don't think so."

He studied her. "When can I see you again?"

"You said you were coming back tomorrow night," she reminded.

"To see Bobby."

"Yes, to see Bobby."

"How will I see *you*?"

They both knew there was no chance of intimacy during Jess's visits to Bobby. And they had both stopped denying that intimacy was what they had to have from each other.

"Perhaps on Friday night. I could probably bring Bobby to the ranch for the night. I'll call my mother and find out for sure."

"Fine. I'll pick you up there."

"Yes, all right. Friday night. If Mom can't watch Bobby for some reason, I'll let you know."

There was so much unsaid between them. But Jess got up, disappeared into the bathroom for a few minutes, then came out and put his clothes on. Casey had donned a robe while he was gone, and she sat on the bed and brushed her hair while he dressed.

Their eyes kept meeting. They both knew their relationship was vastly different from what it had been, but neither felt they could comment on it.

"Walk me to the door?" Jess asked softly.

"All right." Casey put down the hairbrush and got to her feet. It had grown dark and Casey switched on the hall light. In the living room, at the front door, Jess put his arms around her. His kiss was warm and gentle and slightly inquisitive. Casey knew why. He was questioning her change of heart, or more accurately, her aggressive behavior tonight.

Her mouth lingered on his. "I love your taste," she whispered. His hand slid down her back to her hips.

"What else do you love?"

You! All of you! Every masculine inch of you! Your voice, your smile, your smell, your walk!

Deliberately she put on a seductively teasing smile. "What else do you think I love?"

He inched closer, pressing their bodies tightly together. "Casey, we're so right for each other, it boggles my mind."

"In bed."

"In bed, maybe out of bed, too."

Casey's breath caught. Maybe now...

"Well, I'll see you tomorrow night, but I'll be counting the hours until Friday night."

Her smile veiled the sadness in her heart. "I will, too. Good night, Jess."

Twelve

Friday saw the temperature soar. The law offices weren't air-conditioned, and Wes had placed several fans around for some relief from the unusually muggy heat. All morning Casey had battled a rather unique sort of anxiety, which was really a mixture of physical discomfort from the humidity and nervous anticipation of the evening ahead. Lucille and Ben were happy to have Bobby for the night and, Casey suspected, even happier because she was going out with Jess. It was increasingly apparent that her parents would be delighted if she and Jess were to marry.

Which was exactly the matter that had Casey on such pins and needles. She'd decided to talk to Jess about marriage that night. During his visit to Bobby on Wednesday evening, both she and Jess had been in obvious distress over maintaining a respectable distance from each other. Their mutual glances and a long, simmering good-night kiss had contained all sorts of sensual promises for Friday night.

At noon Casey drove home for lunch. She did that often, just to check on Bobby, although Dora Martin was a very

capable sitter. They all had soup and sandwiches together, and
Bobby prattled on about a variety of subjects. The camping
trip was still a point of excitement, and the seven puppies on
Jess's ranch another topic he never tired of discussing.

After kisses and hugs, Casey returned to work. The clock
seemed to move slowly. While typing some letters for Wes,
Casey thought of ways to begin the talk with Jess that evening.
There was no reason to beat around the bush or play coy, she
finally decided. She'd come right out and ask him if he still
wanted to marry her.

The telephone rang a few times during the sluggish afternoon, and when it jangled at four, Casey reached for it as
usual. "Law office," she answered, which was the greeting
Wes had requested she use.

Dora Martin's voice was strangely abnormal. "Casey? I
don't want you to become alarmed or upset. I'm sure he's not
far, but Bobby's wandered out of the yard."

An icy hand clutched Casey's chest. "How long ago? When
did you notice?"

"About a half hour ago. I've been walking around the
neighborhood looking for him."

A lead weight seemed to have invaded Casey's midsection.
"Dora, did you check the Monahans' place? They have three
children that Bobby has played with a few times."

"Yes, and the Cartwrights', too, although their boy is older
than Bobby."

Casey fought the panic closing in on her. Where would
Bobby go? Why had he left the yard? She had laid down one
irrevocable rule, drumming it into her son's head: *You must
never, never leave the yard without asking permission, either
mine or Mrs. Martin's.* She had repeated it until it was coming
out of Bobby's ears. Or, so she'd believed.

"I'll be right there, Dora." In her haste, Casey slammed
the phone down and took her handbag out of the drawer in
one motion. She was on her feet and halfway to the door when
she remembered where she was. Dashing back to Wes's open
office door, she recited breathlessly, "I've got to leave, Wes.
My sitter just called and said she can't find Bobby."

Without waiting to see or hear Wes's startled reaction, Casey ran from the office, down the hall, down the stairs and out to her car. Her driving was based strictly on habit, because her mind was already at home, running through the neighborhood, searching for places that her small son might have gone.

And then Casey remembered the puppy. Was Rusty at home? The fat, waddling little puppy was never more than a foot behind Bobby's energetic movements. Where Bobby went, so did Rusty. It seemed like a critical point to Casey. If the puppy was gone, too, then Bobby had merely taken a notion to go off somewhere. But if the puppy had been left behind...

Shuddering, Casey stopped herself from dwelling on the horrifying possibility of someone taking Bobby. The school! Yes, he might have gone to the grade school. He'd been enthralled with the school's ample playground, its swings and slides, its jungle gym. Periodically Casey had walked the route with Bobby, then let him enjoy the playground for a half hour or so, wanting to completely familiarize him with the three blocks he would be walking every day when school started.

Dora Martin was waiting at the front gate when Casey pulled up. "Is the puppy here?" Casey called as she got out of the car.

"No, the puppy's gone, too."

Casey heaved a relieved sigh. "All right. Tell me exactly what happened."

Dora couldn't quite meet Casey's eyes. "Bobby was playing in the backyard. I could hear him through the windows very well, and I sat down to read the paper. He came in once and got a drink of water and asked if he could have some cookies. I told him yes, and he went back outside. About an hour ago I realized that I hadn't heard him for a little while, so I went out back to check on him."

Casey could see that the older woman was devastated. No one could stare at a child for eight hours a day. Bobby could have wandered out of the yard just as easily with his mother present. "We'll find him, Dora. He couldn't have gone far in an hour. On the way home I thought of the school. That's the first place I'm going to look.''

"I'll come with you."

"No, I'd rather have you check the neighborhood again.''

"All right, Casey. I'll never forgive myself if some harm should come—''

"Don't even think it!'' Casey jumped back into her car and started away. She drove slowly, peering in all directions, taking the same route that she'd taught Bobby to use to reach Blythe's elementary school. Any moment now she'd spot him, Casey told herself. Any second she'd see a small, black-haired boy in jeans and a blue T-shirt, with a fat little rust-colored puppy on his heels.

There were three children playing on the swings at the school's playground. Casey parked and walked over to them. "Hi, kids, I'm looking for my little boy. His name's Bobby and he has black hair. Have any of you seen him?''

The three shook their heads solemnly. Casey smiled tremulously. "Thanks. If you should see a little boy with a reddish-brown puppy, would you tell him that his mother is looking for him?''

The three nodded, and Casey gave the otherwise empty schoolyard a troubled, sweeping glance, then strode back to her car. She sat at the wheel a moment. Where next? Where would he go? What had been in his little-boy mind to take him through that gate and into a world he was just barely becoming familiar with?

He wasn't used to being cooped up, Casey thought with a rapidly sinking heart. On the ranch there had been only a few areas that had been off-limits—the breeding pens, the bulls' pastures—and Bobby had grown up knowing those particular sites were dangerous. Other than those, he'd had free run of the Oliver ranch. He probably didn't understand, despite warnings, why a simple excursion out of his own yard would panic his mother.

And his father!

Jess! She had to call Jess. Quickly Casey started the car and headed back home. Dora was on the street, and Casey stopped to pick her up. "He's not at the school."

"He had a quarter in his pocket, Casey. Would he have gone to the store to spend it?"

Casey remembered the quarter Bobby had found in the grass several days before, and how she'd told him he could keep it. Casey's spirits lifted a notch. "Why, yes, that's a possibility, Dora. We'll go and see."

But a check of the nearest store, and then several others within what Casey considered Bobby's walking distance, proved futile. Casey drove back to her house and parked at the curb. "I don't know where to look next," she said, her voice unsteady from mounting fear. "I've got to talk to... Dora, I'm going in and make some phone calls."

"Call the sheriff, Casey."

The two women's eyes met in a frightened exchange. Casey nodded numbly. "Yes. I should have thought of that myself."

Jess was in the shower, trying to hurry, when he heard the phone ringing. He'd spent the day working outside, and it was getting very close to the time that he was to pick up Casey at the Oliver ranch. Muttering an oath of irritation, he turned the spray off, grabbed a towel and dripped water all the way to the phone on the stand beside his bed. "Hello." It was said none too cordially.

"Jess, this is Casey."

His irritation vanished like a puff of smoke, but before he could say anything, Casey rushed on. "I've been trying to call you for several hours. Jess, I...we...no one... I can't find Bobby."

The words hit him like a ton of bricks, but it took a moment for any real comprehension. "What do you mean, you can't find Bobby? Where is he?"

Casey was so on edge, she let out a rude, disbelieving laugh. "If I knew where he was, I'd know where to find him, wouldn't I? Jess, half the town is looking for him. I've been calling you for..."

"You mean he's gone? How? I thought that sitter you have

is a reliable woman. Wait a minute. Who was supposed to be watching him? Did it just happen, or—''

''Damn you! Don't you dare start looking for someone to blame. At this point I don't care who was supposed to be watching him, and besides, Dora Martin *was* watching him. He simply wandered off. It could have happened with me in the house.''

''Not likely,'' Jess snorted. He was having trouble with the most consuming fury of his life. His son, his beautiful, perfect son was missing? How? Damn it to hell, *why*? ''Where are you calling from?''

''Home. I'm at home.''

''Stay there. I'll be there in ten minutes.''

Casey put the phone down and burst into tears. She'd wept on and off since she'd talked to the sheriff's department. ''We'll alert every car to be on the lookout, Mrs. Maddox,'' she'd been told. Which hadn't been a great deal of comfort. Rationally she understood that the world couldn't come to a halt because one small boy had disobediently sought excitement out of his own yard, but ''rationally'' didn't soothe her aching heart.

She'd called her mother then, and Lucille had immediately organized the family. Dora had gone up and down Third Street again, and within an hour dozens of people were combing the area. Casey heard over and over again, ''We'll find him. How far could a little boy get in a few hours?''

How far? In what direction? For what purpose? Blythe was a small town, easily traversible by an adult on foot in a short period of time. But no one thought that the youngster had gone very far. The consensus was that Bobby was blissfully unaware of the furor he'd caused and was playing in some nearby neighbor's backyard. Casey prayed it was true.

House by house, street by street, the search began. Casey had run back and forth between her family, who were directing the efforts of the concerned volunteers, and her own house, trying again and again to reach Jess. She honestly hadn't expected him to get angry, and his reaction seemed like a final straw in the terrible day. It pointed up, much too clearly, that the two of them weren't even close to the kind of communication it took to make a happy marriage. On top of her almost insane fear for Bobby, the understanding that she'd been hoping for the impossible with Jess was too much to bear with any sort of stiff-upper-lip attitude.

Collapsing onto a kitchen chair, Casey put her head down on her arms on the table and wept with anger and frustration and fear. Where was Bobby? Where was her precious son?

Jess was driving fast, cursing one second, praying the next. His mouth was grim, his eyes full of pain. If something happened to Bobby, he wouldn't be able to deal with it. He'd never accept it, never.

Then his spirit rebelled at such morbid thoughts. Nothing had happened to his son. He'd find Bobby. The little fellow had only gone exploring. It was perfectly natural. Little boys were naturally curious creatures, easily forgetting rules and warnings.

He could remember his own boyhood. No, that wasn't a good example. No one had given a particular damn what he'd done. He could have stayed away from the house for days and no one would have cared. In fact, he'd done exactly that, sometimes sleeping in the streets.

Bobby was different.

No, it wasn't Bobby that was different, it was Casey. Casey was a wonderful, caring mother, unlike the woman Jess had called "Mom." Casey loved Bobby with the protective attention of a she-bear. Casey must be going through hell.

Jess mouthed a vile word, directed at himself. Casey had called, hoping for his support in this frightening situation, and had he given her any? No. He'd started looking for someone to blame!

Striking the steering wheel, Jess cursed his own stupidity. Would he ever learn? How much abuse would a woman take before she found the strength to put a man out of her life for good? Sure, they were great in bed, but a woman needed more than sex from a man. She needed support and confirmation and collaboration. She needed understanding and sustenance and...

She needed love. Casey needed love. She'd said it point-blank several times.

A choking sensation clogged Jess's throat, but along with it he felt as if he'd just been struck a blow. His vision cleared, his *inner* vision. How could he have been so blind? So dense? He loved Casey. *He loved Casey Oliver!*

Something joyous leaped through his system. But it was closely followed by a harsh dose of reality. At this point, nothing else really mattered but Bobby.

Jess rounded a curve in the road, traveling so fast that the tires on the pickup squealed in protest. And then, his eyes bugging out of his head in shock, he slammed the brakes on. The rear of the pickup fishtailed in a screeching stop, and Jess was out of the cab in a flash.

Bobby grinned. "Hi, Jess. Where ya going?"

The little boy's face was dirty and sunburned. He had a plastic bottle tied to his belt and he was carrying his puppy. "Rusty was getting awfully tired, Jess."

So much emotion rocked Jess that he couldn't speak at first. Then he knelt down in the dirt at the side of the road and put his hands on his son's shoulders. "Were you getting tired, too, pardner?"

"A little," Bobby admitted. "I was coming to see you, Jess. It's a long ways to your house, isn't it?"

"A long ways, Bobby." Jess glanced down at the plastic bottle. "I see you brought some water with you. That was smart."

"Uncle Brady told me that a good camper never goes anywhere without a water bottle."

"Well, your Uncle Brady is right. I was on my way to your house. How about you and Rusty coming with me?"

"Sure."

Jess knew his hands were trembling when he took the puppy from Bobby's arms. "Rusty seems all tuckered out."

"He walked an awful long ways, Jess. Then he just sat

wn. I called him and called him, but he wouldn't come. So
had to carry him."

Jess took his son's small hand in his. "Can't leave a friend
hind, pardner." He helped Bobby up into the cab of the
ckup, put Rusty on the seat beside him and climbed in him-
lf. The boy and the fat little puppy, both with droopy eyelids,
ttled down. They were both "all tuckered out."

Jess drove the speed limit now. "So, you were coming to
e me, huh?"

"It didn't seem so far before."

"That's because you rode, Bobby. Your mother's very wor-
ed about you."

Bobby's eyes got big. "Is she home from work?"

"It's getting pretty late, pardner. Didn't you notice the sun
arting to go down?"

"Well, yeah, I was starting to get worried about that. But I
ought I'd be getting to your place pretty soon. Is Mom mad
me?"

"I don't think she's mad, Bobby. But you should never go
f like that without telling someone."

"I was going to, Jess, but..." The little boy looked shame-
ced. "I guess I just forgot."

On the outskirts of Blythe, Jess slowed down, but he drove
e shortest possible route to Casey's house. He spotted Ben
the street with some other people, and he tooted his horn
d stopped. "Ben, he's all right. I've got him right here in
e pickup with me," he yelled out the window.

"Oh, thank God." Ben, Lucille and a small crowd rushed
ver to the truck. After a brief explanation, Jess broke off the
nversation with "I've got to get him home. Casey must be
antic."

"Yes, she is." Ben peered in at his grandson and received
weak smile. Clearly, Bobby was beginning to see the folly
his adventure. "I'll tell everyone and break this up, Jess.
ou go to Casey. And tell her we love her."

"I'll do that, Ben. I'll also tell her that *I* love her."

Ben smiled a slow smile of understanding, and when Jess

drove away, he put his arm around his wife. "I think everything's going to be all right with our Casey, honey."

Casey heard a vehicle stopping out front, and she raised her head, suspecting that Jess had arrived. She didn't want to face his anger or accusations. She didn't want to hear that she'd been neglectful, that their son wouldn't be missing if she hadn't moved to town and put him in the hands of a sitter. She was having trouble enough with guilt-ridden indictments without hearing them from Jess.

And then she heard "Mom?"

"*Bobby!*"

Leaping out of the chair, Casey ran to the front door. "Bobby…oh, Bobby!" Lunging through the door, she caught her son up into her arms. She squeezed his small, solid little body and kissed his dirty face, laughing and crying all the while. Then she swatted his behind and hugged him again. "Where did you go? Where were you?"

"I went to see Jess. Mom, you're squashing me."

Casey let her squirming son slide down until his feet were on the porch floor. Then she looked at Jess. Rusty was in his arms, and for once the wiggly little puppy seemed content to be immobile. Casey avoided looking directly into Jess's eyes. "Where did you find him?"

"On the road, about three miles from town."

"Three miles?" Casey's mouth was dry, although it seemed that her eyes contained another bucket of tears just aching to be spilled. She blinked hard. "Let's go in. Oh! I've got to tell Dad and—"

"I already did. He said he'd let everyone know that Bobby's okay."

It was over. Casey's head was throbbing, her eyes were burning like two live coals from crying, but the nightmare was over. She would have to have a serious talk with her son, but not tonight. He was dirty, tired and had to be hungry. And her emotions hadn't settled down enough to discuss his misconduct with any degree of common sense. One instinct made her

ant to paddle his behind, while another urged her to pick
im up and cradle him as she would an infant.

Maternalism took over. Inside the little house, Rusty padded
o his box and curled up into a fat, rusty ball of exhausted
uppy. Bobby was too dirty and sweaty to either eat or be put
o bed. "I'll run a bath for you," Casey told her son. "Maybe
ess will help you with it while I make some dinner."

"I'll be glad to," Jess agreed quietly. Casey's red eyes and
estless, fretful energy were clear evidence of the anguish
he'd just lived through. He wanted to soothe her, to take her
n his arms and stroke her hair and tell her he loved her, that
e'd finally realized how much she meant to him. He wanted
o beg her forgiveness, plead for an understanding that he was
fraid to really hope for. When she had desperately needed
im, he'd given her negativity, disapprobation. He felt sick to
is stomach with shame and self-reproach.

Bobby was too tired to eat much. Shiny clean, wearing his
ajamas, he was falling asleep at the table. Casey got up.
'Come on, honey. Let's get you tucked in."

Jess stayed seated. He hadn't eaten much, either. He sipped
rom his glass of iced tea while Casey put Bobby to bed. She
adn't invited him to the evening ritual, and he felt he
houldn't intrude. Not tonight.

Casey returned very quickly. "He's already sleeping," she
aid as she began to clear the table.

Jess watched her closely. She was calmer than when he and
Bobby had first arrived, but there was still an underlying ten-
ion in her movements. "Three miles is quite a hike for a little
uy."

Casey carried a stack of dishes to the sink. Then her shoul-
ers squared and she turned. "Jess, I don't want to go on with
ur..."

There was determination in her green eyes, but also a
trange cast of sadness. "Our affair?" he finished softly. "I
ouldn't agree more." He stood up. "Something happened to
ne today. I don't know what to call it, Casey, but a bolt of
ightning couldn't have struck any harder. I was driving fast,

trying to get here. I was furious, raging at fate or whatever it was that was threatening Bobby.''

He moved a step closer. "Then I remembered your call and how I'd reacted." He took another step.

One of Casey's hands came up in a restraining gesture. "Don't, Jess. I don't want you to touch me. This conversation is not going to lead to the bedroom."

His voice dropped. "And if I touch you, it will?"

Casey's chin came up. "It's not enough anymore. All you and I have is sex. There's more to life and relationships, Jess. There's respect and communication, there's..."

"Love?"

The word intruded, almost rudely. Casey hadn't expected it, and it stalled her train of thought. She stared into blue eyes that looked startlingly, rebelliously alive.

"I love you, Casey. That's what I've been trying to tell you. It hit me all of a sudden, from out of nowhere. It was just before I saw Bobby."

Powerful emotions attacked Casey, weakening her, liquefying her bones. She turned to face the sink, and she held on with both hands while her eyes squeezed tightly shut. Her mind wouldn't quite take Jess's words in, and they hovered on the edge of her consciousness. All of the doubts that today's horror had brought so vividly to light again buffeted her. It could be a trick, a ploy. He'd been scared senseless, just as she'd been. He might do anything to get Bobby under his protection.

She felt his hand on her back. "Casey? Look at me."

Her eyes opened listlessly. "Go away, Jess. Please just go away and leave me alone."

"You don't believe me."

"Did you expect I would?"

Her voice was dull, lifeless. He hadn't anticipated out-and-out denial. His feelings were so real now, so defined. But how could he convince *her* of that?

"Go away," she whispered.

"No, I'm not going to go away. I love you, and I'm going to find a way to prove it to you."

She turned then, and a spark of anger showed in her eyes. How?"

"Why would I lie about it?"

"To get Bobby."

"Bobby." Jess's gaze flicked toward the hallway, which led to the bedrooms, and he realized that even if there were no Bobby, God forbid, he would love Casey. This mess was all his doing. He'd all but ruined Casey's life six years ago, and then, when he'd returned and found out he had a son, he'd used any and all means to cajole Casey into marriage. No wonder she wouldn't, or couldn't, believe him now.

His eyes misted. "Is it really that hopeless? Casey, I'm baring my soul to you. I love you with everything I am. Lord help me, I don't know why it took so long to realize it. Or maybe it just happened. I don't know. I don't have any glib answers."

Casey took a shaky breath. There was moisture in Jess's eyes and a stunningly different expression on his face. Her senses warred. She'd wavered back and forth so many times on Jess, and she was afraid to believe him. But she wanted to, she desperately wanted to. She knew she had to guard against her own feelings influencing her. If she were to trust Jess, she must do it because of him, not because she was still putty in his hands.

"We'll talk," she said huskily. "Give me a few minutes alone." Slipping past him, Casey went down the hall to the bathroom. Her hands were trembling while she washed her face and brushed her hair. She took the time to put on just a little makeup, as her face was pale and drawn.

Then she went across the hall to Bobby's room. The little boy was sleeping so soundly, Casey could hear him breathing. He'd walked more than three miles, he and his puppy, trying to pay Jess a visit. Why? What mysterious force of nature had made Bobby disobey explicit orders and set out on a fifteen-mile walk?

Of course Bobby didn't understand distances very well. In a car one made the trip in a very few minutes.

He loved Jess, didn't he? This small boy loved his father,

without even knowing that Jess *was* his father. It was probably a response to what he felt from Jess; no man had ever given him the undivided, unconditional affection that Jess did. Ben and Bobby's uncles were wonderful to the little boy, but Bobby felt the extraspecial emotions he aroused in Jess; he sensed Jess's love for him.

Casey choked on the thought. It was what she had to have from Jess to believe him—that *sense* of love.

She bent over and kissed her son's smooth, warm cheek. The least she owed him—and herself, too—was to make the effort of a completely honest discussion with Jess.

Thirteen

When she walked into the living room, Jess got to his feet. He probed Casey's facial expression, searching for a clue to what she might be thinking after having had some time alone. There was little to be seen in her face, although she did look calmer. "Are you all right?"

"Sit down, Jess." He'd been at one end of the couch, and while he resumed his seat, Casey chose a chair. "I think it's time that you and I stopped even the slightest bit of game playing. I'm going to be totally honest, and I would appreciate the same from you."

"Agreed," Jess said quietly, willing to do whatever she might suggest.

"I had made up my mind to talk to you about marriage tonight." At Jess's startled expression, Casey held up a hand. "Let me finish. From the time you first brought up marriage, I've gone back and forth on it. I fought a dozen emotional battles because of Bobby. He took to you right away, and I went through jealousy, resentment and guilt because of it. I really didn't know that the two of you would become close so quickly, and I didn't like it."

"That's understandable," Jess put in.

"Yes," Casey agreed. "It was understandable. What wasn't quite so easily grasped were my own feelings for you. Under all the hatred and anger and resentment lay something I didn't want to face. I fought it with every ounce of my strength, Jess. I had to ask myself why, when I had such positive proof of the kind of man you are—or were—was I so weak with you? Why, when you touched me, did I forget all the pain and humiliation I went through because of you?"

When her pause stretched on, Jess asked softly, "And did you find an answer to those questions?"

"Yes." Casey lifted her chin. "I fell in love with you at seventeen, Jess, and after you came back, I fell in love with you again. Maybe it never stopped. Maybe, even while I was hating you, I loved you. I don't know. Like you said about yourself a few minutes ago, I don't have all the answers."

Jess wanted to rush across the room and gather her into his arms. But Casey's expression deterred the impulse. She spoke again. "I knew that you didn't love me. No, please don't deny it. You didn't. But we had…other things."

"Sex," Jess interjected in a voice that was beginning to relay the anguish Casey's honesty was creating.

"Yes, sex. I wanted more, Jess. I wanted what my parents have, what my brothers and sister have. I wanted harmony, and closeness. I wanted that special communication that only occurs between people who are really in love with each other. But then I decided to settle for less. I thought all kinds of crazy things. Maybe you'd fall in love with me after we were married, for one."

"Casey…"

"Anyway, I was going to talk to you about it tonight. Then Bobby disappeared. I called you two and three times every hour. I was afraid to leave town and drive out to your place, so I kept calling. I was sure you were working outside and couldn't hear the phone, but I knew you'd want to know. I was scared to death, and the thought of you coming and sharing the agony with me was comforting. I kept calling.''

Jess's skin had paled to a sickly gray. Casey went on. ''You were cruel on the phone, and I knew then that we had no chance of having a stable marriage. I felt it would be a travesty, with no possible conclusion but unhappiness for all three of us.''

Jess slumped back on the sofa, looking at her, staring at her. When she remained silent, he asked, ''Is that all? Are you through?''

''Yes.''

''All right. Your honesty hurts like hell, Casey. I was already so full of self-disgust I didn't think there was room for any more. But there was. I've been the worst kind of jerk there is, and I'm not going to try and soft-pedal anything I've done.'' Rising, Jess restlessly paced the small room.

''When I decided on Blythe, you came to mind. I remembered you as a sexy dish. Yes, I know that's an insult now, but that was what was in my mind. I thought of looking you up, and when I saw you at the rodeo grounds, I was thrilled. You were beautiful—even more beautiful than I remembered. Your hatred baffled me.

''I found out later that day that you'd been married and had a son. But I was glad again, because I also found out you were divorced. I was sure you couldn't possibly hate me—you had no reason to hate me—and I planned to see you again.''

He turned and looked at her. ''Casey, even before I knew Bobby was my son I wanted you. But I won't lie. My feelings were strictly below the belt. You're an arousing, exciting woman, and I wanted to...'' Jess stopped talking and raked his fingers through his hair, then started pacing again.

''Then I figured it all out. Bobby was my son. If you only knew what that did to me. My son.''

Casey heard the emotional cracking of his voice, and she couldn't help a rising empathy. Whatever doubts were tormenting her, she had none where Jess and Bobby were concerned. That bond was firmly set, as surely as if Jess had always been a part of his son's life.

She spoke with more gentleness. "I did know what that did to you. It was the reason why I began to understand you. Then you talked about your childhood, your life, and I realized how different your background was from anything I'd ever known. You were a different kind of man than I'd ever known. It was probably what made you so attractive six years ago. You had a reckless, go-to-hell, cocky attitude, a swagger in your walk. And, oh, you were sexy."

Jess had stopped pacing, his eyes on Casey. They exchanged a long look. "Casey, I love you. I love you so damned much. You just said you love me, too. Let yourself believe me, honey. Please." Closing the gap between them, Jess knelt beside her. His face expressed an impassioned plea. "Look at me. Look at my eyes. Can't you see how much I love you? Casey, it wasn't there before, but it's there now. You've got to be able to see it."

She did look. She studied and probed the depths of his eyes. She was afraid to trust the adoring light she saw, and yet she was moved by it. Her resistance slipped, but a tiny flame of fear still burned. "I won't settle for second best, Jess. I can't. I know that now."

"You won't have second best. You'll have a man who loves you. No one will ever love you more."

She sighed softly. "Oh, Jess, I want to believe you."

She was still wearing the blue dress she'd put on for work that morning. It was rumpled and wrinkled, but she'd forgotten it in the events of the day. Stunned a bit, she realized that Jess's right hand was sliding beneath her skirt, heating the bare skin of her thighs. "That's not going to clarify matters," she protested over a suddenly too rapid heartbeat.

"Maybe it will," Jess whispered, burying his face in the curve of her throat. "Love me, Casey. Let me love you. Let me show you how much I love you."

"Jess, you never play completely fair," she whispered as his hand nested around the mound of her femininity.

"I'm playing for keeps this time." He pressed his lips to the pulse in her throat. "Your heart's beating a mile a minute.

So's mine." Under her skirt he found the top of her panties and pushed his hand down into them.

"Bobby!" she gasped, reaching for the one excuse that might stop this delicious onslaught.

"Bobby's sleeping. And if he should happen to wake up and see his mother and father in each other's arms, it wouldn't be the end of the world. He's got to know, Casey. He's got to be told."

"I know," she moaned. Jess's fingertips were sliding back and forth over her most sensitive spot. "Oh, Jess. What am I going to do with you? You're an incorrigible man."

"You know several things to do with me, honey," he whispered thickly. "I've thought of this ever since Tuesday night. I thought you'd be in my bed, but yours will do just as well."

He was doing it again, making her forget everything else in the heat of his sexuality. That's why she hadn't wanted him to touch her in the kitchen. She knew she couldn't resist his magic. She never had been able to. In despair, Casey began to weep. Tears flooded down her cheeks, and she just let go and sobbed.

Jess froze for a moment, then raised his head. His hand was still under her skirt, and he withdrew it slowly. Strangely, he knew what the problem was. It was almost as if he were reading Casey's mind. He cleared his throat and took her hands in his.

"Casey, look at me."

Sniffling, she brought a watery, resentful gaze to his face. "What for?"

"I love you more than I ever thought it was possible to love someone. I didn't know feelings like this existed. You and Bobby have taught me more about love than anyone else and all of my entire past life has. Will you marry me, Casey? Will you do me the honor of becoming my wife?"

A proposal. A beautifully said, impassioned marriage proposal. Was that what she'd been waiting for? "How...how did you know that's what I was thinking about?" she whispered.

"I sensed it."

He'd said the right thing. He'd unknowingly pushed exactly the right buttons. "Oh, Jess." She slowly slid her hands up his chest and around his neck. "Maybe you do love me."

His eyes were suddenly swimming with tears. "I do, Casey. I love you more than life. I've been the world's biggest idiot. It's so crazy, because I understand why you're afraid of me and yet I can't let it go at that. We're meant to be together. We've always been destined to be together, only I was such a fool. Maybe someday you'll be able to forgive me, but I don't know if I ever will."

Closing her teary eyes, Casey put her forehead against Jess's. She believed him, she realized in a whirling tide of emotions. She believed him. He loved her. She felt it in every fiber of her being, in her very soul. A sense of peace overlaid the desire to weep and laugh and just let go. Her voice was husky with feeling. "I love you. I love you so much I could die from it."

They held each other, and then Jess laughed. It sounded shaky and more filled with emotion than mirth. "Well, don't die, honey. Not when we're just now getting together." He got to his feet, pulled Casey up from the chair, picked her up, carried her to the couch and settled her on his lap. And then they held each other again—silently, tenderly.

Casey finally stirred, feeling reborn, complete. They exchanged sweet kisses interspersed with words of love, until their feelings were no longer soft pastels but brilliant streaks of aroused reds and greens and blues. Jess whispered against her lips with a note of teasing, "We can talk some more or we can make love. Which do you vote for?"

She nibbled his lips with a happy laugh. "Both."

He enclosed her in a fierce embrace and conveyed his love, which was expanding more with each passing second, in a long, hungry kiss. His voice was hoarse when they finally both needed air. "I love you, lady."

"I love *you* cowboy."

"Can I play under your skirt now?"

She laughed gaily, freely. "You're a wicked thing, aren't you?"

His hand snaked under her dress. "Is this so wicked?"

She sighed and relaxed her thighs. "That's wonderful," she murmured, and after a minute, "Oh, Jess, you make me want you so much," she said needfully.

"You make me want you just by being in the same room. You make me want you when I'm miles away and your beautiful face comes to mind. I honestly don't know how we're going to live in the same house and get anything done, do you?"

Casey gave a weak, fluttery little laugh. He was teasing, but there was a lot of truth in it. Their relationship had begun, so long ago, because of their powerful sexual attraction, and if anything, it was even stronger today. She put her mouth to his ear. "I want your body, cowboy," she whispered seductively.

A lazy, slow smile curved his sexy lips. "Honey, you've got it. Forever and ever. This ramblin' man is ready to settle down for good."

"For good," Casey whispered dreamily. "Those are beautiful words, Jess."

"Beautiful words for a beautiful lady. Oh, Casey," he murmured, suddenly staggered by the need to possess her. The past hours had been emotionally strenuous—for her, for him. Jess wanted to bind their love, to prove it with action, and he began with a kiss containing all the heat in his feverish body.

Happiness mingled with Casey's desire as she returned Jess's passion. The sensation of oneness she was feeling with Jess was what she had dreamed of all her adult life. She had somehow always known that real love would feel like this.

She wanted to show him with her body how much she loved him. Her face was flushed, her lips wet and provocatively swollen, when she tilted her head back and began unbuttoning his shirt. Their gazes met and held until the shirt was open, and then she pressed her mouth to his bared chest. "I will want you just as much in ten years, twenty," she told him.

"Yes," he agreed huskily. "This is for keeps, Casey."

She undid the buckle of his belt. "We won't always see eye to eye on everything."

"Undoubtedly."

She slowly slid the tab of his zipper down. "But we'll talk those times out."

"Definitely."

Casey looked down at the impressive display of aroused masculinity she had uncovered, then raised her eyes to Jess's again. "You're a very beautiful man," she whispered. She watched the drift of smoky emotions on his face as she caressed him intimately. Leaning forward, she pressed her lips to his, slipping her tongue into his mouth.

Groaning, Jess clamped his arms around her, holding her to him with mounting desperation. "Maybe we'd better get out of the living room," he murmured shakily. "I'm on the verge of getting very carried away."

Casey got off of his lap and took his hand. Her legs weren't quite steady, and she teetered slightly as Jess got up. He noticed. "Are you all right?" The day had been traumatic, and Casey would have every right to feel shaky.

She wrapped her arms around his waist and laid her cheek on his bare chest. "I'm fine. You affect me so strongly, Jess."

He held her tightly. "We affect each other. We always did, we always will." Moving away, he bent over, placed an arm behind her thighs and lifted her off the floor.

Casey closed her eyes for the short journey to the bedroom. Once inside, Jess let her feet slide to the floor. "Turn on the lights," he instructed as he closed and locked the door. "I want to see you."

She nodded. She wanted to see him, too—every wonderful inch of Jess Lonnigan. They undressed quickly. Casey threw back the covers of the bed, but before she could lie down, Jess came up behind her. He pressed his nakedness against her back, and his hands began moving over her breasts, her stomach, downward to the triangle of auburn hair at her thighs. His lips warmed the side of her throat.

Heat and desire spiraled through Casey. She felt him lift her left foot to the bed, and the erotic position opened her to his searching fingers. The dizzying sensation of unleashed passion ricocheted through her mind and body, taking her to a new plateau of awareness when she felt the hard shaft of his manhood seeking entry.

"Oh, Jess," she moaned hoarsely when they were tightly joined.

"Do you like it this way?" he whispered.

His fingers were a torment of pulsing rhythm, driving her wild. "I won't last," she rasped.

"Don't try, honey. Go with the flow." Slowly, deliciously, he began to move within her. "I want to give you pleasure," he breathed in her ear.

"To make me whimper," she gasped, referring to the day he'd told her he wanted to undress her and make her whimper.

He remembered that day, too, and his responsive chuckle was low and gravelly. "Yes, to make you whimper."

She could barely speak. "You do that...very easily. Oh, Jess...Jess..." The room turned upside down as the rapturous spasms began, and when she was weeping softly and weakly leaning all her weight back against him, he held her until she had calmed.

Then he left her body and turned her around. His gaze moved over her features. "I love you, lady."

She touched his face. "I love you, Jess. So much."

He brushed at a tear on her cheek. "Jade-green eyes that spill pure diamonds," he whispered.

She smiled. "The result of those whimpers you like so well. I expect you will see a lot of them."

He steered her to the bed. "No matter how many times, it will never be enough." With Casey on her back, Jess leaned over her. He touched a nipple, tracing the rosy areola, then fingering the center bud to rigidity. "We're going to be together every day, every night, from now on. It's a fantastic thought, isn't it?"

"Very." She sighed as his mouth opened around the nipple he'd been teasing. "Very fantastic," she repeated huskily.

Sometime in the night Casey awoke. She lay quietly, then realized that Jess wasn't sleeping, either. "You're awake, too?" she whispered.

"Hi." He turned onto his side and pulled her closer. "I've been lying here thinking about Bobby. Are we really going to tell him who I am?"

"I think we have to, don't you?"

"I'd sure like to, but he's just a little kid. Will he understand?"

"Jess, he has to know. Everyone has to know. Lord," Casey groaned, "the gossips will have a field day."

"Exactly. Honey, we know, you and me. And your folks. Why does anyone else have to get in on it? I'll bet that attorney you work for could draw up adoption papers."

Casey bolted upright. "You'd do that?"

"When Bobby's old enough we can tell him the truth. But what's the point of everyone talking it to death? It's no one else's business, Casey, and Bobby doesn't need to grow up with that kind of gossip about his birth. Yes, I'd file for his adoption, if you agree it's best."

Casey nestled back into his arms. "It's best, but I never would have dreamed of asking you to do that. Jess, you're a surprisingly wonderful man."

He grinned. "Yes, by cracky, I am, aren't I?"

"By cracky?" Casey exploded with laughter. "You're also conceited, by cracky," she quipped when she could speak again. "But you have a right to be." She sighed dramatically. "You're only the sexiest guy who ever walked around on two legs."

Jess laughed. "I love you, lady."

Casey yawned and snuggled closer. "I love *you* cowboy." She was almost asleep when she murmured. "Casey Lonnigan. It has a nice ring, Jess."

He smiled and closed his eyes. The future looked bright and beautiful. Casey, Bobby and Jess Lonnigan. Yes, it did have a nice ring. A very nice ring.

* * * * *

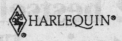

HARLEQUIN®

Not The Same Old Story!

 **PRESENTS®**

Exciting, glamorous romance stories that take readers around the world.

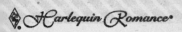 *Harlequin Romance®*

Sparkling, fresh and tender love stories that bring you pure romance.

 HARLEQUIN® *Temptation.*

Bold and adventurous—Temptation is strong women, bad boys, great sex!

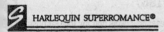 HARLEQUIN SUPERROMANCE®

Provocative and realistic stories that celebrate life and love.

 HARLEQUIN® AMERICAN ROMANCE®

Contemporary fairy tales—where anything is possible and where dreams come true.

 HARLEQUIN® INTRIGUE®

Heart-stopping, suspenseful adventures that combine the best of romance and mystery.

LOVE & LAUGHTER™

Humorous and romantic stories that capture the lighter side of love.

Look us up on-line at: http://www.romance.net   HGENERIC

Take 2 bestselling love stories FREE

Plus get a FREE surprise gift!

Special Limited-Time Offer

Mail to Harlequin Reader Service®

3010 Walden Avenue
P.O. Box 1867
Buffalo, N.Y. 14240-1867

YES! Please send me 2 free Harlequin Presents® novels and my free surprise gift. Then send me 6 brand-new novels every month, which I will receive months before they appear in bookstores. Bill me at the low price of $3.12 each plus 25¢ delivery and applicable sales tax, if any*. That's the complete price, and a saving of over 10% off the cover prices—quite a bargain! I understand that accepting the books and gift places me under no obligation ever to buy any books. I can always return a shipment and cancel at any time. Even if I never buy another book from Harlequin, the 2 free books and the surprise gift are mine to keep forever.

106 HEN CH69

Name	(PLEASE PRINT)	
Address		Apt. No.
City	State	Zip

This offer is limited to one order per household and not valid to present Harlequin Presents® subscribers. *Terms and prices are subject to change without notice. Sales tax applicable in N.Y.

UPRES-98 ©1990 Harlequin Enterprises Limited

Looking For More Romance?

Visit Romance.net

Look us up on-line at: http://www.romance.net

Check in daily for these and other exciting features:

Hot off the press

View all current titles, and purchase them on-line.

What do the stars have in store for you?

Horoscope

Hot deals

Exclusive offers available only at Romance.net

Plus, don't miss our interactive quizzes, contests and bonus gifts.

PWEB

DEBBIE MACOMBER

invites you to the

HEART OF TEXAS

Join Debbie Macomber as she brings you the lives
and loves of the folks in the ranching community
of Promise, Texas.

If you loved Midnight Sons—don't miss
Heart of Texas! A brand-new six-book series
from Debbie Macomber.

Available in February 1998
at your favorite retail store.

Heart of Texas by Debbie Macomber

Lonesome Cowboy	February '98
Texas Two-Step	March '98
Caroline's Child	April '98
Dr. Texas	May '98
Nell's Cowboy	June '98
Lone Star Baby	July '98

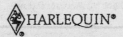

HARLEQUIN®

Act now
to receive these favorite
By Request® collections!

#20114	LEGENDARY LOVERS	$5.50 U.S. ☐	
	by Debbie Macomber	$5.99 CAN.☐	
#20116	SURRENDER!	$5.50 U.S. ☐	
	by Kathleen Eagle	$5.99 CAN.☐	
#20129	ROYAL WEDDINGS	$5.99 U.S. ☐	
		$6.99 CAN.☐	
#20130	HOME FOR CHRISTMAS	$5.99 U.S. ☐	
		$6.99 CAN.☐	
#20133	YOURS, MINE & OURS	$5.99 U.S. ☐	
		$6.99 CAN.☐	
#20135	A MATCH FOR MOM	$5.99 U.S. ☐	
		$6.99 CAN.☐	

(quantities may be limited on some titles)

TOTAL AMOUNT	$
POSTAGE & HANDLING	$
($1.00 for one book, 50¢ for each additional)	
APPLICABLE TAXES*	$ _____
<u>**TOTAL PAYABLE**</u>	$ _____
(check or money order—please do not send cash)	

To order, complete this form and send it, along with a check or money order for the total above, payable to By Request, to: **In the U.S.:** 3010 Walden Avenue, P.O. Box 9047, Buffalo, NY 14269-9047; **In Canada:** P.O. Box 613, Fort Erie, Ontario, L2A 5X3.

Name: _____

Address: _____ City: _____

State/Prov.: _____ Zip/Postal Code: _____

Account Number: _____

*New York residents remit applicable sales taxes.
Canadian residents remit applicable GST and provincial taxes.   075 CSAS

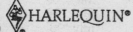 

Look us up on-line at: http://www.romance.net   PBRBL1